# THE BRIDGE KINGDOM

# THE BRIDGE KINGDOM

BY *USA TODAY* BESTSELLING AUTHOR
DANIELLE L. JENSEN

This is a work of fiction. All of the characters, organizations, and events portrayed in this novel are either products of the author's imagination or are used fictitiously.

*THE BRIDGE KINGDOM*



Cover Artwork Illustration: Richard Anderson
Cover Design: Silver Wing Press, LLC
Interior Formatting: Silver Wing Press, LLC

Map designed by Damien Mammoliti

Based on the Audible Originals production of *The Bridge Kingdom*

Published by: Context Literary Agency, LLC
125R Cedarhurst Avenue, Suite B
Cedarhurst, NY 11516

Paperback ISBN: 978-1-7330903-1-5
Hardcover ISBN: 978-1-7330903-2-2

**Also by**

*USA TODAY* BESTSELLING AUTHOR

# DANIELLE L. JENSEN

THE MALEDICTION TRILOGY

*Stolen Songbird*

*Hidden Huntress*

*Warrior Witch*

*The Broken Ones (Prequel)*

THE DARK SHORES SERIES

*Dark Shores*

*Dark Skies*

*Gilded Serpent*

*Tarnished Empire (Prequel)*

THE BRIDGE KINGDOM SERIES

*The Bridge Kingdom*

*The Traitor Queen*

https://danielleljensen.com/

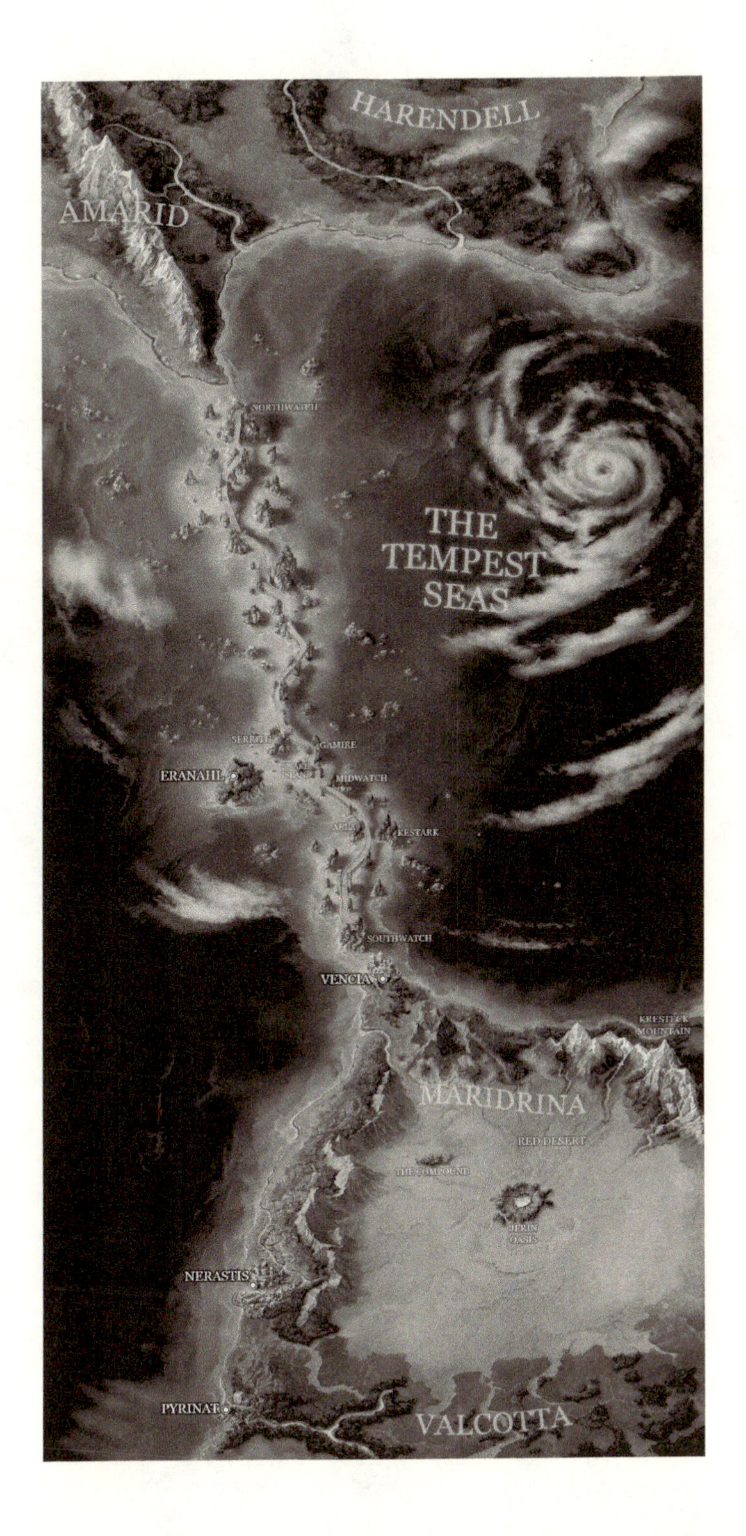
HARENDELL
AMARID
NORTHWATCH
THE
TEMPEST
SEAS
SERRITH
GAMIRE
ERANAHL
MIDWATCH
KESTARK
SOUTHWATCH
VENCIA
KRESTECK
MOUNTAIN
MARIDRINA
RED DESERT
THE COMPOUND
JERIN
OASIS
NERASTIS
PYRINAT
VALCOTTA

# 1
# LARA

LARA RESTED HER elbows on the low sandstone wall, her eyes fixed on the glowing sun descending over the distant mountain peaks, nothing between here and there but scorching sand dunes, scorpions, and the occasional lizard. Impassable for anyone without a good camel, the correct provisions, and a healthy dose of luck.

Not that she hadn't been tempted to try more than once.

A gong was struck, the reverberations echoing over the compound. It had called her to dinner every night for the last fifteen years, but tonight, it rattled through her like a war drum. Lara took a deep breath to steady her nerves, then turned, striding across the training yard in the direction of the towering palms, her rose-colored skirts whispering against her legs. All eleven of her half sisters were converging on the same place, each dressed in a different gown, the color carefully selected by their Mistress of Aesthetics to complement their features.

Lara detested pink, but no one had asked for her opinion.

After fifteen years caged within the compound, tonight would be the sisters' last here together, and their Master of Meditation had ordered them to spend the hour before dinner in a favored location, contemplating all they had learned and all they would accomplish with the tools they'd been given.

Or at least, what *one* of them would accomplish.

The scent of the oasis drifted over Lara on the faintest of breezes. The smell of fruits and leafy things, the char of cooking meat, and, above all, water. Precious, precious water. The compound was located on one of the few springs in the midst of the Red Desert, but far off caravan routes. Isolated. Secret.

Just the way their father, the King of Maridrina, liked it. And from what she'd been told about him, he was a man who always got what he wanted, one way or another.

Pausing at the edge of the training yard, Lara brushed the bottoms of her feet against her calves, dusting off the sand before sliding on delicate, high-heeled sandals, her balance as steady as though she wore combat boots.

*Click, click, click.* Her heels echoed the frantic beat of her heart as she walked down the pathway of mosaic tile and crossed the small bridge, the gentle sound of stringed instruments rising above the gurgle of water. The musicians had arrived with her father's entourage to provide the entertainment for tonight's festivities.

She doubted they'd be making the return journey.

A bead of sweat trickled down her back, the strap holding a knife against her inner thigh already damp. *You will not die tonight*, she silently chanted. *Not tonight.*

Lara and her sisters converged on the center of the oasis, a courtyard encircled by the spring, which turned it into an island of greenery. They walked toward the enormous table draped with silk and heavy with the silverware required for the dozen or more courses waiting in the wings. Servants, all of them mute, stood behind the thirteen chairs, eyes fixed on their feet. As the women approached, they drew the chairs back, and Lara sat without looking, knowing the rose-colored cushion would be beneath her.

None of the sisters spoke.

Underneath the table, Lara felt a hand grip hers. She allowed her eyes to flick to her left, briefly meeting Sarhina's gaze, before returning to her plate. All twelve of them were the King's daughters, now twenty years of age, each born by a different one of his wives. Lara and her half sisters had been brought to this secret place to undergo training that no Maridrinian girl had ever before received. Training that was now complete.

Lara's stomach twisted sour, and she dropped Sarhina's hand, the feel of her closest sister's skin, cool and dry relative to her own, making her want to be sick.

The gong sounded again, and the musicians went silent as the girls rose to their feet. A heartbeat later, their father appeared, his silver hair gleaming in the lamplight as he traversed the path toward them, his azure eyes identical to those of every girl present. Sweat ran in rivulets down Lara's legs even as her training had her take in every detail. The indigo of his coat. The worn leather of his boots. The sword belted at his waist. And, as he turned to walk around the table, the faintest outline of the blade hidden along his spine.

When he sat, Lara and her sisters followed suit, none of them making a sound.

"Daughters." Leaning back in his chair, Silas Veliant, the King of Maridrina, smiled, waited for his taster to nod, then took a long mouthful of wine. All of them mirrored the motion, but Lara barely tasted the crimson liquid as it crossed her tongue.

"You are my most prized of possessions," he said, waving his glass to encompass them all. "Of the twenty of my progeny who were brought here, you are all that survive. That you do, that you *thrive*, is an achievement, for the training you've received would've been a test for the best of men. And you are not men."

It was only that very training that kept Lara from narrowing her eyes. From showing any emotion at all.

"All of you were brought here so that I might determine which of you is best. Which of you will be my knife in the dark. Which of you will become Queen of Ithicana." His eyes had all the compassion of one of the scorpions in the desert. "Which of you will fracture Ithicana's defenses, and, in doing so, allow Maridrina to return to its former glory."

Lara nodded once, all of her sisters doing the same. There was no anticipation. At least, not for their father's choice. It had been made days ago, and Marylyn sat at the opposite end of the table, her golden hair braided like a crown at her brow, her dress lamé to match. Marylyn had been the obvious choice, brilliant, gracious, beautiful as the sunrise—and as alluring as the sunset.

No, the anticipation was for what would come next. The choice had been made as to who would be offered to the crown prince—king, now—of the Kingdom of Ithicana. What remained unknown was what would become of the rest of them. They were of royal blood, and that made them worth something.

All the sisters, Marylyn included, had gathered close on a pile of pillows the last two nights, each of them speculating as to their fates. To whom of the King's viziers might they be wed. To which other realms might they be offered as brides. Neither the man nor the kingdom mattered. What every girl cared about was that it would be freedom from this place.

But all those long nights, Lara had rested on the outskirts, offering nothing, using the time to watch her sisters. To love them. To remember how she had fought each of them as often as she had hugged them tight. Their smiles. Their eyes. The way, even past childhood, they nestled together like a pile of puppies newly away from their mother.

Because Lara knew what the others did not: that their father intended for only *one* sister to leave the compound. And that would be the future Queen of Ithicana.

A salad garnished with cheese and vibrant fruit was placed before her, and Lara ate mechanically. *You will live, you will live, you will live*, she chanted to herself.

"For as long as memory, Ithicana has placed a stranglehold on trade, making kingdoms and breaking them like it were some dark god." Her father addressed them, his eyes flaring bright. "My father, and his father, and his father before him all sought to break the Bridge Kingdom. With assassins, with war, with blockades, with every tool at their disposal. But not one of them thought to use a woman."

He smiled slyly. "Maridrinian women are soft. They are weak. They are good for nothing more than keeping house and raising children. Except for you twelve."

Lara didn't blink. None of her sisters did, and she wondered for a breath whether he realized that every one of them was considering stabbing him in the heart over the insult of his words. He should know well that every one of them was capable of doing it.

Her father continued, "Fifteen years ago, the King of Ithicana demanded a bride for his son and heir as tribute. As *payment*." His lip curled up in a sneer. "The bastard is a year dead, but his son has called in his due. And Maridrina is ready." His eyes went to Marylyn, then to the servants moving to clear the salad plates.

In the shadows of the growing night, Lara sensed movement. Felt the presence of the mass of soldiers her father had brought with him. The servants reappeared with steaming bowls of soup, the scent of cinnamon and leeks drifting ahead of them.

"Ithicana's greed, its hubris, its contempt for *you*, will be its downfall."

Lara allowed her eyes to leave her father's face, taking in each one of her sisters. With all their training, all their knowledge of his plans, he never intended for any of them, save his chosen one, to live an hour past this dinner.

The soups were placed before them, and every one of her sisters waited for their father's taster to take the first mouthful and nod. Then they picked up their spoons and dutifully began to eat.

Lara did the same.

Their father believed that brilliance and beauty were the most important attributes in the daughter he'd select. That she be the girl who'd shown the most acumen for combat and strategy. The girl who'd shown the most talent in the arts of the bedroom. He'd thought he'd known which traits mattered most—but he'd forgotten one.

Sarhina stiffened next to her.

*I'm sorry,* Lara silently whispered to her sisters.

Then Sarhina's body began to spasm.

*I pray that you'll all find the freedom you deserve.*

The soupspoon in Sarhina's hand went flying across the table, but none of the other girls noticed. None of them cared. Because all of them were choking, foam rising to their lips as they twitched and gasped, one by one falling forward or backward or to the side. Then all of them were resting motionless.

Lara set her spoon next to her empty bowl, looking once to Marylyn, who was facedown in her dish. Rising, she rounded the table, lifting her sister's head from the bowl and carefully cleaning away the soup before resting Marylyn's cheek against the table. When Lara looked up again, her father was pale and on his feet, sword half drawn. The soldiers who'd been lurking in the wings rushed forward, corralling the panicked servants into place. But everyone, *everyone*, was staring at her.

"You were mistaken in your choice, Father." Lara stood tall as she addressed her king. She stared him down, allowing the dark, grasping, and selfish part of her soul to climb to the surface and stare out at him. "*I* will be the next Queen of Ithicana. And I will bring the Bridge Kingdom to its knees."

# 2
# LARA

LARA HAD KNOWN what would come next, but it seemed to happen so very quickly. And yet she was certain every detail would be burned into her mind until the day she died. Her father slammed his sword back into its sheath, then reached down to press his fingers against the throat of the nearest girl, holding them there for several moments while Lara watched impassively. Then he nodded once at the soldiers surrounding them.

The men who'd been intended to dispatch Lara and her sisters turned their swords instead on the servants, whose tongueless mouths uttered wordless screams as they tried to flee the massacre. The musicians were cut down, as were the cooks in the distant kitchens and the maids turning down sheets on beds that would never be slept in again. Soon, all who remained were the king's loyal cadre of soldiers, their hands coated with the blood of their victims.

Through this, Lara remained still. Only the knowledge that she was the sole remaining daughter—that she was the last horse *left* to bet on—kept her from fighting her way free of the carnage and fleeing into the desert beyond.

Erik, the Master of Arms, approached through the palms, blade glistening in his hand. His eyes went from Lara to her sisters' still forms, and he gave her a sad smile. "I'm not surprised to find you still standing, little cockroach."

It was the endearment he'd bestowed upon her when she'd arrived, five years old and barely alive, thanks to a sandstorm that had befallen her party on their trek to the compound. "Ice and fire might ravage the world, but still the cockroach survives," he'd said. "Just like you."

Cockroach she might be, but that she still breathed was thanks to him. Erik had dispatched her to the training yard as punishment for a minor transgression two nights prior, and she'd overheard members of her father's cadre plotting the deaths of her and her sisters. A conversation led by Erik himself. Her eyes burned as she regarded him—the man who'd been more a father to her than the silver-haired monarch to her right—but she said nothing, gave him not so much as a smile in return.

"Is it done?" her father asked.

Erik nodded. "All have been silenced, Your Majesty. Save myself." Then his eyes flicked to the shadows not touched by the table's lamps. "And the *Magpie*."

From those shadows stepped her Master of Intrigue, and Lara coolly regarded the wisp of a man who had orchestrated every aspect of the evening.

And in the nasal voice she'd always loathed, the Magpie said, "The girl did most of the dirty work for you."

"Lara should have been your choice all along." Erik's voice was toneless, but grief filled his eyes as they passed over the fallen girls before returning to Lara's face.

Lara wanted to reach for her knife—how *dare* he grieve them when he'd done nothing to save them—but a thousand hours of training commanded her not to move. He bowed low to his king. "For Maridrina." Then he pulled his knife across his own throat.

Lara clenched her teeth, the contents of her stomach rising, bitter and foul and full of the same poison she'd given her sisters. Yet she didn't look away, forcing herself to watch as Erik slumped to the ground, blood pulsing from his throat in great gouts until his heart went still.

The Magpie stepped around the pool of blood and coming fully into the light. "Such dramatics."

Magpie wasn't his real name, of course. It was Serin, and of all the men and women who'd trained the sisters over the years, he was the only one who'd come and gone from the compound at his leisure, managing the king's network of spies and plots.

"He was a good man. A loyal subject." There was no inflection in her father's voice, and Lara wondered if he meant the words, or if they were for the benefit of the soldiers watching the proceedings. Even the most stalwart loyalty had its limits, and her father was no fool.

The Magpie's narrow eyes turned on her. "Lara, as you know, Majesty, was not my first choice. She scored close to the bottom in nearly all things, with the lone exception of combat. Her temper continually gets the better of her. Marylyn"—he gestured to her sister—"was the obvious choice. Brilliant and beautiful. Masterfully in control of her emotions, as she *clearly* demonstrated over the past several days." He made a noise of disgust.

Everything he said about Marylyn was true, but it wasn't the sum of her. Unbidden, memories flooded through Lara's mind. Visions of her sister carefully caring for a runt kitten, which was now the fattest cat in the compound. Of how she'd listen quietly to any of her sisters' troubles, then offer the most perfect advice. Of how, as a child, she'd given names to all the servants, because she'd thought it cruel that they should have none. Then the visions cleared, leaving only a still body before her, golden hair crusted with soup.

"My sister was too kind." Lara turned her head back to her father, her heart skittering in her chest even as she challenged him. "The future Queen of Ithicana must seduce its ruler. Make him believe she is guileless and sincere. She must make him trust her even as she uses her position to learn his every weakness right up to the moment she betrays him. Marylyn was not that woman."

Her father's eyes were unblinking as he studied her, and he gave the faintest nod of approval. "But you are?"

"I am." Her pulse roared in her ears, her skin clammy despite the heat.

"You are not often wrong, Serin," her father said. "But in this, I believe you were mistaken and fate has intervened in order to rectify that mistake."

The Master of Intrigue stiffened, and Lara wondered if he was now realizing that his own life hung in the balance. "As you say, Majesty. It seems Lara possesses a quality that I'd not considered in my testing."

"The most important quality of all: ruthlessness." The king studied her for a moment before turning back to the Magpie. "Ready the caravan. We ride for Ithicana tonight." Then he smiled at her as though she were the most precious of things. "It's time for my daughter to meet her future husband."

# 3
# LARA

FLAMES LICKED THE night sky as the group departed, but Lara only risked one backward glance at the burning compound that had been her home, the blood-spattered floors and walls blackening as the fire consumed all evidence of a plot fifteen years in the making. Only the heart of the oasis, where the dinner table sat encircled by the spring, would remain untouched.

It was still almost more than she could bear to leave her slumbering sisters surrounded by a ring of fire, unconscious and helpless until the concoction of narcotics she'd given them wore off. Already their pulses, which had been slowed to near death for a dangerous length of time, should be quickening, their breathing obvious to anyone who looked closely. If Lara found excuses to linger to ensure their safety, she would only risk discovery, and then all of this would be for naught.

"Don't burn them. Leave them for the scavengers to pick their bones clean," she'd told her father, her stomach twisting into knots until he'd laughed and acceded to her macabre request, leaving her sisters slumped over the table, the slaughtered servants forming a gory perimeter around them.

That was what her sisters would wake to: fire and death. For only if their father believed them silenced did they have any chance at a future. She would carry their mission forward while her sisters made their own lives, now free to be masters of their own fates. She'd explained all of it in the note she'd slipped into Sarhina's pocket while her father ordered the compound swept for survivors. For no one must be left alive who might whisper a word about the deception that now journeyed toward a wedding in Ithicana.

Their journey across the Red Desert would be fraught with hardship and peril. But at that precise moment, Lara was convinced the worst part would be listening to the *Magpie's* chatter the entire way. Lara's mare was laden with Marylyn's trousseau, while she was forced to ride pillion behind the Master of Intrigue.

"From this moment forward, you must be the perfect Maridrinian lady," he instructed, his voice grinding on her nerves. "We cannot risk anyone seeing you behave otherwise, not even those His Majesty believes loyal." He cast a meaningful glance toward her father's guards, who'd formed the caravan with practiced ease.

Not a single one looked at her.

They did not know what she was. What she'd been trained to do. What her purpose was beyond the fulfillment of a contract with the enemy kingdom. But every one of them believed she'd murdered her sisters in cold blood. Which made her wonder how long her father would let them live.

"How did you do it?"

Hours into their journey, the Magpie's question pulled Lara from her thoughts, and she tightened her white silk scarf across her face, despite the fact his back was to her. "Poison." She allowed a hint of tartness to enter her voice.

He snorted. "Aren't we bold now that we believe we are untouchable."

She ran her tongue over her dry lips, feeling the heat of the sun rising behind them. Then she allowed herself to slip into the pool of calm her Master of Meditation had taught her to employ when strategizing, among other things. "I poisoned the soupspoons."

"How? You didn't know where you'd be seated."

"I poisoned all, save those set at the head of the table."

The Magpie was silent.

Lara continued, "I've been taking small doses of several poisons for years to build up my tolerance." Even still, she had purged herself the moment she'd had a chance, vomiting again and again until her stomach was dry, then taking the antidote, the dizzying malaise the only lingering sign she'd ingested a narcotic at all.

The Master of Intrigue's tiny frame tensed. "What if the settings had been altered? You might have killed the king."

"She clearly believed it worth the risk."

Lara tilted her head, having noted the jingle of bells on the horse's bridle as her father had ridden up behind, the creature festooned with silver rather than the tin the guards' mounts wore.

"You guessed that I intended to kill the girls I didn't need," he said. "But instead of warning your sisters or attempting to escape, you murdered them to take the chosen's place. Why?"

Because for the girls to fight their way out would've meant a lifetime on the run. Faking their deaths had been the only way. "I may have spent my life in isolation, Father, but the tutors you selected educated me well. I know the hardship that our people endure beneath Ithicana's yoke on trade. Our enemy needs to be brought low, and of my sisters, I was the only one capable of doing it."

"You murdered your sisters for the good of our country?" His voice was amused.

Lara forced a dry chuckle from her lips. "Hardly. I murdered them because I wished to live."

"You gambled with the king's life in order to save your own skin?" Serin turned to look at her, his expression green. He'd trained her, which meant it was within the king's right to blame him for all that she had done. And her father was known to be merciless.

But the King of Maridrina only laughed with delight. "Gambled and *won*." Reaching over, he pushed aside Lara's scarf to cup her cheek. "King Aren won't see you coming until it's far too late. A black widow in his bed."

King Aren of Ithicana. Aren, her soon-to-be husband.

Lara only vaguely heard her father give the order to his guards to make camp, the group intending to sleep through the heat of the day.

One of the guards lifted her off the back of Serin's camel, and she sat on a blanket while the men set up the camp, using the time to think of what was to come.

Lara knew as much as—probably more than—most Maridrinians did about Ithicana. It was a kingdom as shrouded in mystery as it was in mist: a series of islands stretching between two continents, the land masses guarded by violent seas made more treacherous by defenses the Ithicanians had placed in the waters to ward off infiltrators. But that was not what made Ithicana so powerful. It was the bridge stretching above and between those islands—the only safe way to travel between the continents ten months out of the year. And Ithicana used its asset to keep the kingdoms who depended on trade hungry. Desperate. And most of all, willing to pay any price the Bridge Kingdom demanded for its services.

Seeing her tent was erected, Lara waited until the men had placed her bags inside before slipping into the welcome shade, curbing the urge to thank them as she passed.

She was alone for barely the length of time it took to remove her scarf before her father ducked inside, Serin on his heels. "I'll have to begin training you on the codes now," the Master of Intrigue said, waiting until the king was sitting before ensconcing himself in front of Lara. "Marylyn created this code, and I daresay that teaching it to *you* in such a short time will be a challenge."

"Marylyn is dead," she replied, taking a mouthful of tepid water from her canteen before carefully closing it again.

"Don't remind me," he snapped.

Her smile was filled with a confidence she didn't feel. "Come to terms with the fact that *I* am all who remains of the girls you trained, and then I will not need to refresh your memory."

"Begin," her father commanded, and then he closed his eyes, his presence in her tent for propriety's sake, only.

Serin began his instruction on the code. It needed to be entirely committed to memory, as she couldn't bring notes into Ithicana. It was a code she might never even use, its usefulness entirely predicated on the King of Ithicana allowing her the kindness of corresponding with her family. And kindness, she'd been told, was not an attribute the man was known for.

"As you know, the Ithicanians are exemplary codebreakers, and anything you manage to send out will be subject to intense scrutiny. There's every chance they'll break this one."

Lara held up her hand, ticking off her fingers as she spoke. "I should expect to be completely isolated, from both the Ithicanians and from the outside world. I may or may not be allowed to correspond, and even if I am, there is every chance our code will be broken. There is no way for you to reach me to retrieve a message. No way for me to send something through their people, because you've yet to swing the loyalties of a single one." She balled her hand into a fist. "Other than escaping, which means an end to my ability to spy, just how do you expect me to convey the information to you?"

"If this were an easy task, we'd have accomplished it already." Serin extracted a heavy piece of parchment from his satchel. "There is only one Ithicanian who corresponds with the outside world, and that is King Aren himself."

Taking the parchment, which was embossed with Ithicana's crest of the curving bridge, the edges trimmed with gilt, she examined the precise script, which requested that Maridrina deliver a princess to be his bride in accordance of the terms of the Fifteen Year Treaty, as well as an invitation to negotiate new terms of trade between the kingdoms. "You want me to hide a message within one of his?"

He nodded, handing her a jar of clear liquid. *Invisible ink.* "We'll attempt to entice messages from him to give you the opportunity, but he's not prone to frequent correspondence. For that reason, we should return to studying your sister's code."

The lesson was tedious work and Lara was exhausted. It took all her self-control not to sigh with relief when Serin finally departed to his own tent.

Her father rose, yawning.

"Might I ask a question, Your Majesty?" she asked before he could depart.

At his nod, she licked her lips. "Have you seen him? The new

King of Ithicana?"

"No one has seen him. They wear masks, always, when meeting with outsiders." Then her father shook his head. "But I have met him, once. Years ago, when he was only a child."

Lara waited, her palms soaking the silk of her skirts beneath them.

"He is rumored to be even more ruthless than his father before him. A harsh man, who shows no mercy to outsiders." His gaze met hers, and the uncharacteristic pity in his eyes made her hands turn to ice. "I feel he will treat you cruelly, Lara."

"I have been trained to endure pain." Pain and starvation and solitude. Everything that she could possibly face in Ithicana. Taught to endure it and remain true to her mission.

"It may not come in the form of pain, as you understand it." Her father took her hand and turned it over to reveal her palm, studying it. "Be wary most of all of their kindness, Lara. For above all, the Ithicanians are cunning. And their king will give up nothing without demanding his due."

Her heart skipped.

"The heart of our kingdom is caught between the Red Desert and the Tempest Seas, with Ithicana's bridge the only safe route beyond," he continued. "Neither desert nor sea bends to any master, and Ithicana . . . They'd see our people impoverished, starved, and broken before they'd ever allow trade to flow freely." He dropped her hand. "For generations, we've tried everything to make them see reason. To make them see the harm their greed causes the innocent people of our lands. But the Ithicanians are not men, Lara. They are demons hiding in human form. Which I'm afraid you'll find out soon enough."

Watching her father depart the tent, Lara flexed her hands, wanting to wrap them around weapons. To strike out. To maim. To kill.

Not because of his words.

Dire as her father's warning was, it was one she'd heard countless times before. No, it was the slump of his shoulders. The resignation in his tone. The hopelessness that briefly showed itself in his eyes. All signs that despite everything her father had put into this gambit, he didn't truly believe she'd succeed in her mission. As much as Lara detested being underestimated, she hated those who mattered to her being harmed even more. And with her sisters now free of their shackles, nothing mattered to her more than Maridrina.

Ithicana would pay for its crimes against her people, and by the time she was through with its king, he'd do more than *bend.*

He'd bleed.

Another four nights of travel north saw the red sand dunes giving way to rolling hills covered with dry brush and stubby trees, then craggy mountains that seemed to touch the sky. They followed narrow ravines, and slowly, the climate began to shift, the endless brown dirt broken by patches of green and the occasional brilliant bloom of flowers. The dried creek bed they followed turned muddy, and several hours later, the caravan was splashing through sluggish water, but beyond that, the earth was bone dry. Harsh and seemingly unlivable.

Men, women, and children stopped working in their fields to shield their eyes, watching the group pass. They were all skinny, wearing threadbare homespun clothes and wide-brimmed straw hats that shielded them from the ceaseless sun. They survived on the sparse crops and boney cattle they raised; there was no other choice for them. While, in prior generations, families were able to earn enough at their trades to purchase meat and grain imported from Harendell through the bridge, Ithicana's rising taxes and tolls had changed that. Now only the wealthy could afford the goods, and the working class of Maridrina had been forced to abandon their trades for these dry fields in order to feed their children.

*Barely feed them,* Lara amended, her chest clenched tight as the children ran to line the caravan route, their ribs visibly protruding from beneath their tattered clothes.

"God bless His Majesty," they shouted. "God bless the Princess!" Little girls ran alongside Serin's camel, reaching up to hand her braids of wildflowers, which Lara draped across her shoulders, then across the saddle when they grew too many.

Serin gave her a sack of silver coins to disperse, and it was a struggle to keep her fingers steady as she pressed them into tiny hands.

They learned her name soon enough, and as the muddy creek turned to crystal rapids racing down the slopes toward the sea, they shouted, "Bless Princess Lara! Watch over our beautiful princess!" But it was a growing chant of "Bless Lara, Maridrina's Martyr" that turned her hands cold. That kept her awake long after Serin had finished his lessons each evening, then filled her head with nightmares when sleep finally took her. Dreams where she was trapped by taunting demons, where all her skills had failed her, where no matter what she did, she could not get free. Dreams where Maridrina burned.

And every day, they traveled closer.

As the earth turned lush and moist, the caravan was joined by a larger contingent of soldiers, and Lara was moved from the camel to a blue carriage pulled by a team of white horses, their trappings decorated with the same silver coins as her father's horse. And with the soldiers came a whole retinue of servants tending to Lara's every need, washing and scrubbing and polishing her as they traveled to Maridrina's capital city of Vencia.

Their whispers filtered through her tent walls: that her father had kept the future bride of Ithicana hidden in the desert all these long years for her own safety. That she was a treasured daughter, born of a favored wife, hand-selected by him to unite the two kingdoms in peace, her charm and grace destined to see Ithicana grant Maridrina all the benefits an ally should have, which would allow the kingdom to thrive once more.

The very idea that Ithicana would concede so much was laughable, but Lara felt no amusement at their naiveté. Not as she took in the desperate hope in their eyes. Instead, she carefully stoked her fury, hiding it beneath gentle smiles and graceful waves from the open window of the carriage. It was a strength she needed, given that she'd heard the other whispers, too. "Pity the poor gentle princess," the servants said with sorrow in their eyes. "What will become of her amongst those demons? How will she survive their brutality?"

"Are you afraid?" Her father pulled the carriage curtains closed as they approached the outskirts of Vencia, much to Lara's dismay. It was the city of her birth, and she hadn't seen it since she'd been taken from the confines of the harem and brought to the compound to begin her training at the age of five.

She turned to him. "I'd be a fool not to be afraid. If they discover I'm a spy, they'll kill me and then cancel the trade concessions for spite."

Her father made a noise of agreement, then pulled two knives encrusted with Maridrinian rubies from beneath his coat, handing them to her. Lara recognized them as the ceremonial weapons that Maridrinian women wore to indicate they were wed. They were supposed to be used by a husband in the defense of his wife's honor, but typically they were kept dull. Decorative. Useless.

"They're lovely. Thank you."

He chuckled. "Look more closely."

Pulling them from their sheaths, Lara tested the edges and found them keen, but the balance was off. Then her father reached over and pressed one of the jewels, and the gold casement fell away to reveal a throwing knife.

Lara smiled.

"If they won't allow you to communicate with the outside world, you'll need to bide your time while you learn their secrets, then escape. Perhaps even fight your way free and return to us with what you've learned."

She nodded, flipping the blades back and forth to get the feel of them. There was no chance of her willingly returning to hand-deliver her invasion strategy. To do so would be a death wish.

After learning her father's intention to kill her and her sisters at the dinner, Lara had had time to consider why her father wanted the daughters not destined to be queen dead. It was more than a desire to keep his plot a secret until he'd succeeded in taking the bridge. Her father wanted this plot kept secret *forever*, for if anyone learned of it, his ability to use his other living children as negotiating tools would be negated. No one would ever trust him. Just like he'd never trust her. Which meant if Lara ever returned, successful or not, she too would be silenced.

Her father interrupted her thoughts. "I was there when you girls had your first kills," he said. "Did you know?"

The blades stilled in her hands as Lara remembered. She and her sisters had been sixteen when the line of chained men had been brought to the compound under Serin's watchful eye. They were raiders from Valcotta who'd been captured and brought to test the mettle of Maridrina's warrior princesses. *Kill or be killed*, Master Erik had told them as they were pushed one by one into the fighting yard. Some of her sisters had hesitated and fallen beneath the raider's desperate blows. Lara had not. She would never forget the meaty *thunk* her blade made as it sank into her opponent's throat from across the yard. The way he stared at her in astonishment before slowly collapsing onto the sand, his lifeblood pooling around him.

"I didn't know," she said.

"Knives, as I recall, are your specialty."

*Killing was her specialty.*

The carriage was rumbling over cobbled streets, the horses' hooves making sharp little sounds against the stone. Outside, Lara heard intermittent cheers, and flicking aside the curtain, she tried to smile at the filthy men and women lining the streets, their faces pale from hunger and illness. Worse were the children among them, eyes dull and hopeless, flies buzzing near their eyes and mouths.

"Why don't you do something for them?" she demanded of her father, whose face was expressionless as he stared out the window.

He turned his azure eyes on her. "Why else do you think I created you?" Then he reached into his pocket and gave her a handful of silver to toss from the window, which she did. She closed her eyes as her impoverished people fought each other for the gleaming metal. She would save them. She would wrest the bridge from Ithicana's control, and no Maridrinian would go hungry again.

The horses slowed, making their way down the steep switchbacking streets to the harbor below. Where the ship waited to take her to Ithicana.

She tugged aside the curtain to get her first look at the sea, the scent of fish and brine on the air. There were whitecaps on the water, the rise and fall of the waves stealing her attention as her father plucked the knives from her hands to be returned when the time was right.

The carriage pulled through a market that appeared nearly devoid of life, the stalls empty. "Where is everyone?" she asked.

Her father's face was dark and unreadable. "Waiting for you to open the gates to Ithicana."

The carriage rolled into the harbor, then came to a stop. There was no ceremony as her father helped her out. The ship awaiting them flew a flag of azure and silver. Maridrina's colors.

He led her swiftly down the dock and up a gangplank onto the ship. "The crossing to Southwatch takes less than an hour. There are servants waiting to prepare you below."

Lara cast one backward glance at Vencia, at the sun burning hot and bright above it, then turned her sights on the clouds and mist and darkness that lay across the narrow strait before her. One kingdom to save. One kingdom to destroy.

# 4
# LARA

LARA STOOD ON the ship's deck, which lurched and bucked like a wild horse, digging her fingernails into the railing, fighting to keep the contents of her stomach from spilling out into the sea. To make matters worse, raised in the desert, she had never learned to swim—a weakness that had already begun to haunt her. Every time the ship heeled over in the heavy wind, her breath caught with the certainty they'd capsize and drown. The only things that distracted her from visions of waves closing over her head were the more certain dangers facing her.

By tonight, she'd be married. She'd be alone in a foreign kingdom with a reputation for the worst sort of cruelty. The wife of a young man who was lord over it all. *This* was the life she'd been protecting her sisters from, at the sacrifice of her own, and all of it for the sake of her people. But now the consequences of that choice were terrifyingly imminent. Clouds hung low over the white-capped sea, shifting and moving like sentient beasts, but through them, ever so faintly, she could make out the shadow of an island. *Ithicana.*

Her father joined her at the railing. "Southwatch."

His travel-stained clothing had been replaced with a pristine white shirt and black coat, his polished sword hanging from a belt decorated with silver and turquoise disks. "Aren keeps a full garrison of soldiers there at all times, and they have catapults and other war machines trained on the ocean, ready to sink any who'd attempt to take the island. There are spikes set into the seafloor to spear any ship that manages to approach any point other than the pier, which is itself rigged with explosives should they feel it has been compromised. The bridge cannot be taken at its mouth." His jaw tightened. "It's been tried and tried."

Countless ships and thousands of men lost for every attempt. Lara knew the history of the war that had ended fifteen years ago with Ithicana triumphant, but the specifics rose and fell in her mind like the waves on which the ship rode. Her knees were shaky, her whole body weak with seasickness.

"You are the hope of our people, Lara. We need that bridge."

She was afraid if she opened her mouth, she'd spill whatever remained in her stomach overboard, so she only nodded once. The island was in full view now, twin peaks of stone festooned with lush vegetation rising out of the sea. At their base was a lone pier crusted with armaments, a cluster of unadorned stone buildings, and beyond, a single road leading up to the yawning mouth of the bridge itself.

Her father's sleeve brushed her wrist. "Don't for a heartbeat believe that I trust you," he murmured, stealing back her attention. "I saw what you did to your sisters, and while you might claim to have Maridrina foremost in your heart, I know you were motivated by the desire to save your own life."

If saving her own life had been what she'd cared about, she would have faked her own death. But Lara said nothing.

"While your ruthlessness makes you desirable for this role, your lack of honor makes me question whether you'll put our people's lives above your own." Grabbing her arms, he twisted her toward him, nothing on his face betraying that this was anything more than a conversation between a loving father and his daughter. "If you betray me, I will hunt you down. And what I will do to you will make you wish that you'd died alongside your sisters."

The sound of steel drums danced across the sea and into her ears, punctuated by the distant grumble of thunder.

"And what if I succeed?" Her mouth tasted sour, and she turned her head away, taking in the hundreds of figures on the island waiting for the ship. Waiting for her.

"You'll be the savior of Maridrina. You'll be rewarded beyond your wildest dreams."

"I want my freedom." Her tongue felt strangely thick as she spoke. "I want to be left alone, to my devices. Free to go wherever I choose, to do as I will."

One silver eyebrow rose. "How different you and Marylyn are."

"*Were*."

He inclined his head. "Even so."

"Do we have an agreement then? The bridge in exchange for my freedom?"

His nod was punctuated by a loud boom of thunder. It was a lie, and she knew it. But she could live with his lies because their goals were aligned.

"Drop sails," the captain of the ship bellowed, and Lara gripped the rail as they lost momentum, the sailors running about to make ready to land. The drums continued their beat, pace escalating along with Lara's heart as the ship drifted against the empty pier, sailors leaping the gap to tie off the ship.

The gangplank was lowered, and her father took her arm, leading her toward it. The drumming intensified.

"You have one year." He stepped onto the solid stone of the pier. "Do not falter. Do not fail."

Lara hesitated, dizzy, and, for the first time since the night she'd freed her sisters from their dark fate, desperately afraid. Then she took her first step into the world that was now her new home.

The drums let out a thundering beat, then went still. Holding tight to her father's arm, Lara walked up the pier, biting back a gasp as she took in the masked Ithicanians for the first time.

Their steel helmets were sculpted like raging beasts with mouths full of snarling teeth and brows bearing curved horns. She could see nothing of the men beneath except their eyes, which seemed to glitter with malice as they watched her pass, hands on swords and pikes. No one spoke; the only sounds were the whistle of the wind between the two towers of rock and the call of the storm beyond.

Tearing her eyes from the soldiers, Lara's gaze went down the paved road rising up to the gaping mouth of Ithicana's bridge. It was enclosed like a tunnel, maybe a dozen feet wide and equally as tall, made of a grey stone gone green with exposure to the damp air. A great steel portcullis was raised, the entirety of the bridge's mouth framed by a guardhouse.

A figure stepped out of the dark opening, the steel spikes of the portcullis hanging above him like fangs, and Lara felt her stomach lurch.

*The King of Ithicana.*

Dressed in trousers, heavy boots, and a tunic of drab greenish gray, he was tall and broad of shoulder. Her training told her that he was as much a soldier as any of those lining the road. But those details were lost, her heart beating staccato, as she took in the helmet that concealed his face. It had a snout like a lion's, open to reveal glittering canines, and horns like a bull sprouting from both temples.

Not a man, a demon.

The lingering dizziness from the voyage passed over her in waves, and with it came fear that possessed her like an angry spirit. The heel of her sandal slid on the stone, and Lara stumbled against her father, the ground feeling as though it were moving beneath her like the rocking ship.

*This had been a mistake. A terrible, horrible mistake.*

When only a handful of paces stood between them, her father stopped and turned to her. In his free hand was a jeweled belt with her camouflaged throwing knives hooked on either side. He wrapped it around the waist of her sodden gown, fastening the buckle. Then he kissed both her cheeks before turning back to Ithicana's king. "As was agreed upon, I stand here to offer my most precious daughter, Lara, as a symbol of Maridrina's commitment to its continued alliance with Ithicana. May there ever be peace between our kingdoms."

The King of Ithicana nodded once, and her father gave Lara a gentle shove between the shoulders. With halting steps, she walked toward the king, and as she did, a bolt of lightning lanced through the air, the flash making the visage of his helmet seem to move, like it wasn't metal, but flesh.

The drums resumed, a steady and harsh beat: Ithicana incarnate. The king reached out one hand, and though every instinct told her to turn and run, Lara took it.

For reasons she couldn't articulate, she'd expected it to be cold like metal, and equally unyielding—but it was warm. Long fingers curved around hers, the nails cut short. His palm was calloused, the skin, like hers, covered with tiny white scars. The nicks and cuts that couldn't be avoided when combat was one's way of life. She stared at that hand. It offered some strange comfort; what stood before her was nothing more than a man.

And men could be defeated.

A priestess approached on her left and tied an azure ribbon around their hands, binding them together before belting out the Maridrinian marriage vows so that all could hear over the growing storm. Vows of obedience on her part. Vows to create a hundred sons on his. Lara could've sworn she heard a soft snort of amusement from behind the king's helmet.

But as the priestess raised her hands to proclaim them man and wife, he spoke for the first time. "Not yet."

Waving away the startled priestess, he shook loose the ribbon that Lara was supposed to have worn braided into her hair for the first year of their marriage. The silk flew off toward the sea. One of his helmeted soldiers stepped out of the ranks, coming up to stand before them.

He shouted, "Do you, Aren Kertell, King of Ithicana, swear to fight by this woman's side, to defend her to your dying breath, to cherish her body and none other, and to be loyal to her as long as you both live?"

"I do." The king's words were punctuated by the hammer of a hundred swords and spears against shields, and Lara twitched.

But the shock of the noise was nothing compared to what she felt when the soldier turned to her and said, "Do you, Lara Veliant, Princess of Maridrina, swear to fight by this man's side, to defend him to your dying breath, to cherish his body and none other, and to be loyal to him as long as you both live?"

She blinked. And because there was nothing else for her to say, she whispered, "I do."

Nodding, the soldier pulled out a knife. "Now don't be a baby about this, Majesty," he muttered, and the king answered with a tense chuckle before holding out his hand.

The soldier sliced the knife across the king's palm, then before Lara could pull away, he grabbed her arm and ran the knife across her hand as well. She saw the blood well up before she felt the sting. The soldier pressed their palms together, the King of Ithicana's hot blood mixing with hers before running down their entwined fingers.

The soldier jerked their hands up, almost lifting Lara off her feet. "Behold, the King and Queen of Ithicana."

As if to punctuate his words, the storm finally fell upon them with a resounding clap of thunder that made the ground shudder. The drums took up their frenzied pace, and the King of Ithicana pulled their hands out of the soldier's grip, lowering his arm so Lara wasn't on her tiptoes. "I suggest you board your ship, Your Grace," he said to Lara's father. "This storm will chase you home as it is."

"You could always offer your hospitality," her father responded, and Lara's attention flicked from him to Serin, who stood with the rest of the Maridrinians beyond. "We are, after all, family now."

The King of Ithicana laughed. "One step at a time, Silas. One step at time." He turned and gently tugged Lara into the depths of the bridge, the portcullis rattling its way down behind them. She had only the opportunity for a brief glance back over her shoulder at her father, his expression blank and unreadable. But beyond, Serin met her gaze, inclining his head once in a slow nod before she was pulled out of sight.

It was dark inside, smelling faintly of animal dung and sweat. None of the Ithicanians removed their helmets, but even with their faces concealed, Lara felt their scrutiny.

"Welcome to Ithicana," the king—her husband—said. "I'm sorry to have to do this."

Lara saw him lift a hand holding a vial. She could've dodged it. She could have taken him down with a single blow, fought her way free of his soldiers. But she couldn't let him know that. Instead, she gave him a doe-eyed look of shock as he held it up to her nose, the world spinning around her, darkness rushing in. Her knees buckled and she felt strong arms catch her before she hit the ground. The last thing she heard before she faded from consciousness was the king's resigned voice: "What have I gotten myself into with you?"

# 5
# AREN

AREN, THE THIRTY-SEVENTH ruler of Ithicana, lay on his back, staring up at the soot stains on the roof of the barracks. His helmet rested next to his left hand and, as he turned his head to regard the monstrous steel thing he'd inherited along with his title, he decided that whichever one of his ancestors had come up with the idea of the helmets had been both a genius and a sadist. Genius, because the things put fear in the hearts of Ithicana's enemies. Sadist, because wearing it was like having his head stuffed in a cooking pot that smelled of sweaty socks.

His twin sister's face appeared in his line of sight, her expression amused. "Nana has examined her. Says she's shockingly fit, most certainly healthy, and, barring tragedy, likely to live a goodly long while."

Aren blinked once.

"Disappointed?" Ahnna asked.

Rolling onto one elbow, Aren sat upright on the bench. "Contrary to the opinions of our neighboring kingdoms, I'm not actually so depraved as to wish death upon an innocent girl."

"Are you so sure she's innocent?"

"Are you arguing that she's not?"

Ahnna scrunched up her face, then shook her head. "In true Maridrinian fashion, they've given you a beautiful and sheltered shrinking violet. Good to look at and not much else."

Remembering how the young woman had shaken as she'd walked up the pier, holding tightly to her father's arm, her enormous blue eyes filled with terror, Aren was inclined to agree with his sister's assessment. Yet even so, he fully intended to keep Lara isolated until he could get a grasp on her true nature. And learn exactly where her loyalties lay.

"Have our spies learned anything more about her?"

Ahnna shook her head. "Nothing. He appears to have kept her hidden away in the desert, and until she rode out of the red sands, not even the Maridrinians knew her name."

"Why all the secrecy?"

"They say it was for her protection. Not everyone is pleased about our alliance with Maridrina, Valcotta most of all."

Aren frowned, dissatisfied with the answer, though he could not say why. Maridrina and Valcotta were continually at war over the fertile stretch of land running down the western coast of the southern continent, the border contested by both kingdoms. It was possible the Valcottan Empress might have attempted to disrupt the alliance by assassinating the princess, but he thought it unlikely. For one, Silas Veliant had more daughters than he knew what to do with, and the treaty had not been specific about which girl would be sent. Two, every kingdom north and south knew that Aren's marriage to a Maridrinian princess was nothing more than a symbolic act, all parties involved more interested in the trade terms underpinning the agreement and the peace they purchased. The treaty would have endured even if the princess had not.

But third, and what troubled him most of all, was that it wasn't Maridrinian nature to *hide* from anyone. If anything, Silas would have relished the assassination of a daughter or two because it would renew the flagging support of his people for the war against Valcotta.

"She awake yet?"

"No. I came down as soon as Nana deemed her a fit and healthy wife for you, because I wanted to be the one to share the wonderful news."

His twin's voice dripped with sarcasm, and Aren shot her a warning look. "*Lara* is your queen now. Perhaps try showing her a little respect."

Ahnna responded by flipping him her middle finger. "What are you going to *do* with Queen Lara?"

"With tits like that, I'd suggest bedding her," a gravelly voice interjected.

Aren turned to glare at Jor, the captain of his honor guard, who sat on the far side of the fire pit. "Thank you for the suggestion."

"What were they thinking, dressing her in silk in the pouring rain? Might as well have paraded her naked in front of us all."

Aren *had*, in fact, noticed. Even bedraggled by the rain, she'd been stunning, her form curved, her exquisite face framed by hair the color of honey. Not that he'd expected anything else. Despite being past his prime, the King of Maridrina remained a vital man, and it was known he chose the majority of his wives for beauty and nothing else.

The thought of the other king made Aren's stomach sour. He recalled the smug expression on Silas's face as he handed his *precious* daughter over.

It was an expression the Rat King was entitled to.

While Ithicana was now bound to new and undesirable trade terms, all the King of Maridrina had given up was one of his innumerable children and a promise to continue the peace that had stood between the two kingdoms for the past fifteen years. And not for the first time, Aren cursed his parents for making his marriage to Maridrina part of the agreement.

"A piece of paper with three signatures will do little to unite our kingdoms," his mother had always replied when he complained. "Your marriage will be the first step toward creating a true alliance between peoples. You will lead by example and, in doing so, you will ensure Ithicana does more than just survive by the skin of its teeth. And if that means nothing to you, then remember that your father gave his word on my behalf."

And an Ithicanian always kept his word. Which was why, on the fifteenth anniversary of the agreement, despite his parents being a year dead, Aren had sent word to Maridrina to bring their princess to be wed.

"Can't argue that she's easy on the eyes. I can only hope I'll be so lucky." Though Ahnna's voice was light, Aren didn't miss how her hazel eyes turned dull at the mention of her half of the bargain. The King of Harendell, their neighbor to the north, had yet to send for his son's Ithicanian bride, but with Aren now wed to Lara, it was only a matter of time. Harendell would know by now the terms Maridrina had negotiated, and they'd be keen to extract their own pound of flesh. Both deals would incite retaliation from Amarid. The other northern kingdom's relationship with Ithicana was already fraught with conflict, given that their merchant ships competed for business with the bridge.

Giving Jor a meaningful look, Aren waited until his honor guard made themselves scarce before saying to his sister in a low voice, "I won't make you marry the prince, if you don't wish to. I'll compensate them some other way. Harendell is more pragmatic than Maridrina; they can be bought." Because it was one thing for Aren to take a girl he hadn't chosen and never met as a bride for the sake of peace. Quite another to give his sister to a foreign kingdom, where she'd be alone in a strange place to be used however they willed.

"Don't be an idiot, Aren. You know I'll put the good of our kingdom first," Ahnna muttered, but she leaned against his left shoulder, where she'd stood with him and fought for him all of their lives. "And you didn't answer my question."

That was because he didn't know *what* he was going to do with Lara.

"We can't let our guard down," Ahnna said. "Silas might have promised peace, but don't for a second believe he intends to honor that for the sake of *her*. The bastard would probably sacrifice a dozen daughters if it saw us lowering our defenses."

"I'm aware."

"She might be beautiful," his sister continued, "but never believe for a heartbeat that isn't by design. She's the daughter of our enemy. He *wants* you to be distracted by her. She's probably been instructed to seduce you, to find out what she can about Ithicana's secrets on the hope she'll be able to pass them back to her father. We don't need him holding that kind of bargaining chip."

"How, exactly, would she manage that? It isn't as though we'll be sending her home for visits. She'll have no contact with *anyone* outside of Ithicana. He has to know that."

"Better to be safe. Better that she be kept in the dark."

"So I should keep her locked up in our parents' home on this empty island for the rest of her days?" Aren stared at the glowing embers of the fire. A gust of wind drove rain into the hole in the roof above, the droplets hissing as they struck the charred wood. "And if"—he swallowed hard, knowing he had obligations to his kingdom—"*when* we have a child, should I keep him or her locked up here as well?"

"I never said it would be easy." His sister took his hand, twisting it upright to regard the cut across his palm, bleeding where he'd picked at the scab. "But our duty is to protect our people. To keep Eranahl a secret. To keep it safe."

"I know." But that didn't mean he didn't feel an obligation to his new bride. Whom he'd brought through the dark stretches of the bridge, knowing that when she woke, it would be in a place entirely different than any she'd known. Not the life she'd chosen, but one that had been forced upon her.

"You should go up to the house," Ahnna said. "The sedative will wear off soon enough."

"You go." Aren lay back down on the bench, listening to the thunder rolling over the island, the storm nearly passed, though it would soon be replaced by another. "She's been through enough without waking up in a room with a strange man."

Ahnna looked for a moment like she might argue, then nodded. "I'll send word when she wakes." Rising, she left the barracks on silent feet, leaving him alone.

*You're a coward*, he thought to himself. Because it had only been an excuse to avoid seeing the girl. His mother had believed that this princess was the key to achieving greatness for Ithicana, but Aren wasn't convinced.

Ithicana needed a queen who was a warrior. A woman who'd fight to the death for her people. A woman who was cunning and ruthless, not because she wanted to be, but because her country needed her to be. A woman who'd challenge him every day for the rest of his life. A woman Ithicana would respect.

And there was one thing he was certain: Lara Veliant was *not* that woman.

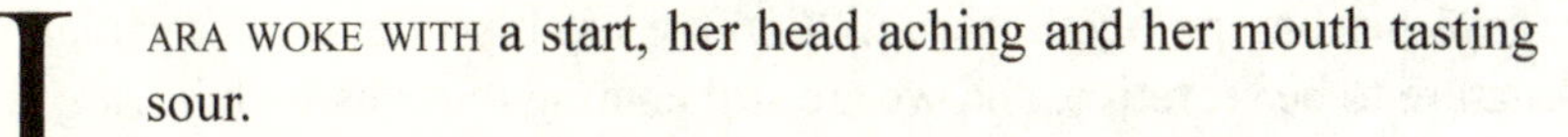

# 6
# LARA

LARA WOKE WITH a start, her head aching and her mouth tasting sour.

Without moving, she opened her eyes, taking in what she could of the bedroom. She spotted an open window, through which poured a humid breeze filled with the scents of flowers and lush greenery she possessed no names for, having spent her life surrounded by sand. The view was of a verdant garden, the light flat and silvery, as though it were filtered through thick clouds. The only sound was the faint pitter-patter of rain.

And that of a female humming.

She relaxed the hand that had instantly balled into a fist, primed to attack, and slowly turned her head.

An extraordinarily striking woman, perhaps five years older than Lara, with long, curling dark hair, stood in the center of the room wearing one of Lara's dresses. *One of Marylyn's dresses*, she realized with a pang.

Seeing the way she'd cocked her head, Lara knew the other woman had heard her move, but she carried on as though she had not, swishing the too-short silken skirts from side to side, continuing with her humming.

Lara said nothing, taking in the carved fruitwood furniture that was polished to a shine and vases of brilliant flowers sat on nearly every flat surface. The floors were made of tiny pieces of wood laid out in elaborate designs; the walls were plastered white and decorated with vibrant artwork. A door led to what appeared to be a bathing chamber and another, shut, which she assumed led to a hallway beyond. Satisfied that she had the lay of her surroundings, Lara asked, "Where am I?"

"Oh, you're awake!" the woman said with feigned surprise. "You're in the king's home on Midwatch Island."

"I see." If Midwatch was, as the name suggested, in the middle of Ithicana, she'd been unconscious for longer than she'd realized. They'd drugged her, which meant they did not trust her. No surprise there. "How did I get here?"

"You arrived at Midwatch by sea."

"How long was I asleep?"

"You weren't precisely asleep. Just not . . . present." The woman gave her an apologetic shrug. "Forgive us. It's in every Ithicanian's nature to be secretive, and we are still coming to terms with having an outsider in our midst."

"So it would seem," Lara murmured, noticing that the woman hadn't answered her question, though she knew *exactly* what they'd dosed her with and why. Keeping a person unconscious for days had consequences—often of the fatal variety. Drugging her to wipe her memory was safer.

But fallible. Especially when the individual being dosed had been exposed in the past. Already, shadows of memory were creeping around the edges of Lara's thoughts. Memories of walking. Walking in ill-fitting footwear on a hard surface. She'd been in the bridge, and at some point along its length, they'd brought her out.

Refocusing her gaze on the woman, she asked, "Why are you wearing my dress?"

"You have a whole chest of them. I was hanging them up for you, and I thought I'd try one on to see if I liked it."

Lara cocked one eyebrow. "And do you?"

"Oh, yes." The stranger arched her back, smiling at her reflection in the mirror. "Entirely impractical, but appealing nonetheless. I could use one or two in my own closet." Reaching up one hand, she pushed the dress's straps off her shoulders, allowing it to slide down her body and pool on the floor at her feet.

She wore not a scrap underneath, her body all curved muscle, her breasts small and pert.

"Gorgeous gown you wore for your wedding, by the way." She pulled a short-sleeved tunic over her head, then tugged a pair of snug trousers on beneath. There were a set of vambraces sitting on the floor, and she buckled those on as though she'd done so a thousand times. "I'd ask to borrow it for my own part in the Fifteen Year Treaty, but I'm afraid it took a bit of wear on your journey."

Lara blinked, realization dawning on her. "You're the Ithicanian Princess?"

"Among other things." The woman grinned. "But I don't want to give away all our secrets. My brother would never forgive me."

"Your brother?"

"Your husband." Picking up a bow and quiver, the woman—the princess—strode across the floor. "I'm Ahnna." She bent down to kiss Lara's cheek. "And I, for one, am so looking forward to getting to know you, sister."

There was a knock at the door, and a servant carrying a platter of sliced fruits entered, setting the food on a table before announcing that dinner would be at the seventh hour.

"I'll leave you alone," Ahnna said. "Give you a chance to get settled. I'm sure waking up here was quite the shock."

After years of Serin's aggressive tutelage, it would take a great deal more than waking in a feather bed to shock Lara, but she allowed a faint tremor into her voice as she said, "The king . . . Is he . . . Will he . . ."

Ahnna shrugged. "Aren is not horribly predictable in his comings and goings, I'm afraid. Better that you make yourself comfortable rather than wait for him to come home. Have a bath. Eat some fruit. Have a drink. Or ten."

A flash of disappointment surged through Lara, but she gave Ahnna a smile before shutting the door and flipping the latch. She stared at the bit of metal for a long moment, surprised the Ithicanians would allow her privacy, then she set aside the thought. Everything she knew about them was more speculation than fact. Better to approach her circumstances as though she knew nothing at all.

After donning the gown Ahnna had discarded and belting on her knives, which she was surprised to find sitting on top of her trunk, Lara circled the room looking for signs she was being spied on, but there were no holes in the walls or the ceiling, no cracks in the floorboards. Picking up her tray of fruit, she wandered into what she'd presumed to be the bathing chamber, only to discover it devoid of anything resembling a bath, despite the wooden shelves laden with soft towels, scrubs, soaps, and whole collection of brushes and combs. However, there was another door.

Lara pushed the solid slab of wood open, revealing a sloped courtyard resplendent with a lushness she had never seen before. The walls of the building were concealed by climbing vines laden with brilliant flowers of pink and purple and orange, and two trees with enormous split leaves climbed toward the sky, several colorful birds sitting on their branches. A pathway made of square cut stones framed by tiny white rocks meandered through the courtyard, but what took her breath away was the stream flowing through the center of everything.

The building, she realized as she stepped into the courtyard, had been constructed almost like a bridge over a small waterfall. The water cascaded over slabs of rock into a pool below, which flowed through a channel to another pool, and then yet another, before running under the far side of the home to whatever lay beyond.

At the base of the waterfall, by the pool, she noted the curved stone benches beneath the water. *This* was where one was intended to bathe. Steam rose faintly from its surface and a quick dip of her toe turned her skin pink with heat. There was only one other entrance to the courtyard, and that was a door opposite to the one leading to her rooms.

Crossing the stream using a small footbridge, Lara walked up to and silently tested the handle. *Locked.* The rooms beyond also had a window that mirrored hers, but it was closed and curtained.

Tilting her head skyward revealed nothing but swirling clouds, and a quick test of the vines on the walls revealed them strong enough to bear her weight, should she choose to climb out. Countless ways to escape, which meant this home was not intended to be a prison.

A voice caught her attention.

"She's awake then?"

*Aren.*

"About a half hour ago."

"And?"

Lara hurried down the path next to the spring, dropping to her knees where the water flowed under the building.

"She was calmer than I anticipated. Mostly she wanted to know why I was wearing one of her dresses. I suppose we all have our priorities."

Silence. Then, "Why *were* you wearing one of her dresses?"

"Because they were pretty and I was bored."

The king snorted, and Lara crawled forward a few feet under the building until she could see their legs. He had a bow held loosely in one hand, which he swung back and forth. She wanted to go farther, to attempt to see his face, but she couldn't risk being heard.

"She say anything of note?"

"I've had more exciting conversations with your cat. Your dinners together are destined to be lively affairs."

"Shocking." The king kicked a rock, sending it bouncing into the stream, splashing Lara in the face. "*Most precious daughter*, my ass. I'd bet he has boots that are more precious to him than that girl."

*I'll take that bet, you self-righteous bastard*, Lara thought.

He added, "These concessions weren't what I wanted out of this treaty, Ahnna. I don't like them, and I don't want to sign the order."

"You have to. Maridrina fulfilled their end of the deal. If we break faith, there will be consequences, the loss of peace being the first of them."

They both started walking, then there was a scrape of boots, the measured thuds of two people walking up stairs, and Ahnna's voice was faint as she said, "Giving the Maridrinian King what he wants will make him depend on us all the more. It might pay off."

And just barely, Lara heard his response: "Maridrina will starve before it ever sees the benefit of this treaty."

The embers of Lara's fury burned hot on the heels of his words, memories of the gaunt children she'd seen on the streets of her kingdom filling her eyes. Straightening, she stormed up the path to her room, intent on finding that asshole of a king and plunging one of her knives into his wicked, Ithicanian guts.

But that would accomplish nothing.

Stopping on the path, she stared up at the sky and took a series of breaths, finding calm in the sea of fire that was her soul. As delightful as gutting her *husband* would be, it wouldn't solve Maridrina's problems. Otherwise, her father would've sent an assassin a long time ago to do that very deed. It was not a matter of bringing down a man, but bringing down a kingdom, and to do that, she needed to play the long game. To delay her strike for when it would be most effective. To remember what she'd been trained for and why. To *be* the woman that her father had created to save their homeland.

A door slammed behind her, and Lara whirled around, expecting one of the servant women had come to offer her services.

She could not have been more mistaken.

The man was naked, save for the towel wrapped around his waist that kept him from being exposed to her entirely. But what she could see was more than enough. Tall and broad-shouldered, his muscled body was as defined as if it were carved from stone, his arms marked with old scars that were white against tanned flesh. And his face . . . Dark hair framed high cheekbones and a strong jaw, which were tempered by full lips. His eyes roved over her, making color rise to her cheeks.

"Of course of all the rooms she could've put you in, she chose *that* one," he said, and the familiarity of his voice was like a pail of icy water being dumped over her head as she realized *who* was standing before her. All she saw now was that wicked mask, and all she heard was *Maridrina will starve*.

he knives at her waist, but she covered
ist of her dress.

even know how to use those?"

kill this arrogant, condescending man
her head, but Lara only gave him a
are of meat."

interest. "So the little princess has a
... Gesturing to her knives, he said, "I meant, do you know how to fight with them?"

To say no meant she could *never* be caught using them in any capacity without outing herself as a liar, so instead Lara cocked one bemused eyebrow. "I was raised to be your queen, not a common soldier."

The interest in his eyes flickered out. Which would not do. She was supposed to seduce him and, in doing so, make him trust her. But for that to happen, he had to want her. The misting rain had made the silk of her dress damp, and she could feel it clinging to her breasts. She'd been trained for this. Had sat through countless lessons where she'd been taught precisely what she needed to do to catch a man's interest. And to keep it. Arching her back, she said, "Are you here to claim what is your due?"

His expression didn't shift. If anything, he appeared bored with her. "The only thing I'm due for is a bath before dinner. Dragging your ass back from Southwatch was sweaty business. You're heavier than you look."

Lara's cheeks flamed.

"That said, if you are inclined to do the same, you are welcome to go first. Given you haven't seen a wash in three days, you probably need it more than I do."

She stared at him, at a loss for words.

"But, if you're only out here to admire the . . . *foliage*, perhaps you might grant me a modicum of privacy." He gave her a lazy smile. "Or not. I'm not shy."

That was what he expected. For her to be dutiful little Maridrinian wife and attend to his needs, whether she wanted to or not.

*It was what he expected*, she thought, watching him watch her,

*but it wasn't what he wanted*. Thoughts flicked through
after another. Of the clothes he wore, the colors intended to
jungle around them. The scars, which had clearly come fro
The bow he'd held in his hand, ready to use at a heartbeat's n
*This man is a hunter*, she decided. *And what he wants is a chase*.

She was more than happy to give him one. Especially if it meant delaying a certain inevitability that she was desperate to avoid.

"Then you can wait." She smiled inwardly at the surprise that lit up his eyes. Unbuckling her belt, she dropped the weapons next to the edge of the pool, then turned her back on the king, pushing the straps of her dress off as she did. Peeling the damp silk from her body, Lara kicked the garment aside, feeling his eyes on her as she stepped into the pool, with only her hair hanging to the small of her back to conceal her naked flesh.

It was scorching hot. A temperature that one needed to ease into, slowly, but Lara gritted her teeth and waded down the steps, only turning when the swirling water covered her breasts.

The king stared at her. She gave him a serene smile. "I'll let you know when I'm finished."

He opened his mouth as though to argue, then shook his head once and turned. Lara allowed him to take three steps before calling out, "Your Majesty."

The King of Ithicana turned to regard her, not quite hiding the anticipation in his expression.

Lara let her head fall back so that the waterfall poured over her hair. "Please leave me the soap. I'm afraid I forgot to bring any out with me." She hesitated, then added, "The towel, too."

The bar landed in the water next to her with a splash. Lara opened her eyes in time to watch him remove the towel from his waist and toss it on a rock, his feet smacking against the path as he strode naked back to his room.

Biting the insides of her cheeks, Lara struggled to contain her grin. This man might be a hunter. But he was mistaken if he believed she was prey.

# 7
# LARA

LARA STAYED IN the hot springs until her skin was pink and wrinkled, half to annoy the King of Ithicana and half because the sensation of being wholly immersed in warm water was an unfamiliar delight. In the oasis, bathing had been limited to a basin, a cloth, and lots of vigorous scrubbing.

Back in her rooms, she took care with her appearance, selecting a sky-blue gown that left her arms and most of her cleavage bare, braiding her wet hair into a coronet that revealed her neck and shoulders. In her trunk was a chest of cosmetics, the false bottom concealing tiny jars of poisons and drugs, from which she tucked a vial into her cleverly designed bracelet. She darkened her lashes and swept gold dust across her skin, staining her lips a rosy pink right as the clock on the desk struck the seventh hour. Then, taking a deep breath, she stepped out into the hallway and followed the smell of food.

The polished floor of the hall reflected the light from beautiful sconces made of Valcottan glass. The walls were covered with a latticework of thin pieces of amber-colored wood, on which several bright paintings framed with bronze were hung. The end of the hallway led to a kitchen, so she took the door leading left, and found herself in a foyer tiled with marble, a heavy exterior door framed with windows revealing nothing in the growing darkness.

"Lara."

Turning her head at the sound of her name, she looked through the open doors into a large dining room, which was dominated by a beautiful table made of wood inset with squares of enamel, around which a dozen chairs were placed. Ahnna sat with her chair pushed back and a glass balanced on one trousered knee.

"How was your bath?" The amusement in Ahnna's eyes suggested she was not unaware of Lara's conversation with her brother.

"Delightful, thank—" She broke off with a surprised gasp. Sitting on a chair across from the princess was the largest cat she'd ever seen, at least the size of a dog. Regarding her with golden eyes, it lifted one paw and licked it, proceeding to groom itself at the dinner table. "Good god," she muttered. "What is that?"

"That's Vitex. He's Aren's pet."

"Pet?"

The other woman shrugged. "Aren found him abandoned when he was just a kitten. Took him into the house and then couldn't get the damned creature to leave. He does keep the snakes out, I'll give him that."

Lara watched the animal warily. It was big enough to take down a human, if it got the jump. "Is he friendly?"

"Sometimes. Best to let him come to you, though. Now shoo, Vitex. Shoo!" The enormous creature gave her a look of disdain, then hopped off the chair and disappeared from the room.

Lara sat down across from the princess, taking in the full wall of windows, which she expected showcased an impressive view in the light of day. "Where is everyone?"

Ahnna took a long mouthful of wine, then picked up the bottle on the center of the table and filled Lara's glass and her own, the act making Lara blink. In Maridrina, only servants handled a bottle. One did not pour for oneself. She rather thought that her countrymen might perish from thirst before ever breaking with the custom.

"This is my parents'"—Ahnna broke off with a wince, then

corrected herself—"*my brother's* private residence, so there isn't anyone here right now but us three, plus the cook and two servants. And I'll be gone tomorrow once my hangover wears off." She lifted her glass. "Cheers."

Lara dutifully lifted her own and took a swallow, noting the stemware was also from Valcotta, the wine from Amarid, and unless she missed her mark, the silverware from her homeland. She catalogued the details away for later consideration. Ithicana made the market for most goods, buying at Northwatch, transporting the products through their bridge, then selling them at a premium at Southwatch, only to reverse the process with the southern kingdoms' exports. Merchants who traveled the length of the bridge paid stiff tolls for the privilege, and they were always kept under guard by Ithicanian soldiers. Ithicana itself exported nothing, but it appeared they had no compunction against importing products from other places.

"Is the entirety of this island the king's private domain, then?" Lara asked, wondering when or if the man in question would make an appearance.

"No. My father built this home for my mother so that she would be comfortable during the times of the year they were here."

"Where were they the rest of the time?"

Ahnna smiled. "Elsewhere."

*Secrets*.

"Are there others living on this island whom I should be aware of?"

"Aren's honor guard is here. You'll meet them at some point, I imagine."

Frustration bit at Lara, and she took another sip of wine to soothe the sensation away. She'd only been here a matter of hours. No one—not even Serin and her father—could expect her to find a way through Ithicana's defenses in the space of a day. "I look forward to meeting them, I'm sure."

Ahnna snorted. "I doubt that. They're a little rough around the edges compared to what you're used to, I expect. Though you are something of a mystery."

The princess was doing her own digging. Lara smiled. "What of you? You say that you will be leaving tomorrow? Is this island not your home?"

"I'm the commander at Southwatch."

Lara choked on her mouthful of wine. "But you're a—"

"Woman?" Ahnna supplied. "You'll find we hold to a different way of life in Ithicana. What's between your legs doesn't determine the path you'll walk in life. Half the garrison at Southwatch is made up of women."

"How liberating." Lara managed to get the words out between coughs even as she envisioned the horror on her father's face should he discover the island he'd failed time and again to beat in battle was defended by women.

"It can be for you, too, should you want it to be."

"Don't make promises we can't keep, Ahnna," a male voice said.

The King of Ithicana strode into the dining room, his dark hair damp from bathing, though she noted his face was still rough with stubble. It gave him a roguish appeal, but she stamped the thought down the moment it rose.

"What's wrong with her learning how to wield a weapon? Ithicana's dangerous. It would be for her own safety."

He eyed the table, then sat at the end of it. "It's not her safety that I'm concerned about."

Lara shot him a look of disdain. "You'd fit in well in Maridrina, Your Grace, if the thought of your wife knowing how to wield a knife puts such fear in your heart."

"Oh my." Ahnna filled her glass up to the brim and leaned back in her chair. "I misjudged your wit, Lara."

"You're wasting your breath, Ahnna," Aren said, ignoring the comment. "Lara believes weapons are the domain of *common* soldiers and not worthy of her time."

"I said no such thing. I said I was trained to be a wife and a queen, not a common soldier."

"And just what *did* that training entail?"

"Perhaps fate will favor you and one day you'll find out, Your Majesty. Although as it stands, you'll need to content yourself with my flawless needlework."

Howling with laughter, Ahnna poured herself yet another glass of wine and then filled one up for her brother. "This might help."

Aren disregarded them both in favor of the servants who appeared bearing trays of food, which they set down on the table, disappearing only to return again with more. There were fresh fruits and vegetables, all brilliantly colored, as well as large fish still in possession of their heads. One fish sat on a bed of steaming rice, which Lara eyed and then dismissed, her attention snapping to the herb-crusted roast beef, the question of its origins tamping down her anger at the excess of food. Food that could've gone to Maridrina.

She waited for one of the servants to serve her, but they all departed. Then the royal siblings began helping themselves, loading their plates with salad and fish and beef all at the same time with no regard to the order of things. "This is more diverse fare than I'm used to," she said. "I've never had fish before, although I suppose it's a staple here."

Aren lifted his head, eyeing the offerings, and Lara saw the corner of his eye tick. "There are some islands with wild boar. Goat. Chicken. Snake is often on the menu. Everything else is an import—usually from Harendell via the market at Northwatch."

Serin's spies reported that not all the goods that entered the bridge at Northwatch exited at Southwatch, indicating that the Ithicanians used the structure to transport products within their own kingdom. *There are ways in and out of the bridge beyond the openings at Northwatch and Southwatch*, Serin had shouted continually at Lara and her sisters. *Those are the weak points. Find your way in.*

Taking healthy servings of everything, Lara cut into her slice of beef, watching the juices pool beneath. Then she took a bite. Smiling at one of the servants who'd reappeared with more wine, she said, "This is delicious."

None of them spoke for a long time, and for her part, Lara's silence was a result of her mouth being full of food. It was better than anything she'd ever had, fresh and seasoned with spices she couldn't even name. *This is what possessing the bridge meant*, she thought, imagining all this food arriving in Maridrina.

"Why did your father keep you in the middle of the Red Desert?" Aren finally asked.

"For our safety."

"Our?"

*Give the truth, when you can*, Serin's voice instructed from her thoughts.

She swallowed a bit of fish that was drenched with a citrus-butter. "Mine and my sisters'. Well, half-sisters."

Both siblings stopped chewing.

"How many children was . . . *is* he hiding out there?" Aren asked.

"Twelve, including myself." Lara took a sip of wine, then refilled her plate. "My father selected from amongst us the girl he believed would be most fitting as your queen."

Aren was staring at her with a blank expression while his twin nodded sagely before asking, "The most beautiful, you mean?"

"No, I'm afraid not."

"The most intelligent?"

Lara shook her head, thinking of how swiftly Sarhina and Marylyn could crack codes. And build them.

"Why you, then?" Aren interjected.

"It wasn't my place to question the reasons behind his decision."

"Surely you have an opinion on the matter?"

"Certainly: that my opinion doesn't matter."

"What if I asked you for it?" He frowned. "I *am* asking for it."

"My father is the longest ruling monarch in Maridrina's history. His wisdom and understanding of the relationship between our two kingdoms is what guided him to choose me to be your wife."

Ahnna abruptly jerked toward her brother, her voice urgent as she said, "Aren, we've been infiltrated. There's a spy amongst us."

Lara felt her stomach drop as Aren's eyes turned on her. Her fingers twitched toward the knives at her waist, ready to fight her way out if she needed to.

"There's no other explanation for it," Ahnna said. "How else could that deceitful prick of a king have known which daughter would make the absolute *worst* wife for you?"

Snorting, Aren shook his head. Lara hid her relief behind another mouthful of fish, which now held the same appeal as swallowing sawdust.

"No wonder he looked so damn smug at the wedding," the princess continued. "He probably figured you'd send her back after a week."

"Ahnna." The King of Ithicana's voice was full of warning.

"It's amazing, really. It's *almost* as though she were *created* to drive you into an early grave."

*More accurate than you know*, Lara thought.

"Ahnna, if you don't shut your mouth, I'm going to drown you in your wine."

Ahnna held up her glass in toast. "You're welcome to try, brother dearest."

Lara chose that moment to interrupt, while at the same time, refilling both the siblings' glasses. Pouring the wine herself made it an easy thing to deposit several drops from the tiny vial hidden in her hand into each, ensuring they'd both sleep heavily tonight. "Speaking of my father, will you allow me to correspond with him?"

They stared at her, their displeasure at her request clear as they both drained their glasses, seemingly unaware of how they mirrored each other. Lara smiled internally, knowing the narcotic mixed with the alcohol would do its duty well.

Finally, Aren asked, "Why would you want to? And please don't tell me it's to sustain what is so obviously *not* a close father-daughter relationship."

A dozen nasty retorts formed in her mind, and Lara bit down on every last one of them. She *did* need the cursed man to fall for her. "It has been made clear to me that to protect the interests of Ithicana, I will never be allowed to see my family, my home, or even my people again. That this house, as lovely as it may be, is to be my prison for as long as you see fit. Pen and paper are all I have left to maintain my connection with all that I have left behind. That is, if you allow it."

He looked away, his jaw working as though he were waging some great internal debate. Then his eyes flicked to his sister, the woman giving him the very faintest shake of her head. Which was interesting.

Ahnna portrayed herself as the lighthearted and compassionate of the pair, but perhaps that was not an accurate assessment of her character.

Yet whatever warning had passed between brother and sister, Aren chose to ignore it. "You are welcome to correspond with your father. But your letters will be read, and if they contain information that jeopardizes Ithicana, you will be asked to remove it. If you're caught using a code, your privileges will be revoked."

*What* he might ask her to remove would reveal a great deal, a concept that was not lost on the Commander of Southwatch. Ahnna's eyes flashed with irritation, and she opened her mouth before shutting it again, unwilling to compromise her performance. Though Lara had no doubt she'd argue against the correspondence once Lara was out of earshot.

"I don't care for having my private letters read," Lara argued, only because he'd expect it.

"And I don't overly care to read them," Aren snapped. "But we must all do things we don't care to do, so I suggest you get used to it." And without another word, he shoved back his chair and exited the room with a slight sway to his step.

Ahnna let loose a world-weary sigh. Pulling the cork from another bottle of wine, she filled Lara's glass to the brim. "At Southwatch, this is what we call an Ahnna pour."

Despite knowing that the woman's behavior was an act to earn her trust, Lara smiled, taking a mouthful of the liquid. "Is he always this quick to temper?" she asked, even as she thought, *Is he always this much of a prick?*

The smile on the other woman's face fell away. "No." There was a slight slur to her voice, and she frowned at her glass. "God, how much of this did I drink?"

"Amarid makes the finest wines in the world—hard not to indulge."

Moments later, Ahnna's chin hit the table with a heavy thud. One of the servants entered at that precise moment, his jaw dropping at the sight of his princess snoring at the dinner table.

"Overindulged," Lara said with a grimace. "Will you help me get her to her room?"

Ahnna was deadweight between the two of them as they half dragged, half carried her down the hallway and into her room, which was as lovely as Lara's own.

"If you hold her, Majesty, I'll check the sheets for snakes."

*Snakes?* The thought distracted Lara enough that she nearly fell sideways under Ahnna's weight when the boy let go. He walked over to the bed and gave it a solid kick before flipping down the bedding, which was thankfully devoid of serpents.

Easing Ahnna onto the bed, Lara dodged a near kick to the face as the taller woman rolled onto her stomach with a muffled grumble. Jerking off her boot, which had a wicked-sharp blade concealed within it, Lara tossed it next to the bed, followed by the other, then dusted off her hands. "Thank you for your assistance," she said to the boy, exiting the room and waiting for him to follow. "What's your name?"

"It's Eli, my lady. I should say, this isn't normal for Ah . . . Her Highness." He bit at his lower lip. "Perhaps I should let His Grace—"

"Let it be." Lara closed the door. "No need to embarrass her further."

The servant looked ready to argue, then Ahnna let out a loud snore, audible through the thick door, and seemed to think better of it. "Do you require anything else this evening, Your Grace?"

Lara shook her head, wanting him gone. "Goodnight, Eli."

Bowing, he said, "Very good. Please check your bed for—"

"Snakes?" She gave him a smile that turned his cheeks pink against the soft brown curls of his chaotic hair. He bowed again before fleeing down the hallway. Lara listened for the clatter of dishes being removed from the dining room, then silently let herself back into Ahnna's room, flipping the latch shut behind her.

The princess did not so much as twitch as Lara methodically searched for any information of use, sighing covetously at the woman's arsenal of weapons, which were all of the finest make. But else of interest, there was nothing beyond a few keepsakes, a jewelry box with some worthless items, and a music box with a false bottom filled with poetry. A childhood bedroom now seldom used.

After turning down the lamp, Lara eased open the door to ensure the hall was empty before striding to her own room. There had been noise of activity at both ends of the hallway; no chance of her making it to the other side of the house without one of the servants noticing. Chewing on her thumbnail, Lara eyed the clock. The narcotic wasn't intended to last long, and the king hadn't indulged in wine to the extent his sister had. Which meant she was running short of time.

Slipping off her dress, Lara retrieved some toweling, along with soaps and scrubs and, lamp in hand, she stepped out into the courtyard. The night air was cool, a light mist of rain dampening her shift as she walked barefoot down the stone path toward the hot spring. Setting her bathing supplies next to the pool, Lara slid off her shift and slipped into the steaming water, taking one of her knives in with her. Then she turned down the lamp to a bare glow and allowed her eyes to adjust to the darkness.

The noise of the jungle managed to be both deafening and soothing, a ceaseless cacophony that settled the rapid patter of her heart as she rested her elbows on the edge of the pool, perusing her surroundings. The chittering of birds merged with the rustle of leaves, the sharp shrieks of monkeys called back and forth through the trees. A creature, perhaps a frog of sorts, made a repetitive rattling noise, insects droned, and mixed with it all was the gurgle of the waterfall behind her.

*Watch. Listen. Feel.*

The latter had always served her best. Master Erik had called it the sixth sense—the unconscious part of the mind that took what all the other senses provided, then added something *more*. An intuition that could be tuned and honed into the most valuable sense of all.

So whether she heard a sound or saw a motion, Lara could not have said, but her attention snapped from the roofline to the opening under the house through which the stream flowed.

*Guard.*

Sure enough, as she stared into the darkness, her eyes eventually picked out the shape of a foot resting against a rock. A flash of irritation that they'd *dare* to watch her while she bathed was erased by the obvious necessity. Aren was the King of Ithicana, and she was the daughter of an enemy kingdom. Of course any avenue between them would be guarded.

After ensuring there were no other guards, she marked the sightlines. Searched for places that would give her cover. She glanced at her white shift resting in clear sight and eased into the stream that drained the pool, crawling on her elbows to keep her body beneath the bank. Warm water caressed her naked body as she crept down to the decorative bridge, which she used as cover to ease out, moving silently behind a bush with wide leaves.

From there, she made quick work of crossing the courtyard, coming up beneath the king's window, which was slightly ajar.

Adjusting a frond to cover her arm, she stretched upward and pulled the window open wider.

*Breathe.*

Reaching up with both arms, she heaved herself through the small gap, the frame scraping over her naked ass as she flipped, landing silently on her feet inside the dimly lit room, knife blade clenched between her teeth.

She was met by Aren's cursed enormous cat staring at her with golden eyes. Lara held her breath, but the animal only leapt onto the windowsill and slipped out into the courtyard.

Her gaze went immediately to the man sprawled across the large, canopied bed. Aren lay on his back, wearing only a pair of undershorts, the sheets tangled around his lower legs.

Knife gripped in her hand, Lara stepped carefully toward the bed, using one of the rugs to clean her feet. No need to leave her tiny footprints.

There'd been no doubt in her mind after seeing him naked earlier that he was an impressive specimen of a man, but this time, she had no fear of being caught staring. Twice her breadth in the shoulders, he was muscled in the way of an individual who pushed his body to the limits on a regular basis. Combat, judging from the scars, but his leanness spoke of an active life, not a man who sat back and ruled from a throne.

Circling the bed, she examined his face: high cheekbones, strong jaw, full lips, and black lashes that a harem wife would die for. Scruff marked the line of his chiseled jaw, and she had to curb the urge to reach out and run her finger along it.

*Maridrina will starve before they ever see the benefit of this treaty.*

His words echoed through her mind, and of its own volition, Lara's hand snaked up, resting the edge of her blade against the steady pulse at his throat. It would be easy. One slice, and he'd bleed out in a matter of moments. He might not even wake long enough to sound the alarm. She'd be gone by the time they even realized he was dead.

And she would have accomplished nothing besides destroying the only chance Maridrina had for a better future.

Lara lowered her knife and made her way to the desk. Her heart skipped as she took in a polished wooden box of heavy parchment embossed with Ithicana's bridge, edges gleaming with gilt. The very same stationery Serin had shown her that Aren used for official correspondence. She immediately searched for anything written on it that was directed to Maridrina. All she found were stacks of short notes on cheap paper, and she flipped through, taking in the reports from spies from every kingdom north and south. More reports from Northwatch and Southwatch islands, revenues, requirements for arms and soldiers and supplies.

*Provisions for Eranahl . . .*

Frowning, she eased the sheet of paper out from under a stack when the bed creaked behind her.

Twisting, her stomach plummeted as her gaze locked with Aren's. He was propped up on one arm, shoulder muscles straining against the sleek golden brown of his skin.

"Lara?" His voice was rough, eyes blurry from narcotics, sleep, and . . . lust. His gaze roved over her naked body, then he rubbed his eyes as though not quite certain whether she was real or an apparition.

*Do something!*

Her training, drilled into her by her masters, finally kicked in. Either she followed through with what her standing there naked promised, or she found a way to get him back to sleep. The former was the safer strategy, but . . . But that wasn't a card she was yet willing to play.

"How did you get in here?" His gaze was sharpening. If she didn't act soon, he'd remember seeing her when he woke, and that was not part of her plan.

*Believe that you are something to be desired,* and he will believe it, too, the voice of Mezat, the sisters' Mistress of the Bedroom, said, invading Lara's thoughts. *Desire is your weapon to wield as wickedly as any sword.*

That had seemed so simple back on the compound. Much less so, now. But she had no other choice.

Slipping the vial from her bracelet, Lara covered her finger with the drug before lifting it to her mouth to coat her lips.

"Shh, Your Grace. Now is not the time for conversation."

"A shame. You have such a pleasant way with words."

"I've other talents."

A slow smirk rose to his face. "Prove it."

A droplet of the narcotic beaded on Lara's bottom lip as she strolled with false confidence toward the bed, feeling Aren drink her in. Watching his arousal take hold. Perhaps there was something to Mezat's teachings after all.

Climbing onto the bed, she straddled him, her pulse roaring in her ears as he reached up one hand to cup her ass. His lips parted as though he'd say something, but she silenced him with a kiss.

The first kiss of her life, and she was giving it to her enemy.

The thought danced away as he groaned into her, his tongue chasing over her drug-laced lips, then delving deeper into her mouth, the sensation opening an unexpected floodgate of heat between her legs.

She silently willed the drugs to work as she kissed him again, hard and demanding, feeling his other hand graze the bottom of her breast until she caught hold of it and pinned it to the mattress. He chuckled softly, but she marked the way his eyelids fluttered, barely conscious, even as his other hand trailed down her bottom, down the back of her leg and then up the inside of her thigh. Up and down. Lara felt the drugs starting to take effect on her even as she felt something else building in her core.

He rolled, catching her other hand and pinning them both to the mattress, his teeth nipping at her earlobe and pulling a gasp from her lips. The room spun above her even as her skin burned hot, his lips kissing her throat. Between her breasts. A singular kiss, just below her navel, turning her breathing to ragged gasps.

Then Aren sighed once, slumped, and went still.

Lara stared unblinking at the ceiling, her heart in her throat. But every beat seemed to grow more sluggish, sleep tugging at her, welcoming her into its warm embrace.

*Move*, she ordered herself, worming her way out from under his weight.

Knowing she had only a matter of minutes before the drug knocked her out, Lara stumbled toward the window, giving the room only a passing glance to ensure it was as she had found it. Her arms shuddered as she eased outside, numb feet finding the cold ground, mud oozing between her toes as she backtracked through the courtyard. Back in the stream, the water danced over her skin, which, despite the narcotic, felt so sensitive that the touch hurt.

The water was warm. Strangely soothing as it pulled her under, welcoming her into its depths.

Soon she was choking. Gasping. Fighting to keep conscious as she reached for the edge and dragged herself out of the pool.

Her body swayed as she pulled the shift over her head. She stumbled up the path, praying the guard would only think her drunk. Her hands hit the solid wood of the door, pushing it in. Shutting it. Turning the bolt.

*Get to the bed. Don't give them a reason to suspect.*

*Get to the bed.*

*Get to the . . .*

# 8

# AREN

AREN PUT AWAY the whetstone he'd been running across the blade of a knife, staring off into the depths of the jungle surrounding his home. Though a hundred sounds emanated from the trees—the trickle of water, the calls of animals, the hum of insects—the island felt quiet. Serene. Peaceful.

A warm furry body rubbed against his arm, and Aren reached up to rub Vitex's ears, the big cat purring contentedly until something in the bushes caught his attention. There'd been a female running about, and even now, Aren spotted her yellow eyes watching them from beneath a large leaf.

"Want to go get her?" he asked his cat.

Vitex only sat on his haunches and yawned. "Good plan. Let her come to you." Aren chuckled. "Let me know how that works out for you."

Behind them, there was the sound of boots against marble and the door swinging open. His sister blinked as she stepped outside.

"You're in better form than I thought you'd be," he said dryly.

Ahnna frowned at him, using one foot to shove the cat inside so she could shut the door. "Why's that?"

"Because the amount of wine you must have consumed to have passed out at the table probably means my cellar's looking lean."

"Good god, did I?"

"If the chatter I heard coming from the kitchen is to be believed." Picking up his bow, Aren stood from where he'd been sitting on the front step, tapping the end of the weapon against his booted toe. "Eli and Lara dragged you back to your room."

Passing a hand over her eyes, Ahnna shook her head as if to clear it. "I remember talking to her and then . . ." She shook her head again. "Sorry. And sorry I'm late. I slept like the dead."

So had he, which was strange, given it had been a clear night. Without a storm to guard Ithicana's shores, Aren normally tossed and turned half the night. He would've been late to rise himself if the damn cat hadn't woken him.

"Good morning, children."

Aren turned to see Jor appear through the mist, a bread roll he'd clearly filched from the kitchen in one hand.

The older man gave Aren a once-over. "You're looking awfully well rested for a man who's just been married."

Ahnna cackled. "I don't think he had much company last night. Or any."

"Pissed the new wife off already?"

Aren ignored the question, a vision of Lara standing at the foot of his bed swimming across his thoughts, her naked body so damnably perfect that it had to have been a dream. The taste of her lips, the feel of her silken skin beneath his hands, the sound of her breath, ragged with desire. It had all been so vivid, but his memory stopped there.

Definitely a dream.

Pulling a folded sheet of paper out of his pocket, Aren handed it to Ahnna. "Your marching orders for Southwatch."

She unfolded it, eyes running over the revised trade terms with Maridrina, brows furrowing with renewed annoyance.

"I'll walk down with you to the barracks," he said. "I need a runner to take Northwatch their copy. Maridrina's already sent buyers through the bridge with gold. They'll be wanting to get underway." To Jor, he said, "Who's on watch?"

"Lia."

"Good. Keep her here. I don't expect Lara to cause any trouble, but . . ."

Jor coughed. "About Lara. Aster's here. He wants a word."

"He's at the barracks?"

"On the water."

"Of course he is." The commander of the Kestark garrison—south of Midwatch —was a member of the old guard. He was appointed near the end of Aren's grandfather's life, and Aren's mother had spent nearly her entire reign looking for a legitimate reason to have him replaced, with no success. The old bastard clung to Ithicanian tradition like a barnacle to a boat, and Aren had not failed to notice that of all the Watch Commanders, Aster had been the only one who hadn't been at his wedding. "I suppose we shouldn't keep him waiting."

The mist hung in the air like a great grey blanket, reducing the sun to a silver orb and making it impossible to see more than a few dozen paces in either direction. Down at the cove, Ahnna's bodyguard awaited her, as did his own, the men and women silently pushing their craft out into the water. Ahnna joined him in one of the Midwatch vessels.

The air was still, not a breeze to fill a sail, and the rattling of the chain rising from where it blocked the cove's entrance felt like a vulgar violation of the silence. Paddles dipped in and out of the water as the group eased around hazards lurking only a few feet beneath the surface, moving out into the open and toward the hulking shadow of the bridge.

"Aren."

Turning to look at his twin, Aren tracked her gaze to the water, where he caught sight of an enormous shape moving beneath them. The shark was longer than the boat he sat in—and more than capable of destroying it, should it feel inclined—but that wasn't why Ahnna had pointed out the predator. Its arrival heralded a calming of the Tempest Seas, and it wouldn't be long before Ithicana's waters were red with blood.

His spine prickled and Aren reached for a spyglass, panning their surroundings, his efforts yielding nothing but grey. A fine thing for hiding the comings and goings of his people, but it served their enemy just as well.

"It's weeks early. Nana hasn't called the end of the season yet." But for all Ahnna's words, he noticed her hand had drifted to the weapon belted at her waist, her eyes watchful. "I need to get back to Southwatch."

Through the mist a pair of vessels appeared. Aster—always one for overt symbolism—having chosen to wait directly beneath the bridge.

"Your Grace." The older man reached out to pull the two boats together. "I'm relieved to see you well."

"Were you expecting otherwise?" The vessels rocked as his guards switched places with the commander, giving the three of them some semblance of privacy.

"Given what you've brought into your house, yes."

"She's little more than a girl, alone, and at our mercy. I think I can handle myself."

"Even a child can slip poison into a cup. And the Maridrinians are known for it."

"Rest easy, Aster, my life is in no danger from Lara. Silas Veliant is no fool—he knows that having his daughter assassinate me would only cost him his new trade deal with Ithicana."

"Lara." Aster spat into the water. "I can hear in your voice that she's already digging in her claws. You must know there's a reason they sent a woman as beautiful as her."

"How would you know what she looks like, Commander?" Ahnna interrupted. "I didn't see you at the wedding, though I suppose it's possible you were hiding in the back."

Aren bit down on his tongue. The Kestark commander was short for an Ithicanian, and he did not like to be reminded of it.

"I've heard what she looks like." Aster's gaze was as dead-eyed as the shark's swimming beneath as he regarded them. "I did not attend, because I did not support your choice in taking her as your wife."

He wasn't alone in that. There were a great many, especially the older generation, who'd protested the union vehemently. "Then why are you here now?"

"To give you some advice, Your Grace. Take the Maridrinian girl down to the water and drown her. Hold her under until you're well and sure she's dead, then feed her corpse to the sea."

For a moment, no one spoke.

"I'm not in the habit of murdering innocent women," Aren finally said.

"Innocent. There's a word." Aster scowled, casting his gaze up at the bridge above them before turning it back on Aren. "I forget how young you are, Your Grace. You were only a boy kept safe in Eranahl the last time we went to war with Maridrina. You didn't fight in those battles where they threw their entire navy against us, blockading Southwatch and stymying trade, all while our people starved. You weren't there when Silas Veliant realized that he couldn't win by force and took his vengeance on the outlying islands, his soldiers slaughtering families and stringing their bodies up for the birds to feast on."

Aren hadn't been old enough to fight, but that didn't mean he didn't remember how desperate his parents had been when they proposed the treaty to Maridrina and Harendell. "We've had fifteen years of peace with them, Aster. Fifteen years of Silas not lifting a hand against Ithicana."

"He's still the same man!" Aster roared. "And you've taken one of his progeny into your bed! I've taken you for many things, Aren Kertell, but not until now did I take you to be a fool."

Ahnna had a knife in her hand, but Aren gave her a warning shake of the head. He'd spent the past year being pushed and questioned by his Watch Commanders and it would take more than a few insults to crack his temper. "I know as well as anyone what sort of man Silas Veliant is, Commander. But this treaty has bought us peace and stability with Maridrina, and I will do nothing to jeopardize that."

Aren waited for the other man to settle, then continued. "While the rest of the world moves forward, Ithicana languishes. Our only industry is the bridge and the fight to keep the bridge. We grow nothing. We create nothing. We know nothing but war and survival. Our children grow up learning a hundred ways to kill a man, but are barely literate enough to write their own names. And that's not good enough."

Aster stared him down, having heard this speech before. But Aren would repeat it a thousand times if that was what it took for men like Aster to accept the change that Ithicana needed.

"We need alliances—true alliances. Alliances that go beyond pieces of paper signed by kings. Alliances that will allow our people opportunities beyond the sword."

"You're a dreamer, just like your mother was." Aster lifted a hand, signaling to the other boats to return. "And it's a beautiful future you envision, I'll give you that, Your Grace. But it's not Ithicana's future."

The boats bumped together, and the commander jumped between them, settling himself among his guards. "And lest your dream turn into our nightmare, do us all a favor, Your Grace, and keep that woman locked up."

# 9
# LARA

LARA SLEPT BETTER than she had in some time, in part due to the narcotics, and in part due to the silence. Her sleep during the journey through Maridrina had been constantly interrupted by ambient noise. Soldiers, servants, horses, camels . . . But here, there were only the faint sounds of birds chirping in the courtyard trees.

It was peaceful.

But that sense of peacefulness was a cloak that hid the violent truth of this place. And the violent truth of herself.

Dressing quietly, Lara ventured out in the direction of the dining room. She braced herself for the possibility that Aren would remember what happened in his room last night. That he'd realize she'd drugged him and her mission would be over before it had even started.

The table was loaded with trays of sliced fruits and meats, creamy yogurt, and tiny little pastries sprinkled with cinnamon and nutmeg. But her eyes were all for the view out the enormous windows. Though it was late morning, the sunlight was dimmed by a filter of clouds, making it no brighter than twilight. Yet it revealed what the darkness last night had hidden: the wild jungle, the trees soaring high, the foliage beneath so dense as to be impenetrable, all of it coated with mist.

"Where is His Majesty?" she asked Eli, hoping he didn't notice the color that had risen on her cheeks. Circumstances had wrested free from her control last night. In more ways than one.

The older servant woman gave Eli a sharp glance. "His Majesty is early to rise. He has gone with the commander to ensure the new trade terms with Maridrina have been conveyed to Northwatch and Southwatch markets."

*Thank god.* She wasn't sure if she was ready to be face-to-face with him. Not after the things they'd done, whether he remembered them or not. Lara gave the woman a grave nod, hoping it hid her discomfort. "The new trade terms will be a godsend for my homeland. Only good can come from it."

A shadow seemed to pass over the older servant's gaze, but she only inclined her head. "As you say, my lady."

"What is your name? I've met Eli, and I should like to know the rest of you better."

"It's Clara, my lady. Eli is my nephew, and my sister, Moryn, is the cook."

"Only you three?" Lara asked, recalling the legion of servants that had accompanied her party from the outskirts of the Red Desert to Ithicana.

A slow smiled worked its way onto Clara's face. "His Majesty was in the habit of staying in the company of his soldiers rather than this house. Though I expect your presence will change that, my lady."

There was a faint glint in the servant's eyes that made Lara's cheeks warm. "Do you know when he will return?"

"He did not say, my lady."

"I see." Lara allowed a hint of disappointment to enter her voice.

Satisfaction filled her as the woman's face softened. "He is kept busy during most days, but his stomach will drive him home for dinner, if nothing else."

"Am I restricted in where I might go?"

"The house is yours, my lady. His Majesty requested that you make yourself comfortable."

"Thank you." Lara then left them to clear the table as she began her tour of the house.

Besides her rooms and Aren's there were four other bedrooms, the dining room, kitchen, and servants' quarters. The entire rear side of the home was filled with overstuffed chairs, a variety of games set on the tables, and walls lined with books. She longed to pick them up, but only trailed a finger along the spines before moving on. Every room was filled with windows, but the view was the same from them all: jungle. Beautiful, but utterly devoid of civilization. *Maybe this is what Ithicana is like*, Lara thought. *The bridge, the jungle, and little else.*

*Or maybe that's just what they wanted her to think.*

Retreating to her rooms, she examined the selection of Ithicanian clothes in the closet, selecting a pair of trousers and a tunic that left her arms bare, as well as a pair of stiff leather boots, and then walked down the hall and out the front door of the house.

*Test your limits in a way that won't make them suspect your capabilities*, Serin silently instructed. *They expect you to be ignorant, helpless, and indulged. Capitalize upon their mistakes.*

Anticipating that she might be followed, Lara started walking. There was a path that lead upward, but instead she chose to follow the spring, knowing that it would eventually deliver her to the sea.

It was only a matter of minutes until she heard the faint tread of someone walking behind her. The crack of a branch. A soft splash of water. Whoever it was had a hunter's stealth, but she'd learned to tell the difference between sand shifting on the wind and that moving beneath a man's weight, so catching the errant sounds of pursuit in this jungle was nothing to her.

Noting the signs of several booby traps in the jungle, Lara continued to follow the stream, soon finding herself drenched with rain and sweat, the humidity of the air making her feel like she was breathing water, but still, she had caught sight of neither bridge nor beach. Nor had her follower made any move to interfere.

She rested a hand against a tree trunk and feigned weariness as she stared up, trying and failing to penetrate the canopy and the mist.

Serin had explained in detail what they knew about the bridge. That the majority of the piers were natural towers of rock jutting out of the sea, holding the spans often a hundred or two hundred feet above the water. There were only a few islands onto which the bridge landed, and those were defended by all manner of hazards designed to sink ships. The most central of her goals was to find out how the Ithicanians accessed the bridge along its length, but she needed to find the thing first.

The stream was flowing down an increasingly steep slope, the now cool water pouring over ledges in tiny waterfalls, filling the air with a gentle roar. Holding onto vines and bracing herself on rocks, Lara picked her way down, already dreading the pain of the climb back up.

Then her boot slipped.

The world turned sideways, a blur of green as she tumbled, her elbow knocking painfully against a rock. Then she was falling.

Lara shrieked once, flailing her arms as she struggled to catch hold of a vine. She slammed into a pool of water, the force driving the wind out of her. Water closed over her head, bubbles streaming from her mouth as she kicked and thrashed her arms. Her boots knocked against the bottom, and she bent her knees to kick off . . .

To find herself only waist deep.

"Bloody hell," Lara snarled, wading to the water's edge. But before she reached shore, a hiss caught her attention.

Freezing where she stood, Lara scanned her surroundings, eyes landing on the brown and black snake shifting angrily in the underbrush. The creature was longer than she was tall, and it was caught between her and the cliff wall. She took a tentative step back into the water, but her motion only seemed to agitate the creature. This is what she got for not heeding Eli's warning.

It took a great deal of self-control not to reach for one of the knives belted to her waist, her ears picking up the scuff of boots and a faintly muttered oath. Throwing knives were her specialty, but her follower was at the top of the cliff and the last thing she needed was to be seen using one of her weapons.

The snake reared up, its head eye level with her. Hissing. Angry. Ready to strike. Lara breathed steadily. In and out. *Come on, whoever you are*, she silently grumbled. *Deal with this creature already*.

The snake swayed from side to side, and Lara's nerve began to fray. Her hand closed over her knife, her finger clicking open the case around the hilt.

The snake lunged.

A bow twanged, a black-fletched arrow spiking the creature's head to the ground. Its body thrashed about violently, then went still. Lara turned.

Aren knelt on the edge of the waterfall she'd so gracelessly toppled off, bow in hand, a quiver full of arrows peeking over his broad shoulders. He straightened. "We have something of a snake problem in Ithicana. Not so bad on this island in particular, but"—he leapt off the edge, landing almost silently next to her—"if she'd sunk her teeth into you, you wouldn't have been long for this world."

Lara glanced at the dead snake and its body twitched. Despite herself, she flinched, and she attempted to conceal the motion with a question. "How can you tell it's female?"

"Size. The males don't get this big." Crouching, he jerked the arrow out of the animal's skull. Wiping blood and bits of scale from the arrowhead, which was three-edged, unlike the barbed broadheads Maridrinians favored, he turned his dark gaze on Lara. "You were supposed to stay in the house."

She opened her mouth, about to tell him that she'd been given no such instruction, when he added, "Don't play the fool. You knew what Clara meant."

She chewed the inside of her cheek. "I don't care for being confined."

He snorted, then jammed the clean arrow back in his quiver. "I would've thought you'd be used to it."

"I am used to it. But that doesn't mean I have to like it."

"You were kept locked up in that desert compound for your own safety. Consider my motivations for keeping you confined here the same. Ithicana is dangerous. For one, the entire island is booby-trapped. And two, you won't walk two paces without passing by some manner of creature capable of putting you in your grave. And three, a coddled little princess like you doesn't know the first thing about taking care of herself."

Lara ground her teeth together. It took every ounce of control in her body to keep from telling him just how wrong he was on that account.

"That said, you did make it farther than I expected you would," Aren mused, his eyes raked over her body, her soaking wet clothes clinging to her skin. "What did they have you and your sisters *doing* on that compound? Running laps and shoveling sand?"

It was an inevitable question. While her frame was small, she was also corded with lean muscle from endless hours of training—hers was not the body of most Maridrinian noblewomen. "Desert living is hard. And my father wanted me prepared for the . . . *vigor* of life in Ithicana."

"Ah." He smiled. "How unfortunate that he didn't also prepare you for the wildlife." Reaching up with his bow, he flicked the tip of it across her shoulder, and out of the corner of her eye, Lara watched a black shape sail through the air.

A spider the size of her palm landed in the dirt before scuttling off into the shadows. She watched it with interest, wondering if it was poisonous. "No worse than the Red Desert's scorpions."

"Perhaps not. But I suspect the Red Desert isn't littered with these." Picking up a rock, he tossed it a dozen paces to the left.

There was a loud crack, and a board covered in wooden spikes snapped up from the ground. Anyone who triggered the device would find themselves sporting half a dozen holes in their body from the waist down. She'd seen the dew clinging to the tripwire a dozen paces back, but in fairness, it would've caught her in the dark. "You've won the pissing contest," she said in a way that implied he really hadn't. "Shall we carry on?"

Instead of snapping back with a witty rejoinder, Aren stepped closer, his hand closing on her wrist. Lara should've recoiled, but instead she froze, remembering the feel of that hand on her naked body, the soft strokes up and down her thigh.

She started to pull away, but he rotated her arm, frowning at the shallow cut on her elbow. Reaching into the pouch on his belt, he extracted a small tin of salve and a roll of bandage and proceeded to tend to the injury with practiced hands. The muscles of his forearms flexed beneath the steel and leather of the vambraces buckled around them. This close, she gained a new appreciation for how much larger he was than her, head and shoulders taller and easily double her weight. All of it lean muscle.

But Erik, her Master of Arms, had been just as big, and he'd trained Lara and her sisters how to fight against those who were larger and stronger. As Aren finished bandaging her arm, she imagined where she would strike. To the arch of his foot or his knee. Knife to open his guts. Another to the throat before he had the chance to get a grip on her.

He tied off the bandage. "I gave up a great deal in this exchange with your father, and all I got in return beyond the promise of continued peace was you. So you'll excuse me for not wanting to see you dead within the first days of your arrival."

"And yet you obviously were content to allow me to wander your dangerous jungles."

"I wanted to see where you'd go." Motioning for her to follow, Aren moved through the deadfall covering the jungle floor, making minimal use of the glittering machete he held in one hand. "Were you trying to escape?"

"Escape to where?" She forced herself to accept his arm as he guided her over a fallen tree. "My father would have me killed for dishonoring him if I returned to Maridrina, and I possess no skills that would allow me to survive elsewhere on my own. Whether I will it or not, Ithicana is where I must remain."

He laughed softly. "At least you're honest."

Lara contained her own laughter. She was many things, but *honest* wasn't one of them.

"Then what were you doing out here?"

*Save the lies for necessity.* "I wanted to see the bridge."

Aren stopped in his tracks, turning to give her a sharp look. "Why?"

She met his gaze unflinchingly. "I wanted to see the bit of architecture that was worth the rights to my body. My loyalty. My life."

He recoiled as though she'd slapped him. "The rights to those things are yours to give, not your father's."

It wasn't what she'd expected him to say. But rather than easing her trepidation about that particular aspect of her mission, it made her skin burn hot with an anger that she couldn't quite explain, so she only gave a curt nod. "So you say."

Smacking a vine out of his way with the machete, Aren strode up a steep incline, not waiting to see if she followed. "You were going the wrong direction, by the way. Now try to keep up. There's only a brief window in which you'll be able to see the bridge through the mist."

They climbed upward, mostly on a narrow trail, during which they said not a word to one another. There was nothing to be seen but endless jungle, and Lara was beginning to believe Aren was toying with her when he walked into a clearing containing a stone tower.

Tilting her face to the sky, she let the endless rain wash the sweat from her face, watching the clouds twist and swirl on winds that didn't breach the tree canopy.

Aren gestured at the tower. "The break in the cloud cover will be brief at this time of year."

The tower smelled of earth and mildew, the stone stairs circling upward worn in the center from countless footsteps. They reached the top—a small empty space open on all sides, revealing misty jungle in every direction. The lookout was at the apex of a small mountain, she realized, and she could only barely make out the grey sea below. There was no beach. No pier. And most importantly, no damned bridge.

"Where is it?"

"Patience." Aren leaned his elbows on the stone wall framing the space.

More curious than annoyed, Lara went to stand next to him, taking in the trees and clouds and sea, but her attention was drawn to him. He smelled of damp leather and steel, of earth and leafy things, but beneath that, her nose picked up the smell of soap and something distinctly, and not unpleasantly, male. Then a blast of wind roared through the tower, chasing away all scents but that of sky and rain.

The clouds parted with incredible speed, the sun burning down upon them with an intensity she hadn't felt since she'd left the desert, turning the swaths of faded green into an emerald so vibrant, it almost hurt her eyes. The mist raced away on the wind, leaving behind sapphire skies. Gone was the mysterious island, and what was left in its place was all brilliant color and light. But no matter how she searched, she could not see anything remotely resembling a bridge.

An amused laugh filled her ears just as fingertips caught her chin, gently lifting her face. "Look further," Aren said, and Lara's eyes went to the now-turquoise seas.

What she saw took her breath away.

# 10
# LARA

ALL THE DESCRIPTIONS given to her during her training paled in comparison to reality. It was not *a* bridge. It was *The Bridge*, for there was nothing that compared with it in the world.

Like a great grey serpent, the bridge meandered as far as the eye could see, joining the continents. It rested on top of naturally formed tower karsts that seemed to have been placed by the hand of God for just such a purpose, defying the Tempest Seas that crashed against their feet. Occasionally, its grey length drifted over the larger islands, resting on thick stone columns built by ancient hands. The bridge was a feat of architecture that defied reason. That defied logic. That should, by all rights, not even exist.

Which was exactly why everyone wanted it.

Tearing her eyes from the bridge, Lara glanced up at Aren whose own gaze was fixed on the stone structure. Though he must have seen it every day of his life, he still exuded a sense of wonder, as though he, too, could hardly fathom its existence.

Before she could look away, he turned his head, and their eyes met. In the sunlight, she saw that his eyes were not black, but hazel, the brown flecked with emerald green that mirrored his kingdom. "Does seeing it bolster your sense of self-worth?"

Her skin burned hot, and she turned away, needing to move. "I am not a commodity."

He huffed out a breath. "That's not what I meant. The bridge, it's . . . For Ithicana, it's everything. And Ithicana is everything to me."

Just as Maridrina was everything to her.

"It's . . . impressive." A weak word for the ancient structure.

"Lara." Out of the corner of her eye, she saw him reach for her, then withdraw his hand as though he thought better of touching her. "I know that you didn't choose to be here."

He scrubbed a hand through his hair, his cheeks clenched as though he were struggling for words, and her heart began to pound anticipating what he would say. "I want you to know that you don't have to do anything you don't want to. That this . . . this is whatever you want it to be. Or don't want it to be."

"What is it to you?"

"The treaty means peace between Ithicana and Maridrina. It means lives saved. Maybe one day it will mean the end to violence on our shores."

"I didn't think we were talking about the treaty." She was intent on understanding what motivated this man, which included his desires.

Aren hesitated. "I hope our marriage will be the first step toward a future where my people's lives aren't tied to this ancient piece of stone."

The statement was so contradictory to what he'd said about the bridge being everything that Lara opened her mouth to ask for him to explain, but she was cut off by the sound of a horn blaring in the distance. It belted out a song, then repeated it twice. Aren swore after the first pass, his hand reaching for the large spyglass mounted at the center of the watchtower. He panned the water, unleashing a tirade of curses when he caught sight of whatever it was he was searching for.

"What is it?"

"Raiders." He flung himself at the stairs, then caught himself on the doorframe, halting his progress. "Stay here, Lara. Just . . . don't move. I'll send someone for you."

She started to argue, but he was already gone. Leaning over the edge of the tower, she watched him exit the base, sprint through the clearing, then disappear from sight.

Standing on her tiptoes, Lara peered through the spyglass. It took her a moment, but she finally caught sight of the ship passing under the bridge toward Midwatch, its deck teeming with armed men in uniforms, the Amaridian flag flying from the mast. A naval vessel. And not, if Aren's words were to be believed, one that had come in peace.

A loud crack split the air. Lara watched as a projectile tore through the rigging, a mast splintering and toppling sideways. It fell, sails and ropes catching on the metal spikes set into the base of one of the bridge piers. The ship keeled over, spilling countless men into the water. Another crack echoed up to her position, and a gaping hole appeared in the hull. A hole that swiftly disappeared as the vessel sank lower in the water.

Hands frozen on the spyglass, Lara held her breath as violent barrage of ammunition methodically destroyed the ship while those still aboard clambered higher, or swam toward shore, fins circling them ominously, no safety within reach. As she watched, one of the sailors was jerked under, and her blood ran cold as a cloud of crimson blossomed where he'd been. After that, it was a frenzy, the sharks attacking one after another after another, the water now more red than blue.

Moving the glass to where the island met the sea, she searched for any sign of Ithicanians, keen to see their defenses in action. But the angle was bad, the jungle obscuring her vision of whatever was happening at the water's edge.

This could be her one chance to see how the Ithicanians repelled invaders from the inside, and she was missing it because of a poor vantage point.

Lara found herself running. Down the stairs and into the clearing, her eyes trained on the path Aren had taken, trusting it would lead her to where she needed to go. The jungle was nothing but a blur of green as she ran, the humid air heavy in her lungs as she leapt over rocks, slid in the mud, caught her balance and kept going. The water wasn't far, and it was downhill.

The path burst out into the open, cutting along the edge of a cliff. Far below, the ocean slammed against sheer rock. She veered around a bend, finding herself at the top of a steep slope. Lara paused, taking cover behind a rock.

She spotted a cove that she hadn't been able to see from the watchtower. With a white sand beach and turquoise waters, it was hidden from the ocean by rocky cliffs, the opening to the sea beyond a gap barely wide enough for a small boat. The gap was currently blocked by a heavy chain connected to stone buildings on each side.

The beach was full of soldiers. Lara's gaze went to the strange boats sitting on the sand, which showed no sign of going anywhere, before shifting her attention to the Ithicanians standing atop the cliffs overlooking the sea, Aren's tall form among them.

Frowning, Lara peered around the boulder, trying to determine where the catapult the Ithicanians had used against the ship was located, when she heard loose gravel sliding down the path behind her. Then a voice: ". . . hardly worth the stones we lobbed at them. A brisk wind would put that decrepit piece of shit on the bottom of the sea."

Her heart skipping, Lara searched for a way to escape, but the beach was crawling with soldiers, to her left was a tangle of jungle vines, and to her right was a sheer drop onto the jagged rocks jutting out of the ocean. The only way to keep from being caught spying was forward.

Stepping out from her cover, Lara picked her way down the steep slope and onto the beach, ignoring the startled expressions of the soldiers.

One man put his fingers to his lips and gave a sharp whistle, causing those standing on the cliffs—including Aren—to turn. He was not so distant that she couldn't make out the surprise, and subsequent irritation, that crossed his face.

Before the soldiers could stop her, Lara circled the cove, climbing the steps carved into the rock that allowed access to the cliff overlooking the sea. Aren met her at the top, clearly not inclined to allow her to watch what was going on. "I told you to stay in the tower, Lara."

"I know, I—" She pretended to lose her balance on the narrow step, hiding a smile as he caught hold of her arm, pulling her onto the clifftop and giving her an unencumbered view of the bridge and the ship sinking next to it. "What's going on?"

"It's no concern of yours. Go down to the beach and someone will take you back up to the house." He motioned to one of his soldiers, and Lara's mind raced, grasping for a reason to linger.

"There are drowning men out there!" She waved away the soldier trying to take her arm. "Why aren't you helping them?"

"Those are raiders." Aren shoved the spyglass he was holding into her hand. "See the flag? That's an Amarid vessel. They were trying to find a way into the bridge under the cover of the fog."

"They could be merchants."

"They aren't. Look at the bridge. See the lines hanging from it?"

Through the glass, Lara pretended to look at the men dangling from ropes when really she was examining the structure itself, searching for openings. This was a vantage point no one but the Ithicanians had, and it was possible she might learn something valuable. But Aren plucked the spyglass out of her hand before she could get more than a quick glance.

"This is an act of war against us, Lara. They deserve what they get."

"No one deserves this," she replied, and though her reaction was an act, her stomach still twisted as the waves pummeled the ship, swallowing the wreckage whole. All the Amaridians were in the water now, some trying to reach the dangling ropes, others swimming in the direction of the island on which she stood. "Help them."

"No."

"Then I will." She whirled around, keen to use a dramatic display of empathy to get a closer look at the small craft on the beach, only to find herself face-to-face with three of Aren's soldiers. "Let me pass."

None of them moved, but neither did they reach for their weapons. Lara glanced over her shoulder, taking in the twin stone structures with solid doors and no windows, which guarded the mechanism for lifting the chain. She suspected they were always guarded. Yet her eyes were drawn from her assessment to the handful of sailors who, against all odds, were within reach of the gap leading to the cove. But several of them were floundering, the heavy waves washing over their heads.

"Please." Lara shouldn't care whether the Amaridians lived or died, but she found that she did, the shake in her voice genuine as she said, "This is cruelty."

Aren's face was dark with anger. "Cruelty is what those men would've done to *my* people if they'd managed to get past our defenses. Ithicana never asked for this. We never invade their lands. Never slaughter their children for sport." He pointed his finger at the sailors, and bile rose in Lara's throat as another was jerked beneath the waves, the water frothing red as the shark tore him apart. "They brought war to us."

"If you let them die, are you any better?" There were only three sailors left, and they were close. Except fins trailed in their wake. "Show some mercy."

"You want mercy?" Aren twisted on his heel, reaching into his quiver even as he turned. Three blurs of black fletching, and the remaining sailors sank beneath the waves. He rotated back to face her, knuckles white where they gripped his bow.

Lara dropped to her knees, closing her eyes and feigning distress even as she sought her own inner focus. Ithicana was showing its true colors. Not peaceful courtyards and soothing hot springs, but violence and cruelty. And Aren was its master.

But she would be his doom.

"Wait for the winds to die, then pick off those hanging from the rock," Aren ordered his soldiers. "The last thing we need is one of them finding their way in at low tide." Then boots thudded past her, and he went down the steps to the hidden beach.

Lara stayed where she was, smiling inwardly as the Ithicanians gave her and her moral outrage wide berth even as she considered Aren's words: *a way in at low tide*. A way into where, was the question. Into the cove? Or had he been referring to a far greater prize?

The winds died, the sun retreated behind another bank of clouds, and the rains returned, soaking her to the bone. But she did not move. In stoic silence, she watched the soldiers push the boats out into the water, sail beneath the bridge, and methodically shoot the sailors who'd managed to cling to the ropes through the entire ordeal, their lifeless bodies falling to the ocean below.

She said nothing as they returned, only marked the meandering route they took, which was too purposeful to be without design, the necessity revealed as the tides reversed, the waters trailing away to reveal the deadly traps beneath the surface. Steel spikes and jagged rocks, all intended to destroy any approaching vessel unaware of the correct path.

The tide hit its lowest point, and Lara started to rise, convinced she'd seen all there was to see. Then a shadow at the base of the nearest bridge pier caught her attention. No, not a shadow. An opening.

Her heart sped, and it was a struggle to keep a smile from her face as elation filled her. She'd found a way into the bridge.

# 11
# AREN

"AMARID'S QUEEN MUST TRULY be desperate to be crewing her ships with this sort." Gorrick flipped over the corpse that had been pulled from the ocean, blood seeping into the white sand. It was missing a leg, courtesy of one of Ithicana's sharks. It was also missing its left thumb, but in that, the sharks were blameless. For the missing digit combined with the brand on the back of his hand indicated that this man had spent some time in one of Amarid's prisons for theft.

Kneeling down, Aren examined the dead soldier's threadbare uniform, the elbows worn through on both arms. "All convicts, you say?"

"Those that we could get a look at."

Standing, Aren frowned at the mist-covered waters of the cove. The Amaridian navy was well acquainted with Midwatch's shipbreakers, but the vessel had sailed right into their path, making them easy pickings. Perhaps an ancient ship with a crew of convicts was all the Amarid Queen had been willing to risk on the tail end of storm season, but still . . . What was the point?

Aren turned back to Gorrick. "Write a report and have it sent to the Watch Commanders informing them that raids have come early." Then he strode up the path toward the barracks, having no interest whatsoever in returning to his house.

"Wife chase you out already, Your Grace?" Jor was lounging next to the fire, a book in one hand. "She didn't seem too pleased with the Ithicanian form of mercy."

That she had not.

Lara had sat and brooded on the cliff edge until he'd wondered if he needed to get someone to drag her back to the house. Then abruptly she'd risen, trotted down the steps to the beach, and stormed past him without a word, the guards he'd posted on her looking as though they'd rather be swimming with sharks than watching over their new queen. About an hour later, Eli had arrived with a letter written by Lara to her father, and now, Aster's comments fresh in his ears, Aren was debating whether or not to send it.

"I doubt she's seen much of the way of violence before." Aren headed toward his bunk before thinking better of it and sitting next to the old soldier. "Read this."

Taking Lara's letter, the older man read it, then shrugged. "Looks to me like a proof of life letter."

Aren was inclined to agree. The letter said little more than that she was well, was being treated kindly, along with a lengthy description of his house, with a great emphasis on the hot spring. Even so, he'd read it over several times looking for code, not sure if he was happy or disappointed when he found none.

"Interesting that she doesn't mention you. Me thinks you have a cold bed in your future."

Aren snorted, the blurry remnants of the dream he'd had of Lara in his room, in his bed, in his arms, flashing across his thoughts. "She seems to take issue with being a treaty prize."

"Maybe she was expecting a better-looking husband. Some people handle disappointment poorly."

Aren lifted one eyebrow. "That's probably the only thing that hasn't been disappointing for her."

Jor shook his head. "Maybe she dislikes cocky little bastards."

"I've heard there are kingdoms where the people show a little respect for their monarchs."

"I can respect you and still think your shit stinks just as bad as the next man's."

Rolling his eyes, Aren accepted the mug that Lia, one of his honor guards, passed him, smiling until she said, "You're just pissed that the Rat King of Maridrina sent you a girl with an opinion rather than a brainless twit who'd"—she made a vulgar gesture—"without question."

"Like you, Lia?" Jor said with a wink, laughing as she tossed the contents of her cup at him. Aren snatched the letter out of the man's hand before it could suffer any further damage.

"You don't actually intend to send it, do you?" Jor asked.

"I told her I would. And besides, if Silas is wanting proof she's alive, it's best we satisfy him. The last thing we need is to give him an excuse to come looking for her."

"Lie. We can get a forger to carry on the correspondence."

"No." Aren's eyes drifted across the lines of neat writing. "I'll either send it or tell her that I chose not to. Is there anything on the surface here that we need to be worried about the Magpie seeing?"

Jor took it back, reading it once more, and not for the first time, Aren cursed having been born those few minutes before Ahnna. Those few damning minutes that made him King and her Commander, when he'd have given anything for their roles to be reversed. He was suited to fighting and for hunting and for sitting around the fire making bad jokes with other soldiers. Not for politics and diplomacy and having his whole goddamned kingdom depending on his choices.

"From the description of your fancy house, they might guess she's at Midwatch with you. They'll realize from her details about the jungle that we're granting her some liberty to move about. Speaking of"—Jor lifted his head—"what *was* she doing running around the island? She came from the same direction as you, which wasn't from the house . . ."

Chance would have it that Aren had arrived at the house right before Lara departed on her unsanctioned exploration of the island, and rather than have Lia stop her, he'd decided to see where his wife intended to go. "She was wandering."

Jor's eyebrows rose. "For what purpose?"

"Looking for the bridge."

All eyes in the common room turned to look at them, and Aren scowled. "It was mere curiosity . . ." He didn't know exactly why he was defending Lara, only that the things she'd said to him had struck a chord. It had been so easy to focus on the sacrifices he was making as part of this marriage that he hadn't stopped to think of what it had cost her. Of what it would continue to cost her. The exact same things he wanted to protect Ahnna from, and why he'd pay Harendell a fortune rather than force his sister into a marriage she didn't want. "Nearly got herself bitten by a snake, so I expect she won't go wandering again anytime soon."

"I wouldn't be so confident about that," Lia said. "When we blocked her from the boats, she looked about ready to punch me in the face. She might not be a warrior, but she's no coward."

"I'm inclined to agree," Jor said. "I'll have a couple extra guards stationed to keep an eye on her when you're not around."

Aren nodded slowly. "Send the letter to Southwatch for Ahnna and our codebreakers to look at and get a forger to transcribe it onto fresh paper. Then send it to Maridrina." His people knew every one of the Magpie's codes. If she was using one, they'd crack it.

"You think she's a spy?"

Exhaling a long breath, Aren considered his new wife, who was nothing like how he'd expected. Maridrinian kings used their daughters as bargaining chips, ways to secure alliances and favors within the kingdom and without. Lara and all of her sisters would have been raised knowing an arranged marriage to him—or someone else—was part of their future. They'd have been trained to do their duty as a wife, regardless of the circumstances.

Yet Lara had made it clear that the treaty secured her presence in Ithicana, not her compliance as a wife, and he respected that. Every woman who'd shared his bed had done so because she'd wanted to, and the idea of spending his life with a woman who was there solely out of duty was unappealing. He'd prefer a cold bed. "I'll give her some space. I think if she's been sent here to spy, she's going to come to me in pursuit of information. Maridrinians aren't known for their patience."

"And if she does?" Jor asked.

"I'll cross that bridge when it comes."

"And if she doesn't?"

In a way, if Lara was, in fact, an innocent girl who'd been sent to secure a peace treaty, it made Aren's task harder than if they exposed her as a spy. Because he had his own agenda when it came to his Maridrinian wife, and he wouldn't get very far with it if she hated his guts. "I'll win her over, I suppose."

Lia's drink sprayed out from between her lips. "Good luck with that, Your Grace."

He gave her a lazy smile. "I won you over."

Lia gave him a look that implied he was the stupidest creature to walk the earth. "She and I are *not* the same."

Yet it wasn't until Lara had continued to give him the cold shoulder for one night, then a week, then two, that he started to think that maybe Lia had been right.

# 12
# LARA

THE WEEKS AFTER the shipwreck and the slaughter on the beach passed without incident. Aren rose at dawn and didn't return until late in the evening, but he didn't leave her unattended. Wise to Lara's prior unsanctioned exploration of the island, the servants kept close watch on her, Clara always seeming to be dusting or mopping nearby, the scent of wood polish perpetually thick on the nose. Though in truth, the storms that passed overhead did more than the servants or guards ever could to keep Lara contained. Violent winds, lightning, and a ceaseless deluge of rain were regular occurrences. Moryn, the cook, told her these were the last gasps of the season and nothing in comparison to the typhoons she'd witness when the next began.

Though she was desperate to get another look at the opening into the pier, Lara, by design, did nothing to provoke interest, using the time to discreetly search the home for any clues that might assist in planning Maridrina's invasion of Ithicana. Maps were her primary goal, and the one thing she failed to find. Serin had countless documents detailing the islands that made up the kingdom, on which a long line depicting the bridge was always drawn, but none with any detail. Lara had now seen for herself—the kingdom was nearly impossible to infiltrate due to the lack of beaches, compounded by the defenses in the water, which the Ithicanians seemed capable of shifting and changing at will.

The other mystery was where the islanders themselves resided. No civilizations of size had ever been spotted from the sea, and successful landings and raids only spoke of small villages, leading Serin and her father both to believe the population small, violent, and uncivilized, dedicated to basic needs, vicious defense of their bridge, and little else. But though she'd only been in Ithicana a short time, Lara was not inclined to agree with that assessment.

It was what Aren had said to her in the tower. *The bridge . . . For Ithicana, it's everything. And Ithicana is everything to me.*

The tone in his voice showed genuine sentiment. There were civilians here. Civilians Aren believed needed protection, and all of her training told her they would be Ithicana's greatest weakness. She need only determine where they were and how to exploit that knowledge. Then pass it back to Maridrina.

She'd sent her first letter to her father already, a code-free missive carefully crafted to ensure it gave no reason for the Ithicanians to detain it. A test to see if Aren would allow her to correspond before she attempted the riskier task of trying to get intel past the codebreakers at Southwatch.

Proof that Aren had been true to his word came in a response from her father. And the letter was delivered by none other than King Aren himself.

She'd seen him arriving home through the window, soaking wet from the most recent downpour, and not for the first time, she wondered what it was he did during his days. More often than not he returned wet, muddy, and smelling of sweat, his face shadowed with weariness. Part of her had wanted to approach him—had feared that she'd erred her strategy of gaining his trust and had alienated him entirely. But another part had told her that she'd made the right choice in forcing him to come to her.

"This arrived in Southwatch for you." He dropped the folded pieces of paper in her lap. He was bathed and changed into dry clothes now, but the exhaustion lingered.

"You read it, I assume." She unfolded the letter, noting Serin's spidery imitation of her father's script and feeling the faintest stab of disappointment. Of course it had been him to write it. He knew the codes, not her father. She set it aside, not wanting to read it just yet.

"You know I did. And to save you the trouble, my codebreakers helpfully translated the piss-poor code. Transcription is on the back. I'll let the deception slide this time because it didn't come from you, but there won't be any second chances."

*So much for Marylyn's unbreakable code*. Flipping over the page, she read aloud, "Relieved that you are well, dearest daughter. Send word if you are mistreated, and we will retaliate."

Aren snorted.

"What did you expect? That he'd marry me off to you and not care what became of me?"

"More or less. He got what he wanted."

"Well, now you know otherwise." And now *she* knew that getting information out of Ithicana would be just as challenging as predicted. "Perhaps you might send him a letter yourself reassuring him of your good intentions."

"I don't have time for carrying on a casual correspondence with your father, or"—he picked up the letter—"the Magpie, judging from the penmanship."

*Bloody hell, the Ithicanians were good.* Lara averted her gaze. "Your time is clearly precious. Please do carry on with whatever it is you need to do."

He started to turn, then hesitated, and from the corner of her eye, she watched him catch sight of the deck of cards she'd left sitting on the table. "You play?"

A mix of nerves and excitement filled her, the same feeling she got before stepping into the training yard to fight. This was a different kind of battle, but that didn't mean she wouldn't win.

"Of course I play."

He hesitated, then asked, "Do you care for a game?"

Shrugging, she picked up the deck and expertly shuffled, the cards making sharp snapping sounds in her hands. "Do you really wish to gamble with me, Your Majesty? I must warn you, I'm quite good."

"One of your many talents?"

Lara's heart skipped, and she wondered if he remembered more from their intimate encounter than she realized. Yet he only eyed her for a moment, then took the seat across from her, resting one booted foot on his knee. "Do you have any coin to bet, or am I risking my money on both sides of every wager?"

She gave him a cool smile. "Pick a different stake."

"How about truths?"

Lara cocked one eyebrow. "That's a children's game. What are we to do next? Dare each other to run around the house naked?"

Because nudity had been more in line with what she'd thought he'd suggest. The cards were a trick of seduction that Mezat, their Mistress of the Bedroom, had taught the sisters. All men, she had told them, were happy to risk their own clothing for a chance to see naked breasts. Except, it turned out, for the King of Ithicana.

"We can save the naked sprints for storm season. It's far more exciting if there's lightning biting at your ass."

Shaking her head, Lara shuffled the cards again. "Poker?" Best to choose a game in which she would not lose.

"How about Trumps?"

"More luck than skill in that game."

"I know." The way he said it was like a dare. And for better or worse, she never turned down a challenge, so she shrugged. "As you like. To nine?"

"Boring. How about a truth for each trump."

Her mind raced with questions she might ask. With questions that *he* might ask, and the answers she'd give.

Reaching over to the corner table, Aren picked up a bottle of amber liquor, took a mouthful, then set it between them. "To make things more fun."

One of her eyebrows rose. "There are glasses on the sideboard, you know."

"Less work for Eli this way."

Rolling her eyes, she took a mouthful. The brandy, as it turned out to be, burned like fire down her throat. Then she dealt the cards, silently cursing when he had the trump. "Well?"

Taking the bottle, Aren eyed her thoughtfully and Lara's heart began to hammer. There were a thousand things he could ask, for which she had no answer. For which she'd have to lie, and then keep that lie alive for the length of her time here. And the more lies she had to balance, the greater chance of getting caught.

"What is"—he took a mouthful"—your favorite color?"

Lara blinked, her heart stuttering and then settling even as she looked away from his hazel eyes, feeling heat rise to her cheeks. "Green."

"Excellent. Plenty of that about, so I need not ply your favor with emeralds."

Giving a soft snort of amusement, Lara handed over the cards, which he swiftly shuffled and then dealt.

She won the next round.

"I'll not ask you nonsense questions," she warned, taking the bottle from him. Her questions needed to be strategic—not intended to uncover the secrets of the bridge, but to understand the man who held those secrets so close to his heart. "Did you take pleasure in killing those raiders? In watching them die?"

Aren winced. "Still angry about that, then?"

"A fortnight is not sufficient time for me to forget the cold-blooded slaughter of a ship full of men."

"I suppose not." Aren leaned back in the chair, eyes distant. "Pleasure." He said the word as though he were tasting it, trying it out, then shook his head. "No, not pleasure. But there is a certain satisfaction to seeing them die."

Lara said nothing, and her silence was rewarded a moment later.

"I've served at Midwatch since I was fifteen. Commanded it since I was nineteen. Over the past ten years, I've lost track of the number of battles I've fought against raiders. But I remember all thirteen times we were too late. When we reached our people after the raiders had their way with them. Families slaughtered. And for what? Fish? They have nothing worth taking. So instead they take their lives."

Lara pressed the palms of her hands to her skirts, sweat soaking through the silk. "Why do they do it, then?"

"They think they can learn ways into the bridge through them. But the civilians don't use the bridge. They don't know its secrets. You'd think after all these years our enemies would have figured that out. Maybe they have." His face twisted. "Maybe they just kill them for *pleasure*."

His fingers brushed hers as he passed over the deck, warm against her icy skin. Aren won the next hand.

"Since we are asking difficult questions . . ." He tapped one finger against his chin. "What's your worst memory?"

She had a hundred worst memories. A thousand. Of abandoning her sisters to fire and sand. Of Erik, the man who'd been like a father to her, taking his own life in front of her because he believed she'd been driven to murder her own sisters. Of being left alone in a pit in the ground for weeks. Of being starved. Of being beaten. Of having to fight for her life, all while her masters told her that it was to make her strong. To teach her to endure. *We do this to protect you*, they had told her and her sisters. *If you need someone to hate, someone blame, look to Ithicana. To its king. If not for them, if not for him, none of this would be necessary. Bring them down, and no Maridrinian girl will ever suffer like this again.*

The memories triggered something deep within her, an irrational wash of rage and fury and fear. A hatred for this place. An even deeper hatred for the man sitting across from her.

Slowly, she shoved the emotions deep down inside her, but as she lifted her head, Lara could tell Aren had seen all of it play across of her face.

*Give him a truth.*

"I was born in the harem in Vencia. I lived there with my mother among all the other wives and younger children. After the treaty was signed, my father had all of his female children of appropriate age taken to the compound for their—for *our*—protection from Valcotta and Amarid and anyone else who sought to disrupt the alliance. I was five years old." She swallowed, the vision of the memory fuzzy, but the sounds and smells sharp as though they were yesterday. "There was no warning. I was playing when the soldiers grabbed me, and I remember kicking and screaming as they dragged me away. They smelled awful—like sweat and wine. I remember more men holding my mother against the ground. Her fighting, trying to get to me. Trying to stop them from taking me." Lara's eyes burned, and she chased away the tears with a mouthful of brandy. Then another. "I never saw her again."

"I wasn't fond of your father before," Aren said quietly. "Less so, now."

"The worst part is . . ." She trailed off, staring at the insides of her eyelids, trying to find what she was looking for. "Is that I can't remember her face. If I met her on a street, I'm not sure I'd even know it was her."

"You'd know."

Lara bit the insides of her cheeks, hating that he, of all people, would say something that would bring her comfort. *It's because of him you were taken from your mother. It's his fault. He is the enemy. The enemy. The enemy.*

A knock sounded loudly against the door, and Lara jumped, ripped from her thoughts by the interruption.

"Come in," Aren said, and the door opened to reveal a beautiful young woman dripping with weapons. Her long black hair was shaved on the sides, the rest pulled into a tail on top of her head—a style that seemed to be favored by the female warriors—and her eyes were a pale grey. Half a head taller than Lara, her bare arms were solid with muscle, her skin marked with old scars.

"This is Lia. She's part of my guard. Lia, this is Lara. She's…"

"Queen." The young woman inclined her head. "It is an honor to meet you, Your Grace."

Lara inclined her head, curious about Ithicana's female warriors. Her father had told Lara and her sisters that they'd be underestimated because they were women, but the women here seemed to be as respected as any man.

Lia had turned her attention back to her king and was handing him a folded piece of paper. "Season's been declared over."

"I heard the horns. Two weeks earlier than last year."

Lara picked up her own letter, hoping they'd say more if they believed her distracted. Serin had written about her eldest brother, Rask, who was heir. He'd apparently fought successfully in some tourney, and the Magpie described the events in vivid detail. Not that she cared, having never had anything to do with her brother. The Ithicanian codebreaker had circled the letters that formed the code, but not, she realized, *Marylyn's code*. Rereading the document with an eye for the code her eldest sister had created, Lara contained a smile as she lifted the pattern from the page. Apparently the Ithicanians were fallible, after all.

Her hidden smile vanished as she parsed the code. *Maridrina receiving only rotten produce. Molding grains. Diseased cattle. Valcottan ships departing with holds full of superior goods.*

Serin had explained the new trade terms that had been negotiated as part of the treaty. The elimination of taxes on goods Maridrina purchased in Northwatch, which would then be shipped to Southwatch with no tolls. On the surface, it was a good deal for Maridrina and a large concession for Ithicana. Unless one considered that it placed all the risk of goods deteriorating during transport on Maridrina's shoulders. If the grain purchased in Northwatch rotted before it reached Southwatch, it was Maridrina's loss and not Ithicana's problem. And what wonder Maridrina was receiving the worst of goods when it was Ithicana who coordinated the transport. The pages crumpled slightly under Lara's grip, and she tore her eyes from the writing as she heard Aren say, "No getting around her request, I suppose."

Lia agreed, then inclined her head. "I'll leave you to it."

Lara watched the other woman leave, struggling to master her expression. Serin's message didn't surprise her, but it was still infuriating to know that the man calmly sitting across from her playing cards was consciously making choices to harm her people.

Cards snapped against the table. Another hand. Another truth.

Picking them up, Lara eyed the hand, knowing they were high and that she should think up a question that gained her something. But when she won, the question that came out was something different. "How did your parents die?"

Aren stiffened, then scrubbed a hand through his hair. Reaching over, he jerked the bottle out of her hand, draining it dry.

Lara waited. In her failed searches for maps, she'd found other things. Personal things. Drawings of the prior king and queen, the resemblance between Aren and Ahnna and their beautiful mother striking. She'd also found a box full of treasures that only a mother would keep. Baby teeth in a jar. Portraits. Notes written in a childish script. There had been rough little carvings, too, with Aren's name scratched on the bottom. A much different family than her own.

"They drowned in a storm," he answered flatly. "Or at least, he did. She was probably already dead."

There was more to that story, but it was clear he had no intention of sharing it. And that he was running out of patience for this horrible game of chance. More cards on the table. Lara won again.

*You rattled him*, she told herself. *He's been drinking. Now is the time to push.*

"What's it like inside the bridge?" Her eyes skipped from the cards, to the empty bottle, to his hands, resting on the arms of his chair. Strong. Capable. The sensation of them running across her body danced across her skin, the taste of his mouth on hers, and she shoved the thoughts away as her cheeks—and other parts of her body—heated.

His eyes sharpened, the haze of brandy wiped away. "You need not concern yourself with what the bridge is or is not like, as you'll never have cause to be in it."

Aren rose to his feet. "My grandmother wishes to meet you, and she is not one to be denied. We'll go tomorrow at dawn. By *boat*." He leaned down, resting his hands on the sides of her chair, the muscles of his arms standing out in stark relief. Invading her space. Attempting to intimidate her the way his damned kingdom intimidated every other.

"Let me make myself abundantly clear, Lara. Ithicana has not held the bridge by spilling its secrets over a bottle of brandy, so if that's your intent, you'll have to get more creative. Better yet, save us all the trouble and forget it even exists."

Lara leaned back in her chair, never breaking eye contact. With both hands, she pulled up the skirt of her dress, higher and higher until her thighs were revealed, seeing the intensity of his gaze shift to a different target. Lifting one leg, she pressed a naked foot against his chest, watching his eyes race from her knee to her thigh to the silken underthings she wore beneath.

"How about you take your bridge," she said sweetly, "and shove it up your ass." His eyes widened right as she straightened her leg, shoving him out of her space. Picking up her book, she tugged her skirt back into place. "I'll see you at dawn. Goodnight, Your Grace."

A faint chuckle filled her ears, but she refused to look up even as he said, "Goodnight, Princess," and disappeared from the room.

# 13
# AREN

VITEX WOVE HIS way in a serpentine pattern between Aren's ankles, purring as he went, seemingly not inclined to desist in his pursuit of attention, despite the fact that Aren had been ignoring him for at least ten minutes.

The nearly blank sheet of paper on the desk taunted him, golden edges glinting in the lamplight. He'd gotten as far as writing out the formal greeting to King Silas Veliant of Maridrina, but not a word further. His intention had been to accede to Lara's request and correspond with her father, to assure the man of his daughter's wellbeing. But now, the pen in his hand on the verge of dripping onto the expensive stationery, Aren found himself at a loss of what to say.

Mostly because Lara remained an enigma. He'd attempted to learn more about her nature during that awful card game, and after hearing how she'd been taken from her mother, it was very clear that if she was a spy, it wasn't out of love for her father. But that didn't mean she was innocent. Loyalty, to a certain extent, could be purchased, and Silas had means.

Irritated with the circular nature of his thoughts, Aren tossed his pen aside. Picking up the box of stationery, he pulled up the false side to reveal the narrow drawer designed to hide documents from prying eyes, and shoved the letter to Lara's father inside. He would complete it once he was more certain that Lara's welfare was something he could assure.

Patting his cat once on the head, he shooed the animal out the door and strode down the hallway. Eli was polishing silverware, but he looked up at Aren's approach. "Going to the barracks, Your Grace?"

It was painfully tempting to escape down to the barracks where he could sit around the fire with his soldiers, drink and properly gamble, but that would raise questions as to why he *wasn't* spending his nights with his new wife. "Just a walk down to the cliffs."

"I'll leave a lamp burning for you, Your Grace." The boy turned back to his work.

Forgoing a lantern, Aren walked down the narrow path to a spot where naked rock overhung the sea. Waves crashed against the black rock of the cliffs below, water rushing as it retreated only to surge forth again, slamming against Midwatch like an implacable, relentless hammer. Ferocious, yet somehow peaceful, the sound lulling Aren's senses as he stared at the blackness over the sea.

Groaning, he laid back, the water pooled on the rocks soaking into his clothes as he stared up into the night, the sky a patchwork of cloud and stars, not a light in any direction to distract from their glimmer. His civilians knew better than that, especially in the shoulder season. The moment in the year when the storms ceased to protect Ithicana, and his kingdom was forced to rely on steel, wits, and secrecy.

Would that ever change? Could it?

Paper crinkled against his chest, the pages tucked inside his tunic what had driven him to seek Lara tonight. They were kill orders.

Two fifteen-year-old girls had stolen a boat in an apparent attempt to escape Ithicana. They'd planned to go north to Harendell, according to the information that had been gleaned from their friends.

The kill order was for them. The charge: treason.

It was forbidden for civilians to leave Ithicana. Only highly trained spies were granted the right to do so, and always on the order that if they were ever caught, they'd die on their own sword before revealing

Ithicana's secrets. Only the career soldiers in his army knew all the ways in and out of the bridge, but it was impossible to keep the island defenses from the civilians who lived on them, and *everyone* knew about Eranahl. Which was why any civilian caught attempting to leave was flogged. And any who succeeded in the attempt were hunted.

And Ithicana's hunters always caught their quarry.

*Fifteen*. Aren clenched his teeth, feeling sickness rising in his guts. The report didn't give a reason for why the girls had fled. It didn't need to. At fifteen, they'd been assigned to their first garrison. It would be their first War Tides, and they'd have no choice but to fight. And rather than doing so, they risked their lives to flee. To find another path. Another life.

And he was supposed to order their execution for the offense.

His parents had rarely fought, but this law had brought out the shouts and slammed doors, his mother pacing the rooms in such fervor that he and Ahnna had both listened in fear of one of her fits taking her, of her heart stopping, never to beat again. Closing his eyes, he heard the echo of her voice, shouting at his father, "We are in a cage, a prison of our own making. Why can't you see that?"

"It's what keeps our people safe," his father would shout back. "Let down our guard, and Ithicana is *done*. They will tear us apart in their fight to possess the bridge."

"You don't know that. It could be different, if we tried to make it so."

"The raiders who come every year say otherwise, Delia. This is how we keep Ithicana alive."

And always, she would whisper, "Alive isn't living. They deserve more."

Aren shook his head to drive away the memory. Except it only receded, content to haunt him.

Allowing civilians to come and go from Ithicana all but ensured every one of the kingdom's secrets would leak. Aren knew that. But if Ithicana had strong alliances with Harendell and Maridrina, the consequences of those leaks would be far more palatable. With the navies of those two kingdoms supporting the bridge's defense, it would give some of his people a chance to pursue paths other than the sword. To leave and educate themselves. To bring that knowledge home and share it. It would mean he'd no longer have to sign kill orders for children.

But the older generations were adamantly against such a move. A lifetime of war had turned them against outsiders, filled them with hate. And filled them with fear. He needed Lara to help him change that, to make them see Maridrinians as friends, not foes. To convince them to fight for a better future, no matter the risks.

Because how things were . . . It couldn't continue forever.

Pulling the papers from his pocket, Aren shredded them, allowing the breeze to carry them out to sea.

Then there was a commotion in the bushes, and Aren was on his feet, blade in hand in time to see Eli burst into the open. The servant boy skidded to a stop, breathless, and said, "It's the queen, Your Grace. She needs your help."

# 14
# LARA

HANDS HELD HER wrists, pinning them to the table. Cloth covered her eyes. Her nose. Her mouth.

Water poured down, an endless torrent.

Only to cease.

"Why were you sent to Ithicana?" a voice whispered in her ear. "What is your purpose? What do you want?"

"To be a bride. To be queen," she choked, fighting her restraints. "I want peace."

"Liar." The voice sent fear through her. "You're a spy."

"No."

"Admit it!"

"There's nothing to admit."

"Liar!"

The water poured, and she drowned all over again. Unable to voice the truth to save herself. Unable to breathe.

There was sand beneath the fingers, cold and dry. She couldn't move, her wrists and ankles bound and tied to her waist. Trussed up like a pig.

Darkness.

She rolled, colliding with a wall, more sand falling onto her head, dragging at her hair. Backward, the same.

No way out.

Except up.

Fear binding her in place, she lifted her head to see faceless figures staring down at her.

So far away. With her wrists tied so tight the skin sloughed off, there was no way to climb.

"Why have you come to Ithicana? What is your purpose? Are you a spy for your father?"

"To be queen." Her throat burned, so dry. So thirsty. "To be a bride of peace. I am no spy."

"Liar."

"I'm not."

Sand struck her in the face. Not just tiny grains, but chunks of rock that bruised and sliced. Forcing her to cringe. To grovel. Eleven shovels flung sand at her from all sides. Striking her. Hurting her. Filling the hole.

Burying her alive.

"Tell us the truth!"

"I am!" The sand was up to her chin.

"Liar!"

She couldn't breathe.

She was seated on a chair, her wrists bound together. Her nails picked and scratched at the ropes, blood trickling down her palms. Fabric covered her eyes, but she could feel the heat of flames.

"They will do worse to you in Ithicana, Lara," Serin's voice crooned in her ear. "Far worse." He whispered the horrors, and she screamed, needing to get away. Needing to escape.

"Worse things will be done to your sisters," he sang, pulling off her hood.

There was fire in her eyes. Burning. Burning. Burning.

"You will not touch my sisters," she screamed. "You cannot have them. You will not hurt them."

Except it was Marylyn holding the coals to her feet, not Serin. Sarhina, tears running down her face, who tightened the noose.

And it was Lara who was burning. Her hair. Her clothes. Her flesh.

She could not breathe.

A hand was gripping her, shaking her. "Lara? Lara!"

Lara reached up, catching hold of the hilt of her knife, remembering herself just in time to stop from stabbing Aren in the face.

"You were having a nightmare. Eli fetched me when they heard you screaming."

*A nightmare.* Lara took a deep breath, digging deep into her core for some semblance of calm. Only then did she see the door hanging crooked on its frame, the latch in pieces scattered across the floor. Aren wore the same clothes he had earlier, his hair damp and clinging to his forehead.

Tearing her eyes away, Lara reached for a water glass, her mouth tasting sour from too much brandy. "I can't remember anything." A lie, given the smell of burning hair still filled her nose. Nightmares that weren't dreams, but memories of her training. Had she said anything incriminating? Had he realized she was reaching for the knife under her pillow?

Aren nodded, but his brow furrowed, suggesting that he didn't quite believe her. The sweat-soaked sheets peeled off her skin as she leaned out of the bed to fill her glass with the water pitcher, knowing the nightgown she wore only barely covered her breasts and hoping the flash of skin would distract him.

"Who did that to you?"

Lara froze, certain in an instant that she *had* shouted something damning while caught in her fugue state. Her eyes skipped to the open door, calculating her chances of escape, but then his fingers grazed the skin of her back, following a familiar pattern. Scars, which her sister Sarhina had rubbed oil into every night for years until they'd faded into thin white lines.

"Who did this?" The heat in his voice made her skin prickle.

Serin had ordered it done after she'd snuck out of the compound and into the desert to watch one of the caravans as it passed, countless camels and men laden with goods to sell in Vencia. For her troubles, she'd received a dozen lashes, Serin screaming the entire time that she'd put *everything* at risk. Lara had never entirely understood why he'd been so angry. There'd been no chance of the caravan catching sight of her, and all she'd wanted was to see what goods they carried.

"My teachers were strict," she muttered. "But it was a long time ago. I almost forget they're there."

Rather than appeasing him, Aren only appeared to grow angrier. "Who treats a child this way?"

Lara opened her mouth, then closed it, no good answer coming to mind. All of her sisters had suffered beatings for infractions, though none as often as she. "I was a disobedient child."

"And they thought to beat the trait out of you?" His voice was icy.

Pulling the sheet up to cover her body, Lara didn't answer. Didn't trust herself to.

"For what it's worth, no one will lay a hand on you in Ithicana. You have my word." Rising, he picked up the lamp. "Dawn is only a few hours away. Try to get some sleep." He left the room, pulling the broken door shut behind him.

Lara lay in bed, listening to the soothing patter of rain against the window, still feeling the trace of Aren's fingers on her bare skin. Still hearing the adamancy in his voice that she'd never be hurt in Ithicana, a promise so entirely at odds with everything she knew about him and his kingdom. *His word means shit,* she reminded herself. He gave his word to allow Maridrina free trade, and all her homeland had to show for it was rotten meat.

Her goal was the bridge. Finding a way past Ithicana's defenses and into the structure coveted by all. And today, Aren was taking her on a tour of his kingdom. With luck, she'd see how they traveled, where and how they launched their boats, where their civilians were located. It was the first step toward a successful invasion. The first step toward Maridrina returning to prosperity.

*Focus on that,* she told herself. *Focus on what this means for your people.*

But no amount of deep breathing steadied the rapid pulse in her throat. Rising from the bed, she went to the doorway to the antechamber. Jumping, she caught hold of the frame, her nails digging into the wood as she pulled herself up and lowered herself down, the muscles in her back and arms flexing and burning as she repeated the motion thirty times. Forty. Fifty. Imagining her sisters doing pull-ups next to her, urging each other on even as they fought for victory.

Dropping to the ground, Lara lay on the floor and moved on to crunches, her abdominals fiery beasts as she passed one hundred. Two hundred. Three hundred. The Red Desert was hotter than Ithicana, but the humidity here was murder. Sweat dripped down her skin as she moved from exercise to exercise, the pain doing more than any meditation to drive away unwanted thoughts.

By the time Clara knocked on the door with a tray full of food and a steaming cup of coffee, Lara was ravenous and beyond caring if the servant noticed her red face and sweaty clothes.

Drinking the coffee, she mechanically shoveled food down her throat, then bathed before donning the same clothes she'd worn during her last trek through the jungle, including the heavy leather boots. She belted her knives at her waist and wove her hair in a tight braid that hung down the center of her back. Light was beginning to glow around the heavy drapes on the window when she left the room.

She found Eli sweeping the hallway. "He's waiting for you out front, my lady."

Aren was indeed waiting, and Lara took a moment to watch him through the glass window before making her presence known. He sat on the steps, elbows resting on the stone behind him, the muscles of his arms bare beneath the short sleeves of his tunic, vambraces buckled onto his forearms. The rising sun, for once not obscured by clouds, glinted off the arsenal of weapons strapped to his person, and Lara scowled at her lone pair of knives, wishing she were similarly armed.

Pushing open the door, Lara took a deep breath of the humid air, tasting the salt of the sea on the soft breeze and smelling the damp earth. A silver mist drifted through the jungle canopy, the air filled with the drone of insects, the call of birds, and the screeches of other creatures for which she had no name.

Aren rose without acknowledging her or her nightmare, and she followed a few steps behind so that she could watch him without scrutiny as they walked down the narrow, muddy trail. He had a predatory grace about him: a hunter, his eyes roving the ground, the canopy, the sky, his bow held loosely in his left hand rather than slung over one shoulder the way her father's soldiers carried them. He would not be caught unaware, and she idly wondered *just* how good a fighter he was. Whether, if it came down to it, she'd be able to best him.

"You always look like you want to kill someone," he remarked. "Possibly me."

Kicking a loose rock, Lara scowled at the muddy pathway. "I hadn't realized the dowager queen still lived." Indeed, she'd been under the impression that all who remained of the royal line were the king and his sister.

"She doesn't. Nana is my father's mother." Aren turned his head as something rustled in the bushes. "My mother, Delia Kertell, was the one born to the royal line. My father's family was common-born, but he rose through the military ranks and was chosen to join her honor guard. Mother took a liking to him and decided to marry him. My grandmother . . . she's a healer, of some renown. Although others might use different words to describe her, my sister included."

"And why does she want to see me, exactly?"

"She's seen you," he said.

Lara narrowed her eyes.

"When you first came and were still asleep. She checked to ensure your health was good. What she wants is to meet you. As to why . . . She's meddlesome and everyone, including me, is too terrified to say no to her."

The idea of a stranger inspecting her body while she was unconscious felt profoundly invasive. Lara's skin crawled, but she covered the reaction with a shrug. "Checking to see if my father had sent a pox-ridden girl to send you to your grave?"

Aren tripped and dropped his bow, swearing as he reached down to retrieve it from the mud.

"Not the swiftest method of assassination, but effective, nonetheless." She added, "And some might say the repugnance of the victim's final years, hours, days, is worth the wait."

The King of Ithicana's eyes widened, but he recovered quickly. "If that's how you intend to do me in, you'll want to move quickly. The pustules and skin rashes will reduce your appeal, I'm afraid."

"Hmm," Lara hummed, then clicked her tongue against her teeth in mock disappointment. "I'd hoped to wait until the dementia had taken over so as to spare myself the memory. But one must do what one must do."

He laughed, the sound rich and full, and Lara found herself smiling. They rounded a bend and came into a clearing dominated by a large building, a group of Ithicanian soldiers loitering in the sunlight.

"Midwatch barracks," Aren said by way of explanation. "Those twelve are my—our—honor guard."

The stone structure was large enough to house hundreds of men. "How many soldiers are here?"

"Enough." He strode through the clearing toward those waiting for them.

"Majesties," one of them said, bowing deeply, although there was amusement in his tone, as though such honorifics were rarely used. Tall and corded with muscle, he was old enough to be Aren's father, his close-cropped brown hair laced with grey. Lara stared into his dark brown eyes, something about his voice familiar, and after a heartbeat, she recognized it as that of the man who'd conducted the Ithicanian portion of her wedding.

"This is Jor," Aren said. "He's the captain of the guard."

"So nice to see you again," she replied. "Do all Ithicanian soldiers have side jobs, or are you an exception?"

The soldier blinked once, then a smile grew on his face, and he gave her an approving nod. "Good ear, princess."

"Poor memory, soldier. I'm a princess no longer—you yourself ensured that." She walked past them all, heading down the narrow path to the sea.

The older man laughed. "I hope you sleep with one eye open, Aren."

"And a knife under your pillow," Lia added, and the whole group laughed.

Aren laughed along with them, and Lara wondered if they knew that he'd yet to consummate their marriage. That by the laws of both kingdoms, they could walk their separate ways. Casting a backward glance over her shoulder, she met Aren's gaze unblinking and he swiftly looked away, giving a root crossing the trail a violent kick.

It didn't take long to reach the tiny cove where they hid the boats, which were a variety of sizes. They resembled canoes, except they had an outboard frame linking them to either one or two additional hulls, which she supposed balanced them in the waves. Some of them were rigged with masts and sails, including the pair into which the group loaded their weapons and gear. A hint of fear grew in Lara's chest. The boats were *tiny* compared to the ship she had taken for the crossing to Southwatch, and the seas beyond the cliff walls protecting the cove suddenly seemed rougher than they had moments ago, the whitecaps rising high and fierce, certain to swamp the flimsy vessels.

A dozen excuses filled her mind as to why she shouldn't, couldn't, leave the shore. But this was why she was in Ithicana—to find a way past their defenses—and Aren was about to reveal the information without any concession on her part. She'd be a fool to pass up the opportunity.

Aren stepped into the boat, then held out a hand for her, easily keeping his balance as the vessel rose and fell beneath him. Lara held her ground, biting the insides of her cheeks as she felt his scrutiny. He opened his mouth, but she beat him to it. "I can't swim, if that's what you're wondering." She hated admitting the weakness, and from the faint smile on his face, he knew it.

"I'm not sure I've ever met anyone who couldn't swim."

She crossed her arms. "It's hardly a necessary skill in the middle of the Red Desert."

All the soldiers studiously busied themselves with various tasks, every one of them clearly listening.

"Well." Aren turned to squint at the sea. "You've seen what prowls these waters. Drowning might be the easier way to go."

"How comforting." She ignored his hand and stepped into the boat before she could lose her nerve. It swayed beneath the added weight, and Lara dropped to her knees, clinging to the edge.

Laughing softly, Aren knelt next to her, holding up a black piece of fabric. "Sorry for this, but some secrets must be kept." Not waiting for assent, he blindfolded her.

*Shit*. She should've known it wouldn't be this easy. But sight wasn't the only way to discover information, so she kept her mouth shut.

"Let's go," he ordered, and the boat surged away from the beach.

For a moment, Lara thought it wouldn't be that bad, and then they must have slipped out of the cove, because the boat began to buck and plunge like a wild horse. Lara's heart thundered in her chest, and she clung to the bottom, not caring what Aren or the rest of the Ithicanians thought of her as water splashed her clothes, soaking them through. If they tipped over, or if one of them threw her in, none of her training would help her. She'd be dead.

*And then eaten.*

On the heels of her terror came a wave of nausea, her mouth filling with sour saliva no matter how many times she swallowed. *You can do this. Get control of yourself.* She clenched her teeth, fighting against the rising contents of her stomach. *Do not throw up,* she ordered herself. *You will not throw up.*

"She's going to puke," Jor said.

As if on cue, Lara's breakfast rose fast and violent, and she leaned blindly toward the edge right as the boat tipped sharply in the same direction. Her grip on the boat slipped even as she vomited, and she fell face first into the water. The cold sea closed over her head, and she flailed, imagining the water filling her lungs, fins circling around her. Teeth rising up to jerk her under.

She'd been here before. Drowned. Smothered. Strangled.

An old terror with a new face.

She could not breathe.

Hands grabbed at her tunic, hauling her back into the boat. She slammed into something solid and warm, then someone peeled up the edge of the fabric covering her face, and she found herself staring into the depths of Aren's hazel eyes.

"I've got you." His grip on her was so fierce it should've hurt, but was instead almost as comforting as being on dry land. Behind him was the bridge pier with the opening at its base, so tantalizingly close that her fear eased. But Aren pulled the blindfold back down, plunging her back into darkness.

The loss of her sight sent a wave of dizziness through her. Sweat mixed with the water dripping down her face, her breath coming in frantic little gasps.

She inhaled a ragged breath, fighting for the calm void she'd been trained to find if tortured when one of the guards said, "We could take the bridge. This seems cruel."

"No," Jor snapped. "Not happening."

But Lara felt Aren still. He was considering the idea. Which he'd only be doing if he, too, believed unnecessarily terrifying her was cruel. So she let her fear take hold.

Once she did, there was no turning back. Her terror was a wild beast of a thing bent on consuming her. Her chest clenched, her lungs paralyzed, and stars danced across her vision.

The waves tossed the boat up and down, the spikes set into the sea scraping along the metal-lined hull. Lara clung to Aren, the strength of his arm holding her against his chest and her fingernails digging into his shoulders the only things keeping her from falling into madness.

Vaguely, she heard the group arguing, but their words were a dull drone of noise, as unclear as a foreign language. But Aren's command, "Just do it!" cut through the fog.

The soldiers around her grumbled and swore. The steel plates on the hull ground against rock, and a second later, the violent buck and swell of the sea ceased. They were inside the bridge pier, but her panic didn't ease, for there was still water everywhere. She could still drown.

A crackle of a torch. The smell of smoke. The boat shifting as the soldiers disembarked. Lara fought to take note of these details, but her focus centered on the water surrounding her, on what was lurking within it.

"There's a ladder." Aren's chin, rough with stubble, brushed against her forehead as he shifted. "Can you reach up and grab it? Can you climb?"

Lara couldn't move. Her chest felt like bands of steel were wrapped around it, every exhalation painful. There was a faint repetitive thumping against the bottom of the boat, and it took her far too long to realize that it was because she was shaking and her boot was hitting the hull. But she couldn't seem to stop it. Couldn't seem to do anything but cling to Aren's neck, her knees clamped around his thighs like a vise.

"I promise I won't let you fall in." His breath was warm against her ear, and very slowly, she mastered enough of her panic to let go of his neck with one hand, reaching up to find the cold metal of the ladder. But it took all the bravery she possessed to let go of him, to pull herself up, blindly reaching for the next rungs.

Aren stood with her, gripping her waist with one arm, his other braced on the steel. He lifted her up, holding her steady until her feet found the ladder.

"How far?" she whispered.

"Sixty more rungs, from where your hands are now. I'll be right beneath you. You won't fall."

Lara's breath was deafening in her ears as she went up, rung by rung, her whole body quivering. She'd never felt like this before. Never been so afraid—not even when she'd stared death in the eye when her father had come to take Marylyn from the compound. She continued up and up, until someone grabbed her by the armpits, hauling her sideways, and set her down on solid stone.

"We'll keep that blindfold on only a little longer, Majesty," Jor said, but Lara hardly cared. There was a solid surface beneath her hands, and the ground wasn't moving. She could breathe.

Rock scraped against rock, boots thudded softly, then strong hands gripped her shoulders. Her blindfold was peeled back, and Lara found herself looking up into the King of Ithicana's worried face. Around them stood the soldiers, three of them holding torches that flickered yellow and orange and red. But beyond them yawned a darkness deeper than a moonless night. A blackness so complete, it was as though the sun itself had ceased to exist.

They were inside the bridge.

# 15
# LARA

"ARE YOU ALL RIGHT, Lara?"

It took several seconds for Aren's question to register, Lara's attention all for the grey stone beneath her, which was stained dark with dirt and lichen. The bridge wasn't made from blocks, as she had thought, but rather a smooth and unblemished material. Like mortar . . . but stronger. She'd never seen anything like it. The air was musty and ripe with the smell of mildew and moisture and manure. Aren's voice echoed off the walls, asking after her well-being over and over before the sound disappeared into the endless corridor of black.

"Lara?"

"I'm fine." And she was, in the sense that her panic had settled with the solidness of the bridge beneath her feet, excitement slowly bubbling up to take its place. She had done it. She'd found a way into the bridge.

Everyone was staring at her, shifting their weapons and supplies with obvious unease. Aren had caved to her fear, and in doing so, had revealed one of Ithicana's secrets. Jor, in particular, did not look pleased.

Aren's face was unreadable. "We need to get moving. I don't want to miss the tide on our return." He frowned. "Not while they're running cattle."

*Cattle. Food.* According to Serin's letter, the best of it was finding its way into the holds of Valcottan ships, not Maridrinian stomachs.

Jor held up her blindfold. "Best we put this back on."

The group's footfalls reverberated as they walked, Lara's hand resting on Aren's arm for guidance, the wind and sea only faintly audible. The bridge bent and curved, rising on gentle inclines and dipping down on declines as it meandered through the islands of Ithicana. It was a ten-day journey at walking speed between Northwatch and Southwatch islands, and she could scarcely imagine what it would be like to be enclosed within the bridge for so long. With no sense of day or night. With no way to get out other than to run toward the mouths of this great beast.

Though there *were* ways out; she knew that with certainty now. But how many? How were they accessed from the interior of the bridge? Were the openings only to the piers, or were there others? How did the Ithicanians know where they were?

Foreigners from every kingdom, merchants and travelers, traversed the bridge regularly. They were always under Ithicanian escort, but she knew for fact they weren't blindfolded. Serin had told her and her sisters that the only markers in the bridge were those stamped in the floor indicating the distance between the beginning and end. There were, to his knowledge, no other signs or symbols, and the Ithicanians were apparently fastidious in removing any marks anyone attempted to place. Those caught doing so were forever forbidden from entering the bridge, no matter how much money they offered to pay.

Answers would not be easily gained. She needed to earn Aren's trust, and to do that, she needed him to think he was winning her over.

"I'm sorry for my . . . loss of composure," she murmured, hoping the others wouldn't overhear, though the acoustics made it impossible that they would not. "The sea is . . . I'm not . . ."

She struggled to articulate an explanation for her fear, settling with, "Thank you. For not letting me drown. And for not mocking me mercilessly."

With the blindfold in place, Lara had no way to judge his reaction, and the silence stretched before he finally answered. "The sea is dangerous. Only war takes more Ithicanian lives. But it's unavoidable in our world, so we must master our fear of it."

"You don't appear to fear it at all."

"You're wrong." He was silent for a dozen strides. "You asked me how my parents died."

Lara bit her lip, remembering: *They'd drowned.*

"My mother had been sick for years with a bad heart. She was taken by a fit one night. A bad one. One she wouldn't come back from. Though there was a storm blowing in, my father insisted on taking her to my grandmother on the slim hope she could help." Aren's voice shook, and he coughed once. "No one could say for certain, but I was told my mother wasn't even breathing when he loaded her into the boat and set sail. The storm came in fast. Neither of them was seen again."

"Why did he do it?" She was both fascinated and horrified. This hadn't been just any pair, but the king and queen of one of the most powerful kingdoms in the known world. "If she was already gone, why risk it? Or at the very least, why didn't he have someone else take her?"

"Moment of stupidity, I suppose."

"Aren." Jor's voice was chiding from where he walked behind them. "Tell it right or don't tell it all. You owe them that much."

Lara considered the older guard, curious about their relationship. Her father would've had the head of anyone who'd dare speak to him in such a way. Yet Jor seemed to do so without fear; and indeed, she felt nothing more than mild irritation from the king striding on her left.

Aren huffed out a breath, then said, "My father didn't send her with someone else, because he wasn't the sort of man to put his well-being ahead of another. As to why he risked it at all . . . I suppose it was because he loved my mother enough that the hope of saving her was worth his own life."

To risk everything for the slim chance of saving those you loved . . . Lara knew that compulsion because that was how she felt about her sisters. And it might cost her her own life just yet.

"Ill-fated romance aside, my point is, I know what it's like to lose something to the sea. To hate it. To fear it." He kicked a bit of rock, sending it rattling ahead of them. "It knows no master, most certainly not me."

He said nothing more on the issue, or on anything else.

There was no sense of time in the bridge, and it seemed they'd been striding down the path for eternity, when Aren finally came to a halt.

Blind, Lara stood utterly still, relying on her other senses as the soldiers shifted about. Boots scuffed against stone, the echoes making it difficult for her to tell from which direction they were working, but then a breeze brushed against her left hand at the same time it hit her cheek, fresh air filling her nostrils. The opening was in the wall, not the floor.

"The stairs are too steep to navigate blind." Aren flipped her over his shoulder, his hand warm against her thigh as he balanced her weight. Instinct had her grip him by the waist, her fingers digging into the hard muscles of his stomach as he stooped down. Only at the last second did she think to reach out, her hand running the length of a solid slab that must have made up the door. A door that, unless she missed her mark, blended seamlessly into the wall of the bridge.

The sounds of the jungle grew as they went down a curved staircase, then the soft light of the sun filtered through her blindfold.

Aren set her back onto her feet without warning. Lara swayed as the blood rushed from her head, his hand on her back, guiding her forward before she could find her bearings.

"Good enough," Jor announced from somewhere ahead, and the blindfold was tugged from her eyes. Lara blinked, looking around, but there was only jungle, the canopy blocking even the bridge from sight.

"It's not far," Aren said, and Lara silently trailed after him, careful to keep to the narrow path. The guards encircled them, weapons held loosely in their hands, their eyes watchful. Unlike her father, who was constantly surrounded by his cadre of soldiers, this was the first time since their wedding that she'd seen Aren treated like a king. The first time she'd seen them protect him so aggressively. What was different?

Was this island dangerous? Or was it something else? There was a crackle in the trees, and both Jor and Lia stepped closer to her, hands going to their weapons, and Lara realized it wasn't the king they were worried about protecting. It was her.

They skirted the edge of a cliff overlooking the sea, the water thirty feet below crashing violently against the rocks. Lara searched in both directions for a spot where men could land, but there was none. On the assumption it was the same way all around the island, she could see why the builders had chosen it as a pier. It was nearly impenetrable. Yet, given Aren had intended to come by boat, there must be a way.

The house appeared out of nowhere. One minute it was trees and vines and vegetation, the next, a solid stone structure, the windows flanked with the ubiquitous storm shutters that all buildings on Ithicana likely possessed. The stone was coated with green lichen, and as they approached, Lara determined it was made of the same material as the bridge, as were the outbuildings in the distance. Built to withstand the lethal tempests that battered Ithicana ten months of the year.

Coming around the house, she caught sight of a stooped figure working in a garden fenced by stone.

"Brace yourself," Jor muttered.

"Finally deigned to grace me with your presence, Your Majesty?" The old woman didn't rise or turn from her plants, but her voice was clear and strong.

"I only received your note last night, Grandmother. I came as soon as I could."

"Ha!" The woman turned her head and spit, the glob flying clear over the garden wall to smack against a tree trunk. "Dragged your heels all the way here, I suspect. Either that or the weight of your crown is making you sluggish."

Aren crossed his arms. "I don't have a crown, which you well know."

"It was a metaphor, you fool."

Lara lifted a hand to her mouth, trying not to laugh. Somehow, the motion caught the old woman's attention despite her back being turned. "Or is my grandson's tardiness the result of him tarrying to wipe puke off your face, little princess?"

Lara blinked.

"Smelled you from a hundred paces away, girl. All those years in the dunes gave you no stomach for the waves, I take it?"

Flushing, Lara glanced at her clothes, which were still damp from falling out of the boat. When she looked back up, Aren's grandmother was on her feet, an amused smile on her face. "It's your breath," she explained, and Lara struggled not to stomp on Aren's foot when he covered his own mouth to hide a smirk. The old woman noticed.

"A little seasickness wouldn't have killed her, you idiot. You shouldn't have caved."

"We took precautions."

"Next time let her puke." Her gaze shifted back to Lara. "They all call me Nana, so you can, too." Then she pointed a finger at one of the guards. "You, pluck and dress that bird. And you two"—she jerked her chin at another pair—"finish picking these and then wash them up. And you." She leveled a steely gaze at Lia. "There's a basket of laundry that needs scrubbing. See it done before you go."

Lia opened her mouth to protest, but Nana beat her to it. "What? Too good to scrub the skids from an old woman's drawers? And before you say yes, remember that I wiped your shitty ass more times than I care to count when you were a babe. Be grateful that I can at least still do that much for myself."

The tall guardswoman scowled but said nothing, only collected the basket and disappeared down the slope to retrieve water.

"I assume Jor has gone off to bother my students." It took Nana pointing it out for Lara to realize with a start that the man had abandoned them without her noticing. "It still hasn't sunk in that they aren't interested in an old lecher like him."

"Your girls can take care of themselves," Aren replied.

"That wasn't my point, now was it?" Nana pulled the gate to the garden shut, then shuffled in their direction. Her hair was solid silver, and her skin wrinkled, but her eyes were shrewd and discerning as she squinted at her grandson. "Teeth!"

The barked command made Lara jump, but without hesitation, Aren bent over and opened his mouth, allowing his grandmother to inspect his straight white teeth. She grunted with satisfaction and then patted his cheek. "Good boy. Now where's your sister been? Avoiding me?"

"Ahnna's teeth are fine, Grandmother."

"Not her teeth that concern me. Has Harendell asked for her yet?"

"No."

"Send her anyway. It shows good faith."

"No." The word came out of Aren as a growl, which surprised Lara. Surely he didn't intend to break his contract with the northern kingdom? Not when he'd been willing to fulfill his half without argument?

"Ahnna doesn't need your coddling, boy. She can take care of herself."

"That's between me and her."

Nana grunted and spit before turning her attention to Lara. "So this is what Silas sent us, is it?"

"Pleased to make your acquaintance." Lara inclined her head with the same respect she'd have given a Maridrinian matron.

"We'll see how long that pleasure lasts." Faster than Lara would've believed an old woman could move, Nana reached over and gripped her by the hips, twisted her this way and that, before running her hands up Lara's sides, laughing when Lara batted them away. "Built for bedding if not breeding." She leveled a stare at her grandson. "Which I'm certain you've noticed, even if you haven't availed yourself."

"Grandmother, for the love of god—"

Reaching up, Nana flicked his earlobe hard. "Mind your tongue, boy. Now as I was saying"—she turned back to Lara—"you'll labor hard, but you'll deliver. You've the willpower." She ran a quick finger down an old scar on Lara's arm, one she'd earned in a knife fight against a Valcottan warrior. "And you've known pain."

This woman was too shrewd. Too close. Lara snapped, "I'm not a broodmare."

"Thank goodness for that. We've little time for horses here in Ithicana. What we need is a queen who'll produce an heir. Unlike your father, my grandson won't have an entire harem to ensure the royal line continues. Just. You."

Lara crossed her arms, annoyed though she had no right to be. There was zero chance of her producing *anything*. She'd been supplied with a year's worth of contraceptive tonic. There would be no surprises on that front.

"Come with me, I'll give you something for the seasickness. Boy, you go find something else to keep you busy."

Lara followed her inside. She expected the interior of the home to be damp and musty like the bridge, but instead it was dry and warm, the polished wooden panels on the walls reflecting the flames in the fireplace. One wall hosted floor-to-ceiling shelves filled with jars packed with plants, powders, colored tonics, and what appeared to be insects of various sorts. There were also several long glass cages, and Lara shivered as she saw coiled forms move within them.

"Don't like snakes?"

"I have a healthy respect for them." This earned a cackle of approval.

After rooting around in her shelves, Nana produced a twisted root, which she passed to Lara. "Chew this before and while you're on the water. It will help keep the nausea at bay." Lara sniffed it uncertainly, relieved to discover the smell, at least, was not disagreeable.

"I've got nothing for overcoming fear, though. That's your own problem to manage."

"Given I can't swim, I feel my fear of water is as healthy as my respect for snakes."

"Learn." The curtness of the old woman's tone conveyed a lack of tolerance for complaint that reminded Lara briefly, painfully, of Master Erik.

With a jerk, Nana opened the curtains covering one of the windows, allowing the sunlight to spill inside, then beckoned Lara closer. "You've your father's eyes. And your grandfather's."

Lara shrugged. "The color is some small proof that I'm a true princess of Maridrina."

"I wasn't talking about the color." Quick as the snakes in the cages, Nana caught Lara by the chin, fingers pressing painfully against her jaw. "You're a sly little thing, just like them. Always searching for an advantage."

Resisting the urge to pull away, Lara stared back into the woman's eyes, which were hazel. Like Aren's. But what she saw within them was very different from what she saw in his. "You speak as though you know my family."

"I was a spy when I was young. Your grandfather recruited me into his harem. He had the foulest breath of any man I've ever met, but I learned to hold my breath and think of Ithicana."

Lara blinked. This woman had infiltrated the harem as a spy? That it could be done was alarming of itself, but only the loveliest girls were brought into the King's harem, and Nana was . . .

"Ha, ha!" Nana's laugh made her jump. "I didn't always look like the last prune left in the bowl, girl. In my day, I was quite the beauty." Her fingers tightened. "So don't think I don't know firsthand how you use your fair face to achieve your own ends. Or the ends of your country."

"I am here to nurture the peace between Ithicana and Maridrina," Lara replied coolly, considering whether she'd have to find a way to see this woman put down. While she was confident in her ability to manipulate Aren and those close to him, Nana was quite another story.

"This kingdom wasn't built by fools. Your father sent you to make trouble, and if you think we aren't watching you, you're wrong."

Unease flickered in Lara's chest.

"Aren cares a great deal for honor and he'll keep his word to you no matter what it costs him." Nana's eyes narrowed. "But I don't give a squirt of piss for honor. What I care about is family, and if I think you are a true threat to my grandson, don't think for a heartbeat that I won't arrange for an *accident* to occur." The woman's smile was all straight white teeth. "Ithicana is a dangerous place."

*And I'm a dangerous woman,* Lara thought before answering, "He seems more than capable of taking care of himself, but I appreciate your candor."

"I'm sure." Nana's eyes seemed to delve straight into Lara's soul, and she felt no small amount of relief when the old woman twitched the curtains shut and gestured to the door. "He won't want to miss the tides. Harendell is running cattle and he hates cows in the bridge."

*Because they're not making him any money*, Lara thought bitterly. But she couldn't help asking, "Why is that?"

"Because he got trampled during one of the annual runs when he was fifteen. Three cracked ribs and a broken arm. Though he'd tell you the worst was having to stay with me while he recovered."

*Annual runs? What the hell was the old woman talking about? The only reason there was cattle in the bridge was because her father had arranged to have them purchased at Northwatch.* Not for the first time, unease flickered through her at the disconnect between what she knew to be true and what she was seeing and hearing in Ithicana. *They must have been sold to Valcotta or another nation*, she decided. *Loaded onto ships so that Maridrina was bypassed entirely.* Though given Valcotta's enormous herds, she didn't see why they'd be importing them.

Pushing the thought aside, Lara followed Nana outside where she was blinded for a few paces by the brilliant sunlight, but when her vision cleared, it revealed Aren frowning as he haphazardly hung laundry on a line, a glowering Lia crouched next to a washbasin by his feet.

"I see there have been gaps in your education, boy." Nana scowled at a dripping sheet.

"I'm willing to accept certain personal failings." Aren jerked his hand away in horror from a voluminous pair of undergarments that Lia was trying to hand to him.

Nana rolled her eyes. "Useless child." But Lara didn't miss the faint smile that grew on the old woman's face as Aren dried his hands on his trousers.

"You intend to elaborate on why you had me drag Lara all the way here? I assume it wasn't for a five-minute conversation."

"Oh, Lara and I will be talking a great deal over the coming weeks, because you're going to leave her here with me."

Lara's mouth dropped open in horror, no amount of training enough to hide her dismay over this development.

Aren rocked from his heels to his toes, eyes narrowed. "Why would I do that?"

"Because she's the Rat King's spawn, and I'll not have her roaming

Midwatch while you're distracted with more important matters. Here I can keep an eye on her."

*And probably arrange an accident within the week.*

"No."

Nana planted her wrinkled hands on her hips. "I wasn't giving you the choice, boy. Besides, what need have you of her? Despite all the practice you've had over the years, you haven't had her on her back once, by my reckoning. And you aren't going to have time for it over the next two months, so she might as well be here where I can put her to use."

Aren exhaled a long, slow breath, casting his eyes up to the sky as though searching for patience. Lara bit her tongue, waiting for his response. Knowing she was screwed if he acceded to his grandmother's request.

"No. I didn't bring her to Ithicana to keep her locked up as a prisoner, and I certainly didn't bring her so you could keep her as a servant. She's coming with me."

Nana's jaw hardened, her muddy fingernails digging into the fabric of her tunic. *He's never said no to her before*, Lara thought, amazed.

"You've too much of your mother in you, Aren. Both of you blind, idealistic fools."

Silence.

"We're done here. Lara, come on." Aren twisted on his heel, and Lara scampered after him, half convinced that Nana would stick a knife in her back in a last-ditch effort to keep her from Aren. From behind, she heard the old woman snap, "Jor, you keep that boy safe or I'll cut your balls off and feed them to my snakes."

"Always do, Nana," Jor drawled, then trotted past Lara and Aren. "I'd walk faster. She's not a woman used to being denied."

Aren snorted, but kept to his measured pace. "I should've guessed this is what she wanted. Controlling old bat."

Controlling, yes, but also far too canny for her own good. Lara might be walking away with Aren, but he'd heard Nana's warnings. If Lara wasn't careful, he might begin to take those warnings to heart.

"You can't fault her for trying to protect her grandson. She's fond of you." Lara shied away from a tree hosting an enormous spider.

"Most people are. I'm quite charming, or so I'm told."

Lara shot him a pitying look. "A king should rarely take a compliment at face value. Sycophants, and all that."

"How fortunate that I now have you to give me the unvarnished truth."

"Would you prefer varnished lies?"

"Possibly. I'm not certain my untested ego is ready for so much abuse. My soldiers might not follow me if they're subjected to night after night of me crying in my cup."

"Try sobbing into your pillow—it muffles the noise."

Aren laughed, then glanced backward at the house. "What did she say to you?"

Holding up the root she'd been given, Lara paused, realizing that Nana had suspected Aren would refuse. Which begged the question: Why had he? The reason, she guessed, was more complicated than a desire to get her between the sheets. "Apparently she takes offense to the idea of me puking on your boots."

He rewarded her with a low chuckle that sent an unexpected thrill racing through her. Then he extracted the blindfold from where it had been tucked into his belt, her shoulders tightening reflexively as he wrapped it around her face, his fingers smelling like soap. "Do you want to walk or be carried?"

"Walk." Though she came to regret the decision when she'd tripped for about the dozenth time, relief filling her when they stepped into the cool darkness of the pier, Aren holding her elbows to steady her as she climbed the steps. She counted them, calculating the distance.

Back inside the bridge, the group moved at speed, no one speaking. So it was unmistakable when the faint sound of a horn, long and mournful, pierced the thickness of the stone encasing them. Aren and the rest stopped in their tracks, listening. It sounded again, the same long note, followed by a pattern of short peals that repeated three times in rapid succession before cutting off in the middle of the fourth, as though the horn had been ripped from the blower's lips.

"That's Serrith's call for aid," Jor said.

"Have its civilians departed for War Tides yet?" Aren demanded.

*War Tides?*

"No." Even with the blindfold on, Lara felt the tension running through the group crackling like an electric storm.

"Who's closest?" There was a shake to Aren's voice. A hint of something Lara had yet to see in him: *fear*.

Jor cleared his throat. "We are."

Silence.

"We can't leave her alone in the bridge," Aren said.

"We can't spare anyone to stay with her, and we don't have time to bring her back to Nana."

Lara bit her tongue, wanting to weigh in but knowing she was best served in saying nothing.

"No helping it. We'll have to bring her with us." Aren's hands brushed against the side of her face as he pulled off the blindfold. "Keep up. Keep silent. And when the fighting starts, stay out of the way."

Praying he'd mistake her excitement for fear, she nodded once. "I will."

The group broke into a run.

# 16
# LARA

LARA STRUGGLED TO keep pace with the Ithicanians, the stale air burning in her chest as the group sprinted through the bridge. Only luck allowed her to notice when Lia planted a foot square on a mile marker, her mouth moving silently as she began counting her strides.

Lara picked up Lia's count, storing away the number when the other woman held up a hand and skidded to stop. Jor boosted her on his shoulders while the rest prepared their gear. None of them spoke, and Lara kept to the shadows as she watched Lia reach up to press her palm against what appeared to be smooth stone. There was a heavy click, then, with a heave of effort, she lifted up a hinged hatch in the ceiling of the bridge.

*Another way in.*

Triumph rushed through Lara even as cool air gusted inside, catching at the loose strands of her hair as Jor and Aren lifted the other soldiers into the opening. Then Jor was up, and only she and Aren remained.

"You ever reveal any of this to anyone, I'll kill you myself."

Without waiting for a response, he grabbed Lara by the waist and raised her up into the opening.

Jor caught hold of her arms, lifting her onto the top of the bridge before leaning down to haul Aren up as well, the two of them flipping the hatch shut. But it was hard for Lara to focus on what the men were doing, because she stood on a bridge through the clouds.

Wet mist had settled back on Ithicana while they'd been inside, and it whirled and gusted, pulling at her clothes before spinning away in violent little eddies. Below, the sea crashed against a pier or an island or maybe both—she couldn't tell. Couldn't see more than a dozen paces in either direction, and it was like being in a totally different world. Like being in a dream that stood on the brink of a nightmare.

"Be careful," Aren warned, taking her hand. "It's slippery, and we're at a high point. You wouldn't survive the fall."

She followed him at a slow run, everyone struggling to keep their balance on the slick surface as the bridge sloped down toward the next pier, which Lara could only faintly see through the mist. But before they reached it, the guards all dropped as though given an invisible cue, Aren hauling her down with him.

As Lara's hands pressed against the wet stone, her eyes landed on a mile marker, the wheels in her mind turning as a strategy for invasion began to form.

Jor had a spyglass out, which panned this way and that before freezing in place. "Amarid naval vessel." He passed the glass to Aren, who looked once, then swore.

"We should wait for reinforcements," Jor continued, taking the glass back and crawling to the opposite side of the bridge, staring out in the same direction as the rest of the soldiers. The mist swirled, revealing an island for a heartbeat before obscuring it again. "Once they get their whole crew on land, we'll be badly outnumbered."

No one spoke, and it was then that the winds shifted direction. With them came the screams.

"We go now," Aren ordered.

None of the guards argued. One of them attached a cable to a thick metal ring embedded in the bridge, the other end fixed to a heavy bolt that was fitted into a weapon designed like a crossbow. Then he handed it to Aren. "You do the honors, Your Grace?"

Aren took the weapon, kneeling on the stone. "Come on," he muttered. "Let me see."

The winds stalled, and no one seemed to breathe. Lara dug her fingers into the stone, watching and waiting, the anticipation making her heart race. Then the air roared against them, sweeping away the clouds, and Aren smiled once.

He released the bolt with a loud twang, grunting against the force of the recoil. The bolt soared toward the island, trailing the slender cable after it, and with a loud crack audible even from the distance, it spiked through one of the trees.

The soldier who'd given him the weapon tightened up the slack on the cable and knotted it off. Then, with seemingly no fear, he pulled on a heavy glove, attached a hook over the cable, and swung out into the open air. Lara watched in amazement as the man shot along the wire over the open sea, going faster and faster until he was over land, and then reached up with the glove and slowed himself, dropping like a cat into the brush beneath the tree.

The rest of the soldiers followed swiftly, but as Lara glanced over her shoulder, she determined Aren wasn't paying them the slightest bit of attention. Instead, he was mixing powders into a small bladder. As she watched, he added water to the mixture, then, very carefully, attached the device to an arrow with a bit of twine. He lifted it to his bow and shot it at the ship anchored below.

Seconds later, an explosion shook the air, the ship visible through the mist as flames climbed the rigging. "That ought to keep them busy."

Slinging his bow over his shoulder, he removed a hook and glove like the others had used. "I'm going to need you to hold onto me."

Wordlessly, Lara wrapped her arms around his neck and her legs around his waist. Heat rushed through her as he pulled her tight against him with his free hand.

"Don't scream." He flipped the hook over the line and jumped.

Lara barely contained her shriek, clinging to him as they dropped, soaring downward at incredible speed. Below, the surf broke against the island cliffs, and she could make out the longboats retreating from a small cove to the burning ship to assist their comrades. Wind roared in her ears, and then they were above green jungle.

"Hold on tight," he said into her ear, then he let go of her, reaching up with a gloved hand to grip the cable, checking their speed until they hung safely above the others.

Lara let go, landing among them, and she purposely wobbled and fell on her ass even as Aren landed with predatory grace next to her. In a practiced move, he extracted a leather mask identical to those all the guards were now wearing and pulled it over his face.

"Stay here," he whispered. "Keep out of sight and watch out for snakes."

Then they were gone.

Lara waited until the count of fifty, then went after them, knives in hand. She moved carefully, trusting that their passage would have sent any snakes racing away. It wasn't difficult to determine the direction they'd gone; she only had to follow the screams.

A battle waged in a village, the interiors of the stone houses ablaze, countless dead and dying lying on the paths running between them. Some had been armed, most had not. Families. Children. All cut down by the Amaridian soldiers fighting Aren and his guards. Keeping behind a tree, Lara watched the King of Ithicana hurl himself against the other men, machete in one hand, dagger in the other, leaving only corpses in his wake. He fought like he'd been born to it, fearless, but clever, and she found herself unable to look away.

Until shouts from the beach caught her attention. Abandoning her position, Lara retreated in that direction, her stomach tightening as she caught sight of the Amaridian soldiers moving up the trail toward the village. The ship was fully engulfed with fire, which meant these were desperate men with no avenue for escape. And Aren and his bodyguard were outnumbered three to one. Unless she wanted Amarid to be the kingdom taking control of the bridge, she needed to even the odds.

Lara picked a point just around the corner from a gap in a towering pair of rocks through which the soldiers would have to pass.

Two soldiers rounded the bend, starting in surprise at the sight of her standing in their path. "It's her. The Maridrinian girl."

She waited for them to rush her, these men as much Maridrina's enemy as they were Ithicana's, but they stood their ground, gaping at her as if uncertain what to do next. "You're not supposed to be here."

Lara shrugged. "Your bad luck, I suppose." Then she threw her knives in rapid succession. The soldiers dropped, blades in their throats. Three more came, and Lara snatched up one of the dead men's swords and launched herself forward, slashing one man's gut even as she dove under the blade of another, hamstringing him as she rolled. His comrade swung at her and she parried, then kicked him in the knee, burying her blade in his chest as he fell.

Taking up his weapon as she rose, Lara attacked the third, driving him back before slicing off his hand at the wrist. The soldier screamed, his blood splattering her in the face even as he collided with the soldiers who'd come up from behind.

It was screaming and chaos. Men tripping over the bodies of their companions as they tried to squeeze through the narrow pass, Lara killing them when convenient, maiming them when it wasn't, her goal to keep them from joining the battle and from overwhelming Aren and his soldiers.

But when a pair of arrows whistled over her head, she threw herself into the jungle, hiding in the underbrush as the rest of the Amaridian soldiers rushed past. Once they were gone, she retrieved her throwing knives and sheathed them in favor of using one of the Amaridians' heavier weapons. Slicing throats as she went, Lara ran up the trail to the village.

There was blood everywhere. Bodies everywhere. Several of the honor guard had fallen, and Lara's stomach plunged as she searched those remaining for Aren.

She found him fighting an enormous man wielding a chain. Aren's clothes were bloody, his once sharp movements now sluggish and sloppy. The Amaridian warrior swung his chain hard, and Lara hissed as it caught Aren in the ribs, doubling him over. She instinctively took several steps in their direction, knife in hand, ready to intervene, but Aren came up swinging, catching the big man in the face with his fist, then plunging a knife into his gut. They both went down in a heap.

Before Aren could get back to his feet, another Amaridian soldier charged toward his exposed back.

Without thinking, Lara threw herself between them, her knife sinking in beneath the sternum, angling up to pierce the soldier's heart.

His momentum knocked her over, the wind rushing out of her lungs as her shoulders hit the ground, the dying soldier falling on top of her. He was flailing and thrashing, the hilt of the knife digging into her stomach, and she couldn't get out from under him.

Couldn't breathe as the meaty bulk of his chest pressed down against her face.

The weight abruptly lifted.

Lara gasped, sucking in air, before rolling onto her hands and knees, watching as Aren unnecessarily slid a knife across the dead soldier's throat. Hands slick with the other man's blood, Aren grabbed hold of her arms, pulling her close. "Are you all right? Are you hurt?" He was pulling at her clothes, the blood of the dead sailor mercifully concealing that from her victims on the pathway.

"I'm fine," she gasped, finally able to breathe. "You're not." He was bleeding heavily from a gash on his forearm, but she suspected that wasn't the worst of it.

"It's nothing. Stay back. Stay out of sight." He tried to push her behind one of the village homes, but she clung to his shoulders, desperate to keep him out of the fray. If he died, *everything* was for naught.

He hesitated, and she buried her face in his shoulder, certain he'd set her aside and reenter the battle. But he was injured and spent, and it would not end well. Panic rose in her throat, and she whispered the only thing she could think of that would get him to stay: "Please. Don't leave me."

His hands were hot against her back, both of them soaked with the blood of their enemies. "Lara . . ." His voice was pained, and she knew he was seeing the bodies of his people. That he was seeing his bodyguards, fighting and faltering against the enemy.

*You could fight.*

*You could fight for him and save these people.*

The thought danced across her mind, but she was saved from having to make a decision by the arrival of reinforcements.

Ithicanian soldiers poured into the village, Aren's bodyguards falling back, encircling him and Lara as the others cut down the Amaridian soldiers, ruthlessly dispatching the injured until the only sound was the moans and cries of the villagers.

Aren didn't let go of her until it was over.

Smoke burned Lara's eyes as she looked around. As she saw, for the first time, what war really looked like. Not just dead soldiers, but unarmed civilians lying on the ground. The still forms of children.

*Do you think it will be any different when your father comes with his army? Do you think they'll show any more mercy?*

Villagers who had fled began to return to the village, mostly older children clutching babies and the hands of small children. Some of them began to sob as they found the still forms of their parents. But far too many just stood frozen, faces lost and hopeless.

"Still believe those Amaridian sailors deserved mercy?" Aren said softly from behind her.

"No," she whispered as she strode toward the nearest injured Ithicanian, ripping strips of fabric from her tunic as she dropped to her knees. "I don't."

# 17
# AREN

AREN STARED INTO the basin of water, its contents slowly turning red as he washed away the blood crusting his fingernails. His blood. The blood of his enemies.

The blood of his people.

The water trembled and he jerked his hands out of the basin, wiping them dry on a piece of toweling that had been left for him. Every inch of him ached, especially his ribs where that big bastard had caught him with the chain. Nana had informed him nothing was broken, but his side was already a livid bruise, and experience told him that tomorrow would be worse. Yet he'd take the pain a thousand times over if it meant arriving at Serrith sooner. Twenty minutes earlier. Ten. Five. Even a heartbeat sooner might have allowed him to save at least one of the villagers who'd been killed today.

"The call to assemble the council in Eranahl has been sent and replies received. Everyone will be there by nightfall."

He turned to find Jor standing behind him, the bandage wrapped around his head concealing the deep gash he'd taken in the fighting. A gash that Lara, of all people, had stitched up. Of their own accord,

Aren's eyes drifted to where his wife knelt among the wounded, silently taking direction from Nana and her students. Her honey-colored hair was crusted dark with blood, as were her clothes, but rather than detracting from her beauty, it only made her seem fierce. Like a warrior. Half a day ago, the notion would've been laughable.

But not anymore.

Jor tracked his gaze, giving a deep sigh when he saw whom Aren was staring at. "She's in possession of a problematic amount of information."

"There was no helping it."

"Doesn't mean it isn't a problem."

"She saved my life."

Jor sucked in a deep breath, then blew it out slowly. "Did she now."

"I was down and one of them came at my back. She got in the way and stuck a knife in him." Every time he blinked, Aren saw Lara beneath that brute of an Amaridian, blood everywhere. Felt the fear of certainty that all the blood was hers. "Sort of ruins the theory that she's here to assassinate me, don't you think?"

"Maybe she wants to do it herself," Jor replied, but his voice was unconvinced.

Lara lifted her head, as though sensing their scrutiny. Aren turned away before their eyes could meet, and the pile of dead Amaridians came into his line of sight. He'd pulled the bastard off her and slit his throat, but the man had been already dead, the knife Lara had picked up somewhere embedded with precision in his heart.

*Luck*, he told himself. But Aren's instincts were telling him something else.

"If anything, we need to keep a closer eye on her now," Jor said. "If the Maridrinians determine where she is and come for her, that little lass's head is full of enough bridge secrets to cause us some serious trouble."

"What are you suggesting?"

"I'm suggesting that maybe she's more trouble than she's worth. Accidents happen. Snakes find their way into beds. The Maridrinians could hardly hold it against us—"

"No."

"Then keep pretending she's alive." Jor had mistaken the reason for Aren's refusal. "Get a forger to fake her letters to her father. They never have to know."

Aren turned on the man who'd watched over him since he was a child. "I will say this once and never again. If anyone harms her, they lose their head. That goes for you, it goes for Aster, and it goes for my grandmother, too, lest she think me ignorant to her ways. Understood?"

Without waiting for a response, Aren walked to the pyres that had been hastily assembled on the outskirts of the village, the air thick with the smell of the oil drenching the wood. Dozens of bodies, big and small, were laid out in even rows, and the survivors stood around it, some weeping, some staring into nothingness.

Someone passed him a torch and Aren stared at the flickering flames, knowing that he should say something. But any words he might offer these people that he was supposed to protect—that he had *failed* to protect—seemed empty and meaningless. He couldn't promise it wouldn't happen again, because it would. He couldn't promise revenge, because even if raiding Amarid were a possibility for his already strained army, he wouldn't lower himself to harming Amaridian civilians just because their queen was a vindictive bitch. He *could* tell them that he fully intended to send a crate full of heads along with the charred remains of the ship's flag back to their mistress, but what did that even mean? It wouldn't bring back the dead.

So he said nothing, only leaned forward to touch the torch to the oil-soaked wood. Flames tore along the branches, the air growing hot, and it wasn't long until his nose filled with the awful smell of burning hair. Charring blood. Cooking flesh. It made his stomach churn, and he gritted his teeth, wanting to flee but forcing himself to hold his ground.

"The ships are here from Eranahl," Jor said. "We need to start loading the survivors or we'll lose the weather." As if to emphasize the point, a droplet of rain smacked against Aren's forehead. Then another and another.

"Give them a minute." He couldn't tear his gaze from a sobbing mother standing too close to the now hissing flames. This morning she would've woken believing that by nightfall she and her family would be on the way to the safety of Eranahl, and now she'd be making the journey alone.

"Aren . . ."

"Give them a goddamn minute." Heads turned at the sharpness of his tone, and he strode away from the flames. Past the injured whom Nana and her students were preparing for the journey, and down the path to the cove where the ships waited.

Rounding the bend, he frowned at the dozen or so dead enemy soldiers that had been dragged to the side of the path when something caught his eye: a man with an Amaridian blade embedded in his chest. Backtracking, Aren examined the corpses more closely.

Most of his soldiers fought hand-to-hand with knives and the machetes they needed to move through the dense jungle underbrush, and the wide blades made for distinct injuries. But most of these men bore wounds inflicted by the slender swords favored by Amarid, and several of them had the eight-inch knives these soldiers carried embedded in their bodies.

They were killed by their own weapons.

Aren stepped back a few paces to examine the scene, eyes drifting over the pools of blood mixing with rain to create growing puddles. These men had been killed by individuals they'd encountered coming up the path, not from behind by his reinforcements.

*But by whom?* All of his guard had been with him in the village, as were the civilians who could fight.

A prickle rose on the back of Aren's neck. Hand going to the blade at his waist, he whirled around. Only to find Lara standing in the middle of the path.

Her eyes drifted to where his hand lingered on his weapon and one of her eyebrows rose, but for reasons Aren couldn't articulate, he couldn't let go of the hilt. *She'd killed that soldier with an Amaridian blade . . .*

But her only visible injury was a bruise on her cheek. Never mind that Maridrinian women were forbidden from fighting, the very idea that she could've accomplished this on her own was utter lunacy—his best fighters couldn't have done it alone.

"Where will they go?" Her voice cut through his thoughts.

"There are safer places." He wondered why he was being so cagey when now she knew so much. But it was one thing for her to know about the bridge. Quite another for her to know about Eranahl.

*Without the bridge, Eranahl doesn't exist,* his father's voice whispered in his ear. *Ithicana doesn't exist. Defend the bridge.*

"If there are safer places, why don't you keep your civilians there?"

There were practical reasons. Keeping every Ithicanian civilian within Eranahl year-round was impossible, but that wasn't the reason he gave. "Because that would be like keeping them in cages. And my people are . . . free." The word caught in his throat, a sudden understanding of what his mother had been fighting for slapping him in the face. For what was Ithicana but a larger prison, those born to it forbidden to ever leave.

Lara went very still, her head cocked and eyes unblinking, as though his answer had dug deep into her thoughts, leaving no space for anything else. "Their freedom seems to come at a significant cost."

"Freedom always has a price." How much larger would the price be to allow his people the freedom of the world?

"Yes." The word seemed to stick in her throat, and she shook her head once, her eyes going to the dead men lining the path. Aren watched her closely, searching her expression for any clue that she was somehow complicit in their deaths, but she only appeared deep in thought.

"You should head down to the cove. The boats are waiting."

Tearing her eyes from the corpses, Lara walked toward him, silent as any Ithicanian as she navigated the slick slope. His heart skipped then accelerated, the steady *thump thump* rhythm it took when he was heading into battle or trying to outrun a storm. The thrill that, despite knowing he should not, Aren had sought all his life.

Lara stopped in front of him. Her hair was wet from the rain, a stray lock plastered against her cheek. It took all his self-control not to brush it away.

"Once the boats are loaded, I'm leaving for a . . . meeting. You'll stay with my grandmother until I return for you."

Lara frowned, but rather than arguing, she reached up and placed her hand on his, her skin feverishly hot. Then, with surprising strength, she pushed down, snapping his blade back into its sheath.

"I'll wait by the water." Without another word, she stepped over a puddle and made her way down the path toward the beach.

# 18
# LARA

War Tides.

That's what the villagers on Serrith Island had called it. The two coldest months of the year when the Tempest Seas were calm enough for Ithicana's enemies to attack.

And this year War Tides had come early.

So early that the villagers had not yet been evacuated to the mysterious location where they spent the season, which was probably why the Amaridian navy had twice risked getting caught in a late storm. For while a well-defended singular location could be protected, countless little civilian outposts were another matter.

*It was the best time to attack*, the cold, strategic part of Lara thought. When Ithicana's army would be forced to split their efforts between protecting dozens of small villages and protecting the bridge. And if it came to it, she *knew* Aren would put his people's lives first. It had been written on his face when those horns had sounded, the panic and desperation. The willingness to risk *everything* to save them. And the dead look in his eyes as he'd surveyed the massacred village and known that he'd failed.

*They aren't your responsibility*, she viciously reminded herself. *Your loyalty is to Maridrina. To the civilians of your homeland who suffer under Ithicana's monopoly on trade. To the Maridrinian children who have nothing on their plates but rotting vegetables and rancid meat, if they have anything to eat at all. They are dying as surely as if Ithicana were slitting their throats.*

The thoughts were enough to turn her mind to the matter of smuggling information out of Ithicana. While it might be possible for her to code short messages into her letters to her father, she didn't dare attempt to include any of the details she'd learned about the bridge. If the codebreakers noticed them, she'd be lucky to get out of Ithicana alive, and everything that she'd done would be for naught. Aren knew where she'd been and what she'd learned. It would be easy for them to shore up the defenses, and there would be no catching them by surprise.

No, she had to gather the information she needed, and then smuggle it out all at once. The question was how.

Instinctively, she knew that the way had to be through the King of Ithicana himself. Her thoughts went to her cosmetics box, within which the ink Serin had given her was hidden. Not only did she need to entice Aren to write a message to her father, she needed to steal it for long enough to write her own, never mind the problem of resealing it without anyone noticing that it had been tampered with.

"Quit plotting and help Taryn with the dishes, you lazy tit."

Nana's voice ripped Lara from her thoughts, and she turned to scowl at the old woman. "What?"

"Did you not hear, or did you not understand?" Nana's hands were on her hips, a large snake wrapped around her neck and shoulders. It lifted its head to regard Lara, and she shivered.

"This is my island," Aren's grandmother barked. "And on my island, if you wish to eat, you work. On your feet." She clapped her hands sharply.

Lara rose, instantly annoyed with having obeyed, but to sit back down would be childish.

"Out."

Glowering, she stepped out into the morning air, catching sight of

Taryn, who sat next to a washtub, up to her elbows in soapy water. The young woman was the only one of Aren's guards to remain with her—the one to have drawn the short straw, she'd readily griped to Lara on her blindfolded walk back through the bridge to Nana's island, which was called Gamire. A group of unfamiliar soldiers silently trailed them. Lara had thought it Taryn's reluctance to spend time with her, or perhaps disappointment over not going to wherever Aren had scuttled off to, that had made the role undesirable, but after a night spent in Nana's house, the real reason was apparent.

The old witch was an obnoxious, bullying harridan, and Lara had no idea how she was going to keep from murdering the bloody woman in her sleep.

"You'll get used to her, after a while." Taryn dunked a plate into the steaming basin. "Helps that most of us have been patched back together by her at least once." Letting go of the dish, the woman lifted up her undershirt to reveal an oval-shaped series of scars that covered the better half of her ribs. "I fell into the water during a skirmish and a shark had a go at me. If not for Nana, I'd be dead."

A knife or a sword or an arrow—those were wounds Lara could fathom, but that . . . "Nasty creatures."

"Not really." Taryn dropped her undershirt and returned to the plate. "They've been trained to be man-eaters, but it's not their preference."

Taking the dripping plate and rubbing it with a towel, Lara thought of the Amaridian sailors being dragged beneath the surface. The blooms of blood. "If you say so."

Pushing back her long dark ponytail, Taryn smiled, revealing straight white teeth that must please Nana greatly. "They are brilliant creatures. There are a few who stay with us always, but most of them are only here during War Tides. That, more than the weather, is how Nana knows when storm season is coming or going. The fishermen notice their numbers."

*Did her father and Serin know that?* Lara chewed the insides of her cheeks, considering the information. One of the risks of attacking at the beginning of the calm season was that there was no way to predict exactly when it would begin.

"They always congregate at the places where raiders attack the most, like at Midwatch." Taryn swirled a rag inside a chipped mug before handing it over. "There are myths that say they are guardians of Ithicana's people, which is why it is forbidden to harm them unless absolutely necessary." She laughed. "It's just a myth, though. They come to be fed, and they don't discern between us or our enemies. Anyone in the water is fair game."

Lara shivered, setting the dry cup in a clean basin with the rest.

"Quit your chattering," Nana barked from a distance. "There's other chores that need doing."

Taryn rolled her eyes. "Want to escape?"

"Is escape from Nana possible?"

A wink. "I've had lots of practice."

True to her word, after the clean dishes were put away, Taryn managed to have them assigned to a task that sent them down into a village Lara hadn't even realized was there. She took in the Ithicanians bustling about between the stone houses or cajoling children who were shirking their chores. "Why isn't it evacuated?"

"They don't need to be. Gamire Island is safe."

*Find the civilians.* Lara remembered Serin's words, the back of her neck prickling as two children ran past her, sacks of oats in their arms. Her eyes took in the village again. There were groups of men gutting fish, but her nose picked up the scent of baking bread, of red meat on the grill, and the faint tang of lemon, though not once had she seen a fruit tree in this place. Which meant it had all come as an import via the bridge.

"Those living on the other islands . . . where do they go for War Tides?" she asked, because *not* asking would be more suspicious. And because she was deeply curious where this mystery location might be.

"That's for the king to tell you." Taryn gave her a sideways glance. "Or not, as the case may be."

"He's not particularly forthcoming."

Shrugging as a way to silence that line of questioning, Taryn led Lara down a narrow path through the jungle. They walked until the breeze rose and the scent of salt filled the air, waves loud where they crashed against the cliff walls. Lara didn't see the shipbreaker until the older soldier manning it shifted next to it. Pleased recognition gleamed in his eyes at the sight of Taryn, but his gaze hardened as it landed on Lara.

"We're your relief for the next hour," Taryn said. "Use it wisely and get yourself some of that meat I smelled cooking."

After the soldier had departed, she said, "Don't take it personally. Most everyone above a certain age lost a loved one or two to the war with Maridrina. Even after fifteen years of peace, it's hard for them to see you as anything other than the enemy."

*I am the enemy*, Lara thought. "You don't?"

"I did, at first." Taryn's grey eyes stared off into the distance. "Until you saved my cousin's life."

"Cousin?" Lara blinked, eyeing the muscular brunette in a different light. "Aren is your cousin?"

"I see that surprises you." Huffing out an amused breath, Taryn said, "My father was Aren's father's brother, which makes Nana my grandmother, too, if you're keeping track."

She hadn't been, but perhaps she should. The female guard was not exactly royalty, but very nearly. And there was nothing about her that had even hinted it was so. Taryn wore the same drab gear as the rest of the guards, lived in the spare accommodations of the barracks, cooked and cleaned with the rest of her comrades. Other than her weapons, which were quality, there was nothing about her that suggested wealth or privilege. *Where does all the money go?* Lara wondered, remembering the incredible revenue numbers she'd seen on the pages in Aren's desk. As a child, she'd believed Ithicana must have palaces made of gold filled with everything they took from Maridrina and the other kingdoms, but so far she'd seen only modest luxury.

"You could have stood by and let him be killed, but instead you risked your life to save him. That's not the act of an enemy."

*If only you knew.* Lara's stomach hollowed, her breakfast no longer sitting quite so well.

Picking up a spyglass, Taryn panned the ocean, allowing Lara the opportunity to examine the shipbreaker. The catapult was large, made of solid wood and steel and mounted to a base that was bolted to the rocky ground beneath it. There were a number of levers and gears, and to either side of it were two identical, yet much smaller devices. A glance over her shoulder revealed a lumpy pile covered with grey-green canvas, which were undoubtedly the projectiles.

Easing up the corner of the tarp, Lara eyed a stone that might've weighed fifty pounds. It didn't seem big enough to have done the damage she'd seen enacted at Midwatch, but combined with enough force . . . She turned back to the shipbreaker to find Taryn watching her.

The other woman grinned. "We launched Aren, once."

"Pardon?"

"Lia and I. Though it was *his* idea, lest you think us total idiots." Taryn patted the machine. "We were maybe twelve or thirteen, and he got the grand notion that it would be fun to see how high we'd fly. Though he was the only one who got to try it out."

"Did it . . . work?"

"Oh, he flew all right. But what he didn't account for was how much the landing would hurt." She cackled merrily. "Thankfully there was a fishing boat nearby to pull him out. Nana had us lugging rock for *weeks* as punishment, and that was after Jor screamed at us up and down the entire island."

"He's lucky not to have gotten himself killed." And how different would Lara's life have been if he had? Or would she even have a life at all? She could easily imagine her father receiving the news of the Prince of Ithicana's untimely death only to turn around and exterminate all those involved in the plot that had depended on the Fifteen Year Treaty.

Taryn grinned. "You could say that about half the things he does." She patted the weapon again. "Want to give it a try?"

Gasping out a laugh, Lara said, "And now I see to the heart of the ploy of bringing me down here."

"Not *you*. A rock."

"Oh." Lara eyed the machine in a whole new light. "Yes. Yes, I would."

It was an incredible piece of machinery, able to be operated by a single individual, but given the weight of the stones, Lara was glad there were two of them. It rotated silently on its base, and various cranks allowed the user to adjust it to change the distance a stone could be thrown. The smaller catapults, she learned, were intended to mark distance, everything finely calibrated.

"We'll try to hit that piece of driftwood." Under Taryn's watchful eye, Lara lobbed small rocks at the floating debris until she struck it.

"Nicely done, Your Majesty. Now we adjust the big one to the same distance like so." The woman turned the cranks and Lara watched intently until she stepped back. "Now you do the honors."

Hands sweating with excitement, Lara took hold of the biggest lever of all and pulled. The catapult released with a tremendous crack, and they both stepped around the machine to watch as the rock sailed through the air and crashed into the driftwood.

Taryn punched her fist into the air. "You sank your first ship!"

There was a commotion behind them, and the soldier they'd relieved raced up next to them. "Raiders?" he demanded.

"Tests." Taryn's voice was cool. "His Majesty ordered that all the shipbreakers be tested again. This one appears to be fine order." Taryn nodded at Lara. "Shall we carry on, Your Grace?"

Lara hid a smile. "By all means."

They spent the day touring the island *testing* the shipbreakers, and then found themselves back at the village for dinner, which they took standing around an open fire with nearly all the villagers in attendance. It was, Taryn told her, to honor those lives lost on the neighboring island of Serrith. Lara ate grilled meat and vegetables from the sticks on which they were skewered, drank the frothy beer from a mug that never seemed to empty, and warmed her hands against the flames when the night breeze turned cool.

The villagers were wary of her at first, and Lara stood somewhat apart, listening as they told stories about the myths of Ithicana, of serpents and storms that defended the emerald isles. Of the ancient bridge itself, which their legends said was not built, but had grown out of the earth like a living thing. Their words rose and fell until children dozed off in their parents' arms and were tucked under woolen blankets. Then instruments were brought out, drums and guitars and pipes, the music accompanying the men and women as they sang and danced, Taryn joining in with a surprisingly lovely soprano voice.

They cajoled Lara to join in the singing, but she begged off, pleading a terrible singing voice, but it was mostly because she wanted to watch. And listen. And learn.

When the gathering began to quiet, couples slipping off into the darkness hand in hand, the older folk forming circles where they gossiped and complained, passing around a smoking pipe from person to person, Taryn finally rested a hand on Lara's shoulder. "We should get back before Nana comes looking for us."

Guided by the faint light of a lantern, they made their way up the narrow path, the sounds of the jungle wild and riotous around them.

"I didn't want to be a soldier, you know."

Lara cast a sideways glance at Taryn. "I'm not surprised. You strike me as more of a fisherwoman."

Taryn spat out a laugh, but her tone turned serious. "I wanted to go to one of the universities in Harendell to study music."

The universities in Harendell were renowned throughout all the kingdoms, north and south, but the idea that an Ithicanian would wish to attend struck Lara as odd, because it was . . . impossible. "But Ithicanians never leave?"

"Because it's forbidden." Taryn waved her hand. "Oh, there are spies who go, of course, but it's not the same. It's a false life where you aren't yourself, and I couldn't abide that. To follow my dream as someone else—" She broke off. "I never told my parents, because I knew they wished for me to train as a warrior and eventually be named to Aren's council. But I told my Aunt Delia."

*Aren's mother*, Lara thought. *The queen.*

"My aunt believed that the surest way to earn trust was to give it." Taryn pulled on Lara's arm, stopping her to allow something to slither across their path before carrying on. "Everyone supported the treaty to end the war with Maridrina, but no one supported the inclusion of a marriage clause. No one wanted Aren to marry an outsider, especially a Maridrinian. But Aunt Delia believed it was the only way for us to ever have peace with our neighbors. The only way for people to stop seeing an enemy when we sat across the table to trade."

*It's a lie*, Serin's voice shrieked inside Lara's head. *Using kindness to get you to reveal what you should not*. But Lara silenced the voice.

"If she believed this marriage would stop Maridrinians from viewing Ithicana as an enemy, she was mistaken."

Taryn shook her head. "She didn't want to change your kingdom's beliefs. She wanted to change *ours*."

No more could be said, as they had reached Nana's home, the old woman standing in the doorway, watching them approach. "The wayward children return."

"We kept busy, Nana."

"Busy drinking, from the smell of it."

A somewhat hypocritical comment given Lara could smell alcohol on the woman's breath, a bottle and a half-filled glass sitting on the table behind her.

"I'm off to bed," Lara said, in no mood to be berated, but Nana caught Lara's arm in an iron grip. With the other hand, she held out a bag that twitched and squeaked. "First you feed the snakes."

Lara eyed the bag with distaste. Not because she had any particular aversion to mice, but because she was sick of the old witch ordering her about like a servant. What she wanted to do was sneak out tonight to have a look at the bridge pier, but Nana probably intended to sit up watching her. "No."

Nana's eyebrows rose. "No? Is the little princess too good to feed an old woman's pets?"

Lara's fingers tightened reflexively. Then her eyes lighted upon the shelves above the snake cages, and an idea began to form. "I'm afraid of mice," she lied, flinching away from the bag as Nana swung it her direction.

"Get over it."

Lara was forced to catch the bag or have the mice scatter everywhere. Silently cursing the old woman, Lara plucked a mouse out of the bag by its tail, carefully unlatched one of the cages, and tossed the creature inside before moving onto the next.

The snakes were all poisonous. Taryn had told her that Nana harvested their venom and used it to create antidotes, as well as medicines for various natural afflictions. There were dozens of vials of foggy liquid stored above the cages, and above those, countless more plants and remedies, all clearly labeled. Between each cage, Lara scanned the contents, smiling when she found what she was looking for.

Dropping the still wriggling bag of mice, Lara shrieked, "It bit me!"

"Which snake?" Nana demanded, a hint of panic in her voice.

"Not a snake," she sobbed, sticking one of her fingers into her mouth and biting down to create a realistic injury. "A mouse!"

"Dammit, girl!" Nana snatched up the bag, but it was too late. The remaining mice were running every which way. "Taryn, catch the damn things before they get into my larder."

Lara wailed, climbing onto a chair while the rodents took advantage of their freedom. But the second Nana's back was turned, she snatched a small jar from the shelves.

"Catch them, catch them!"

Taryn was dutifully chasing after the mice, but she'd drank enough that night that her movements were too slow, the rodents dodging easily until she turned to stomping on them with her heavy boots. Lara took the moment to uncork the jar.

"Don't kill them!" Nana had two mice by the tails and was shoving them into the bag. "The snakes won't eat them if they're dead!" She lunged for another mouse, and Lara leaned sideways and dumped a generous splash of the jar's contents into Nana's cup, once again grateful for the Ithicanian preference for strong drink.

"Got one!" Taryn tossed the mouse into Nana's sack. Lara corked the vial and shoved it back in its place on the shelf, then stood on her chair watching, uselessly, as the two women collected the remaining mice.

Muttering under her breath, Nana proceeded to finish feeding the snakes, then she grabbed hold of Lara's hand, examining the tiny bleeding wound. "Idiot. Will serve you right if it festers."

Jerking her hand out of the old woman's grip, Lara glared at her. "I'm going to bed." Her boots thudded imperiously as she made her way over to the cot that had been made up for her, and she curbed a smile as, from the corner of her eye, she watched Nana down the contents of her cup.

Now to wait.

# 19
# LARA

NOT AN HOUR later, the home dark, Nana's groan split the silence. A moment later, the old woman climbed from her bed and staggered out the door. On her feet in a flash, Lara went to the wall of vials, plucking up one she'd noticed earlier. Measuring out a drop, she held it beneath Taryn's nostril, silently apologizing for the headache it would cause in the morning as the gently snoring woman snorted it up.

Lara stepped outside into a pool of lantern light. A gentle breeze tugged at her hair, smelling of jungle and rain, the stars overhead only visible in patches through the growing cloud cover. Lara took the lantern, turned the flame up as high as it would go, then strode toward the small outbuilding where the toilet was located.

Stopping outside, she smirked at the sounds coming from within, then rotated in a circle, peering into the darkness. As predicted, a tall Ithicanian man appeared. "Is there something I can help you with, Your Grace?" He hooked his thumb on his belt as he eyed her.

"Oh!" Lara jumped, then pressed a hand to her mouth as though startled. "Well, I needed to . . ." She gestured at the building right as a tremendous fart reverberated from within, followed up by a groan of dismay. Lara might be out of her element in Ithicana, but when it came to narcotics, she was right at home. Nana was exactly where she expected her to be.

The guard's eyes widened in the lantern light. "Right." He was obviously trying not to laugh. "I see. Well, perhaps you could . . ."

"A bush will do." Lara giggled, pushing the lantern at him. "Can you hold this for me?"

Relieving herself behind the cover of a tree, Lara returned to the guard and retrieved the lantern. Holding it up, she marked how he squinted and blinked from the brightness. "Do you suppose she'll be all right?" Lara gestured to the outhouse. "Do you think we should . . . ?"

"No!" The thought of interrupting Nana in the toilet was clearly not something he cared to risk. "I'm sure she'll be fine."

"I hope so." Lara gave him a winning smile, then retreated to the house. Nana would be shitting for hours, but she'd be fine come morning. Snuffing the lantern, she hung it on the hook and went inside.

But she didn't shut the door all the way.

Counting to five, she eased it back open, greeted by nothing but blackness. Her eyes hadn't adjusted from the brilliant light of the lantern, but that meant neither would have the guard's. Moving blind, Lara edged around the corner of the house where she waited until she could make out the shadows of the trees, then she dropped to the ground, crawling silently next to Nana's garden wall until she was in the jungle.

The trees on this island weren't nearly as thick as they were on Midwatch, faint moon and starlight filtering through the leaves, allowing Lara to move at a slow trot up the path toward the bridge pier. Any sound she made was covered by the ocean breeze, but she paused occasionally to listen for sounds of pursuit. There were none.

The faint scent of wet rock drifted over her nose, strange and yet familiar, and after a heartbeat, Lara recognized it as the unique odor of the bridge stone. Moving more cautiously, lest there be guards, she crept up the path until, through the trees, she made out the large shadow of the pier rising up into the night. A shadow that spread out north and south: the bridge.

Picking her way through the trees, Lara searched for any sign of a guard, but there was none, so she made her way to the base of the pier. It was constructed from the combination of a natural rock outcropping and bridge stone, and it held the bridge perhaps twenty feet above the ground. The terrain around it was rocky, so there was no obvious path leading to the entrance she knew was there. Lara ran her fingernail against the expanse of bridge stone that made up the pier, searching the base for the outline of the door, but she soon gave up. There were too many scratches and marks, and she didn't have that much time. So she resorted to pushing on the surface, throwing her weight against the stone in the hopes it would open.

Nothing.

Swearing, Lara went to the part of the pier that was natural stone. Kicking off her heavy boots and tucking them into a shadow, she started climbing. Higher and higher she rose, back and shoulders burning from the effort. She reached the bottom of the bridge, feeling along the side of it and smiling as she found linear striations in the stone that provided just enough handholds for her to climb. Her fingers screaming at her, Lara scrambled up the side of the bridge, rolling onto the top.

Darkness spread out beneath her in an endless sea of night, only a few pinpricks of light from the island's interior breaking the velvety blackness. Moving slowly, Lara trailed her fingers down the middle of the bridge, knowing that she'd eventually find a mile-marker twin to the one inside.

Sweat dribbled down her back, her internal clock telling her that she needed to get back to Nana's house, but she pressed on until she found it. Then she strode back to the pier, counting her carefully measured paces.

Only to hear voices coming from the opposite direction.

"Goddamn idiots. What were they thinking parking a whole merchant party above Gamire for the night?"

It was Jor. He and who knew how many others were on top of the bridge with her.

Heart thudding, Lara dropped to her stomach, crawling to the edge and peering over. Below, a group exited from the trees, one of them carrying a jar of a faintly glowing substance.

"They don't know they're above Gamire, Jor." Lia's voice. "That's the whole damn point."

"Doesn't make it less of a pain in our asses."

Lara rolled to the opposite edge from the party below, then carefully lowered herself down the side, her sweating fingers quivering from the effort.

"Are you two about finished up there?"

Aren's voice. One of Lara's hands slipped, and she gasped, dangling from one hand until she regained her grip.

"We had a look. There's a merchant party camped for the night right below us, and the topside hatch is too close for us to enter undetected. It's a three-mile walk either direction to the next hatch, and with those winds blowing in, I wouldn't advise it. No one is looking to spend the night tied to the bridge top in the pouring rain."

Aren let out a weary sigh. "By boat it is, then."

"And rough waters. I hope whatever Nana gave your lovely bride will settle her stomach enough for the journey. Though something strong might be in order to deal with her damned panic."

"Leave Lara alone." Aren's voice wasn't amused. "She was raised in the desert, and she can't swim. Falling in the water is a valid fear."

"Yeah, yeah," Jor muttered, and Lara used the sound to clamber down farther. When she was ten feet from the bottom, she jumped, her bare feet making only the faintest slap as she hit the ground and rolled, taking five long steps until she was out of sight in the trees. Mud squished between her toes as she circled around, watching as Aren rested his hands against the pier, one above the other, and pressed twice. A faint click, and a panel of rock swung open. He went inside.

Above, Jor and Lia had looped a rope through one of the many rings embedded in the bridge and were climbing down the pier side by side. Lia was pulling the rope through the loop when Aren reemerged and said, "There's someone sleeping right against the bloody door."

"Like I said," Jor replied. "Idiots."

"It is what it is. Let's go." Aren started down the path toward

Nana's home. To retrieve *her*, she realized.

*Shit*. Lara waited until the others had followed before creeping up to the pier to retrieve her boots from their hiding place. It was going to be a mad dash to get back to Nana's ahead of them undetected, but she couldn't leave without having a look inside. Pressing her hands twice in the same spot Aren had, Lara grinned as the door swung open.

She'd expected it to be entirely dark inside, but the curved stairs leading upward were illuminated by more glowing jars. Taking the steps three at a time, she reached a smooth stone wall. Knowing there was a risk of being caught, but judging it worth the reward, she pressed her hands against it twice.

*Click*.

She winced at the sound, then eased the door open a crack, the heavy block moving on silent hinges. There was indeed a man sleeping in front of it, his snores likely all that had kept the masked Ithicanian soldiers sitting guard inside from hearing the noise.

The doorway needed to be marked so her father's soldiers could find it from the inside. Yet she knew the Ithicanians swept the bridge for any signs of tampering, so it had to be something they wouldn't notice.

Her mind raced through the years of Serin's lessons, knowing she needed a solution and that it needed to present itself immediately or Aren was going to reach Nana's before her and find her missing.

An idea sprung into her thoughts. Pulling out her knife, Lara sliced open a shallow wound on her forearm then tucked away the blade. Covering her fingers in blood, she carefully traced the outer rim of the door. Once dry, it wouldn't be noticeable against the stone. But if sprayed with the right compound, it would react.

There was no time to do anything else.

Carefully closing the door, Lara flew down the stairs and pushed the door in the base shut. Then she was running as fast as she dared, her bare feet scraping against roots and rocks. But she couldn't move this swiftly in her heavy Ithicanian boots while maintaining any level of silence.

Ahead, she picked out the faint glow of the jar Aren carried, and she slowed her speed, moving up as close behind them as she dared.

She considered trying to pass them in the trees, but there was no chance of them not hearing her. Not in the dark, at this pace.

Nana's house appeared ahead.

*Think of a plan*, she silently screamed at herself even as she watched Aren round the house. Open the door. He was back out in a flash shouting, "Where is she?"

Tugging on her boots, Lara cut into the trees, then stepped out into the clearing, walking through it toward Aren. "I'm right here, so quit yelling."

He stared at her, as did his bodyguard and the guard tasked with watching the house. Nana chose that moment to fling open the door to the outhouse clad only in a nightdress and boots.

"What," Aren demanded, "are you doing wandering the woods in the middle of the night?"

Serin's voice echoed through her head: *Most people lie to avoid embarrassment. Very few people lie to embarrass themselves, which inclines others to believe them.*

Lara looked at the ground, knowing that the sweat running down her face and her ruddy complexion would only add truth to the lie. "I wasn't feeling well, and the facilities were"—she gestured at Nana—"occupied."

Aren turned to his grandmother. "Are you ill?"

"The shits. I'll live."

"It must've been something we ate." Lara pressed a hand to her stomach as though it pained her. "Or perhaps some filth on those mice you made me touch."

"Mice? You made her feed your snakes?" Shaking his head, Aren rounded on the guard. "Where the hell were you?"

"Here. I didn't see her leave. I was watching."

"Not very well."

"I was trying to be discreet," Lara snapped, kicking the toe of her boot into the dirt. "Now if you're all finished gaping at me, I'd like to go back to sleep."

Aren exhaled a long breath.

"What?" Lara folded her arms under her breasts and looked up at him.

"A fleet of thirty Amaridian ships is lurking off Ithicana's coast. There's a squall blowing in that might buy us some time, but Midwatch is under my command, and I need to get back to prepare our defenses."

"They intend to raid?"

"Likely." He exhaled. "You can come back with us or stay here with Nana for War Tides. Your choice."

"I'll go back to Midwatch." There was no bloody way in hell she was spending another day with that awful woman. Never mind that judging from Nana's narrow-eyed expression, the old woman wasn't entirely fooled by her deception. No doubt she'd tie Lara to the bed every night and triple her guard. And because she needed to step forward with her plan to lure Aren in, Lara added, "I want to go with you."

His brow furrowed, and he glanced away. "We can't go through the bridge. There's a merchant party on their way to Southwatch camped above this pier for the night, and we can't get in without them seeing. It will have to be by boat."

Lara swallowed the unease that burned in her stomach, hearing the rising winds. *Control your fear,* she commanded. *There is much to be gained here if you keep your wits about you.*

"I'll manage," she muttered.

Aren turned on Taryn, who was rubbing her temples. "Not your finest hour, soldier. Jor will deal with your punishment once we're home."

"Sorry, Your Grace," Taryn said, and guilt briefly rose in Lara before she swallowed it away.

Aren led Lara by the hand through the darkness, Jor in the lead and the groggy Taryn behind, the other woman carrying something bulky that bumped against her shoulder as she ran.

The winds were rising higher by the second, but over them, the surf slamming against the cliff walls filled Lara's ears, and her heart thundered riotously knowing they intended to sail upon it. Sweat rolled in beads down her back as they reached the cliff tops overlooking the sea, nothing visible in the blackness, the moon and stars obscured by clouds.

It began to rain.

A cold drizzle that soaked her hair and trickled down the back of her tunic as she watched the soldiers stationed on the island strain to lift what appeared to be an enormous wooden ladder up into the air. The end of it was attached to ropes, and it took eight of them to lower it over the edge of the cliff into the darkness below.

"There's a large rock outcropping below," Aren shouted into her ear. "We'll climb down, then wade over to the islet where we have the boats moored. It's low tide, but the water will still be up to your knees."

"Let's go!" Jor was on the ladder and climbing down toward the crashing sea below, Lia following him.

"I'll go first. Then you, then Taryn."

Lara nodded wordlessly, unable to speak around the chatter of her teeth. Aren swung onto the ladder and clambered down, but when Lara gripped the rungs, her fingers felt numb. Her arms and legs trembled, and it took all her willpower to descend. Down and down toward the water.

*If they can do it, so can you.* She repeated the chant, her lips moving silently, her hands slick with sweat, spray drenching her clothes as wave after wave hammered the outcropping below. Finally, Aren's hands closed around her waist, steadying her as she stepped onto the slimy rocks. Taryn was down a moment later, and when she gave the call, there was a creak as the soldiers lifted the ladder back onto the island.

Lara could see nothing. *Nothing*. But all around her, water roared. One step in the wrong direction and she was done for. The thought had her dropping to her knees, her fingers clutching at the rocks.

"We don't have time for you to crawl," Aren shouted over the noise. "We'll be in a far worse spot if we're stuck out here when the tide turns."

Her knees trembled as she rose, her breath coming in great gasping whooshes as she took one step, then two, allowing Aren to guide her.

"Jor's marked the path." Aren lifted her hand, using it to point, because she couldn't so much as see his outline in the blackness.

*There*.

Smears of glowing algae were faintly visible every few paces. Her heart steadied, and she pressed forward, her confidence growing with each step.

"There's about a ten foot stretch here that's submerged. You'll be up to your knees, but the current is strong, so hold on to me."

"Damn you for making me do this."

Aren laughed, which pissed her off enough to take the first step.

Lara's boot filled with water, the current shoving against her leg, then dragging her in the opposite direction as it surged. She clung to Aren's belt, feeling Taryn's steadying hand on her shoulder from behind.

Step.

Step.

Her toe caught on a rock, and Lara stumbled, a sob tearing from her throat as she caught her balance.

Step.

Step.

A large wave surged against her, and she slid sideways, her legs washing out from under her. She was up to her waist in water, only her grip on Aren's belt keeping her upright. Her scream cut the night, frantic and desperate and primal, then his hands closed around her arms, dragging her from the water.

"You're out. It's all right. Worst is over."

"The second I'm on dry land, I'm going to gut you like a pig!" She hated being afraid and the only thing strong enough to chase the emotion away was anger. "I am going to smother you in your sleep!"

A dozen voices laughed, Jor's voice the loudest of them all. "And she finally shows her true intentions."

Aren snorted. "You might want to curb your vitriol until you're in a place where I can't pick you up and toss you into the drink." Then Aren stomped to the far side of the islet.

Taryn's hand caught her elbow, helping her up. "It will only take us an hour to get to Midwatch." She pressed a strap into Lara's hand. "I had one of the villagers make this for you. If something happens, it will keep you afloat until one of us can get you back in the boat."

Lara ran her hands along the object, which was a looped strap secured to a cask. A small act, but an enormous kindness. And one Lara didn't deserve. "Thank you."

The Ithicanians deposited her in one of the boats, and she cowered there, clinging with one hand to her cask and the other to the edge as they pushed out into the water. Their voices were unconcerned, despite this being madness that no sane individual would undertake under any circumstances.

The boat rose and fell on waves, and her stomach did the same, but Lara couldn't let go long enough to dig the root Nana had given her out of her pocket. She was busy puking over the edge when the group went silent, their hands still on ropes and rudders and lines.

"There they are." Lia's voice.

Jor cursed under his breath. "I hope this storm turns nasty and puts them at the bottom of the sea."

Lifting her head, Lara stared blearily out over the water. Bobbing in the distance were dozens, no, hundreds of lights. And carrying on the wind toward them was the sound of music and singing voices.

*Ships.*

*The Amaridian fleet.*

"We should go light a few of them up," Lia snapped. "That would put a damper on their party."

As one, all heads turned in Aren's direction. Fingernails digging into the edge of the boat, Lara waited to see how he would respond.

"Keep on to Midwatch." His voice was low.

"But we could sink a few of them," Lia argued. "We have the supplies."

"Midwatch," Aren repeated. "They haven't attacked, and we do not instigate."

"But they will! You know as soon as the weather turns, they'll raid!"

"When they do, we'll fight them. Same as always."

There was no emotion in Aren's voice, but Lara could feel frustration and anger coming off him in waves.

"Or we could stop them now." Lia was not giving up.

"They're outside our waters and they've shown no aggression." Aren shifted restlessly, his knee brushing against Lara's back. "If we attack unprovoked, Amarid will have cause to declare war against us. This is a few ships—*a raid.* We can deal with that. The full force of Amarid's navy against us is quite a different matter. Ithicana does not instigate conflict—we can't afford to. Now get us back to Midwatch."

Wordlessly, everyone began to move and the boats regained their speed, skipping across the waves. Yet Lara couldn't tear her gaze from the fading light of the fleet, her father's speech from that fateful dinner shifting and rattling through her head. *For as long as memory, Ithicana has placed a stranglehold on trade, making kingdoms and breaking them like it were some dark god.*

She'd believed that. Believed *him* without question. Yet Aren's words . . . they weren't those of a ruler with god-like power. Quite the opposite. They were the words of a leader of a kingdom fighting to survive.

# 20
# AREN

AREN RUBBED HIS eyes, which felt like they'd been filled with sand and then left to bake in the summer sun for a week. His ribs throbbed, his back ached, and his palms were marked with blisters from too many days of overuse. The worst was the tooth he was fairly certain had been knocked loose when Lara accidentally smacked his face after she'd been almost swept into the ocean. He prayed it resolved itself, or Nana would never let him hear the end of it.

"We're as ready as we can be." Jor drank deeply from a silver flask he took from a pocket before passing it across the firepit to his king. "You look like you need this."

He probably did need it, but Aren waved the flask away. His team, the green-faced Lara in tow, had returned to Midwatch just prior to dawn, and the entire day had been spent in preparation for the inevitable Amaridian attack. Now, there was little to do but watch the weather. With the winds still high, the raiders would be unlikely to attempt a landing, but a light squall like this one wouldn't last. And it certainly wouldn't be enough to drive the ships back to the safety of

Amaridian harbors. "I'm going to take the next patrol."

Jor lifted one eyebrow. "You already did your shift."

"I need to move. You know the sitting drives me to madness."

"It's a cold rain. You'll be regretting your decision halfway around the island."

"Regret," Aren said, picking up his cloak, "is currently my middle name."

"You're particularly whiney tonight."

Scratching his cheek with his middle finger, Aren lifted a hand to acknowledge the soldier who'd just come in from walking the perimeter, then started to the door.

"Might as well go with you. Just in case you give up halfway and run to the comfort of the fancy house."

"I wouldn't count on it."

The driving rain was, in fact, freezing, the wind tearing at the hood of Aren's cloak until he gave up on covering his head. They walked in silence for a long time, more focused on keeping their footing on the slick rocks and mud as they traversed the cliffs overlooking the sea. More than a few soldiers had fallen to their deaths, and despite the series of shitty days he'd had, Aren didn't care to join their ranks.

When they reached the first lookout, both of them casting their eyes out over the storm-tossed waters, Jor finally said, "You were right to stand your ground with them yesterday."

"Maybe." Aren's thoughts drifted to the meeting at Eranahl, to the hard faces of his Watch Commanders as they had arrived, weaving their way through the evacuees disembarking from their ships, supplies and crying children everywhere. *Most disorganized evacuation in recent history*, he'd heard muttered more times than he could count. He was inclined to agree with the sentiment.

"It's the council's duty to question you. They pushed your mother constantly, especially about this. She learned to know when they were giving good advice and when it was their fear talking—when to stand her ground and when to concede."

Aren extracted his spyglass, scanning the blackness for any lights on the horizon marking a ship. "You think I was right to stand my ground on this?"

The only sound was the wind howling and the waves slamming against the cliffs below. "I don't know. I'm not sure there is a *right* choice in this, Aren. All paths lead to war." Jor leaned back on his hands. "But what's done is done, at least so far as the battle facing us is concerned. Now if you'll excuse me, I need to take a piss."

The older man silently disappeared into the jungle and then not so silently did his business. Aren remained crouched on the rocks, shoving his hands in his pockets to warm them. With the evacuation mostly complete, his people had answered the annual call to arms, everyone between fifteen and fifty either at or on their way to their assigned garrison, the only exception being families with small children, who only sent one parent. Able bodies fought. Those unable played other roles, whether it be watch duties, dispatching signals, organizing supply drops, or managing the complex task of ensuring every one of the hundreds of outposts were appropriately manned. Ithicana didn't have civilians during War Tides. It had an army.

An army that was furious that Amarid had caught them with their trousers down at Serrith. An island that just happened to be under Aren's watch.

Over and over, he replayed the War Tides council meeting in his head, seeing a hundred things he could've done differently. Said differently.

"I understand you took heavy losses at Serrith, Your Grace." Watch Commander Mara's voice echoed in his head. "That's twice Amarid has sneaked up on you, and War Tides has only just begun. The pretty Maridrinian girl must be *quite* distracting."

Everyone in the room had shifted uneasily, *Lara* the crux of the barb, not the losses. They knew that Serrith was a nightmare to defend, the proximity of the bridge to the beach allowing vessels to hide beneath it while launching landing craft, rendering the shipbreakers useless. It took manpower and preparation to hold off an attack, and even then, with heavy fog, the soldiers stationed there would only have had a few minutes—the time it took for the longboats to reach the beach—to mount their defense. Which would've been enough if the man on watch hadn't fallen asleep at his post. A mistake the soldier had paid for with his life.

"I understand she was with you when the attack happened. In the bridge."

There'd been no hope of keeping that quiet. Not with all the evacuees from Serrith now in Eranahl. Gossip moved faster than a tempest in Ithicana. The only saving grace was that Aster was late to the meeting. If the Watch Commander knew what Lara had seen, the old bastard would burst a blood vessel. "It's never been my intention to keep Lara locked up. You all know that."

Yet neither had it been his intention to bring her into the bridge or for her to see how his military used it to fight their enemies. But watching her panic in the boat, gasping for breath and shaking uncontrollably . . . He hadn't been able to take it. He wasn't about to admit *that* in front of these battle-hardened men and women whose respect he needed to earn.

"Knowing your intentions isn't the same as agreeing with them. The Maridrinians are rats. Let one loose, and soon all of Ithicana will be infested with them."

"The Maridrinians are our allies," Ahnna said from where she stood at the far end of the large replica of Ithicana, her hand resting protectively on Southwatch island.

Mara made a face. "The Maridrinians are our *business partners* at best, Ahnna. We pay them for peace. That's not an alliance."

*But it could be*, Aren thought before he interjected. "They gave us fifteen years of peace in exchange for nothing, *Mara*. They proved their commitment to the treaty, and now it's time for us to do the same."

"But at what cost?" Mara gestured to the middle of the map, where model Amaridian ships sat to represent the lurking enemy fleet. The Amaridians were always Ithicana's worst raiders, primarily because they were competitors for the same business: trade between the continents. Amaridian merchant vessels took the greatest risks, making the crossing north and south even during storm season, primarily trafficking goods Ithicana wanted no part of in its markets. Maridrina had made heavy use of their services. Until now. And the Amaridian Queen clearly intended to make her displeasure over that fact known.

"Once terms are negotiated with Harendell they'll check Amarid's navy," said Aren. For while Amarid might risk quarrelling with Ithicana, picking battles with their enormous neighbor was another thing entirely.

"Has Harendell sent for Ahnna yet?"

Aren sensed his twin shifting nervously behind him. "No."

"Begun trade negotiations?"

"Not yet." Sweat dribbled down Aren's back, and it was a struggle not to grind his teeth. "Which isn't surprising. They'll be waiting to see how the peace stands in the south before they start making demands."

"Doesn't smell like peace." Everyone turned to watch Commander Aster enter the room. "Smells to me like war."

He handed Aren a folded letter sealed with amethyst-colored wax stamped with the Valcottan emblem of crossed staffs. "Ran into the mail runner in the bridge and thought to bring this to you directly."

*You mean you thought to have me read it in front of everyone*, Aren thought, cracking the wax with more force than was necessary, reading the few lines and struggling to keep a grimace from his face as he set the page down on the replica of Midwatch. The Empress of Valcotta was a reasonable woman. The Valcottans were reasonable people. But both *hated* Maridrina in a way that bordered on religion. It was a sentiment that the Maridrinians returned.

"Well?" Mara demanded at the same time Aster blurted out, "Has Valcotta declared war on us?"

Eyes on the page, Aren read: "*To His Royal Majesty, King Aren Kertell, King of Ithicana, Ruler of the Tempest Seas and Master of the Bridge*."

Everyone in the room seemed to hold their breath, and he knew why. Until today, the Empress had always addressed him as Dearest Aren, beloved son of my friend, God keep her soul in peace. The use of his titles was *not* a good sign.

He continued. "Long have Valcotta and Ithicana been friends—"

"Friends who raid when the weather's nice," Jor muttered from where he stood at Aren's left.

"All friends quarrel on occasion," Aster said. "Will you continue,

Your Grace?"

Aren coughed. "Long have Valcotta and Ithicana been friends, and it grieves us terribly to learn that you have chosen to betray that friendship by siding with Maridrina against us."

Someone in the room let out a low whistle, but Aren didn't lift his head from the page. "It breaks our heart to know that our dear friend Ithicana now supplies our mortal enemy in their unjust attacks against our lands. And all our dead we shall lay at your feet."

No one spoke.

"Strong is our desire to maintain our friendship with Ithicana, but this affront cannot go unanswered. Once the calm is upon us, we shall deploy our fleets to blockade our foe, Maridrina, from reaching your markets at Southwatch island until this offensive alliance is broken."

He was prevented from reading the rest, as both Aster and Mara broke into laughter, much of the room echoing them. "Good fortune favors us after all," Aster finally managed to get out. "Silas thought he was so clever. Thought he'd managed to extract the one thing from us that we didn't want to give, but neither he nor Maridrina will see *any* of it."

Aren hadn't laughed then, and he certainly wasn't laughing now. A twig snapped, and he jerked from his thoughts, turning to watch Jor step back out onto the rocks, still in the process of buckling his belt.

"Winds are strengthening," Jor said. "Storm is going to rage harder before it gives its last gasp. Amarid will have to cool its heels for a few days before they come for blood." The old soldier smirked at Aren. "It's an opportune moment for you to go spend some time with that pretty wife of yours. She's starting to take a shine to you, I can tell."

"You came to all those realizations while you were taking a shit?"

"It's when I do my best thinking. Now go. I'll finish the patrol."

Rising to his feet, Aren cast his gaze in the direction of his house, then shook his head. Lara was supposed to be the first step toward a better future for Ithicana. But with Amarid about to wage war and Valcotta doing its best to destroy the treaty, a better future no longer felt like a dream.

It felt like a delusion.

# 21
# LARA

LARA RESTED HER chin on her forearms, one eye on the faint glow in the east and the other on the Ithicanians grouped in the clearing in front of the barracks. Rainwater dripped down the back of her neck, but after three nights spent spying from the roof of the large stone structure, she barely noticed the endless damp anymore.

The population of Midwatch had grown by four, if not five, times in the past few days, men and women arriving by boat to join the ranks. They were civilians—or at least had been until War Tides began—but calling them such seemed a misnomer, as they fell into the efficient routine of Midwatch with practiced ease. Even the youngest, who couldn't have been more than fifteen, seemed to have arrived fully trained.

Still, the ranking officers—who were all career soldiers at Midwatch—ran them through drill after drill, day and night, leaving nothing to chance.

And anything that happened in the midnight hours, Lara was witness to.

Sneaking out of the Midwatch house was no great challenge

despite the number of guards Aren now had posted around the home. For one, she'd earned a bit of trust from them by saving Aren's life during the battle on Serrith Island, so they were no longer waiting for her to do something nefarious. Two, the clouds from the rainstorms made for the darkest of nights, giving her perfect cover for escape. And three, the Ithicanians were distracted by what they perceived as a far greater threat than a young woman soaking herself in a hot spring:

The Amaridians.

The fleet remained off the coast of Ithicana, though there had been no attacks since Serrith. Eli, the source of much of Lara's information, had told her that they were unlikely to make a move until the weather cleared. The waters were shallow and full of rocks and shoals, as well as the man-made defenses Ithicana was known for, and unpredictable winds and poor visibility made attacking during foul weather inadvisable.

But the storm wouldn't last forever, and Midwatch seethed with anticipation of the battles to come. Which served Lara's purposes well.

Already her head was full with what she'd learned during her venture off Midwatch with Aren, and the past three nights had yielded even more. From her perch, she'd learned much about how the bridge was patrolled, inside and out, where sentries were stationed on the surrounding islands, and the signals they used to communicate with Midwatch, which seemed to function as a central control point for this area of Ithicana. She'd learned about the explosives they used to destroy enemy ships, shot by arrow or launched by shipbreaker and, if the story she'd overheard was true, occasionally planted by hand under the cover of night.

She'd watched them train, working in the rain with only faint lantern light to avoid the attention of anyone on the water. Hand to hand, with blades, and with bow, the worst of them were at least proficient. The best of them . . . well, she wouldn't want to go up against the best of them unless she had to. Their weapons were all of fine make, every one of them armed to the teeth, the garrison stockpiled with enough to supply them with spares.

Midwatch was only one piece of the puzzle, but if it was the standard that Ithicana held itself to, then what Serin and the rest of her masters had told Lara and her sisters about Ithicana being impenetrable had been alarmingly accurate.

But as to the rest of what she and her sisters had been told about Ithicana . . . that, Lara was questioning. Questioning what was truth and what was lies, because it was impossible that all parties had been honest with her. Not with everyone claiming to be the victim and no one the aggressor.

*Someone was deceiving her.*

Or everyone was. Pushing back a strand of wet hair from her face, Lara wished, not for the first time, that she'd been allowed to spend time away from the compound. Everything she knew had come from books and from her masters. Outside of combat, she was like a scholar who studies the world but never leaves the library. It was a limitation, and one she'd pointed out to Serin several times, much to his endless irritation.

"It's not worth the risk," he had snapped. "All it would take is one slip on your part, and everything that we've worked for, fought for, would be undone. Is your desire for a sojourn worth losing the only chance Maridrina has at escaping Ithicana's yoke?" He'd never waited for a response, only slapped her cheek and said, "Remember your purpose."

Master Erik had given her a different answer when she'd pressed. "Your father is a man who needs *control*, little cockroach," he said, passing a whetstone up and down a blade. "Here, he can control every variable, but outside"—he used the weapon to gesture to the desert—"true control is beyond even a king's power. Your life is as it is out of necessity, my girl. But it won't be this way forever."

His words had infuriated her at the time—a vague non-answer, in her childish opinion—but now . . . Now she wondered if there was more depth to his response than she'd once realized.

Now she wondered if the variable her father had most wanted to control was her.

The main door to the barracks opened and shut beneath her, and Lara's attention perked as a tall figure exited the building. He had his hood pulled up against the rain, clothing identical to that of every other soldier, but she knew instinctively it was Aren. Something about his stride. The way he held his shoulders. The hint of pride that radiated from him as he surveyed the troops. And something else that she couldn't quite put a finger on . . .

She knew that what her father and Serin had told her about the King of Ithicana had been a lie—though she understood why. It was easier to stab a demon in the back. A much harder thing to betray a man whose actions and choices were driven by a desire to do right by his people. But she also knew that her homeland and Ithicana were at odds, and what would save one would damn the other. The welfare of her people was her priority, her mission to give them the one thing that would ensure their future. And for that reason, Aren could never be anything to her but the enemy.

Aren stepped closer to the training soldiers to say something to the woman leading the exercises, and Lara leaned forward to catch what it was. When she did, a piece of debris slipped off the roof of the barracks, landing with a soft thud on the ground.

Aren turned on his heel, one hand going to the weapon belted at his waist, the other shoving back his hood.

Lara froze. Dressed in black clothes, she was hidden in the darkness atop the roof. *Unless* someone held up a lantern to investigate a noise.

With the toe of his boot, Aren nudged the fallen bit of branch and leaves. Lara silently willed him to look away. *It's nothing. Just foliage knocked loose by the wind. Happens a hundred times a day.* But even as she did, she could relate to the sixth sense that was telling him something wasn't right.

"Someone bring a lantern over here. And a ladder. I think we've got snakes on the roof again."

Pulse roaring in her ears, Lara eased backward, her fingers clutching the slimy stone of her perch. He'd hear even the slightest noise, but if she didn't move fast . . .

A horn sounded in the distance, and the Ithicanians—Aren included—stopped what they were doing and turned in the direction of the water. Another horn sounded, this one closer, and Aren gave a sharp nod. "Amaridians are on the move." He started shouting out orders, but Lara couldn't afford to stay to listen. Dawn was approaching, and she needed the cover of night to get back into the house undetected. And she needed to be inside by the time the sun was up, or her absence would be noted.

Easing around the back of the barracks, she jumped, catching hold of a tree branch that really needed to be cut back. From tree to tree, she climbed, then dropped into the shelter of the jungle. Using the route she'd established on her first night, she cut over to the path leading up to the house, moving as fast as she dared on the muddy earth.

Gorrick and Lia were guarding the exterior, and she silently circled until she found a place out of sight of both of them, then scaled the wall, crawled over the roof, and dropped into the courtyard. Easing inside through her cracked window, she swiftly scrubbed the mud from her boots and clothes, putting everything back in the wardrobe where it could dry undetected.

A knock sounded at the door, the lock rattling. "Your Grace? It's dawn."

Taryn. The woman was like damned clockwork. Since her perceived failure to watch Lara while they were staying at Nana's house, Taryn was intent on redeeming herself by monitoring Lara like a hawk. She slept in the hall outside Lara's door—would've slept right next to her bed if Lara hadn't gently noted that Taryn's snoring rivaled the thunderstorms for volume.

If she didn't answer, Taryn would likely break down the door. "Coming!"

Throwing on a robe and wrapping a towel around her hair, Lara trotted across the floor and opened the door. "Is something wrong? I heard horns?"

"Amarid," Taryn replied vaguely, then her eyes narrowed. "Why is there mud on your face?"

"I was just washing it off. Certain muds are good for the skin. They cleanse the pores."

"Mud?" Taryn gave her a dubious frown, then shook her head, passing a weary hand over her eyes before stepping into the room, giving it a once-over. "I've told you not to leave your window open. You're asking to wake up with a snake under the covers with you."

"I only opened it just now," Lara lied. "It was stuffy in here."

Taryn checked under the bed. "The storm's blown over, so you can go outside if you want fresh air." Then she flipped back the cover and swore, stepping back several paces. "What did I tell you?"

A small snake, black with yellow bands, was coiled in the center of the bed, hissing angrily at them. Muttering under her breath, Taryn stepped in the hallway and shouted for Eli, who appeared moments later, a long stick with a loop of rope at one end. He deftly caught the creature, the loop tightening around its neck, then departed as quickly as he'd come, snake in tow.

Apparently, Lara needed to add *check room for snakes* to her routine when returning from a reconnaissance mission.

Though there wasn't much more to be gained from the roof of the barracks. Or from Midwatch, for that matter. It was a nearly impossible nut to crack unless her father could get someone on the inside. Ideally, that would be her, but she fully intended to be long gone before Maridrina invaded, her life as much in danger from her father's soldiers as it would be from the Ithicanians once they realized she'd betrayed them. Which meant she needed to find an entry point other than Midwatch for her father to exploit.

"I'm going to nail your window shut." Taryn stepped aside so that Eli's aunt could enter with the breakfast tray, which was deposited on the small table. "Or else start locking Vitex in here with you at night."

The thought of sleeping with the enormous cat watching gave Lara the shivers. "I'll keep it shut. I promise."

Sitting at the table, Lara loaded two plates full of food and then gestured at the other woman to join her, both of them drinking deeply from their steaming coffees. They'd grown increasingly familiar in their time together, Taryn easy to be around in a way that reminded Lara of her sisters. "Has Amarid attacked?"

"Not yet. They know they no longer have the element of surprise, so they'll look for points of weakness."

"Is Aren . . ."

"He'll be on the water, making sure we have no points of weakness. Why?" Taryn smirked. "Miss him?"

Lara gave a snort of amusement that could be taken either way, but the wheels were turning in her head. Aren gone meant there was no one on Midwatch to tell her *no*. "I wanted to ask him something . . ."

"Oh?"

"I want to get used to being on the water."

Taryn paused in her chewing of a mouthful of ham, then swallowed. "War Tides isn't exactly the ideal time for sailing aimlessly about, Lara."

Lara gave her a gentle kick under the table. "I *know* that. I was thinking I could sit in a boat in the cove. Then perhaps by the end of War Tides, I'll have adjusted to the water enough that I might venture further without subjecting everyone to my vomiting."

Taryn took another bite of meat, her brow furrowed. "There's a lot of comings and goings right now . . ."

"Is there another location that would work better? I don't want to be in the way." And if there was another landing point on the island—perhaps one with fewer defenses —it might mitigate her need to find another entrance to the bridge.

"Nowhere with a proper beach."

Lara exhaled in disappointment. "It's only that I feel so trapped. I want to see more of Ithicana, but with my seasickness and my . . . fear, it seems impossible."

Trapped the way Taryn felt trapped. Limited in where she might go and what she might do by circumstance and necessity. Lara watched her words strike home, the other woman setting down her fork, eyes distant as she thought. "I suppose we could try it for an hour and see if anyone takes issue."

Lara grinned. "Let me wash the rest of this mud off my face, and then we can go."

Three hours later, the two of them sat in a bobbing canoe, Lara trying to keep track of the goings-on in the cove while periodically leaning over the side to empty her guts.

Taryn had taken her to another building not far from the barracks, which was filled with a variety of vessels that weren't currently in use. She'd selected a small canoe that wouldn't fit more than the two of them, so old it barely appeared seaworthy. No one would miss this particular vessel. As they carried it down to the beach, Lara silently considered how she might secret it away for her eventual escape.

She rested her forearms on the edge of the canoe and watched the chain guarding the mouth to the cove rise so that vessels could ferry goods from the pier to the shore. Crates of food, supplies, and weapons, all hailing from Harendell. There were cages of clucking chickens, three live pigs, and a dozen sides of beef, the Ithicanians' movements concealed by heavy mist.

The signal horns never seemed to cease their blowing. Ripples of sound that conveyed countless different messages, judging from the various reactions they incited, and not something that could be mimicked by an untrained Maridrinian soldier. Lara suspected her father would need to enlist musicians should he wish to turn the form of communication to his advantage. Taking a sip from a canteen of water, Lara rubbed her throbbing temple as she listened to the notes, attempting to memorize patterns and responses, though it would take days, probably weeks of listening and watching for her to make any sense of them.

The canoe had swung around so she was facing away from the cliffs guarding the cove from the sea, but the rattle of the chain caught her attention and she turned to watch a series of vessels enter, her eyes immediately finding Aren in one of them.

And his finding her.

She watched him exchange words with Jor, then the vessel altered its course from the beach to Lara's little canoe. Standing, he held onto the mast as the two boats came alongside. "I suppose there's an interesting explanation for this?"

Taryn rose, the canoe rocking, and Lara's stomach rocked along with it. "Her Grace is of the opinion that exposure will cure her seasickness."

"How's that working out?"

Taryn gestured at the school of tiny fishes circling the boat, and Lara felt her cheeks warm as they both laughed at her expense. Then Aren said, "Go get some rest, Taryn. I'll take over for a bit."

Lara's heart skipped as Aren settled on the seat facing Lara. He waited until the other boat was nearly to the beach before asking, "Why exactly have you volunteered yourself for this particular misery?"

Lara stared at the bottom of the canoe, which was taking on a bit of water through a tiny crack that she'd need patch. "Because. If I don't learn to master the sea, I'll never be able to go anywhere with you."

"Master?" He leaned forward, and her eyes, of their own accord, fixed on his lips, heat rising to her cheeks as she remembered the feel of them against her own.

"Perhaps tolerate is a better word," she murmured, noticing a nasty scrape on the inside of his forearm. "You're hurt."

"It's nothing. I had an altercation with a rock, and the rock came out better in the exchange."

Part of her was afraid to move closer to him, already aware that in his presence, she'd stopped seeing and hearing what was going on around them. But, she told herself, he was also the key to seeing more of Ithicana, and that was a necessary part of her plan. "Let me have a look."

He shifted nearer, unbuckling the greave that protected the backside of his arm. "See? Nothing of consequence."

"It should still be bandaged."

It didn't need to be bandaged. Both of them knew it. But that didn't stop her from taking hold of his wrist. Or him from supplying her with salve and a roll of fabric. The boat rocked on a series of larger waves, and his knee bumped against the side of her thigh, sending a surge of heat the rest of the way up her leg, filling her with a sensation that was decidedly distracting.

Forcing her attention on the injury, Lara picked out a few bits of rock, smeared the raw spots with salve, then carefully wrapped the bandage, but it was impossible not to notice how his breath moved the errant wisps of hair on her forehead. The way the muscles in his forearm flexed when he moved. The way his other hand brushed her hip as he gripped the side of the canoe.

"You're knowledgeable in the healing arts."

"Any idiot can wind a bandage around an arm."

"I meant more what you did on Serrith."

Lara shrugged, tying off the bandage. "All Maridrinian women are expected to be able to put their husbands back together. I received the appropriate training."

"Practicing stitches on a cloth isn't the same as running a needle and thread through a person's bleeding skin. I nearly fainted the first time I had to do it."

A smile rose on her face, and she unfastened the bandage knot, unsatisfied with it. "Women haven't the luxury of such squeamishness, Your Grace."

"You're avoiding the question, *Your Grace.*" His voice was light, teasing, but beneath she sensed a seriousness, as though he were searching for a lie.

"My sisters and I practiced on the servants and guards whenever there was an injury. On the horses and camels, too." That was the truth. What she didn't tell him was that her true training came from trying to save the lives of the Valcottan warriors she and her sisters fought on the training yard. It had been a twisted way to learn. In one heartbeat, trying to take a man's life. In the next, trying to save it. Only to take it again.

"It's a useful skill to have around here. That is, if you're willing."

Buckling the greave over the bandage, the back of her hand brushed his palm, and he closed his fingers around hers. Her train of thought vanished. "I'll help as much as I'm able to. They're my people now."

His expression softened. "That they are."

Both of them jumped as something rapped sharply against the hull of the canoe, and Lara looked up to see Jor standing in the boat next to them, paddle in hand. "You ready?"

"For what?"

The older man gave him an incredulous look. "The horns, Aren. Amarid is moving south."

Lara hadn't heard any horns blow. Hadn't seen the other canoe approach. Hadn't noticed a goddamned thing while bandaging that arm. And neither, it appeared, had Aren.

He clambered out of her canoe and into the other vessel, setting them both to rocking, and then they were on the move toward the entrance to the cove. Lara stared after them, finally shouting, "How am I supposed to get back to shore?"

"You have a paddle," he shouted back, a wild grin on his face as the wind caught at his hair. "Use it!"

From that moment, a pattern formed of Lara and Taryn coming down after breakfast to float on the water, rain or shine. At first, it was misery. The incessant bobbing up and down made Lara's head spin and her stomach heave, but gradually the sickness began to ease, as did the surge of fear she felt stepping off dry land and into the boat.

The raids were endless, the music of the horns so constant, it seemed an endless song of war. Aren and his soldiers were continuously on the move, chasing off raiders, reinforcing defenses, and ensuring the countless watch stations and outposts were kept supplied. More often than not, their excursions turned into skirmishes, the boats returning full of wounded men and women, the faces of their comrades drawn and exhausted.

The worst of the injured went to the dozen healers stationed at Midwatch, but those needing only stitches or bandages were left in Lara's boat for her to tend to. More often than not, one of her patients was Aren, which was the *only* time Taryn left her side.

"I'm starting to wonder," she said as she applied a leech to the swelling on his cheek, smirking when he recoiled from the creature, "if you are purposefully trying to get yourself injured or if you are just that inept."

He cringed as she lifted another leech out of the jar. "Is there a third option?"

"Sit still." She applied the leech the way the healers had shown her, marveling at the way the swelling almost instantly reduced on his cheekbone, the engorged creatures dropping into her hands when they'd finished. Along with supplies, the healers had also insisted that she be given a better boat, returning her little canoe to its dry dock. She'd been sneaking out at nights to slowly move the vessel to the hiding place she'd selected near one of the cliffs, along with a number of stolen supplies, ready to facilitate her escape when the time was right.

"You seem to be doing better with the water."

"I don't get sick anymore. Though I suppose it might be different out in the open where the waves are larger."

"Perhaps someday we'll test that theory."

*Someday*. Which meant no time soon. It was a struggle to keep the frown from her face because she was running out of ideas for winning him over. She had won his lust, that much was clear from the way his eyes skimmed over the unlaced neckline of her tunic. Winning his trust, however, was proving to be far more of a challenge.

She'd thought, for a time, it was because their marriage had yet to be consummated. That maybe he needed that step before he'd hand her the metaphorical keys to the kingdom, but she had since rejected that theory. Aren was not, judging from the offhand comments she'd heard from his soldiers, inexperienced with women, so it would take more than skill in the bedroom to make him fall for her.

And it would take more than him falling for her to make him trust her.

For as much as he might come to care for her, he loved his people more. His trust would only come if he believed she was as loyal to his people as he was.

"I'm not certain that leech deserves so much of your attention." Aren's voice pulled Lara from her thoughts, and she blinked, realizing that she'd been regarding the squirming creature in her hand for far too long.

"They just gave you back your handsome face, so perhaps you should give them the credit they deserve."

Aren smiled and Lara realized what she'd said. With everyone else, she was strategic, but Aren flustered her. Things had a way of slipping out when he was around.

"It's going to rain tonight. I thought I might take the opportunity to have a proper dinner at the house. With you."

Her face was burning, heart a riot in her chest. "Tonight?"

He looked away from her. "My ability to predict the weather has its limits. But yes, tonight looks promising."

*Say yes*, her inner voice screamed. *Do what you need to do.* Except being alone with him . . . Lara wasn't sure what would happen. Or rather, she *was* sure and wanted to avoid it at all costs.

Not because she didn't want him to kiss her, because she did.

And not because she didn't want him to peel the clothes from her body, because god, she'd envisioned that more than once.

It was because she *did* want him that she needed to avoid this situation, because betraying him was already going to be hard enough.

Horns blasted, and this time the rhythm wasn't music, but an anxious rippling blare that tore at her ears. Aren stiffened, his expression intent. "What is it?" she demanded.

"Aela."

"Who?"

"It's one of the islands under Kestark's watch. It's being attacked."

"Kestark?"

"The garrison south of us." His eyes were distant, listening. "But Aela's outpost is calling for Midwatch's aid."

Already soldiers were pouring down the beach, pushing boats out into the water. More horns sounded, and Aren's face paled.

"What's happening?"

"Their shipbreaker is jammed." He stood, gesturing to his guards, who were paddling hard toward them. "The outpost is going to be slaughtered. Amarid will take the island, and it will be a bloody nightmare to dig them out."

Lara's mind raced, deciding on a plan even as it formed in her mind. She caught his hand. "Take me with you. If there are injured, I can help."

"That's what we have healers for."

"Five of which are elsewhere, two of which are injured themselves. Which leaves you only five to bring with you. It's not enough to deal with slaughter."

"Others will come."

The boat was only yards away. She had seconds to convince him.

"And how many of your people will die in the time it will take for them to arrive?" She tightened her fingers on his. "I can help them."

Indecision ricocheted across his face, then he nodded. "Follow orders. No arguments." The other boat came alongside, and he hauled Lara and her box of supplies in with him. "Go!" he shouted.

Paddles drove them toward the gap, the chain already up, the ocean covered with whitecaps beyond. Wild and unpredictable. A prickle of fear crawled down Lara's spine as she sat in the bottom of the boat.

"Time to put your experiment to the test," Aren said as they passed between the towering cliffs, the vessel bucking and plunging the moment they hit the open sea.

"To Aela!" Jor roared. "Let's give these Amaridians a taste of Midwatch steel!"

"To Aela!" The soldiers on the other vessels echoed the chant, and behind them, horns called over the water. Not the musical ripple of a signal, but a violent blast of rage.

A battle cry.

# 22
# LARA

The boats barely seemed to touch the water as they skated across the sea, a strong north wind filling the sails. Lara's heart was in her throat, but with her nausea under control, she was able to study the bridge as they followed its great grey length south, eyes picking out scouts perched on its top and the glints of spyglasses on the islands to either side.

"How long until we reach Aela?" she shouted over the wind.

"Not long," Aren replied. "The closest Midwatch teams will already be there."

Time seemed to both fly and crawl. A thousand details flooded her mind even as her heartbeat moved into the swift but steady thud it always did before battle. *You aren't here to fight,* she reminded herself. *You're here to observe under the cover of helping the healers, nothing more.* The words did nothing to calm her anticipation.

When they rounded an enormous limestone karst tower, all the Ithicanians pulled their masks from their belts and donned them. Weapons loosened. Eyes intent.

Then she saw it.

The ship was larger than any she'd seen before, a great three-masted monstrosity as tall as the bridge itself. She picked out the Amaridian flag, countless soldiers scurrying about its deck. Beyond, a half dozen longboats were moving toward a narrow beach on which a battle was being waged, the sand soaked with blood.

Swiftly she saw the reason the Amaridians had chosen Aela Island beyond the relatively easy landing the beach provided them. There was a pier on the western edge of the island, the bridge curving inland before heading back out to sea. And if the Ithicanians were fighting this hard to defend it, she'd bet that pier had an opening in its base. "How many men are on that ship?"

"Four hundred," Jor replied. "Perhaps a few more."

"And us?"

No one answered.

Aren caught her hand, pulling her close. "See the line of rock and trees?" He pointed. "We'll get you and the other healers past that line. You stay there and the injured will be brought to you, understood?"

"Yes."

His hand tightened. "Keep your hood up so the Amaridians don't recognize you. And if things go badly, go with the other healers. They know how to make a retreat."

And she'd bet that retreat was into the bridge. But gaining that information wasn't worth the cost of Aren's life.

Her heartbeat was no longer steady, but a wild and chaotic beast. "Don't let it go badly," she whispered. "I need you to win this."

But Aren was already shouting orders. "Bring down those longboats. The rest of you, to the beach!"

The boats flanked the enormous ship, the air thick with arrows shot from both sides. Aren knelt in the boat next to her, emptying a quiver into the backs of the Amaridians climbing into longboats, their corpses falling into the water below. Lara's fingers itched to snatch up a weapon, to fight, but she forced herself to cower low in the boat, flinching every time an arrow thudded into the thick wood.

Then they were past the ship.

Four of the Ithicanian vessels veered away from the pack, skipping over the surf to slam into the longboats full of soldiers heading to shore. Wood splintered and cracked, men toppling into the water. The Ithicanians boarded the longboats with lethal grace, blades flashing, the sun glinting off sprays of blood.

The rest of the boats drove toward the carnage on the beach. There were bodies everywhere, the sand more red than white. Maybe two dozen Ithicanians were holding the enemy to the waterline, using the narrow access and higher ground to their advantage, but they were falling back. Dying beneath the Amaridian onslaught.

They had to hurry, or the island would be lost.

The Midwatch boats dropped their sails, riding the waves as they were launched onto the shore. At the last second, Aren snatched up Lara's hand. "Jump!" he shouted.

Lara leapt, her boots sinking into the sand, the momentum nearly sending her sprawling. Then they were running toward the Amaridians, who were now sandwiched between two forces.

Screams shattered the air, bodies and limbs hitting the sand, the stench of blood and opened guts oppressive. Lara held tight to her box of supplies, keeping behind Aren as he pushed up the hill, stepping over his victims as she went. The weapons of the fallen littered the sand, and every instinct demanded she pick one up. That she fight.

*You mustn't,* she commanded herself. *Not unless you have no choice.*

But the warrior in her railed against the limitation, so when a soldier got past the Ithicanian line, she slammed her supply box into his face, watching with satisfaction as he toppled backward, the point of Aren's blade appearing through his chest.

The King of Ithicana used one booted foot to shove the dead man off his weapon, the leather of his mask coated with gore. Catching her hand, he drew her at a run, dodging around the few remaining Amaridians who were on their knees begging for their lives.

"Show them no mercy!" he shouted, then pulled Lara behind a series of boulders. An older Ithicanian woman, her face drawn, clothes drenched with blood, was closing the lids of a young man, his body marked with several mortal wounds. Three other soldiers lay on the ground, wounds bandaged, their faces tight with pain.

The healer's eyes widened at the sight of her king. "Explain to Lara what you need her to do," Aren told her. Then he was back around the rock, shouting, "Taryn, get that shipbreaker working and sink that bitch!"

The Midwatch healers appeared, their escorts already having abandoned them. "What do you want me to do?" Lara asked.

"Wait for them to bring us the injured. What do you have for supplies? I'm short."

Lara handed her the box, then scampered up the back of one of the boulders to watch the battle unfolding below. Her blood ran cold at the sight.

Aren stood on the beach with maybe a hundred Ithicanians, but beyond, the water was full of longboats. Dozens of them, all bursting with heavily armed soldiers, and more still waiting on the ship's deck to be unloaded. There were hundreds of them. And no way to stop them.

The Ithicanians were firing arrows at the front-runners, but it wasn't long until they were spent, leaving nothing for them to do but wait.

The old healer had climbed up next to her, expression grim as she took in the scene.

Lara dug her nails into the rock. "We can't win this. Not against these odds."

"We've won against worse. Though this one will cost us."

*Was it still a victory if everyone was dead?* Lara thought.

It must've shown on her face, because the older woman sighed. "Have you ever seen a battle before, Your Majesty?"

Lara swallowed hard. "Not like this."

"I'd tell you to prepare yourself, but you can't." The old woman rested her hand on Lara's. "This moment will change you." Then she climbed down the rocks to join the Midwatch healers.

The scene was eerily silent, the only sound the roar of the surf and the occasional cry of pain, the wounded left on the beach until the battle was won. So quiet. Too quiet.

Then the first of the longboats hit the shore, and everything turned to chaos.

The two forces slammed into each other, the air filling with shouts and screams, the clash of metal against metal and weapons against flesh.

Wave after wave of boats hurtled into shore, the heavy vessels crushing and killing Amaridians and Ithicanians alike, the waterline a teeming mass of humanity. The sailors struggled to withdraw, to get back to the ship to retrieve more soldiers, but Aren's men flung themselves at the sailors, cutting them down. Pulling the vessels onto the sand.

Yet still more came.

The Ithicanians fought with vicious efficiency, better trained and better armed, but grossly outnumbered. They fought until they couldn't stand, taking injury after injury until they collapsed on the beach or were pulled under waves that were more blood and bodies than water.

And still the enemy came.

It was the perfect opportunity to sneak away. To go look at the bridge pier and determine whether she could use it in her strategy, but her body remained rooted in place.

*You have to do something*. The voice rose up from the depths of Lara's mind, incessant and tenacious. *Do something. Do something.*

But what could she do? There were no injured behind these rocks for her to tend, and there wouldn't be until the battle was over. She could take a weapon and fight, but this wasn't the same circumstances as Serrith. In this madness, she couldn't turn the tide.

*Do something.*

Her eyes flicked back to the wounded bleeding out on the beach. Drowning in the waves. And then she was over the rocks and running.

Lara had been the fastest of her sisters—*built for speed*, Master Erik had always said. Today she ran like she never had before.

Her thighs burned as she sprinted down the beach, arms pumping, eyes fixed on her target. Skidding to a stop next to a young woman who'd taken two arrows in the back and one in the thigh, Lara bent and heaved her over one shoulder, then raced back to the boulders.

Rounding them, Lara carefully deposited the injured soldier on the ground in front of the startled healers. "Help her."

Then she was back on the beach and running.

Necessity compelled her to choose those with injuries they might survive. As it was, most of those farther up the beach were long past saving, eyes staring blankly at the gray sky.

So she edged closer to the battle.

The soldiers able to fight were doing so on top of the bodies of the fallen. Amaridians and Ithicanians, both tangled in the mess of limbs, dead hands seeming to grasp and trip them as the crimson waves pulled and tugged on carnage.

Most everyone on the ground was dead. Either from their original injuries, or from being crushed and drowned, but still Lara prowled the rear of the Ithicanian line, water filling her boots as she searched.

"Get back," someone shouted at her, but she ignored them, catching sight of a man, younger than her, choking as he tried to climb out of the battle, the waves rolling over his head, boots stomping on his back.

Lara dove, catching hold of his hand and holding tight so that the water wouldn't pull him farther out.

Someone kicked her in the side.

Another stomped on the back of her leg, and she cried out.

They were pressing in on her, driving her down into the sand, but the boy was looking at her and she at him, and Lara refused to let go.

Inch by inch, she dragged him back, then a hand closed on her belt and pulled her and the injured soldier the rest of the way free.

"What are you doing?"

Aren's voice. His face hidden behind his mask.

Over his shoulder, she saw an Amaridian raising a cudgel. Snatching up a rock, she threw it hard, shattering the soldier's face. "Fight," she screamed at Aren, then scrambled to her feet.

Holding the injured boy under the armpits, she dragged him up the beach and out of harm's way. Then she threw herself back into the carnage.

The Ithicanians saw what she was doing, and they fought to

give her openings. Called her name when someone fell. Guarded her back while she dragged their comrades out of the water because they couldn't afford to stop fighting.

And the enemy kept coming.

Pushing them farther up the sand.

Step by step, the Ithicanians retreated, and Lara howled in fury, because all those she'd pulled onto the beach were now in danger of being trampled once more. Her body screamed with pain and exhaustion, her sides cramping as her lungs struggled to draw in enough air to fuel her thundering heart.

Then a familiar crack echoed across the island, along with the whistle of something large flying through the air.

Splintering wood and screams filtered up from the deeper water, and Lara lifted her head to see a large hole in the side of the ship. Someone had repaired the shipbreaker.

Another crack split the air, and this time the projectile hit one of the masts. It shattered, falling sideways, the ropes and sails falling to the deck.

Another crack, this time a hole opening in the hull, water pouring in with every wave.

The weapon didn't stop. Boulder after boulder was thrown at the ship, then Taryn turned on the longboats, hitting them with deadly accuracy.

The Amaridians began to panic, lines breaking as they fought to save their own skins. But there was no retreat, and the Ithicanians would show them no mercy.

"For Ithicana!" someone roared, and the chant raced down the beach until it drowned out all other noise as the soldiers rallied around their king, pressing forward.

So there was no one to hear when Lara whispered, "For Maridrina," and dove back into the chaos.

# 23
# AREN

Aren found Lara crouched next to a tide pool washing blood from her hands and arms. Her clothing was soaked in gore, and as she lifted her head to regard him, he noted the red streaks on her cheeks from where she'd pushed aside the strands of hair that had tugged loose from her thick braid.

His soldiers were talking about her; and not, for once, about how she was a useless Maridrinian, good for nothing but bedding. Today had changed that. Time and again, she'd sprinted onto the beach to pull an injured Ithicanian back behind their lines, showing no regard for her own life as the Amaridians had fought their way forward, the battle pitched and desperate.

And once the battle was won, she'd treated the wounded with speed and efficiency, packing wounds and tying tourniquets, buying them time until the healers could reach them. Saving lives, one soldier at a time, her face tight with determination.

Today she'd won Ithicana's respect.

And his own.

"Are you all right?" He crouched down to submerge his own

hands in the water. He'd done it earlier, but his skin still felt sticky and stained.

"Tired." She sat back on her haunches, eyes going to the corpses floating amidst the debris of the shattered ship, the water still crimson. "How many died?"

"Forty-three. Another ten aren't likely to make it through the night."

Lara squeezed her eyes shut, then snapped them open. "So many."

"Would have been more if you hadn't convinced me to bring you. Or if you hadn't ignored my orders." He didn't add that he'd spent a good portion of the battle afraid that the decision would see her dead on the sand, an Amaridian sword in her back.

"It feels like I accomplished nothing in the scheme of things," she murmured.

"The men and women whose lives you saved would beg to differ, I suspect."

"Lives I saved." She shook her head. "I should go back to help."

Aren caught her wrist as she rose, his fingers wrapping around the slender bones, which seemed too delicate to have accomplished what she had. "We need to go."

"Go?" Spots of anger rose on her cheeks. "We can't leave them like this."

He wanted to abandon this beach and his injured people no more than she did, but the defense of his kingdom was a finely oiled machine with a thousand different pieces. Pulling one out of place, even for a matter of hours, put the whole works at risk, and right now, his piece was very much out of place. "I moved significant numbers from the defense of Midwatch and its surrounding islands. We need to return."

"No." She pulled out of his grip. "Fewer than a dozen of the soldiers here are unscathed. We can't leave them undefended. What if the Amaridians attack again?"

Out of the corner of his eye, Aren could see his guard standing by the boats, Jor giving him a pointed glare. Several of the other Midwatch teams were at the ready on the beach, waiting for his order to depart. "There are no Amaridian ships on the horizon, and reinforcements are already on the way. They'll be here within the hour."

"I'm not leaving until they arrive."

She crossed her arms, and it occurred to him that he might have to drag the woman every soldier on this beach was lauding as a hero into a boat if he ever wanted to depart. Which wasn't exactly the visual he wished to present to them.

Huffing out a breath, Aren pulled a knife from his belt and knelt in the sand, drawing a snaking line representing the bridge. "The defense of the bridge is broken into sections led by Watch Commanders, each with a subset of the Ithicanian military under his or her control. The Midwatch garrison is here"—he made a hole in the sand—"and the Kestark garrison is here. Four Amaridian ships were making motions to attack here." He made four holes south of Kestark Island.

"The healers could use my assistance," Lara interrupted. "So perhaps get to the point."

"I *am* getting to the point," he grumbled, hoping a convoluted explanation would convince her to leave rather than provoke questions. "Kestark moved their reserves to reinforce the locations most likely to come under attack, while at the same time, the Amaridians attacked here at Aela Island. Kestark couldn't risk pulling back their reserve, nor could they redeploy the teams making up the net of defense through here"—he drew an oval—"so they called for assistance from Midwatch. But now Midwatch is down the majority of its reserves, so if there are any attacks here"—he drew another oval—"we won't be able to come to their aid in a timely fashion."

Lara stared at the drawing, blinking only once in apparent confusion. Then she pressed her fingers to her temples. "For the love of God, Aren, none of this justifies abandoning these soldiers." She started to pull away, but he tugged her back.

"Listen. The four Amaridian ships that were expected to attack instead withdrew —probably because they saw it wouldn't be an easy fight—and they've moved east and out of sight of our scouts. So now there will be a wave of signals, with teams shifting one position north and west in order to allow the Kestark teams closest to us to move to reinforce. As I said, they'll be here within the hour."

"Fine." Moving out of reach, she started up the sand to where the wounded were laid out in rows.

"Insufferable woman," he muttered, then a whistle caught his attention. Aren turned to see Jor gesturing at a pair of Kestark boats flying across the water on a violent gust of wind that smelled like rain. He turned back to point them out to Lara, but she was already out of earshot.

Growling out a few choice curses, he strode down to the water. "Everyone go. I want you back at Midwatch before this squall hits."

His soldiers immediately pushed off from the beach, but instead of watching them, Aren found his eyes drawn to where Lara walked among the injured, occasionally bending down to speak with one of them. The growing winds caught at the loose strands of her hair, the fading sunlight making it glow like tendrils of honey. His soldiers moved aside for her, inclined their heads to her. Respected her.

The image juxtaposed that of her walking up the road at Southwatch on her father's arm, silk clad and eyes wide: the portrait of a queen he'd worried Ithicana would never accept. Turned out, he'd been wrong.

"And when will we be departing, Your Grace?" Jor asked, coming up to stand next to him. "When your little wife says it's time to go?"

"We'll go when the *Queen of Ithicana* says it's time to go."

The older man chuckled, then clapped him on the shoulder.

The first of the Kestark boats reached shore, and Aren recognized Commander Aster even as the man's eyes lighted upon him, apprehension filling them. "Your Grace. I didn't realize you'd come yourself."

"The benefit of being at the Midwatch garrison. Like I was supposed to be."

Aster's face lost more of its color, and rightfully so. That he was arriving now meant he hadn't been at Kestark garrison, or even with the bulk of his forces warding off the anticipated attack. And Aren was quite certain he knew exactly where the other man had been.

"As you can see, *Commander*, things almost didn't go Ithicana's way today. Aela is a weak point, its outpost was undermanned, and the shipbreaker hadn't been recalibrated after storm season, leaving those who were here sitting ducks for an entire ship full of Amaridians."

"We're behind on inspections, Your Grace," Aster blurted out.

"The season came early . . ."

"Which doesn't explain why you over-deployed to the southeast and left your northern end exposed. Perhaps you'll enlighten me?"

"There were four naval ships. We needed to be ready to defend—"

"To defend a series of islands that wouldn't be assailable if the Amaridians attacked with twenty ships!" Aren snarled. "Which if you'd been paying attention, you would've known. Which suggests to me that you were *distracted* when you gave the order."

"I was *not* distracted, Your Grace. I've been commanding Kestark since you were a child."

"And yet . . ." Aren gestured at the rows and rows of dead faces staring sightlessly at the sky. Then he leaned forward. "Evacuations are complete, so that means your lovely wife and children are safely ensconced in Eranahl, leaving you with all the time in the world to screw your mistress in the house I know you had built for her just west of here."

Aster's jaw tightened, but he didn't deny it. He couldn't, not with his own personal guard listening from where they stood next to their boats. Then his eyes drifted past Aren's shoulder. "What is *she* doing here?"

Turning, Aren saw that Lara stood behind him, a surviving officer—a girl who was only eighteen—at her elbow. He started to defend Lara's presence, but the girl beat him to it.

"Respectfully, Commander, a hell of a lot more of us would be dead if our queen hadn't come."

Lara said nothing, but her blue eyes were cold and eviscerating as she stared Aster down. Then her gaze shifted to Aren and she nodded once.

"No more mistakes, Commander." Aren took her arm and stepped toward the boat where his own guard waited. "And do us all a favor and keep your cock in your trousers and your eyes on the enemy for the rest of War Tides."

"My eyes are on the enemy. She's standing right there."

Temper frayed past repair, Aren turned and slugged the man in the face, knocking him out cold. Then he turned to the girl-soldier. "You've just been promoted to Acting Commander of Kestark until another can be chosen. Do let me know if anyone gives you any trouble."

Lara helped him and the guard push the boat out into the water, then hopped in, sitting in her usual spot, the most out of the way she could be in the small vessel. Aren sat next to her, but there was no space for conversation, all of them forced to row hard to get past the break line, the wind against them.

The squall was coming in hard from the north, lightning dancing across the blackening sky, and the vessel rose and fell on swells that grew with every passing minute. Lara's back was to him, but Aren could feel the fear radiating from her, knuckles white where she gripped the edge of the boat. She kept her composure until a freak gust caught the sail. Lia and Gorrick flinging their weight onto the outrigging was the only thing keeping them from capsizing. That tore a scream from her throat. Lara had thrown herself unarmed into battle, but this . . . this was what terrified her. And Aren found himself unwilling to subject her to it.

"We need to get off the water!" he shouted at Jor, spitting out a mouthful of seawater as a wave washed over them. Jor signaled to the boat carrying the rest of his guard, then he scanned their surroundings and pointed.

Sail lowered, they rowed hard, heading for one of the countless landing points hidden throughout Ithicana.

The rain fell in a deluge, making it almost impossible to see as they wove between two towers of limestone and into a tiny cove with cliffs on all sides. From the top of one of the cliffs two heavy wooden beams reached out over the water, ropes with hooks dangling from each of them. Lia lunged, catching hold of one of the hooks and clipping it to the ring mounted at the stern of the vessel.

Aren passed his paddle to a white-faced Lara. "If we get too close to the walls, push the boat away."

She nodded, holding the wooden paddle like a weapon. Behind him, Taryn waited until the boat swung around to the right angle, then jumped, catching hold of a rope hanging from the cliff, climbing swiftly to the top.

"Aren, get over here and help." Jor and Gorrick had removed the pin holding the mast in place and were struggling to heave it out of its base. Aren stumbled over a seat, then caught hold of the mast and added his strength to the effort. The mast popped out right as a violent swell lifted the boat, sending both mast and Gorrick tumbling into the water.

Aren fell backward on his ass, leaving only Jor standing, the old man shaking his head in disgust. "Why does this never get easier?" He reached down and clipped the other line to the boat, while Aren helped the swimming Gorrick lash the mast to the side.

An exhausting eternity later, they finally lifted the second boat onto shore with the winch, where they tied it down, the lot of them trudging around the bend of rock to where the safe house waited.

The interior of the stone building was mercifully dry and free from gusting wind. After assigning two of the men to first watch, Aren slammed the wooden door shut with more force than was necessary. Without fail, his eyes went immediately to Lara, who stood at the center of the room holding the bag full of supplies.

"Are there many of these places?" She turned in a circle.

There wasn't much to see. Bunks made of wood and rope lined two of the walls. Crates of supplies were piled against the third wall, and the fourth was mostly taken up by the door. His guards were all pulling off their boots and tunics to dry, then turning their attention to their weapons, which all needed to be sharpened and oiled.

"Yes." He tugged off his own tunic and tossed it on a bunk. "But as you noticed, they're a damned pain in the ass to use in the middle of a storm."

"Will the storm sink the rest of the Amaridian fleet?" she asked, and the guard chuckled, reminding him that everyone was listening.

"No. But they'll move out into open water rather than risk being driven up onto a shoal or against any rocks. Will give us a bit of respite."

One of her eyebrows rose. "Not the most comfortable respite."

"Now, now," Jor said. "Don't be so swift to discount the comforts of a safe house. Particularly a *Midwatch* safe house." He went over to one of the crates, prying open the lid and looking inside. "His Grace has fine tastes, so he ensures anywhere he might have to spend a night is stocked with only the best."

"Are you complaining?" Aren sat on the bottom bunk and leaned back against the wall.

Jor extracted a dusty bottle. "Amaridian fortified wine." He held it closer to the lantern on the singular table and read the label. "No, Your Grace, I am most certainly *not* complaining."

Popping the cork, Jor poured a measure into the tin cups Lia set out, handing one to Lara. He held one up. "Cheers to the Amarid vintners who make the finest drink of the known world, and to their fallen countrymen, may they rot in the depths of the Tempest Seas." Then the old soldier cleared his throat. "And to our own fallen, may the Great Beyond gift them clear skies and smooth seas and endless women with perfect tits."

"Jor!" Lia jabbed him in the arm. "A goodly number of our fallen were women. I'm sure at least a few of them liked men. At least let them be surrounded by—"

"Perfect cocks?" Nine sets of surprised eyes turned to look at Lara, who shrugged.

"Where mortal life fails, the Great Beyond delivers," Jor intoned, and Aren flung his boot at him.

Lia threw up her hands. "People died. Show respect."

"I *am* respecting them. Disrespecting them would've been toasting their sacrifice with this sludge." Jor plucked a bottle of foggy Maridrinian wine from the crate. It rattled, and he gave it an incredulous glare, eyeing what appeared to be a rock sitting in the bottom of the bottle. "Not bad enough by itself, they need to put bits of rock in it?" His eyes flicked to Lara. "Is this some strange test of the fortitude of Maridrinian stomachs that I haven't heard about?"

Everyone smirked, then Gorrick roared, "To Ithicana!" They all repeated him, lifting their glasses.

As Aren swallowed the wine, which was very good, he heard Lara murmur, "To Ithicana," and take a small sip from her glass.

Refilling the glasses, Aren stood. "To Taryn, who slaughtered our enemy. And to our queen," he pulled Lara forward, "Who saved our comrades."

"To Taryn!" everyone shouted. "To Her Majesty!"

The wine disappeared within minutes, for despite the flippancy, today had left its mark. It was how they managed—by pretending not to care, but Aren knew that Jor would make time for each of them, helping them come to terms with what they'd witnessed. And with what they had done. He was captain of the guard for a reason.

Lara was hugging her arms around her body, shivering despite the wine. The wind and rain had been colder than Ithicana normally saw, and her clothes were soaked through. He watched her eye the other women, who were stripped down to trousers and undershirts, and then her hand went to her belt.

His heart skipped, then raced as she unbuckled it, setting it aside along with the Maridrinian marriage knives she habitually wore. Then she unfastened the laces of her tunic at her throat and pulled the garment over her head.

The safe house went completely silent for a heartbeat, then filled with the over-loud clatter of weapons being cleaned and mindless chatter, everyone looking anywhere but at their queen.

Aren could not seem to do the same. While the other women wore thick standard-issue fabrics, Lara's undergarments were the finest ivory silk, which was soaked, rendering it effectively transparent. The full curves of her breasts pressed against the fabric, her rose-colored nipples peaked from the cold. *There was*, Aren thought, *nothing the Great Beyond could offer that would be more perfect than her.*

Realizing he was staring, Aren jerked his gaze away. Snatching up a thin blanket folded at the end of the bunk, he handed it to Lara, careful to keep his eyes on her face. "It will warm up in here with all the bodies—I mean, people. Soon. It will be warmer soon."

Her smile was coy as she wrapped the blanket around her shoulders, but her mirth at his discomfort fell away as she caught sight of Jor examining one of her knives.

He had the jeweled thing out of its sheath and was testing the edge. "Sharp." He used it to cut the wax off a wheel of Harendellian cheese. "I thought these were supposed to be ceremonial?"

"I thought it wise to render them somewhat useful," Lara replied, expression intent.

"Barely." Jor balanced the weapon, the gem-crusted hilt making it heavy and cumbersome, though the blade itself looked well made.

"We could sell these for a fortune up north and get you something you might actually be able to use."

Lara was shifting and swaying as though she wanted nothing more than to reach over and snatch the knife back, so Aren did it for her, wiping the cheese off the blade with the side of his trousers before returning it to her.

"Thank you," she murmured. "My father gave them to me. They're the only thing he ever gave to me."

Aren wanted to ask why that mattered. Why she cared at all for anything to do with the greedy, sadistic creature who'd sired her. But he didn't. Not with everyone listening.

Jor picked up the bottle of Maridrinian wine. "Desperate times. Desperate times." Then he popped the cork and poured, something landing with a splash in his tin cup. "Now what do we have here?"

"What is it?" Lia asked.

"It appears a smuggler's prize has lost its way." The old soldier held up something that glittered red in the lamplight, then he tossed it Aren's direction. "There's a buyer at Northwatch who's going to be very dissatisfied with his wine purchase."

Aren held up the large ruby. He was no expert on gemstones, but judging from the size and color, it was worth a small fortune. A very unhappy smuggler, indeed. Shoving it in his pocket, he said, "This should cover the taxes the individual was trying to evade."

Everyone laughed then dug into the supplies, all of them battered and half-starved after a day of fighting and rowing and almost dying, more interested in shoveling food down their throats than in conversation. Lara sat next to Aren on the bunk, balancing on her knees a spread of cured meats, cheeses, and a tin cup of water as she ate.

Her slender hands and fingers had an assortment of old scars, nicks and lines, and one knuckle that was slightly larger, suggesting it had been broken at one point. Not the hands one would expect of Maridrinian princess, but whereas before he'd questioned what sort of life she'd been living in the desert to earn those scars, now he was having very different thoughts about those hands.

Of how it would feel to hold them.

Of how it would feel to be touched by them.

Of how it would feel—

"Lights out!" Jor announced. "The wind tells me this storm will break overnight, and we'll want to be back on the water at dawn."

All eyes shifted to the eight bunks, then to the ten people in the room.

"Either double up or draw straws for the floor."

Gorrick climbed to the top of one of the bunks, then pulled Lia up with him, and Aren winced, hoping they'd keep their hands to themselves for once.

"I'll take the floor," he said. "But I'm damn well going up for a nap in my feather bed once we get home tomorrow."

"We appreciate your hardship, Your Majesty." Jor reached over and turned down the lamp, plunging the safe house into near darkness.

Aren lay on the stone floor, one arm folded under his head for a pillow. It was cold and uncomfortable, and despite his exhaustion, sleep wouldn't come as he listened to the deepening breathing of those around him, a thousand thoughts filling his head.

When something cold brushed against his chest, Aren almost jumped out of his skin before realizing it was Lara. She was leaning out of the bunk next to him, her eyes lambent in the faint glow of the lamp. Wordlessly she caught hold of his hand with hers and tugged him upward, drawing him onto the bunk.

Pulse roaring in his ears, Aren climbed over her, his back resting against the cold wall, unsure of what to do with his arms and his hands or any part of himself until she curled against him, her skin icy.

*She's just cold,* he told himself, *and you need to keep your hands to yourself.*

Which might well have been the hardest thing he'd ever done, with one of her knees between his, her arms tucked against his chest, her head resting on his shoulder, and her breath warm against his throat. He wanted nothing more than to roll onto her, to taste those lips and peel that taunting bit of silk from her chest, but instead he pulled the blanket over her naked shoulder, then rested his hand against her back.

The room was humid with breath and heavy with the smell of

sweat and steel. Taryn was snoring as though her life depended on it, Gorrick was jabbering in his sleep, and someone—probably Jor—was farting at regular intervals. It was very likely the least desirable situation to share a bed with his *wife* for the first time. But even as her hair tickled his nose, his arm fell asleep under her head, and a crick formed in his neck, it occurred to Aren, as he drifted off, that there was nowhere else he'd rather be.

Hours later, Aren awoke to a rhythmic thumping. Frowning, he turned his head and found Lara's eyes open and gleaming in the faint light. Pulling one hand from under the blanket, she pointed upward and cocked her eyebrow with an amused smirk.

Gorrick and Lia. Likely warming themselves up after their turn at watch.

He winced, whispering, "Sorry. It's a soldier's life." Then he mentally ran through the watch, realizing that Jor had skipped him over and that Taryn was gone, which meant it was almost sunrise.

"Want to go outside?" Relief filled him when Lara nodded.

They pulled on boots and clothes and weapons in near silence, Lara taking food from one of the crates and following him out into the night. The storm had blown over, the sky a riot of silver stars, the only sound the crashing of the waves against the island's cliffs.

Taryn was perched on a rock in the shadows, but he heard her murmured thanks when Lara went over and gave her some of the food.

"Aren, take her to the east side."

"Why?"

Even in the darkness, he felt Taryn smile. "Trust me."

"All right." He took Lara's hand. "We'll be back at sunrise."

Aren hadn't been to this particular island many times, so he went slowly. He managed to find his way to the eastern lookout by memory, a flat bit of rock that hung out over the ocean. A sea of blue starlight stretched before them.

Lara stepped ahead, still holding on to his hand. "I've never seen anything so beautiful."

Neither had he, but Aren forced his eyes from her face to the calm water below. "We call it Sea of Stars. It doesn't happen often, and always during War Tides, so it doesn't get much appreciation."

Glowing strands of algae covered the water, the clusters forming brilliant blue spots of light on the sea, making him feel as though he stood between two planes of starlight. It rippled on the gentle waves, casting shadows on the rocks that seemed to dance to the rhythm of the swells. They stood watching for a long time, neither of them speaking, and it occurred to Aren that he should kiss her, but instead he said, "What changed?"

Because something had. Something had shifted, softening her toward him, perhaps to all of Ithicana, and he wasn't sure what it was. For near as he could tell, most of her experiences since she'd arrived hadn't been particularly good. She was the daughter of a man who was more Aren's enemy than his ally, and he shouldn't trust her. Didn't trust her. But with every passing day he spent with her, he found himself *wanting* to trust her. With everything.

Lara swallowed audibly, pulling her hand from his grip and crossing her legs on the ground, waiting until he sat next to her. The blue light from the sea illuminated her face, making her seem otherworldly and untouchable. "When I was growing up, I was told many times the amount of revenue Ithicana was rumored to make in a year off the bridge."

"How much?" He shook his head at the number when she answered. "It's more."

"Are you bragging?"

"Just being truthful."

The corner of her mouth quirked, and she was quiet for a moment before she continued. "To me, the amount was staggering. And I thought . . . I was told that Ithicana played and manipulated the market, gouged travelers afraid to tempt the seas, and exacted heavy taxes and tolls from merchants who wished to transport and market their own goods. That you decided who had the right to buy and sell in your markets, and that you'd take away that privilege if they crossed you in any way. That you controlled nearly all the trade between two continents and eleven different kingdoms."

"Accurate." He didn't bother to add that Ithicana paid in blood for that right, because she'd seen the evidence herself.

"What wasn't accurate . . . was the reason *why*."

"What did they tell you?"

"Greed." Her eyes were unblinking as she stared over the ocean. "When I was young, I believed you must live in enormous palaces filled with all the greatest luxuries the world had to offer. That you sat on a throne of gold."

"Ah, yes. My throne of gold. I keep it on another island and visit it when I need to reaffirm my sense of self-worth and entitlement."

"Don't mock me."

"I'm not." He picked at the top of his boot where the leather had split from too much exposure to salt water. "It must have been quite disappointing to discover the truth."

Lara made a sound that was a half-laugh, half-sob. "Midwatch is just as luxurious as my home in the Red Desert, and my time spent here relaxing by comparison. I was raised hard, Aren."

"Why were they so hard on you?"

"I thought I knew, but now . . ." She lifted her chin from her knees, turning her head to look at him. "You ask me what changed? What changed is that now I know you use that money to feed and protect your people."

There had been a certain inevitability to her learning that truth. Maybe if he'd kept her locked up in the Midwatch house, with no contact with anyone but the staff and his guard, he might have kept it from her. But he'd wanted his marriage to Lara to be a symbol for change in Ithicana, a new direction. And for that to happen, they'd needed to see her, and there had always been consequences to that path, and the revelation of Ithicana's secrets was one of them.

And he so badly wanted to trust her.

"The truth is, Ithicana isn't survivable without the bridge," he said. "Or rather, it is survivable, but only if every minute of every waking day is dedicated to survival." Pivoting on the ground so they were facing each other, he stared into her eyes. The sun was rising, the light shifting from blue to gold, and it was like waking from a dream and being plunged back into reality. If Aren could have stopped it, he would've. "Imagine a life where you had to fight these storms and these waters to feed your family. To clothe your children. To shelter them. Where weeks might pass when you couldn't take a boat on the water. Where a series of days might pass when it would verge on suicide to step outside your home. What else is there but survival in a world like that?"

Aren hadn't realized he'd taken her hands, but she squeezed them tightly then, and he paused, his thumbs trailing lightly over her scars. "The bridge changes that. It allows me to give my people what they need so that some small part of their days might be dedicated to more than just survival, even if it's only an hour. So that my people might have a chance to read, to learn, to make art. To sing or dance or laugh."

He broke off, realizing that he'd never explained this to anyone. Explained what it was like to rule this place. The constant fight to give his people lives worth living. And it wasn't enough. He wanted them to have *more*.

"You could feed every one of them like kings with that kind of money." Lara wasn't questioning his word, but driving him forward, extracting the whole of the truth.

"That's true. But having those things—having the bridge—comes with a cost. Other kingdoms know what sort of revenue the bridge earns, and that makes them want to possess it. Pirates believe we have stockpiles of gold hidden throughout the islands, so they raid us to find it. So we have to fight. My standing army isn't enormous, but during War Tides, nearly two thirds of my people drop their trades and take up arms to defend the bridge. I have to buy them weapons. I have to pay them for their service. And I have to compensate their families when they die."

"So despite everything, Ithicana is only surviving after all."

He tightened his grip on her hands. "But maybe someday it could be something better."

Neither of them spoke, and when a soft breeze blew strands of hair across her face, Aren reached up to brush them away. Lara didn't flinch from his touch. Didn't look away. "You're beautiful." He tangled his fingers in her hair. "I've thought so since the moment I saw you, but I don't think I've ever said it."

Lara lowered her eyes, pink rising to her cheeks, although it might've just been the glow of the sun. She gave the slightest shake of her head.

"I should have." He lowered his head, intent on kissing her, but instead a sharp noise made him jump.

Hand going to his weapon, Aren turned to see Jor coming around the corner, his face filled with amusement. "I hate to break up your picnic, Your Majesties, but dawn is upon us, and we need to be on our way."

As if to punctuate his words, horns sounded out over the water announcing ships on the horizon. "Does this change things for you?" he asked Lara, helping her to her feet.

She closed her eyes, her face clenching for a moment as though she were in pain, then she opened them and nodded. "It changes everything."

Hope, and something else, something uniquely reserved for her, flooded his heart and, taking Lara by the hand, Aren led her back to the boats at a run.

# 24
# LARA

EVERYTHING HAD CHANGED.

And nothing.

It wasn't lust. Lara wasn't so weak as to abandon a lifetime of planning and preparation for the sake of a man too handsome and charming for his own good. If that had been the sum of it, she'd have sated her curiosity, then carried on with as clear a conscience as any spy could have. No, it was her admiration for Aren that was becoming increasingly problematic, as was her grief over what would happen to Ithicana once she was through with it.

Lara and her sisters had been taught to despise Ithicana for a reason. Their purpose had been to infiltrate the defenses of a nation so that it could, at best, be conquered. At worst, be destroyed. An easy thing to envision when the enemy had been nothing more to her than masked demons using their might to keep her people oppressed.

But now they had faces. And names. And families.

All of whom were annually attacked by kingdoms and pirates alike. Perhaps the Ithicanians were cruel and merciless, but now Lara found she couldn't fault them for that. They did what they needed to *survive*, and with every piece of information she stored away about them, her guilt swelled, because she knew Ithicana wouldn't survive *her*. While that knowledge might have once brought her satisfaction, it was now nothing but an inescapable fact that seemed destined to plague her every waking moment with self-loathing.

Her actions on Aela Island had accomplished what she'd feared impossible: earning Aren's trust. And not just his trust, but that of all the soldiers who'd fought in the battle. Their expressions in her presence had gone from distrustful to respectful, and as one, they'd stopped questioning her right to go where she pleased. A right she'd instantly abused. No one had questioned her when she'd stepped away from the healers and the injured after the battle. No one had stopped her or followed her when she'd walked to the base of the bridge pier, where she'd found the nearly invisible entrance, which she marked with a few carefully placed stones that would mean nothing to the Ithicanians and everything to the Maridrinian soldiers when they took Aela Island.

Inside the pier she'd also hidden three of the horns she stolen off corpses on the beach, ready to misdirect Ithicanian reinforcements when the time was right. A strategy that Aren had practically explained to her in his attempts to coax her away from the injured and into a boat. Which he'd only done because he believed she was coming to love them the way he did.

*Do not falter,* she silently chanted, eyes fixed on the sky as she floated her still aching body in the hot spring. *Do not fail.*

Biting at a hangnail on her thumb, Lara considered what she'd learned. Considered whether it was *enough* for Maridrina to take Ithicana. Enough to conquer the unconquerable, and enough to give Maridrina the bridge that would be its salvation.

*It was enough.*

All that was left was to get the details of her invasion plan to Serin and her father, then for her to fake her death and escape Midwatch and Ithicana and, hopefully, her father's inevitable assassins. Where she'd go, she didn't know. To Harendell, perhaps. Maybe once the dust had settled, she'd try to find her sisters. Make a life for herself. Though try as she might, she couldn't envision what a life beyond Ithicana might look like. A life without *him*.

Lara's eyes stung, and in a flurry of motion, she climbed out of the spring, reaching for the towel sitting on the rock. Over a week had passed since the attack on Aela, and yet she hadn't taken one step further to putting her plan into motion. She'd told herself it was because the muscle she'd torn in her shoulder during the battle needed time to heal before she would be strong enough to make her escape. But her heart told her that she was delaying for other reasons. Reasons that put her whole mission in jeopardy.

But tonight was the night.

Aren had sent word from the barracks via Eli that there was going to be a storm this evening, and that he planned to dine with her. And if he was with her, that meant Taryn, who still insisted on sleeping outside her door, would take a break from her bodyguard duties. A double dose of a sleeping narcotic in Aren's wine after dinner, and then she'd have the whole night in his bedchamber to work with no fear of interruptions.

Already clouds were rolling in, the wind blowing, for even in the calm season, the Tempest Seas were not without teeth. Lara worked methodically on her appearance, drying her hair, then using a hot iron to create coils that hung down her back. She darkened her eyes with kohl and powders until they smoldered, and stained her lips a pale pink. She chose a dress she hadn't worn before: dark purple, the silk scandalously sheer, her body revealed beneath whenever she passed in front of a light. On her ears, she wore black diamonds, and on her wrist, the clever bracelet that concealed the vials of narcotics.

Stepping out into the hallway, she made her way down to the dining room, her sandals feeling strange after so many weeks of wearing heavy boots. The room was lit with candles, the shutters on the large windows open despite the risk the wind posed to the expensive glass. And a soaking wet Eli stood in close conversation with Taryn, whom Lara was surprised to find still in the house. They both turned to look at her, expressions grim, and Lara's heart skipped. "Where is he?"

"They went on patrol late morning." Taryn scrubbed a hand along the shaved sides of her head. "No one has seen or heard from them since."

"Is that normal?" Lara couldn't control the shake in her voice.

The other woman exhaled a long breath. "It's not abnormal for Aren to decide there's somewhere he needs to be other than Midwatch." Then her eyes gave Lara a once-over. "But I don't think that's the case tonight."

"So where is he?"

"Could've been trouble with one of the boats. Or maybe they decided to wait out the storm. Or—"

Horns sounded, and Lara no longer needed Taryn to tell her what they meant: *raiders*.

"I'm going down to the barracks." Running to her rooms, Lara replaced her sandals with boots and pulled a cloak over her dress.

Outside, the rain was falling steadily, but the wind wasn't high enough to cause the Ithicanians any trouble on the water. Taryn at her arm, and the rest of her bodyguard before and behind her, Lara hurried down the dark path toward the barracks.

Where the tension was higher than she'd ever seen it.

"I'll find out what they know." Taryn left Lara with the other two guards, who followed her as she skirted the cove, climbing the carved stone steps to the cliff tops, where she could see the sea. Several soldiers knelt behind the boulders they used for cover, spyglasses in hand.

"Anything?" But they only shook their heads.

*What if he didn't come back?*

It would throw her plan to shit. Without Aren to write a letter to her father, she had no way to get a detailed message past Ahnna and her codebreakers at Southwatch. Her only option would be to fake her death and escape, then send the information to her father from outside of Ithicana. But then he and Serin would know she was alive, and that meant a lifetime of assassins chasing at her heels. Yet, as she crouched on the ground to watch the blackness of the ocean, it wasn't solutions to her dilemma that filled her thoughts.

It was fear.

She'd seen so many Ithicanians die in combat, in so many different ways. Run through or gutted. Crushed or strangled. Beaten or drowned. Their corpses danced through her thoughts, all of them now wearing Aren's face.

"They haven't sent any word." Taryn appeared at Lara's elbow. "But that doesn't necessarily mean anything other than that they don't want to announce their presence to the enemy."

*Or they were all dead,* Lara thought, her chest tightening painfully.

Taryn handed her a folded packet of papers. "This came for you."

Holding the paper next to one of the jars of algae, Lara scanned the contents. Serin, pretending to be her father, discussed his disappointment in her second-eldest brother, Keris, who was demanding to attend university in Harendell rather than take command of Maridrinian forces like her eldest brother. *He wishes to study philosophy! As though there is time to sit around contemplating the meaning of life when our enemies continue to bite at our flanks!*

Some of the soldiers stirred, pulling her attention from the letter, and it was some moments before she could refocus. Marylyn's code felt elusive. Lara's eyes continually dragged out to sea. But eventually her mind pulled Serin's message from the drivel. *Valcotta has blockaded our access to Southwatch. Famine on the rise.*

A wave of nausea passed over Lara, and she shoved the pages into her cloak's pocket. With its shipbreakers, Southwatch was capable of running Valcotta off, but she could understand their reluctance to antagonize the other nation. Understood what it would cost them for Valcotta to join the ranks of kingdoms raiding Ithicana. But it was her people who paid the price.

They sat in the rain for hours, but no horns sounded. No boats appeared below requesting access to the cove. Nothing even moved in the darkness.

Eventually Taryn shifted next to her. "You should go back to the house, Lara. There's no telling when they'll return, and you'll catch a chill sitting in this cold rain."

She should go. She knew she should go. But the idea of having to wait for one of them to bring her news . . . "I can't." Her tongue felt thick.

"The barracks, then?" There was a plea to the other woman's voice.

Reluctantly, Lara nodded, but every few paces up the trail, she cast a backward glance toward the sea, the roar of it beckoning, drawing her back.

"This is Aren's bunk," Taryn said, once they were in the confines of the stone building. "He won't mind if you sleep here."

Shutting the door to the tiny room, Lara set her lamp on the rough wooden table next to the narrow bed, then sat, the mattress rock hard and the blanket rough compared to her soft sheets at the house. It reminded her of the cot she'd shared with him at the safe house. How she'd fallen asleep in his arms, listening to the beat of his heart.

She pulled off her cloak and curled on her side, her head resting on the pillow.

It smelled like him.

Squeezing her eyes shut, Lara drew upon every lesson her Master of Meditation had ever taught her, measuring her breath and clearing her mind, but sleep wouldn't come, so she sat, the blanket wrapped around her legs.

There was nothing in the room to distract her. No books or puzzles. Not even a deck of cards. The sparse quarters of a soldier, not a king. Or at least, not of the sort of king she'd believed existed. The quarters of a leader who did not hold himself above his people. Who wore their hardships like his own. Because they were his own.

*Please be alive.*

The door swung open, and Lara jerked around to find Taryn standing in the doorway. "They're back."

She followed the other woman at a run down to the cove, her chest tight with fear. It was fear for herself, her mind screamed. Fear for her mission. Fear for the fate of her people.

But her heart told her otherwise.

The sand of the beach shifted beneath her feet, and Lara squinted into the darkness. A faint voice called out, then the chain rattled, clearing the entrance to the cove.

More splashing, waves thudding against hulls and paddles carving through the water. But above all of that, Lara picked out groans of pain. Her heart skipped.

Please let him be alive.

The cove turned into a flurry of activity, boats full of bloodied men and women drifting in, those on shore tying them off and helping the injured onto land. Her eyes skipped over their shadowed faces, searching. Searching.

"Will you goddamned hurry it up?" Jor's voice. Lara wove through the efficient traffic, trying to find the soldier. Finally, she spotted both him and Lia crouched in the bottom of a boat, a slumped figure between them.

"Aren?" Her voice came out as a croak, her feet abruptly rooted on the spot.

The pair reached down, and relief flooded her veins as Aren batted their hands away. "Get off me. I can damn well get out myself."

He stood and the boat wobbled, both Jor and Lia easily catching their balance, but Aren nearly going over the side.

"Enough of your pride, boy," Jor barked, and between him and Lia, they dragged their king onto land.

Lara couldn't see what was wrong with him in the dark, the lanterns casting shadows that appeared like bloodstains, only they shifted and moved. Then Aren turned, and the lantern behind him revealed the outline of an arrow embedded in his upper arm.

"Get out of my way." She shoved two soldiers to the side and ran toward Aren.

"What the hell are you doing down here?" Aren pushed Jor away even as he stumbled. Lara lurched forward and caught his weight, the hot tang of blood filling her nose. "I can walk on my own," he muttered.

"Clearly." Lara's body quivered with the effort of holding him upright as they navigated the sloped beach to the treeline, the path leading to the barracks dimly lit with jars of algae.

Dragging Aren into the barracks, she eased him down on a bench. Throwing aside her sodden cloak, she pulled one of her knives and cut away his tunic, dropping the ruined garment on the floor. Then she knelt next to him, her eyes taking in the injury.

The arrowhead was buried deep in the muscle of his upper arm, the shaft having been broken in half by someone at some point, the wood stained dark with blood.

"Goddamned Amaridians." Jor's voice seemed distant to Lara, every part of her focused on Aren's breath against her neck, hot and ragged.

Lifting her face, she met his pain-hazed gaze. "We can't pull it out—we have to push it all the way through."

"Every moment with you is such a delight." A faint spark returned to Aren's eyes. "Sorry I missed dinner."

"You should be." She struggled to keep her voice even. "It smelled very good."

"Missing the food isn't the part I'm sorry about." He lifted his uninjured arm, fingers brushing against the large diamond still adorning her ear, sending a tremble racing through her.

"Brace yourself on me." She pushed his hand away before her composure was totally shot. "The last thing we need is you squirming and making the injury worse."

Aren huffed out a pained laugh, but took hold of her waist with the hand of his uninjured arm, his fingers digging into the muscles of her back.

"This will hurt," Jor warned, taking a firm grip on the arrow. Swearing, Aren dropped his head against Lara's shoulder and she pulled him against her, knowing she wasn't strong enough to keep him steady if he struggled.

"Relax," Jor said. "You're being a baby."

Lara murmured into Aren's ear, "Breathe." His shoulders trembled as he inhaled and exhaled, and she knew his attention was on her. His fingers flexed, then slid from her waist to her hip. "Breathe," she repeated, her lips grazing the lobe of his ear. "Breathe." As she said the word the third time, she met Jor's gaze.

He pushed.

Aren screamed into her shoulder, shoving against her so hard that Lara almost went over backward, her boots skidding against the barracks floor. Blood splattered her face, but she held on, refusing to let go of him.

"Got it!" Jor said, and a second later, Lara's knees buckled and she fell back, Aren landing on top of her. For a heartbeat, neither of them moved, Aren's breathing labored in her ear, his body pressed against hers. She held him, clung to him, an irrational desire to hunt down and destroy those who'd done this consuming all other thought. Then Jor and Lia were hauling him off her.

Scrambling upright, Lara wiped the blood off her face, her heart hammering as Jor examined the injury. "You'll mend," he said, then moved aside as one of Nana's students arrived.

All around were bloodied soldiers. Some gritted their teeth against the pain. Some screamed as their comrades tried to staunch horrific wounds. Some lay motionless.

Every one of them injured in defense of their home.

Lara's eyes fell on Taryn, tears dribbling down the woman's face as she pressed her hands against a young man's stomach, trying to hold his guts inside. "Don't you die on me." Her whispered voice somehow cut through the din. "Don't you dare die."

But as Lara watched, the young man's chest went still.

How many more hearts would still when her father made his move?

*They are your enemy,* she chanted. *Your enemy. Your enemy*. But the words were profoundly hollow in her mind.

Lara took one step back. Then two. Three. Until she was out of the barracks and on the empty path.

"Lara!"

She turned. Aren stood a dozen paces behind her on the path, the bandage on his arm half falling off as though he'd pushed away the healer working on him before she could finish.

"Wait."

She couldn't. She shouldn't. Not when every bit of resolve she possessed was crumbling to the ground. Yet her feet remained fixed to the earth as Aren slowly made his way toward her, blood running down his arm and dripping from his fingertips.

"I'm sorry." His voice was shaky. "I'm sorry that all you've seen since you've been here is violence."

*All she had ever known was violence. It was nothing to her. And everything.*

"I wish it was different. I wish it wasn't like this."

He swayed, dropping to his knees, and Lara didn't realize she'd also knelt until the mud soaked through her dress. Didn't realize she'd reached out to steady him until the hand of his uninjured arm caught hold of her hip for balance. A dance where she led and he followed.

"Eyes just like your damnable father. That's what I thought when I first saw you. We call it Maridrinian bastard blue."

He must have felt her flinch, because his grip on her hip tightened, drawing her closer. She didn't fight him.

"But I was wrong. They're different. They're . . . deeper. Like the color of the sea around Eranahl."

*Eranahl?* She'd seen that name before, written on one of the pages in his desk . . . Heard it when he'd berated Commander Aster on the beach at Aela Island. Revealing it was a slip on his part, she was sure of it. But she couldn't bring herself to care as his hand slid to the small of her back. It took all the willpower she had to keep from slipping her arms around his neck, to keep from kissing those blasted perfect lips of his, never mind the blood and gore.

Lara withdrew her hand from his shoulder, but he caught it with his own. Folding her fingers into a fist, he kissed her knuckles, eyes burning into hers. "Don't go."

Everything was burning.

Lara's heart beat frantically, her breathing unsteady, her skin so sensitive that the press of her clothes almost hurt.

*Stop!* The warning shrieked inside her head. *You're losing control.* She tuned the voice out, shoved it away.

Aren's thumb brushed the inside of her wrist, her knuckles still pressed to his lips, and it sent rivers of sensation running over her skin, the desire to have his hands elsewhere making her legs weak. She swayed and he pulled her against him, both of them unsteady.

"You need to go back to the healers," she whispered. "You need to let them stitch that up before you bleed to death."

"I'll be fine." He lowered his head even as she lifted hers, sharing the same air, the same breath, the rapid rise and fall of his chest belying his words. *He was not fine.*

The thought of it filled her with terror. Terror that turned instantly to rage. Why did she care what happened to him beyond the success of her mission? Why did she care whether he lived or died? This was the man who willfully made decisions that caused great harm to the people of her homeland. Perhaps he did so for the sake of his own people, but that did not excuse the complete lack of empathy and guilt he felt in the doing. *He was her enemy, and she needed to get free of him before she made a mistake.*

Then his lips brushed softly against hers, and it undid her entirely. Her fingers tangled in his hair, and she wanted more. More of this and more of him. But instead of giving it to her, he pulled back. "I need you to help me make this stop. I'm tired of fighting against the world, when what I want is to fight to make Ithicana part of it."

And it was as though reality slapped her across the face.

Lara pulled away from him. "It's never going to stop, Aren." Her voice was barren. Dead. Which was strange, because inside her head was a chaos of emotion. "You have what *everyone* wants, and they're never going to stop trying to take it. This *is* Ithicana, and it's all it will ever be. Live with it."

"This isn't living, Lara." He coughed, then winced, pressing his hand against the wound. "And I intend to keep fighting for a better future even if it kills me."

Irrational fury surged through her veins at his words. "Then you might as well lay down and die!" She needed to be away from this situation because it was tearing her apart. Rising in a flurry of motion, Lara turned and ran, up the dark path, slipping on the mud and roots, to the house.

She waited in her rooms until the halls were silent, until there was no chance of anyone disturbing her, then crept through the dark hallways and picked the lock to Aren's room. Vitex sat on the bed, but he only slunk outside, ignoring her as he passed.

Closing the door behind her, Lara brightened her lamp and went to Aren's desk. She extracted the jar of invisible ink Serin had given her, then drew the stationery box of heavy official parchment next to her left hand, flipping open the lid. Taking the top page, she turned it over so the embossed shape of the bridge was facedown, then she dipped a pen into the ink and began to write in tiny script, the liquid drying invisible as she detailed everything she'd learned about Ithicana and a strategy for taking, and breaking, the Bridge Kingdom. Her hand shook as she reached the bottom, but she only set aside the paper to dry and retrieved another, repeating her message. Then another, and another, until all twenty-six pages in the box contained identical damning words.

It took all her strength not to tear them to pieces as she set everything back and retreated to her own room. Exhaustion weighing her limbs, she buried her face in the pillows of her bed, tears soaking the feathers within. *It's the only way,* she told herself. *It's the only way to save Maridrina.*

Even if it meant damning herself.

# 25
# LARA

War Tides ended with a typhoon that came in fast and violent, the seas so rough that not even the Ithicanians would venture out on them. Even the bridge was likely empty, Eli told her, the storm too intense for merchant ships to brave the short crossing to Northwatch and Southwatch islands. Midwatch felt profoundly isolated as a result, cut off entirely from the world, and made worse by the fact that Lara was stuck in the house alone with the servants.

Though the fighting was over, Aren was avoiding her. He spent all his days with his soldiers and his nights on the narrow cot in the barracks, not once coming up the path to the Midwatch house.

Even so, she checked the number of pages of stationery in his room nightly, but every last page of the condemning words remained in Ithicana.

As did she.

On the morning after the storm broke, Lara decided it was time. Dressing in her Ithicanian clothes, she filled her pockets with jewels and some of her more favored narcotics, ate as much as she could stuff in her stomach, then told Eli she was going to go outside for some fresh air.

Attempting the seas during a storm would see her dead in truth, so she'd waited for clear skies before enacting her plan to fake her death, knowing that honor would drive Aren to send a formal letter informing Lara's father of her demise. That Serin, ever watchful, would check the page and discover what she'd written. Then she could only hope and pray that, when she hadn't shown up after a time in Vencia, her father and Serin would believe she was dead in truth. Then no assassins would come searching for her in Harendell, which was where she planned to go. She could live her life knowing that she'd given her people a chance for a better future.

At the cost of the futures of everyone living in Ithicana.

With the storms to watch over the island, Taryn and the rest had been given respite from guard duty, and there was no one to evade as she followed a trail to the cliffs overlooking the sea, cutting down the northern side until she came to the spot she'd selected long ago.

It was a high spot, the water forty feet below, but what had drawn her to it was the series of flat rocks jutting out of surf. They were suitable for her to lower her little canoe onto with ropes, and equally suitable for staging what would appear an accidental fall and a tragic death. From there, she intended to hop from island to island, using safe houses as she found them, slowly making her way to Harendell during the breaks in the storm.

It was a plan fraught with peril, yet it wasn't fear that sat heavy in her gut as she stared down at the rocks.

"Don't fall."

Startled, Lara lost her balance, and Aren reached out and caught hold of her arm, hauling her away from the edge.

He made a noise of exasperation, then kept pulling on her arm. "Come with me. You have duties to attend to."

"What duties?"

"A queen's duties."

She dug in her heels, leaving twin trails in the mud until he stopped and gave her a look of disgust. "*That's* not a duty, Lara. Supervising the return of the Midwatch evacuees is. So either start walking, or I'm going to drag you down to the water and toss you in a boat."

"I'll walk." She was furious that her plan was being disrupted, but also furious at the small kernel of relief that she felt knowing she'd likely have to wait for another storm to pass before leaving Ithicana.

Ensconced in her usual spot in the boat, she waited until they were out of the cove before asking, "Where are we going?"

"Serrith." Aren hunched over, his back to her.

"Just a charming day on the water," Jor said from behind her as he put up the sail. After that, no one said anything more.

The cove at Serrith Island was dominated by two of the large twin-hulled vessels she'd seen during the evacuation, but they were already empty of civilians and supplies, their crews readying to depart. *To depart to Eranahl*, she mused, watching them. Though where exactly that was remained a mystery to her despite all her weeks of spying.

Her skin prickled as she followed Aren up the path through the gap in the rock where she'd killed all those soldiers. They continued on until they reached the village. It was an entirely different sight than the last time they'd been here. Instead of blood and bodies, dead-eyed children and weeping parents, it was bustling with industry. Women opened up the shuttered windows and doors to their homes to air them out, and children ran wild between them.

There was a flood of greetings and well wishes, proud introductions of new babies to their rulers, and children trailing in their wake, desperate for a moment of attention. Aren's tactic was obvious. Trying to pull on her heartstrings by pushing chubby babies into her arms or by giving her sweets to hand out to the children.

And it was effective. She wanted to drop to the ground and weep, because their world was going to be torn asunder. But it was between them and the Maridrinians. Maridrina's starving people *needed* the bridge, needed the revenues, needed the goods that came through it. So she would sacrifice these people for her own and then pray that guilt and grief didn't kill her.

Lara would have given anything to have her sisters here to share the burden, because they would understand. They were the *only* people who would understand. But she was alone, and every minute that passed felt like she was closer to the breaking point of what she could endure.

Only when they returned to the boats did she feel like she could breathe again, sitting with her face in her hands as they sailed back to Midwatch.

"Looks like the guardians have had some visitors," Jor said, breaking the silence.

Lara lifted her head, eyes landing on a small island with gentle white beaches that faded into rock and greenery. Looming above it was the bridge, its length resting on a pier centered on the island. It wasn't that the island itself was unique, only that it appeared remarkably easy to access relative to the others the builders had used as piers.

*Because they'd had no choice*, she determined, eyeing the distance. The largest bridge span she'd seen was a hundred yards between piers, and to bypass this island would've required a longer stretch than was possible. Her eyes then landed on the three human-shaped forms lying halfway up the beach, bloated and rotting in the sun. "What is this place?"

"Snake Island."

She thought of the countless serpents she'd seen since arriving. "A name that describes most of Ithicana."

"This one in particular." Aren motioned for Jor to lower the sails, allowing the boat to drift over the shallow bottom toward the beach. "Look."

She stared, seeing shifting movement beneath the ledge of rock overhanging the beach, but unable to make out details.

Aren stood up in the boat next to her, a still moving fish that had been caught earlier in one hand, waiting as the waves washed them gently to shore. When they were about a dozen feet out, Jor stuck a paddle in the water, bracing the boat from moving farther. Aren threw the fish.

It landed about midway up the beach, and Lara watched in horror as dozens upon dozens of snakes shot out of the overhang, flying toward the fish with their jaws open. They were big, the average of them longer than Aren was tall, and some much larger than that.

The front-runner snapped its jaws around the fish as the others piled on top of one another, struggling and snapping until the fish disappeared down a gullet, the snake's neck distended to contain its prize.

"Good God." Lara pressed her hand against her mouth.

"One of them gets its teeth into you, you'll find yourself paralyzed within minutes. Then it's a matter of time before one of the big ones comes along to finish the job."

"Big ones . . ." The island became impossibly more forbidding as Lara searched for signs of said snakes. She caught sight of a stone path leading up to the base of the pier. It was overgrown, but compared to all the other piers, it seemed almost welcoming. "Please don't tell me you use this as a route into the bridge?"

Aren shook his head. "Red herring. Does its job well, it's so inviting."

"Too inviting," Jor added. "How many of ours have those blasted serpents fed upon?"

Lara looked askance at Aren.

"It's a game our young people play, though it's forbidden. Two people bait the snakes away from the path, and the runner must make it to the pier, climb up and out onto the bridge, then drop back into the water. A test of bravery."

"More like a proof of idiocy," Jor snapped.

"Certainly a good way to get oneself killed." Lara chewed the inside of her cheeks, debating the usefulness of this particular place. It would be easy to anchor ships and ferry men in, if something could be done about the snakes.

Lara was so caught up in her thoughts she didn't notice Aren had stripped down to his trousers until he hopped over the edge of the boat, standing in the hip-deep water. "Hold this for me." He handed her his bow. "Don't let it get wet."

"What do you think you're doing?"

He cracked his knuckles. "It's been a long time, but I'm sure I can still do it."

"Get back into the boat, Aren," Jor said. "You're not a fourteen-year-old boy anymore."

"No, I'm not. Which should only be to my advantage. Lia and

Taryn, you bait. Do a good job of it unless you want to spend your days watching Ahnna's ass."

"You'll do no such thing," Jor ordered the two women. "Stay put."

Aren twisted round in the water, resting his hands on the boat. "Do I need to remind you who is king here, Jor?"

Lara felt her jaw drop. Never in her time in Ithicana had she seen him pull rank. Give orders, yes, but this was different.

The two men glared at each other, but Jor threw up his free hand in defeat. "Do as *His Majesty* orders."

With grim faces, the two women retrieved a pair of fish each, then jumped into the water. *They've done this before*, Lara thought. *They've done this before for him.*

Lara's heart was pounding in a staccato beat. "Get in the boat. Your arm isn't healed."

"It's healed well enough."

"This is madness, Aren! What are you trying to prove?"

Aren didn't answer, wading until he stood only a few feet back from the water line, then standing utterly still while the two soldiers splashed noisily in opposite directions, drawing the attention of the snakes. The ground beneath the ledge was a twisting mass of bodies, the creatures moving away from the path, watching the women.

*This is because of what you said*, a voice in her head whispered. *You told him to lay down and die.*

"Aren, get back in the boat." Her voice was unrecognizably shrill. "You don't need to do this."

He ignored her.

*Tell him you care. Tell him his life matters to you. Say what you need to say to get him back in the boat.*

Except she couldn't. Couldn't tell him a lie like that only to stab him in the back.

*But is it a lie?*

"Aren, I . . ." Lara's throat strangled the rest of the words.

Jor nodded at the guards in the boat, and those carrying bows silently knocked arrows, but somehow, Aren sensed what they were doing. "If any of you shoots one of those arrows, you're done in my guard."

They lowered their bows. "You can't be serious," Lara snarled. "Aren, get back in the boat, you—"

"Go!"

At his command, the women threw flopping fish onto the beach. Once again, snakes shot out from the under the ledge, dozens upon dozens. More than Lara could count. And just as the frontrunners were about to snap up their prize, Aren broke into a sprint, feet sinking into the deep sand. He only made it halfway up the beach when the snakes saw him, several of them rearing up high to regard the intruder before launching themselves his direction.

He was fast.

But the snakes were faster.

"They're coming!" Lara screamed, watching in horror as the wicked creatures flew across the sand. Aren was on the path, racing toward the towering pier, sweat gleaming on his bare shoulders. He had thirty yards to go.

He wasn't going to make it.

The snakes were throwing themselves through the air, their jaws snapping only paces behind him. And they were closing in.

"Run!"

Lara stood, not even noticing how the boat rocked beneath her. He could not die. Not like this.

Jor was on his feet, too. "Run, you little shit!"

Only a dozen yards. *Please*, she prayed. *Please, please*.

She and Jor saw it before Aren did. An enormous beast of a snake rounding the base of the pier, drawn by the commotion of its smaller brethren. It saw Aren the same time he saw it, the snake rearing even as the king skidded, caught between death on both sides.

Without thinking, Lara lifted Aren's bow and tore an arrow out of the hand of the nearest guard. Nocking the arrow even as she whirled, she let it fly. The black fletching shot through the air, barely missing Aren's shoulder, catching the man-eater square in its open mouth.

Aren reacted instantly, leaping over the fallen snake and jumping to catch handholds in the worn rock, jerking his heels out of reach of the lunging snakes just in time. He climbed to the midway point in a matter of seconds, then turned his head to look at the boat, likely to see who'd disobeyed his orders.

Lara let the bow slip from her fingers, but it didn't matter. He'd seen. They'd all seen. And now she'd have to deal with the consequences.

No one spoke as he climbed, and Lara's heart didn't slow for a moment of it, knowing full well that a fall from that height would kill him. The wound on his arm had broken open, and blood was dripping off him as he climbed, but if it bothered him, he didn't show it. Reaching the top of the bridge, Aren loped down the span until he was back over deep water, then without hesitation, dove into its depths.

Lara held her breath, searching the sea for any sign of him. But there was nothing.

His shoulder was bleeding.

What if there were sharks nearby?

Jor was moving behind her, kicking off his boots, the boat drifting. "Lia, Taryn! Get over here."

Then Aren broke the surface, hauling himself into the boat in one smooth motion. Water glistened on his tanned skin, muscles rippling as he caught his balance, his soldiers half falling out to clear a path as he stepped toward her. "What the hell was that?"

Lara stood her ground, not caring that he loomed over her. "Me saving your childish ass, that's what it was."

"I didn't need saving."

Jor's subsequent cough sounded a great deal like "bullshit." Aren glared at Jor once, before turning back to Lara. "You never said you could use a bow. Would've been a useful thing for you to mention in recent months."

"You never asked." Rising on her toes, she glared at him until he took a step back, the boat rocking as it drifted closer to shore. "And if you *ever* scare me like that again, don't think I won't hesitate to use one on you."

"And here I thought you didn't care."

"I don't! You can walk back onto that beach and bed down with one of those snakes for all the difference it makes to me."

"Is that so?" And quick as the serpents on the island, he picked her up and tossed her into the water.

Lara landed on her ass on the sandbar, the water only up to her waist, but her clothing soaked. "Asshole!" She clambered to her feet, the waves lapping at her knees.

"Says the woman who's been nothing but a thorn in my—" He cut off with a yelp as Jor leaned back in the boat and kicked him solidly in the ass.

Aren landed on his hands and knees with a splash, nearly knocking Lara over. Regaining his footing faster than she had, Aren shouted, "Goddammit, Jor. What the hell was that for?"

But the boat was already sailing away. "We'll be back," Jor shouted, "Once you two work out this little marital spat." Then the vessel rounded the pier and they were out of sight.

Unleashing a string of blistering curses, Aren smacked his hand against the surface of the water. Lara hardly noticed. Instead she watched the snakes making their way down the sand, stopping at the waterline. Several of them reared, swaying back and forth as they watched the two of them. And behind her . . . open ocean. Even if she could swim, Lara damn well knew what lurked within those waters.

She was trapped.

The sun beat down on her head, and her brow prickled as beads of sweat formed, mixing with the seawater drenching her hair.

Her growing panic must have been written all over her face, because Aren said, "The snakes won't come out here. They can swim, but they don't like to. Jor will come back. He's just being an asshole. There's nothing to be afraid of."

"Easy for you to say." Lara's teeth clattered together as though she were cold, but she wasn't. "You can swim away if you want to."

"It's tempting."

"I'm not surprised. Given how little worth you place on Maridrinian lives." The words had crept out, but perhaps it was time they did. Perhaps it was time that she called him out for Ithicana's villainy.

Aren stared at her, jaw open. "Perhaps you might explain to me just what *I* have done to elicit a comment like that from you? I've done nothing but treat you with courtesy, and the same goes for your countrymen."

"Nothing?" Lara knew she was allowing her temper to get the better of her, but anger tasted better than fear. "You think allowing my people to starve because it's good for your coffers is *nothing*?"

Silence.

"You think Ithicana is responsible for Maridrina's troubles?" His voice was incredulous. "We're goddamned allies."

"Ah, yes. *Allies*. Which is why *everyone* knows the majority of the food sold at Southwatch goes to Valcotta."

"Because they buy it!" He threw up his hands. "Southwatch is a free market. Whoever offers the most for the goods gets them. No bias. No favoritism. That's how it works. Ithicana is neutral."

"How easily you wash your hands of all culpability." She was growing furious that he'd spent the day trying to elicit her sympathy for his people, then turned a blind eye on hers. "And how can you claim an alliance in one breath and neutrality in the next?"

Aren swore, shaking his head. "I can't. I can't anymore." He pressed a thumb into his temple. "Why do you think Amarid has been breathing down our necks? It's because they're angry about the concessions we gave Maridrina, and which we will give Harendell if Ahnna ever decides to go marry their prince."

"And what impact have your so-called concessions made? Maridrina is starving, caught between Ithicana and the Red Desert, and I've yet to see you show the slightest bit of empathy."

"You have no idea what you're talking about."

"No? I *heard you* the day I was brought here. Heard you say that concessions you gave to my father were not what you wanted, and that Maridrina would starve before it ever saw the benefit of this treaty!"

He stared at her, face tight with fury. "You're right. I did say that. But if you and the rest of your people want to cast blame for Maridrina's famine, it's best you look to your father."

Lara opened her mouth to retort, but nothing came out.

"Have you read the treaty?" he asked.

"Of course I have. If Maridrina kept the peace with Ithicana for fifteen years, you'd marry a princess of the realm and offer significant concessions to tariffs and tolls on the bridge for as long as the peace between our kingdoms held."

"That's the sum of it. And when it came time to negotiate those concessions, I offered to eliminate all costs associated with a singular imported good, believing that I could force your father toward a choice that would culture peace. Cattle. Wheat. Corn. But you know what he demanded? Harendellian steel."

Her chest tightened. "You're lying. Everything my father has done is for the good of our people."

Aren laughed but there was no humor in it. "Everything your father does is for the good of *his* coffers. And for his pride." He shook his head. "Our taxes on steel and weapons have always been prohibitively exorbitant because the trafficking of weapons has political ramifications we'd prefer to avoid. Never mind that those weapons were often used, in turn, against us."

She couldn't breathe.

"Maridrina has no ore mines, which means the steel for its weapons must be sourced elsewhere. And because your father won't give up his endless war with Valcotta, he has been forced to import his weapons by ship at great cost. Until now."

The sun was too bright, everything a blur.

"I'll continue, since it seems your education in the desert had some gaps." Aren's hazel eyes glinted with anger. They were the only thing she could seem to focus on. "War costs money, believe me, I know. But your father doesn't have the bridge, so he pays for it with heavy taxes that have crippled Maridrina's economy. So even when its merchants dock at Southwatch's *open market*, they are unable to bid competitively. And so they set sail with what no one else will buy."

Diseased meat. Rotten grain. Lara closed her eyes. If he was telling the truth, it meant that everything that had been fueling her desire to capture the bridge had been false. And all that would remain to justify the fall of Ithicana was the very thing she'd railed against her entire life: greed.

"I'm not the one who has been lying to you. Not that I expect you to believe me."

Jor and the others chose that moment to circle back around, and the expression on Aren's face was enough to wipe the amusement off the older man's. The boat drew closer, and Aren grabbed the edge, hauling himself in. Once Lara did the same, Aren ordered, "Put up the other sail."

Jor winced. "That eager to get home?"

"We aren't going home."

"Oh? Where to?"

Aren cast a glance at the darkening skies in the east, then turned back around. But it wasn't Jor his eyes went to.

Lara's stomach flipped as Aren stared her down. Challenged her. "We're going to pay a visit to Maridrina."

# 26
# LARA

THAT HE WAS willing to risk stepping into enemy territory, that he was willing to bring her—who knew so many of Ithicana's secrets—into that territory, should've convinced Lara that Aren's words were true. That her father, Serin, and all her masters at the compound were liars.

But it didn't.

Stories of Ithicana's villainy had been burned into Lara's soul. Whispered in her ears all of her life. Chanted like a mantra through hours, days, *years* of grueling training that had nearly broken her. That had broken many of her half-sisters, sending them, one way or another, to their deaths.

*Take the bridge and you will be the savior of Maridrina.*

To believe Aren would mean changing that chant to something very different. *Take the bridge and you will be the destroyer of a nation. Take the bridge and you will prove yourself your father's pawn.* For that reason, she, like a coward, immediately argued against going.

"We are in the middle of storm season." Lara pointed at the darkness in the east. "What sort of madman takes to the seas to prove a point?"

"This sort of madman." Aren pulled the line Lia passed him tight. "Besides, the skies are clear in the direction we're going. And if the storm does catch us, we are rumored to be *very* adept sailors."

"We are in a canoe!" Lara despised the shrillness in her voice. "I fail to see how your *skill* will come into play in the middle of a typhoon!"

Aren laughed, sitting down on one of the benches. "We're hardly going to sail into the capital of Maridrina in an Ithicanian vessel."

"How then?" she demanded. "The bridge?"

Jor snorted and gave Aren a meaningful look. "Better to bypass Southwatch, isn't it, Your Majesty?"

Aren ignored him, putting his heels up and leaning back against a pack. "You'll see soon enough."

Soon enough she was clinging to the edge of the vessel as it skipped across the waves, heeled over so far she was certain a strong gust of wind would capsize them, drowning them in the open sea.

Lara reminded herself to pay attention to where they were going. *This is how they infiltrate your homeland, how they spy.* Yet as the bridge and its mist faded into the distance and more islands rose up ahead, all she cared to learn was the depths of Serin and her father's deception.

The Ithicanians dropped one of the sails, the boat easing from its terrifying angle to settle on the sea, and Lara took stock of where Aren had taken her. Columns of rock crusted with green rose out of blue seas so clear that the bottom seemed only an arm's reach away. Birds filled the air in enormous flocks, some diving into the water only to emerge with a fish clutched in their beaks, which they gulped down before one of their fellows could steal it away. Some of the larger islands had white beaches that beckoned invitingly, and nowhere, nowhere, was there any sign of the defenses that turned the waters around Ithicana's bridge red with enemy blood.

Lara rose onto her knees to look up as they passed between two towers of limestone. "Do people live here?"

As if to answer her question, when they rounded another island, several fishing boats appeared, the men and women aboard them stopping what they were doing to lift their hands in greeting, many of them calling out to Aren by name.

"Some live here," he responded slowly, as though the admission cost him something. "But it's dangerous. If they are attacked, we can't come to their aid until it's too late to matter."

"Are they attacked often?"

"Not since the treaty was signed, which is why more people have settled their families here."

"Do they leave during War Tides?"

His jaw tightened. "No."

Lara turned away from the fishing boats to look up at him, a sickening feeling filling her guts. What were the chances that Serin and her father didn't know these people were here? And what were the chances Aren wouldn't do everything in his power to help them if they were attacked?

Even if it meant weakening the bridge's defenses.

They meandered through the islands in silence before sailing beneath a natural stone arch into a hidden cove that dwarfed the one at Midwatch where, to Lara's surprise, several large ships were anchored.

"They're mostly naval vessels that we've captured. We've refit several to pass as merchant ships. This one's mine." Aren pointed at a mid-sized vessel painted with blue and gold.

"Aren't they all yours?" Lara replied sourly, accepting Jor's arm for balance before taking hold of the rope ladder dangling off the side of the ship.

"They all belong to King Aren of Ithicana. But this one is under the command of Captain John, merchant of Harendell. Now come on. That storm's going to chase us into Vencia if we delay much longer."

The hold, as it turned out, was full of the very product that Ithicana had been trying to keep from Maridrina: steel. "Can't keep a hold full of cattle sitting around for these situations," Aren said. "Plus, steel's the only commodity worth the risk of a storm season crossing. Or at least it was."

As they retreated back on deck and into the captain's quarters, Lara broke off a tiny piece of the root Nana had given her, then chewed on it vigorously, hoping it would quell the nausea inflicted by more than just seasickness.

Opening a chest, Aren riffled around and extracted a set of clothes and a floppy cap, which he tossed her way. "Disguises. If you pretend to be a boy, you'll have more liberty once we arrive in the city."

Scowling at him, Lara took the clothes and waited for him to turn his back before shedding her Ithicanian garments. After a bit of thought, she wrapped a scarf tightly around her chest, binding her breasts as well as she could, then donned the baggy shirt and voluminous trousers apparently favored by sailors from Harendell. She twisted her long braid into a coil on top of her head, securing it tightly, then tugged the cap over the whole affair and turned around.

Aren was already dressed in his Harendell attire, a similar floppy hat perched on his head. He frowned. "You still look like a woman."

"Shocking." She crossed her arms.

"Hmm." He turned in a circle, then walked to a corner and rubbed a hand across the floor. "This ship hasn't gone anywhere for over a year, and I don't think anyone's been in to clean." Retreating across the room, he reached for her.

Lara recoiled in alarm. "What are you doing?"

"Finishing your disguise." Holding the back of her head, he rubbed a hand that smelled like dirt and mouse shit across her face, ignoring her protests. Stepping back, Aren eyed her up and down. "Slouch a bit. And keep that frown on your face. It suits that of a thirteen-year-old boy forced into the service of his roguish-yet-charming older cousin."

Lara lifted her hand in a gesture that was universally insulting.

Aren laughed, then shouted out the door. "All hands on deck. We set sail for Maridrina."

With practiced efficiency, the soldiers-turned-Harendellian-sailors were readying the ship, Jor in conversation with a dozen Ithicanians she didn't recognize, but who must have been on the island.

"What's the story, Captain?" Jor called out as Aren and Lara came on deck.

"We saw a break in the storms and risked the crossing for a quick profit. Last chance to make a pretty penny while steel prices are high."

Everyone nodded in agreement, and it dawned on Lara that they'd done this before. That the most sought-after man in Ithicana had waltzed beneath her father's nose with no one, not even Serin, so much the wiser. Aren took hold of the wheel at the helm, shouting orders. The anchor was raised, sails dropped into place, then the ship was drifting out of the cove.

"Do you go to Maridrina often?"

Aren shook his head. "Not anymore. Before my coronation, I spent a great deal of time in other kingdoms furthering my education on trade economics."

"Is that what you were doing?" Jor said as he walked by. "And here I thought all those ventures out of Ithicana were to give you an opportunity to gamble, chase skirts, and piss away money on cheap booze."

"That too." Aren had the decency to look embarrassed. "Regardless, all of it ended when I was crowned, but for *Lara*, I'm going to make an exception."

She rested her elbows on the rail. "How long will it take us to get there?"

"Either ahead of this storm"—he grinned—"or not at all."

"This is unnecessary." She was more worried about what she'd find when they arrived than whether he'd get her there alive.

"That's my call to make. Now, why don't you go find something useful to do?"

Because she knew Aren wouldn't expect her to listen, Lara did just that. Armed with a bucket, a mop, and a filthy brush, she scrubbed the deck before moving into the captain's quarters where she pilfered some gold she found in the drawer of a desk, pausing in her cleaning only to toss the blackened water and haul in fresh. From the corner of her eye, she saw Aren open his mouth each time she passed before snapping it shut and glowering at the sea ahead of them.

Which was satisfying in and of itself, but more than that, the cleaning gave her uninterrupted time to think. As Lara saw it, she had three options once they made port. The first was that she ran. There was no doubt in her mind that she could escape Aren and his guard, and with the jewels she had in her pocket along with the gold she'd already pilfered from the captain's quarters, she'd be able to set up a life for herself wherever she saw fit. She'd have her freedom, and on the assumption that Aren would eventually write to her father on the marked paper, she'd have done her duty to her people.

The second was that she made her way to her father's palace and used the codes Serin had given her to gain admittance. That she'd tell them all that she knew in detail in exchange for her freedom, as had been promised. Though doing so risked her father cutting her throat a heartbeat after she'd given him what he needed. And the third . . .

The third was that everything Aren had told her was true. That her father had been given the opportunity to improve the lives of the Maridrinian people, but had chosen not to. That her father, not Ithicana, was the oppressor of her homeland. Yet Lara's mind balked, unwilling to accept that explanation. Certainly unwilling to accept it without proof.

Clutching a bucket of dirty water in one hand and the railing with the other, she turned to watch Aren sail the ship, her heart lurching despite the ridiculous cap he wore.

*What if her life had been dedicated to a lie?*

Lara was saved from thinking on it further as a wave washed over the deck, rendering her efforts unnecessary. The seas had grown rough and, lifting her face to the sky, she watched as lightning crackled through the clouds, wind tugging at her foolish hat. Aren was skirting the edge of the storm, which was almost upon them. Squinting, Lara took in the shadow of the continent ahead of them. What were the chances they'd make it?

Dropping her mop and bucket, she staggered across the rocking deck and up the steps to where Aren stood at the helm. "You need to turn west and get ahead of this typhoon, you mad fool," she shouted over the wind, gesturing at the black clouds.

"It's just a little storm," he said. "I'll beat it. But you should hold on."

Clinging to the railing with one hand and her hat with the other, Lara watched as Vencia and its sheltered harbor grew on the horizon, barely visible as the rain began to fall. Unlike the day she'd left, the sky over the city of her birth was black and ominous, the whitewashed buildings rising up from the harbor a dull grey. Lording over it all was the Imperial Palace, its walls washed a brilliant blue, its domes made of bronze. It was where her father kept his harem of wives, one of whom was her mother, if she was still alive.

Dimly, she heard Aren order his crew to drop some of the sails, the ship barely slowing as it raced toward the breakwater protecting the harbor. Lightning flashed, and a heartbeat later, thunder shook the ship. Wave after wave swamped the deck, the Ithicanians holding tight to lines to keep from being washed overboard.

Only Aren appeared unperturbed.

Fighting her growing nausea, Lara dug her fingers into the railing. Surf smashed against the high breakwater like a ceaseless battering ram, froth and spray flying fifty feet in the air. Each time it sounded like an explosion, and sweat poured down her back as she envisioned what would happen to the ship if it ran against the structure.

With a grunt of effort, Aren turned the wheel, his gaze fixed on the seemingly tiny gap through which they would pass.

A wave rose to nearly the height of the breakwater. "This is insanity." Lara barely kept her balance as the vessel swung round and straightened, sliding through the gap with unerring precision. A loud breath of air expelled from her lungs, the wood of the railing digging into Lara's forehead as she rested against it, rain splattering against her forehead.

"I told you we'd make it," Aren said, but she didn't answer, only took in the crowded harbor, the waters smooth relative to those of the open sea they'd left behind.

During storm season, she knew the majority of merchant vessels remained close to the coast, able to duck into a harbor if dark skies threatened, so heads turned at the sight of a Harendellian ship coming in. The likely contents of their hold enticed the harbormaster enough to wave them into the docks ahead of the queue, much to the obvious disgust of those captains and crews.

"It's been a long time, you brave bastard," the man shouted as the ship bumped against the dock, Jor and several of the others leaping over the rail to secure the vessel.

Aren waited until they dropped the gangplank before motioning for Lara to follow him down, the rain growing heavier by the minute. "You say brave, but my grandmother uses quite another word to describe me."

The harbormaster laughed. "Greedy?"

Aren clapped a hand to his chest and staggered sideways. "You wound me!"

They laughed as though they were old friends. Aren extracted a handful of coins and passed them over to the harbormaster, then another golden one, which the man slipped into his pocket while his assistant was recording the details on a piece of paper.

"You're well to have arrived when you did," the harbormaster said. "Steel prices won't hold for long with Ithicana shipping the cursed metal without tax or toll. It's piling up on Southwatch. Not that the Valcottans are giving King Silas much chance to retrieve his prize." He spat into the water.

Aren made a noise of commiseration. "So I've heard."

"Ithicana's new queen has done us no favors. All the gold Silas taxed out of our pockets has been spent on steel, and yet we've seen nothing in return."

"Beautiful women have a way of costing men money," Aren responded.

Lara bristled, and the harbormaster's eyes left Aren to land on her. "Don't much like the way you're looking at me, lad."

Aren clapped Lara on the shoulder hard enough to make her stagger. "Don't mind my cousin. He's only sour as he spent the entire crossing swabbing the deck rather than lazing about, as he's wont to do."

"Family makes for the worst crew."

"Don't it just. Was half tempted to chuck him overboard half a dozen times, but to do so would mean I could never go home."

"More than a few ladies in Vencia would be happy to put you up, I should think."

"Don't tempt me."

A fourth plan, which involved sticking a knife deep into Aren's guts, began to evolve as Lara followed the two men off the docks.

The harbormaster's voice dragged her attention back to the conversation. "I've heard Amarid spent the calm season showing the Bridge Kingdom exactly what they thought of Ithicana stealing away the business of supplying Maridrina with Harendellian weapons."

"Ithicana isn't supplying weapons."

Lara detected the heat in Aren's voice, but the harbormaster didn't seem to notice.

"Same is same. Shipping them for free. Getting them into our hands. Or would be, if Valcotta weren't risking their fleet to keep us from making port." The bitterness in his voice was palpable. "King Silas should've bargained for cattle."

"Cows don't win wars," Aren replied.

"Neither do half-starved soldiers. Or those dead from plague." The harbormaster spat on the ground. "The only good our princess's marriage has done for Maridrina was line the pockets of the beggars the king paid to sit on the street and cheer her name as she passed."

Aren and the man turned to the details of offloading the ship. It was nothing but a drone in Lara's ears as what she'd heard sank deep into her soul. What Serin had told her in his letter about the famine and plague was true, yet . . . Yet if what this man said had any verity to it, she'd been much deceived about who was to blame. Sweat rolled in little beads down her back, making her skin itch.

It couldn't be true. Aren had hired this man to say these things. It was all lies intended to trick her. A band of tension wrapped around Lara's chest, every breath a struggle as she attempted to reconcile a lifetime of teaching with what she was seeing. What she was hearing.

With what she had done.

"Have your crew offload it first thing in the morning. This storm is going to make it next to impossible to do it now."

Lara blinked, focusing on Aren as he shook the harbormaster's hand, waiting until the man was out of earshot before saying, "Proof enough for you?"

Lara didn't answer, pressing a hand to her aching temple, hating how it shook.

"Are we going back to the ship now?" Her tongue was thick in her mouth, her own voice distant.

"No."

There was something in his tone that pulled her from her fugue. Water sluiced down the hard angles of Aren's face, little beads collecting on his dark lashes. His hazel eyes searched hers for a moment, then he scanned the wharf. "We'll need to wait out the storm in Vencia. Best to do it in a bit of comfort."

Her pulse thudded like a drum in her skull as she walked through the market, following on Aren's heels, the Ithicanians casually walking around them. *Run*. The word repeated in her head, her feet flexing in her boots, desperate to take her away from this situation. She didn't want to hear any more. She didn't want to face the fact that she might not be a liberator. She might not be a savior. Not even a martyr.

She wanted to run from these shards of truth telling her she was something else entirely.

Aren climbed the narrow switchback streets, two-story buildings crammed together on both sides, windows shuttered against the storm. He stopped in front of a door with a sign that said *The Songbird* over top of it. Music, the clink of glasses, and the collective murmur of voices seeped onto the street. He hesitated with one hand on the handle, then pulled open the door with a sigh.

The scent of woodsmoke, cooking food, and spilled ale washed over Lara, and she took in the common room filled with low tables, most of them claimed by merchant class patrons. Jor and Aren sat at a table in the corner, the other guards taking places at the bar. Fighting to control the turbulent emotions shifting through her heart, Lara took a seat at Aren's right, slouching in the chair and hoping the rain hadn't washed away the dirt completing her disguise. A female voice caught her attention.

"Well now, look what the cat dragged in."

A young woman, perhaps in her early-twenties, had approached the table. She had long hair, a lighter and more golden shade of blond than Lara's, and a good portion of her generous cleavage was revealed by the low-cut bodice of her dress.

Aren picked up one of the small glasses of amber liquid that a serving girl had brought to the table. "How are you, Marisol?"

"How am I?" The woman—Marisol—planted her hands on her

hips. “It’s been over a year since you showed your sorry face in Vencia, John, and you ask how I am?”

“Has it been that long?”

“You damn well know it has been.”

Aren lifted his hands in an apology, giving the woman a charming smile that Lara had never seen before on his face. Flirtatious. Familiar. The nature of their relationship dawned on Lara, her skin turning hot.

“Circumstances beyond my control. But it’s good to see you.”

The woman pushed out her bottom lip and gave him a long look. Then she sat on his knee and wrapped an arm around his neck. Lara’s fingers twitched toward the knives hidden in her boots, fury bubbling in her veins. What was he thinking, parading his mistress in front of her? Was this some sort of punishment? Was he making a point?

The woman then greeted Jor and waved at one of the servers to bring another round.

Jor drained his glass, plucking the next from the server before she’d even had a chance to set it down. “Good to see you, Marisol.”

The woman’s gaze landed on Lara. “Who’s the sullen one?”

“My cousin. He’s learning the trade.”

Marisol tilted her pretty head, eyeing Lara as though she were trying to place her face. “Eyes like that, your mother must’ve been dallying with King Silas himself.”

Aren choked on his drink. “Now wouldn’t that be something?”

“You might have more fun if you smiled a bit more, boy. You could learn more from your cousin than how to sail a ship.”

Lara gave her a smile that was all teeth, but the woman only laughed, her attention back on Aren. “How long are you here?”

“Only until tomorrow, assuming the storm breaks.”

Her jaw tightened in obvious disappointment. “So soon.”

“My presence is required back home.”

“That’s what you always say.” Marisol exhaled softly, then shook her head. “You’ll be needing rooms for your crew for the night, then? And your cousin?”

Lara’s stomach flipped. *But not for him.* Surely he didn’t intend . . .

"For them. And one for me as well."

One of Marisol's eyebrows rose, and Lara fought the urge to punch her in her pretty little nose.

Jor cleared his throat. "He's gotten himself married off, Marisol."

The woman stood so abruptly that she knocked against the table, sending liquid sloshing out of the glasses.

Setting down his drink, Aren gave Jor a black glare, but the older man only shrugged. "No sense belaboring the conversation. Now she's been told, so we can get on with business."

Marisol's eyes glittered, and she blinked rapidly. "Congratulations. I'm sure she's charming."

"She has a temper like wildfire and a sharp tongue to go along with it."

Marisol's gaze shifted to Lara, far too many realizations flashing through her eyes. Rather than staring her down like she wanted to, Lara fixed her attention on a crack in the table. "I'm sure she's very beautiful," the other woman said.

Aren was quiet for a moment. "As beautiful as clear skies over the Tempest Seas. And equally as elusive."

Lara's stomach flipped as his words registered, a compliment wrapped in a dark truth that she couldn't deny.

"Well, that explains why you're in love with her, then," Marisol said softly. "You've always been enthralled by challenges."

Lara snatched up one of the little glasses and downed the contents, her ears buzzing even as she looked anywhere but at Aren.

Jor coughed loudly, then waved his arms in the air. "We need a round of drinks over here."

"Perhaps more than one." Marisol sat at the table, giving the slightest of nods to the musicians. They set aside the stringed instruments, retrieving drums and tambourines, filling the room with rhythm. Young women dressed in bright-colored dresses danced through the tables, the bracelets of bells around their wrists and ankles jingling as their voices accompanied the music. Moments later, the patrons began to clap, the din making it hard for Lara to hear herself think.

Marisol clapped along. "There is no evidence the king is building up his fleet in an effort to fight the Valcottan blockade. Not even any sign that he *intends* to. I have informants up and down the coast, and not a single shipyard boasts a commission from the crown."

Lara blinked. *This woman was a spy?*

"The prices of imports have skyrocketed. Food is limited to what Maridrina can produce itself, which is little given all our farmers have been turned to soldiers, and famine is on the rise in the cities. It's only expected to worsen."

Aren clapped along in time to the music. "Amarid isn't picking up the slack? I would've thought they'd be clamoring for the opportunity."

Marisol shook her head. "Amaridian sailors are crying in every port that the alliance between Ithicana and Maridrina has destroyed their incomes." Her eyes flicked to Aren. "And now that the alliance isn't working out as intended, they seem happy for Maridrina to pay the price."

"Vindictive of them."

Marisol took a sip from her drink, then nodded. "The support of the Maridrinian people for the conflict with Valcotta had been on the wane for years, because no one believed there was anything to be gained from it. But since the wedding and Valcotta's subsequent retaliation, favor for all-out war with Valcotta has grown tenfold. Men and boys both are throwing themselves at army recruiters, fancying themselves the saviors of their people, and—" Marisol broke off, casting a quick glance at Lara.

"And?" Aren prompted.

"And there is a growing number of voices suggesting that the alliance of the Fifteen Year Treaty should be broken. That while Maridrina starves, Ithicana continues to profit off trade with Valcotta. That if the Bridge Kingdom were a true ally, they would deny our enemies port at Southwatch."

Lifting one shoulder, Marisol let it fall. "The concessions Ithicana granted Maridrina haven't benefited our people in the slightest. But rather than blaming King Silas, they blame Ithicana for the hardship. The people are itching for a fight."

*Maridrina will starve before they ever see the benefit of this treaty.*

Aren's words echoed through Lara's skull. How right he'd been.

The song ended, the dancers faded back to their other posts, and the musicians chose a more subdued song for their next piece. Marisol stood. "I need to get back to work. I'll have food sent over and rooms made up for you and your crew."

Her father, Serin . . . all her masters. They'd lied to Lara and her sisters. That in itself was no great revelation—she'd realized that Ithicana's villainy had been exaggerated and expounded upon in order to turn the girls into fundamentalists with one clear goal: the destruction of Maridrina's oppressor. But until this precise moment, she had believed that while her father's methods had been vile, his motivation had been pure. To save Maridrina's people. To feed them and protect them.

Except Ithicana wasn't the oppressor. Her father was.

Lara and her sisters hadn't been isolated in the desert compound for their safety. They hadn't even been kept there to conceal her father's plans from Ithicana, not really. It had been to keep Lara and her sisters from the truth. Because if they'd known that their mission was driven not by the need to right a wrong, but by their father's endless greed, how willing would any of them have been to betray a husband? To tear apart a nation? To see a people slaughtered? Promises and threats and bribes were paltry motivators compared to the fanaticism that had been burned into her and her sisters' souls.

But for Lara, that fanaticism burned no longer.

# 27
# AREN

"WHY ARE WE HERE?" Jor motioned for one of the girls to bring another round of drinks. "What are we risking wild seas and enemy territory for?"

Pushing his food around on the plate in front of him, Aren didn't answer. Lara had gone upstairs to their room an hour ago, silent, her face pale. He'd told her to remain there until he returned for her own safety. He had no expectations that she'd listen.

He'd known. Standing in the water with her next to Snake Island, he'd known. All the little peculiarities about his Maridrinian wife, the little things that had struck him as odd, had accumulated until there was no denying it.

Lara was a spy.

The woman he'd goddamned fallen in love with was a spy.

In the early days of their marriage, he'd believed Lara's apparent disdain for him was driven by her discomfort of being forced into a marriage that she didn't want. A life she hadn't chosen. But the shock on her face when he told her that her father had been given the chance to feed his starving people and had bought weapons instead signaled she'd been *lied* to on top of everything else.

Aren employed enough spies of his own to know the best of them believed that the work they did was for a greater good. The Rat King would be hard-pressed to find a spy who believed Ithicana was the cause of Maridrina's plight, so he'd created one: a daughter raised in total isolation to implant a false sense of righteousness.

Except now she knew the truth.

"Aren?" Jor's voice was unconcerned, but Aren had never heard the captain of his guard slip on a pseudonym, particularly that of his king. The older man was worried. And rightly so. Ithicana was caught between a rock and a very hard place.

Before Aren had a chance to answer, one of his crew stepped inside the tavern and nodded once. Aren's heart sank. "You're about to find out."

Outside, his guard reported, "She's walking up the main boulevard. Gorrick is tailing her." He handed Aren his bow and quiver.

Aren took the weapons without comment and started up the street, Jor on his heels. Vencia was crowded as always, and it took him a bit of time to find the tall Ithicanian tailing his wife. "Go back," he muttered to Gorrick once he had Lara in his sights. "We'll take it from here."

The man opened his mouth to argue, then saw the expression on Aren's face, and faded into the crowd.

Lara strode up the center of the street, still wearing her disguise, which meant the drunks and rabble-rousers left her alone. Yet as they tailed her, he wondered how the disguise fooled anyone at all. Every time she turned her head to regard something that had caught her interest, torchlight framed the delicate lines of her face, her full lips, the long column of her neck, the rounded curve of her ass. The slight sway to her step. No Harendellian ship boy he'd ever met walked like *that*.

She was so painfully beautiful, and even knowing that she'd used it against him didn't lessen how powerfully he was drawn to her.

He silently pleaded: *Please let me be wrong about what you intend to do.*

But there was no denying the route Lara was taking, up the

switchback streets in the direction of her father's palace, that blue and bronze testament to his hubris and greed.

Jor cursed as he, too, realized which way Lara was going. "We need to stop her."

Aren sidestepped a drunken pair and moved into the shadows closer to the buildings. "Not yet."

The farther they climbed, the fewer people filled the street, but Lara hadn't once looked back. As though it hadn't even occurred to her that he might have her watched.

"What are you doing, Aren?" Jor hissed.

"I need to see if she'll betray me if given the chance."

But what he hoped was that the truth had turned her. That, now awake to her father's deception, she'd turn her back on whatever purpose she'd been set to. If she was the sort of woman he believed, no, *prayed*, her to be.

She kept walking toward the gate, the guards flanking it regarding her with bored interest, a lone youth of no concern to them. Aren stopped in the shadows where the guards wouldn't see him, pulling a single arrow from his quiver. The bow was his own, but the wood felt strange and unfamiliar beneath his sweating fingers.

Jor reached for his weapon. "Let me do this for you."

Aren stepped sideways, nocking the arrow as he shook his head. "No. I brought her into Ithicana. She's my responsibility." Lara wasn't slowing, and the guards at the gate perked up as she approached.

One of the guards called out to her. "What are you about, boy?" Lara didn't answer.

Again, Jor tried to take the weapon. "You're half in love with the girl. You don't need this on your conscience."

"Yes, I do."

She stopped a dozen paces from the heavy iron gates.

"State your purpose or be on your way," the guard shouted.

Aren slowly drew the bow, aiming the arrow at the center of her slender back. At this range, it would punch straight through her heart. She'd be dead before she could damn him, and Ithicana, more than she already had.

Aren's heart was wild and frantic in his chest, hot sweat mixing with the rain running down his back. As he blinked, he saw her fall. Saw her blood spill out in a pool around her. Saw those cursedly beautiful eyes of hers lose their spark. Then he blinked again and she was standing motionless in the darkness. She took a hesitant step forward. His arm quivered.

Another step.

The bowstring dug into his fingers as he slowly began to straighten them, knowing that despite having no choice, he'd never forgive himself for killing her.

Her body rocked and his heart skipped. Then lightning flashed and Lara whirled, sprinting away from the gates. Jor jerked Aren deeper into the shadows as she passed, heading back into the city. He took a step to follow before everything he'd eaten for dinner rose in his throat. Bracing a hand against the wall of the building, Aren puked his guts out onto the street.

"Follow her," he managed to get out. "Make sure she gets back safe."

Only when Jor had disappeared down the street did Aren rest his head against the slimy wet stone. A half a second. That had been the difference between her running into the night and her lying dead on the street. Half a second.

The stench of vomit filled his nose, but that wasn't what made his eyes burn. He scrubbed at them furiously, hating the King of Maridrina to the depths of his soul. The alliance between Maridrina and Ithicana made a mockery of the word, for it felt Aren had no greater enemy than Silas Veliant.

"You," someone shouted. "No loitering. Get on your way!"

Casting one backward glance at the palace where Lara's father slept, Aren melted into the night.

# 28
# LARA

"WHISKEY," LARA MUTTERED AT the barkeep, easing onto a stool back at *The Songbird*, water dripping from her clothing to pool on the floor beneath her.

The barkeep eyed her with amusement. "Can you pay, boy?"

"No," she snapped. "I intend to drink it and then run out the back."

The amusement in his eyes fled, and he leaned over the bar. "Listen, you little—"

"Darling, can you bring up some more wine from the cellar?" Marisol appeared from nowhere. "I'll handle this."

Shrugging, the barkeep strode toward an open door behind the bar. Once he was gone, Marisol pulled a bottle from beneath the bar and poured a generous measure into a glass, which she pushed in front of Lara. "I don't know how they do things in Harendell, but I'm not in the habit of getting children drunk in my establishment."

Lara gave her a cold stare, drained the glass, then pushed it back in front of the other woman. Then she reached into her pocket and retrieved a gold Harendellian coin and slammed it on the bar. "Make an exception."

One eyebrow rose. "You are a charmer, aren't you, Your Majesty."

"Do you bestow titles on all your patrons?"

"Only on women with eyes of Veliant blue who travel in the company of Ithicanian spies."

There seemed little point in trying to dissuade her. "Either pour and talk at the same time, or shut up. I'm in no mood." No mood for anything but to silence the questions that spun wild through her thoughts as she tried to come to terms with a world that seemed turned upside down. And certainly in no mood to make small talk with Aren's former lover.

Marisol poured, then set the bottle down next to the glass. "I saw you when you passed through Vencia on your way to Ithicana." She rested her elbows on the polished wood. "The curtain was pulled back in the carriage, and I caught just a glimpse. You looked like you were going to war, not to be married."

Lara *had* been going to war. Or so she'd thought at the time.

"The king ordered the streets cleared. No one was allowed out of their homes until you'd boarded the ship. For your protection, they said."

It had nothing to do with her protection. It was one last step to ensure that Lara boarded the ship convinced Maridrina was in the direst of straits and that Ithicana was to blame. One last piece of deception.

"Then they loaded you onto the ship, and you were gone. Off to Ithicana and off, unbeknownst to me at the time, to steal away my favorite lover."

Lara gave her a sweet smile. "Given you hadn't seen him in over a year, I'm not sure you had much claim to him at that point. If ever."

"You are quite the little bitch, aren't you?"

Lara plucked the glass Marisol was polishing from her hands, filled it, waited for the other woman to raise it, then clinked hers against it. "Cheers to that."

Swallowing the liquid in one mouthful, Marisol set aside the glass. "We expected things to change. For your father to ease his filthy taxes or at least to use the money for something better than his ceaseless war with Valcotta."

"But nothing changed."

Marisol shook her head. "If anything, it's only gotten worse."

"Makes one wonder why I bothered going." Except Lara knew exactly why she'd gone to Ithicana. To save her sisters. To save her kingdom. To save herself. In this precise moment, she half wondered if she'd damned them all.

"Not your choice, I suppose." Marisol's eyes drifted over Lara's shoulder, taking in the comings and goings of the common room. "What I do know is that you married the best man I've ever had a privilege to meet, so perhaps instead of drowning your sorrows, you ought to consider a better use of your time." She inclined her head. "Either way, I hope you enjoy your evening, Your Majesty."

"Good night," Lara muttered, refilling her glass. She *knew* Aren was a good man. Her instincts, which she should've trusted, had been screaming it at her for longer than she'd cared to admit, but she'd ignored them in favor of what she'd been *told.* She'd been duped. Manipulated. Played.

She'd gone to the palace to kill her father.

Her plan had been to use the codes she'd been given to gain access, then wait for them to bring her to her father—and kill him. With her bare hands, if she needed to. It wasn't as though she hadn't been trained to do it. They'd kill her afterward, but his death would be worth it. Worth that moment when her father realized that she, his prized weapon, had turned on him instead.

But as Lara had stood there in the pouring rain, her father's soldiers watching her with bored interest, Master Erik's voice had filled her ears: *Do not let your temper get the better of you, little cockroach. For when you do, you risk your enemies getting the better of you.*

It would be one thing if her loss of temper only cost *her*. But as she stood there, skin prickling with some sixth sense warning her of danger, it occurred to Lara that it would be Ithicana—and Aren—who would pay the price. The sheets of paper in Aren's rooms at Midwatch still bore all of the bridge's secrets. If even one of them reached Serin's hands . . . that was damage that could never be undone. She needed to ensure they were destroyed. Once that was accomplished, she could turn to vengeance with a clear conscience.

She'd returned, intending to leave Aren a note explaining everything and instructing him to destroy the papers, but the vision of Aren's face when he read it kept spinning across her thoughts. He, who was loyal to his very core, would take her act of disloyalty personally. He'd *hate* her. Lara swallowed the contents of her glass in big gulps, wishing the alcohol would work faster. Wishing it would numb her traitorous heart.

Filling her glass again and again, she ruminated until the bottle was empty, the whiskey doing *nothing* to numb the dull ache in her chest. She would've ordered another and kept on drinking, but there was no one left to serve her, all the bottles and glassware put away for the night, the room silent and still.

Rising to her feet, Lara turned to discover the common room empty of patrons and staff, chairs pushed into tables, floors swept, and door latched. Devoid of life. Except for Aren, who sat at the table behind her.

She stared blearily at him, her heart feeling as though it had been torn into a thousand pieces, then set aflame.

"Waiting for me to go to bed so you can go find Marisol?" The words were slurred. Spiteful. But she almost wished he'd do it if for no other reason than it would give her a valid reason to hate him. A valid reason to leave and never look back.

The corner of his mouth turned up. "Who do you think came to find me to *deal with my shit-mouthed little cousin?*"

Lara made a face. "She knows I'm not your cousin. She knows exactly who I am, and, by extension, who you are."

"Clever Marisol."

"You aren't concerned?"

Aren shook his head, then rose to his feet. His clothes were wet, but whatever rainwater he'd tracked in had long since dried. *How long had he been sitting there?*

"She's been spying for Ithicana for almost a decade—since your father hung hers and then spiked his head on Vencia's gates. She's loyal."

Jealous words danced on Lara's tongue, but she swallowed them. "She's beautiful. And kind."

"Yes." His gaze was intense. "But she's not you."

Her body swayed, the room spinning. Aren closed the distance between them in two strides, hands catching her sides. Steadying her. Lara closed her eyes to try to stop the spinning, but the rotating room was replaced with the memory of his hard, muscled body, his tanned skin beneath her fingers. Heat blossomed low in her belly.

*You can't,* she told herself. *You're a liar and a traitor. You aren't the woman he believes you to be, and you never can be. You can never be yourself.* Not without risking him discovering the truth. If she couldn't find the courage to tell him the truth, then she needed to get back to Ithicana to destroy all evidence of her betrayal, and then disappear. Fake her death. Return to Maridrina for vengeance.

*And never see Aren again.*

Her eyes burned, her breath threatening to catch in a sob and betray her.

"Are you all right?"

She clenched her teeth. "I don't feel well."

"Not surprising given the amount you drank. You have a royal's taste, by the way. That's not a cheap bottle."

"Paid for it myself." She said the words slowly in attempt to make them clearer.

"You mean with the coins you stole from *my* ship."

"If you're stupid enough to leave them lying around, you deserve to lose them."

"I'm sorry. I didn't catch that through all the slurring."

"Asshole."

He laughed. "Can you walk?"

"Yes." Untangling herself from his grip, she staggered toward the stairs, when all of a sudden, the bottom step was flying up to meet her. But before Lara's face could slam against the wood, Aren caught hold of her, swinging her up into his arms. "Let's not tempt fate."

"Just need water."

"You need a pillow. Maybe you'll get lucky and the storm will linger long enough for you to sleep this off. But I doubt it."

Lara made an angry sound against his chest, but it was more

for herself. At the ease with which she curled against him. At how appealing a few more nights with him would be, despite knowing that it was only delaying the inevitable.

"Did the whiskey help?"

"No."

"It's never helped me much, either."

A tear leaked onto her cheek, and she turned her face into his chest to hide it. "I'm sorry I've been so terrible. You deserve someone better than me."

Aren exhaled, but said nothing. The methodical movement of him climbing the stairs lulled her, consciousness slowly fading away. She didn't fight it, because against all the odds, she trusted him implicitly. Still, she was aware enough to hear him, his voice hoarse as he said, "Since the moment I set eyes on you in Southwatch, there's been no one but you. Even if I'm a goddamned fool for it, there will never be anyone but you."

*You are a fool,* she thought as darkness took her.

And that made two of them.

# 29
# AREN

HE'D NEVER BEEN able to sleep past dawn on a clear day.

How his sleeping body knew the winds had died and the rain ceased was a mystery. A sixth sense from a lifetime in Ithicana that warned him when the Tempest Seas lowered their guard, and that it was time to raise his. So when his eyes snapped open with the faintest glow on the horizon, Aren rose from where he'd slept on the floor, dressed silently so as not to disturb Lara, who was still faintly snoring into her pillow, then ventured downstairs for something to eat.

It was as though a burden had lifted from his shoulders. Coming to Vencia was always a risk, but it had been a thousandfold more so with Lara in tow. Yet it had been worth it. Worth having her discover the truth of the circumstances in Maridrina with her own eyes and ears. Having her understand that it was her *father*, not Ithicana, who was the oppressor of her homeland. Having Lara finally see with eyes unclouded by whatever bullshit her mind had been filled with over the years.

Those things had been worth the risk that she'd turn on him and spill every cursed secret she'd learned. Worth those torturous moments when Aren had believed he'd have to stop her.

Worth the moment when Aren became certain that her allegiance had, if not entirely turned to Ithicana, at least abandoned his enemy.

That she'd made that choice had been clear from the time he'd watched her sitting at the bar, drinking whiskey like her life depended on it. Aren knew his wife well enough to tell when she was pissed off. That silent simmering burn that caused any sane individual to give her a wide berth, whether they realized it or not. Last night, she'd been furious. But for the first time, it wasn't at him. No, when she'd turned around and saw him, her anger had been vanquished by another emotion entirely. One that he'd been desperate to see in her eyes for longer than he cared to admit.

Down in the common room, Jor was seated with Gorrick, but Aren only gave them a nod and took a seat in the corner by himself, content to watch the comings and goings while sipping the coffee that Marisol brought him, his friend and former lover too busy with the rush to do more than squeeze his shoulder in passing.

The room was half filled with traveling merchants. Some wore the clear gaze of those keen to make a profit once the markets opened. Others wore the blurry eyes and green faces of those who'd enjoyed a night out in Vencia and were awake only because they feared their masters' wrath.

Aren had far more in common with the latter group. Since he was fifteen, he'd been venturing out of Ithicana. Ostensibly, it was to spy. To learn the ways of his kingdom's pseudo-allies and clear-cut enemies, but there was no denying that he also used the trips to step away from the ceaseless burdens that came with his title. Vencia had always been his favorite, and he'd rode out a dozen or more typhoons drinking and gambling and laughing in one common room or another, more often than not with a local girl to warm his bed, no one believing him to be anything other than a son of a successful merchant.

While the Kingdom of Maridrina was a thorn in Ithicana's backside, the Maridrinian people had long been friends to Aren, which created a certain conflict. He was not supposed to like them, but he did. Liked how they haggled and argued about every damned thing; how they were brash and brave, even the most cowardly of them prone to picking fistfights to defend a friend's honor; how they sang and laughed and lived, every one of them with grand ambitions for *more*.

Vencia itself was a beautiful place, a hillside of whitewashed buildings with blue roofs that always seemed to gleam as he approached from the sea, its streets thrumming with people hailing from every nation, north and south. A metropolis that thrived *despite* its king, who ruled with an iron fist and who used taxes to all but plunder his own people.

No, if Maridrina found itself a new ruler and Aren wasn't the king of his own kingdom, he'd be happy to make a life in Vencia. Sometimes he wondered if that was half of what his council feared about opening up Ithicana's borders and allowing its citizens to leave: that they'd see how bloody *easy* life was in other kingdoms, and never come back. That Ithicana wouldn't be conquered, but rather slowly fade from existence.

Except he didn't think that was how it would go. There was something about the wild thrill of living in Ithicana that spoke to the souls of those born to it, and neither people nor kingdom would ever willingly let each other go.

Aren's thoughts were interrupted by a shadow falling across his table.

"Good morning, Your Grace," a nasally voice said. "I hope you'll forgive me for interrupting your breakfast."

Aren's fork hesitated halfway to his mouth, and it took a great deal of effort to swallow his mouthful of eggs. He lifted his head. "I've been called a great many things in this room, but never that."

The Magpie gave a thin smile and took the seat across from Aren. "I appreciate the game as much as anyone, Your Grace, but perhaps we might forgo the pretense that you are anyone other than the King of Ithicana." His smile grew. "For expedience's sake."

Aren set down his fork and leaned back in his chair. Out of the corner of his eye, he saw Jor and Gorrick lift their heads, Serin's face deeply familiar to them. But they'd only seen Maridrina's spymaster from afar, because never, *never*, had their cover been compromised.

Every Ithicanian spy knew going into enemy territory that if they were caught they should fall on their own sword before giving up their kingdom's secrets, and Aren had no doubt that everyone with him would do just that. Except, perhaps, for the woman upstairs.

"It's the scar on your hand that gave you away." Serin jerked his chin toward Aren's left hand, which rested on the table, the curved white scar from an old knife fight clearly visible. "Along with the mask, you always wore gloves when you met with outsiders. But not at your wedding, which of course I was in attendance for. Such a dramatic ceremony it was."

Gorrick stood, yawning, then strolled over to the bar as though to sweet-talk Marisol. His friend smiled and laughed as she polished the glass she was holding, but a heartbeat later, she'd disappeared from the room. To find Taryn, who'd secure Lara.

If that was even a possibility.

God, he was a fool for lowering his guard. For believing that it had ended last night when Lara hadn't gone into the palace. Perhaps that had only been a ruse, and even now, his Maridrinian wife was spilling out everything she'd learned to her father's lackeys.

"Not like you Ithicanians to make a mistake." Serin lifted his hand to get a servant girl's attention. "We, of course, suspected that you paid our shores visits from time to time, but not until now did you so blatantly announce your arrival."

Aren's eyebrow rose.

"It was the steel, you see. It was marked at Northwatch for transport through the bridge over a year ago, and yet the load somehow arrived in Vencia only yesterday, offloaded only this very morning. And via a ship claiming to have come from Harendell, not from a Southwatch ferry."

*Fuck.* Ahnna was going to kill him if he managed to survive this.

"I'd suggest that it was an amateur mistake, but this isn't your first visit to Vencia, is it, Your Grace?" Serin accepted a coffee from one of Marisol's girls. "You seem far too comfortable for it to be your first time."

Aren picked up his cup, eyeing the spymaster. "I've always had a fondness for Vencia. Plenty of attractive women."

Serin gave an amused sniff. "I would've thought those days would be behind you now that you're a married man."

"Perhaps they would be if you hadn't sent me such a harridan."

The coffee in Serin's cup quivered, and the tiny man set it down swiftly to hide the reaction. Apparently, Lara had not stuck to the spymaster's plan in her methods of seduction. Which was probably a good thing, because Aren suspected he and Serin had quite different tastes when it came to women.

"We could send you another . . . perhaps one with a kinder, gentler disposition." Serin's eyes flicked to Marisol. "I see you have a fondness for blondes. I can think of just the princess for you. She was my first choice, but fate conspired against me. Against both of us, it would appear."

Aren's curiosity over why Lara had been chosen flared once again before being pushed aside by concern for his friend. Marisol had been linked to him; that meant she was in danger. "Tempting. Unfortunately, such practices are frowned upon by my people. I'll have to content myself with what you sent me."

"Speaking of Lara, how is she? It's been some time since we received word from her, and her father has grown . . . concerned."

Aren's mind raced. If the steel hadn't been unloaded and processed until this morning, it was possible they'd only been under the Magpie's scrutiny for a matter of hours, all of which Lara had spent passed out in a bed upstairs. Alternatively, this could be a ruse to distract Aren while the Maridrinians secured their princess. "She's well enough."

"Her father would like some proof of that."

"When I return home, I'll suggest she put pen to paper. But I must warn you, Lara isn't the most . . . *obedient* of wives. She's more likely to tell me to shove both pen and paper up my ass."

Serin's brow crinkled. "Perhaps remind her of her father's enduring concern for her welfare."

Aren rested his elbows on the table. "Cut the shit, Magpie. We both know your master cares nothing for his daughter. He got what he wanted, which was free trade on steel and weapons. So what else is it you're after?"

Waving his hand as though to dispel the tension, Serin gave him an apologetic smile. "Appearances must be maintained, you understand. Frankly, you can slit the little bitch's throat and my master would care not; what he *does* care about is your commitment to the alliance between our kingdoms."

"He has his steel, as per our agreement. What more does he feel he deserves?"

A sage nod. "It's true you've held to the letter of the agreement, as have we. What I'm referring to is more . . . the *spirit* of the agreement. The treaty was for an alliance of peace between Ithicana and Maridrina, and yet you continue to host and trade with our greatest enemy in your market at Southwatch, allowing *them* to purchase the goods Maridrina so desperately needs. My master asks that you reconsider this practice."

"You want me to cut ties with Valcotta?" Cut ties with the kingdom that provided close to a third of the bridge's revenues every year? Valcotta was no ally, but neither were they Ithicana's sworn enemy the way Maridrina had been in the past. Yet if Aren did what Serin was asking . . . "I've no interest in going to war against Valcotta."

"Nor is my master asking you to." Serin slid an embossed silver cylinder across the table, the lacquered seal Maridrinian blue. "He merely requests that you cease supplying them in their war against us."

"They'll retaliate, and war will be on my doorstep whether I asked for it or not."

"Perhaps." Serin took a mouthful of his coffee. "But if Valcotta attacks your lands, rest assured that Maridrina will retaliate against them tenfold. We do not take kindly to those who interfere with our friends and allies."

Words of support, but Aren heard the threat beneath them. *Do as my master says, or face the consequences.*

"Think on it, Your Grace." Serin rose to his feet. "My master looks forward to your written response detailing your commitment to our friendship." The thin smile returned. "Safe travels back to your homeland, and *please*, do give Lara my regards."

Without another word, the Spymaster of Maridrina left the common room, the door slamming shut in his wake. Picking up the message tube, Aren quickly scanned the contents before shoving it into the bag by his feet, then met Jor's eyes from across the room.

*Time to go.*

# 30
# LARA

LARA WOKE JUST before dawn, a blanket covering her from toe to chin, a glass of water sitting on the bedside table, and her head throbbing with the worst headache of her life.

Moaning, she rolled over to bury her face in the pillow. The events of the prior night were hazy, but she remembered them well enough for her cheeks to burn as she recalled Aren catching her before she could fall smack on her face. The way she'd curled into his arms as he'd carried her up the stairs. The things she'd said. The things *he'd* said.

Sitting upright, Lara eyed her boy's clothes, which she'd slept in, the boots sitting on the floor next to her bed the only garment that Aren had removed from her after she'd passed out.

*Her knives.*

Looking around frantically, Lara threw the pillows onto the floor, her heart settling and a faint smile rising to her lips as she saw the blades resting there. Apparently Aren had noticed more of her habits than she'd realized.

Picking up the water, she opened the shuttered windows and

looked outside: clear skies and only a light breeze ruffling the laundry hanging from the line across the street. *They could go home today.*

*Home.* Shaking her head sharply at the slip, Lara drained the glass in several long gulps, and pulled on her boots. The room was decidedly devoid of dirt, so she used a bit of soot from the lamp to complete her disguise before shoving her few belongings into her bag and stepping out into the hallway.

To find herself face-to-face with half of Aren's guard.

"What's going on?" she asked Taryn, who looked strange in the simple dress she wore as disguise.

"Weather's going to turn. Time to go."

*She was lying.* There were very few things that put fear into the eyes of the Ithicanians, and the promise of a storm certainly wasn't one of them.

Downstairs was already busy with the early-rising merchant class who were breaking their fast, but her eyes immediately found Aren sitting at the bar. Behind it stood Marisol, who, for once, wasn't polishing a glass, her focus entirely on the man in front of her. Lara's jaw tightened, but her jealousy fled as she remembered Aren's words. *There will never be anyone but you.*

Except with all the lies she'd told, all the ways she'd manipulated him, how could she stay with him?

As Lara stood frozen in the entrance to the common room, Aren turned and caught sight of her. What looked like relief spread across his face. With a final word to Marisol, he dumped a handful of coins on the bar. *Something was very wrong.*

He strode across the room. "Finally decided to show yourself, cousin? Barely going to have enough time to make the run to Southwatch as it is without waiting on your primping."

She glowered at him because other patrons were watching, but once he was within arm's reach, he muttered, "We've been compromised. We need to go."

Jor and the rest of the Ithicanians were outside leaning against the wall with false nonchalance. Despite their apparel, no one with half an eye would believe them sailors. They were too alert, and not a one of them appeared hungover. Unlike her.

"Don't want to miss the tide," Aren announced, and immediately they were on the move.

In the harbor, they wove through the crowd at a near run, down to the wharf and onto the dock where their vessel was moored. The Ithicanians who'd remained with the ship were already scurrying about on the deck, readying to set sail. Readying to flee. Lara's focus sharpened, and she scanned the docks and crowds for any sign of pursuit. Aren had said their cover had been compromised, but there were levels to that statement. If the Maridrinians had discovered they were from Ithicana, that was one thing. If they'd discovered Aren's identity—or worse, Lara's—then they were in serious trouble.

"You're mad, John." The harbormaster's paunch shook as he scuttled toward them. "There's a storm brewing."

Aren paused at the base of gangplank, using one hand to push Lara up. "Nothing but a squall. It will keep the Valcottans off my heels."

"Insanity," the man grumbled. "I'll keep a space open for you."

"We'll be back before lunch. You can buy me a drink or two on my return."

"More likely that I'll be toasting your memory."

Aren's laugh cut off abruptly. Her hackles rising, Lara turned from her inspection of the darkness swirling in the east to find Serin standing a dozen paces or so behind the harbormaster, his arms crossed behind his back. Watching.

The ship rocked on a swell, and Lara staggered, her shoulders colliding with Aren's chest, his arm reflexively wrapping around her to catch her balance, holding her against him.

Serin's eyes widened.

"Go," she whispered, seeing the realization dawn on the spymaster's face. Realization that her presence in Maridrina meant she knew the truth. That the gambit fifteen years in the making had played itself out too soon. The realization that if Lara made it out of this harbor, so would any chance of her father ever taking the bridge. "Go!" she screamed.

"Raise the sails!" Aren roared.

The Ithicanians surged into action, and in a heartbeat, the ship was drifting away from the dock, the gangplank landing in the water with a splash. Aren dragged her with him as he raced to the helm, shouting orders even as swarms of soldiers descended upon them.

"Hurry!" The gap between ship and dock was widening, but not swiftly enough. "Aren, I can't let them take me alive." Lara pulled one of her knives from her boot. "They'll make me talk."

He caught sight of her knife, realizing her intentions. "Put it away, Lara! I won't let them take you."

"But—"

He tore the jeweled blade from her hand and threw it, the weapon flipping end over end to land on the dock. Which was filled with sprinting soldiers, the front-runners preparing to leap.

"Come on, wind!" Aren shouted. "Don't let this be the one damned time you refuse to blow."

As if answering the call of its master, the wind howled in from the east, the sails snapping taut. The ship lurched as three of the soldiers jumped, their arms flailing as they fell into the water instead of onto the deck.

The ship collided with another vessel with a loud crunch, the other crew shouting and swearing as they scraped the length of it, slamming into another ship, then another, as Aren used the strength of the wind to force their way through.

Soldiers ran in all directions, leaping onto ships in an attempt to reach their target, but they were too slow. Except in the distance, naval vessels were swarming with sailors making ready for pursuit.

"Can you outrun them?" Lara demanded.

Aren nodded, his eyes fixed on their progress through the crowded harbor.

Bells clanged riotously in the city.

"Shit!" Aren shouted. "We need to get past the breakwater before they lift the chain."

Lara's gaze skipped across the water to the twin towers flanking the gap in the breakwater, to the heavy steel chain that was creaking upward.

"Full sail!"

The deck was organized chaos as the Ithicanians hauled on lines, white canvas streaming skyward. The ship leapt across the waves toward the gap, but the chain was rising just as fast. Even if they managed to get across, it would tear loose the rudder and they'd be easy pickings for the Maridrinian navy.

"We can't hit that gap with full sail," Jor shouted. "We'll be tossed up on the rocks."

"Get them up," Aren ordered. "All of them."

Lara clung to the rail, her hair whipping out behind them with the speed of their progress. Yet the expressions on the crews' faces told her it wasn't enough. That they were headed toward a disaster that would see them all drowned or captured, which would amount to the same thing.

And there was nothing she could do to save them. Even if she jumped overboard, the ship would be trapped. Serin and her father would never let them go free.

Slamming her fists on the rail, Lara snarled in wordless fury, despair carving her insides hollow. Despite *everything*, her father was going to win.

Aren's hand caught hers. "The wind—it gusts around the hill and through the gap in the breakwater. If we time this just right, it might work."

"What might work?" The chain was perilously close.

"You'll see." He shot her a grim smile. "Hold on to the rail, and for the love of god, don't let go!" Then he let go of her hand and heaved on the wheel.

As he did, an enormous gust of wind struck them broadside. The rigging groaned, ropes and wood and canvas straining, on the verge of snapping, and the ship heeled over. Further and further and Lara shrieked, clinging to whatever she could, certain the vessel would capsize.

The ship shuddered, a loud scraping filling Lara's ears as the chain dragged along their port side. The noise was horrific, wood splintering and cracking, their speed flagging even as the wind eased, the ship slowly righting itself.

"Come on!" Aren shouted while Lara stared up at the soldiers manning the breakwater towers, their eyes wide with astonishment.

Then they were through.

Regaining her footing, Lara stumbled to the side of the ship to look back. Arrows rained down on their wake, fired more in desperation than at any chance of hitting a mark. Nor, she thought, would they risk the catapults mounted on the hills. Her father wanted them captured, not dead. The Maridrinian vessels were crowded up behind the now fully raised chain, the captains shouting at those manning the towers.

"It will take them a bit of time to get the chain reversed. They might chase us all the way to Southwatch." Aren's eyes shifted to the black clouds hanging over the dark ocean, promising wild seas. "The race is on."

# 31
# LARA

THE NAVAL VESSELS gave up chase halfway to Southwatch, though whether it was for fear of the storm brewing in the east or the dozen shipbreakers on the fortified island, it was impossible to say.

Docking the ship at the Southwatch wharf was no mean feat, and Lara's whole body ached with tension as Aren eased the battered ship against the stone, Ithicanian crews on land using rigging attached to the wharf to tie the rocking ship down. She, Aren, and the rest of the crew disembarked swiftly, meeting an older Ithicanian man at the guardhouse mounted where the wharf met the island.

"We did not realize you were in Vencia, Your Grace." The man bowed with more formality than anyone at Midwatch ever used. His gaze skipped past his king to land on Lara, his eyes widening as he inclined his head to her.

"Unplanned trip. Where's the commander?"

Aren's voice was crisp and unwavering, but his left hand clenched and then opened in a repetitive motion that betrayed him. He was *not* looking forward to justifying himself to his sister, that much was certain.

"Off island, Your Grace. She left this morning to deal with a conflict on Carin Island, and I expect she'll need to ride out this storm there."

Aren's hand relaxed. "Tell her I'm sorry to have missed her, but we cannot linger. Have the ship stripped, then sink it."

"As you say, Your Grace." Bowing once again, the man continued down toward the ship, shouting orders as he went.

Lara cast a backward glance at the battered vessel. "Why sink it? Can't you just . . . repaint it?"

"No time to return it to safe harbor before this storm hits. The sea will tear it apart and sink it anyway if we leave it here, which could cause problems with other ships trying to make port. Ahnna will cut my balls off if she has to deal with cleaning up that sort of mess."

"I get the impression that she'll be reaching for her knife anyway when she discovers where you've been."

He laughed, his hand falling against her lower back to guide her up the path. "A little luck on our side that we missed her, then."

"Will she let it go?"

"Not a chance, but hopefully she won't feel inclined to follow us all the way to Midwatch to voice her opinion on the matter."

"Your bravery is inspiring."

"We all have our fears. Now let's get inside before the rain hits."

They didn't linger in the Southwatch market, which would've been a disappointment to Lara if she'd hadn't burned with urgency to return to Midwatch. The market was a series of large stone warehouses, plus one smaller building that Taryn told her was where all the trade was conducted. She longed to see what was inside those buildings, what sort of goods had come from Harendell, Amarid, and beyond, and what would depart from her own homeland. Just as she now found herself longing to talk to the Ithicanians who lived and worked here on Southwatch. To *know* them in a way she, out of necessity, hadn't allowed herself to before.

Because now they felt as much her people as the Maridrinians she'd left behind. On the heels of that realization came a deep and unceasing shame that she, who was their queen and whom they believed to be their defender, had nearly put them on the funeral pyre. Men, women, and children. Families and friends. Most who were innocents dedicated to no more than living their lives—those people, as much as Aren, would've been the individuals she'd have betrayed if her words had reached Serin and her father.

With that knowledge burning in her heart, she was glad when Aren and his guards led her into the yawning black mouth of the bridge.

The Bridge. How she hated the cursed thing, which was the source of every bit of despair in her life. With every step she took down its stinking length, she wished it didn't exist. Wished she'd been sent to Ithicana with no agenda beyond being a wife. Wished she was not her wicked, lying, and traitorous self. But wishes were for fools. Which was perhaps fitting, because her foolish self lost all grasp of logic whenever her sleeve brushed against Aren's, every time his gaze fell upon her, every time she remembered the feel of his hands on her body and how much she desired them there again.

There was no day or night in the bridge. Only endless musty darkness. The storm caused a moaning sound within the tunnel, sometimes little more than a whisper, and other times a deafening roar that forced the group to stuff cotton into their ears. It was like a living beast, and by the end of their first day of walking, Lara was half convinced she'd been consumed.

She could not stay in Ithicana, even if she wanted to. And she did want to. More than anything. But her entire relationship with Aren had been built on a lie, and if she told him the truth, what were the chances he'd forgive her? He loved his people too much to allow someone like her to remain his queen. Neither was keeping it a secret an option. Her father would make her pay for her betrayal. There would be no happily-ever-after. Not for her.

Reluctantly, a plan formed in Lara's mind. Her first order would be to destroy the papers with her planned invasion. Then she'd wait for a clear night, and make a run for her hidden canoe and supplies. All that would be left would be to sail toward revenge. Because she fully intended to make her father pay for what he'd done to Maridrina. What he'd intended to do to Ithicana. And what he'd done to her. Plotting the variables distracted her. Took away the tightness that gripped her chest every time she realized she'd never see Aren again.

From time to time they encountered groups transporting goods. Bored donkeys pulled carts filled with steel, fabrics, and grain southward. Men with handcarts transported crates of Valcottan glassworks northward. And once, after following a stream of spilled ale for several miles, they passed a wagon full of barrels headed north. Jor had jokingly put his head under the leaky barrel until Aren kicked his feet out from under him, then informed the man driving to quit making a mess of his bridge.

Sometimes there were merchants in the caravans, but always they were flanked by Ithicanian guards wearing masks. Before encountering any of them, her own group would don identical masks, and Lara idly wondered what the merchants would think if they knew the rulers of Ithicana had passed them in the darkness.

They made camp in the bridge two nights in a row, eating cold rations they'd picked up at Southwatch with only water to drink. The guards took rotating shifts on watch, everyone sleeping with only their pack for a pillow and their cloaks for blankets. Privacy was nonexistent, and by the third day of walking, Lara was almost frantic to be free of the place.

"Home sweet home," Jor said, and the rest of the group stopped, silently watching while the captain rested both hands against pressure points on the bridge wall. A soft click filled the air, and a door-sized block of stone swung inward on silent hinges, revealing a small chamber with an opening in the floor.

Jor stepped inside and looked down. "Tide's still too high. We'll have to wait a bit."

"I'm taking Lara topside," Aren abruptly stated. "The rest of you wait down here."

No one said anything, Taryn and Jor silently opening the hatch in the ceiling. Aren boosted Lara up, then hauled himself outside. Leaving the hatch open, he walked several dozen paces down the length of the bridge. Lara followed, stopping next to one of the thick steel rings embedded in the rock that the Ithicanians used for their zip lines.

The storm had been short, ending on their second day in the bridge, although another was brewing on the horizon. For now, the sky around Midwatch was clear and sunny, the water below a tranquil blue. The fresh air and open space instantly relieved the oppressive pall the bridge had cast.

"We need to talk, Lara."

Her heart skittered, her veins flooding with trepidation.

"I know you're a spy for your father."

Her stomach hollowed. "I *was* a spy for my father. I am no longer."

"I'm going to need more proof than just your word."

"The proof is that I'm here. With you."

Silence.

When Lara's nerve finally frayed, she asked, "Aren't you going to say something?"

Aren turned to face Midwatch, tension radiating off him. "I suppose one question is obvious: Did you pass any information back to him that I should know about?"

"I've given him nothing." Because she hadn't. Not one single thing. Not with all those damnable pieces of paper still sitting in his desk, waiting for her to destroy them.

He exhaled a long breath. "I suppose that's something."

*Something.*

The need for him to know the reason behind her actions burned in Lara's chest. "Serin and my other teachers, they lied to me. All my life, they lied about the nature of Ithicana, about the relationship between your kingdom and mine. They painted you as a dark oppressor that used its power over trade to suppress my people. To control them. To starve them. All for the sake of profit. They told me that you killed merchants and sailors for no reason other than that they'd come too close to your shores. Not just killed, but maimed and tortured for sport. That you were a demon."

Aren said nothing, so she continued. "They made me believe

that doing this would save my people. That it was righteous. Now I understand that that's why they kept me locked up in the compound—so I might never learn the truth. And they believed you would keep me similarly contained so that I would have no chance to learn the truth until it was too late."

"And what is the truth?"

What was the truth? Lara had no delusions that she was a good person in the way of someone like Marisol. She'd killed Valcottan warriors brought to her compound for no reason other than it was their lives or hers. Learned countless ways to torture, maim, and kill. She'd stood by while the servants who'd cared for her and her sisters since they were children were murdered in cold blood. Had watched while the man who'd been like a father to her slit his own throat out of misplaced guilt. She'd lied and deceived and manipulated, and nearly doomed an entire nation. *Good*, she was not.

Yet neither did she believe that she was evil. She'd condemned herself to this fate in order to save the lives of her sisters, whom she loved above all things. And once here, she'd followed through with her mission on the belief she was saving her people. Noble motivations, perhaps, except she wasn't entirely certain that they absolved her of guilt. Knowing what would happen to Ithicana, she'd still written instructions on how to destroy it. She'd made that choice. All she could do now was try to atone. "The truth is . . . the truth is that *I* am the villain." But she would play that part no longer.

More silence.

"What are you going to do with me?" she asked.

"I don't know, Lara." With his words, the tension between them ratcheted up. "I've . . . suspected for some time now, but hearing you say it . . . I don't know."

A frantic fear fluttered in her chest. A fear that she'd lost him. That he hated her. That he'd never forgive her.

"I didn't give him anything, Aren." She so desperately wanted to salvage what was left between them. "I haven't done anything."

"Haven't done anything?" He whirled around to face her. "How can you claim that? How can you say you've done *nothing* when, from the moment we were married, you've been plotting to stab me in the back? Everything you've said, everything you've done, everything between us has been a damned lie. A way to manipulate me into trusting you so that you could learn Ithicana's secrets, then use them against us. All while I, like a bloody fool, was trying to win you over."

It was the truth, but it wasn't the sum of it. Because during that time, she'd grown to care about him and his kingdom, to understand their plight, and still she'd chosen to destroy them. Had written every detail she'd learned on those pages, a strategy for invading Aren's homeland and stealing away the bridge his people so desperately needed. It had only been sheer *luck* that one of those pages hadn't made it into her father's hands.

"Did you care at all?" he demanded.

"Yes. More than you know. More than I can explain." She shoved the hair that had blown into her face out of her way, grasping for words to make him understand. "But I didn't think there was another way. I believed the only chance my people had was for me to win them the bridge. My whole life has been dedicated to giving them a better future, no matter the cost to me. Surely you of all people can understand that?"

"It's not the same." His voice was cold. "The better future you envisioned was built on the backs of Ithicanian corpses."

Lara closed her eyes. "Then why didn't you just kill me once you knew? Why did you bring me to Vencia, if you suspected? Why did you risk so much?"

Aren scuffed his boot against the bridge, staring at Midwatch. "I realized that you'd been misled. And if the truth gave us a chance, then it was a risk I was willing to take." He let out a ragged breath. "I followed you that night when you walked up to the palace gates. I pointed an arrow at your back, and I . . . I almost did kill you. If you'd taken one more step, I would've." His hands were shaking, the tremor of movement holding her attention like a vice. "But then you turned around and came back. Back to me."

"I couldn't do it." Lara closed her hands over his, needing to stop them from shaking. "And I won't. Not ever. Not even if he tracks me down and kills me for betraying him."

Aren went very still. "Did he threaten you?"

She swallowed hard. "He told me on the ship to Ithicana that if I failed or if I betrayed him, he'd hunt me down."

"If he thinks—"

A scuffle of sound interrupted him, causing them both to jump. Seconds later, with a muttered oath, Ahnna pulled herself out of the hatch, her face a storm cloud.

Aren stepped in front of Lara, walking toward Ahnna even as his sister closed the distance with rapid strides.

"What the hell were you thinking?" Ahnna snapped. "Going into Maridrina yourself? Have you lost your bloody mind?"

"I've been dozens of times before. What of it?"

"Not as king you haven't. You have a responsibility to our people. Plus, you nearly got caught. What the hell would've happened if you had?"

"Then you'd have your chance at the crown."

"You think that's what I want?" Her eyes went past her brother, landing on Lara. "And there stands the worst of it. Bad enough that *you* went, but you took the daughter of our enemy, the woman who, if all the rumors are true, you've been supplying with all of Ithicana's secrets, back to her homeland?"

"I took my *wife* to her homeland for reasons that are none of your goddamned business."

Ahnna's face took on a ghastly pallor, but she balled her hands into fists, and for a heartbeat, Lara thought she'd strike her brother. Strike her king. But all she said was, "There is no reason good enough. She knows enough to allow Maridrina to bring us to our knees, and you practically delivered her to its king. She could've run straight into the Magpie's arms."

"She didn't."

"But what if she had? This wasn't the plan. You were supposed to—"

"I was supposed to what?" Aren lunged forward, looming over his sister. "Keep her locked up here forever? She's my damned wife, not my prisoner."

"Wife? In name only, from what I hear. And don't think that

*everyone* doesn't realize that you're risking your entire kingdom just to get between her legs."

No one spoke. Not Aren or Ahnna. Not the soldiers who'd come topside and were now looking anywhere but at their leaders. And not Lara whose heart felt like it was about to burst from her chest. Because Ahnna's fears were valid. Yet Aren was defending her. Despite knowing she'd come to Ithicana with ill intentions, he was defending her right to a life. Her right to a home. Her right to freedom. And she didn't deserve it. Didn't deserve him.

Before Lara could think through the consequences of what she intended to say, she stepped forward, her boots sliding on the slick surface of the bridge. "Ahnna—"

"Stay out of this." Without looking, the other woman swung an arm to block Lara's path.

The blow caught Lara in the chest and she stumbled back, feet scrabbling.

She was falling.

"Lara!" Aren reached for her, but it was too late.

She screamed, arms flailing as the air rushed past her, but there was nothing to grab. Nothing that would stop the inevitable.

She slammed against the water, the force driving the wind out of her in a rush of bubbles even as she plunged down and down.

Panic raced through her, wild and unchecked, and on its heels came the desperate need to *breathe*. She kicked, thrashing her arms, fighting toward the surface that seemed impossibly far away.

*You will not die.*

*You will not die.*

*You will not* . . . The thought faded and the light of the surface began to dim as she sank into the depths.

Until something grabbed her around the waist.

Lara struggled, reaching blindly for her knife until her face broke the surface and Aren was shouting in her ear, "Breathe, Lara!"

She sucked in a desperate mouthful of air. And another. A wave rolled over her head, and fear filled her anew.

Clawing and grasping, she tried to climb. Tried to get above the water.

Then Aren's face was in front of hers. "Quit fighting me. I've got you, but you need to be still."

It was an impossible request. She was drowning. She was dying.

"I need you to trust me!" His voice was desperate, and somehow it cut through her fear. Brought her back to herself. She quit fighting him.

"Good. Now hold on to me and don't move."

Grasping his shoulders, Lara forced her shaking legs to still. They were not quite beneath the bridge, perhaps two dozen yards from the nearest pier: the narrow one with no access to the bridge. And the shore . . .

"Can we make it?" she asked, spitting out a mouthful of water as another wave splashed her in the face.

"No."

"What do we do?" She twisted, looking up at the bridge. She could hear the soldiers shouting, see Jor hanging off the side from a rope, his finger pointing at the water.

"Quit moving, Lara!"

She froze. Because in that moment, she saw what Jor was pointing at. What had Aren's attention—and his fear.

Grey fins cut through the water.

Circling them.

Moving closer.

"We have to last until they can reach us in a boat."

Her eyes jerked to the distant pier, the opening still concealed by the tide. Then to the cove where two boats had been launched. There was no way they'd make it in time.

As if to punctuate her thought, one of the sharks darted toward them before veering off at the last second.

"Shit," Aren snarled.

The creatures were swimming closer, and Lara sobbed as something smacked against her foot.

The soldiers above began firing arrows, the bolts slicing into the water all around them, blood blossoming when they struck true. Then, seemingly as one, the fins disappeared.

"Aren!" Ahnna's scream echoed from above, and a second later, an enormous fin was slicing through the waves toward them.

"Let me go." Lara made the decision because she knew he wouldn't. "Without you, I'll drown. But if you let it have me, you'll have a chance."

"No."

"Don't be a fool. We don't both have to die."

"Quiet."

Aren's eyes were fixed on the circling shark. "I know you, old girl," he muttered at it before glancing up. "You'll come in for a taste before you come from below for the kill."

"Let me go!"

"No."

Lara shoved away from him, tried to swim, but Aren dragged her back, kicking hard. Pulling her with him.

The shark darted toward them. So fast. Too fast to dodge. Infinitely too fast to out-swim. Fear, primal and base, took hold of her, and Lara screamed.

"Now!"

A steel bolt attached to a cable sliced through the air from above, exploding through the shark's side, but the creature kept coming as though the instinct to hunt mattered more than the wound it had been dealt.

Lara screamed again, choking on water, watching it drive toward them, mouth opening to reveal row after row of razor-sharp teeth.

The cable attached to the bolt went taunt.

In one violent motion, the shark was ripped out of the water, its enormous body thrashing through the air before it slammed down against the sea, fighting against the cable leashing it to the bridge.

Water surged over Lara's head, and the shark's tail slammed against her with the force of a battering ram, tearing her from Aren's grasp.

She floundered, not knowing which way was up. Not knowing where the shark was. Where Aren was. Bubbles raced past her face, obscuring her vision while she kicked and fought. Then hands closed on her wrist, pulling her to the surface.

"Swim!" It wasn't Aren's voice, but those from the soldiers above, Ahnna's voice loudest of all. "All the blood is drawing them in! Swim, goddamned you!"

He dragged her through the water, the waves growing more violent with every surge. And above, the skies grew darker. Lightning flashed in the distance.

Aren stopped swimming.

He treaded water, his breathing ragged with the effort of supporting them both.

Lara saw what he was looking at.

The nearest pier, bristling with metal spikes, the ocean slamming against it with the ferocity of the coming storm.

"You need to . . . grab . . . one of the spikes," he gasped. "Don't let go."

And without waiting for her to respond, he hauled her toward the pier.

The waves caught hold of them with irreversible momentum, launching her and Aren at the stone and steel.

There would be one chance. Only one chance.

Lara sucked in a deep breath, marking the spike she'd reach for. The steel that would be her salvation or her damnation.

Aren twisted at the last minute, taking the impact. Lara fumbled blind, knowing she had only a second.

Her hand closed on the spike even as she felt Aren let her go.

Holding on took all her strength as the water dragged at her legs, her arms shaking with the effort. For a moment, her body hung out of the water, then the waves crashed into her again. She clung to the metal, managing to get her legs over and around it, breathing as the water retreated again.

"Aren!" She searched the water for him, terror filling her heart.

"Here!"

He was dangling from the spike where it was embedded in the rock. But he wouldn't last long.

The water pummeled them again, then above the noise, Lara heard her name. Looking up, she saw Ahnna dangling from a rope above, another line in her hand. She swung it in Lara's direction. "Grab hold!"

The heavy rope whipped past, and Lara reached for it, nearly losing her grip as she did. Again and again the rope swung past her, but she couldn't reach it.

And Aren was running out of time.

So when the rope swung past once more, Lara lunged, knowing that if she missed, she'd fall in the water and that Aren was past the point where he could help her. But that he'd try anyway.

Her balance wavered, her fingers reaching and grasping and catching hold of the rope.

Lara's legs slipped and she was dangling. Silently thanking Erik for every pull-up he'd forced her to do during training, she hauled herself up, hooking the loop under her armpits.

Swinging hard, she caught hold of the spike and crawled hand over hand toward Aren, barely keeping her grip as the water surged against her, drowning her with every pass.

"Grab on to me," she screamed even as a wave knocked her free from her perch.

She swung and slammed against Aren. Instinct had her wrapping her legs around his waist, her arms protesting as his weight dragged against her. Then he was reaching up and gripping the rope.

The sea hurled against them once more, driving them both against rock, and Lara choked and sobbed, knowing she couldn't hold on any longer. Knowing that one more wave would pull her free.

And it was coming, froth flying toward her. Just before it reached them, the rope jerked and they were rising. Faster and faster. They rotated and swung, Aren pulling himself up so that her legs, still wrapped around him, eased the pressure on her arms.

"Do not let go." Blood trickled down a cut on his temple. "You will not let go."

They bumped against the side of the bridge, and Lara whimpered as she was dragged along the rock, but the pain fled in the face of relief as hands grabbed hold of her clothing, hauling her up, laying her down on the solid surface of the bridge. Gasping, she rolled on her side, puking up endless amounts of seawater until all she had the strength for was resting her forehead against the wet stone.

"Lara." Arms pulled her upright, and she turned only to collapse against Aren's chest, clinging to his neck. He was shaking, yet the feel of him against her was more comfort than the solid land beneath her feet.

No one spoke. There were men and women all around them, she knew, but it was as though she were alone with him, the rain from the coming storm pattering against her cheek.

"Aren?" Ahnna's voice broke the silence, the distant boom of thunder echoing his name. "I didn't mean . . . It was . . ."

Lara felt him stiffen, felt his anger even as he said, his voice cold, "Get back to Southwatch, *Commander*. And if I see your face before War Tides, rest assured that I won't hesitate to fulfill Ithicana's contract with Harendell."

Lara turned in his grip in time to see Ahnna jerk as though she'd been slapped. "Yes, Your Majesty." Without another word, she walked away, her soldiers following on her heels.

Rising on shaking legs, Aren pulled Lara with him. "We need to get back to Midwatch. The storm is coming."

But as her heart thudded inside her chest, Lara knew that he was wrong.

The storm was already here.

# 32
# AREN

PULLING OFF THE boots he'd borrowed at the barracks, Aren slowly stripped his sodden and torn clothing, leaving it in a pile on the floor while he eased across the dark room to the wardrobe to retrieve dry trousers. The shutters rattled against the windows as the wind attacked, the rain drumming furiously against the roof, all of it drowned out by bursts of thunder that shook the house to its foundation. The air was full of the sharp, fresh smell of ozone, blending with the ever-present scent of damp earth and greenery that he associated with home.

*Boom*. The ground beneath his feet reverberated, the pressure changing as the typhoon descended in full force. This was a beast of a storm—the sort that gave the Tempest Seas their name. With winds so wild and feral they seemed almost sentient, this storm would leave swaths of destruction in its wake, and anyone or anything caught out in the water would be wiped from the face of the earth. Ithicana was built to endure the worst the sea and sky could unleash, and indeed it was only during these tempests that Aren ever truly breathed easy, certain that his kingdom was safe from its enemies.

But not tonight.

Exhaling, he rested a hand against the post of his bed, searching for some sense of equilibrium, but it was a lost cause. Like so many other things.

Lara hadn't said a word since they'd been pulled from the sea. He couldn't blame her. She'd been nearly drowned. Nearly eaten. Nearly pummeled against rock. She hadn't broken down entirely, which should've felt like a small miracle except that he would've preferred that to the emotionless silence.

Face blanched so white her lips were gray, Lara had followed numbly where she'd been led, her arms limp in his grasp as she'd been examined for injuries. No sign of her dry humor or the venomous tongue that he simultaneously loved and loathed. Just . . . nothing.

Closing his eyes, Aren rested his forehead against the bedpost because the other option was to rip it free and smash it against the wall. Fury, unbridled and burning, rushed through his veins. At Ahnna. At the bridge. At himself.

A sound more animal than human rose in his throat, and in a flurry of motion, he twisted and slammed his fist against the wall. Pain blossomed in his knuckles, and he dropped into a crouch, wanting to explode, wanting to run. Knowing none of it would do any good.

*Boom*. The house shuddered, and his thoughts went to the Rat King's letter, shoved into his bag, wherever that was. The ultimatum was clear: ally with Maridrina against Valcotta or face war and blockades like those Maridrina had imposed fifteen years prior, lifted only with the signing of the treaty.

They had been the darkest of times. Maridrina had kept *anyone* from landing at Southwatch for two years, completely shutting down trade. Nothing was shipped through the bridge, and Ithicana's revenues dried up entirely. Without them, there had been no way to feed his people. To keep them provisioned. To keep them alive. Not with violent storms driving fishermen from the seas more days than not. Famine had swept Ithicana. Plague, too. And the idea of going back to that . . .

The alternative was to join with a man who'd been plotting against him in the worst sort of ways. To join a war he wanted no part of. It was profoundly tempting to formally ally with Valcotta for spite. Ithicana's coffers were strong enough to buy what the kingdom needed for a year or more with no additional revenue from the bridge. Between Southwatch's shipbreakers and the strength of Valcotta's fleets, Silas's armies wouldn't have a chance.

Yet such an action would place all the suffering on Maridrina's people. *Lara's* people.

Condemning them to starvation would make him the villain the Magpie had painted. Aren would become the man Lara had been raised to hate. But to cede to her father's request would mean jeopardizing Ithicana when Valcotta came for retribution. There was no solution.

His father's voice danced through Aren's head, words shouted at his mother. *Ithicana makes no alliances. We are neutral—we have to be, or war will come for us.* But like his mother before him, Aren now believed the time for neutrality had come to an end. Except there was a difference between desiring an alliance and allowing its terms to be dictated by another man.

Aren wavered, then in two strides, he was at his desk. Flipping open the hidden compartment, Aren extracted the letter he'd started to Silas those months ago. Staring at the polite greeting and appropriate honorifics, he shoved the page aside, reaching for a clean sheet.

*Silas,*

*Ithicana will not cease trade with Valcotta. Should you wish to see an end to their naval aggression, I suggest you desist in your attacks on Valcotta's northern border. Only with peace between your two nations does Maridrina have the chance to return to health and prosperity. As to your insinuation that Ithicana has not held to the spirit of the agreement between our nations, we feel it necessary to point out your hypocrisy in making such a claim. In the best interests of both our peoples, we will forgive your schemes and allow Maridrina to continue to trade at Southwatch market under the terms agreed upon. Let it be said, however, that should you seek to retaliate against your spy, Ithicana will take it as an act of aggression against its queen, and the alliance between our kingdoms will be irrevocably severed.*

*Choose wisely.*

*Aren*

He stared at the letter, knowing he could never tell Lara what he had written. Her life had been dedicated to easing the plight of her people, and she wouldn't forgive him threatening those very same people for the sake of protecting her. Yet there could be no other way to ensure Silas wouldn't harm her. God help him if he was forced to follow through.

Rising, Aren stepped out into the hallway, walking until he found Eli.

"Bring this to the barracks when the storm eases. Tell Jor it's to be sent immediately to the King of Maridrina."

Retreating to his rooms, Aren opened the door to the courtyard. And stepped out into the storm.

# 33
# LARA

LARA LANDED WITH a thump on her knees, knife gripped in one hand. Darkness surrounded her. Thunder rumbled through the room, followed by two flashes of lightning that faintly illuminated the outline of a window. The wood floor beneath her was polished smooth, and the air was thick with moisture and the earthy scent of jungle.

Hot tears ran down her face, and she scrubbed them off her cheeks. The moment she'd returned to Midwatch, she intended to find her way into Aren's room to destroy the damnable proof of her betrayal before it could go any further. To do it without him knowing because she could never let him read those words.

It was one thing for him to know that she'd lied to him. Manipulated him. Deceived him. Quite another to read the proof of it. For him to see every moment that he'd believed a connection was growing between the two of them had been a strategy to gain the information she needed. That, after all they'd been through, she had still made the choice to destroy him that fateful night he'd kissed her in the mud.

Not only was it unforgivable, the amount of hurt it would cause him to read it . . . She couldn't let that happen. Not when simply destroying the pages would eliminate all the evidence. Her plan had been to lightly drug Aren at dinner, then to sneak into his room and start a small fire on his desk that could easily be blamed on a candle left too close to a piece of paper. She could then claim to have smelled the smoke, her screams and pounding on the door enough to wake him and alert the staff. Between the flames and the water it would take to douse them, all the stationery bearing her invisible message would be ruined beyond use. It was a dangerous, damaging plan, but she'd rather chance burning the Midwatch house to the ground than risk Aren questioning why all of his stationery had mysteriously gone missing.

But while Lara had waited for the dinner hour, exhaustion had taken over, and she'd fallen asleep on the clean soft sheets of her bed. Now the scents of dinner were wafting under the door, and she wasn't the least bit prepared.

"You can fix this," she muttered, climbing to her feet. Pulling on one of her silken Maridrinian dresses and running a brush through her hair, Lara's mind raced as she shoved a vial of narcotic into her bracelet. Out in the hallway, she hurried toward the shuttered dining room, certain she'd find Aren there. He was not one to neglect his stomach.

But there was only Eli, who started at the sight of her. "We thought you'd want dinner in your room, my lady," he said. "Do you wish to eat in here instead?"

"Thank you, but I'm not hungry. Do you know where he is?" There was only one *he* in this house.

"His rooms, my lady. He didn't want dinner."

Logic and her training whispered that she should wait for another night. Another opportunity. Better to do that than risk being caught. Yet Lara found herself instead hurrying down the opposite hall to Aren's room, her bare feet silent on the cool floor.

She knocked, then waited. No answer.

She tried the handle and, for once, found it unlocked. "Aren?"

Aren was nowhere in sight. *This was her chance. She could pretend she found the fire burning.*

Securing the door, Lara bolted to the heavy desk, immediately spying the open stationery box. And the beginnings of a letter composed to her father.

Her heart in her throat, Lara stared at the few lines of dried ink addressed to her father. How Aren could stomach being so polite to his enemy was beyond her. Though perhaps that he couldn't stomach it was the reason the letter wasn't finished.

A purr caught her attention, and she looked down as Aren's cat began to wind his huge body between her legs, nearly knocking her over. An idea, one better and far less damaging than a fire, jumped into her head. "Sorry for this Vitex. But I need your help."

She staged the scene, placing the box on its side on the floor, then splattering the letter with ink, leaving the well overturned on the rest of the pages so they were soaked through and unusable. But not before counting the stack. Twenty-five blank pages plus the unfinished letter made for twenty-six.

Luring Vitex over, she scratched his ears, gently taking hold of one of his paws and using it to make distinctive prints through the ink. Realizing what she was doing, the cat hissed at her and pulled away, leaving a trail across the room as he went.

Every muscle in her body twitched, and with a ragged gasp, Lara sank to her knees, staring at what had been the culmination of all her efforts. Of all her training. Of her life. Remembering the way she'd felt the last time she held those pages, knowing that the damning words she'd written would save her people. How wrong she'd been.

Yet with them gone so went the weight she'd been carrying since she'd learned the truth of her father's deception. What she'd done before . . . It had been awful. The worst sort of betrayal. But it had been motivated by lies that had filled her ears almost her entire life. Whereas turning on her father now was an act driven by the truth. What she was doing now was her own choice.

And though Lara knew that she'd painted a target on her back, that her father's assassins would never stop hunting her, for the first time in her life, she felt free.

Driven by some strange sixth sense, she drifted into the antechamber and opened the door to the courtyard, the wind buffeting her with the force of a giant. Stepping outside, she found herself in a hell of wind and rain.

The air shrieked as it circled the courtyard, carrying leaves and branches and rain that bit into her bare arms and slapped her cheeks. The tempest was deafening in its fury, multipronged bolts lancing across the sky, the thunder battering her eardrums.

In the midst of it stood Aren.

He was shirtless and barefoot, staring up at the sky, seemingly heedless of the tempest circling around him. Or of the danger he was in.

A branch ripped from one of the trees to hurtle across the yard, exploding against the side of the house. "Aren!" But the storm drowned out her voice.

It was impossible to keep her feet as she struggled down the path, knocked over time and again by gusts of wind that threatened to lift her into the air. Her hair whipped in a wild frenzy, blinding her, but not for a heartbeat did she consider turning back. Regaining her feet on the slick stones, she lunged.

The winds died as her hands closed on Aren's arms, as though the world itself gave a sigh and relaxed, the debris falling softly to the ground and the rain easing into a gentle patter against her skin.

"Lara?"

Releasing a ragged breath, she tilted her face up to find Aren staring down at her, his expression bewildered, as though he couldn't comprehend how she'd come to be standing before him.

"Is it over?" she asked, finding it difficult to breathe. And even more difficult to think. "The storm?"

"No. We're in the eye of it now."

*The eye of the storm.* Her chest tightened. "What are you doing out here?"

The hard muscles of his forearms flexed beneath her grip. "I needed it."

Instinctively, she understood what he meant. Most people sought solace from danger, but for him, the danger was solace. The rush of adrenaline that cleared his mind, that wiped away the uncertainty that plagued every decision he made as king. The fear of erring. The consequences of doing so. In the storm, he knew his path.

She understood, because she felt the same way. "You could've died today. Doing what you did."

"You would've died if I hadn't."

His hands closed around her arms, and though his palms were feverishly hot, Lara shivered. "You might have been better off if I had."

His grip tightened. "Do you honestly believe that I could have ever forgiven myself if I'd stood there and watched you drown?"

"But what I did—"

"Is in the past. It's behind us now."

Her pulse was a dull roar in her ears as his words sank in. Aren had forgiven her. How he'd found it in his heart to do so, she couldn't understand, but there it was. What she'd wanted more than anything, but hadn't had the hope to wish for.

"Do you want to leave Ithicana? Because if that's what it takes for you to be happy, I'll set you on any shore you wish with everything you need to make a life for yourself."

Lara had planned to leave. Her father's assassins would soon been on her heels, and she hadn't believed there was anything to be gained by staying. A relationship between the two of them would never have a chance—Aren would inevitably discover the truth about her and would never forgive her for it.

But Aren knew the truth. And against all odds, he had forgiven her. Now . . . now the thought of turning her back on this place, of turning her back on *him*, was the worst future she could imagine.

"You can't let me leave Ithicana." Her throat felt tight, and the words came out breathy and strange. "I know too much. You'd be risking too much."

His eyes burned into hers, and never in her life had she felt like someone else saw her so perfectly. "I can let you go, because I trust you."

She couldn't breathe.

"I don't want to leave." The words were a truth dug from the depths of her heart. She did not want to leave Ithicana. She did not want to leave *him*. She wanted to stay, to fight and sweat and bleed for him and his harsh, wild, and beautiful kingdom.

The storm circled, watching but leaving them untouched for this one moment.

Aren's hands loosened on her arms, and for one terrifying heartbeat, she thought he'd let her go. That he wanted her to go.

Instead his fingers traced up the backs of her arms, the light touch leaving rivers of sensation in their wake. Gentle strokes up and down, as though he were calming some wild thing that was apt to bite.

Or testing the waters.

His hands grazed the sides of her breasts, and Lara exhaled a soft breath as his thumbs hooked on the straps of her dress, easing them down as he bent, his lips brushing one naked shoulder. Then the other.

A whimper escaped her as Aren pulled her damp hair away, exposing her neck and kissing her collarbone, her throat, the line of her jaw. Only his grip on her dress kept it from falling away and leaving her naked before him.

Lara wanted to touch him.

Wanted to feel his sleek skin stretched over hard muscles, but she was afraid, because she knew to do so would be her undoing. There would be no turning back.

Aren's lips paused, and she held her breath, waiting for them to descend on her own even as she wondered whether, if she allowed herself to sink into this hot pool of desire, she'd ever surface again. Whether she'd want to.

But he only rested his forehead against hers. "I need you to say that you want this, Lara. That you're allowing this because you choose to, not because it was forced upon you."

Her chest burned, and emotion so intense it hurt surged through her. She pulled back so their eyes locked. "I want this." And because that wasn't the sum of it, she added, "I want you."

The storm returned with a vengeance as their lips collided, but Lara barely felt the winds as Aren lifted her against him, his hands gripping her hips as she wrapped her legs around his waist, her arms sliding around his neck. His mouth was hot, his tongue slick against hers, the rain drenching their skin as he carried her through the tempest and into the shelter of the house.

Inside, his feet slid on the wet tile and they slammed against the wall, knocking what remained on the shelves to the floor. He braced himself, his hands to either side of her, his breath hot against her throat as Lara ground against him. Her heels dug into his back as she pulled him closer, wanting nothing between them, even as the friction of his belt against her dragged a moan from her lips.

Her back arched until only her head touched the wall behind her, and her dress, the skirt already bunched around her waist, was pulled down to expose the top of her breasts. She felt Aren's breath catch.

"God, you're beautiful," he growled. "Insufferable and venom-tongued and the most incredible woman I've set eyes on."

His words made her thighs slick and she gasped. "Door. Shut the damned door."

"Yes, Your Majesty." He slipped his tongue into her mouth, tasting her, before allowing her to slide to the ground, the hardness of him pressing against her stomach before he turned to wrench on the door and shut out the storm.

The heavy bolt in place, Aren stalked toward her, his hazel eyes predatory, ever the hunter. Lara stepped backward into the bedroom, daring him to follow. Luring him in because she was not, and never would be, anyone's prey. Her calves hit the solid wood of his bed, and she stared him down, stopping him in his tracks.

The howl of the wind was muffled now, and over it, she could hear him breathing. Each inhale and exhale ratcheted up her need as her eyes roved over his body, marking the way the muscles in his jaw flexed as he watched her with equal focus.

Reaching blindly for the lantern, Lara turned the flame up high, then set it to one side, her eyes never leaving his. Clasping hold of the sodden bodice of her dress, the neckline clinging to her peaked nipples, she slowly peeled the silk from her body, discarding the garment on the floor. Then she lay back on the bed, resting her weight on her elbows. With deliberate slowness, Lara allowed her knees to fall open.

She watched his control snap, watched as he held his ground only because of the strength of her stare, his desire apparent against the rain-soaked trousers that were all he wore. "Take them off," she commanded, his low laugh making her skin prickle with the need to have his hands on her once more.

He unbuckled his belt, then hooked his thumbs over it and pushed, the weight of the knife fastened to it dragging his trousers to the floor, where he kicked them aside. This time it was Lara's turn to catch her breath as she took in the hard length of him, for while she'd seen him naked before, it had never been like *this*. Her thighs trembled beneath the floodgate of her *need* to have him, and she nodded once.

In three strides, he was across the room, but rather than pinning her to the bed, as she'd thought he would, he fell to his knees before her. Ithicana—and its king—bent to nothing and no one. But he bent for her.

Aren kissed the inside of her left knee. Then her right knee, lingering on an old scar that ran halfway up her inner thigh. His hands, rough with callouses earned defending his kingdom, caught hold of her legs. And with her quivering beneath his grip, he lowered his face and slid his tongue inside of her.

Her hips bucked, but he held her against the bed, licking and sucking at the apex of her thighs until a moan tore from her lips. She fell back against the sheet, hands reaching for him, pulling at him, but he only lifted his head long enough to give her a feral smirk before sliding his fingers into the spot his tongue had just vacated.

Lara's back bowed and she grabbed at the edge of the bed, the world tilting as he caressed the inside of her, his mouth consuming her again, the pressure building deep in her core. Lightning flashed as his teeth grazed her and the world shattered, her vision fracturing as waves of pleasure washed over her until she was left gasping and trembling.

Aren didn't move for a long moment, then with tenderness that broke her heart, he kissed her stomach before resting his cheek against it, her fingers tangling in his hair.

But she wasn't done with him. Nor he with her.

He climbed over her with the grace of a panther on the hunt. Catching hold of her hands, he pinned her arms over her head, his knuckles digging into the mattress. For a heartbeat, she resisted, pushing against his far superior strength. And then her body yielded. Not to him, but to herself. To what she wanted. Her life had been spent as an unwitting pawn in her father's machinations, but no longer. Every victory or mistake, every tender touch or fit of violence . . . They would be hers now. She would own them. She would own this moment.

Lifting her head, she kissed him and felt him shudder as she locked her legs around his waist, drawing him down so their bodies pressed together. The kiss deepened, all tongues and teeth, heavy breaths more felt than heard over the rumble of thunder.

The tip of him brushed against her, and Lara moaned into his mouth, her body knowing what it wanted, desperate for him to fill her. She ground her hips against him, gasping as his cock teased inside of her before pulling away.

"Not everything will be on your terms, love," he growled into her ear. "I will not be rushed."

"You are a demon after all," she whispered, but her ability to speak vanished as he released his grip on her wrists and his face lowered to her breast, mouth sucking and teasing her nipple, his hand back between her legs. Her own hands drifted to his shoulders, fingers trailing over the hard curves of his muscles, tracing the lines of old scars and new, then down his spine, relishing the way he shivered beneath her touch.

But it wasn't enough. She bit at his neck, wanting him closer, wanting their bodies and souls to merge, never again to part.

"Aren. *Please*."

He reared back, taking her with him. On his knees, he held her against him, eyes locked on hers as he slowly lowered her onto his length. Head falling back, Lara shrieked into the storm, clawing at his shoulders as he sank into her and then stilled.

"Look at me."

She did, pressing her cheek against his hand as he reached up to cup the side of her head. "I love you," he said, his lips grazing against hers. "And I *will* love you, no matter what the future brings. No matter how hard I need to fight. I will always love you."

The words undid her, broke her apart completely, then forged her into something new. Something stronger. Something better. She kissed him, long and hard and deep, their bodies rocking together.

Lowering her back to the sheets, he pulled out, then thrust back in with torturous slowness. Then again. And again. With each pounding stroke, their bodies grew slick with sweat. She gripped his hand, her other hand dragging through his hair, down his back, needing to possess every inch of him as her own body tightened, burning, burning toward release.

She would fight for him.

She would bleed for him.

She would die for him.

Because he was her king, and even if it meant assassins hunting her for the rest of her days, she would damned well be Ithicana's queen.

Release washed over her, violent as the tempest battering her kingdom, and she felt her body's pleasure pull Aren over the edge. He buried himself to the hilt, howling her name as the room shuddered beneath the onslaught of the storm, then collapsed, his breath ragged pants in her ear.

They barely moved for what seemed hours. Lara curled into the warmth of his arms, her mind drifting as he stroked her naked back, as he covered her with a sheet when the sweat on their bodies began to cool. It was only when his breathing turned to the soft measure of slumber that she lifted her head.

Brushing the hair back from his forehead, she gently kissed him. And because she needed to say it, but wasn't ready for him to hear, she whispered, "I love you."

With her head resting against his chest and his heartbeat in her ear, she finally allowed sleep to take her.

# 34
# LARA

THE TYPHOON RAGED for four days, most of which Lara and Aren spent in bed. Very little of it did they spend sleeping.

Moments outside the bedroom were spent playing cards and peculiar Ithicanian board games, for which Aren was a terrible cheater. Hours of her reading aloud while his head rested in her lap, his eyes distant as he listened, his fingers interlocked with hers. He told stories of his childhood in Ithicana, which mostly seemed to involve avoiding his tutors in favor of running amok through the jungle until Jor chased him down. He told her about the first time he, Taryn, and Lia had raced for their lives on Snake Island, taking turns while their friends watched from boats on the water.

"What about Ahnna?"

Aren snorted. "She isn't stupid enough for such stunts."

There was an edge to his voice that caused Lara to set her glass of juice down on the table with a loud clink. "You need to apologize to your sister for what you said. It was uncalled for."

Aren turned away, shoving a book back on the shelf and draining his own drink. "She almost got you killed."

"It was an accident. And lest you weren't paying attention, she was also the one to save both our asses."

"Noted."

"Aren."

He refilled his drink. "I've said worse to her, and she to me. She'll get over it."

Lara chewed the insides of her cheeks, understanding that it was not reluctance to apologize, but rather the knowledge that he'd be asked to justify his actions as pertained to *her*. "There is a substantial difference between cruel words exchanged between siblings and threats uttered by a king to the commander of his armies."

He gave her a belabored sigh. "Fine, fine. I'll apologize when I see her next."

"Which will be when?"

"God, but you are persistent."

Lara gave him her sweetest smile.

"The council meeting before the beginning of War Tides when we discuss our strategy. Ahnna represents Southwatch, so she has to be there."

Her mouth opened to ask *where* precisely the meeting would take place, but then she shut it again. These past days Lara had been careful not to pry into any details a spy might be interested in, cautious of giving Aren any reason to doubt her loyalty. Part of her wondered if that would ever change, or if her past would always tarnish their relationship.

"Why don't you ever talk about your sisters?"

*Her sisters*. Lara closed her eyes, fighting the unexpected burn of tears. It was a conscious effort on her part to think of them as little as possible. In part, it was to avoid the pain in her chest that came with remembrance, the gut-wrenching sense of loss that came every time she realized that she'd likely never see them again. The other part was her fear that if she kept them too close to mind, she might accidentally reveal they were still alive, and that information might get back to her father. And for their sakes, she couldn't even trust Aren with the truth, for if he ever found cause to turn on her, he might do so by turning on them. "They're dead."

The glass slipped from his hand to smash against the floor. "You aren't serious?"

Lara dropped to her knees to pick up the fragments. "Everyone who knew about my father's plot was killed, with the exception of Serin."

"All of them? Are you sure?"

"I left them facedown on the dinner table, surrounded by flames." She remembered the feel of Marylyn's golden blond hair beneath her fingers as she had moved her sister's head out of the soup bowl. The way she, her father, and all of their party had ridden away from the compound, her sisters abandoned to luck and their own wits. A bit of glass pricked her finger and she hissed, sucking the blood from the wound before returning to the task.

Aren's hands closed over hers. "Leave it, love. Someone else will clean it up."

"I don't want Eli doing it." She picked up another fragment of glass. "He tries to do everything too quickly, and he's sure to cut himself."

"Then I'll do it myself."

The shards of glass fell from her hands, and she watched how the bits of amber liquid on them caught the light. There was still so much she hadn't told him.

"My childhood was ugly. They tried to turn us into monsters. It might be that they succeeded."

The only sound was the rain outside.

"That day of the attack on Serrith Island . . . There were a dozen or so dead Amaridians on the path leading up from the cove."

"I killed them, if that's what you're asking."

"All of them?"

"Yes. You were outnumbered, and your death wasn't . . . It wasn't part of my plan."

He exhaled a long breath, then repeated, "Wasn't part of your plan."

Though Aren knew the truth and had forgiven her for it, part of Lara still feared that he'd change his mind. That these past few days were nothing but a trick: a way to show her what might have been if she'd come to this marriage without betrayal in her heart.

He drew Lara to her feet. "No one can know. About any of it. Too many of my people were against this union to begin with. If they learned you were a spy—and a trained assassin—sent to infiltrate our defenses, they'd never forgive it. They'd demand your execution, and if I didn't agree to it . . ."

Lara felt the blood drain from her face. Not because of the threat to her life, but because of the threat to his. "Is it better for you if I go? We can fake my death, and all the troubles my being here present will be solved."

Aren didn't respond, and when she finally found the nerve to lift her head, it was to find him staring off into the distance, eyes unfocused. Then he shook his head sharply. "I swore a vow to you, and I intend to keep it."

Lara's chest tightened. "My father will send assassins for me. Anyone close to me will be in danger."

"Not if they don't know where you are."

"They know I'm at Midwatch, Aren. And it's not as impenetrable as you seem to think. My father won't let my betrayal go easily."

"I'm aware of Midwatch's limitations, which is why we won't be staying here." He pulled her into his arms. "And your father *will* let it go if he believes the cost of revenge more than he wishes to pay."

Revenge was worth any price to her father. "Let me go back to Maridrina. Let me kill him and end this."

"I'm not using you to murder my enemies."

"He's my enemy, too. And the enemy of the Maridrinian people."

"I don't disagree." Aren's hand moved up and down her spine. "But assassinating your father will accomplish the exact opposite of what we're working toward. Even if Serin can't prove it was Ithicana, he'll cast the blame at our feet, and it won't be long until the Maridrinian people forget Silas the tyrant and start demanding vengeance for Silas the martyr. Your eldest brother is cut from the same cloth as your father, and I don't intend to hand him an army set on Ithicanian blood.

"If they attacked," he continued, "we could likely convince

Valcotta to ally with us and crush them, but it would be *your* people who suffered. And at the end of it, we'd be back to the same place as we were fifteen years ago, our peoples hating each other."

"So we do nothing, then?" Everything he said was true, but Lara couldn't keep the bitterness from her voice.

"We watch. We prepare. But . . ." He shrugged one shoulder. "Any action we might take at this point would cause more harm than good."

"With Valcotta attacking Maridrinian merchants attempting to land at Southwatch, my homeland will continue to go hungry."

"It would all resolve if your father would give up the war with Valcotta. Let farmers return to their fields and tradesmen to their trades."

But he wouldn't. Lara knew that for certain because her father would never concede defeat.

"As it is, storm season will help by chasing the Valcottan's back to their harbors. Vencia's harbor is the closest of any to Southwatch, and your people will capitalize on the short breaks in the storms. Impossible as it is to believe, the storm season is better for your countrymen than the calm. Food *will* arrive on Maridrina's shores."

Aren wouldn't lie to her—Lara believed that. She trusted him. Even if it killed her to do nothing.

He was quiet for a long time, then he said, "But there are two sides to this, Lara. Very few Ithicanians have ever left our shores. Very few of them have ever met a Maridrinian. The result is that they believe your father is the sum of your people. I need you to help me change that. I need you to make them see that Maridrinians are not our enemies. To make them want more than just an alliance of paper and words between kings, but an alliance between our people. Because that's the only way we'll ever find peace."

"I don't see how that can happen while he lives."

"He won't live forever."

Lara exhaled a long breath. "But my brother, as you say, is just like him. He'll take advantage of the utopia you envision."

"I don't envision a utopia, Lara. Just something better." He kissed her shoulder, his lips warm. "It's past time we stopped allowing our enemies to dictate our lives and start living them for those we love.

And for ourselves."

"A dream."

"Then make it reality." Reaching into his trouser pockets, he extracted a small silken pouch. "I have something for you."

Lara's head turned, her eyes widening as he extracted the delicate links of gold, emeralds and black diamonds flashing in the light. "You mentioned a fondness for green."

Carefully, he brushed her hair to one side and fastened the necklace around her neck. "It was my mother's. My father had it made for her years ago, and she almost never took it off. The servants found it in their rooms after—" He broke off, shaking his head to clear the emotion. "She always said it was meant to be worn."

Lara trailed one finger down the gold and jewels, then pulled it away, her hand balling into a fist. "I can't take this. Ahnna should have it."

"Ahnna hates jewelry. And besides, you're Queen of Ithicana. You're the one who should wear it."

Taking her hands in his, Aren turned her toward the large mirror on the wall and pressed the fingers of her hand against the large black diamond resting at the center of her collarbone, her pulse throbbing beneath. "Northwatch." Then he moved down the necklace, naming the larger islands as he went.

"Serrith." He paused there, kissing her shoulder, grazing his teeth against her neck, feeling her body hitch, then press against him, her head falling back against his shoulder. "Midwatch." Their fingers trailed over the slope of her right breast, pausing on a large emerald. He made a humming noise of consideration, then continued down the jeweled map, stopping at Southwatch, the emerald nestled in her cleavage.

"It's yours," he murmured into her ear. "Ithicana. Everything that I have is yours. To protect. To make better."

"I will," she whispered. "I promise." Turning, Lara rested her forehead against his chest, focusing on the feel of his hands. On the sound of his heart.

Then he went still. "Listen."

"I don't hear anything."

"Exactly. The storm has passed. Which means it will have ended south of here, so the Vencia ferrymen will already be on the water heading to Southwatch."

So strange that she had to put her faith in the Tempest Seas, which she feared more than anything else, to protect both her peoples. Slowly, the tension seeped out of her. "Since it's safe to go outside, I find myself fancying a proper bath."

"Your wish is my command, Your Majesty," he growled into her ear, flipping her over his shoulder and heading to the door. In the hallway, they encountered Eli, who bore a stuffed satchel on one shoulder.

"I'm doing a run to the barracks, Your Graces. Any messages you wish to relay?"

Aren hesitated. "Yes. Tell Jor I want to see him. *After* lunch." He patted Lara meaningfully on the ass, laughing when she kneed him in the chest. "But for now, I need a bath."

Several hours later, they were finishing a meal of grilled fish and citrus sauce when the door to the house slammed open.

Heedless of his mud-splattered boots, Jor tromped into the dining room and took a seat across from them. "Majesties." His twinkling eyes moved back and forth between Lara and Aren as he snaked a cake from the tray. "How nice to see the two of you finally playing nice."

Lara's cheeks warmed, and she took a mouthful of fruit juice, hoping the glass would hide her embarrassment.

"And all it took to earn your affection was the poor boy jumping into shark-infested waters to save your ass." He sighed dramatically. "I'm not sure I'm up for such acts of heroism. I suppose I'll have to put aside the dream of taking you on when Aren gets himself killed with one of his stupid stunts."

"Piss off, Jor."

Lara only smiled. "Fortunately for you, I have a soft spot for elderly men."

"Elderly?" Bits of cake flew from the guard's mouth. "I'll have you know, little miss, that I'm . . ."

"Enough, enough." Aren filled the cup in front of Jor. "That's not why you're here."

"Yes, do tell me why I had to drag my *elderly* ass up the hill to visit you two lovebirds."

Lara turned in her chair to eye Aren, curious.

"How do the skies look?" he asked.

"Stick your head out the door and see for yourself."

"Jor."

"Clear." The guard chewed slowly on another cake, brow furrowed with suspicion. "Why?"

Aren's hand closed over Lara's, his thumb tracing a circle against her palm. "Tell everyone to pack their things and ready the boats. I think it's time we went home."

# 35
# LARA

HOME.

To Lara, Midwatch was home, with its quiet serenity. But there was no mistaking the excitement on the faces of the guards as they tied their packs and loads of provision into a trio of boats, nearly tripping over each other in their haste. Wherever they were going was home for them, too, and the flurry of activity only bolstered Lara's curiosity. There were no civilizations of size in Ithicana, nothing bigger than a fishing village, and the Maridrinian in her struggled to believe that the King of the Bridge Kingdom would call one of those home.

"Where are we going?" she asked Aren for the hundredth time.

He only gave her an amused smile and tossed her bag of possessions into the canoe. "You'll see."

She'd barely been allowed to take anything, only a set of her Ithicanian clothes, a selection of undergarments, and, at Aren's request, one of her silk Maridrinian dresses, though of what use that would be in a fishing village, she didn't know.

Nibbling on a fresh piece of root to help keep her stomach calm,

Lara settled into the boat, staying out of the way as they exited the cove. Though the skies were relatively calm, the sea was full of branches and debris, and through the mist draping Midwatch, Lara noted the jungle had been severely damaged by the storm, trees felled and plants stripped of flowers and leaves.

The boats passed under the bridge, the island fading from sight, and Lara turned her gaze ahead as the sail was lifted, the brisk winds whisking them across the surf. They veered west, away from the snaking bridge, passing innumerable tiny landmasses, all which appeared uninhabited, although well she knew that in Ithicana, appearances could be deceiving.

They sailed for an hour when, rounding a smaller island, Lara's eyes fell upon a veritable mountain rising out of the ocean. *Not a mountain,* she silently corrected herself. *A volcano.* The island itself was several times the size of Midwatch, the slopes of the volcano, which reached up to the sky, thick with verdant jungle. Azure waters slammed against cliff walls fifty feet high, with no signs of a beach or a cove. Impenetrable and, if the smoke rising from the peak was any indication, a dangerous place to inhabit.

Yet as they curved around the monolith, Jor lowered a sail, easing their speed even as Lia rose to her feet, hand balanced against Taryn's shoulder as she scanned their surroundings. "No sails on the horizon," she declared, and Aren nodded. "Run up the flag then."

The bright green flag bisected by a curved black line was unfurled and raised to the top of the mast, the wind catching at it with an eagerness that was reflected on the faces of all the Ithicanians. They drew closer to the island and, shading her eyes with her hand against the glare off the water, Lara picked out a dark opening in the otherwise solid cliff walls.

The entrance to the sea cave grew as the boats approached, barely enough clearance for the masts as they drifted inward, the darkness obscuring whatever lay within.

Lara's heart thundered in her chest, realizing that she was witnessing something that no other outsider had seen. A place that was wholly the domain of Ithicana. A secret greater, perhaps, than even those of its precious bridge.

A deafening rattle made Lara jump. Aren's hand rested against her back to steady her as everyone's eyes adjusted to the dimness. Blinking, she watched in awe as a steel portcullis covered with seaweed and barnacles lifted into a narrow gap in the rock of the ceiling and the three boats were gently washed into a tunnel that bent to the right. Gripping the sides of the boat, Lara held her breath as Taryn and Lia rowed them inward, the tunnel opening into an enormous cavern. Sunlight filtered down through small openings in the ceiling to dance across the smooth water, and the floor of the cave seemed within arm's reach, though Lara suspected it was far deeper.

Moored to the walls were dozens of boats, including the large ones she'd seen evacuating the village on Serrith Island. Half-dressed children swam among them, their shrieks of laughter audible as the rattle of the portcullis descending behind them faded away. There were shouts of recognition as the children caught sight of Aren and his guards, and the lot of them fell in like a school of fish around the boats. Jor laughed, pretending to swat at them with a paddle as they made their way to the far end of the cavern where steps carved into the dark rock led upward.

The children's voices filling her ears, Lara allowed Aren to help her out of the boat, her legs unsteady beneath her. *What was this place?*

Her sweating hand resting on Aren's arm, Lara walked up the stairs toward the sunlit opening, her heart pounding in her chest. Together, they stepped out, and a gust of briny wind caught at Lara's hair, tearing it loose from its braid. The brightness bit at her eyes, and she blinked, half to clear the tears and half because she couldn't believe what she was seeing.

It was a city.

Covering the steep slopes of the volcano crater, the city's streets and houses and gardens all wove seamlessly into the natural vegetation, all of it reflected in an emerald lake which pooled in the basin. Releasing Aren's arm, Lara turned in a circle, struggling to take in the magnitude of this place that shouldn't, that couldn't, possibly exist.

Men and women dressed in tunics and trousers went about their business, and countless children ran amok, likely enjoying the respite from poor weather. There were hundreds of people, and she had no doubt that many more could be found within the structures that were built into the slope, made from the same solid material as the bridge. Trees and vines wrapped around the homes, their roots digging deep into the earth, the greys and greens broken by countless blooms every color of the rainbow. Metal chimes hung from tree branches, and with every breath of wind, their delicate music filled the air.

Every bit a king surveying his kingdom, Aren said, "Welcome to Eranahl."

# 36
# AREN

IT WAS THE worst storm season Aren had ever seen.

Typhoon after typhoon lashed Ithicana, sea and wind and rain battering the fortress that was Eranahl, keeping it even more isolated than normal. The city was forced to dig into its supplies, and it would be a mad dash to restock the vaults before War Tides descended and the city's population tripled, those living on the islands close to the bridge coming to take shelter from the inevitable raiders. They'd bring supplies with them, but with months of only limited clear days to fish and gather, they'd be running lean themselves.

Which meant the bridge would need to provide.

Yet it had been painfully easy not to think about the looming dangers in the intervening months since he'd brought Lara home to Eranahl. Easy to sit around the table with his friends, drinking and eating, laughing and telling stories into the darkness of the night. Easy to lose himself in a book without the anticipation of horns calling warnings of raiders. Easy to sleep late in the morning, his arms wrapped around his wife's slender form. To wake and worship the curves of her body, the taste of her mouth, the feel of her hands on his back, in his hair, on his cock.

There were days it felt like Lara had been with him all his life, for she had wholly immersed herself in every aspect of his being. In every aspect of Eranahl. He'd feared that she'd struggle to integrate herself with his people and them with her. But within a month, she'd learned the name of every citizen and how each of them was related, and Aren often found her working with the people, helping them when they were sick and injured. Most of Lara's time was spent with the youth of Ithicana, partially because they held fewer of the biases against Maridrinians than their parents and grandparents and partially, he thought, because it gave her a sense of purpose. She started a school, for while her asshole of a father might have treated her poorly, he hadn't scrimped on her education, and her efforts to share that knowledge won her more hearts than even her heroics at Aela Island.

Lara made his friends hers, going toe to toe with Jor over who could tell the worst jokes, drinking and eating and laughing as she delved into their lives, her hand tucked in Aren's as they waited out storm after storm. Never did she reveal more than cursory details about her own life, but if anyone noticed, they did not comment. And Aren himself had stopped digging, had stopped asking who had inflicted her scars, inside and out, content that if she wished to tell him, she would.

With much cajoling and prodding, the Ithicanian children had convinced Lara to wade into the cavern harbor, teaching her to float and to paddle about, but she was out in a flash if a fish bumped her and she refused to put her head under the surface. The few times someone had been brave—or foolish—enough to dunk her had been the *only* times Aren had seen her lose her temper at the children, screaming bloody murder. Then she'd stormed half naked and dripping back to the palace, where she refused to speak to anyone, including him, for the balance of the day, only to go right back into the water with them during the next storm break.

Coming to Eranahl had changed his wife. It hadn't softened her, exactly, for she still had the wickedest temper of anyone he'd ever met, but it seemed to Aren that being here had pulled her out of her shell. Out of the fortress she'd constructed to protect herself. She was happier. Brighter. Content.

Except every storm season came to an end, and this one would be no different.

Heaving in a sigh, Aren eyed the sky, the rain pattering gently against his skin. There was only the faintest breeze, the squall barely deserving the name, and he suspected it would only be a matter of days before Nana ruled the season over. Which is why his war council had convened.

For the last hour, Watch Commanders had been arriving by boat: battle-hardened men and women who had seen the worst their enemies had to offer, and had dealt worse in return. Each of the nine, including him at Midwatch, was responsible for the defense of certain portions of the bridge and the islands flanking it, and all of them had arrived ready to discuss what the season would bring. Save one.

Ahnna was late.

Stepping into the shelter of Eranahl's cavern harbor, Aren sat on the steps to wait, annoyed at the anxiety building in his gut. This would be the first time he'd seen his twin since Lara's fall from the bridge. First time they'd spoken since he'd threatened to ship her off to Harendell. Ahnna had been adamantly against Lara being anything more than a glorified prisoner kept at Midwatch, and he couldn't help but wonder how she would react to Lara being in the heart of Ithicana.

The gates began their slow rattle upward, startling Aren from his thoughts. One of the Southwatch boats drifted around the bend, and he squinted into the dim light, trying to make out his twin. Ahnna sat at the stern, rudder in hand, expression unreadable.

The boat bumped against the stone steps, one of the soldiers hopping out and mooring it while the others unloaded supplies. Ahnna flipped her pack over her shoulder, calling to her crew to enjoy their few hours of liberty before taking the steps two at the time.

"Your Majesty," she said, and his heart sank. "I apologize for being late. With the state of relations between the southern kingdoms, Southwatch requires my full attention."

"It's fine." He tried to come to terms with the wedge between them that might never be removed. "We've time."

Ahnna's eyes turned skyward, then she shook her head. "I'm not sure that we do."

The palace was silent as he and Ahnna entered, everyone who wasn't needed having vacated the premises and those who were needed busy with their tasks. It made for a strange quality of sound, as though the absence of people changed the building, causing footsteps to echo and voices to carry.

Not that either of them felt inclined to speak.

Turning down the hall, Aren caught sight of Lara sitting on a padded bench outside the council chambers, shoulders squared, eyes fixed on the solid doors. She wore a silken gown of blues and greens, her hair braided into a coronet that revealed the long column of her neck. High-heeled sandals, the leather inlaid with lapis lazuli, were strapped to her feet, and from here, he could see her cheeks and brow bones shone with golden dust.

"I see she hasn't given up her expensive tastes," Ahnna muttered.

Lara hadn't, and Aren indulged her, but not for the reasons his sister thought. Lara would've forgone the luxuries, would've blended in with his people to the point they forgot she hadn't been born among them, but both of them understood the importance of the people remembering she was Maridrinian. Of them coming to love her as a Maridrinian, which they had.

Lara rose at their approach, and as she turned to face them, Aren heard the soft catch of Ahnna's breath. She was staring at the jewels around Lara's neck, the emerald and black diamond necklace that had been their mother's. "How could you?" Her words came out as a hiss between her teeth. "Of all the things you could have given her, why that?"

"Because Lara is queen. And because I love her."

A thousand retorts flashed through his sister's eyes, but she said none of them. Only bowed to Lara. "I'm glad to see you well, Your Grace." Then she extracted the key marking her as a Watch Commander, unlocked the council chamber, and went inside.

"I told you it would be a mistake not to talk to her sooner." Lara rested her hands on her hips, giving him a slow shake of her perfect head. "You slap her in the face with everything she doesn't want to see and then expect her to grit her teeth and bear it."

Closing the distance between them, Aren pulled Lara against him, her arms slipping around his neck. "Why are you always right?" he asked, closing his eyes and kissing her throat.

"I'm not. It's only that you are so often wrong."

He chuckled, feeling some of his tension dispel only for it to return when she said, "It's too soon, Aren. Let me go get Jor."

"No. You are Queen of Ithicana and that makes you my second in command. That is how it has always been, and for me to take Jor in there with me instead would send a message to the Watch Commanders and the people that I don't see you as capable. That I don't trust you. It would undo everything we've accomplished since you came to Eranahl."

"As far as they know, I *am* incapable."

"I know otherwise." But he was the only one who knew; Lara's past, her training, her deadliness a secret Aren kept from everyone. And would continue to keep in order to protect both his wife and the tenuous peace their marriage symbolized. "Besides, there is more to running a kingdom than martial prowess."

"This is War Tides council meeting," she said between her teeth, eyes shifting down the corridor to ensure they were alone. "The *only* thing that matters is martial prowess. Let me get Jor."

Aren shook his head. "You're the only one who knows all the stakes." He rested his forehead against hers. "I need you at my side."

And before she could argue further, he unlocked the door and tugged Lara inside Ithicana's war room.

# 37
# LARA

Aren dropped her arm the moment they entered, the intimacy that had thickened the air between them moments ago gone. And replaced with something else entirely.

Here, they were not husband and wife. Not King and Queen of Ithicana. In this room, Aren was Commander of Midwatch and she was his second, and Lara instinctively mimicked his squared shoulders and grave expression, following at his heels to the elevated replica of Midwatch, the island one part of an enormous map of Ithicana. The only complete map of Ithicana in existence.

No one was allowed in this room but Watch Commanders and their seconds. Not even servants were admitted to clean, the group taking care of the duty with typical Ithicanian efficiency. That she, a Maridrinian, stood in this room was unprecedented, a fact made clear when every head turned toward her, their eyes wide with shock.

"Where's Jor?" Ahnna's voice cut through the silence from where she stood next to the replica of Southwatch, her hand resting possessively on the large island.

"Downstairs." Aren's voice was curt, though Lara suspected the tone had more to do with nerves than with irritation. He'd known her presence would be questioned.

"Commander, perhaps we might discuss whether Her Majesty's presence is appropriate," Mara said. Which was unsurprising. The woman had made no secret of her distaste for Lara, barely speaking to her whenever she was in Eranahl.

Aren turned cool eyes on the commander of Northwatch. "We choose our seconds. Our choices are not questioned." He jerked his chin toward Aster, whom Mara had taken on as her second after his dismissal from the Kestark command. "Unless you'd care to change that protocol?"

Mara held up her hands in defense. "I only thought you'd wish to have someone with experience as your second, Commander. Emra"—she gestured at the young commander of Kestark—"selected someone with age to compensate for her youth."

Emra had chosen her mother—a battle-hardened warrior whom Lara liked immensely—as her second, and the woman in question rolled her eyes skyward as her daughter replied, "I chose someone I could trust."

A small beacon of solidarity, but what relief Lara felt at the young woman's words was washed away when Ahnna said, "Since when don't you trust Jor?"

Aren shifted next to Lara, his legs brushing her skirts. She knew that not having his sister's support hurt. From what she'd gleaned from Taryn, Jor, and the rest of the guards, the twins had been close, fighting at each other's backs until Ahnna had moved to Southwatch. She'd been the key vote of support in this council chamber in Aren's marriage to Lara, but judging from the princess's expression, she deeply regretted that decision.

"Lara is my wife. She is Queen. I trust her, and she is my second." Lara held her breath as Aren's gaze roved around the room. "Anyone who has a problem with that can get the fuck out now."

Mara snorted, but everyone else held their tongues. "Let's begin, shall we? I want to be on the water before nightfall."

It was a long process of Mara detailing the developments that had taken place over the storm season. What the Northwatch spies had learned about Harendell and Amarid's intentions. Where their armies and navies were located. The number of ships that had been built or destroyed. Lara listened intently; it was not lost on her that every ruler in the world would kill to have a spy in her shoes.

"Amarid is replacing the ships they lost raiding last year," Mara said. "But we've tracked their progress, and none will be ready by the beginning of War Tides, so we may see some respite."

"All of them?" Aren asked. "With what funds? Amarid is nearly bankrupt."

A bankruptcy that Lara knew had been cemented by Ithicana taking the income Amarid usually received for shipping steel across the Tempest Seas. Of all the kingdoms, north and south, her marriage to Aren had cost Amarid the most.

"Straight from the coffers, near as we can tell," Aster answered. "It's not on credit. No one will lend to them anymore." The older man lifted the page in his hand. "There's a rumor the ships were financed with gemstones, but that seems unlikely."

*Gemstones*. The word plucked at Lara's mind, important somehow, though she couldn't think of why. "What sort of gemstones?"

Every pair of eyes in the room shifted to her before moving to Aren. His jaw tightened with obvious irritation. "Answer the question."

"Rubies," Aster said. "But Amarid has no mines, so it's likely nothing more than a rumor."

Lara's fingers went to the knife belted at her waist, trailing over the crimson stones embedded in the hilt.

"I'm not interested in rumors," Aren said. "I'm interested in facts. Find out how Amarid's paying for the ships. If they're in bed with someone, I want to know who it is. And what their intentions are." He waved a hand at Mara to continue, but Lara's mind stayed with the ships. With the idea that there might be someone outside of Amarid interested in financing further attacks against Ithicana.

". . . a marked increase in Amarid's import of certain Maridrinian goods." Mara's words stole back Lara's attention.

"What manner of goods?"

Mara's expression was unamused. "Cheap wine, mostly."

"Why, given that Amarid makes the best wines and is known the world over for their distilleries, would they import Maridrinian wine?"

"Clearly a few Amaridians have a taste for cloudy swill," Mara snapped. "Now moving on."

"Commander, watch yourself." Aren's voice was cold.

The older woman only threw up her hands in exasperation. "I assume the Maridrinians are selling what they can in order to buy what they need—I only noted them as they were unusual and it might be a market we can exploit in the future."

"It wasn't a large shipment," Ahnna interrupted. "Our tolls would have eaten up half the profit, it was such cheap stuff. I snaked a crate of it and included it with the supplies for Midwatch."

Lara's pulse was roaring in her ears now, the memory of the bottle of Maridrinian wine in the safe house supplies dancing in front of her eyes, along with the smuggler's ruby they'd found in it. A ruby that was sitting in her jewelry box at Midwatch. How better to smuggle gemstones than in cheap wine that the Ithicanians were unlikely to touch, that they wouldn't have even noticed, if Ahnna hadn't played a prank? If Aren had made the connection, Lara couldn't tell—he was guarding his reactions too closely.

"May I continue?" Mara demanded, and at Aren's nod, she gave a swift rundown of Northwatch's defenses, then passed the meeting to the next commander.

The islands both north and south of Midwatch suffered most of the attacks during the past War Tides, and much of the conversation turned to speculation of whether this year would be the same. Lara listened with one ear, but her mind would not let go of the notion that someone in Maridrina was financing the Amaridian navy.

The conversation moved progressively south, the meeting stopping only when someone needed to relieve themselves and resuming immediately upon the individual's return. There was no time. Lara could feel it: the galloping thrum of adrenaline that usually preceded a storm, but this time it whispered *war*. Aren took his turn for Midwatch, barely referring to the notes Lara passed him.

"Midwatch Island itself was only attacked once. On the shoulder season, and obviously by an inexperienced captain, as they sailed directly into the path of our shipbreakers. It was as though they were asking to be sunk. Even still, we had little respite, the other islands under our watch were attacked repeatedly."

They turned to the particulars, but Lara scarcely heard the conversation, her skin ice-cold. Key to her father's plan had been Lara witnessing Ithicana's military tactics from the inside, her training allowing her to understand those tactics and how they could be exploited. All of War Tides, she'd believed every opportunity she had to watch the Ithicanians in action had been luck, but what if it hadn't been? What if it had been by design? What if it had been ordered by the individual financing the rebuilding of those ships?

What if that individual was her father?

"The Amaridian attack on Serrith was the only occasion where we took significant losses . . ."

*Serrith.* Unbidden, the memory of the attack surfaced in her mind. Of the way the Amaridian sailors had recognized her, but instead of attacking, had backed off until it became clear it was her life or theirs. Which made no sense at all, given that Lara and the treaty she represented were the cause of all of Amarid's woe.

"You're up, Emra," Aren said. "How fares Kestark?"

The paper in the young woman's hands trembled as she spoke, but her voice was clear and steady as she summarized the state of her watch, which had taken heavy losses during War Tides. Reaching the end of her notes, she paused before saying, "An Amaridian merchant vessel passed through Kestark two days past."

"Keep to the important details, girl," Aster said, and Lara curbed the urge to throw the glass in her hand at his head. "We don't have time to discuss every merchant vessel blown into our waters during a storm season crossing."

Emra's eyes flashed with irritation, but she shut her lips in habitual deference to the older man.

Anything to do with Amarid was important now, and Lara opened her mouth to ask Emra to elaborate, but Aren beat her to it. "Why do you mention it?"

"I was on Aela Island doing an inspection of the outpost, Commander. We noticed the vessel anchored on the east side out of the wind, the crew making a show of doing some repairs."

"And?"

"And I noticed it was sitting high in the water. Which, given she'd come in from the north, seemed odd. So we boarded her to see what was what."

"You *boarded* an Amaridian ship?"

"Peacefully boarded. Hold was empty, and when I inquired their business, the captain told me they were transporting a wealthy noblewoman."

"Such an exciting tale this is," Aster said dryly, but Aren waved him silent, which was well timed, as Lara was considering ways to poison the man's drink to get him to shut up. "Did you see the woman?"

"Yes, Commander. A very beautiful woman with golden hair. She had a maid with her, along with some military types for escort."

"Did you speak to them?"

Emra shook her head. "No. But I noticed her dress was the same style as those Her Majesty sometimes wears."

"She was Maridrinian?"

Emra shrugged, her cheeks reddening. "I've not enough experience to say. Her Majesty is the only Maridrinian I've ever met."

"Perhaps you ought to have consulted your mother, *Commander*," Mara interjected. "She, after all, fought in the war against Maridrina and is thus well aware of what they look and sound like. Either way, it matters little. Maridrinians who can't afford bridge passage often risk the voyage on Amaridian vessels. They're cheap."

"And I wouldn't have thought much more of it, Commander," Emra replied, "except we passed through Midwatch territory on our way to Eranahl, and we spotted the same vessel. And a merchant tub like that wouldn't make it to Maridrina and back to Midwatch in less than two days."

Lara's skin pricked with goosebumps as though she were being watched, despite there being no windows in the room. Her father didn't use women in battle or as spies, the only exception being Lara and her sisters. And she'd paid for her sisters' freedom in blood.

"Anyone else notice the same?" Aren asked.

Heads shook, but the commander of the garrison north of Midwatch said, “Our scouts caught sight of an Amaridian merchant vessel heading south and east, past Serrith and Gamire Islands, but it looked to be sailing ahead of a squall forming in the west.”

“Is there something we should know about?” Mara asked.

The *something* was that Lara’s father was hunting for her. Lara knew it and, judging from the tension she felt radiating from Aren, he suspected it as well. But neither of them could say so without raising the question of *why* Silas was so interested in tracking down his wayward daughter.

Aren shook his head. “Carry on.”

It was Ahnna’s turn at Southwatch.

The princess rubbed her chin, then reached to touch the replica of the island she guarded so fiercely. “All of Southwatch’s defenses are in good order. What damage was inflicted during the storm season we were able to repair during the breaks.” Referring to the page in her hand, Ahnna detailed the numbers of soldiers stationed, the weapons cache, the food and water supplies.

“You all know”—she set the papers down—“that Valcotta was able to maintain a partial blockade of Maridrina’s access to Southwatch, despite the toll it took on their fleet. We’d expected to take a hit to our profits, but the Valcottan Empress is too savvy to give us a reason to complain. We had Valcottan merchant ships lined up ten deep during every storm break, and they bought everything, often at a premium. When the Maridrinian vessels did have the chance to make port, there was little for them to buy. Though, to his credit, King Silas has them prioritizing food, not his precious steel and weapons.”

“It’s all still at Southwatch?” Aren asked.

“We’ve a whole warehouse full of weapons,” Ahnna replied. “It’s all going to turn to rust by the time he ever sees them at the rate things are going. And yet they keep arriving.”

“His buyers take all the steel and weaponry the Harendellians offer at Northwatch,” Mara said. “And the Valcottan buyers know that.”

Ahnna nodded. “But he doesn’t dare use his resources to retrieve it. Not with his people rioting in the streets. They’re starving. And they're desperate. And they blame Ithicana for all of it."

Lara's heart seemed to come to a standstill as a sudden understanding took hold of her. She'd been a fool, imagining it might be over. Had believed, with delusional hope, that without the efforts of her spying, her father would have no way of infiltrating Ithicana's defenses.

Her father had waited *fifteen years*, invested a fortune and the lives of twenty of his daughters in his bid for the bridge. He'd lied and manipulated and murdered to keep it all a secret. There was no chance that he'd ever let it go.

No matter what it cost Maridrina.

She needed to speak with Aren alone. Needed to warn him that Ithicana was in as much danger as it ever had been. Needed to do it before this meeting ended, so that these individuals who protected Ithicana's shores would go back to their watch prepared to fight.

But she couldn't very well ask to speak to him privately without everyone questioning what she and Aren were keeping from the council.

Picking up Aren's stack of notes, Lara fanned herself vigorously enough that eyes shifted to her. Then she reached for her glass of water, purposefully knocking it to the floor, the glass shattering.

Aren broke off in his argument with Mara, twisting to look at her.

"Sorry," she murmured.

His eyes narrowed as Lara swayed on her feet. "It's very hot in here."

"Are you well?"

"I think I need to sit down," she said, then fell sideways into his arms.

# 38
# AREN

"THIS BETTER BE GOOD," Aren said through his teeth as he carried her down the corridor. "Because I sure as shit don't believe you fainted."

"Get us somewhere we can talk," was her whispered response, confirming his supposition.

Kicking open the door to their rooms, Aren waved away the wide-eyed servants who'd scurried up behind him. "Too long on her feet." Then he elbowed the door shut, Lara sliding nimbly from his arms the moment the latch clicked.

"We only have a few minutes," she said, "so listen carefully. My father's formed an alliance with Amarid."

Silence.

"Ithicana has spies throughout both kingdoms, Lara, and *none* of them have reported even a hint of an alliance between Maridrina and Amarid. Quite the opposite, in fact."

"Yes, no doubt that's what my father wishes you to believe."

Aren listened silently as Lara explained the connections between the focused attacks on the Midwatch area, the Maridrinian wine and the smuggled ruby, and the ships being financed in Amarid with the very same gemstones. A stream of small details and coincidences that he might have passed off as nothing, except for the fact he *knew* why Lara had been sent to Ithicana. Knew Silas was his enemy.

"And there's the ships lurking around Midwatch. The noblewoman—" She broke off, hesitating. "The noblewoman is only an excuse for the soldiers to be aboard. You know they're looking for me."

It was there Aren interrupted. "Of course he's looking for you, Lara, because without you, his plots, his alliance with Amarid—everything—it amounts to nothing."

"But—"

Aren gripped her shoulders. "Without you, he has nothing."

Lara hadn't betrayed him, Aren believed that. Trusted her with his heart, with the bridge, with his people. Yet the frantic gleam in her eye formed a seed of doubt in his chest. "You're certain you didn't give him any clues in your letters?"

Lara met his gaze unblinking. "I am certain. Just as I'm certain that he's creating a situation in which he no longer needs me to take the bridge. He's going to do it by force."

Exhaling a long breath, Aren said, "Lara, he's tried it before. Tried and failed, and took catastrophic losses. The Maridrinians remember what it was like to come against our shipbreakers. To see their comrades drowned in the waves, pummeled into rocks, and torn apart by sharks. Silas can hire out all the Amaridian vessels he wants to—it's not a fight your people will support."

"Why do you think he's starving them?"

His blood abruptly chilled. "To try to get us to break off trade with Valcotta."

Lara slowly shook her head. "That's the last thing he wants. My father doesn't want Ithicana as an ally; he wants you as his enemy." Her eyes were bright with unshed tears. "And he's done it. My father has turned you into Maridrina's villain, and very soon, they'll come for your blood."

Even as the words poured from Lara's throat, Aren knew they were true. That despite everything he'd done, everything he'd dreamed of for Ithicana's future, war would be on his doorstep. Twisting away from Lara, he gripped the foot of the bed he shared with her, the wood groaning under his grip.

"Can you defend Ithicana against both nations?" Lara's voice was soft.

Slowly, he nodded. "This year, yes. But I expect our losses will be catastrophic. Both kingdoms have far more soldiers to throw against us than Ithicana has to lose."

And what were his options? The surest way to stop Silas would be to join forces with Valcotta, but that would be disastrous for Maridrina. Lara's people would die by the thousands, cut down by blades or starved to death. Innocent lives lost—all because of the greed of one man. But to do otherwise would likely mean the end of Ithicana unless Harendell intervened, which past behavior indicated unlikely.

"There is no solution," he said.

Silence.

"Stop trade with Valcotta." Lara's words were so quiet, he barely heard them. "Attempt to undercut support for this war with Maridrina. Make Ithicana the hero."

"If I break trade relations with Valcotta and use my resources to crack their blockade on Maridrina, it will decimate our profits. Ithicana needs the income Valcotta brings in at Southwatch in order to survive. Never mind that they'll likely retaliate. You want me to risk that on speculation? On coincidences?"

"Yes."

Silence.

"Aren, you brought me here because you believed your people needed to know Maridrina in order for there to be peace between our people. In order for them to see Maridrina as an ally, not as the enemy of old." Her voice was choked. "It goes both ways. Maridrina also need to see Ithicana as an ally. As a friend."

Aren's shoulders bowed. "Even if I agree with you, Lara, I'll never get the council to go along with it. They believe we've bought peace with Maridrina—that we gave your father what he wanted, so he has no reason to attack us. They won't jeopardize the Valcottan revenue based on the supposition that your father might want more."

"Then maybe it's time you told them the truth about me. Maybe that will be enough to prove to them the gravity of our situation."

Aren felt the blood drain from his face. "I can't."

"Aren—"

"I can't, Lara. Ithicana's reputation for cruelty isn't entirely undeserved. If they discover you were a spy . . ." His mouth felt dry as sand. "It wouldn't be a merciful execution."

"So be it."

"No." He crossed the space between them in three strides, pulling her into his arms, his lips pressing against her hair. "No. I refuse to turn you over to be slaughtered. I'll damn well let them feed me to the sea before I ever agree to that. I love you too much."

And because Aren knew she was brave enough to sacrifice herself whether he willed it or not, he added, "If they learned the truth about you, the last thing they'd do is help your people. They'll force me to ally formally with Valcotta, and what would happen . . . I'm not sure Maridrina would survive it."

Her shoulders started to shake, and then sobs tore from her throat. "It's impossible. Impossible to save both. It always has been."

"Maybe not." Aren pushed her toward the bed. "I need you to stay here and keep up your performance."

Lara wiped a hand across her cheek. "What are you going to do?"

Stopping with his hand on the door, Aren turned to look at his wife. "Your father sent you to Ithicana for a purpose. He failed. But I also brought you here for a reason, Lara. And I think it's time to see if my gambit worked."

She didn't stop Aren as he exited, his long strides eating up the corridors of the palace as he formed the words. A speech he'd used countless times, but now turned to a different purpose. Reaching the council chambers, Aren extracted his key, unlocked the door, and entered.

Conversation froze, then Ahnna said, "Nana sent word. Storm season is over. War Tides has begun."

There was a shifting and gathering in the room, every one of the commanders and seconds present now keen to return to their watch. To prepare to repel their enemies, whoever they might be. To be through with this meeting.

But Aren wasn't through with them.

"There's one more matter we need to discuss," he said, the tone of his voice causing all heads to turn. "Or rather, finish discussing. And that is the matter of the plight of the Maridrinian people."

"What's there to say?" Aster said, exchanging a chuckle with Mara. "They made their bed."

"As did we."

The smile fell away from Aster's face.

"Sixteen years ago, Ithicana signed a treaty of peace with Maridrina and Harendell. A treaty that both of those kingdoms have held to, neither of them attacking our borders in the intervening period. Our terms with Maridrina have all been met. They provided me with my lovely wife, and we have eased the costs of using the bridge."

"I assume you're driving to a point, Your Grace," Mara said.

"The terms have been met," Aren interrupted, "but the question of the nature of the agreement between our two nations remains unanswered. Is it, as Commander Mara so eloquently described, a *business contract*, where Ithicana has paid Maridrina for peace? Or is it an alliance, where our two kingdoms use the terms of the treaty to foster a relationship beyond the exchange of services and products and coins?"

No one spoke.

"The people of Maridrina are starving. Little of their land is suited to produce, and of that which is suited, more than half rests fallow for lack of hands to work it. The wealthy are still able to import, but the rest? Hungry. Desperate. All while we, their so-called allies, do business with their enemy, filling Valcottan holds with the goods Maridrina desperately needs because the Valcottans pay the most. Sitting idly by while Valcottan ships deny Maridrina the steel they've rightfully paid for. No wonder they call this treaty a farce."

"What's happening in Maridrina is Silas's doing," Ahnna said. "Not ours."

"It *is* Silas's doing. But are we any better for sitting back and watching while innocent children go to their graves when we have the power to save them? Silas is no more the sum of his kingdom than I am the sum of ours, and neither of us is immortal. There is a larger picture."

"Just what are you suggesting, Aren?" Ahnna asked, her voice toneless.

"I'm suggesting Ithicana demand Valcotta drop its blockade. And should they refuse, that they be denied port at Southwatch. That we prove ourselves allies to Maridrina."

The room broke into a flurry of voices, Aster's the loudest of all. "These sound like your wife's words, Your Grace."

"Do they really?" Aren leveled the man with a glare. "How long have I been pushing for us to form unions with other kingdoms so that our people have opportunities beyond war? For us to turn Ithicana into something more than just an army viciously guarding its bridge? How long did my mother push for it before me? These are not Lara's words."

Though in a way they were, because before, he'd only cared about protecting his own kingdom. About how Ithicana might benefit from an alliance. Now Aren saw both sides, and he believed he was a better man for it.

"But to have an alliance that would allow our people these opportunities, we cannot just *take*. We have to give something in return. Maridrina's plight? It's an opportunity to show Ithicana's worth. Our worth."

"Is this to be a proclamation, then?" Aster spat. "For us to risk our own children and have no say in the risking?"

If Aren could've made it an order, he would've, for no reason other than that he would be the one to bear the guilt if things went wrong. But such was not Ithicana's way. "We vote."

Slow nods, then Emra's mother said, "All right, then. Hands for those in favor."

Hers went up immediately, as did Emra's and four of the other younger commanders. Including Aren's vote, that made seven, and he needed nine. It was one of the reasons he hadn't asked Lara to come back here with him. Odd numbers ensured the vote wouldn't hang. And having her absent meant no one could hold her accountable.

Several of the old guard, including Aster, stepped back, shaking their heads. But Aren almost fell over in surprise when Mara lifted her hand. Seeing his shock, the commander of Northwatch said, "Just because I question you doesn't mean I don't believe in you, boy."

All who remained to cast their vote was his sister.

Ahnna trailed a finger over Southwatch, her brow furrowed. "If we do this, it will mean the destruction of our relationship with Valcotta. It means war for Ithicana."

Aren cast his gaze over the replica of his kingdom. "Ithicana has always been at war, and what do we have to show for it?"

"We're alive. We have the bridge."

"Don't you think it's time we fight for something more?"

Ahnna didn't answer, and sweat trickled down Aren's back as he waited for his twin to cast her vote. Waited to see if she could move past her distrust of Lara and Maridrina. If she'd risk taking a chance, this leap of faith. If she'd fight at his side the way she always had.

Ahnna gave her island one last affectionate pat, and then she nodded once. "I swore long ago to fight by your side, no matter the odds. Now is no different. Count Southwatch in."

# 39
# LARA

EIGHT WEEKS LATER, Lara clunked her mug against Jor's over the fire pit, shrieking with laughter when a log burst, spraying sparks at their hands.

For the first time in living memory, the months of respite from storms hadn't meant war for Ithicana, though it felt as though the entire nation had held its breath until the season was declared over.

After a strongly worded warning from Aren to drop the blockade or risk losing the right to trade at the Southwatch market—which the Valcottan Empress had ignored—Ithicana had driven the Valcottan navy ships lurking around Southwatch back, allowing Maridrinian vessels full access. Aren had then proceeded to load Ithicana's own vessels full of food and supplies, which were delivered into Vencia and distributed to the poor. Again and again, Aren had used Ithicana's coffers and resources to supply the belabored city until the Maridrinian people were cheering his name in the streets.

Whether it was because he'd lost the support of his people for war or because Lara hadn't given him the intelligence he'd needed, her father hadn't lifted a hand against Ithicana. Neither had Amarid, which seemed to still be licking its wounds. And now that the storms were rolling in, both kingdoms had lost the chance for another year. Or perhaps forever, if the strength of the relationship between the Ithicanian and Maridrinian people were any indication.

Not that there hadn't been consequences. The empress had responded with a letter telling Aren he deserved whatever he got for bedding down with snakes, turning her armada entirely to merchant transport in an attempt to further undercut the bridge's revenues, which were already halved by the loss of trade with the southern nation. The coffers were drained. But in Lara's mind, both Maridrinian and Ithicanian civilians were alive. They were safe. Nothing else mattered.

She had done her duty as both princess and queen.

"Your brother should be passing by Midwatch right now," Jor said, handing her another full mug of ale. "Tide's low. We could take a stroll through the bridge and pay him a visit. Have a little family reunion."

Lara rolled her eyes. "I'll pass." Her brother Keris had finally convinced their father to allow him to attend university in Harendell to study philosophy, and he was traveling through the bridge with his entire retinue of courtiers and attendants to start his first semester. One of the mail runners had come ahead of them, and he said the party looked like a flock of birds, everyone bedecked in silks and jewels.

"Let's go," Aren murmured into her ear. "I'm looking forward to a night with you in a real bed."

"You're going to fall asleep the second your head hits the pillow." She relished the rising heat of desire between her legs as his fingers traced along the veins in her arms. She'd stayed with him at the barracks all through War Tides, but the narrow soldier's cot had *not* been conducive to romance. Although they'd made do.

"I'll take that bet. Come on."

He led her out into the gentle rain, the worst of the squall already over. One of Aren's soldiers was outside, and he looked at her with surprise. "Thought you already went up to the house."

"Not yet. Jor kept refilling my mug. I expect they'll be out of ale by the time your shift is up."

"Thought I saw you, was all." The big guard frowned, then

shrugged. "They're signaling for a supply pickup at the pier, so we might have more drink arriving."

"I'll send some down from the house," Aren assured the man, tugging on Lara's arm.

"Thank you, Your Grace." But Aren was already towing her up the path, the chain in the cove rattling upward behind them. Mud squelched beneath their boots as they made their way up the trail to the house they'd barely visited over the prior eight weeks, neither of them able to relax enough to step away from the barracks.

"A bath, first," Lara said, thinking dreamily about the steaming hot springs. "You smell like soldier."

"You're not so fresh yourself, Majesty." Aren swung her up into his arms, the lantern light dancing wildly where it hung from her hand. She twisted in his grip, wrapping her legs around his waist. A soft moan escaped her lips as she pressed against him, his hands gripping her ass.

Lara kissed him hard, sliding her tongue into his mouth, then laughed when he slipped, the lantern falling from her hands and going dark. "Don't you dare drop me."

"Then quit distracting me," he growled. "Or I'll be forced to take you in the mud."

She slid to the ground and took his hand, leading him at a perilous run up the slope until she caught sight of Aren's cat, Vitex, sitting on the front step, tail twitching angrily.

"What are you doing out here?" Aren reached for the cat and it hissed and leapt away, limping slightly as it bolted into the trees.

Lara watched him go. "He's hurt."

"The female he's been chasing probably got a piece of him. He likely deserved it." Catching her by the waist, Aren lifted her up the stairs and shoved open the door to the house.

It was dark.

"Not like Eli not to set out a lamp." Lara's skin prickled as she stared into the yawning blackness. Aren had sent word up to the house that War Tides was over, instructing Eli to select an expensive bottle of wine from the cellar for his mother and aunt. But the Ithicanian boy *never* shirked his duties.

"Maybe he drank the wine instead," Aren murmured, raining kisses onto her throat, his hands finding her breasts. "Will do him good."

"He's fourteen." The house was silent. Which wasn't precisely unusual, but there was something about the *nature* of the silence that rubbed Lara the wrong way. As though no one breathed.

"Exactly. Do you know the sorts of things I was doing at fourteen?"

Lara stepped away, listening. "I should check on him."

An aggrieved sigh exited Aren's throat. "Lara, relax. The storms are here and they will do their duty." Pulling her into his arms, he kissed her. Slowly. Deeply. Driving all thought from her head as he gently pushed her down the dark corridor into their room, where, thankfully, there was a lamp burning. The yellow flame pushing back the darkness eased Lara's agitation, and she let her head fall back as her husband's teeth grazed her neck, feeling the faint breeze from the open window.

"Bathe later," he growled.

"No. You stink. Get outside and I'll be there in a moment."

Grumbling, he shucked off his tunic and vambraces, tossing both on the floor, starting toward the antechamber and the door to the courtyard beyond.

Peeling off her hooded cloak, Lara hung the damp garment on a hook to dry and was unfastening the top lace of her tunic when her heart skittered, her eyes falling on a letter with a familiar seal. Next to it, a knife twin to the one at her waist sat in a small pile of crimson sand, its rubies glittering in the light. The knife Aren had thrown on the docks in Vencia. Dread filled her stomach as she walked over to the table, picking the heavy paper up with numb fingers, and breaking the wax.

*Dearest Lara,*

*Even in Vencia, we have heard talk of the affection between the Ithicanian King and his new queen, and how it fills our heart to know that you have, however improbably, found love in your new home. Please accept our most sincere well-*

*wishes for your future, however short that future might be.*

*Father*

"Aren." Her voice shook. "Why wasn't this letter delivered at the barracks? Who brought it?"

No answer.

A scuffle of motion.

A muffled curse.

Whirling, she reached for the knife at her waist. Then froze. Aren was on his knees on the far side of the room. A hooded figure dressed in clothing identical to Lara's own held a glittering blade to his throat. And beneath the bed next to them, a young man's hand protruded, fingers covered in drying blood. *Eli . . .*

"Hello, little sister," a familiar voice said, and the woman reached up and pulled back her hood.

# 40
# LARA

"MARYLYN." THE NAME CROAKED out of Lara's throat, her chest a riot of emotion at seeing her sister again, even as she knew what the other woman's presence meant. Beautiful, with golden blond hair.

Marylyn had been the noblewoman on the ship Emra had boarded.

"Lara."

Aren started to struggle, snapping Lara out of her trance. "Don't move," Lara warned him. "Her blade will be poisoned."

"You do know my tricks."

"Let him go."

"We both know that's not likely to happen, little cockroach."

The old nickname burned in her ears, while her eyes searched for a way to disarm Marylyn without getting Aren killed. But there was none.

"Who is this woman?" Aren demanded.

"Lara is my little sister. My lying, thieving, little bitch of a sister."

The words were a slap to the face. "Marylyn, I came here to spare you."

"Liar." Marylyn's voice was pure venom. "You stole what was rightfully mine, then left me to rot in the desert. Do you have any idea how long it took me to get to Vencia to explain to Father what you'd done?"

"I did it to protect you!"

"Lara, the martyr." Marylyn's lip turned up in a sneer. "Only I saw through to your true intentions, you lying whore."

Lara stared at her, dumbfounded. The letter she'd left in Sarhina's pocket had explained everything. Her father's intention to have the rest of them killed. That Lara faking their deaths and then taking Marylyn's place as Queen of Ithicana was the only way to save all their lives, except for perhaps her own. She'd given them their freedom. "He was going to kill our sisters. It was the only way. Why don't you understand?"

"I understand perfectly." Marylyn shifted the blade pressed to Aren's throat, angling the tip upward. "Do you think I didn't know that Father intended to kill the rest of you?" She laughed. "Do you think I cared?"

This wasn't her sister. It couldn't be. Marylyn had always been the sweetest. The kindest. The one who needed to be protected.

*The best actress.*

"You said your sisters were dead." Aren's voice jerked her back into the moment.

"What now, has she been keeping secrets?" Marylyn stroked his cheek with her free hand, laughing as he recoiled. "Allow me to bring you into the fold, Majesty. No one forced Lara to come to Ithicana to spy, she *chose* to. Except 'chose' isn't even a strong enough word. Lara conspired against us all in order to ensure *she* would be Queen of Ithicana so that *she* would have the glory of throwing your people on Maridrinian blades."

"That's not true," Lara whispered.

"That's the woman you married, Majesty. A liar like none I've ever known. Worse than that, she's a murderer. I've seen her kill. Maim. Torture. All in cold blood. All practice for what she intended to do to your people."

That part was true. Painfully and horribly true. "We all did it, Marylyn. None of us had a choice."

Her older sister rolled her eyes. "There was always a choice." Her eyes turned on Aren. "What do you think he would've done in the same position? Do you think he'd have slaughtered an innocent man just to save himself?"

*No.*

"Selfish little cockroach, always putting herself first. Although I can see *why* you decided to remain around after you plunged the knife in his back." She trailed a finger down Aren's bare chest. "What a prize he is. They didn't tell us *that* during our lessons at the compound. I might have put him through his paces a few times myself before slitting his throat."

Fury seared through Lara's chest, and she unclipped her knife from its jeweled hilt, though the thought of hurting her sister made her sick. "Don't touch him."

Marylyn pursed her lips. "Why? Because he's yours? For one, he's rightfully mine. Two, even if I intended to leave him alive, which I don't, do you really think he's going to want anything to do with you now that he understands what kind of woman you are? When he finds out what you've *done?*"

"I've done nothing."

Reaching into her pocket, Marylyn extracted a heavy piece of parchment edged with gold.

*No.*

"Recognize this, Your Majesty?" Marylyn held it in front of Aren's face. "You wrote it last fall in response to my father's request you hold true to the *spirit* of the Fifteen Year Treaty. Not the most charitable of responses, although I suppose you did deliver, in the end." Her whole body shook with laughter.

*Not possible.*

*She'd destroyed all the pages.*

"There is a type of ink that is invisible until sprayed with another agent. At that point, it becomes quite visible. If you look in Lara's quarters, I'm certain you'll find a jar of it, somewhat depleted."

Marylyn flipped the letter around, and Lara could do nothing as Aren took in line after line of her neat writing laying out every one of Ithicana's secrets, a strategy to infiltrate the bridge that was damning in its details.

*She'd brought Ithicana to its knees.*

"Lara?" Aren's eyes burned into hers, and the anguish in them was like having her heart carved out of her chest.

"I didn't . . ." *She had.* "I wrote it before. Before I knew the truth." Before he'd risked his life to save hers. Before he'd taken her into his bed. Before he'd trusted her with *everything.* "I thought I'd destroyed all the copies. This is . . . this is a mistake. I love you."

*She'd never said it before. Never told him she loved him. Why had she never said it before?*

"You love me." His voice was hollow. "Or were you only pretending to?"

"How tragic this is." The clock chimed, punctuating Marylyn's words. "Though I suspect it is about to get so much worse given that Keris's party of *courtiers* has crossed paths with a weapons shipment from Harendell."

A horn sounded. A call for aid. Then another and another until the notes were nothing more than a garbled mix of noise.

"Those courtiers exited piers on Aela and Gamire Islands and attacked your guard posts from the rear, disabling their shipbreakers so that Amaridian vessels loaded with hundreds of our soldiers could land unmolested. Even now, many of them are moving on to Northwatch and Southwatch to attack them from behind. And we have men using Ithicana's own signal horns to ensure no one will come to their aid. That's only the beginning, of course. Lara's instructions were *quite* detailed. Especially in how we might take Midwatch."

Panic flared in Aren's eyes, and she knew what he was thinking: All his soldiers—all his friends—were sitting in the barracks, their guard down.

Marylyn continued to prattle, but Lara's mind raced. If they could get down to the barracks, maybe they could get the chain closed in time. Send a signal to Southwatch warning them. But that was impossible unless she disarmed Marylyn.

"Don't do this. Don't be our father's pawn any longer."

Her sister's face darkened. "I'm no one's pawn."

"Aren't you? You do his bidding, and for what? Everything we were told as children was a lie intended to fuel an irrational hatred of Ithicana. To turn us into fanatics who'd stop at nothing to bring our enemy down. But Father was the villain. He is the oppressor Maridrina needs to rid itself of. We were deceived, Marylyn. Why can't you see that?"

"No, Lara. You were deceived." Marylyn gave a pitying shake of her head, the back of her leg knocking against the bed. "I've always seen clearly. You ask what I have to gain? I bring your heads back to Vencia, and Father has promised to shower me with riches. If I hunt down our other wayward sisters, he will make me heir. I will be Queen of Maridrina and master of the bridge." She smiled. "Ithicana will be no longer."

Rage consumed Lara like a sentient beast, prowling through muscle and tendon, making her fingers flex on the knife in her hand. Master Erik had always warned her that anger would make her sloppy. Cause her to make mistakes. But he was a liar. Rage gave her focus. And it was that focus that caught the faint shifting of the sheets on the bed behind Marylyn. That allowed her to hear the faint hiss over the rapid beat of her heart. Aren, born and bred to this wild kingdom, heard it, too.

"You're deluding yourself." Lara watched the shifting shape. "Father knows that you're a mad dog. And once you've done his dirty work for him, he will have you put down. Or I could do it for him."

She threw the knife.

The blade sliced through the air, missing Marylyn, but sinking deep into the bed, the sheets now a flurry of motion.

"Lost your touch." Her sister cackled even as Aren leaned back, shoving his weight against her. They toppled against the bed and the injured snake struck. Marylyn screamed as its teeth sank into her shoulder. Twisting, she released Aren and stabbed her blade into the snake, pinning its body to the mattress.

Lara was already across the room. She slammed into Marylyn, sending them both rolling. They grappled, fists and feet flying with the intent to injure. Maim. Kill. Blow after blow, both of them equally well trained. Yet when it came to this one thing, to violence, Lara had always been better.

Catching Marylyn's head in a lock, Lara whispered, "You are queen of nothing," then jerked her arms and snapped her sister's neck.

The light went out of the other woman's eyes, and time seemed to stand still.

How had it come to this? It seemed a lifetime ago that she'd made the decision to sacrifice herself in order to save her sisters. To be Maridrina's champion. To break the Bridge Kingdom. Everything had changed since then. Her beliefs. Her allegiance. Her dreams. Yet now one of her sisters lay dead at her hands, and Ithicana was on the brink of falling beneath Maridrina's yoke.

Despite everything, her father had still won.

"What have you done?"

The horror in Aren's voice made her teeth clench. "I didn't intend for this to happen."

He had a machete in his hand, but his arm shook as he leveled it at her. "Who are you? What are you?"

"You know who I am."

His breathing was ragged. Eyes never leaving her, he reached to retrieve the piece of paper that was Ithicana's damnation, rereading the lines, his thoughts scorched across his face. *They couldn't fight this.*

There was a commotion outside. The sounds of men shouting.

"I'm not leaving you behind to damn me further," Aren hissed.

Lara didn't fight as he bound her wrists with the tie for one of the drapes. Or when he pulled a pillowcase over her head and dragged her out of the room, even as soldiers spilled into the house. Ithicanian voices, at first. Then Maridrinian. Then chaos.

Screams cut the air, blades against blades, and she was jerked this way and that. Horns still sounded, filling the air with the call for aid that would never come. Night air filled her nose, and she was falling, knees banging painfully against the steps. Arms pulling her upright, then they were running.

Branches whipping her face, roots tripping her feet, the ground slick with mud.

Hissed voices. "This way, this way."

The shouts of pursuit.

"Down, down. Did you gag her?"

Her face was pressed against the ground, wet earth seeping through the pillowcase. A rock dug into her ribs. Another pressed sharply against her knee. All of it felt distant, as though it were happening to her in a dream. Or to someone else.

They carried on through the night, the heavy rain helping them avoid what seemed like countless Maridrinian soldiers hunting them across Midwatch, though logically she knew it couldn't be so many. By now her father's elite would've discovered Marylyn's body—and the absence of hers and Aren's—and there was no doubt that finding them would be nearly the same priority as taking the bridge itself.

Only as dawn came, filtered grey through clouds and the sodden fabric covering her face, did they take cover. There were familiar voices in the group. Jor and Lia. Others from the honor guard. Her ears strained for Aren's, but not once did she pick it out amongst the whispers.

Still, she was certain he was there. Sensed his presence. Felt the guilt and anger and defeat radiating from him in waves as he came to terms with the fall of his kingdom. Knew, instinctively, when he sent everyone away so that he was alone with her.

Lara waited for a long time for him to speak, braced herself for the blame and accusations. Aren remained silent.

When she could take it no more, Lara pushed upright, lifting her bound wrists to tug the pillowcase from her head, blinking in the dim light.

Aren sat on a rock a few paces away, elbows braced on his knees, head hanging low. He was still shirtless, and the rain ran in torrents down his muscled back, washing away smears of blood and mud. A bow and quiver rested under the shelter of an overhang. A machete was belted at his waist. In his hand he held her knife—the one she'd thrown at the snake—and he was turning it over and over as though it were some artifact he'd never seen before.

"Did anyone get out?" Her voice rasped like sandpaper over rough wood. "To warn Southwatch?"

"No." His hands stilled, the blade's keen edge glittering with rain. "Taryn tried. The Maridrinians used our own shipbreakers with shocking proficiency. She's dead."

Sharp pain dug into Lara's stomach, her mouth tasting sour. *Taryn was dead. The woman who hadn't even wanted to be a soldier was dead, and it was because of her.* "I'm so sorry."

He lifted his head, and Lara recoiled from the fury in his eyes. "Why? You got everything you wanted."

"I didn't want this." Except she had, at one point. Had wanted to shatter Ithicana. That desire had gotten them to this point, no matter how much she regretted it.

"Enough of your lies." He was on his feet in one smooth motion, stalking toward her, knife in hand. "I may not have a full report yet, but I know the bridge has fallen to your father using a plan to infiltrate our defenses that was better than I could've come up with myself. Your plan." As he raised his voice, she couldn't help but flinch, knowing they were still being hunted.

"I thought I'd destroyed all the evidence. I don't know how it got away from me—"

"Shut up!" He lifted the blade. "My people are dead and dying because of you." The knife slipped from his fingers. "Because of *me*."

Wrenching the damning piece of paper out of his pocket, he held it up to her face. Not the side she'd written on, but the one *he'd* written, the script flowing and neat. Words persuading her father to reconsider his war with Valcotta and to put his people before his pride. Her chest hollowed as she read the end.

*Let it be said, however, that should you seek to retaliate against your spy, Ithicana will take it as an act of aggression against its queen, and the alliance between our kingdoms will be irrevocably severed.*

Aren dropped to his knees in front of her, gripping the sides of her face, his fingers tangling in her hair. Tears glinted in his eyes. "I *loved* you. I trusted you. With myself. With my kingdom."

Loved. Past tense. Because she'd never deserved his love, and now she'd lost it for good.

"And you were only using me. Only pretending. It was all an act. A ploy."

"No!" She wrenched the word from her lips. "At first, yes. But after . . . Aren, I love you. Please believe that, if nothing else."

"I used to wonder why you never said it. Now I know." His grip on her face tightened, then he jerked his hands away. "You say it now only because you're trying to save your own skin."

"That's not true!"

Explanations fought each other to make it out of her mouth first. Ways to make him understand. Ways to make him believe her. They all died on her lips as he fished the knife out of the mud.

"I should kill you."

Her heart fluttered in her chest like a caged bird.

"But despite everything, *everything*, you've done, I don't have the balls to stick this blade in your black Maridrinian heart."

The knife sliced between her wrists, cutting the cord in one clean jerk. He pressed the hilt into the palm of her hand.

"Go. Run. I've no doubt that you'll make it off this island." His jaw tightened. "It's in your nature to survive."

Lara stared at him, her lungs paralyzed. He wasn't letting her go, he was . . . banishing her. "Please don't do this. I can fight. I can help you. I can—"

Aren shoved her shoulders with enough force to send her stumbling back. "Go!" Then he reached down and retrieved his bow, nocking one of the black-fletched arrows.

Holding her ground, she parted her lips, desperate not to lose the chance to undo the damage that she'd done. The chance to fight back against her father. To liberate Ithicana.

To win Aren back.

"Go!" He shouted the word at her, leveling the arrow at her forehead even as tears poured down his cheeks. "I never want to see your face. I never want to hear your name. If there were a way to scour you from my life, I'd do it. But until I find the strength to put you in a goddamned grave, this is all I have. Now run!"

His fingers quivered on the bowstring. *He would do it. And it would kill him.*

Lara twisted in the mud, sprinting up the slope, her arms pumping. Her boots slipped and slid as she jumped over fallen trees and slapped aside ferns.

And stopped. Bracing a hand against a tree, she turned. In time to see his arrow shoot past her face, thudding into the tree next to her.

She pressed a shaking hand against the line scraped against her cheek, a trickle of blood running between her fingers. Eyes fixed on her, Aren pulled another arrow from his quiver, nocked it, and aimed the barbed tip. His lips moved. *Run.*

She ran, never looking back again.

# 41
# LARA

"ANOTHER."

The barkeep raised one eyebrow over the mug he was polishing with a dirty rag, but made no comment as he refilled her glass with the swill this tap house passed off as wine. Not that it mattered; it wasn't as though she intended to savor it.

Downing the contents in three gulps, Lara pushed the glass back across the bar. "Fill it."

"Pretty girl like you could get herself in a bit of trouble drinking the way you do, miss."

"Pretty girl like me will cut the throat of anyone who gives her trouble." She gave him a smile that was all teeth. "So how about you don't tempt fate and you just hand over the bottle." She shoved a few coins stamped with the Harendell King's face in the man's direction. "Here. Saves us having to exchange any more words tonight."

Wiser than he looked, the barkeep only shrugged, took the coins, and handed her a full bottle of swill. But even drunk, she marked his words. Her face was familiar here. It was time to find a new watering hole to drown herself in every night.

Which was a shame. It smelled like spilled beer and vomit, but she'd grown fond of this place.

Drinking directly from the bottle, she blearily scanned the room, tables full of Harendell sailors dressed in baggy trousers and those stupid floppy hats that never ceased to remind her of Aren. A trio of musicians played in the corner. No-nonsense serving women carried trays of steaming roast beef and rich soups to the patrons, the smell making her mouth water. A nod at one of the women had a bowl of soup arriving in front of her moments later.

"Here you are, Lara."

*Shit*. It was time for her to move on. How long had she been in this town? Two months? Three? In the haze of alcohol, she'd lost track of days, it feeling both like a lifetime and just yesterday that she'd dragged her battered boat onto a Harendell beach, half-starved and her clothes still red with the blood of the Maridrinian soldiers she'd slaughtered to get herself off Midwatch.

The smell of soup tickled her nose, but her stomach soured, and she shoved the bowl away, drinking from the bottle instead.

The smart thing would be to move inland, north and away from all those who knew and cared about Lara, The Traitor Queen of Ithicana. Her father's agents would be looking for her—maybe another one of her sisters, for all she knew—and a drunken wreck like her was an easy mark.

But she kept finding excuses not to go. The weather. The ease of stealing coin. The comfort of this shithole of a tap house. Except she knew the reason she stayed was because here, the news from Ithicana was on everyone's lips. Night after night she sat at the bar, listening to the sailors chatter about this battle and that, hoping and praying that the tides would turn. That, rather than grumbles about the growing dominion of Maridrina, she'd hear that Aren was back in power. That Ithicana held the bridge once more.

Wasted hopes.

With every passing day, the news grew worse. No one in Harendell was particularly pleased that Maridrina now controlled the bridge—already the old men were bemoaning the good old days of Ithicanian efficiency and neutrality—and there was much chatter over the likelihood of the Harendellian King taking action. Except even if he did, Lara knew it wouldn't be until after storm season, six months from now. And by then . . . by then, it would be too late.

". . . battle with the Ithicanians . . . the king . . . prisoner."

Lara's ears perked, unease pushing aside the haze of the wine. Turning to the table behind her, which was filled with a group of heavyset men with equally heavy mustaches, she asked, "What was that you said about the Ithicanian King?"

One of the men grinned lasciviously at her. "Why don't you come over here and I'll tell you everything there is to know about the sorry sot." He patted one knee, which was coated with grease stains.

Picking up her bottle, Lara swayed over to the table and set it down among their mugs. "Here I am. Now, what was it you were saying?"

The man patted his knee. She shook her head. "I'm fine on my feet, sir."

"I'd be better with that fine ass of yours on my lap." His hand swung in a wide arc, cracking against her bottom, where it remained, his meaty fingers digging into her flesh.

Lara reached behind, taking a firm grip on his wrist. The idiot had the nerve to smile. Pulling hard, she twisted, slamming his palm against the table and, a heartbeat later, embedding her dagger in it.

The man squealed and tried to pull away, but the knife blade was stuck in the wood beneath his hand.

One of the others reached for it, but fell back, nose broken.

Another swung his fist at her face, but she dodged easily, the toe of her boot catching him in the groin.

"Now." She rested one hand on the knife and gave it a gentle twist. "What was it you were saying about the King of Ithicana?"

"That he was captured in a skirmish with the Maridrinians." The man was sobbing, squirming on his seat. "He's being held prisoner in Vencia."

"Are you certain?"

"Ask anyone! The news just came in from Northwatch. Now please!"

Lara eyed him thoughtfully, nothing on her face betraying the terror rising in her guts. Jerking the knife free, she leaned down. "You slap another ass, I'll personally track you down and cut that hand off."

Spinning on her heel, she nodded at the barkeep and strode out the door, barely feeling the rain that drove against her face.

*Aren had been captured.*

*Aren was a prisoner.*

*Aren was her* father's *hostage.*

The wind ripped and tore at her hair. The last thought replayed endlessly in her mind as Lara strode toward the boarding house, people leaping out of her way as she passed. There was only *one* reason her father would keep Aren alive: to use him as bait.

Taking the steps two at a time, she unlocked the door to her room, slamming it behind her. Guzzling water straight from a pitcher, she stripped off the simple blue dress she wore and donned her Ithicanian clothes, swiftly packing her meager belongings into a sack. Then, a chip of charcoal in hand, she sat down at the table.

The necklace was warm from resting against her skin, the emeralds and diamonds glittering in the candlelight. She had no right to wear it, but the thought of the necklace being stolen, of it being worn by anyone else, was unbearable, so she never took it off.

She did so now.

Laying the necklace on the paper, Lara traced the jewels with the charcoal, the haze from the wine slowly receding as she worked. When the drawing was complete, she returned the necklace to her throat and held up a complete map of Ithicana, her gaze fixed on the large circle to the west of the rest.

*This is madness,* the logical part of her mind screamed. *You can barely swim, you're a shit sailor, and it's the middle of storm season.* But her heart, which had been a cold, smoldering thing since she'd run from Aren on Midwatch, now burned with a ferocity that would not be denied.

Tucking the map into her pocket, she belted on her weapons and stepped out into the storm.

It took Lara three weeks to get there, and she nearly died a dozen times or more during the journey. Violent storms chased her onto tiny islands, her screaming into the wind as she dragged her little boat above the storm surge. She fought off snakes who thought to hide under the cover of her boat; freak gusts of wind that tore at her singular sail; and waves that swamped her, stealing away all her supplies.

But she was called the little cockroach for a reason, and here she was.

The skies were crystal clear, which likely meant the worst sort of storm was imminent, and the sun nearly blinded her with the glare off the waves. Her boat, the sail lowered, bobbed just beyond the shadow of the enormous volcano, the only sound the waves crashing against the cliffs.

Lara stood, her knees shaking as she held on to the mast for balance. There was a glint of sunlight hitting glass from the depths of the jungle slopes, but even without it, she knew they were watching.

"Open up," she shouted.

In answer, a loud crack split the air. Lara swore, watching as the boulder flew through the air toward her. It hit the water a few paces away, soaking her, the waves nearly flipping her boat.

Climbing back to her feet from where she'd been cowering in the bottom, she dug her fingers into the mast, fighting to master her fear of the water all around.

"Hear me out, Ahnna!" The other Ithicanians would've hit her on the first shot. Only the princess would bother to terrorize her first. "If you don't like what I have to say, you can throw me back into the sea."

Nothing stirred. There was no sound other than the roar of the ocean.

Then, a rattle split the air, the distinctive sound of the gates to Eranahl opening. Picking up her paddle, Lara maneuvered her way inside.

Familiar faces filled with cold fury met her as the boat knocked against the steps. She didn't fight as Jor jerked her out by the hair, the stone stairs biting into her shins as he dragged her up, snarling, "I'd cut your heart out here and now if not for the fact Ahnna deserves the honor." He pulled a hood over her head, obscuring her vision.

They took her to the palace, the sounds and smells painfully familiar, and as she counted the steps and turns, Lara knew she was being taken to the council room. Someone, probably Jor, kicked the backs of her knees once they entered, and she fell, palms slapping against the ground.

"You have a lot of nerve coming back, I'll give you that."

The hood was ripped from her head. Pushing upright, Lara met Ahnna's gaze, her stomach tightening at the cruel scar that now ran from the midpoint of the woman's forehead down to her cheekbone. That she hadn't lost her eye was a miracle. Surrounding her were some half a dozen soldiers, all who bore the marks of having barely escaped Southwatch with their lives. And behind them, hanging on the wall, was a large map of Maridrina.

"Give me one good reason why I shouldn't slit your throat, you traitorous bitch."

Lara forced a smile onto her face. "It's not very creative."

A boot caught her in the ribs, flipping her over. Pressing a hand against her side, Lara cast a dark look at Nana, whose boot it had been, before returning her attention to the woman in power. "You won't slit my throat because my father has Aren as his prisoner."

Ahnna's jaw tightened. "A fact that does not help your cause."

"We need to get him back."

"We?" The princess's voice was incredulous. "Your father has Aren inside his palace in Vencia, which I'm sure you know is a veritable fortress guarded by the elite of the Maridrinian army. My *best* haven't been able to so much as get inside. Every one of them has died trying. By all means, humor me with why *you* will be any help at all. Will you *seduce* your way in, whore?"

Lara stared her down, the silence hanging in the room stifling.

For fifteen years, she'd been trained how to infiltrate an impenetrable kingdom.

How to discover weaknesses and exploit them.

How to destroy her enemies.

How to be merciless.

She'd been born for this.

Yet Lara said nothing because words would not convince these people who believed—rightly—that she was a liar.

*Breathe in. Breathe out.*

She moved.

These were battle-hardened warriors, but the element of surprise was hers. And she was what she was. Holding nothing back, she whirled, fists and feet a blur as she disarmed the soldiers around her, knocking them down. Driving them back.

Ahnna launched at her with a scream, but Lara snaked a foot around her leg, and rolled with her, coming up with the tall princess in a chokehold, the other woman's knife in her free hand.

Silence filled the room, the warriors regaining their feet and eyeing her with a new and healthy respect even as they considered how they could disarm her.

Lara cast her eyes around the room, meeting each gaze individually before releasing Ahnna's throat. The other woman rolled away, gasping, eyes full of shock. Lara rose to her feet.

"You need me, because I know our enemy. I was raised by them to be their greatest weapon, and you've seen firsthand what I can do. What they never considered is that their greatest weapon might turn on them." And Lara wasn't the only weapon they'd created: There were ten other young women out there who owed her a life debt, which she fully intended to call due.

"You need me because I am the Queen of Ithicana." Twisting, she threw the knife in her hand, watching as it embedded in the map, marking Vencia—and Aren—with perfect precision. "And it's time my father was brought to his knees."

***The story continues in...***

Want to make sure you never miss a giveaway, cover reveal, or release day?

*Sign up for Danielle L. Jensen's mailing list on her website:*

**https://danielleljensen.com/**

**Want more from Danielle L. Jensen?**
**Step into the magical and action-packed world of...**

**Start reading book one now: https://danielleljensen.com/dark-shores/**

"Richly-woven, evocative, and absolutely impossible to put down—I was hooked from the first lines! *Dark Shores* has everything I look for in a fantasy novel: fresh, unique settings, a cast of complex and diverse characters, and an unflinching boldness with the nuanced world-building. I loved every word."—Sarah J. Maas, #1 *New York Times* bestselling author

"The book grabs readers from the beginning with its stellar worldbuilding and multidimensional characters, and the mythical elements are truly believable within the constructs of the story. The perspective shifts between the viewpoints of Teriana and Marcus from chapter to chapter, offering readers greater insights into each. ...A gripping introduction to a new series."—*Kirkus Reviews* (starred)

"The plot's twists and turns and fantastical elements add to the allure of this thrilling story. VERDICT Exhilarating fantasy-adventure romance for fans of Tricia Levenseller's *Daughter of the Pirate King*, Alexandra Christo's *To Kill a Kingdom*, or Natalie C. Parker's *Seafire*. Readers will eagerly await the next book in the series."—*School Library Journal*

"This is a lush, imaginative world, and as the focus shifts between Teriana and Marcus, it becomes clear that the readers are only getting a glimpse of its complicated history and mythology. ...Their secrets don't, of course, stop Teriana and Marcus from embarking on a steamy romance, and fans of Rutkoski's sighworthy *The Winner's Kiss* and the high-stakes sea adventure of Levenseller's *Daughter of the Pirate King* will want to know where Marcus and Teriana journey to next." —*Bulletin of the Center for Children's Books*

**Enjoy Lara and Aren's story?**
**Fans of THE BRIDGE KINGDOM also enjoy...**

# THE MALEDICTION NOVELS

**About book one, STOLEN SONGBIRD...**

A USA Today bestseller and finalist in the 2014 Goodreads Choice Awards for Best Debut Author.

For five centuries, a witch's curse has bound the trolls to their city beneath the mountain. When Cécile de Troyes is kidnapped and taken beneath the mountain, she realises that the trolls are relying on her to break the curse.

Cécile has only one thing on her mind: escape. But the trolls are clever, fast, and inhumanly strong. She will have to bide her time…

But the more time she spends with the trolls, the more she understands their plight. There is a rebellion brewing. And she just might be the one the trolls were looking for…

**Get book one: https://danielleljensen.com/books-2/stolen-songbird/**

# ABOUT THE AUTHOR

Danielle L. Jensen is the *USA Today* bestselling author of The Malediction Novels: *Stolen Songbird*, *Hidden Huntress*, *Warrior Witch*, and *The Broken Ones*, as well as the Dark Shores Series. She lives with her family in Calgary, Alberta.

**Follow her on the web at:**

https://daniellejensen.com/
*Twitter:* https://twitter.com/dljensen_
*Facebook:* https://www.facebook.com/authordanielleljensen/
*Instagram:* https://www.instagram.com/danielleljensen/

CPSIA information can be obtained
at www.ICGtesting.com
Printed in the USA
LVHW041253150323
741601LV00006B/451

# *From the Pages of*
# Germinal

No dawn whitened the dead sky. The blast furnaces alone flamed, and the coke ovens, making the darkness sanguinary without illuminating the unknown. And the Voreux, at the bottom of its hole, with its posture as of an evil beast, continued to crunch, breathing with a heavier and slower respiration, troubled by its painful digestion of human flesh. (page 14)

"It is because of mother that I didn't like being turned into the street." (page 43)

On the next day, and the days that followed, Étienne continued his work at the pit. He grew accustomed to it; his existence became regulated by this labour and to these new habits which had seemed so hard to him at first. (page 125)

Étienne summed up the situation in a word: if the Company really wanted a strike, then the Company should have a strike. (page 170)

"But you see I don't care a damn for your ideas, I don't! Politics, Government, and all that, I don't care a damn for it! What I want is for the miner to be better treated. I have worked down below for twenty years, I've sweated down there with fatigue and misery, and I've sworn to make it easier for the poor buggers who are there still; and I know well enough you'll never get anything with your ideas, you'll only make the men's fate more miserable still." (page 218)

"Now it is for us to have power and wealth!" (page 261)

The women had appeared, nearly a thousand of them, with outspread hair dishevelled by running, the naked skin appearing through their rags, the nakedness of females weary with giving birth to starvelings. A few held their little ones in their arms, raising them and shaking them like banners of mourning and vengeance. Others, who were younger, with the swollen breasts of amazons, brandished sticks; while frightful old women were yelling so loudly that the cords of their fleshless necks seemed to be breaking. (page 320)

Since the anarchists had triumphed in it, chasing out the earlier evolutionists, everything was breaking up; the original aim, the reform of the wage-system, was lost in the midst of the squabbling of sects; the scientific framework was disorganised by the hatred of discipline. And already it was possible to foresee the final abortion of this general revolt which for a moment had threatened to carry away in a breath the old rotten society.

(page 367)

"There's no pleasure in life when hope goes. Yes, that might have gone on longer; we might have breathed a bit. If we had only known! Is it possible to make oneself so wretched through wanting justice?" (page 408)

It was done for; the evil beast crouching in this hole, gorged with human flesh, was no longer breathing with its thick, long respiration. The Voreux had been swallowed whole by the abyss.

(page 438)

And these two men, who felt contempt for each other—the rebellious workman and the sceptical master—threw themselves on each other's necks, sobbing loudly in the deep upheaval of all the humanity within them. It was an immense sadness, the misery of generations, the extremity of grief to which life can fall. (page 473)

Men were springing forth, a black avenging army, germinating slowly in the furrows, growing towards the harvests of the next century, and this germination would soon overturn the earth.

(page 484)

# *Germinal*

Émile Zola

*Translated by Havelock Ellis*

*With an Introduction and Notes*
*by Dominique Jullien*

George Stade
Consulting Editorial Director

BARNES & NOBLE CLASSICS
NEW YORK

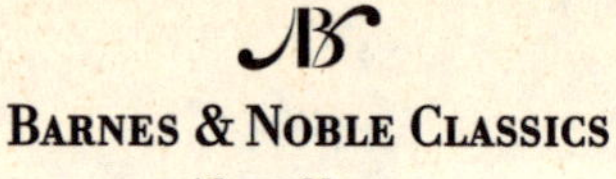

**BARNES & NOBLE CLASSICS**

NEW YORK

Published by Barnes & Noble Books
122 Fifth Avenue
New York, NY 10011

www.barnesandnoble.com/classics

*Germinal* was first published in French in 1885.
Havelock Ellis's translation first appeared in 1894.

Published in 2005 by Barnes & Noble Classics with new Introduction, Notes, Biography, Note on the Translation, Chronology, Inspired By, Comments & Questions, and For Further Reading.



*Germinal*
ISBN-13: 978-1-59308-291-8
ISBN-10: 1-59308-291-6
LC Control Number 2005927044

Produced and published in conjunction with:
Fine Creative Media, Inc.
322 Eighth Avenue
New York, NY 10001

Michael J. Fine, President and Publisher

Printed in the United States of America

QM

1 3 5 7 9 10 8 6 4 2

FIRST PRINTING

# *Émile Zola*

Émile Zola was born in Paris on April 2, 1840. In 1843 his family moved to Aix-en-Provence, where his father, Francesco, a civil engineer of Italian origin and meager means, had found work planning a new waterworks system. Four years later, he contracted a fever and died, leaving his widow, Émilie, and Émile in acute financial peril. With the help of family and friends, Émile studied at the Collège Bourbon in Aix, where he became a close friend of the future painter Paul Cézanne. After he and his mother moved to Paris in 1858, he continued his studies, with the help of a scholarship, at the Lycée Saint-Louis. Though he had won academic awards at school in Aix, his performance at the Lycée was undistinguished. He failed the *baccalauréat* exam twice and could not continue his studies, instead sinking into a grim state of unemployment and poverty.

In 1862 Zola was hired by the publisher Hachette, and he rose quickly through the ranks of the advertising department to earn a decent living. At the same time, he began to write journalistic pieces and fiction. In the latter, he sought to truthfully depict life and not censor the experiences of brutality, sex, and poverty. His explicit autobiographical novel, *Claude's Confession* (1865), created such a scandal that the police searched his house for pornographic material. Zola left Hachette in 1866 to work as a freelance journalist, and he inflamed readers with his opinionated critiques of art and literature. In 1867, he published his first major work, *Thérèse Raquin*. In his preface to this novel about adultery and murder, Zola introduced the term "naturalist" to describe his uncompromisingly "clinical" portrayals of human behavior.

A year after his marriage in 1870 to a former seamstress, Gabrielle Alexandrine Meley, Zola began publishing a series of novels that was to occupy him for more than twenty years.

Under the umbrella name *Les Rougon-Macquart,* the series details the fortunes of three branches of a French family during the Second Empire (1852–1870). Among the twenty volumes are several masterpieces, including *The Drunkard* (1877), *Germinal* (1885), *The Earth* (1887), and Zola's greatest commercial success, *Nana* (1880). As Zola's fame grew, he often retired to his second home in the countryside, where he was surrounded by fellow writers and literary disciples. As he claimed in his aesthetic manifesto, *The Experimental Novel* (1880), he and his friends created groundbreaking narratives that proudly defied the conventions of Romantic fiction.

While Zola was at work on a new series, *The Three Cities,* France was shaken by a scandal in the highest ranks of the military. In 1894 a Jewish officer, Alfred Dreyfus, was convicted of leaking secret military information to a German military attaché. When it became clear that Dreyfus had been framed by French officials under a cloud of anti-Semitism, Zola wrote "J'accuse"—an open letter excoriating the military and defending the wrongfully convicted officer. Then Zola himself was convicted of libeling the military and sentenced to prison; he fled to England but returned the next year for Dreyfus's second court martial. The subsequent years were relatively much quieter for Zola as he worked to finish a new series of novels, *The Four Gospels.*

In 1902 Émile Zola died from carbon monoxide poisoning that some said was planned by fanatics offended by his role in the Dreyfus Affair. At Zola's funeral, which was attended by some 50,000 people, Anatole France eulogized him as "a moment in the history of human conscience." Zola was buried at Montmartre Cemetery, but in 1908 his remains were moved to a place of honor in the Panthéon in Paris.

# *Table of Contents*

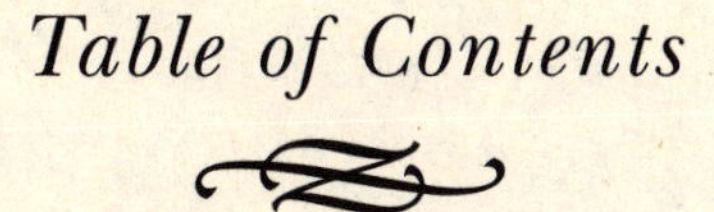

# *The World of Émile Zola and* Germinal

**1840** Émile Zola is born on April 2 in Paris, to Francesco Zola, an Italian civil engineer, and Émilie Zola, née Aubert.

**1843** The Zolas move to Aix-en-Provence, where Francesco engineers and executes a plan to supply drinking water to the town.

**1844** *Le Comte de Monte Cristo* (*The Count of Monte Cristo*), by Alexandre Dumas (*père*), is published.

**1847** Francesco dies of illness brought on by work-related exposure to bad weather, leaving his wife and son in dire financial straits.

**1848** The Revolution of February 24 leads to the fall of the July Monarchy and the establishment of the Second Republic. Louis-Napoléon Bonaparte is elected president.

**1852** Émile enrolls at the Collège Bourbon in Aix, where he wins prizes of distinction in several subjects. He and fellow student and future painter Paul Cézanne form what will be a longstanding friendship. A love of the work of Alfred de Musset and Victor Hugo reflects Émile's early affinity for Romanticism. Louis-Napoléon becomes emperor as Napoléon III.

**1853** Baron Georges Haussmann begins his large-scale redesign of Paris. The Crimean War begins.

**1856** Gustave Flaubert's novel *Madame Bovary* is published.

**1857** Charles Baudelaire's poetry collection *Les Fleurs du mal* (*The Flowers of Evil*) is published.

**1858** When they can no longer afford to live independently in Aix, Émilie and Émile move to Paris, hoping for assistance from friends. Émile receives a bursary (scholarship) that allows him to begin school at the prestigious Lycée Saint-Louis.

**1859** Émile fails the *baccalauréat,* the test required for university study. His limited options for employment lead to a two-year period of destitution that will deeply influence his writing. Living the bohemian life in Paris's Latin Quarter, he writes poems, many of which have not been recovered.

**1862** Zola is hired as a clerk by the publisher Hachette and advances in the advertising department. In his free time, he reads contemporary fiction and writes journalistic pieces and fiction. Victor Hugo's *Les Misérables* (*The Miserable Ones*) is published.

**1863** Édouard Manet's painting *Le Déjeuner sur l'herbe* (*Luncheon on the Grass*), which depicts a nude and a partially nude woman picnicking with two dressed men, is exhibited in the *Salon des Refusés* and creates a scandal.

**1864** A book of Zola's short stories, *Les Contes à Ninon* (*Tales for Ninon*), is published. The author corresponds with the brothers Edmond and Jules de Goncourt, who publish the naturalistic novel *Germinie Lacerteux* (*Germinie*). The International Workingmen's Association is founded.

**1865** Zola meets and sets up a household with his future wife, Gabrielle Alexandrine Meley, a working-class seamstress. He publishes a sexually explicit memoir, *La Confession de Claude* (*Claude's Confession*), to considerable scandal and a great deal of publicity. A book that will substantially influence Zola's thinking, Claude Bernard's *Introduction à l'étude de la médecine expérimentale* (*An Introduction to the Study of Experimental Medicine*), is published. Zola later argues that the novelist, like the scientist, can bring the scientific method to his work, and that the novelist can experiment with as well as observe his characters.

**1866** Zola meets Édouard Manet, whose portrait of Zola will eventually hang in the Musée d'Orsay in Paris. Zola resigns from Hachette and writes highly opinionated art and literary criticism for the newspaper *L'Événement. Mes*

*Haines* (*My Hates*) and *Mon Salon* (*My Salon*), two volumes of essays on art and literature, are published.

**1867** Zola's compelling novel of murder, *Thérèse Raquin,* is published, to many hostile reviews; in the book's preface, Zola uses the term "naturalist" to describe a new form of writing that unites scientific observation and literary depiction. The first International Exhibition of Paris opens.

**1868** In the novel *Madeleine Férat,* published this year, Zola explores the concept of heredity.

**1869** Gustave Flaubert's *L'Éducation sentimentale* (*Sentimental Education*) is published. Zola writes a letter introducing himself to the author. Coal miners strike in Aubin and La Ricamarie. Zola presents the master plan of *Les Rougon-Macquart,* his richly detailed twenty-novel portrait of a family, to his publisher.

**1870** Meley and Zola marry. The Franco-Prussian War begins, which leads to the Siege of Paris and the fall of the Second Empire. Zola flees to Marseilles. During the 1870s, Zola will meet often with influential authors Flaubert, Edmond de Goncourt, and Ivan Turgenev.

**1871** Zola returns to Paris and publishes *La Fortune des Rougon* (*The Fortune of the Rougons*), the first of the Rougon-Macquart cycle; the novel enjoys only modest success. The Franco-Prussian War ends. Adolphe Thiers, president of France's newly formed Third Republic, suppresses the Commune of Paris.

**1872** Zola publishes *La Curée* (*The Kill*), a novel about real estate dealings during the years when Paris was being redesigned.

**1873** Zola publishes *Le Ventre de Paris* (*The Belly of Paris*), a novel that takes place in the central food markets of Paris. Arthur Rimbaud's *Une Saison en enfer* (*A Season in Hell*) and Jules Verne's *Le Tour du monde en quatre-vingts jours* (*Around the World in Eighty Days*) are published. Napoléon III dies, and Patrice de MacMahon becomes president of the French republic, following the resignation of Thiers.

**1874** *La Conquête de Plassans* (*The Conquest of Plassans*), the fourth novel of the Rougon-Macquart series, is published. The first Impressionist art exhibition is held.

**1875** *La Faute de l'abbé Mouret* (*The Sin of the Abbé Mouret*), Zola's novel about a priest in love, is published and is a commercial success.

**1876** Another novel in the Rougon-Macquart series, *Son Excellence Eugène Rougon* (*His Excellency Eugène Rougon*), is published.

**1877** Zola's *L'Assommoir* (*The Drunkard*), an authentic portrait of working-class life and the effects of alcoholism, is denounced by the left and the right but meets with great commercial success. Now financially well-off, the Zolas move to the rue de Boulogne.

**1878** *Une Page d'Amour* (*A Love Affair*), about the guilty passions of an adulterous couple, is published. The Zolas buy a cottage at Médan, near Paris. Coal miners strike at Anzin.

**1879** A theatrical production of *The Drunkard* is a huge success. Jules Grévy, a moderate, is elected president of the Third Republic. Jules Guesde founds the French Socialist Workers Party.

**1880** Zola has his greatest commercial success with his ninth Rougon-Macquart novel, *Nana.* His influential treatise on naturalism, *Le Roman Expérimental* (*The Experimental Novel*), is published. *Les Soirées de Médan* (*Evenings at Médan*), a collection of stories by Zola and fellow authors, is published. Zola's mother dies. Flaubert dies.

**1882** Zola publishes the novel *Pot-Bouille* (*Restless House*).

**1883** *Au Bonheur des Dames* (*A Ladies' Paradise*), about how a new enterprise, the department store, effects smaller merchants, is published. Guy de Maupassant's *Une Vie* (*A Life*) is published.

**1884** Zola's novel *La Joie de vivre* (*The Joy of Life*) is published. The Waldeck-Rousseau law legalizes labor unions. Coal miners strike at Anzin. J.-K. Huysmans publishes *À rebours* (*Against the Grain*), an attack on naturalism.

**1885** *Germinal,* thought by many to be Zola's greatest work, is published; it depicts the hard life of coal miners in northern France.

**1886** *L'Oeuvre* (*The Masterpiece*) is published; the novel describes an Impressionist painter resembling Cézanne.

**1887** The next Rougon-Macquart novel, *La Terre* (*The Earth*), is published.

**1888** A "fairy tale" novel, *La Rêve* (*The Dream*), is published. While still married, Zola begins an affair with a young housekeeper, Jeanne Rozerot, that will continue until the end of his life.

**1889** Rozerot gives birth to Zola's first child, Denise. Construction of the Eiffel Tower, begun in 1887, is completed.

**1890** *La Bête Humaine* (*The Beast in Man*), considered by some to be Zola's most pessimistic book, is published.

**1891** Jacques, Rozerot and Zola's second child, is born. Zola and his wife travel through the Pyrenees. *L'Argent* (*Money*) is published.

**1892** *La Débâcle* (*The Debacle*), a war novel that also traces the rise of the Paris Commune, is published.

**1893** Zola publishes *Le Docteur Pascal* (*Doctor Pascal*), the final Rougon-Macquart work.

**1894** *Lourdes*, the first installment of Zola's idealistic trilogy *Les Trois Villes* (*The Three Cities*), is published. Sadi Carnot, president of the French republic, is assassinated, and Jean Casimir-Périer becomes president. Spurred by virulent anti-Semitism in the military, the public, and the press, the French government without clear justification convicts Alfred Dreyfus, an officer in the French army, of giving secret information to a German military attaché.

**1896** *Rome*, the next book in the *Three Cities* trilogy is published.

**1897** Edmond Rostand's *Cyrano de Bergerac* debuts.

**1898** *Paris*, the last book of the *Three Cities* trilogy, is published. New evidence leads to the reopening of the Dreyfus case, and Zola publishes his famous open letter in defense of Dreyfus, "J'accuse," in the newspaper *L'Aurore*. He accuses the army of deception and cover-up; found guilty of libeling the army; he is fined 3,000 francs and sentenced to a year in prison. He flees to England.

**1899** Zola returns to Paris. Dreyfus is reconvicted at a second court martial but is granted a presidential pardon. Zola publishes *Fécondité* (*Fecundity*), the first installment of a new series, *Les Quatre Évangiles* (*The Four Gospels*).

**1901** *Travail* (*Labor*), the next in the *Four Gospels* series, is published.

**1902** Zola dies, asphyxiated by carbon monoxide fumes resulting from a blocked chimney in his Paris apartment building. Many speculate that he was deliberately killed because of his involvement in the Dreyfus Affair. When he is buried at Montmartre Cemetery, his funeral is attended by 50,000 people, including a delegation of miners.

**1903** *Vérité* (*Truth*), the last of the *The Four Gospels* novels that Zola completed, is published. The final volume, *Justice,* was not finished at the time of his death.

**1906** Dreyfus is exonerated from any wrongdoing.

**1908** In recognition of Zola's achievements, his remains are transferred to the Panthéon in Paris.

**1937** *The Life of Émile Zola,* a film directed by William Dieterle, wins three Academy Awards.

# *Introduction*

On October 5, 1902, a crowd of fifty thousand escorted Émile Zola's body to Montmartre Cemetery. Among them were a delegation of coal miners from Denain rhythmically chanting "Germinal! Germinal! Germinal!" And in 1908 Zola's remains would be transferred to the Panthéon, the repository of official French literary glories. Yet when he died, probably murdered (his bedroom chimney was found blocked, and he was asphyxiated by fumes during the night), Zola was a highly controversial figure, a hero on the left for the working classes, intellectuals, and Dreyfus supporters, and a notorious villain to conservatives, anti-Semites, and defenders of the army's national pride. To this day, Zola is best known for two of his writings. The first is "J'accuse," his high-profile defense of Captain Alfred Dreyfus, whose condemnation to hard labor on fabricated treason charges sparked a gigantic controversy, split the nation into two enemy camps, and provided the first modern example of widespread anti-Semitism. In "J'accuse," his open letter to President Félix Faure, Zola proved an expert at using modern media for a political campaign, and he was a key factor in Dreyfus's subsequent retrial and eventual rehabilitation, although Dreyfus was fully exonerated only in 1906, almost four years after Zola's death. His other great claim to fame is the novel *Germinal* (1885). Set in a small mining town during the last years of the Second Empire, it helped draw the public's attention to the plight of the modern working classes. *Germinal* is widely regarded as Zola's masterpiece, and to this day it is by far the best-selling of Zola's novels, both in France and internationally.

## BIOGRAPHY

Émile Zola was born in Paris on April 2, 1840, the son of an Italian engineer, Francesco Zola, and Émilie Aubert. The family soon moved to Aix-en-Provence but was left destitute by the father's death in 1847. Zola would grow up in straitened circumstances and would have to fight for his living. He moved to Paris to complete high school. Although once he was there his performance in school was mediocre (he failed the *baccalauréat* exam twice in 1859), he formed lasting friendships with some classmates who would also eventually achieve fame in the art world—in particular, painter Paul Cézanne (1839–1906), who would enter Zola's fictional world in the novel *L'Oeuvre* (1886; *The Masterpiece*), written directly after *Germinal*.

Like a character in a Balzac novel, Zola came to Paris equipped only with his talent, his ambition, and a few *sous*. Without a degree or a job, life was difficult indeed, and Zola knew times of bitter poverty. But his bohemian lifestyle also afforded him time to read and to begin writing. However, the life of the Romantic outcast was not meant for Zola. Rather, he would become one of the first modern, professional writers, writing simultaneously as a journalist and a novelist. After landing a job with the publishing house Hachette, where he quickly rose to become head of the advertising department, he formed connections in the Parisian literary world and began publishing: first press chronicles and then short stories—*Les Contes à Ninon* (1864; *Tales for Ninon*)—and an autobiographical novel, *La Confession de Claude* (1865; *Claude's Confession*). In 1865 he declared his literary principles in favor of realism defined as "a piece of nature seen through a temperament." He also met Gabrielle Alexandrine Meley, who would become his wife in 1870.

Zola soon became notorious for his vehement articles in favor of Édouard Manet and the painters who would soon be known as the Impressionists. At a time when these painters were systematically denied admission to the Salon (an annual, juried art exhibit presented by the French Academy), Zola led press campaigns to defend their revolutionary work. He mercilessly attacked academic painting, denouncing it as a prettified lie for the bourgeoisie's consumption. A now-famous portrait of Zola (1868) by Manet shows him seated at his desk, surrounded by a reproduction of Manet's scandalous *Olympia* (1863) and a Japanese print depicting a wrestler. From that early period and for the rest of his life, Zola would be that fighter, throwing all his weight into the battle at hand, whether in favor of modern painters, the working poor, or the victims of anti-Semitism. His attacks on the imperial regime, voiced in the Republican press, as well as in his satirical novel *La Fortune des Rougon* (1871; *The Fortune of the Rougons*) became ever more virulent, and he was eventually saved from prosecution by the demise of the Empire following the Franco-Prussian war (1870–1871). After the National Assembly's suppression of the Paris Commune of 1871, Zola would criticize the Assembly's conservatism and its bloody repression of the insurgents, demand an amnesty for the Communards, and stigmatize the greed and selfishness of the rich. Forced to step down as parliamentary reporter, he channeled his formidable energy into his novels. Until the end of the Rougon-Macquart cycle, the saga of a French family living during the reign of Napoléon III, he would publish a novel every year: *The Fortune of the Rougons* was followed by *La Curée* (1872; *The Kill*), on the real estate boom during the time when city planner Georges Haussmann was building modern Paris; *Le Ventre de Paris* (1873; *The Belly of Paris*), set in the city's central food markets; *La Conquête de Plassans* (1874; *The Conquest of Plassans*), a story of church politics; *La Faute de l'abbé Mouret* (1875; *The Sin of the Abbé Mouret*), about a priest in love; *Son Excellence Eugène Rougon* (1876; *His Excellency Eugène Rougon*), a novel of justice and corruption; and *L'Assommoir* (1877; *The Drunkard*), on alcoholism among the working classes.

Novels kept appearing: A story of adulterous love, *Une Page d'amour* (*A Page of Love*) was published in 1878. A novel on prostitution (*Nana*, 1880), brought more scandal and yet more fame. Zola was now famous—or infamous, to some who caricatured him mercilessly as dipping his pen in a chamber pot, or as a pig groveling in the mud of lowly instincts, or as a rag picker impaling his characters on his stick, and so forth—and well-off, if not exactly rich. He bought a villa at Médan in 1878. Friends, admirers, and disciples who would gather at his villa eventually published, with Zola, a collective volume of "naturalist" stories, *Les Soirées de Médan* (1880; *Evenings at Médan*). Zola was now hailed as a leader of the naturalist school; he defined his aesthetic principles in *Le Roman expérimental* (1880; *The Experimental Novel*). Naturalism involved the application to literature of two scientific principles: determinism, or the belief that character, temperament, and ultimately behavior are determined by the forces of heredity, environment, and the historical moment; and the experimental method, which entailed the objective recording of precise data in controlled conditions.

Profoundly saddened by the deaths of his mother and his friend Gustave Flaubert in 1880, Zola sought refuge in his work. He published in close succession several more novels: on the hypocrisy of the middle classes, *Pot-Bouille* (1882; *Restless House*); on a young tycoon who builds his fortune on the first modern department store, *Au Bonheur des Dames* (1883; *A Ladies' Paradise*); about unhappy love, *La Joie de vivre* (1884; *The Joy of Life*); on the coal mines, *Germinal* (1885); about the art world, *L'Oeuvre* (1886; *The Masterpiece*); and on the peasantry, *La Terre* (1887; *The Earth*); followed by a romantic love story, *La Rêve* (1888; *The Dream*). By the mid-1880s, the tide of naturalism was about to turn. Already, J.-K. Huysmans had published *À rebours* (1884; *Against the Grain*), an attack on naturalism. And soon Zola's personal life also would be turned upside down. In 1888 he fell in love with a young laundress, Jeanne Rozerot, who would make him extremely happy and bear him two children. After a lifetime devoted to work, Zola was belatedly discovering the joys of "autumn love" and fatherhood. He took up bicycling and photography. He was eager to finish the Rougon-Macquart cycle and move on: *La Bête humaine* (1890; *The Beast in Man*), a novel in which the mechanical violence of the train is a metaphor for the human instinct of violence, was followed by: *L'Argent* (1891; *Money*), a novel on the financial world; *La Débâcle* (1892; *The Debacle*), a novel on the empire's demise; and finally *Le Docteur Pascal* (1893; *Doctor Pascal*), a book that ends the cycle on a note of a "passion for life."

Zola's last years were devoted to a political fight (the Dreyfus

Affair) and idealistic, utopian novels. The cycle of *Les Trois Villes* (1894–1898; *The Three Cities*: one book each for Lourdes, Rome, and Paris) aims to show the failure of traditional Catholicism in the face of modern problems and offers an optimistic vision of the future inspired by a faith in science and the utopian principles of French socialism. After he finished *Paris*, Zola threw himself into the battle in defense of Dreyfus. Convinced of Dreyfus's innocence, he launched a press campaign that culminated with the open letter "J'accuse," published in the popular daily *L'Aurore* (January 13, 1898). Fined 3,000 francs and sentenced to a year in prison, Zola fled to London for a year; he continued to fight for a retrial for Dreyfus until his death. As a novelist, Zola had always been a figure of scandal. But his political activism against anti-Semitism and the miscarriage of military justice won him bitter enemies and passionate hatred. He began a final cycle of novels, *Les Quatre Évangiles* (1899–1903; *The Four Gospels*), which portrays a utopian society regenerated after a nonviolent revolution: *Fécondité* (1899; *Fecundity*), *Travail* (1901; *Labor*), and *Vérité* (1903; *Truth*, a transposition of the Dreyfus affair into a child rape case) were to be followed by *Justice*, which Zola's death left unfinished. During the Dreyfus Affair, Zola had moved closer to socialist leader Jean Jaurès and his party, but his last works reflect a kind of utopian anarchism (including Charles Fourier's theories on the reorganization of labor and distribution of wealth) rather than the orthodox Marxist views of class struggle.

## THE ROUGON-MACQUART CYCLE

In 1868 Zola conceived the project of his great Rougon-Macquart cycle, "the Natural and Social History of a Family under the Second Empire." The idea was to take an extended family and tell the stories of its different members as they unfold in a specific historical and social moment. The influence of positivist philosophy—with Hippolyte Taine's definition of heredity, environment, and the historical moment as the three forces determining human behavior—was explicit in Zola's naturalist aesthetic. "If my work must have a purpose," wrote Zola, programmatically, in preliminary notes that predate the first volume of the Rougon-Macquart by two years, "it shall be to tell *human truth,* to dismantle the human machine, and, by using heredity, to reveal its concealed springs" ("Notes generales sur la direction du travail" [1869; "General Notes on the Direction of the Work"]). Heredity, as a modern-day version of fate, was a major element of the project and provided a kind of pseudoscientific backbone to the entire cycle. Zola thought of himself as a scientist, "an anatomist of the soul and the flesh," an "observer" whose only concern was truth, and who borrowed analytic and experimental methods from the modern sciences ("Deux definitions du roman" [1866; *Two Definitions of the Novel*]; "Le Roman expérimental" [1880; *The Experimental Novel*]). If Balzac's ambition had been to compete with the social registry, Zola's was to emulate science. The middle of the nineteenth century was abuzz with theories of heredity, and Dr. Prosper Lucas's *Traité philosophique et physiologique de l'hérédité naturelle* (1850; *Philosophical and Physiological Treatise of Natural Heredity*) found its most creative reader in Zola. Alcoholism, violence, madness, and degenerative diseases travel in the blood of the Rougon-Macquarts, producing geniuses as well as criminals. Étienne Lantier, *Germinal*'s hero, is overwhelmed by murderous urges when he drinks a single drop of liquor. His brother Claude, the hero of *The Masterpiece*—after *Germinal,* the next novel in the cycle—turns his genetic inheritance into creativity (he starts out as a great painter) but succumbs in the end to madness and suicide. Nana, the prostitute heroine of the eponymous 1880 novel, is Étienne and Claude Lantier's half-sister; in her the hereditary alcoholism has turned into a propensity for "vice."

Of greater interest to readers of today, however, is the historical value of Zola's fictional cycle. The twenty novels that make up the Rougon-Macquart series, each exploring a specific milieu, form a fascinating and vividly detailed document on all facets of Second Empire French society. Upper- and lower-middle-class Frenchmen, priests and prostitutes, real-estate tycoons and kitchen maids, the world of high finance and modern department stores, urban slums and mining tenements, small-town politicians and Parisian socialites—all are featured in turn in Zola's oeuvre. Zola was particularly keen to represent the people, who were, as he saw it, the "great absentee" from Balzac's collection of short stories and novels, *La Comédie humaine* (*The Human Comedy*), the otherwise comprehensive panorama of French society during the Restoration and the July Monarchy, in the first half of the nineteenth century. Working-class Paris was thus given pride of place in Zola's 1877 *The Drunkard*. The novel tells the story of Gervaise Macquart, whose efforts to rise to even a modest level of middle-class comfort and respectability are crushed by alcoholism. The novel was a huge success (and a huge scandal) and established Zola as the people's novelist. But left-wing readers criticized Zola for showing what they saw as a negative image of the people, portrayed at best as the hapless victims of a selfish and greedy bourgeoisie, at worst as animalistic brutes plagued by all manner of vices.

*Germinal* would attempt to rise above the despair of the characters' immediate circumstances, show workers in social and political roles, and offer a vision of a better future. Although the strike fails tragically, and the miners are worse off at the end of the novel than they are at the beginning (in particular the Maheus, who lose four members to the strike, leaving the widow, Maheude, and the crippled boy, Jeanlin, as the sole breadwinners in the end), the growing politicization of the miners, which develops through the shared experience of the strike and in response to the hero's leadership, is meant to be taken as a sign of progress.

The novel ends on a note of revolutionary hope, which fulfills the promise concealed in the metaphorical title, *Germinal*. Nineteenth-century readers in France would have been immediately familiar with the resonances of that title, and its political suggestions. "Germinal" was the name of the "seedtime" month in the Revolutionary calendar. It went from March 21 to April 19 and corresponded to the spring rebirth of plants. Images of renewal and resurrection are found in Étienne Lantier's final vision of the town of Montsou reviving in the spring sun: "Men were springing forth, a black avenging army, germinating slowly in the furrows, growing towards the harvest of the next century, and this germination would soon overturn the earth" (p. 484).

Another, more specific historical allusion is present as well: Just as there had been bread riots in Paris during the Revolution, on 12 and 13 Germinal, *an* (year) III (April 1 and 2, 1795), in the novel the miners, and particularly their wives, take to the streets demanding bread (part five, chapters IV–VI). And the bread riots also remind us of another famous revolutionary episode, when a starving mob led by the women of Paris marched to Versailles to capture the "Baker" (the king) and his family, in 1789. The end of *Germinal* indulges in a bit of "retrospective foresight" as it prophesies a revolution in the making: Since the story is supposedly set in the final years of the Second Empire, this is an easily identifiable allusion to the 1871 Commune; although the Paris Commune had been a failure and had ended in a bloodbath, it had nonetheless shown that the working classes were a force to be reckoned with and had opened the way to the social, economic, and political improvements of the late century. Early readers of the novel—in a century when revolutions broke out on average every twenty years—would have been left with the sense of the inevitable recurrence of revolution. In *Germinal*, the people are no longer just suffering victims of capitalism; they have begun, however ineffectually, to awaken to political consciousness and are thus key to the irreversible movement of progress. In this sense *Germinal* anticipates Zola's later utopian novels; it looks to the future more than it echoes the past.

What makes *Germinal* so compelling is the combination of symbolic force and factual accuracy. Zola approached each one of his novels with extensive research; he was particularly thorough in this and complemented his factual research with a visit to the real location of his story. He first read extensively—on the mining industry, the mining regions of northern France, the daily lives of miners, technical innovations in the pits, and working-class political movements. Then, at the end of February 1884, for about a week he visited the mining country. He talked to engineers, entered miners' houses, went deep down into the mining tunnels, and observed the small mining town of Anzin, where a strike had just begun. His voluminous "Notes sur Anzin" ("Notes on Anzin"; see the Gallimard edition of *Les Rougon-Macquart*, listed in "For Further Reading") form an extraordinary record of personal impressions and factual information. Zola was very careful to avoid anachronism. Between the late 1860s, when the novel takes place, and 1884, when Zola took notes for his novel, things had been changing in the coal mines, although the technical methods of extraction hadn't altered dramatically, and the miners' living conditions remained miserable and were made worse by rising prices and an economic slump. In *Germinal* we find women, as young as twelve and as old as forty, working in the mines. Women were paid half of a man's wages. Children of eleven worked fourteen-hour days. Strikes were illegal and often ended in bloody confrontations with the army. But miners were beginning to agitate for better conditions. A series of dramatic strikes in the last years of the Second Empire shocked public opinion and inspired the strike scenes in *Germinal.* In 1869 the army fired into the crowd of striking miners at La Ricamarie, killing thirteen, including two women. Another fourteen died later in similar circumstances at Aubin. But slowly miners, like workers elsewhere, were organizing to improve their lot. Little by little, the labor laws restricting workers' rights were relaxed. Workers' associations gradually became more tolerated. Protective laws were implemented: For example, in 1874 women could no longer be employed underground, and children under twelve were not allowed to work in the mines at all. Solidarity among workers improved, as support for ill, injured, and striking workers was more effectively organized. Karl Marx's *Manifest der Kommunistischen Partei* (*Manifesto of the Communist Party*) was published in 1848. In 1864 Marx helped found the International Workingmen's Association in London; this "First International" helped radicalize workers' movements in France. And the French translation of *Das Kapital* (1867, first volume) was published beginning in 1875. Hard-line Marxism, with its intransigent theory of class warfare, came to dominate Labor-Capital relations. This is clearly shown in the novel. *Germinal* weaves the story of the hero's political education into the background story of the miners' plight. When Étienne Lantier first comes to Montsou, he is poor and ignorant. His mind is as barren as the dark plain of the mining country. But when he emerges from the flooded mine at the end of the novel, Étienne is poised to become a professional revolutionary, leaving behind both nihilistic terrorism and conciliatory reformism.

Zola's novel is a fascinating document on the political movements of the time. Rasseneur, who owns the café where miners gather to drink and talk, embodies the moderates, the supporters of cooperation between Labor and Capital. The moderates are pitted against socialist politicians like Pluchart, the hero's role model, who is sent by the International to organize and indoctrinate miners of the northern region of France. At the heart of the novel lies the ideological rivalry between Rasseneur and Étienne and their battle for the miners' hearts and minds. Étienne's superior education and rousing rhetorical skills soon give him precedence over Rasseneur, who is booed by the miners when he tries to speak against the strike (part four, chapter VII). But after the catastrophic failure of the strike, it is Étienne's turn to experience loss of popularity. When the enraged miners throw bricks at him, he is rescued by Rasseneur, who calms the mob with his soothing eloquence, and who is once again cheered as its leader. Later, the two men have a drink together and bond over their shared disillusionment with the savagery of the crowd (part seven, chapter I). Yet in the last chapter, Étienne, called to Paris by Pluchart to join the Paris section of the International, is once again reconciled with the miners. The silent handshakes he exchanges with them on the morning of his departure acknowledge that they once again accept him as their leader and count on him, rather than Rasseneur, to lead them to victory (part seven, chapter VI). Zola's portrayal of his hero as a Marxist revolutionary in the making is masterful. He shows Étienne's transformation from a young and rather incompetent worker to a self-taught zealot and an ambitious *déclassé,* who fights for the working classes but feels superior to them. (Étienne's culture is a medley of popularized Darwinism, undigested Marxism, and elements of anarchism lifted from social theorist Pierre-Joseph Proudhon and Russian anarchist Mikhail Bakunin.) Zola's ambivalence toward professional revolutionaries is obvious—Pluchart, the elusive and ambitious apparatchik, who uses the miners' discontent for his own political promotion and spends barely enough time in Montsou to collect party memberships (part four, chapter IV), is hardly idealized. But, curiously, Étienne is not idealized either. He is "intoxicated with this first enjoyment of popularity" (p. 159), and later he hardens into a sectarian collectivist when he convinces the miners at a secret meeting in the woods that the new communist society is around the corner (part four, chapter VII). He is too pleased with his own pedantry (p. 260). He is an irresponsible revolutionary whose fiery speeches about a better future bring tragedy to his comrades.

Equally at odds with the moderates, the socialists, and the capitalists are the terrorists, or "nihilists," as they were called then by their Russian name. The chilling Souvarine is one of them. By birth he is a Russian aristocrat, whose sympathy for the poor has turned into an apocalyptic conception of class struggle. For Souvarine, the prerequisite for any revolutionary progress is the total annihilation of society by fire and blood. Anything short of that is "foolery": "'Set fire to the four corners of the towns, mow down the people, level everything, and when there is nothing more of this rotten world left standing, perhaps a better one will grow up in its place'" (p. 132). In the 1880s, anarchists were a source of concern and a hot topic of debate among intellectuals. Zola had extensive conversations about the nihilists with his friend, Russian writer Ivan Turgenev, who had met the famous anarchist Bakunin. A few years before the publication of *Germinal*, Zola wrote an article describing the Russian nihilists' "revolutionary hysteria" and their "mystical" goal as regeneration by fire, extermination, and disaster. Anarchy, for them, would lead to a new equilibrium ("La République en Russie" ["The Republic in Russia"], *Le Figaro*, March 20, 1881).

The fictional Souvarine was inspired by the historical Bakunin, whose quarrel with Karl Marx split the European revolutionary movement for many years. Bakunin's appeal for a violent overthrow of the social order, the antithesis of Marx's communism in that it rejects centralized political control, inspired a large and diverse following. Europe at the end of the century was shaken by terrorist attacks: In 1878 General Mezentsov, head of the Russian police, and Prince Kropotkin, governor of Kharkov, were murdered. Assassination attempts were made on the King of Spain, Alfonso XII, and the King of Italy, Umberto I, who was eventually assassinated in 1900. In 1881 a fourth attempt on the life of Czar Alexander II was successful. In 1883 the French prime minister, Jules Ferry, was attacked. Fear generated by anarchist violence mixed with a dread of a popular uprising resulted in a vague but overwhelming sense of anxiety about impending apocalypse. An echo of this angst is clearly heard in *Germinal*: "It was the red vision of the revolution, which would one day inevitably carry them all away, on some bloody evening at the end of the century" (p. 321). Even Christian socialism makes a token appearance in the novel, embodied by the inflammatory and ineffectual priest abbé Ranvier, who raves against bourgeois selfishness in the pulpit but is unable to help the striking miners and is promptly sent away by the authorities at the end of the strike (part seven, chapter I).

"A great fresco": This is how Zola described *Germinal*. Perhaps more than any other Rougon-Macquart novel, this one is a potent mixture of documentary accuracy and visionary imagination. "I have enlarged upon the facts," Zola wrote in a famous letter to fellow naturalist Henry Céard about *Germinal*, "and taken a leap towards the stars on the trampoline of precise observation. Truth soars upon the wing of the symbolic." We do not look to Zola for subtle psychological nuances; his characters belong to the old forms of epic and myth. His is an art of mass movements and murals, highly dramatic and visual. Over a relentlessly flat, black and grey landscape, where the only vertical dimension is provided by the pits, two groups of enemies face off: The wretched, destitute Maheus, with their tribe of sickly children, and the pampered and overfed Hennebeaus and Grégoires, whose daughter Cécile is strangled by the Maheu patriarch, old Bonnemort ("Good Death"), who has left his lungs, his legs, and his sanity in the mine. Although Cécile is an innocent victim, her murder at the hands of Bonnemort makes sense in the symbolic context of the novel. The mob's rampage across the mining country at the height of the strike reaches the ferocity and stark retributive justice of a Greek tragedy with the death and subsequent mutilation of the grocer Maigrat—gruesomely punished by the furious women (they stuff dirt into his mouth and tear off his genitals) for having starved and raped them for years. Scenes underground conjure up visions of hell, with naked black creatures crawling through narrow, muddy, or burning hot bowels. Hell is followed by apocalypse when the Russian terrorist Souvarine calmly sabotages the mine, trapping his fellow miners under torrents of water and debris. The last scenes nightmarishly link Eros and Thanatos as Étienne finally murders his rival, Chaval, and makes love to the dying Catherine in the flooded mineshaft. Presiding over the destruction of her family, Maheude is like an allegory of human suffering and destruction. Hunger, lust, and rage, the primeval passions of humanity at a basic survival level, are played out on this barren stage. And over all these episodes stands the aptly named mine, Le Voreux, an anthropomorphic monster of a mine that devours human flesh, like some modern-day Minotaur devouring its daily ration of men, women, and children.

This almost mythical view of the human condition would seem to work almost at cross-purposes with the novel's political message. Étienne's journey toward socialist militancy consists of several heroic descents into hell, which take on the archetypal significance of encounters with the underworld. He is first greeted by old Bonnemort upon his arrival on a cold winter night. Bonnemort, the third generation of men devoured by Le Voreux, is already a ghost. As the spirit of the mine, he is an intermediary who will facilitate Étienne's entry into this hellish world. At the other end of the Maheu family chain, little Jeanlin, the goblin-like perverted child who takes pleasure in tormenting gentler creatures (his friends Lydie and Bébert are his favorite victims, along with Souvarine's pet rabbit), also provides Étienne with an underground episode, when he hides him in the abandoned mineshaft after the strike. Étienne's final descent to the underworld, on the day of Souvarine's terrorist attack on Le Voreux, leaves him prematurely aged, his hair all white after his nine days trapped underground. Thus his emergence and departure for a new quest on a glorious spring day reveals an unstable combination of political optimism, historically anchored in a concrete situation (Étienne's future is as a socialist politician fighting for the workers in Paris), and the cyclical timelessness of ritualistic initiation (the hero's wisdom is acquired through suffering). Maheude herself, even though she undergoes a radical political change during the course of the novel, seems to revert back to political apathy at the end. The novel concludes, significantly, with the parting dialogue between Étienne and Maheude. Earning only 30 sous for her ten hours of back-breaking work in more than 100 degrees of heat, she looks forward to the time when her youngest children will be old enough to start working: "'They after the others. They have all been done for there; now it's their turn'" (p. 478). Initially skeptical of political action, unwilling to rebel, and suspicious of Étienne's socialist theories both out of common sense and a habit of docility in the face of the powers that be, Maheude is gradually brought around to becoming one of the most intransigent strikers. Cruelly defeated (her husband has been shot by the soldiers; her oldest son and daughter die in the mine's destruction; and eight-year-old Alzire starves to death during the strike), she reverts to a resignation of almost mythical proportions. Maheude, it would seem, is Zola's response to Victor Hugo's Michelle Fléchard, the peasant woman symbolizing the people in his allegorical novel of the Revolution, *Quatre-vingt-treize* (1874; *Ninety-three*). But while Michelle Fléchard, a quasi-animalistic mother figure, is all instinct and no thought, hopelessly closed to any political ideas, entirely uncomprehending of her own situation, and exclusively focused on preserving the lives of her three small children, Maheude learns to rise above this instinctive survival stage to become an active subject in her own story—but she pays a terrible price for it. As she prepares to return to hell, grotesquely bundled in miners' trousers, she resembles nothing more than Bataille, the old horse who lives and dies at the bottom, an exemplary and heart-breaking figure of patience without hope.

Sadness, then, the "terrible sadness" that Huysmans noted in a letter to Zola, when he received the novel, rather than revolutionary optimism, is the pervasive feeling in the novel. Beyond the revolutionary call for the *Grand Soir* (the mythical night when, according to popular belief, all labor would stop in a general strike that would mark the apocalyptic beginning of the revolution), the tale told is the timeless one of human exploitation. The Étiennes and the Souvarines of the world will continue their separate ways, whether fomenting strikes or blowing up workplaces, while the Maheus of the world keep on feeding the beast. Their enemy is not the Grégoires or even the Hennebeaus, but an "inaccessible" divinity, "an unknown god," removed at a "terrible distance," who sits "on his throne crouching down at the bottom of his tabernacle" (p. 204)—whether this figure is an allegory of capitalism or (detached from any historical moment) an allegory of human greed. The struggle depicted in the novel reaches far beyond the Marxist class struggle "between Capital and Labor," as Zola described the subject of his future novel in his preliminary sketch, it grows to cosmic proportions, a mythical fight between light and darkness. Étienne's arrival on a cold winter night forms a vivid counterpoint to his departure in the bright sunshine of an April morning. The plight of the miners is poetically structured by the title metaphor, which starts out as a political reference, setting up expectations of a revolutionary story, yet develops into a mythic image of natural regeneration.

According to Greek myth, an army is born of a dragon's teeth. The *Metamorphoses*, by Ovid (43 B.C.–A.D. 18), contains several variants: The best known tells of the mythical foundation of Thebes by Cadmos, who kills a dragon and sows its teeth, from which sprout armed men who fight one another; the survivors help found the city (book 3). In the story of the Argonauts, Jason forms an army by sowing a dragon's teeth, from which armed men spring (book 7). Seen through the prism of this myth, *Germinal*'s uprising is a complex combination of germination (the dragon teeth; the city's founding) and struggle (the fighting armies). This motif illuminates the political and ideological divisions among the miners, which were "a blind force which constantly devoured itself" (p. 411), as Étienne says, and also, more generally, the typical nineteenth-century ambivalence about the working classes, who are seen either as the People, in their virtuous and politically responsible incarnation, or as a dangerous mob, threatening chaos. For all his sympathy for the poor and his hostility toward the bourgeoisie, Zola is not immune to this double vision of the working class—a class of which he, of course, was not a member. The miners, especially Jeanlin, the degenerate son of Maheu, whose ugliness is both physical and moral, are constantly described with natural metaphors: Individually they are compared to animals, and collectively to mindless, terrifying natural forces. The rage of the mob is irrational; Étienne can stir it up but he cannot control it. A telling episode is the destruction of Deneulin's Jean-Bart mine, whose ruin does not make sense: It is a small, privately owned mine whose owner is losing money. Its workers, moreover, are treated somewhat better than at Le Voreux, and yet the miners destroy it and leave Le Voreux (the Company mine) intact. Jeanlin's murder of the little soldier makes no more sense: Jules is just as poor as the miners he is in charge of containing, and all he does is dream of returning to his village in Brittany when his time in the army is over. The people of *Germinal* are a subterranean force that is violent and coarse in its justice, whose instinct prevails over reason, and whose final victory is both desired and feared. An epic myth, that of an army germinating in the dark, intersects a cosmic myth, the killing of the dark god of Capital crouching in his labyrinthine recess: *Germinal*, Zola's naturalistic story about a coal miners' strike, expands into a tale of human strife.

---

**Dominique Jullien** (Ph.D. 1987, Paris III-Sorbonne) is a professor of French at Columbia University and the University of California, Santa Barbara, and the editor in chief of the *Romanic Review.* Her research interests center on nineteenth- and twentieth-century French and comparative literature, Proust and Borges studies, the presence of *The Arabian Nights* in modern literature, and more generally, questions of intertextuality and rewriting. Her books include *Proust et ses modèles: Les Mille et une Nuits et les Mémoires de Saint-Simon* (1989) and *Récits du Nouveau Monde: les Voyageurs français en Amérique de Chateaubriand à nos jours* (1992). She is the editor of *Aragon, Elsa Triolet: Love and Politics in the Cold War* (2001). She has published numerous articles on nineteenth- and twentieth-century literature, including several on Émile Zola.

# *A Note on the Translation*

Zola's reception in the English-speaking world was even more contentious than in France. Victorian England was not ready to welcome a naturalist writer who exposed humanity with all its instinctive and crude tendencies. Yet, paradoxically, Zola's novels sold very well in England, although critical reception remained almost uniformly negative. The situation was further complicated by the fact that British readers fell into two distinct categories. Educated Victorians could read the books in the original French, since books from the Continent were sold freely and were not subject to censorship; for the less cultured, Zola was deemed to be a corrupting influence and dangerous reading.

The history of Zola's English reception is linked with the fortunes of his London publisher, Vizetelly and Company. Henry Vizetelly (1820–1894) marketed Zola as the French Dickens and offered Zola's novels in affordable one-volume editions. Translations of *L'Assommoir* (*The Drunkard*) and *Nana* were published in 1884, to great success, and Henry Vizetelly promptly bought the translation rights to all of Zola's novels, believing that he had found a rich and steady market in his Zola translations. However, in spite of the fact that the English versions had been preemptively expurgated in order to make them suitable for the Victorian audience and outfitted with prefaces assuring the readers of the books' morality, Henry Vizetelly would soon face scandals, accusations of pornography, and obscenity trials as a result of his work.

On October 31, 1888, following the publication of Zola's *La Terre*, translated as *The Soil* (later translators used the title *Earth* or *The Earth*), Henry Vizetelly was tried and found guilty of purveying obscene publications. He was ultimately sentenced to three months of imprisonment and given a fine that brought the ruin of his publishing company. These events, compounded by Vizetelly's age and frail health, would hasten his death in 1894. Zola's novels, which had been best-sellers, had become a liability for British publishers. Henry's son, Ernest Vizetelly (1853–1922), who had been collaborating with his father on the Zola projects since 1887 as an editor and translator, took over the business and attempted to put the novels back on the market after they had been "adequately expurgated." For instance, the 1889 Vizetelly catalog lists several Zola novels—among them *Nana*, the notorious story of a prostitute—as "undergoing revisions." To pass an increasingly puritanical censorship, the translations were once again revised and toned down, often considerably. Although sometimes presented as "unabridged," they were in fact nothing of the sort. Thus at the hands of Ernest Vizetelly, who had been deeply affected by the obscenity trial, Zola's novels underwent an even more radical process of expurgation.

In the case of *Germinal*, anything sexual was expurgated from the Vizetelly translation—Maigrat's fate, Catherine's menstruation, Jeanlin's precocious games with Lydie, sex scenes involving Maheude, Mouquette, or Pierronne, and so on. In the French original, the most graphic scene in *Germinal*, the death of Maigrat, is recounted in horrifyingly vivid detail over two and a half pages. In Vizetelly's translation the episode is reduced to a single, modest paragraph in which the reader is informed that the women "heaped every indignity upon it, they dragged it hither and thither, they stamped on it, they spat on it, they stripped it, they mutilated it even, in abominable fashion, amidst the wildest, the most ferocious glee." Altogether, the revised Vizetelly version of *Germinal* runs to just 443 pages, as opposed to the 532 pages of Havelock Ellis's literal translation.

As a result, the Vizetelly translation is unacceptably bowdlerized for today's readers. In spite of its literary quality and its historical interest—Ernest Vizetelly was Zola's friend and correspondent and was indefatigably helpful and supportive during Zola's exile in London—it is not the one we have chosen for this edition. Instead, we are using Havelock Ellis's 1894 translation. An early advocate of sexual liberation and a champion of women's rights and sex education, Ellis (1859–1939) opened the way for the likes of Alfred Kinsey. His groundbreaking books—*The Dance of Life* (1923), *The Erotic Rights of Women* (1918), and, above all, the six-volume *Studies in the Psychology of Sex,* published between 1897 and 1928—caused tremendous controversy and were banned for several years in England.

It was only natural that as a translator, Havelock Ellis, who also wrote a book of essays on French literature, *From Rousseau to Proust* (1935), would be drawn to Zola's works and welcome the challenge of publishing a literal and unexpurgated version of *Germinal* in English. "It is only the great men," wrote Ellis, "who are truly obscene. If they had not dared to be obscene, they could never have dared to be great." In his preface to *Germinal,* the translator recalls with tender fondness the nights spent translating the novel with the help of his wife:

> So, in the little Cornish cottage over the sea we then occupied, the evenings of the early months of 1894 were spent over Germinal, I translating aloud, and she with swift efficient untiring pen following, now and then bettering my English dialogue with her pungent wit. In this way I was able to gain a more minute insight into the details of Zola's work, and a more impressive vision of the massive structure he here raised, than can easily be acquired by the mere reader. That joint task has remained an abidingly pleasant memory. It is, moreover, a satisfaction to me to know that I have been responsible, however inadequately, for the only complete English version of this wonderful book, 'a great fresco,' as Zola himself called it, a great prose epic, as it has seemed to some, worthy to compare with the great verse epics of old.

Havelock Ellis was also among the group of writers who signed an unsuccessful petition in support of Henry Vizetelly at the time of the trial. Reissued today in the Barnes & Noble Classics edition, his translation serves as a reminder of the courage it took to translate and publish a writer whose books were considered pornography and could bring dishonor and ruin upon a well-established publishing house. Émile Zola was vilified, exiled, and perhaps murdered for his courageous defense of the downtrodden of late-nineteenth-century French society: His early British translators were not unworthy of him.

—Dominique Jullien

*Germinal*[1]

# *PART ONE*

## CHAPTER I

OVER THE OPEN PLAIN, beneath a starless sky as dark and thick as ink, a man walked alone along the highway from Marchiennes to Montsou,[2] a straight paved road ten kilomètres in length, intersecting the beetroot-fields. He could not even see the black soil before him, and only felt the immense flat horizon by the gusts of March wind, squalls as strong as on the sea, and frozen from sweeping leagues of marsh and naked earth. No tree could be seen against the sky, and the road unrolled as straight as a pier in the midst of the blinding spray of darkness.

The man had set out from Marchiennes about two o'clock. He walked with long strides, shivering beneath his worn cotton jacket and corduroy breeches. A small parcel tied in a check handkerchief troubled him much, and he pressed it against his side, sometimes with one elbow, sometimes with the other, so that he could slip to the bottom of his pockets both the benumbed hands that bled beneath the lashes of the wind. A single idea occupied his head—the empty head of a workman without work and without lodging—the hope that the cold would be less keen after sunrise. For an hour he went on thus, when on the left, two kilomètres from Montsou he saw red flames, three stoves burning in the open air and apparently suspended. At first he hesitated, half afraid. Then he could not resist the painful need to warm his hands for a moment.

The steep road led downwards, and everything disappeared. The man saw on his right a paling, a wall of coarse planks shutting in a line of rails, while a grassy slope rose on the left surmounted by confused gables, a vision of a village with low uniform roofs. He went on some two hundred paces. Suddenly, at a bend in the road, the fires re-appeared close to him, though he could not understand how they burnt so high in the dead sky, like smoky moons. But on the level soil another sight had struck him. It was a heavy mass, a low pile of buildings from which rose the silhouette of a factory chimney; occasional gleams appeared from dirty windows, five or six melancholy lanterns were hung outside to frames of blackened wood, which vaguely outlined the profiles of gigantic stages; and from this fantastic apparition, drowned in night and smoke, a single voice arose, the thick, long breathing of a steam escapement that could not be seen.

Then the man recognised a pit. His despair returned. What was the good? There would be no work. Instead of turning towards the buildings he decided at last to ascend the pit-bank, on which burnt in iron baskets the three coal fires which gave light and warmth for work. The labourers in the cutting must have been working late; they were still throwing out the useless rubbish. Now he heard the landers push the waggons on the stages. He could distinguish living shadows tipping over the trams or tubs near each fire.

"Good-day," he said, approaching one of the baskets.

Turning his back to the stove, the carman stood upright. He was an old man, dressed in knitted violet wool with a rabbit-skin cap on his head; while his horse, a great yellow horse, waited with the immobility of stone while they emptied the six trams he drew. The workman employed at the tipping-cradle,* a red-haired lean fellow, did not hurry himself; he pressed on the lever with a sleepy hand. And above, the wind grew stronger—an icy north wind—and its great, regular breaths passed by like the strokes of a scythe.

"Good-day," replied the old man. There was silence. The man, who felt that he was being looked at suspiciously, at once told his name.

"I am called Étienne Lantier.[3] I am an engine man. Any work here?"

The flames lit him up. He might be about twenty-one years of age, a very brown, handsome man, who looked strong in spite of his thin limbs.

The carman, thus re-assured, shook his head.

"Work for an engine man? No, no! There were two came yesterday. There's nothing."

A gust cut short their speech. Then Étienne asked, pointing to the sombre pile of buildings at the foot of the platform:

"A pit, isn't it?"

---

*Also known as a "tippler" or "tumbler," this device allowed the miner to unload the tub of coal with less effort, by turning it upside down.

The old man this time could not reply: he was strangled by a violent cough. At last he expectorated, and his expectoration left a black patch on the purple soil.

"Yes, a pit. The Voreux.[4] There! The settlement is quite near."

In his turn, and with extended arm, he pointed out in the night the village of which the young man had vaguely seen the roofs. But the six trams were empty, and he followed them without cracking his whip, his legs stiffened by rheumatism; while the great yellow horse went on of itself, pulling heavily between the rails beneath a new gust which bristled its coat.

The Voreux was now emerging from the gloom. Étienne, who forgot himself before the stove, warming his poor bleeding hands, looked round and could see each part of the pit: the shed tarred with siftings, the pit-frame,* the vast chamber of the winding machine, the square turret of the exhaustion pump. This pit, piled up in the bottom of a hollow, with its squat brick buildings, raising its chimney like a threatening horn, seemed to him to have the evil air of a gluttonous beast crouching there to devour the earth. While examining it, he thought of himself, of his vagabond existence these eight days he had been seeking work. He saw himself again at his workshop at the railway, delivering a blow at his foreman, driven from Lille, driven from everywhere. On Saturday he had arrived at Marchiennes, where they said that work was to be had at the Forges, and there was nothing, neither at the Forges nor at Sonneville's. He had been obliged to pass the Sunday hidden beneath the wood of a cartwright's yard, from which the watchman had just turned him out at two o'clock in the morning. He had nothing, not a penny, not even a crust; what should he do, wandering along the roads without aim, not knowing where to shelter himself from the wind? Yes, it was certainly a pit; the occasional lanterns lighted up the square; a door, suddenly opened, had enabled him to catch sight of the furnaces in a clear light. He could explain even the escapement of the pump, that thick, long breathing

---

*Also known as "headgear"; the rigging for hauling or lifting located at the head of a mine shaft.

that went on without ceasing, and which seemed to be the monster's congested respiration.

The workman, expanding his back at the tipping-cradle, had not even lifted his eyes on Étienne, and the latter was about to pick up his little bundle, which had fallen to the earth, when a spasm of coughing announced the carman's return. Slowly he emerged from the darkness, followed by the yellow horse drawing six more laden trams.

"Are there factories at Montsou?" asked the young man.

The old man expectorated, then replied in the wind:

"Oh, it isn't factories that are lacking. Should have seen it three or four years ago. Everything was roaring then. There were not men enough! there never were such wages. And now they are tightening their bellies again. Nothing but misery in the country; everyone is being sent away; work-shops closing one after the other. It is not the Emperor's fault, perhaps; but why should he go and fight in America?[5] without counting that the beasts are dying from cholera, like the people."

Then, in short phrases and with broken breath, the two continued to complain. Étienne narrated his vain wanderings of the past week: must one, then, die of hunger? Soon the roads will be full of beggars.

"Yes," said the old man, "this will turn out badly, for God does not allow so many Christians to be thrown on the street."

"We haven't got meat every day."

"But if one had bread!"

"True, if one only had bread."

Their voices were lost, gusts of wind carrying away the words in a melancholy howl.

"Here!" began the carman again very loudly, turning towards the south. "Montsou is over there."

And stretching out his hand again he pointed out invisible spots in the darkness as he named them. Below, at Montsou, the Fauvelle sugar works were still going, but the Hoton sugar works had just been dismissing hands; there were only the Dutilleul flour mill and the Bleuze rope walk for mine-cables which kept up. Then, with a large gesture he indicated at the north half the horizon: the Sonneville workshops had not received two-thirds of their usual orders; only two of the three blast furnaces of the Marchiennes Forges were alight; finally, at the Gagebois glass works a strike was threatening, for there was talk of a reduction of wages.

"I know, I know," replied the young man at each indication. "I had been there."

"With us here things are going on at present," added the carman; "but the pits have lowered their out-put. And see opposite, at the Victoire, there are also only two batteries of coke furnaces alight."

He expectorated, and set out behind his sleepy horse, after harnessing it to the empty trams.

Now Étienne could oversee the entire country. The darkness remained profound, but the old man's hand had, as it were, filled it with great miseries, which the young man unconsciously felt at this moment around him everywhere in the limitless tract. Was it not a cry of famine that the March wind rolled up across this naked plain? The squalls were furious: they seemed to bring the death of labour, a famine which would kill many men. And he tried to pierce the shades, tormented at once by the desire and by the fear of seeing. Everything was hidden in the unknown depths of the gloomy night. He only perceived, very far off, the blast furnaces and the coke ovens. The latter, with their hundreds of chimneys, planted obliquely, made lines of red flame; while the two towers, more to the left, burnt blue against the blank sky, like giant torches. It resembled a melancholy conflagration. No other stars rose on the threatening horizon except these nocturnal fires in a land of coal and iron.

"You belong to Belgium, perhaps?" began again the carman, who had returned behind Étienne.

This time he only brought three trams. Those at least could be tipped over; an accident which had happened to the cage, a broken screw nut, would stop work for a good quarter of an hour. At the bottom of the pit-bank there was silence; the landers no longer shook the stages with a prolonged vibration. One only heard from the pit the distant sound of a hammer tapping on an iron plate.

"No, I come from the South," replied the young man.

The workman, after having emptied the trams, had seated himself on the earth, glad of the accident, maintaining his savage silence; he had simply lifted his large, dim eyes to the carman, as if annoyed by so many words. The latter, indeed, did not usually talk at such length. The unknown man's face must have pleased him that he should have been taken by one of these itchings for confidence which sometimes make old people talk aloud even when alone.

"I belong to Montsou," he said, "I am called Bonnemort."[6]

"Is it a nickname?" asked Étienne, astonished.

The old man made a grimace of satisfaction and pointed to the Voreux:

"Yes, yes; they have pulled me three times out of that, torn to pieces, once with all my hair scorched, once with my gizzard full of earth, and another time with my belly swollen with water, like a frog. And then, when they saw that nothing would kill me, they called me Bonnemort for a joke."

His cheerfulness increased, like the creaking of an ill-greased pulley, and ended by degenerating into a terrible spasm of coughing.[7] The fire basket now clearly lit up his large head, with its scanty white hair and flat, livid face, spotted with bluish patches. He was short, with an enormous neck, projecting calves and heels, and long arms, with massive hands falling to his knees. For the rest, like his horse, which stood immovable, without suffering from the wind, he seemed to be made of stone; he had no appearance of feeling either the cold or the gusts that whistled at his ears. When he coughed his throat was torn by a deep rasping; he spat at the foot of the basket and the earth was blackened.

Étienne looked at him and at the ground which he had thus stained.

"Have you been working long at the mine?"

Bonnemort flung open both arms.

"Long? I should think so. I was not eight when I went down into the Voreux and I am now fifty-eight. Reckon that up! I have been everything down there; at first trammer, then putter, when I had the strength to wheel, then pikeman* for eighteen years. Then, because of my cursed legs, they put me into the earth cutting, to bank up and patch, until they had to bring me up, because the doctor said I should stay there for good. Then, after five years of that, they made me carman. Eh? that's fine—fifty years at the mine, forty-five down below."

While he was speaking, fragments of burning coal, which now and then fell from the basket, lit up his pale face with their red reflection.

"They tell me to rest," he went on, "but I'm not going to; I'm not such a fool. I can get on for two years longer, to my sixtieth, so as to get the pension of one hundred and eighty francs. If I wish them good-evening to-day they would give me a hundred and fifty at once. They are cunning, the buggers. Besides, I am sound, except my legs. You see, it's the water which has got under my skin through being always wet in the cuttings. There are days when I can't move a paw without screaming."

A spasm of coughing interrupted him again.

"And that makes you cough so," said Étienne.

But he vigorously shook his head. Then, when he could speak:

"No, no! I got cold a month ago. I never used to cough; now I can't get rid of it. And the queer thing is that I spit, that I spit——"

The rasping was again heard in his throat, followed by the black expectoration.

"Is it blood?" asked Étienne, at last venturing to question him.

Bonnemort slowly wiped his mouth with the back of his hand.

"It's coal. I've got enough in my carcass to warm me till I die. And it's five years since I put a foot down below. I stored it up, it seems, without knowing it. Bah, it keeps you!"

There was silence. The distant hammer struck regular blows

---

*A *trammer* or a *putter* is a worker whose job is to push the carts, or trams, filled with coal, in the tunnels. A *pikeman*, also called a "hewer," is a miner who extracts the coal by hewing the rock. Bonnemort has been, in succession, a pit boy, a trammer or putter, a hewer, a repairman, and a driver.

in the pit, and the wind passed by with its moan, like a cry of hunger and weariness coming out of the depths of the night. Before the flames which grew wild, the old man went on in lower tones, chewing over again his old recollections. Ah, certainly: it was not yesterday that he and his began hammering at the seam. The family had worked for the Montsou Mining Company since it started, and that was long ago, a hundred and six years already. His grandfather, Guillaume Maheu, an urchin of fifteen then, had found the rich coal at Réquillart, the Company's first pit, an old abandoned pit to-day down below near the Fauvelle sugar works. All the country knew it, and as a proof, the discovered seam was called the "Guillaume," after his grandfather. He had not known him—a big fellow, it was said, very strong, who died of old age at sixty. Then his father, Nicolas Maheu, called the Rouge, when hardly forty years of age had died in the pit, which was being excavated at that time: a landslip, a complete downfall, and the rocks drank his blood and swallowed his bones. Two of his uncles and his three brothers, later on, also left their skins there. He, Vincent Maheu, who had come out almost whole, except that his legs were rather shaky, was looked upon as a knowing fellow. But what could one do? One must work; one worked here from father to son, as one would work at anything else. His son, Toussaint Maheu, was being worked to death there now, and his grandsons, and all his people, who lived opposite in the settlement. A hundred and six years of mining, the youngsters after the old ones, for the same master. Eh? there were many *bourgeois* that could not give their history[8] so well!

"Anyhow, when one has got enough to eat!" murmured Étienne again.

"That is what I say. As long as one has bread to eat one can live."

Bonnemort was silent; and his eyes turned towards the settlement, where lights were appearing one by one. Four o'clock struck in the Montsou tower, and the cold became keener.

"And is your company rich?" asked Étienne.

The old man shrugged his shoulders, and then let them fall as if overwhelmed beneath an avalanche of gold.

"Ah! yes. Ah! yes. Not perhaps so rich as its neighbour the Anzin Company. But millions and millions all the same. They can't count it. Nineteen pits, thirteen at work, the Voreux, the Victoire, Crèvecoeur, Mirou, St. Thomas, Madeleine, Feutry-Cantel, and still more, and six for pumping or ventilation, like Réquillart. Ten thousand workers, concessions reaching over sixty-seven communes, an out-put of five thousand tons a day, a railway joining all the pits, and workshops, and factories! Ah! yes, ah! yes! there's money there!"

The rolling of trams on the stages made the big yellow horse prick his ears. The cage was evidently repaired below, and the landers had got to work again. While he was harnessing his beast to re-descend, the carman added gently, addressing himself to the horse:

"Won't do to chatter, lazy good-for-nothing! If Monsieur Hennebeau knew how you waste your time!"

Étienne thoughtfully looked into the night. He asked:

"Then Monsieur Hennebeau owns the mine?"

"No," explained the old man, "Monsieur Hennebeau is only the general manager; he is paid just the same as us."

With a gesture the young man pointed into the darkness.

"Who does it all belong to, then?"

But Bonnemort was for a moment so suffocated by a new and violent spasm that he could not get his breath. Then, when he had expectorated and wiped the black froth from his lips, he replied in the rising wind:

"Eh? all that belong to? Nobody knows. To people."

And with his hand he pointed in the darkness to a vague spot, an unknown and remote place, inhabited by those people for whom the Maheus had been hammering at the seam for more than a century. His voice assumed a tone of religious awe; it was as if he were speaking of an inaccessible tabernacle containing a sated and crouching god to whom they had given all their flesh and whom they had never seen.

"At all events, if one can get enough bread to eat," repeated Étienne, for the third time, without any apparent transition.

"Indeed, yes; if we could always get bread, it would be too good."

The horse had started; the carman, in his turn, disappeared, with the trailing step of an invalid. Near the tipping-cradle the workman had not stirred, gathered up in a ball, burying his chin between his knees, with his great dim eyes fixed on emptiness.

When he had picked up his bundle, Étienne still remained at the same spot. He felt the gusts freezing his back, while his chest was burning before the large fire. Perhaps, all the same, it will be as well to enquire at the pit, the old man might not know. Then he resigned himself; he would accept any work. Where should he go, and what was to become of him in this country famished for lack of work? Must he leave his car-case behind a wall, like a strayed dog? But one doubt troubled him, a fear of the Voreux in the middle of this flat plain, drowned in so thick a night. At every gust the wind seemed to rise as if it blew from an ever-broadening horizon. No dawn whitened the dead sky. The blast furnaces alone flamed, and the coke ovens, making the darkness sanguinary without illuminating the unknown. And the Voreux, at the bottom of its hole, with its posture as of an evil beast, continued to crunch, breathing with a heavier and slower respiration, troubled by its painful digestion of human flesh.

## CHAPTER II

IN THE MIDDLE OF the fields of wheat and beetroot, the Deux-Cent-Quarante settlement[9] slept beneath the black night. One could vaguely distinguish four immense blocks of small houses, back to back, barracks or hospital blocks, geometric and parallel, separated by three large avenues which were divided into gardens of equal size. And over the desert plain one heard only the moan of squalls through the broken trellises of the enclosures.

In the Maheus' house, No. 16 in the second block, nothing was stirring. The single room that occupied the first floor was drowned in a thick darkness which seemed to overwhelm with its weight the sleep of the beings whom one felt to be there in a mass, with open mouths, overcome by weariness. In spite of the keen cold outside, there was a living heat in the heavy air, that hot stuffiness of even the best kept bedrooms, the smell of human cattle.

Four o'clock had struck from the clock in the room on the ground floor, but nothing yet stirred; one heard the piping of slender respirations, accompanied by two series of sonorous snores. And suddenly Catherine got up. In her weariness she had, as usual, counted the four strokes through the floor without the strength to arouse herself completely. Then, throwing her legs from under the bedclothes, she felt about, at last struck a match and lighted the candle. But she remained seated, her head so heavy that it fell back between her shoulders, seeking to return to the bolster.

Now the candle lighted up the room, a square room with two windows, and filled with three beds. There could be seen a cupboard, a table, and two old walnut chairs, whose smoky tone made hard, dark patches against the walls, which were painted a clear yellow. And nothing else, only clothes hung to nails, a jug placed on the floor, and a red pan which served as a basin. In the bed on the left, Zacharie, the eldest, a youth of one-and-twenty, was asleep with his brother Jeanlin, who had completed his eleventh year; in the right-hand bed two urchins, Lénore and Henri, the first six years old, the second four, slept in each other's arms, while Catherine shared the third bed with her sister Alzire, so small for her nine years that Catherine would not have felt her near her if it were not for the little invalid's humpback, which pressed into her side. The glass door was open; one could perceive the lobby of a landing, a sort of recess in which the father and the mother occupied a fourth bed, against which they had been obliged to instal the cradle of the latest comer, Estelle, aged scarcely three months.

However, Catherine made a desperate effort. She stretched herself, she fidgeted her two hands in the red hair which covered her forehead and neck. Slender for her fifteen years, all that showed of her limbs outside the narrow sheath of her chemise were her bluish feet, as it were tattooed with coal, and her slight arms, the milky whiteness of which contrasted with the sallow tint of her face, already spoilt by constant washing with black soap. A final yawn opened her rather large mouth, with splendid teeth against the chlorotic pallor of her gums; while her grey eyes were crying in her fight with sleep, with a look of painful distress and weariness which seemed to spread over the whole of her naked body.

But a growl came from the landing, and Maheu's thick voice stammered:

"Devil take it! It's time. It is you lighting up, Catherine?"

"Yes, father; it has just struck downstairs."

"Quick then, lazy. If you had danced less on Sunday you would have woke us earlier. A fine lazy life!"

And he went on grumbling, but sleep returned to him also. His reproaches became confused, and were extinguished in fresh snoring.

The young girl, in her chemise, with her naked feet on the floor, moved about in the room. As she passed by the bed of Henri and Lénore, she replaced the coverlet which had slipped down. They did not wake, lost in the strong sleep of childhood. Alzire, with open eyes, had turned to take the warm place of her big sister without speaking.

"I say, now, Zacharie—and you, Jeanlin; I say, now!" repeated Catherine, standing before her two brothers, who were still wallowing with their noses in the bolster.

She had to seize the elder by the shoulder and shake him; then, while he was muttering abuse, it came into her head to uncover them by snatching away the sheet. That seemed funny to her, and she began to laugh when she saw the two boys struggling with naked legs.

"Stupid, leave me alone," growled Zacharie in ill-temper, sitting up. "I don't like tricks. Good Lord! Say it's time to get up?"

He was lean and ill-made, with a long face and a chin which showed signs of a sprouting beard, yellow hair, and the anæmic pallor which belonged to his whole family.

His shirt had rolled up to his belly, and he lowered it, not from modesty but because he was not warm.

"It has struck downstairs," repeated Catherine; "come! up! father's angry."

Jeanlin, who had rolled himself up, closed his eyes, saying:

"Go and hang yourself; I'm going to sleep."

She laughed again, the laugh of a good-natured girl. He was so small, his limbs so thin, with enormous joints, enlarged by scrofula, that she took him up in her arms. But he kicked about, his apish face, pale and wrinkled, with its green eyes and great ears, grew pale with the rage of weakness. He said nothing, he bit her right breast.

"Beastly fellow!" she murmured, keeping back a cry and putting him on the floor.

Alzire was silent, with the sheet tucked under her chin, but she had not gone to sleep. With her intelligent invalid's eyes she followed her sister and her two brothers, who were now dressing. Another quarrel broke out around the pan, the boys hustled the young girl because she was so long washing herself. Shirts flew about; and, while still half-asleep, they eased themselves without shame, with the tranquil satisfaction of a litter of puppies that have grown up together. Catherine was ready first. She put on her miner's breeches, then her canvas jacket, and fastened the blue cap on her knotted hair; in these clean Monday clothes she had the appearance of a little man; nothing remained to indicate her sex except the slight roll of her hips.

"When the old man comes back," said Zacharie, mischievously, "he'll like to find the bed unmade. You know I shall tell him it's you."

The old man was the grandfather, Bonnemort, who, as he worked during the night, slept by day, so that the bed was never cold; there was always someone snoring there. Without replying, Catherine set herself to arrange the bedclothes and tuck them in. But during the last moments sounds had been heard behind the wall in the next house. These brick buildings, economically put up by the Company, were so thin that the least breath could be heard through them. The inmates lived there, elbow to elbow, from one end to the other; and no fact of family life remained hidden, even from the youngsters. A heavy step had tramped up the staircase; then there was a kind of soft fall, followed by a sigh of satisfaction.

"Good!" said Catherine. "Levaque has gone down, and here is Bouteloup come to join the Levaque woman."

Jeanlin grinned; even Alzire's eyes shone. Every morning they made fun of the household of three next door, a pikeman who lodged a worker in the cutting,* an arrangement which gave the woman two men, one by night, the other by day.

"Philomène is coughing," began Catherine again, after listening.

She was speaking of the eldest Levaque, a big girl of nineteen, and the mistress of Zacharie, by whom she had already had two children; her chest was so delicate that she was only a sifter at the pit, never having been able to work below.

"Pooh! Philomène!" replied Zacharie, "she cares a lot, she's asleep. It's hoggish to sleep till six."

He was putting on his breeches when an idea occurred to him, and he opened the window. Outside in the darkness the settlement was awakening, lights were dawning one by one between the laths of the shutters. And there was another dispute: he leant out to watch if he could not see, coming out of Pierron's opposite, the captain† of the Voreux, who was accused of sleeping with the Pierron woman, while his sister called to him that since the day before the husband had taken day duty at the pit-eye, and that certainly Dansaert could not sleep there that night. Whilst the air entered in icy whiffs, both of them, becoming angry, maintained the truth of their own information, until cries and tears broke out. It was Estelle, in her cradle, vexed by the cold.

Maheu woke up suddenly. What had he got in his bones, then? Here he was going to sleep again like a good-for-nothing. And he swore so vigorously that the children became still. Zacharie and Jeanlin finished washing with slow weariness. Alzire, with her large, open eyes, continually stared. The two youngsters, Lénore and Henri, in each other's arms, had not stirred, breathing in the same quiet way in spite of the noise.

"Catherine, give me the candle," called out Maheu.

She finished buttoning her jacket, and carried the candle

---

*Also called "stoneman"; the person in charge of clearing away the rubble in the galleries.

†The man in charge of overseeing operations at the pit head.

into the closet, leaving her brothers to look for their clothes by what light came through the door. Her father jumped out of bed. She did not stop, but went downstairs in her coarse woollen stockings, feeling her way, and lighted another candle in the parlour, to prepare the coffee. All the sabots of the family were beneath the sideboard.

"Will you be still, vermin?" began Maheu, again, exasperated by Estelle's cries which still went on.

He was short, like old Bonnemort, and resembled him, with his strong head, his flat, livid face, beneath yellow hair cut very short. The child screamed more than ever, frightened by those great knotted arms which were held above her.

"Leave her alone; you know that she won't be still," said his wife, stretching herself in the middle of the bed.

She also had just awakened and was complaining how disgusting it was never to be able to finish the night. Could they not go away quietly? Buried in the clothes she only showed her long face with large features of a heavy beauty, already disfigured at thirty-nine by her life of wretchedness and the seven children she had borne. With her eyes on the ceiling she spoke slowly, while her man dressed himself. They both ceased to hear the little one, who was strangling herself with screaming.

"Eh? You know I haven't a penny and this is only Monday: still six days before the fortnight's out.[10] This can't go on. You, all of you, only bring in nine francs. How do you expect me to go on? We are ten in the house."

"Oh! nine francs!" exclaimed Maheu. "I and Zacharie three: that makes six, Catherine and the father, two: that makes four; four and six, ten, and Jeanlin one, that makes eleven."

"Yes, eleven, but there are Sundays and the off-days. Never more than nine, you know."

He did not reply, being occupied in looking on the ground for his leather belt. Then he said, on getting up:

"Mustn't complain. I am sound all the same. There's more than one at forty-two who are put to the patching."

"Maybe, my old man, but that does not give us bread. Where am I to get it from, eh? Have you got nothing?"

"I've got two coppers."

"Keep them for a half pint. Good Lord! where am I to get it from? Six days! it will never end. We owe sixty francs to Maigrat, who turned me out of doors day before yesterday. That won't prevent me from going to see him again. But if he goes on refusing——"

And Maheude continued in her melancholy voice, without moving her head, only closing her eyes now and then beneath the dim light of the candle. She said the cupboard was empty, the little ones asking for bread and butter, even the coffee was done, and the water caused colic, and the long days passed in deceiving hunger with boiled cabbage leaves. Little by little she had been obliged to raise her voice, for Estelle's screams drowned her words. These cries became unbearable. Maheu seemed all at once to hear them, and, in a fury, he snatched the little one up from the cradle and threw it on the mother's bed, stammering with rage:

"Here, take her; I'll do for her! Damn it all, child! it wants for nothing: it sucks, and it complains louder than all the rest!"

Estelle began, in fact, to suck. Hidden beneath the clothes and soothed by the warmth of the bed, her cries subsided into the greedy little sound of her lips.

"Haven't the Piolaine people told you to go and see them?" asked the father, after a period of silence.

The mother bit her lip with an air of discouraged doubt.

"Yes, they met me; they were carrying clothes for poor children. Yes, I'll take Lénore and Henri to them this morning. If they only gave me a few pence!"

There was silence again.

Maheu was ready. He remained a moment motionless, then added, in his hollow voice:

"What is it that you want? Let things be, and see about the soup. It's no good talking, better be at work down below."

"True enough," replied Maheude. "Blow out the candle: I don't need to see the colour of my thoughts."

He blew out the candle. Zacharie and Jeanlin were already going down; he followed them, and the wooden staircase creaked beneath their heavy feet, clad in wool. Behind them the closet and the room were again dark. The children slept; even

Alzire's eyelids were closed; but the mother now remained with her eyes open in the darkness, while, pulling at her breast, the pendent breast of an exhausted woman, Estelle was purring like a kitten.

Down below, Catherine had at first occupied herself with the fire, which was burning in the iron grate, flanked by two ovens. The Company distributed every month, to each family, eight hectolitres of a hard slaty coal,[11] gathered in the passages. It burnt slowly, and the young girl, who piled up the fire every night, only had to stir it in the morning, adding a few fragments of soft coal, carefully picked out. Then, after having placed a kettle on the grate, she sat down before the sideboard.

It was a fairly large room, occupying all the ground floor, painted an apple green, and of Flemish cleanliness, with its flags well washed and covered with white sand. Besides the sideboard of varnished deal the furniture consisted of a table and chairs of the same wood. Stuck on to the walls were some violently-coloured prints, portraits of the Emperor and the Empress, given by the Company, of soldiers and of saints speckled with gold, contrasting crudely with the simple nudity of the room; and there was no other ornament except a box of rose-coloured paste-board on the sideboard, and the clock with its daubed face and loud tick-tack, which seemed to fill the emptiness of the place. Near the staircase door another door led to the cellar. In spite of the cleanliness, an odour of cooked onion, shut up since the night before, poisoned the hot, heavy air, always laden with an acrid flavour of coal.

Catherine, in front of the sideboard, was reflecting. There only remained the end of a loaf, cheese in fair abundance, and a fragment of butter; and she had to provide bread and butter for four. At last she decided, cut the slices, took one and covered it with cheese, spread another with butter, and stuck them together; that was the "brick," the bread and butter sandwich taken to the pit every morning. The four bricks were soon on the table, in a row, cut with severe justice, from the big one for the father down to the little one for Jeanlin.

Catherine, who appeared absorbed in her household duties, must, however, have been thinking of the stories told by

Zacharie about the head captain and the Pierron woman, for she half opened the front door and glanced outside. The wind was still whistling. There were numerous spots of light on the low fronts of the settlement, from which arose a vague tremor of awakening. Already doors were being closed, and black files of workers passed into the night. It was stupid of her to get cold, since the porter at the pit-eye was certainly asleep, waiting to take his duties at six. Yet she remained and looked at the house on the other side of the gardens. The door opened, and her curiosity was aroused. But it could only be one of the little Pierrons, Lydie, setting out for the pit.

The hissing sound of steam made her turn. She shut the door, and hastened back; the water was boiling over, and putting out the fire. There was no more coffee. She had to be content to add the water to last night's dregs; then she sugared the coffee-pot with brown sugar. At that moment her father and two brothers came downstairs.

"Faith!" exclaimed Zacharie, when he had put his nose into his bowl, "here's something that won't get into our heads."

Maheu shrugged his shoulders with an air of resignation.

"Bah! It's hot! It's good all the same."

Jeanlin had gathered up the fragments of bread and made soup of them. After having drunk, Catherine finished by emptying the coffee-pot into the tin-jacks. All four, standing up in the smoky light of the candle, swallowed their meal hastily.

"Are we at the end?" said the father; "one would say we were people of poverty."

But a voice came from the staircase, of which they had left the door open. It was Maheude, who called out:

"Take all the bread: I have some vermicelli for the children."

"Yes, yes," replied Catherine.

She had piled up the fire, wedging the pot that held the remains of the soup into a corner of the grate, so that the grandfather might find it when he came in at six. Each took his sabots from under the sideboard, passed the strings of his tin over his shoulder and placed his brick at his back, between shirt and jacket. And they went out, the men first, the girl, who came last, blowing out the candle and turning the key. The house became dark again.

"Ah! we're off together," said a man who was closing the door of the next house.

It was Levaque, with his son Bébert, an urchin of twelve, a great friend of Jeanlin's. Catherine, in surprise, stifled a laugh in Zacharie s ear.

"Why! Bouteloup didn't even wait until the husband had gone!"

Now the lights in the settlement were extinguished, and the last door banged. All again fell asleep; the women and the little ones resuming their slumber in the midst of wider beds. And from the extinguished village to the roaring Voreux a slow filing of shadows took place beneath the squalls, the departure of the colliers to their work, bending their shoulders, and trying to protect their arms, while the brick behind formed a hump on each back. Clothed in their thin jackets they shivered with cold, but without hastening, straggling along the road with the tramp of a flock.

## CHAPTER III

ÉTIENNE HAD AT LAST descended from the platform and entered the Voreux; he spoke to men whom he met, asking if there was work to be had, but all shook their heads, telling him to wait for the captain. They left him free to roam through the ill-lighted buildings, full of black holes, confusing with their complicated storeys and rooms. After having mounted a dark and half-destroyed staircase, he found himself on a shaky footbridge, then he crossed the screening shed, which was plunged in such profound darkness that he walked with his hands before him for protection. Suddenly two enormous yellow eyes pierced the darkness in front of him. He was beneath the pit-frame in the receiving room, at the very mouth of the shaft.

A captain, Father Richomme, a big man with the face of a good-natured gendarme, and with a straight grey moustache, was at that moment going towards the receiver's office.

"Do they want a hand here for any kind of work?" asked Étienne again.

Richomme was about to say no, but he changed his mind and replied like the others, as he went away:

"Wait for Monsieur Dansaert, the head captain."

Four lanterns were placed there, and the reflectors which threw all the light on to the shaft vividly illuminated the iron rail, the levers of the signals and bars, the joists of the guides along which slid the two cages. The rest of the vast room, like the nave of a church, was obscure, and peopled by great floating shadows. Only the lamp-cabin shone at the far end, while in the receiver's office a small lamp looked like a fading star. Work was about to be resumed, and on the iron pavement there was a continual thunder, trams of coal being wheeled without ceasing, while the landers, with their long, bent backs, could be distinguished amid the movement of all these black and noisy things, in perpetual agitation.

For a moment Étienne stood motionless, deafened and blinded. He felt frozen by the currents of air which entered from every side. Then he moved on a few paces, attracted by the winding engine, of which he could now see the glistening steel and copper. It was twenty-five mètres beyond the shaft, in a loftier chamber, and placed so solidly on its brick foundation that though it worked at full speed, with all its four hundred horse power, the movement of its enormous crank, emerging and plunging with oily softness, imparted no quiver to the walls. The engine-man, standing at his post, listened to the ringing of the signals, and his eye never moved from the indicator where the shaft was figured, with its different levels, by a vertical groove traversed by shot hanging to strings, which represented the cages; and at each departure, when the machine was put in motion, the drums—two immense wheels, five mètres in radius, by means of which the two steel cables were rolled and unrolled—turned with such rapidity that they became like grey powder.

"Look out, there!" cried three landers, who were dragging an immense ladder.

Étienne just escaped being crushed; his eyes were soon more at home, and he watched the cables moving in the air, more than thirty mètres of steel ribbon, which flew up into the pit-frame where they passed over pulleys to descend perpendicularly into the shaft, where they were attached to the cages. An iron frame, like the high scaffolding of a belfry, supported the pulleys. It was like the gliding of a bird, noiseless, without a jar, this rapid flight, the continual come and go of a thread of enormous weight, capable of lifting twelve thousand kilogrammes at the rate of ten mètres a second.

"Attention there, for God's sake!" cried again the landers, pushing the ladder to the other side in order to climb to the left-hand rowel. Slowly Étienne returned to the receiving room. This giant flight over his head took away his breath. Shivering in the currents of air, he watched the movement of the cages, his ears deafened by the rumbling of the trams. Near the shaft the signal was working, a heavy-levered hammer drawn by a cord from below and allowed to strike against a block. One blow to stop, two to go down, three to go up; it was unceasing, like blows of a club dominating the tumult, accompanied by the clear sound of the bell; while the landers, directing the work, increased the noise still more by shouting orders to the engine-man through a trumpet. The cages in the middle of the clear space appeared and disappeared, were filled and emptied, without Étienne being at all able to understand the complicated proceeding.

He only understood one thing well: the shaft swallowed men by mouthfuls of twenty or thirty, and with so easy a gulp that it seemed to feel nothing go down. Since four o'clock the descent of the workmen had been going on. They came to the shed with naked feet and their lamps in their hands, waiting in little groups until a sufficient number had arrived. Without a sound, with the soft bound of a nocturnal beast, the iron cage arose from the night, wedged itself on the bolts with its four decks, each containing two trams full of coal. Landers on different platforms took out the trams and replaced them by others, either empty or already laden; and it was into the empty trams that the workmen crowded, five at a time, up to forty. When they filled all the compartments, an order came from the trumpet—a hollow indistinct roar—while the signal cord was pulled four times from below, "ringing meat," to give warning of this burden of human flesh. Then, after a slight leap, the cage plunged silently, falling like a stone, only leaving behind it the vibrating flight of a cable.

"Is it deep?" asked Étienne of a miner, who waited near him with a sleepy air.

"Five hundred and fifty four mètres," replied the man. "But there are four levels, the first at three hundred and twenty." Both were silent, with their eyes on the returning cable. Étienne said again:

"And if it breaks?"

"Ah! if it breaks——"

The miner ended with a gesture. His turn had arrived; the cage had re-appeared with its easy, unfatigued movement. He squatted in it with some comrades; it plunged down, then flew up again in less than four minutes to swallow down another load of men. For half-an-hour the shaft went on devouring in this fashion, with more or less greedy gulps, according to the depth of the level to which the men went down, but without stopping, always hungry, with its giant intestines capable of digesting a nation. It went on filling and still filling, and the darkness remained dead. The cage mounted from the void with the same voracious silence.

Étienne was at last seized again by the same despair which he had experienced on the pit bank. What was the good of persisting? This head captain would send him off like the others. A vague fear suddenly decided him: he went away, only stopping before the building of the engine room. The wide open door showed seven boilers with two furnaces. In the midst of the white steam and the whistling of the escapes a stoker was occupied in piling up one of the furnaces, the heat of which could be felt as far as the threshold; and the young man was approaching, glad of the warmth, when he met a new band of colliers who had just arrived at the pit. It was the Maheu and Levaque set. When he saw Catherine at the head, with her gentle boyish air, a superstitious idea caused him to risk another question.

"I say there, mate! do they want a hand here for any kind of work?"

She looked at him surprised, rather frightened at this sudden voice coming out of the shadow. But Maheu, behind her, had heard and replied, talking with Étienne for a moment. No, no one was wanted. This poor devil of a man who had lost his way here interested him. When he left him he said to the others:

"Eh! one might easily be like that. Mustn't complain; everyone hasn't the chance to work himself to death."

The band entered and went straight to the shed, a vast hall coarsely boarded and surrounded by cupboards shut by padlocks. In the centre an iron fire-place, a sort of closed stove without a door, was red and so stuffed with burning coal that fragments flew out and rolled on to the trodden soil. The hall was only lighted by this stove, from which sanguinary reflections danced along the greasy wood-work up to the ceiling, stained with black dust. As the Maheus went into the heat there was a sound of laughter. Some thirty workmen were standing upright with their backs to the fire, roasting themselves with an air of enjoyment. Before going down, they all came here to carry away a little warmth in their skins, so that they could face the dampness of the pit. But this morning there was much amusement: they were joking Mouquette, a putter girl of eighteen, whose enormous breasts and flanks were bursting through her jacket and breeches. She lived at Réquillart with her father, old Mouque, a groom, and Mouquet, her brother, a lander; but their hours of work were not the same, and in the middle of the wheat fields in summer, or against a wall in winter, she took her pleasure with her lover of the week. All in the mine had their turn; it was a perpetual round of comrades without further consequences. One day, when reproached about a Marchiennes nail-maker, she was furiously angry, exclaiming that she respected herself far too much, that she would cut her arm off if anyone could boast that he had seen her with anyone but a collier.

"It isn't that big Chaval now?" said a miner, grinning, "that little fellow must have needed a ladder. I saw you behind Réquillart, a token that he got on to a milestone."

"Well," replied Mouquette, in a good humour, "what's that to do with you? You were not asked to push."

And this gross good-natured joke increased the laughter of

the men, who expanded their shoulders, half cooked by the stove, while she herself, shaken by laughter, was displaying in the midst of them the indecency of her costume, embarrassingly comical, with her masses of flesh exaggerated almost to disease.

But the gaiety ceased; Mouquette told Maheu that Fleurance, big Fleurance, would never come again; she had been found the night before stiff in her bed; some said it was her heart, others that it was a pint of gin she had drunk too quickly. And Maheu was in despair; another piece of ill-luck; one of the best of his putters gone without any chance of replacing her at once. He was working in a set; there were four pikemen associated in his cutting, himself, Zacharie, Levaque, and Chaval. If they had Catherine alone to wheel, the work would suffer.

Suddenly he called out:

"I have it! there was that man looking for work!"

At that moment Dansaert passed before the shed. Maheu told him the story, and asked for his authority to engage the man; he emphasised the desire of the company to substitute men for women, as at Anzin. The head captain smiled at first; for the scheme of excluding women from the pit was not usually well received by the miners, who were troubled about placing their daughters, and not much affected by questions of morality and health. But after some hesitation he gave his permission, reserving its ratification for Monsieur Négrel, the engineer.

"All very well!" exclaimed Zacharie; "the man must be far away by this time."

"No," said Catherine. "I saw him stop at the boilers."

"After him, then, lazy," cried Maheu.

The young girl ran forward; while a crowd of miners proceeded to the shaft, yielding the fire to others.

Jeanlin, without waiting for his father, went also to take his lamp, together with Bébert, a big, stupid boy, and Lydie, a small child of ten. Mouquette, who was in front of them, called out in the black passage that they were dirty brats, and threatened to box their ears if they pinched her.

Étienne was, in fact, in the boiler building, talking with a stoker, who was charging the furnaces with coal. He felt very cold at the thought of the night into which he must return. But he was deciding to set out, when he felt a hand placed on his shoulder.

"Come," said Catherine; "there's something for you."

At first he could not understand. Then he felt a spasm of joy, and vigorously squeezed the young girl's hands.

"Thanks mate. Ah! you're a good chap, you are!"

She began to laugh, looking at him in the red light of the furnaces, which lit them up. It amused her that he should take her for a boy, still slender, with her knot of hair hidden beneath the cap. He also was laughing, with satisfaction, and they remained, for a moment, both laughing in each other's faces with radiant cheeks.

Maheu, squatting down before his box in the shed, was taking off his sabots and his coarse woollen stockings. When Étienne arrived everything was settled in three or four words: thirty sous a day, hard work, but work that he would easily learn. The pikeman advised him to keep his shoes, and lent him an old cap, a leather hat for the protection of his skull, a precaution which the father and his children disdained. The tools were taken out of the chest, where also was found Fleurance's shovel. Then, when Maheu had shut up their sabots, their stockings, as well as Étienne's bundle, he suddenly became impatient.

"What is that ass Chaval up to? Another girl turned up on a pile of stones? We are half-an-hour late to-day."

Zacharie and Levaque were quietly roasting their shoulders. The former said at last:

"Is it Chaval you're waiting for? He came before us, and went down at once."

"What! you knew that, and said nothing? Come, come, look sharp!"

Catherine, who was warming her hands, had to follow the band. Étienne allowed her to pass, and went behind her. Again he journeyed through a maze of staircases and obscure corridors in which their naked feet produced the soft sound of old slippers. But the lamp cabin was glittering—a glass house, full of hooks in rows, holding hundreds of Davy lamps,[12] examined and washed the night before, and lighted like candles in a chapel. At the barrier each workman took his own, stamped with his number; then he examined it and shut it himself, while the marker, seated at a table, inscribed on the registers the hour of descent. Maheu had to intervene to obtain a lamp for his new putter, and there was still another precaution: the workers defiled before an examiner, who assured himself that all the lamps were properly closed.

"Golly! It's not warm here," murmured Catherine, shivering.

Étienne contented himself with nodding his head. He was in front of the shaft, in the midst of a vast hall swept by currents of air. He certainly considered himself brave, but he felt a disagreeable emotion at his chest amid this thunder of trams, the hollow blows of the signals, the stifled howling of the trumpet, the continual flight of those cables, unrolled and rolled at full speed by the drums of the engine. The cages rose and sank with the gliding movement of a nocturnal beast, always engulfing men, whom the throat of the hole seemed to drink. It was his turn now. He felt very cold, and preserved a nervous silence which made Zacharie and Levaque grin; for both of them disapproved of the hiring of this unknown man, especially Levaque, who was offended that he had not been consulted. So Catherine was glad to hear her father explain things to the young man.

"Look! above the cage there is a parachute with iron grapnels to catch into the guides in case of breakage. Does it work? Oh, not always. Yes, the shaft is divided into three compartments, closed by planking from top to bottom; in the middle the cages, on the left the passage for the ladders——"

But he interrupted himself to grumble, though taking care not to raise his voice much:

"What are we stuck here for, blast it? What right have they to freeze us in this way?"

The captain, Richomme, who was going down himself, with his free lamp fixed by a nail into the leather of his cap, heard him.

"Careful! look out for ears," he murmured paternally, as an old miner with an affectionate feeling for comrades. "Workmen must do what they can. Hold! here we are; get in with your people."

The cage, provided with iron bands and a small meshed lattice work, was in fact awaiting them on the bars. Maheu, Zacharie and Catherine slid into a tram below, and as all five had to enter, Étienne in his turn went in, but the good places were taken; he had to squeeze himself near the young girl, whose elbow pressed into his belly. His lamp embarrassed him; they advised him to fasten it to the button-hole of his jacket. Not hearing, he awkwardly kept it in his hand. The embarkation continued, above and below, a confused packing of cattle. They did not, however, set out. What, then, was happening? It seemed to him that his impatience lasted for many minutes. At last he felt a shock, and the light grew dim, everything around him seemed to fly, while he experienced the dizzy anxiety of a fall contracting his bowels. This lasted as long as he could see light, through the two reception storeys, in the midst of the whirling flight of the scaffolds. Then, having fallen into the blackness of the pit, he became stunned, no longer having any clear perception of his sensations.

"Now we are off," said Maheu, quietly.

They were all at their ease. He asked himself at times if he was going up or down. Now and then, when the cage went straight without touching the guides, there seemed to be no motion, but rough shocks were afterwards produced, a sort of dancing amid the joists, which made him fear a catastrophe. For the rest he could not distinguish the walls of the shaft behind the lattice work, to which he pressed his face. The lamps feebly lighted the mass of bodies at his feet. Only the captain's free light, in the neighbouring tram, shone like a lighthouse.

"This is four mètres in diameter," continued Maheu, to instruct him. "The tubbing wants doing over again, for the water comes in everywhere. Stop! we are reaching the bottom: do you hear?"

Étienne was, in fact, now asking himself the meaning of this noise of falling rain. A few large drops had at first sounded on the roof of the cage, like the beginning of a shower, and now the rain increased, streaming down, becoming at last a deluge. The roof must be full of holes, for a thread of water was flowing on to his shoulder and wetting him to the skin. The cold became icy, and they were buried in black humidity when they passed through a sudden flash of light, the vision of a cavern in which men were moving. But already they had fallen back into darkness.

Maheu said:

"That is the first main level. We are at three hundred and twenty mètres. See the speed."

Raising his lamp he lighted up a joist of the guides which fled by like a rail beneath a train going at full speed, and beyond, as before, nothing could be seen. They passed three other levels in flights of light. The deafening rain continued to strike through the darkness.

"How deep it is!" murmured Étienne.

This fall seemed to last for hours. He was suffering for the wrong position he had taken, not daring to move, and especially tortured by Catherine's elbow. She did not speak a word; he only felt her against him and it warmed him. When the cage at last stopped at the bottom, at five hundred and fifty-four mètres, he was astonished to learn that the descent had lasted exactly one minute. But the noise of the bolts fixing themselves, the sensation of solidity beneath, suddenly cheered him; and he was joking when he said to Catherine:

"What have you got under your skin to be so warm? I've got your elbow in my belly, sure enough."

Then she also burst out laughing. Stupid of him, still to take for a boy! Were his eyes stopped?

"It's in your eye that you've got my elbow!" she replied, in the midst of a storm of laughter which the astonished young man could not explain.

The cage voided its burden of workers, who crossed the pit-eye hall, a chamber cut in the rock, vaulted with masonry, and lighted up by three large lamps. Over the iron flooring the porters* were violently rolling laden trams. A cavernous odour exhaled from the walls, a freshness of saltpetre in which mingled

---

*Also called "onsetters" and "pit boys"; workers who load the cages at the bottom of the shaft.

hot breaths from the neighbouring stable. The openings of four galleries yawned here.

"This way," said Maheu to Étienne. "You're not there yet. It is still two good kilomètres."

The workmen separated, and were lost in groups in the depths of these black holes. Some fifteen went off into that on the left, Étienne walked last, behind Maheu, who was preceded by Catherine, Zacharie, and Levaque. It was a large gallery for waggons, through a bed of solid rock, which had only needed walling here and there. In single file they still went on without a word, by the tiny flame of the lamps. The young man stumbled at every step, and entangled his feet in the rails. For a moment a hollow sound disturbed him, the sound of a distant storm, the violence of which seemed to increase and to come from the bowels of the earth. Was it the thunder of a landslip bringing on to their heads the enormous mass which separated them from the light? A gleam pierced the night, he felt the rock tremble, and when he had placed himself close to the wall, like his comrades, he saw a large white horse close to his face, harnessed to a train of waggons. On the first, and holding the reins, was seated Bébert, while Jeanlin, with his hands fastened to the edge of the last, was running barefooted behind.

They again began their walk. Farther on they reached cross ways, where two new galleries opened, and the band divided again, the workers gradually entering all the stalls of the mine.

Now the waggon-gallery was constructed of wood; props of timber supported the roof, and made for the crumbly rock a shirt of scaffolding, behind which one could see the plates of schist glimmering with mica, and the coarse masses of dull, rough sandstone. Trains of tubs, full or empty, continually passed, crossing each other with their thunder, borne into the shadow by vague beasts trotting by like phantoms. On the double way of a shunting line a long, black serpent slept, a train at standstill, with a snorting horse, his crupper looking like a block fallen from the roof. Doors for ventilation were slowly opening and shutting. And as they advanced the gallery became more narrow and lower, and the roof irregular, forcing them to bend their backs constantly.

Étienne roughly struck his head; without his leather cap he would have broken his skull. However, he attentively followed the slightest gestures of Maheu, whose sombre profile was seen against the glimmer of the lamps. None of the workmen knocked themselves; they evidently knew each boss, each knot of wood or swelling in the rock. The young man also suffered from the slippery soil, which became damper and damper. At times he went through actual marshes, only revealed by the muddy splash of his feet. But what especially astonished him were the sudden changes of temperature. At the bottom of the shaft it was very fresh, and in the waggon-gallery, through which passed all the air of the mine, an icy breeze was blowing, with the violence of a tempest, between the narrow walls. Afterwards, as they penetrated more deeply along other passages which only received a small disputed share of air, the wind fell and the heat increased, a suffocating heat as heavy as lead.

Maheu had not again opened his mouth. He turned down another gallery to the right, simply saying to Étienne, without looking round:

"The Guillaume seam."

It was the seam which contained their cutting. After the first steps, Étienne hurt his head and elbows. The sloping roof descended so low that, for twenty or thirty mètres at a time, he had to walk bent double. The water came up to his ankles. After two hundred mètres of this, he saw Levaque, Zacharie, and Catherine disappear, as though they had flown through a narrow fissure which was open in front of him.

"We must climb," said Maheu. "Fasten your lamp to a buttonhole and hang on to the wood." He himself disappeared, and Étienne had to follow him. This chimney-passage left in the seam was reserved for miners, and led to all the secondary passages. It was about the thickness of the coal-bed, hardly sixty centimètres. Fortunately the young man was thin, for, as he was still awkward, he hoisted himself up with a useless expense of muscle, flattening his shoulders and hips, advancing by the strength of his wrists, clinging to the planks. Fifteen mètres higher they came on the first secondary passage, but they had to continue, as the cutting of Maheu and his mates was the sixth passage in the hell, as they said; every fifteen mètres the passages were placed over each other in never-ending succession through this cleft, which scraped back and chest. Étienne groaned as if the weight of the rocks had pounded his limbs; with torn hands and bruised legs, he also suffered from lack of air, so that he seemed to feel the blood bursting through his skin. He vaguely saw in one passage two squatting beasts, a big one and a little one, pushing trams: they were Lydie and Mouquette already at work. And he had still to climb the height of two cuttings! He was blinded by sweat, and he despaired of catching up the others, whose agile limbs he heard brushing against the rock with a long gliding movement.

"Cheer up! here we are!" said Catherine's voice.

He had, in fact, arrived, and another voice cried from the bottom of the cutting:

"Well, is this the way to treat people? I have two kilomètres to walk from Montsou and I'm here first."

It was Chaval, a tall, lean, bony fellow of twenty-five, with strongly marked features, who was in a bad humour at having to wait. When he saw Étienne he asked with contemptuous surprise:

"What's that?"

And when Maheu had told him the story he added between his teeth:

"These men are eating the bread of girls."[13]

The two men exchanged a look, lighted up by one of those instinctive hatreds which suddenly flame up. Étienne had felt the insult without yet understanding it. There was silence, and they got to work. At last all the seams were gradually filled, and the cuttings were in movement at every level and at the end of every passage. The devouring shaft had swallowed its daily ration of men: nearly seven hundred hands, who were now at work in this giant ant-hill, everywhere making holes in the earth, drilling it like an old worm-eaten piece of wood. And in the middle of the heavy silence of the crushing of these deep strata, one could hear, by placing one's ear to the rock, the movement of these human insects at work, from the flight of the cable which moved the cage up and down to the biting of the tools cutting out the coal at the end of the stalls. Étienne, on turning round, found himself again pressed close to Catherine. But this time he caught a glimpse of the developing curves of her breast: he suddenly understood the warmth which had penetrated him.

"You are a girl, then!" he exclaimed, stupefied.

She replied in her cheerful way, without blushing:

"Of course. You've taken your time to find it out!"

## CHAPTER IV

THE FOUR PIKEMEN HAD spread themselves one above the other over the whole face of the cutting. Separated by planks, hooked on to retain the fallen coal, they each occupied about four mètres of the seam, and this seam was so thin, scarcely more than fifty centimètres thick at this spot, that they seemed to be flattened between the roof and the wall, dragging themselves along by their knees and elbows, and unable to turn without crushing their shoulders. In order to attack the coal, they had to lie on their sides with their arms raised, brandishing, in a sloping direction, their short-handled picks.

Below there was, first, Zacharie; Levaque and Chaval were on the stages above, and at the very top was Maheu. Each worked at the slaty bed, which he dug out with blows of the pick; then he made two vertical cuttings in the bed and detached the block by burying an iron wedge in its upper part. The coal was rich; the block broke and rolled in fragments along their bellies and thighs. When these fragments, retained by the plank, had collected round them, the pikemen disappeared, buried in the narrow cleft.

Maheu suffered most. At the top the temperature rose to thirty-five degrees, and the air was stagnant, so that in the long run it became fatal. In order to see, he had been obliged to fix his lamp to a nail near his head, and this lamp, close to his skull, still further heated his blood. But his torment was especially aggravated by the moisture. The rock above him, a few centimètres from his face, streamed with water, which fell in large continuous rapid drops with a sort of obstinate rhythm, always at the same spot. It was vain for him to twist his head or bend back his neck. They fell on his face, dropping unceasingly. In a quarter of an hour he was soaked, and at the same time covered with sweat, smoking as with the hot steam of a laundry. This morning a drop beating upon his eye made him swear. He would not leave his picking, he dealt great strokes which shook him violently between the two rocks, like a grub taken between two leaves of a book and in danger of being completely flattened.

Not a word was exchanged. They all hammered; one only heard these irregular blows, which seemed veiled and remote. The sounds had a sonorous hoarseness, without any echo in the dead air. And it seemed that the darkness was an unknown blackness, thickened by the floating coal dust, made heavy by the gas which weighed on the eyes. The wicks of the lamps beneath their caps of metallic tissue only showed as reddish points. One could distinguish nothing. The cutting opened out above like a large chimney, flat and oblique, in which the soot of ten years had amassed a profound night. Spectral figures were moving in it, the gleams of light enabled one to catch a glimpse of a rounded hip, a knotty arm, a vigorous head, besmeared as if for a crime. Sometimes, blocks of coal shone suddenly as they became detached, illuminated by a crystalline reflection. Then everything fell back into darkness, pickaxes struck great hollow blows; one only heard panting chests, the grunting of discomfort and weariness beneath the weight of the air and the rain of the springs.

Zacharie, with arms weakened by a spree of the night before, soon left his work on the pretence that more timbering was necessary. This allowed him to forget himself in quiet whistling, his eyes vaguely resting in the shade. Behind the pikemen nearly three mètres of the seam were clear, and they had not yet taken the precaution of supporting the rock, having grown careless of danger and miserly of their time.

"Here, you swell," cried the young man to Étienne, "hand up some wood."

Étienne, who was learning from Catherine how to manage his shovel, had to raise the wood in the cutting. A small supply had remained over from yesterday. It was usually sent down every morning ready cut to fit in the bed.

"Hurry up there, damn it!" shouted Zacharie, seeing the new putter hoist himself up awkwardly in the midst of the coal, his arms embarrassed by four pieces of oak.

He made a hole in the roof with his pick-axe, and then another in the wall, and wedged in the two ends of the wood, which thus supported the rock. In the afternoon the workers in the earth cutting took the rubbish left at the bottom of the gallery by the pikemen, and cleared out the exhausted section of the seam, in which they destroyed the wood, being only careful about the lower and upper roads for the haulage.

Maheu ceased to groan. At last he had detached his block, and he wiped his streaming face on his sleeve. He was disturbed as to what Zacharie was doing behind him.

"Let it be," he said, "we will see after breakfast. Better go on hewing, if we want to make up our share of trams."

"It's because it's sinking," replied the young man. "Look, there's a crack. It may slip."

But the father shrugged his shoulders. Ah! nonsense! Slip! And if it did, it would not be the first time; they would get out of it all right. He grew angry at last, and sent his son to the front of the cutting.

All of them, however, were now stretching themselves. Levaque, resting on his back, was swearing as he examined his left thumb which had been grazed by the fall of a piece of sandstone. Chaval had taken off his shirt in a fury, and was working with bare chest and back for the sake of coolness. They were already black with coal, soaked in a fine dust diluted with sweat which ran down in streams and pools. Maheu first began again to hammer, lower down, with his head level with the rock. Now the drop struck his forehead so obstinately that he seemed to feel it piercing a hole in the bone of his skull.

"You mustn't mind," explained Catherine to Étienne, "they are always howling."

And like a good-natured girl she went on with her lesson. Every laden tram arrived at the top in the same condition as it left the cutting, marked with a special metal token so that the receiver might put it to the reckoning of the stall. It was necessary, therefore, to be very careful to fill it, and only to take proper coal, otherwise it was refused at the receiving office.

The young man, whose eyes now became accustomed to the darkness, looked at her, still white with her chlorotic complexion, and he could not have told her age; he thought she must be twelve, she seemed to him so slight. However, he felt she must be older, with her boyish freedom, a simple audacity which confused him a little; she did not please him: he thought her too roguish with her pale Pierrot head, framed at the temples by the cap. But what astonished him was the strength of this child, a nervous strength which was blended with a good deal of skill. She filled her tram faster than he could, with quick small regular strokes of the shovel; she afterwards pushed it to the inclined way with a single slow push, without a hitch, easily passing under the low rocks. He tore himself to pieces, got off the rails, and was reduced to despair.

It was certainly not a convenient road. It was sixty mètres from the cutting to the upbrow, and the passage, which the miners in the earth cutting had not yet enlarged, was a mere tube with a very irregular roof swollen by innumerable bosses; at certain spots the laden tram could only just pass; the putter had to flatten himself, to push on his knees, in order not to break his head, and besides this the wood was already bending and yielding. One could see it broken in the middle in long pale rents like an over-weak crutch. One had to be careful not to graze one's self in these fractures; and beneath the slow crushing, which caused the splitting of billets of oak as large as the thigh, one had to glide almost on one's belly with a secret fear of suddenly hearing one's back break.

"Again!" said Catherine, laughing.

Étienne's tram had gone off the rails at the most difficult spot. He could not roll straight on these rails which sank in the damp earth, and he swore, became angry, and fought furiously with the wheels, which he could not get back into place in spite of exaggerated efforts.

"Wait a bit," said the young girl. "If you get angry it will never go." Skilfully she had glided down, had buried her buttocks backwards beneath the tram, and by putting the weight on her loins she raised it and replaced it. The weight was seven hundred kilogrammes. Surprised and ashamed, he stammered excuses.

She was obliged to show him how to separate his legs to support his feet against the planking on both sides of the gallery, in order to give himself a more solid fulcrum. The body had to be bent, the arms made stiff so as to push with all the muscles of the shoulders and hips. During the journey he followed her and watched her proceed with tense back, her fists so low that she seemed trotting on all fours, like one of those dwarf beasts that perform at circuses. She sweated, panted, her joints cracked, but without a complaint, with the indifference of custom, as if it were the common wretchedness of all to live thus bent double. But he could not succeed in doing as much; his shoes troubled him, his body seemed broken by walking in this way with lowered head. At the end of a few minutes the position became a torture, an intolerable anguish, so painful that he got on his knees for a moment to straighten himself and breathe.

Then at the upbrow there was more labour. She taught him to fill his tram quickly. At the top and bottom of this inclined plane, which served all the cuttings from one level to the other, there was a trammer—the breaksman above, the receiver below. These scamps of twelve to fifteen years shouted abominable words to each other, and to warn them it was necessary to yell still more violently. Then, as soon as there was an empty tram to send back, the receiver gave the signal and the putter embarked her tram, the weight of which made the other ascend when the breaksman loosened his break. Below, in the bottom gallery, were formed trains which the horses drew to the shaft.

"Here, you confounded rascals," cried Catherine in the inclined way, which was entirely wooded, about a hundred mètres long, and resounded like a gigantic trumpet.

The trammers must have been resting, for neither of them replied. On all the levels haulage had stopped. A shrill girl's voice said at last:

"One of them must be on Mouquette, sure enough!"

There was a roar of laughter, and the putters of the whole seam held their sides.

"Who is that?" asked Étienne of Catherine.

The latter named little Lydie, a scamp who knew more than she ought, and who pushed her tram as stoutly as a woman, in spite of her doll's arms. As to Mouquette she was quite capable of being with both the trammers at once.

But the voice of the receiver arose shouting out to load. Doubtless a captain was passing beneath. Haulage began again on the nine levels, and one only heard the regular calls of the trammers, and the snorting of the putters arriving at the upbrow and steaming like overladen mares. It was the element of bestiality which breathed in the pit, the sudden desire of the male, when a miner met one of these girls on all fours, with her flanks in the air and her hips bursting through her boy's breeches.

And on each journey Étienne found again at the bottom the stuffiness of the cutting, the hollow and broken cadence of the axes, the deep painful sighs of the pikemen persisting in their work. All four were naked, mixed up with the coal, soaked with black mud up to the cap. At one moment it had been necessary to free Maheu, who was gasping, and to remove the planks so that the coal could fall into the passage. Zacharie and Levaque became enraged with the seam, which was now hard, they said, and which would make the condition of their account disastrous. Chaval, turned, lying for a moment on his back, abusing Étienne, whose presence decidedly exasperated him.

"A sort of snake; hasn't the strength of a girl! Are you going to fill your tub? It's to spare your arms, eh? Damned if I don't keep back the ten sous if you get us one refused!"

The young man avoided replying, too happy at present to have found this convict's labour and accepting the brutal rule of the worker by master worker. But he could no longer walk, his feet were bleeding, his limbs torn by horrible cramps, his body confined in an iron girdle. Fortunately it was ten o'clock, and the stall decided to have breakfast.

Maheu had a watch, but he did not even look at it. At the bottom of this starless night he was never five minutes out. All put on their shirts and jackets. Then, descending from the cutting they squatted down, their elbows to their sides, their buttocks on their heels, in that posture so habitual with miners that they keep it even when out of the mine, without feeling the need of a stone or a beam to sit on. And each, having taken out his brick, bit seriously at the thick slice, uttering occasional words on the morning's work. Catherine, who remained standing, at last joined Étienne, who had stretched himself out farther along, across the rails, with his back against the planking. There was a place there almost dry.

"You don't eat," she said to him, with her mouth full and her brick in her hand.

Then she remembered that this youth, wandering about at night without a sou, perhaps had not a bit of bread.

"Will you share with me?"

And as he refused, declaring that he was not hungry, while his voice trembled with the gnawing in his stomach, she went on cheerfully:

"Ah! if you are fastidious! But here, I've only bitten on that side. I'll give you this."

She had already broken the bread and butter into two pieces. The young man, taking his half, restrained himself from devouring it all at once, and placed his arms on his thighs, so that she should not see how he trembled. With her quiet air of good comradeship she lay beside him, at full length on her stomach, with her chin in one hand, slowly eating with the other. Their lamps, placed between them, lit up their faces.

Catherine looked at him a moment in silence. She must have found him handsome, with his delicate face and black moustache. She vaguely smiled with pleasure.

"Then you are an engine-driver, and they sent you away from your railway. Why?"

"Because I struck my chief."

She remained stupefied, overwhelmed, with her hereditary ideas of subordination and passive obedience.

"I ought to say that I had been drinking," he went on, "and when I drink I get mad—I could devour myself, and I could devour other people. Yes; I can't swallow two small glasses without wanting to kill someone. Then I am ill for two days."

"You mustn't drink," she said, seriously.

"Ah, don't be afraid. I know myself."

And he shook his head. He hated brandy with the hatred of the last child of a race of drunkards, who suffered in his flesh from all those ancestors, soaked and driven mad by alcohol to such a point that the least drop had become poison to him.

"It is because of mother that I didn't like being turned into the street," he said, after having swallowed a mouthful. "Mother is not happy, and I used to send her a five-franc piece now and then."

"Where is she, then, your mother?"

"At Paris. Laundress, Rue de la Goutte-d'or."[14]

There was silence. When he thought of these things a tremor dimmed his dark eyes, the sudden anguish of the injury he brooded over in his fine youthful strength. For a moment he remained with his looks buried in the darkness of the mine; and at that depth, beneath the weight and suffocation of the earth, he saw his childhood again, his mother still beautiful and strong, forsaken by his father, then taken up again after having married another man, living with the two men who ruined her, rolling with them in the gutter in drink and ordure. It was down there, he recalled the street, the details came back to him; the dirty linen in the middle of the shop, the drunken carousals that made the house stink, and the jaw-breaking blows.

"Now," he began again, in a slow voice, "I haven't even thirty sous to make her presents with. She will die of misery, sure enough."

He shrugged his shoulders with despair, and again bit at his bread and butter.

"Will you drink?" asked Catherine, uncorking her tin. "Oh, it's coffee, it won't hurt you. One gets stupid when one drinks like that."

But he refused; it was quite enough to have taken half her bread. However, she insisted good-naturedly, and said at last:

"Well, I will drink before you since you are so polite. Only you can't refuse now, it would be rude."

And she held out her tin to him. She had got on to her knees and he saw her quite close to him, lit up by the two lamps. Why had he found her ugly? Now that she was black, her face powdered with fine charcoal, she seemed to him singularly charming. In this face surrounded by shadow, the teeth in the broad mouth shone with whiteness, while the eyes looked large and gleamed with a greenish reflection, like cat's eyes. A lock of red hair which had escaped from her cap tickled her ear and made her laugh. She no longer seemed so young, she might be quite fourteen.

"To please you," he said, drinking and giving her back the tin.

She swallowed a second mouthful and forced him to take one too, wishing to share, she said; and that little neck that went from one mouth to the other amused them. He suddenly asked himself if he should not take her in his arms and kiss her lips. She had large lips of a pale rose colour, made vivid by the coal, which tormented him with increasing desire. But he did not dare, intimidated before her, only having known girls on the streets at Lille of the lowest order, and not realising how one ought to behave with a work-girl still living with her family.

"You must be about fourteen then?" he asked, after having gone back to his bread.

She was astonished, almost angry.

"What? fourteen! But I am fifteen! It's true I'm not big. Girls don't grow quick with us."

He went on questioning her and she told everything without boldness or shame. For the rest she was not ignorant concerning man and woman, although he felt that her body was virginal, with the virginity of a child delayed in her sexual maturity by the environment of bad air and weariness in which she lived. When he spoke of Mouquette, in order to embarrass her, she told some horrible stories in a quiet voice, with much amusement. Ah! she did some fine things! And as he asked if she herself had no lovers, she replied jokingly that she did not wish to vex her mother, but that it must happen some day. Her shoulders were bent. She shivered a little from the coldness of her garments soaked in sweat, with a gentle resigned air, ready to submit to things and men.

"People can find lovers when they all live together, can't they?"

"Sure enough!"

"And then it doesn't hurt anyone. One doesn't tell the priest."

"Oh! the priest! I don't care for him! But there is the Black Man."

"What? Black Man?"

"The old miner who comes back into the pit and wrings naughty girls' necks."

He looked at her, afraid that she was making fun of him.

"You believe in those stupid things? Then you don't know anything."

"Yes, I do. I can read and write. That is going on among us; in father and mother's time they learnt nothing."

She was certainly very charming. When she had finished her bread and butter, he would take her and kiss her on her large rosy lips. It was the resolution of timidity, a thought of violence, which choked his voice. These boy's clothes—this jacket and these breeches—on the girl's flesh excited and troubled him. He had swallowed his last mouthful. He drank from the tin and gave it back for her to empty. Now the moment for action had come, and he cast a restless glance at the miners further on. But a shadow blocked the gallery.

For a moment Chaval stood and looked at them from afar. He came forward, having assured himself that Maheu could not see him; and as Catherine was seated on the earth he seized her by the shoulders, drew her head back and tranquilly crushed her mouth beneath a brutal kiss, affecting not to notice Étienne. There was in that kiss an act of possession, a sort of jealous resolution.

However, the young girl was offended.

"Let me go, do you hear?"

He kept hold of her head and looked into her eyes. His moustache and small red beard flamed in his black face with his large eagle nose. He let her go at last, and went away without speaking a word.

A shudder had frozen Étienne. It was stupid to have waited. He could certainly not kiss her now, for she would, perhaps, think that he wished to behave like the other. In his wounded vanity, he experienced real despair.

"Why did you lie?" he said, in a low voice. "He's your lover."

"But no, I swear," she cried. "There is not that between us. Sometimes he likes a joke, he doesn't even belong here; it's six months since he came from the Pas-de-Calais."

Both rose; work was about to be resumed. When she saw him so cold she seemed annoyed. Doubtless she found him handsomer than the other; she would have preferred him perhaps. The idea of some amiable, consoling relationship disturbed her; and when the young man saw with surprise that his lamp was burning blue with a large pale ring, she tried at least to amuse him.

"Come, I will show you something," she said, in a friendly way.

When she had led him to the bottom of the cutting, she pointed out to him a crevice in the coal. A slight bubbling escaped from it, a little noise like the warbling of a bird.

"Put your hand there; you'll feel the wind. It's fire-damp."*

He was surprised. Is that all? Is that the terrible thing which blew everything up? She laughed, she said there was a good deal of it today to make the flame of the lamps so blue.

"Now, if you've done chattering, lazy louts!" cried Maheu's rough voice.

Catherine and Étienne hastened to fill their trams, and pushed them to the upbrow with stiffened back, crawling beneath the bossy roof of the passage. Even after the second journey, the sweat ran off them and their joints began to crack.

The pikemen had resumed work in the cutting. The men often shortened their breakfast to avoid getting cold; and their bricks, eaten in this way, far from the sun, with silent voracity, loaded their stomachs with lead. Stretched on their sides they hammered more loudly, with the one fixed idea of filling a large number of trams. Every thought disappeared in this rage for gain which was so hard to earn. They no longer felt the water

---

*Methane gas; highly flammable and explosive, it is one of the worst hazards the miners face. Zacharie—among others—dies in a firedamp accident while attempting to save his sister.

which streamed on them and swelled their limbs, the cramps of forced attitudes, the suffocation of the darkness in which they grew pale, like plants put in a cellar. Yet, as the day advanced, the air became more poisoned and heated with the smoke of the lamps, with the pestilence of their breaths, with the asphyxia of the fire-damp—painful to the eyes like spiders' webs—which only the aëration of the night could sweep away. At the bottom of their mole-hill, beneath the weight of the earth, with no more breath in their inflamed lungs, they went on hammering.

## CHAPTER V

MAHEU, WITHOUT LOOKING AT his watch which he had left in his jacket, stopped and said:

"One o'clock directly. Zacharie, is it done?"

The young man had just been at the planking. In the midst of his labour he had been lying on his back, with dreamy eyes, thinking over a game of la crosse of the night before. He woke up and replied:

"Yes, it will do; we shall see to-morrow."

And he came back to take his place at the cutting. Levaque and Chaval had also dropped their picks. They were all resting. They wiped their faces on their naked arms and looked at the roof, in which slaty masses were cracking. They only spoke about their work.

"Another chance," murmured Chaval, "of getting into earth that slips. They didn't take account of that in the bargain."

"Rascals!" growled Levaque. "They only want to bury us in it."

Zacharie began to laugh. He cared little for the work and the rest, but it amused him to hear the Company abused. In his placid way Maheu explained that the nature of the soil changed every twenty mètres. We could not foresee this, and we must be just. Then, when the two others went on talking against the masters, he became restless, and looked around him.

"Hush! that's enough."

"You're right," said Levaque, also lowering his voice; "it isn't wholesome."

A morbid dread of spies haunted them, even at this depth, as if the shareholders' coal, while still in the seam, might have ears.

"That won't prevent me," added Chaval loudly, in a defiant manner, "from lodging a brick in the belly of that damned Dansaert, if he talks to me as he did the other day. I won't prevent him, I won't, from buying pretty girls with a white skin."

This time Zacharie burst out laughing. The head captain's love for Pierronne was a constant joke in the pit. Even Catherine rested on her shovel at the bottom of the cutting, holding her sides, and in a few words told Étienne the joke; while Maheu became angry, seized by a fear which he could not conceal.

"Will you hold your tongue, eh? Wait till you're alone if you want to get into trouble."

He was still speaking when the sound of steps was heard in the upper gallery. Almost immediately the engineer of the mine, little Négrel, as the workmen called him among themselves, appeared at the top of the cutting, accompanied by Dansaert, the head captain.

"Didn't I say so?" muttered Maheu. "There's always someone there, coming out of the earth."

Paul Négrel, M. Hennebeau's nephew, was a young man of twenty-six, refined and handsome, with curly hair and brown moustache. His pointed nose and sparkling eyes gave him the air of an amiable ferret of sceptical intelligence, which changed into an abrupt authoritative manner in his relations with the workmen. He was dressed like them, and like them smeared with coal; to make them respect him he exhibited a dare-devil courage, passing through the most difficult spots and always first when landslips or fire-damp explosions occurred.

"Here we are, are we not, Dansaert?" he asked.

The head captain, a coarse-faced Belgian, with a large sensual nose, replied with exaggerated politeness:

"Yes, Monsieur Négrel. Here is the man who was taken on this morning."

Both of them had slid down into the middle of the cutting. They made Étienne come up. The engineer raised his lamp and looked at him without asking any questions.

"Good," he said at last. "But I don't like unknown men to be picked up from the road. Don't do it again."

He did not listen to the explanations given to him, the necessities of work, the desire to replace women by men for the haulage. He had begun to examine the roof while the pikemen had taken up their picks again. Suddenly he called out:

"I say there, Maheu; have you no care for life? By heavens! You will all be buried here!"

"Oh! it's solid," replied the workman, tranquilly.

"What! solid! but the rock is giving already, and you are planting props at more than two mètres, as if you grudged it! Ah! you are all alike. You will let your skull be flattened rather than leave the seam to give the necessary time to the timbering! I must ask you to prop that immediately. Double the timbering—do you understand?"

And in face of the unwillingness of the miners who disputed the point, saying that they were good judges of their safety, he became angry.

"Go along! when your head is smashed, is it you who will have to bear the consequences? Not at all! it will be the Company which will have to pay you pensions, you or your wives. I tell you again that we know you; in order to get two extra trams by evening you would sell your skins."

Maheu, in spite of the anger which was gradually mastering him, still answered steadily:

"If they paid us enough we should prop it better."

The engineer shrugged his shoulders without replying. He had descended the cutting, and only said in conclusion, from below:

"You have an hour. Put yourselves to the work, all of you; and I give you notice that the stall has a fine of three francs."

A low growl from the pikemen greeted these words. The force of the system alone restrained them, that military system which, from the trammer to the head captain, ground one beneath the other. Chaval and Levaque, however, made a furious gesture, while Maheu restrained them by a glance, and Zacharie shrugged his shoulders chaffingly. But Étienne was, perhaps, most affected. Since he had found himself at the bottom of this hill a slow rebellion was rising within him. He looked at the resigned Catherine, with her lowered back. Was it possible to kill one's self at this hard toil, in this deadly darkness, and not even to gain the few pence to buy one's daily bread?

However, Négrel went off with Dansaert, who was content to approve by a continual movement of his head. And their voices again rose; they had just stopped once more, and were examining the timbering in the gallery, which the pikemen were obliged to look after for a length of ten mètres behind the cutting.

"Didn't I tell you that they care nothing?" cried the engineer. "And you! why, in the devil's name, don't you watch them?"

"But I do—I do," stammered the head captain. "One gets tired of repeating things."

Négrel called loudly:

"Maheu! Maheu!"

They all came down. He went on:

"Do you see that? Will that hold? It's a twopenny-halfpenny construction! Here is a beam which the posts don't carry already, it is done so hastily. By Jove! I understand how it is that the mending costs us so much. It'll do, won't it? if it lasts as long as you have the care of it; and then it may go smash, and the Company is obliged to have an army of repairers. Look at it down there; it is mere botching!"

Chaval wished to speak, but he silenced him.

"No! I know what you are going to say. Let them pay you more, eh? Very well! I warn you that you will force the managers to do one thing: They will pay you the planking separately, and proportionately reduce the price of the trams. We shall see if you will gain that way! Meanwhile, prop that over again, at once; I shall pass to-morrow."

Amid the dismay caused by this threat he went away. Dansaert, who had been so humble, remained behind a few moments, to say brutally to the men:

"You get me into a row, you here. I'll give you something more than three francs fine, I will. Look out!"

Then, when he had gone, Maheu broke out in his turn:

"By God! what's fair is fair! I like people to be calm, because that's the only way of getting along, but at last they make you mad. Did you hear? The tram lowered, and the planking separately! Another way of paying us less. By God it is!"

He looked for someone upon whom to vent his anger, and saw Catherine and Étienne swinging their arms.

"Will you just fetch me some wood! What does it matter to you? I'll put my foot into you somewhere!"

Étienne went to carry it without rancour for this rough speech, so furious himself against the masters that he thought the miners too good-natured. As for the others, Levaque and Chaval had found relief in strong language. All of them, even Zacharie, were timbering furiously. For nearly half an hour one only heard the creaking of wood wedged in by blows of the hammer. They no longer spoke, they snorted, became enraged with the rock, which they would have hustled and driven back by the force of their shoulders if they had been able.

"That's enough," said Maheu at last, worn out with anger and fatigue: "An hour and a half! A fine day's work! We shan't get fifty sous! I'm off. This disgusts me."

Though there was still half an hour of work left he dressed himself. The others imitated him. The mere sight of the cutting enraged them. As the putter had gone back to the haulage they called her, irritated at her zeal: let the coal go out alone. And the six, their tools under their arms, set out to walk the two kilomètres back, returning to the shaft by the road of the morning.

On the way Catherine and Étienne were delayed while the pikemen slid down. They met little Lydie, who stopped in a gallery to let them pass, and told them of the disappearance of Mouquette, whose nose had been bleeding so much that she had been away an hour, bathing her face somewhere, no one knew where. Then, when they left her, the child began again to push her tram, knocked up and muddy, stiffening her insect-like arms and legs like a lean black ant: struggling with a load that was too heavy for it. They let themselves down on their backs, flattening their shoulders for fear of scratching the skin on their foreheads, and they walked so closely to the polished rock at the back of the stalls that they were obliged from time to time to hold on to the woodwork, so that their backsides should not catch fire, as they said jokingly.

Below they found themselves alone. Red stars disappeared afar at a bend in the passage. Their cheerfulness fell, they began to walk with the heavy step of fatigue, he in front, she behind. Their lamps were blackened. He could scarcely see her, drowned in a sort of smoky mist; and the idea that she was a girl disturbed him because he felt that it was stupid not to embrace her, and yet the recollection of the other man prevented him. Certainly she had lied to him: the other was her lover, they lay together on all those heaps of slaty coal, for she had a loose woman's gait. He sulked without reason, as if she had deceived him. She, however, every moment turned round, warned him of obstacles, and seemed to invite him to be affectionate. They were so lost here, it would have been so easy to laugh together like good friends! At last they entered the large haulage gallery; it was a relief to the indecision from which he was suffering; while she once more had a saddened look, the regret for a happiness which they would not find again.

Now the subterranean life rumbled around them with a continual passing of captains, the come and go of the trains drawn by trotting horses. Lamps starred the night everywhere. They had to efface themselves against the rock to leave the path free to shadowy men and beasts, whose breath came against their faces. Jeanlin, running barefooted behind his train, cried out some naughtiness to them which they could not hear amid the thunder of the wheels. They still went on, she now silent, he not recognising the turnings and roads of the morning, and fancying that she was leading him deeper and deeper into the earth; and what specially troubled him was the cold, an increasing cold which he had felt on emerging from the cutting, and which caused him to shiver the more the nearer they approached the shaft. Between the narrow walls the column of air now blew like a tempest. He despaired of ever coming to the end, when suddenly they found themselves in the pit-eye hall.

Chaval cast a sidelong glance at them, his mouth drawn with suspicion. The others were there, covered with sweat in the icy current, silent like himself, swallowing their grunts of rage. They had arrived too soon and could not be taken to the top for half an hour, more especially since some complicated manœuvres were going on for lowering a horse. The porters were still rolling the trains with the deafening sound of old iron in movement, and the cages were flying up, disappearing in the rain which fell in the black hole. Below, the sump, a cesspool ten mètres deep, filled with this streaming water, also exhaled its muddy moisture. Men were constantly moving around the shaft, pulling the signal cords, pressing on the arms of levers, in the midst of this spray in which their garments were soaked. The reddish light of three open lamps cut out great moving shadows and gave to this subterranean hall the air of a villainous cavern, some bandits' forge near a torrent.

Maheu made one last effort. He approached Pierron, who had gone on duty at six o'clock.

"Here! you might as well let us go up."

But the porter, a handsome fellow with strong limbs and a gentle face, refused with a frightened gesture.

"Impossible: ask the captain. They would fine me."

Fresh growls were stifled. Catherine bent forward and said in Étienne's ear:

"Come and see the stable, then. That's a comfortable place!"

And they had to escape without being seen, for it was forbidden to go there. It was on the left, at the end of a short gallery. Twenty-five mètres in length and nearly four high, cut in the rock and vaulted with bricks, it could contain twenty horses. It was, in fact, comfortable there. There was a pleasant warmth of living beasts, the good odour of a fresh and well-kept litter. The only lamp threw out the calm rays of a night-light. There were horses there, at rest, who turned their heads, with their large infantine eyes, then went back to their hay, without haste, like fat well-kept workers, loved by everybody.

But as Catherine was reading aloud their names, written on zinc plates over the mangers, she uttered a slight cry, seeing something suddenly rise before her. It was Mouquette, who emerged in fright from a pile of straw in which she was sleeping. On Monday, when she was overtired with her Sunday's spree, she gave herself a violent blow on the nose, and left her cutting, under the pretence of seeking water, to bury herself here with the horses in the warm litter. Her father, being weak with her, allowed it, at the risk of getting into trouble.

Just then Mouque, the father, entered, a short, bald, worn-out looking man, but still stout, which is rare in an old miner of fifty. Since he had been made a groom, he chewed to such a degree that his gums bled in his black mouth. On seeing the two with his daughter, he became angry.

"What are you up to there, all of you? Come! up! The jades, bringing a man here! It's a fine thing to come and do your dirty tricks in my straw."

Mouquette thought it funny, and held her sides. But Étienne, feeling awkward, moved away, while Catherine smiled at him. As all three returned to the pit-eye, Bébert and Jeanlin arrived there also with a train of tubs. There was a stoppage for the manœuvring of the cages, and the young girl approached their horse, caressed it with her hand, and talked about it to her companion. It was Bataille, the dean of the mine, a white horse who had lived below for ten years. These ten years he had lived in this hole, occupying the same corner of the stable, doing the same task along the black galleries without ever seeing daylight. Very fat, with shining coat and a good-natured air, he seemed to lead the existence of a sage, sheltered from the evils of the world above. In this darkness, too, he had become very cunning. The passage in which he worked had grown so familiar to him that he could open the ventilation doors with his head, and he lowered himself to avoid knocks at the narrow spots. Without doubt, also, he counted his turns, for when he had made the regulation number of journeys he refused to do any more, and had to be led back to his manger. Now that old age was coming on, his cat's eyes were sometimes dimmed with melancholy. Perhaps he vaguely saw again, in the depths of his obscure dreams, the mill at which he was born, near Marchiennes, a mill placed on the edge of the Scarpe, surrounded by large fields over which the wind always blew. Something burnt in the air—an enormous lamp, the exact appearance of which escaped his beast's memory—and he stood with lowered head, trembling on his old feet, making useless efforts to recall the sun.

However, the manœuvres went on in the shaft, the signal hammer had struck four blows, and the horse was being lowered; there was always excitement at such a time, for it sometimes happened that the beast was seized by such terror that it was landed dead. When put into a net at the top it struggled fiercely; then, when it felt the ground no longer beneath, it remained as if petrified and disappeared without a quiver of the skin, with enlarged and fixed eyes. This animal, being too big to pass between the guides, it had been necessary, when hooking it beneath the cage, to bind back the head and attach it to the flanks. The descent lasted nearly three minutes, the engine being slowed as a precaution. Below, the excitement was increasing. What then? Was he going to be left on the road, hanging in the blackness? At last he appeared in his stony immobility, his eye fixed and dilated with terror. It was a bay horse hardly three years of age, called Trompette.

"Attention!" cried Father Mouque, whose duty it was to receive it. "Bring him here, don't undo him yet."

Trompette was soon placed on the metal floor in a mass. Still he did not move: he seemed in a nightmare in this obscure infinite hole, this deep hall echoing with tumult. They were beginning to unfasten him when Bataille, who had just been unharnessed, approached and stretched out his neck to smell this companion who lay on the earth. The workmen jokingly enlarged the circle. Well! what pleasant odour did he find in him? But Bataille, deaf to mockery, became animated. He probably found in him the good odour of the open air, the forgotten odour of the sun on the grass. And he suddenly broke out into a sonorous neigh, full of musical gladness, in which there seemed to be the emotion of a sob. It was a greeting, the joy of those ancient things of which a gust had reached him, the melancholy of one more prisoner who would not ascend again until death.

"Ah! that animal Bataille!" shouted the workmen, amused at the antics of their favourite, "he's talking with his mate."

Trompette was unbound, but still did not move. He remained on his flank, as if he still felt the net straining him, garroted by fear. At last they got him up with a lash of the whip, dazed and his limbs quivering. And Father Mouque led away the two beasts, fraternising together.

"Here! Is it ready yet?" asked Maheu.

It was necessary to clear the cages, and besides it was yet ten minutes before the hour for ascending. Little by little the stalls emptied, and the miners returned from all the galleries. There were already some fifty men there, damp and shivering, their inflamed chests panting on every side. Pierron, in spite of his mawkish face, struck his daughter Lydie, because she had left the cutting before time. Zacharie slily pinched Mouquette, with a joke about warming himself. But the discontent increased; Chaval and Levaque narrated the engineer's threat, the tram to be lowered in price, and the planking paid separately. And exclamations greeted this scheme, a rebellion was germinating in this little corner, nearly six hundred mètres beneath the earth. Soon they could not restrain their voices; these men, soiled by coal, and frozen by the delay, accused the Company of killing half their workers at the bottom, and starving the other half to death. Étienne listened, trembling.

"Quick, quick!" repeated the captain, Richomme, to the porters.

He hastened the preparations for the ascent, not wishing to be hard, pretending not to hear. However, the murmurs became so loud that he was obliged to notice them. They were calling out behind him that this would not last always, and that one fine day the whole affair would be smashed up.

"You're sensible," he said to Maheu; "make them hold their tongues. When one hasn't got power one must have sense."

But Maheu, who was getting calm, and had at last become anxious, did not need to interfere. Suddenly the voices fell; Négrel and Dansaert, returning from their inspection, entered from a gallery, both of them sweating. The habit of discipline made the men stand in rows while the engineer passed through the group without a word. He got into one tram, and the head captain into another, the signal was sounded five times, ringing for big meat, as they said, for the masters; and the cage flew up in the air in the midst of gloomy silence.

## CHAPTER VI

As HE ASCENDED IN the cage heaped up with four others, Étienne resolved to continue his famished course along the roads. One might as well die at once as go down to the bottom of that hell, where it was not even possible to earn one's bread. Catherine, in the tram above him, was no longer at his side with her pleasant enervating warmth; and he preferred to avoid foolish thoughts and to go away, for with his wider education he felt nothing of the resignation of this flock; he would end by strangling one of the masters.

Suddenly he was blinded. The ascent had been so rapid that he was stunned by the daylight, and his eyelids quivered in the brightness to which he had already grown unaccustomed. It was none the less a relief to him to feel the cage settle on to the bars. A lander opened the door, and a flood of workmen leapt out of the trams.

"I say, Mouquet," whispered Zacharie in the lander's ear, "are we off to the Volcan to-night?"

The Volcan[15] was a café-concert at Montsou. Mouquet winked his left eye with a silent laugh which made his jaws gape. Short and stout like his father, he had the impudent face of a fellow who devours everything without care for the morrow. Just then Mouquette came out in her turn, and he gave her a formidable smack on the flank by way of fraternal tenderness.

Étienne hardly recognised the lofty nave of the receiving-hall, which had before looked imposing in the ambiguous light of the lanterns. It was simply bare and dirty; a dull light entered through the dusty windows. The engine alone shone at the end with its copper; the well-greased steel cables moved like ribbons soaked in ink, and the pulleys above, the enormous scaffold which supported them, the cages, the trams, all this prodigality of metal made the hall look sombre with their hard grey tones of old iron. Without ceasing, the rumbling of the wheels shook the metal floor; while from the coal thus put in motion there arose a fine charcoal powder which powdered black the soil, the walls, even the joists of the steeple.

But Chaval, after glancing at the table of counters in the receiver's little glass office, came back furious. He had discovered that two of their trams had been rejected, one because it did not contain the regulation amount, the other because the coal was not clean.

"This finishes the day," he cried. "Twenty sous less again! This is because we take on lazy rascals who use their arms as a pig does his tail!"

And his sidelong look at Étienne completed his thought.

The latter was tempted to reply by a blow. Then he asked himself what would be the use since he was going away. This decided him absolutely.

"It's not possible to do it right the first day," said Maheu, to restore peace, "you'll do better to-morrow."

They were all none the less soured, and disturbed by the need to quarrel. As they passed to the lamp cabin to give up their lamps, Levaque began to abuse the lamp-man, whom he accused of not properly cleaning the lamp. They only slackened down a little in the shed where the fire was still burning. It had even been too heavily piled up, for the stove was red and the vast room, without a window, seemed to be in flames, to such a degree did the reflection make bloody the walls. And there were grunts of joy, all the backs were roasted at a distance till they smoked like soup. When their flanks were burning they cooked their bellies. Mouquette had tranquilly put down her breeches to dry her chemise. Some lads were making fun of her; they burst out laughing because she suddenly showed them her posterior, a gesture which in her was the extreme expression of contempt.

"I'm off," said Chaval, who had shut up his tools in his box.

No one moved. Only Mouquette hastened, and went out behind him on the pretext that they were both going back to Montsou. But the others went on joking; they knew that he would have no more to do with her.

Catherine, however, who seemed preoccupied, was speaking in a low voice to her father. The latter was surprised; then he agreed with a nod; and calling Étienne to give him back his bundle:

"Listen," he said: "you haven't a sou; you will have time to starve before the fortnight's out. Shall I try and get you credit somewhere?"

The young man stood for a moment confused. He had been just about to claim his thirty sous and go. But shame restrained him before the young girl. She looked at him fixedly; perhaps she would think he was shirking the work.

"You know I can promise you nothing," Maheu went on. "They can but refuse us."

Then Étienne consented. They would refuse. Besides, it would bind him to nothing, he could still go away after having eaten something. Then he was dissatisfied at not having refused, seeing Catherine's joy, a pretty laugh, a look of friendship, happy at having been useful to him. What was the good of it all?

When they had put on their sabots, and shut their boxes, the Maheus left the shed, following their comrades, who were leaving one by one, after they had warmed themselves. Étienne went behind. Levaque and his urchin joined the band. But as they crossed the screening place a scene of violence stopped them.

It was in a vast shed, with beams blackened by the powder, and large shutters, through which blew a constant current of air. The coal trams arrived straight from the receiving-room, and were then overturned, by the tipping-cradles, on to hoppers, long iron slides; and to right and to left of these the screeners, mounted on steps and armed with shovels and rakes, swept together the clean coal, which afterwards fell through funnels into the railway waggons beneath the shed.

Philomène Levaque was there, thin and pale, with the sheeplike face of a girl who spat blood. With head protected by a fragment of blue wool, and hands and arms black to the elbows, she was screening beneath an old witch, the mother of Pierronne, the Brûlé, as she was called, with terrible owl's eyes, and a mouth drawn in like a miser's purse. They were abusing each other, the young one accusing the elder of raking her stones so that she could not get a basketful in ten minutes. They were paid by the basket, and these quarrels were constantly arising. Hair was flying, and hands were making black marks on red faces.

"Give it her bloody well!" cried Zacharie, from above, to his mistress.

All the screeners laughed. But the Brûlé turned snappishly on the young man.

"Now, then, dirty beast! You'd do better to own the two kids you have filled her with. If it's possible, a slip of eighteen, who can't stand straight!"

Maheu had to prevent his son from descending to see, as he said, the colour of this carcass's skin.

A foreman came up and the rakes again began to move the coal. One could only see, all along the hoppers, the round backs of women eagerly disputing the stones.

Outside, the wind had suddenly quieted; a moist cold was falling from a grey sky. The colliers thrust out their shoulders, crossed their arms and set forth irregularly, with a rolling gait which made their large bones stand out beneath their thin garments. In the daylight they looked like a band of negroes thrown in to the mud. Some of them had not finished their bricks; and the remains of the bread carried between the shirt and the jacket made them hump-backed.

"Hullo! there's Bouteloup," said Zacharie, grinning.

Levaque without stopping exchanged two sentences with his lodger, a big brown fellow of thirty-five with a placid honest air:

"Is the soup ready, Louis?"

"I believe it is."

"Then the wife is good-humoured to-day."

"Yes, I believe she is."

Other miners bound for the earth cutting came up, new bands which one by one were engulfed in the pit. It was the three o'clock descent, more men for the pit to devour, the gangs who would replace the sets of the pikemen at the bottom of the passages. The mine never rested; day and night human insects were digging out the rock six hundred mètres below the beetroot fields.

However, the youngsters went ahead. Jeanlin confided to Bébert a complicated plan for getting four sous' worth of tobacco on credit, while Lydie followed respectfully at a distance. Catherine came with Zacharie and Étienne. None of them spoke. And it was only in front of the Avantage inn that Maheu and Levaque rejoined them.

"Here we are," said the former to Étienne, "will you come in?"

They separated. Catherine had stood a moment motionless, gazing once more at the young man with her large eyes full of a greenish limpidity like spring water, the crystal deepened the more by her black face. She smiled and disappeared with the others on the road that led up to the settlement.

The inn was situated between the village and the mine, at the crossing of two roads. It was a two-storeyed brick house whitewashed from top to bottom, enlivened around the windows by a broad pale-blue border. On a square sign-board nailed above the door, one read in yellow letters: *À l'Avantage,* licensed by Rasseneur. Behind stretched a skittle-ground enclosed by a hedge. The Company, who had done everything to buy up the property placed within its vast territory, was in despair over this inn in the open fields, at the very entrance of the Voreux.

"Go in," said Maheu to Étienne.

The little parlour was quite bare with its white walls, its three tables and its dozen chairs, its deal counter about the size of a kitchen dresser. There were a dozen glasses at most, three bottles of liqueur, a decanter, a little zinc box with a pewter tap to hold the beer; and nothing else—not a figure, not a little table, not a game. In the metal fire-place, which was bright and polished, a coal fire was burning quietly. On the flags a thin layer of white sand drank up the constant moisture of this water-soaked land.

"A glass," ordered Maheu of the big fair girl, a neighbour's daughter who sometimes took charge of the place. "Is Rasseneur in?"

The girl turned the tap, replying that the master would soon return. In a long, slow gulp, the miner emptied half his glass to sweep away the dust which filled his throat. He offered nothing to his companion. One other customer, a damp and besmeared miner, was seated before the table, drinking his beer in silence, with an air of deep meditation. A third entered, was served in response to a gesture, paid and went away without uttering a word.

But a stout man of thirty-eight, with a round shaven face and a good-natured smile, now appeared. It was Rasseneur,[16] a former pikeman whom the Company had dismissed three years ago, after a strike. A very good workman, he could speak well, put himself at the head of every opposition, and had at last become the chief of the discontented. His wife already held a licence, like many miners' wives; and when he was thrown on to the street he became an inn-keeper himself; having found the money, he placed his inn in front of the Voreux as a provocation to the Company. Now his house had prospered; it had become a centre, and he was enriched by the animosity which he had gradually fostered in the hearts of his old comrades.

"This is a lad I hired this morning," said Maheu at once. "Have you got one of your two rooms free, and will you give him credit for a fortnight?"

Rasseneur's broad face suddenly expressed great suspicion. He examined Étienne with a glance, and replied, without giving himself the trouble to express any regret:

"My two rooms are taken. Can't do it."

The young man expected this refusal; but it hurt him nevertheless, and he was surprised at the sudden grief he experienced in leaving. No matter; he would go when he had received his thirty sous. The miner who was drinking at a table had left. Others, one by one, continued to come in to clear their throats, then went on their road with the same slouching gait. It was a simple washing without joy or passion, the silent satisfaction of a need.

"Then, there's no news?" Rasseneur asked in a peculiar tone of Maheu, who was finishing his beer in small gulps.

The latter turned his head, and saw that only Étienne was near.

"There's been more squabbling. Yes, about the timbering."

He told the story. The innkeeper's face reddened, swelling with emotion, which flamed in his skin and eyes. At last he broke out:

"Well, well! if they decide to lower the price they are done for."

Étienne constrained him. However he went on, throwing side-long glances in his direction. And there were reticences, and implications; he was talking of the manager, M. Hennebeau, of his wife, of his nephew, the little Négrel, without naming them, repeating that this could not go on, that things were bound to smash up one of these fine days. The misery was too great; and he spoke of the workshops that were closing, the workers who were going away. During the last month he had given more than six pounds of bread a day. He had heard the day before, that M. Deneulin, the owner of a neighbouring pit, could scarcely keep going. He had also received a letter from Lille full of disturbing details.

"You know," he whispered, "it comes from that person you saw here one evening."

But he was interrupted. His wife entered in her turn, a tall woman, lean and keen, with a long nose and violet cheeks. She was a much more radical politician than her husband.

"Pluchart's letter," she said. "Ah! if that fellow was master things would soon go better."

Étienne had been listening for a moment; he understood and became excited over these ideas of misery and revenge. This name, suddenly uttered, caused him to start. He said aloud, as if in spite of himself:

"I know him—Pluchart."

They looked at him. He had to add:

"Yes, I am an engine-man: he was my foreman at Lille. A capable man. I have often talked with him."

Rasseneur examined him afresh; and there was a rapid change on his face, a sudden sympathy. At last he said to his wife:

"It's Maheu who brings me this gentleman, one of his putters, to see if there is a room for him upstairs, and if we can give him credit for a fortnight."

Then the matter was settled in four words. There was a room; the lodger had left that morning. And the inn-keeper, who was very excited, talked more freely, repeating that he only asked possibilities from the masters, without demanding, like so many others, things that were too hard to get. His wife shrugged her shoulders and demanded justice, absolutely.

"Good evening," interrupted Maheu. "All that won't prevent men from going down, and as long as they go down there will be people working themselves to death. Look how fresh you are, these three years that you've been out of it."

"Yes, I'm very much better," declared Rasseneur, complacently.

Étienne went as far as the door, thanking the miner, who was leaving; but the latter nodded his head, without adding a word, and the young man watched him painfully climb up the road to the settlement. Madame Rasseneur, occupied with serving customers, asked him to wait a minute, when she would show him his room, where he could clean himself. Should he remain? He again felt hesitation, a discomfort which made him regret the freedom of the open high-road, the hunger beneath the sun, endured with the joy of being one's own master. It seemed to him that he had lived years since his arrival on the pit-bank, in the midst of squalls, to those hours passed under the earth on his belly in the black passages. And he shrank from beginning again; it was unjust and too hard. His man's pride revolted at the idea of becoming a crushed and blinded beast.

While Étienne was thus debating with himself, his eyes, wandering over the immense plain, gradually began to see it clearly. He was surprised; he had not imagined the horizon was like this, when old Bonnemort had pointed it out to him in the darkness. Before him he plainly saw the Voreux in a fold of the earth, with its wood and brick buildings, the tarred screening shed, the slate-covered steeple, the engine-room and the tall, pale red chimney, all massed together with that evil air. But around these buildings the space extended, and he had not imagined it so large, changed into an inky sea by the ascending waves of coal soot, bristling with high buttresses which carried the rails of the foot bridges, encumbered in one corner with the timber supply, which looked like the harvest of a mown forest. Towards the right the pit-bank hid the view, colossal as a barricade of giants, already covered with grass in its older part, consumed at the other end by an interior fire which had been burning for a year with a thick smoke, leaving at the surface in the midst of the pale grey of the slates and sandstones long trails of bleeding rust. Then the fields unrolled, the endless fields of wheat and beetroot, naked at this season of the year, marshes with scanty vegetation, cut by a few stunted willows, distant meadows separated by slender rows of poplars. Very far away little pale patches indicated towns, Marchiennes at the north, Montsou at the south; while the forest of Vandame at the east bordered the horizon with the violet line of its leafless trees. And beneath the livid sky, in the faint daylight of this winter afternoon, it seemed as if all the blackness of the Voreux, and all its flying coal dust, had fallen upon the plain, powdering the trees, sanding the roads, sowing the earth.

Étienne looked, and what especially surprised him was a canal, the canalised stream of the Scarpe, which he had not seen in the night. From the Voreux to Marchiennes this canal ran straight, like a dull silver ribbon two leagues long, an avenue lined by large trees raised above the low earth, threading into space with the perspective of its green banks, its pale water, into which glided the vermilion of the boats. Near one pit there was a wharf with moored vessels which were laden directly from the trams at the foot-bridges. Afterwards the canal made a curve, sloping by the marshes; and the whole soul of that smooth plain appeared to lie in this geometrical stream, which traversed it like a great road, carting coal and iron.

Étienne's glance went up from the canal to the settlement built on the height, of which he could only distinguish the red tiles. Then his eyes rested again at the bottom of the clay slope, towards the Voreux, on two enormous masses of bricks made and burnt on the spot. A branch of the Company's railroad passed behind a paling, for the use of the pit. They must be sending down the last miners to the earth cutting. Only one shrill note came from a truck pushed by men. One felt no longer the unknown darkness, the inexplicable thunder, the flaming of mysterious stars. Afar, the blast furnaces and the coke kilns had paled with the dawn. There only remained, unceasingly, the escapement of the pump, always breathing with the same thick, long breath, the ogre's breath of which he could now see the grey steam, and which nothing could satiate.

Then Étienne suddenly made up his mind. Perhaps he seemed to see again Catherine's clear eyes, up there, at the entrance to the settlement. Perhaps, rather, it was the wind of revolt which came from the Voreux. He did not know, but he wished to go down again to the mine, to suffer and to fight. And he thought fiercely of those people Bonnemort had talked of, the crouching and sated god, to whom ten thousand starving men gave their flesh without knowing it.

# *PART TWO*

## CHAPTER I

THE GRÉGOIRES' PROPERTY, PIOLAINE, was situated two kilomètres to the east of Montsou, on the Joiselle road. The house was a large square building, without style, dating from the beginning of the last century. Of all the land that once belonged to it there only remained some thirty hectares, enclosed by walls, and easy to keep up. The orchard and kitchen garden especially were everywhere spoken of, being famous for the finest fruit and vegetables in the country. For the rest, there was no park, only a small wood. The avenue of old lines, a vault of foliage three hundred mètres long, reaching from the gate to the porch, was one of the curiosities of this bare plain, on which one could count the large trees between Marchiennes and Beaugnies.

On that morning the Grégoires got up at eight o'clock. Usually they never stirred until an hour later, being heavy sleepers; but last night's tempest had disturbed them. And while her husband had gone at once to see if the wind had made any havoc, Madame Grégoire went down to the kitchen in her slippers and flannel dressing-gown. She was short and stout, about fifty-eight years of age, and retained a broad, surprised, dollish face beneath the dazzling whiteness of her hair.

"Mélanie," she said to the cook, "suppose you were to make the brioche this morning, since the dough is ready. Mademoiselle will not get up for half an hour yet, and she can eat it with her chocolate. Eh? It will be a surprise."

The cook, a lean old woman who had served them for thirty years, laughed.

"That's true! It will be a famous surprise. My stove is alight, and the oven must be hot; and then Honorine can help me a bit."

Honorine, a girl of some twenty years, who had been taken in as a child and brought up in the house, now acted as housemaid. Besides these two women, the only other servant was the coachman, Francis, who undertook the heavy work. A gardener and his wife were occupied with the vegetables, the fruit, the flowers and the poultry-yard. And as service here was patriarchal, this little world lived together, like one large family, on very good terms.

Madame Grégoire, who had planned this surprise of the brioche in bed, waited to see the dough put in the oven. The kitchen was very large, and one guessed it was the most important room in the house by its extreme cleanliness and by the arsenal of saucepans, utensils, and pots which filled it. Provisions abounded, hanging from hooks or in cupboards.

"And let it be well gilt, won't you?" Madame Grégoire said, as she passed into the dining-room.

In spite of the hot-air stove which warmed the whole house, a coal-fire enlivened this room. In other respects it exhibited no luxury: a large table, chairs, a mahogany sideboard; only two deep easy-chairs betrayed a love of comfort, long happy hours of digestion. They never went into the drawing-room, they remained here in a family circle.

Just then M. Grégoire came back, dressed in a thick fustian jacket; he also was ruddy for his sixty years, with large, good-natured, honest features beneath the snow of his curly hair. He had seen the coachman and the gardener; there had been no damage of importance, nothing but a fallen chimney-pot. Every morning he liked to give a glance round Piolaine, which was not large enough to cause him anxiety, and from which he derived all the happiness of ownership.

"And Cécile?" he asked, "isn't she up yet then?"

"I can't make it out," replied his wife. "I thought I heard her moving."

The table was set; there were three cups on the white cloth. They sent Honorine to see what had become of mademoiselle. But she came back immediately, restraining her laughter, stifling her voice, as if she had been talking aloud in the room above.

"Oh! if monsieur and madame could see mademoiselle! She sleeps; oh! she sleeps like an angel. One can't imagine it! It's a pleasure to look at her."

The father and mother exchanged tender looks. He said, smiling:

"Will you come and see?"

"The poor little darling," she murmured. "I'll come."

And they went up together. The room was the only luxurious one in the house. It was draped in blue silk, and the furniture was lacquered white, with blue tracery—a spoilt child's whim, which her parents had gratified. In the vague whiteness of the bed, beneath the half-light which came through a curtain that was drawn back, the young girl was sleeping with her cheek resting on her naked arm. She was not pretty, too healthy, in too vigorous condition, fully developed at eighteen; but she had superb flesh, the freshness of milk, with her chestnut hair, her round face and little wilful nose lost between her cheeks. The coverlet had slipped down, and she was breathing so softly that her respiration did not even lift her bosom.

"That horrible wind must have prevented her from closing her eyes," said the mother, softly.

The father imposed silence with a gesture. Both of them leant down and gazed with adoration on this girl, in her virgin nakedness, whom they had desired so long, and who had come so late, when they had no longer hoped for her. They found her perfect, not at all too fat, and could never feed her sufficiently. And she went on sleeping, without feeling them near her, with their faces against hers. However, a slight movement disturbed her motionless face. They feared that they would wake her, and went out on tip-toe.

"Hush!" said M. Grégoire, at the door. "If she has not slept we must leave her sleeping."

"As long as she likes, the darling!" agreed Madame Grégoire. "We will wait."

They went down and seated themselves in the easy chairs in the dining-room; while the servants, laughing at mademoiselle's sound sleep, kept the chocolate on the stove without grumbling. He took up a newspaper; she knitted at a large woollen quilt. It was very hot, and not a sound was heard in the silent house.

The Grégoires' fortune, about forty thousand francs a year, was entirely invested in a share of the Montsou mines. They would complacently narrate its origin, which dated from the very formation of the Company.

Towards the beginning of the last century, there had been a mad search for coal between Lille and Valenciennes. The success of those who held the concession, which was afterwards to become the Anzin Company, had turned all heads. In every commune the ground was tested; and societies were formed and concessions grew up in a night. But among all the obstinate seekers of that epoch, Baron Desrumaux had certainly left the reputation for the most heroic intelligence. For forty years he had struggled without yielding, in the midst of continual obstacles: early searches unsuccessful, new pits abandoned at the end of long months of work, land-slips which filled up borings, sudden inundations which drowned the workmen, hundreds of thousands of francs thrown into the earth; then the squabbles of the management, the panics of the shareholders, the struggle with the lords of the soil, who were resolved not to recognise royal concessions if no treaty was first made with themselves. He had, at last, founded the association of Desrumaux, Fauquenoix and Co. to exploit the Montsou concession, and the pits began to yield a small profit when two neighbouring concessions, that of Cougny, belonging to the Comte de Cougny, and that of Joiselle, belonging to the Cornille and Jenard Company, had nearly overwhelmed him beneath the terrible assault of their competition. Happily, on the 25th August, 1760, a treaty was made between the three concessions, uniting them into a single one. The Montsou Mining Company was created, such as it still exists to-day. In the distribution they had divided the total property, according to the standard of the money of the time, into twenty-four sous, of which each was sub-divided into twelve deniers, which made two hundred and eighty-eight deniers; and as the denier was worth ten thousand francs, the capital represented a sum of nearly three millions. Desrumaux, dying but triumphant, received in this division six sous and three deniers.

In those days the baron possessed Piolaine, which had three hundred hectares belonging to it, and he had in his service as steward Honoré Grégoire, a Picardy lad, the great-grandfather of Léon Grégoire, Cécile's father. When the Montsou treaty was made, Honoré, who had laid up savings to the amount of some fifty thousand francs, yielded tremblingly to his master's unshakable faith. He gave up ten thousand francs in fine crowns, and took a denier though with the fear of robbing his children of that sum. His son Eugène, in fact, received very small dividends; and as he had become a bourgeois and had been foolish enough to throw away the other forty thousand francs of the paternal inheritance in a company that came to grief, he lived meanly enough. But the interest of the denier gradually increased. The fortune began with Félicien, who was able to realise a dream with which his grandfather, the old steward, had nursed his childhood—the purchase of dismembered Piolaine, which he acquired as national property[1] for a ludicrous sum. However, bad years followed. It was necessary to await the conclusion of the revolutionary catastrophes, and afterwards Napoleon's bloody fall;[2] and it was Léon Grégoire who profited at a stupefying rate of progress by the timid and uneasy investment of his great-grandfather. Those poor ten thousand francs grew and multiplied with the Company's prosperity. Since 1820 they had brought in cent. for cent., ten thousand francs. In 1844 they had produced twenty thousand; in 1850, forty. During two years the dividend had reached the prodigious figure of fifty thousand francs; the value of the denier, quoted at the Lille bourse at a million, had centupled in a century.

M. Grégoire, who had been advised to sell out when this figure of a million was reached, had refused with his smiling paternal air. Six months later an industrial crisis broke out; the denier fell to six hundred thousand francs. But he still smiled; he regretted nothing, for the Grégoires had maintained an obstinate faith in their mine. It would rise again: God himself was not so solid. Then with this religious faith was mixed profound gratitude towards an investment which for a century had supported the family in doing nothing. It was like a divinity of their own, whom their egoism surrounded with a kind of worship, the benefactor of the hearth, lulling them in their great bed of idleness, fattening them at their gluttonous table. From father to son it had gone on. Why risk displeasing fate by doubting it? And at the bottom of their fidelity there was a superstitious terror, a fear lest the million of the denier might not suddenly melt away if they were to realize it and to put it in a drawer. It seemed to them more sheltered in the earth, from which a race of miners, generations of starving people, extracted it for them, a little every day, as they needed it.

For the rest, happiness rained on this house. M. Grégoire, when very young, had married the daughter of a Marchiennes druggist, a plain, penniless girl, whom he adored, and who repaid him with happiness. She shut herself up in her household, and worshipped her husband, having no other will but his. No difference of tastes separated them, their desires were mingled in one idea of comfort; and they had thus lived for forty years, in affection and little mutual services. It was a well-regulated existence; the forty thousand francs were spent quietly, and the savings expended on Cécile, whose tardy birth had for a moment disturbed the budget. They still satisfied all her whims—a second horse, two more carriages, toilets sent from Paris. But they tasted in this one more joy; they thought nothing too good for their daughter, although they had such a horror of display that they had preserved the fashions of their youth. Every unprofitable expense seemed foolish to them.

Suddenly the door opened, and a loud voice called out:

"Hullo! What now? Having breakfast without me!"

It was Cécile, just come from her bed, her eyes heavy with sleep. She had simply put up her hair and flung on a white woollen dressing-gown.

"No, no!" said the mother; "you see we are all waiting. Eh? has the wind prevented you from sleeping, poor darling?"

The young girl looked at her in great surprise.

"Has it been windy? I didn't know anything about it. I haven't moved all night."

Then they thought this funny, and all three began to laugh; the servants who were bringing in the breakfast also broke out laughing, so amused was the household at the idea that mademoiselle had been sleeping for twelve hours right off. The sight of the brioche completed the expansion of their faces.

"What! Is it cooked, then?" said Cécile; "that must be a surprise for me! That'll be good now, hot, with the chocolate!"

They sat down to table at last with the smoking chocolate in their cups, and for a long time talked of nothing but the brioche. Mélanie and Honorine remained to give details about the cooking and watched them stuffing themselves with greasy lips, saying that it was a pleasure to make a cake when one saw the masters enjoying it so much.

But the dogs began to bark loudly; perhaps they announced the music mistress, who came from Marchiennes on Mondays and Fridays. A professor of literature also came. All the young girl's education was thus carried on at Piolaine in happy ignorance, with her childish whims, throwing the book out of the window as soon as anything wearied her.

"It is M. Deneulin," said Honorine, returning.

Behind her, Deneulin, a cousin of M. Grégoire's, appeared without ceremony; with his loud voice, his quick gestures, he had the appearance of an old cavalry officer. Although over fifty, his short hair and thick moustache were as black as ink.

"Yes! It is I. Good-day! Don't disturb yourselves."

He had sat down amid the family's exclamations. They turned at last to their chocolate.

"Have you anything to tell me?" asked M. Grégoire.

"No! nothing at all," Deneulin hastened to reply. "I came out on horseback to rub off the rust a bit, and as I passed your door I thought I would just look in."

Cécile questioned him about Jeanne and Lucie, his daughters. They were perfectly well, the first was always at her painting, while the other, the eldest, was training her voice at the piano from morning till night. And there was a slight quiver in his voice, a disquiet which he concealed beneath bursts of gaiety.

M. Grégoire began again:

"And everything goes well at the pit?"

"Well, I am upset over this dirty crisis. Ah! we are paying for the prosperous years! They have built too many workshops, put down too many railways, invested too much capital with a view to a large return, and to-day the money is asleep. They can't get any more to make the whole thing work. Luckily, things are not desperate; I shall get out of it somehow."

Like his cousin he had inherited a denier in the Montsou mines. But being an enterprising engineer, tormented by the desire for a royal fortune, he had hastened to sell out when the denier had reached a million. For some months he had been maturing a scheme. His wife possessed, through an uncle, the little concession of Vandame, where only two pits were open—Jean-Bart and Gaston-Marie—but in an abandoned state, and with such defective material that the output hardly covered the cost. Now he was meditating the repair of Jean-Bart, the renewal of the engine, and the enlargement of the shaft so as to facilitate the descent, keeping Gaston-Marie only for exhaustion purposes. They ought to be able to shovel up gold there, he said. The idea was sound. Only the million had been spent over it, and this damnable industrial crisis broke out at the moment when large profits would have shown that he was right. Besides, he was a bad manager, with a rough kindness towards his workmen, and since his wife's death he allowed himself to be pillaged, and also gave the rein to his daughters, the elder of whom talked of going on the stage, while the younger had already had three landscapes refused at the Salon,[3] both of them joyous amid the downfall, and exhibiting in poverty their capacity for good household management.

"You see, Léon," he went on, in a hesitating voice, "you were wrong not to sell out at the same time as I did; now everything is going down. You run risk, and if you had confided your money to me you would see what we should have done at Vandame in our mine!"

M. Grégoire finished his chocolate without haste. He replied peacefully:

"Never! You know that I don't want to speculate. I live quietly, and it would be too foolish to worry my head over business affairs. And as for Montsou it may continue to go down, we shall always get our living out of it. It doesn't do to be so diabolically greedy! Then, listen, it is you who will bite your fingers one day, for Montsou will rise again, and Cécile's grandchildren will still get their white bread out of it."

Deneulin listened with a constrained smile.

"Then," he murmured, "if I were to ask you to put a hundred thousand francs in my affair you would refuse?"

But seeing the Grégoires' disturbed faces he regretted having gone so far; he put off his idea of a loan, reserving it until the case was desperate.

"Oh! I have not got there! it is a joke. Good heavens! Perhaps you are right; the money that other people earn for you is the best to fatten on."

They changed the conversation. Cécile spoke again of her cousins, whose tastes interested, while at the same time they shocked her. Madame Grégoire promised to take her daughter to see those dear little ones on the first fine day. M. Grégoire, however, with a distracted air, did not follow the conversation. He added aloud:

"If I were in your place I wouldn't persist any more; I would treat with Montsou. They want to, and you will get your money back."

He alluded to an old hatred which existed between the concession of Montsou and that of Vandame. In spite of the latter's slight importance, its powerful neighbour was enraged at seeing, enclosed within its own sixty-seven communes, this square league which did not belong to it, and after having vainly tried to kill it had plotted to buy it at a low price when in a failing condition. The war continued without truce. Each party stopped its galleries at two hundred mètres from the other; it was a duel to the last drop of blood, although the managers and engineers maintained polite relations with each other.

Deneulin's eyes had flamed up.

"Never!" he cried, in his turn. "Montsou shall never have Vandame as long as I am alive. I dined on Thursday at Hennebeau's, and I saw him fluttering around me. Last autumn, when the big men came to the administration building, they made me all sorts of advances. Yes, yes, I know them—those marquises, and dukes, and generals, and ministers! Brigands who would take away even your shirt at the corner of a wood."

He could not cease. Besides, M. Grégoire did not defend the administration of Montsou—the six stewards established by the treaty of 1760, who governed the Company despotically, and the five survivors of whom on every death chose the new member among the powerful and rich shareholders. The opinion of the owner of Piolaine, with his reasonable ideas, was that these gentlemen were sometimes rather immoderate in their exaggerated love of money.

Mélanie had come to clear away the table. Outside, the dogs were again barking, and Honorine was going to the door, when Cécile, who was stifled by heat and food, left the table.

"No, never mind! it must be for my lesson."

Deneulin had also risen. He watched the young girl go out, and asked, smiling:

"Well! and the marriage with little Négrel?"

"Nothing has been settled," said Madame Grégoire; "it is only an idea. We must reflect."

"No doubt!" he went on, with a gay laugh. "I believe that the nephew and the aunt—— What baffles me is that Madame Hennebeau should throw herself so on Cécile's neck."

But M. Grégoire was indignant. So distinguished a lady, and fourteen years older than the young man! It was monstrous; he did not like joking on such subjects. Deneulin, still laughing, shook hands with him and left.

"Not yet," said Cécile, coming back. "It is that woman with the two children. You know, mamma, the miner's wife whom we met. Are they to come in here?"

They hesitated. Were they very dirty? No, not very; and they would leave their sabots in the porch. Already the father and mother had stretched themselves out in the depths of their large easy chairs. They were digesting there. The fear of change of air decided them.

"Let them come in, Honorine."

Then Maheude and her little ones entered, frozen and hungry, seized by fright on finding themselves in this room, which was so warm and smelled so nicely of the brioche.

## CHAPTER II

The room remained shut up and the shutters had allowed gradual streaks of daylight to form a fan on the ceiling. The confined air stupefied them so that they continued their night's slumber: Lénore and Henri in each other's arms, Alzire with her head back, lying on her hump; while Father Bonnemort, having the bed of Zacharie and Jeanlin to himself, snored with open mouth. No sound came from the closet where Maheude had gone to sleep again while suckling Estelle, her breast hanging to one side, the child lying across her belly, overcome also and stifling in the soft flesh of the bosom.

The clock below struck six. Along the front of the settlement one heard the sound of doors, then the clatter of sabots along the pavements; the screening women were going to the pit. And silence again fell until seven o'clock. Then shutters were drawn back, yawns and coughs were heard through the walls. For a long time a coffee-mill scraped, but no one awoke in the room.

Suddenly a sound of blows and shouts, far away, made Alzire sit up. She was conscious of the time, and ran bare-footed to shake her mother.

"Mother, mother, it is late! You have to go out. Take care, you are crushing Estelle."

And she saved the child, half-stifled beneath the enormous mass of the breasts.

"Good gracious!" stammered Maheude, rubbing her eyes, "I'm so knocked up I could sleep all day. Dress Lénore and Henri, I'll take them with me; and you can take care of Estelle; I don't want to drag her along for fear of hurting her, this dog's weather."

She hastily washed herself and put on an old blue skirt, her cleanest, and another garment of grey wool in which she had made two patches the evening before.

"And the soup! Good gracious!" she muttered again.

When her mother had gone down, hustling everything, Alzire went back into the room taking with her Estelle, who had begun screaming. But she was used to the little one's rages; at eight she had all a woman's tender cunning in soothing and amusing her. She gently placed her in her still warm bed, and put her to sleep again, giving her a finger to suck. It was time, for now another disturbance broke out, and she had to make peace between Lénore and Henri, who at last awoke. These children could never get on together; it was only when they were asleep that they put their arms round one another's necks. The girl, who was six years old, as soon as she was awake, set on the boy, her elder by two years, who received her blows without returning them. Both of them had the same kind of head, which was too large for them, as if blown out, with disorderly yellow hair. Alzire had to pull her sister by the legs, threatening to take the skin off her bottom. Then there was stamping over the washing, and over every garment that she put on to them. The shutters remained closed so as not to disturb Father Bonnemort's sleep. He went on snoring amid the children's frightful clatter.

"It's ready. Are you coming, up there?" shouted Maheude.

She had put back the blinds, and stirred up the fire, adding some coal to it. Her hope was that the old man had not swallowed all the soup. But she found the saucepan dry, and cooked a handful of vermicelli which she had been keeping for three days in reserve. They would swallow it with water, without butter, as there could not be any remaining from the day before, and she was surprised to find that Catherine in preparing the bricks had performed the miracle of leaving a piece as large as a nut. But this time the cupboard was indeed empty: nothing, not a crust, not an odd fragment, not a bone to gnaw. What was to become of them if Maigrat persisted in cutting short their credit, and if the Piolaine people would not give them the five francs? When the men and the girl returned from the pit they would want to eat, for unfortunately it had not yet been found out how to live without eating.

"Come down, will you?" she cried out, getting angry. "I ought to be gone by this!"

When Alzire and the children were there she divided the vermicelli in three small portions. She herself was not hungry, she said. Although Catherine had already poured water on the coffee-dregs of the day before, she did so over again, and swallowed two large glasses of coffee so clear that it looked like rusty water. That would keep her up all the same.

"Listen!" she repeated to Alzire. "You must let your grandfather sleep; you must watch that Estelle does not knock her head; and if she wakes, or if she howls too much, here! take this bit of sugar and melt it and give it her in spoonfuls. I know that you are sensible and won't eat it yourself."

"And school, mother?"

"School! well, that must be left for another day: I want you."

"And the soup? would you like me to make it if you come back late?"

"Soup, soup: no, wait till I come."

Alzire, with the precocious intelligence of a little invalid girl, could make soup very well. She must have understood, for she did not insist. Now the whole settlement was awake, bands of children were going to school, and one heard the trailing noise of their clogs. Eight o'clock struck, and a growing murmur of chatter arose on the left, among the Levaque people. The women were commencing their day around the coffee-pots, with their fists on their hips, their tongues turning without ceasing, like mill-stones. A faded head, with thick lips and flattened nose, was pressed against a window-pane, calling out:

"Anything new? Stop a bit."

"No, no! later on," replied Maheude. "I have to go out."

And for fear of giving way to the offer of a glass of warm coffee she pushed Lénore and Henri, and set out with them. Up above, Father Bonnemort was still snoring with a rhythmic snore which rocked the house.

Outside, Maheude was surprised to find that the wind was no longer blowing. There had been a sudden thaw; the sky was earth coloured, the walls were sticky with greenish moisture, and the roads were covered with pitch-like mud, a special kind of mud peculiar to the coal country, as black as diluted soot, thick and tenacious enough to retain her sabots. Suddenly she boxed Lénore's ears, because the little one amused herself by piling the mud on her clogs as on the end of a shovel. On leaving the settlement she had gone along by the pit-bank and followed the road of the canal, making a short cut through broken-up paths, across rough country shut in by mossy palings. Sheds succeeded one another, long work-shop buildings, tall chimneys spitting out soot, and soiling this ravaged suburb of an industrial district. Behind a clump of poplars the old Réquillart pit exhibited its crumbling steeple, of which the large skeleton alone stood upright. And turning to the right, Maheude found herself on the high road.

"Stop, stop, dirty pig! I'll teach you to make mincemeat."

Now it was Henri, who had taken a handful of mud and was

moulding it. The two children had their ears impartially boxed, and were brought into good order, looking out of the corner of their eyes at the mud pies they had made. They draggled along, already exhausted by their efforts to unstick their shoes at every step.

On the Marchiennes side the road unrolled its two leagues of pavement, which stretched straight as a ribbon soaked in cart grease between the reddish fields. But on the other side it went down like a braid through Montsou, which was built on the slope of a large undulation in the plain. These roads in the Nord, drawn like a string between manufacturing towns gradually built up, with their slight curves, their slow ascent, tend to make the department one laborious city. The little brick houses daubed over to enliven the climate, some yellow, others blue, others black—the latter, no doubt, in order to reach at once their final shade—went serpentining down to right and to left to the bottom of the slope. A few large two-storeyed villas, the dwellings of the heads of the workshops, made holes in the serried line of straight façades. A church, also of brick, looked like a new model of a large furnace, with its square tower already stained by the floating coal dust. And amid the sugar works, the rope works, and the flour mills, there stood out ballrooms, restaurant and beershops, which were so numerous that to every thousand houses there were more than five hundred inns.

As she approached the Company's yards, a vast series of storehouses and workshops, Maheude decided to take Henri and Lénore by the hand, one on the right, the other on the left. Beyond was situated the house of the director, M. Hennebeau, a sort of vast châlet, separated from the road by a grating, and then a garden in which some lean trees vegetated. Just then, a carriage had stopped before the door and a gentleman with decorations and a lady in a fur cloak alighted: visitors just arrived from Paris at the Marchiennes station, for Madame Hennebeau, who appeared in the shadow of the porch, was uttering exclamations of surprise and joy.

"Come along, then, dawdlers!" growled Maheude, pulling the two little ones, who were standing in the mud.

When she arrived at Maigrat's, she was quite excited. Maigrat lived close to the manager; only a wall separated the latter's grounds from his own small house, and he had there a warehouse, a long building which opened on to the road as a shop without a front. He kept everything there, grocery, pork, fruit, and sold bread, beer, and saucepans. Formerly an overseer at the Voreux, he had started with a small canteen; then, thanks to the protection of his superiors, his business had enlarged, gradually killing the Montsou retail trade. He centralised merchandise, and the considerable custom of the settlements enabled him to sell more cheaply and to give longer credit. Besides, he had remained in the Company's hands, and they had built his small house and his shop.

"Here I am again, Monsieur Maigrat," said Maheude, in her humble way, finding him standing in front of his door.

He looked at her without replying. He was a stout, cold, polite man, and he prided himself on never changing his mind.

"Now you won't send me away again, like yesterday. We must have bread from now to Saturday. Sure enough, we owe you sixty francs these two years."

She explained in short, painful phrases. It was an old debt contracted during the last strike. Twenty times over they had promised to settle it, but they had not been able; they could not even give him forty sous a fortnight. And then a misfortune had happened two days before; she had been obliged to pay twenty francs to a shoemaker who threatened to seize their things. And that was why they were without a sou. Otherwise they would have been able to go on until Saturday, like the others.

Maigrat, with protruded belly and folded arms, shook his head at every supplication.

"Only two loaves, Monsieur Maigrat. I am reasonable, I don't ask for coffee. Only two three-pound loaves a day."

"No," he shouted at last, at the top of his voice.

His wife had appeared, a pitiful creature who passed all her days over a ledger, without even daring to lift her head. She moved away frightened at seeing this unfortunate woman turning her ardent beseeching eyes towards her. It was said that she yielded the conjugal bed to the putters among the customers. It was a known fact that when a miner wished to prolong his credit, he had only to send his daughter or his wife, plain or pretty, it mattered not, provided they were complacent.

Maheude, still imploring Maigrat with her look, felt herself uncomfortable under the pale keenness of his small eyes, which seemed to undress her. It made her angry; she would have understood before she had had seven children, when she was young. And she went off, violently dragging Lénore and Henri, who were occupied in picking up nut-shells from the gutter where they were making investigations.

"This won't bring you luck, Monsieur Maigrat, remember!"

Now there only remained the Piolaine people. If these would not throw her a five franc piece she might as well lie down and die. She had taken the Joiselle road on the left. The administration building was there at the corner of the road, a veritable brick palace, where the great people from Paris, princes and generals and members of the Government, came every autumn to give large dinners. As she walked she was already spending the five francs: first bread, then coffee, afterwards a quarter of butter, a bushel of potatoes for the morning soup and the evening stew; finally, perhaps, a bit of pigs' chitterlings, for the father needed meat.

The Curé of Montsou, Abbé Joire, was passing, holding up his cassock, with the delicate air of a fat well-nourished cat afraid of wetting her fur. He was a gentleman who pretended not to interest himself in anything, so as not to vex either the workers or the masters.

"Good-day, Monsieur le Curé."

Without stopping he smiled at the children, and left her planted in the middle of the road. She was not religious, but she had suddenly imagined that this priest would give her something.

And the journey began again through the black, sticky mud. There were still two kilomètres to walk, and it was necessary to drag the little ones more, for they were frightened, and no longer amused themselves. To right and to left of the path the same vague landscape unrolled, enclosed within mossy palings, the same factory buildings, dirty with smoke, bristling with tall chimneys. Then the flat land was spread out in immense open fields, like an ocean of brown clods, without a tree-trunk, as far as the violet line of the forest of Vandame.

"Carry me, mother."

She carried them one after the other. Puddles made holes in the pathway, and she pulled up her clothes, fearful of arriving too dirty. Three times she nearly fell, so sticky was that confounded pavement. And as they at last arrived before the porch, two enormous dogs threw themselves upon them, barking so loudly that the little ones yelled with terror. The coachman was obliged to take a whip.

"Leave your sabots, and come in," repeated Honorine.

In the dining-room the mother and children stood motionless, dazed by the sudden heat, and very constrained beneath the gaze of this old lady and gentleman, who were stretched out in their easy chairs.

"Cécile," said the old lady, "fulfil your little duties."

The Grégoires charged Cécile with their charities. It was part of their idea of a good education. One must be charitable. They said themselves that their house was the house of God. Besides, they flattered themselves that they performed their charity with intelligence, and they were exercised by a constant fear lest they should be deceived, and so encourage vice. So they never gave money, never! Not ten sous, not two sous, for it is a well-known fact that as soon as a poor man gets two sous he drinks them. Their alms were, therefore, always in kind, especially in warm clothing, distributed during the winter to needy children.

"Oh! the poor dears!" exclaimed Cécile, "how pale they are from the cold! Honorine, go and look for the parcel in the cupboard."

The servants were also gazing at these miserable creatures with the pity and vague uneasiness of girls who are in no difficulty about their own dinners. While the housemaid went upstairs, the cook forgot her duties, leaving the rest of the brioche on the table, and stood there swinging her empty hands.

"I still have two woollen dresses and some comforters," Cécile went on; "you will see how warm they will be, the poor dears!"

Then Maheude found her tongue, and stammered:

"Thank you so much, mademoiselle. You are all too good."

Tears had filled her eyes, she thought herself sure of the five francs, and was only pre-occupied by the way in which she would ask for them if they were not offered to her. The housemaid did not reappear, and there was a moment of embarrassed silence. From their mother's skirts the little ones opened their eyes wide and gazed at the brioche.

"You only have these two?" asked Madame Grégoire, in order to break the silence.

"Oh, madame! I have seven of them."

M. Grégoire, who had gone back to his newspaper, sat up indignantly.

"Seven children! But why?[4] good God!"

"It is imprudent," murmured the old lady.

Maheude made a vague gesture of apology. What would you have? One doesn't think about it at all, they come quite naturally. And then, when they grow up they bring something in, and that makes the household go. Take their case, they could get on, if it was not for the grandfather who was getting quite stiff, and if among the lot only two of her sons and her eldest daughter were old enough to go down into the pit. It was necessary, all the same, to feed the little ones who brought nothing in.

"Then," said Madame Grégoire, "you have worked for a long time at the mines?"

A silent laugh lit up Maheude's pale face.

"Ah, yes! ah, yes! I went down till I was twenty. The doctor said that I should stay there for good after I had been confined the second time, because it seems that made something go wrong in my inside. Besides, then I got married, and I had enough to do in the house. But on my husband's side, you see, they have been down there for ages. It goes up from grandfather to grandfather, one doesn't know how far back, quite to the beginning when they first took the pick down there at Réquillart."

M. Grégoire thoughtfully contemplated this woman and these pitiful children, with their waxy flesh, their discoloured hair, the degeneration which stunted them, gnawed by anæmia, and with the melancholy ugliness of starvelings. There was silence again, and one only heard the burning coal as it gave out a jet of gas. The moist room had that heavy air of comfort in which our middle-class nooks of happiness slumber.

"What is she doing, then?" exclaimed Cécile impatiently. "Mélanie, go up and tell her that the parcel is at the bottom of the cupboard, on the left."

In the meanwhile, M. Grégoire repeated aloud the reflections inspired by the sight of these starving ones.

"There is evil in this world, it is quite true; but, my good woman, it must also be said that work-people are never prudent. Thus, instead of putting aside a few sous like our peasants, miners drink, get into debt, and end by not having enough to support their families."

"Monsieur is right," replied Maheude sturdily. "They don't always keep to the right path. That's what I'm always saying to the ne'er-do-wells when they complain. Now, I have been lucky; my husband doesn't drink. All the same, on feast Sundays he sometimes takes a drop too much; but it never goes farther. It is all the nicer of him, since before our marriage he drank like a hog, begging your pardon. And yet, you know, it doesn't help us much that he is so sensible. There are days like to-day when you might turn out all the drawers in the house and not find a farthing."

She wished to suggest to them the idea of the five-franc piece, and went on in her low voice, explaining the fatal debt, small at first, then large and overwhelming. They paid regularly for many fortnights. But one day they got behind, and then it was all up. They could never catch up again. A gulf was formed, and the men became disgusted with work which did not even allow them to pay their way. Do what they could, there were nothing but difficulties until death. Besides, it must be understood that a collier needed a glass to wash away the dust. It began there, and then he was always in the inn when worries came. Without complaining of anyone it might be that the workmen did not earn as much as they ought to.

"I thought," said Madame Grégoire, "that the Company gave you lodging and firing?"

Maheude glanced sideways at the flaming coal in the fireplace.

"Yes, yes, they give us coal, not very grand, but it burns. As to lodging, it only costs six francs a month; that sounds like nothing, but it is often pretty hard to pay. To-day they might cut me up into bits without getting two sous out of me. Where there's nothing, there's nothing."

The lady and gentleman were silent, softly stretched out, and gradually wearied and disquieted by the exhibition of this wretchedness. She feared she had wounded them, and added, with the stolid and just air of a practical woman:

"Oh, I don't want to complain. Things are like this, and one has to put up with them; all the more that it's no good struggling, perhaps we shouldn't change anything. The best is, is it not, to try and live honestly in the place in which the good God has put us?"

M. Grégoire approved this emphatically.

"With such sentiments, my good woman, one is above misfortune."

Honorine and Mélanie at last brought the parcel.

Cécile unfastened it and took out two dresses. She added comforters, even stockings and mittens. They all fitted beautifully; she hastened and made the servants put on the chosen garments; for her music mistress had just arrived; and she pushed the mother and children towards the door.

"We are very short," stammered Maheude; "if we only had a five-franc piece——"

The phrase was stifled, for the Maheus were proud and never begged. Cécile looked uneasily at her father; but the latter refused decisively, with an air of duty.

"No, it is not our custom. We cannot do it."

Then the young girl, moved by the mother's overwhelmed face, wished to do all she could for the children. They were still looking fixedly at the brioche; she cut it in two and gave it to them.

"Here! this is for you."

Then, taking the pieces back, she asked for an old newspaper:

"Wait, you must share with your brothers and sisters."

And beneath the tender gaze of her parents she finally pushed them out of the room. The poor starving urchins went off, holding the brioche[5] respectfully in their benumbed little hands.

Maheude dragged her children along the road, seeing neither the desert fields, nor the black mud, nor the great livid sky. As she passed through Montsou she resolutely entered Maigrat's shop, and begged so persistently that at last she carried away two loaves, coffee, butter, and even her five-franc piece, for the man also lent money by the week. It was not her that he wanted, it was Catherine; she understood that when he advised her to send her daughter for provisions. They would see about that. Catherine would box his ears if he came too close under her nose.

## CHAPTER III

ELEVEN O'CLOCK STRUCK AT the little church in the Deux-Cent-Quarante settlement, a brick chapel in which Abbé Joire came to say mass on Sundays. In the school beside it, also of brick, one heard the faltering voices of the children, in spite of windows closed against the outside cold. The wide passages, divided into little gardens, back to back, between the four large blocks of uniform houses, were deserted; and these gardens, devastated by the winter, exhibited the destitution of their marly soil, lumped and spotted by the last vegetables. They were making soup, chimneys were smoking, a woman appeared at distant intervals along the fronts, opened a door and disappeared. From one end to the other, over the pavement, the pipes dripped into tubs, although it was no longer raining, so charged was this grey sky with moistness. And the village, built altogether in the midst of the vast plain, and edged by its black roads as by a mourning border, had no touch of joyousness about it save the regular bands of its red tiles, constantly washed by showers.

When Maheude returned, she went out of her way to buy potatoes from an overseer's wife whose crop was not yet exhausted. Behind a curtain of sickly poplars, the only trees in these flat regions, was a group of isolated buildings, houses placed four together, and surrounded by their gardens. As the Company reserved this new experiment for the captains, the work-people called this corner of the hamlet the settlement of the Bas-de-Soie, just as they called their own settlement Paie-tes-Dettes, in good-humoured irony of their wretchedness.

"Eh! Here we are," said Maheude, laden with parcels, pushing in Lénore and Henri, covered with mud, and with faltering steps.

In front of the fire Estelle was screaming, cradled in Alzire's arms. The latter, having no more sugar and not knowing how to soothe her, had decided to pretend to give her the breast. This ruse often succeeded. But this time it was in vain for her to open her dress, and to press the mouth against the lean breast of an eight year old invalid; the child was enraged at biting the skin and drawing nothing.

"Pass her to me," cried the mother as soon as she found herself free; "she won't let us say a word."

When she had taken from her bodice a breast as heavy as a leather bottle, to the neck of which the brawler hung, suddenly silent, they were at last able to talk. Besides, everything was going on well; the little housekeeper had kept up the fire and had swept and arranged the room. And in the silence they heard upstairs the grandfather's snoring, the same rhythmic snoring which had not stopped for a moment.

"What a lot of things!" murmured Alzire smiling at the provisions. "If you like, mother, I'll make the soup."

The table was encumbered: a parcel of clothes, two loaves, potatoes, butter, coffee, chicory, and half a pound of pig's chitterlings.

"Oh! the soup!" said Maheude with an air of fatigue. "We must gather some sorrel and pull up some leeks. No! I will make some for the men afterwards. Put some potatoes on to boil; we'll eat them with a little butter and some coffee, eh? Don't forget the coffee!"

But suddenly she thought of the brioche. She looked at the empty hands of Lénore and Henri who were fighting on the floor, already rested and lively. These gluttons had slily eaten the brioche on the road! She boxed their ears, while Alzire, who was putting the saucepan on the fire, tried to appease her.

"Let them be, mother. If it was for me, you know the brioche is all the same to me. They were hungry, walking so far."

Mid-day struck; they heard the clogs of the children coming out of school. The potatoes were cooked, and the coffee, thickened by a good half of chicory, was passing through the percolator with the singing noise of large drops. One corner of the table was free; but the mother only was eating there. The three children were satisfied to be on their knees; and all the time the little boy with silent voracity looked, without saying anything, at the chitterlings, excited by the greasy paper.

Maheude was drinking her coffee in little sips, with her hands round the glass to warm them, when Father Bonnemort came down. Usually he rose late, and his breakfast waited for him on the fire. But to-day he began to grumble because there was no soup. Then, when his daughter-in-law said to him that one cannot always do what one likes, he ate his potatoes in silence. From time to time he got up to spit in the ashes for cleanliness, and, settled in his chair, he rolled his food round in his mouth, with lowered head and dull eyes.

"Ah! I forgot, mother," said Alzire. "The neighbour came——"

Her mother interrupted her.

"She bothers me!"

There was a deep rancour against the Levaque woman who had pleaded poverty the day before to avoid lending her anything; while she knew that she was just then in comfort, since her lodger, Bouteloup, had paid his fortnight in advance. In the settlement they did not usually lend from household to household.

"Here! you remind me," said Maheude. "Wrap up a millfull of coffee. I will take it to Pierronne; I owe it to her from the day before yesterday."

And when her daughter had prepared the packet she added that she would come back immediately to put the men's soup on the fire. Then she went out with Estelle in her arms, leaving old Bonnemort to chew his potatoes leisurely, while Lénore and Henri fought for the fallen parings.

Instead of going round, Maheude went straight across through the gardens, for fear lest Levaque's wife should call her.

Her garden was just next to that of the Pierronnes, and in the dilapidated trellis-work which separated them there was a hole through which they fraternised. The common well was there, serving four households. Beside it, behind a clump of feeble lilacs, was situated the shed, a low building full of old tools, in which were brought up the rabbits which were eaten on feast days. One o'clock struck; it was the hour for coffee, and not a soul was to be seen at the doors or windows. Only a workman belonging to the earth-cutting, waiting the hour for descent, was digging up his patch of vegetable ground without raising his head. But as Maheude arrived opposite the other block of buildings, she was surprised to see a gentleman and two ladies in front of the church. She stopped a moment and recognised them; it was Madame Hennebeau bringing her guests, the decorated gentleman and the lady in the fur mantle, to see the settlement.

"Oh! why did you take this trouble!" exclaimed Pierronne, when Maheude had returned the coffee. "There was no hurry."

She was twenty-eight, and was considered the beauty of the settlement, dark, with a low forehead, large eyes, straight mouth, and coquettish as well; with the neatness of a cat, and with a good figure, for she had had no children. Her mother, Brûlé, widow of a pikeman who died in the mine, after having sent her daughter to work in a factory, swearing that she should never marry a collier, had never ceased to be angry since she had married, somewhat late, Pierron, a widower with a girl of eight. However, the household lived very happily, in the midst of chatter, of scandals which circulated concerning the husband's complacency and the wife's lovers. No debts, meat twice a week, a house kept so clean that one could see one's self in the saucepans. As an additional piece of luck, thanks to favours, the Company had authorized her to sell bon-bons and biscuits, jars of which she exhibited, on two boards, behind the windowpanes. This was six or seven sous profit a day, and sometimes twelve on Sundays. The drawback to all this happiness was only Mother Brûlé, who screamed with all the rage of an old revolutionary, having to avenge the death of her man on the masters, and little Lydie, who pocketed, in the shape of frequent blows, the passions of the family.

"How big she is already!" said Pierronne, simpering at Estelle.

"Oh! the trouble that it gives! Don't talk of it!" said Maheude. "You are lucky not to have any. At least you can keep clean."

Although everything was in order in her house, and she scrubbed every Saturday, she glanced with a jealous housekeeper's eye over this clean room, in which there was even a certain coquetry, gilt vases on the sideboard, a mirror, three framed prints.

Pierronne was about to drink her coffee alone, all her people being at the pit.

"You'll have a glass with me?" she said.

"No, thanks; I've just swallowed mine."

"What does that matter?"

In fact, it mattered nothing. And both began drinking slowly. Between the jars of biscuits and bon-bons their eyes rested on the opposite houses, of which the little curtains in the windows formed a row, revealing by their more-or-less whiteness the virtues of the housekeepers. Those of the Levaques were very dirty, veritable kitchen clouts, which seemed to have wiped the bottoms of the saucepans.

"How can they live in such dirt?" murmured Pierronne.

Then Maheude began and did not stop. Ah! if she had had a lodger like that Bouteloup she would have made the household go. When one knew how to do it, a lodger was an excellent thing. Only one ought not to sleep with him. And then the husband had taken to drink, beat his wife, and run after the singers at the Montsou café concerts.

Pierronne assumed an air of profound disgust. These singers gave all sorts of diseases. There was one at Joiselle who had infected a whole pit.

"What surprises me is that you let your son go with their girl."

"Ah, yes! but just stop it then! Their garden is next to ours. Zacharie was always there in summer with Philomène behind the lilacs, and they don't put themselves out on the shed; one couldn't draw water at the well without surprising them."

It was the usual history of the promiscuities of the settlement;

boys and girls became corrupted together, throwing themselves on their backsides, as they said, on the low, sloping roof of the shed when twilight came on. All the putters got their first child there when they did not take the trouble to go to Réquillart or into the cornfields. It was of no consequence; they married afterwards, only the mothers were angry when their lads began too soon, for a lad who marries no longer brings anything into the family.

"In your place I would have done with it," said Pierronne, sensibly. "Your Zacharie has already filled her twice, and they will go on and join themselves. Anyhow, the money is gone."

Maheude was furious and raised her hands.

"Listen to this: I will curse them if they get joined. Doesn't Zacharie owe us any respect? He has cost us something, hasn't he? Very well. He must return it before getting a wife to hang on him. What will become of us, eh, if our children begin at once to work for others? Might as well die!"

However, she grew calm.

"I'm speaking in a general way; we shall see later. It is fine and strong, your coffee; you make it proper."

And after a quarter of an hour spent over other stories, she ran off, exclaiming that the men's soup was not yet made. Outside, the children were going back to school; a few women were showing themselves at their doors, looking at Madame Hennebeau, who, with lifted finger, was explaining the settlement to her guests. This visit began to stir up the village. The earth-cutting man stopped digging for a moment, and two disturbed fowls were frightened in the gardens.

As Maheude returned, she ran against the Levaque woman who had come out to stop Dr. Vanderhagen, a doctor of the Company, a small hurried man, overwhelmed by work, who gave his advice as he walked.

"Sir," she said, "I can't sleep; I feel ill everywhere. I must tell you about it."

He spoke to them all familiarly, and replied without stopping:

"Just leave me alone; you drink too much coffee."

"And my husband, sir," said Maheude in her turn, "you must come and see him. He always has those pains in his legs."

"It is you who take too much out of him. Just leave me alone!"

The two women were left to gaze at the doctor's retreating back.

"Come in, then," said the Levaque woman, when she had exchanged a despairing shrug with her neighbour. "You know, there is something new. And you will take a little coffee. It is quite fresh."

Maheude refused, but without energy. Well! a drop, at all events, not to disoblige. And she entered.

The room was black with dirt, the floor and the walls spotted with grease, the sideboard and the table sticky with filth; and the stink of a badly-kept house took you by the throat. Near the fire, with his elbows on the table and his nose in his plate, Bouteloup, a broad stout placid man, still young for thirty-five, was finishing the remains of his boiled beef, while standing in front of him, little Achille, Philomène's first-born, who was already in his third year, was looking at him in the silent, supplicating way of a gluttonous animal. The lodger, very kind behind his big brown beard, from time to time stuffed a piece of meat into his mouth.

"Wait till I sugar it," said the Levaque woman, putting some brown sugar beforehand into the coffee-pot.

Six years older than he was, she was hideous and worn out, with her bosom hanging on her belly, and her belly on her thighs, with a flattened muzzle, and greyish hair always uncombed. He had taken her naturally, without choosing, the same as he did his soup in which he found hairs, or his bed of which the sheets lasted for three months. She was part of the lodging; the husband liked repeating that good reckonings make good friends.

"I was going to tell you," she went on, "that Pierronne was seen yesterday prowling about on the Bas-de-Soie side. The gentleman that you know was waiting for her behind Rasseneur's, and they went off together along the canal. Eh! that's nice, isn't it? A married woman!"

"Gracious!" said Maheude, "Pierron, before marrying her, used to give the captain rabbits; now it costs him less to lend his wife."

Bouteloup began to laugh enormously, and threw a fragment

of sauced bread into Achille's mouth. The two women went on relieving themselves with regard to Pierronne—a flirt, not prettier than anyone else, but always occupied in looking after every freckle of her skin, in washing herself, and putting on pomade. Anyhow, it concerned the husband, if he liked that sort of thing. There were men so ambitious that they would wipe the masters' behinds to hear them say thank-you. And they were only interrupted by the arrival of a neighbour bringing in a little urchin of nine months, Désirée, Philomène's youngest; Philomène, taking her breakfast at the screening-shed, had arranged that they should bring her little one down there, where she suckled it, seated for a moment in the coal.

"I can't leave mine for a moment, she screams directly," said Maheude, looking at Estelle, who was asleep in her arms.

But she did not succeed in avoiding the domestic affair which she had read in the other's eyes.

"I say, now we ought to get that settled."

At first the two mothers, without need for talking about it, had agreed not to conclude the marriage. If Zacharie's mother wished to get her son's wages as long as possible, Philomène's mother was enraged at the idea of abandoning her daughter's wages. There was no hurry; the second mother had even preferred to keep the little one, as long as there was only one; but when it began to grow and eat and another one came, she found that she was losing, and furiously pushed on the marriage, like a woman who does not care to throw away her money.

"Zacharie has drawn his lot," she went on, "and there's nothing in the way. When shall it be?"

"Wait till the fine weather," replied Maheude, constrainedly. "They are a nuisance, these things! As if they couldn't wait to be married before going together! My word! I would strangle Catherine if I knew that she were to do that."

The other woman shrugged her shoulders.

"Let be! she'll do like the others."

Bouteloup, with the tranquillity of a man who is at home, searched about on the dresser for bread. Vegetables for Levaque's soup, potatoes and leeks, lay about on a corner of the table, half-peeled, taken up and dropped a dozen times in the midst of continual gossiping. The woman was about to go on with them again when she dropped them anew and planted herself before the window.

"What's that there? Why, there's Madame Hennebeau with some people. They are going into Pierronne's."

At once both of them started again on the subject of Pierronne. Oh! whenever the Company brought any visitors to the settlement they never failed to go straight to her place, because it was clean. No doubt they never told them stories about the head captain. One can afford to be clean when one has lovers who earn three thousand francs, and are lodged and warmed, without counting presents. If it was clean above it was not so clean underneath. And all the time that the visitors remained opposite, they went on chattering.

"There, they are coming out," said Levaque at last. "They are going all round. Why, look, my dear—I believe they are going into your place."

Maheude was seized with fear. Who knows whether Alzire had sponged over the table? And her soup, also, which was not yet ready! She stammered a good-day, and ran off home without a single glance aside.

But everything was bright. Alzire, very seriously, with a cloth in front of her, had set about making the soup, seeing that her mother did not return. She had pulled up the last leeks from the garden, gathered the sorrel, and was just then cleaning the vegetables, while a large kettle on the fire was heating the water for the men's baths when they should return. Henri and Lénore were good by chance, being absorbed in tearing up an old almanac. Father Bonnemort was smoking his pipe in silence. As Maheude was getting her breath Madame Hennebeau knocked.

"You will allow me, will you not, my good woman?"

Tall and fair, a little heavy in her superb maturity of forty years, she smiled with an effort of affability, without showing too prominently her fear of soiling her bronze silk dress and black velvet mantle.

"Come in, come in," she said to her guests. "We are not disturbing anyone. Now, isn't this clean again! And this good woman has seven children! All our households are like this. I ought to explain to you that the Company rents them the house at six francs a month. A large room on the ground floor, two rooms above, a cellar, and a garden."

The decorated gentleman and the lady in the fur cloak, arrived that morning by train from Paris, opened their eyes vaguely, exhibiting on their faces their astonishment at all these new things which took them out of their element.

"And a garden!" repeated the lady. "One could live on that! It is charming!"

"We give them more coal than they can burn," went on Madame Hennebeau. "A doctor visits them twice a week; and when they are old they receive pensions, although nothing is held back from their wages."

"A Thebaid! a real land of milk and honey!" murmured the gentleman in delight.

Maheude had hastened to offer chairs. The ladies refused. Madame Hennebeau was already getting tired, happy for a moment to amuse herself in the weariness of her exile by playing the part of exhibiting the beasts, but immediately disgusted by the sickly odour of wretchedness, in spite of the special cleanliness of the houses in which she ventured. Besides, she was only repeating odd phrases which she had overheard, without ever troubling herself further about this race of work-people who were labouring and suffering beside her.

"What beautiful children!" murmured the lady, who thought them hideous, with their large heads beneath their bushy, straw-coloured hair.

And Maheude had to tell their ages; they also asked her questions about Estelle, out of politeness. Father Bonnemort respectfully took his pipe out of his mouth; but he was not the less an object of uneasiness, so worn out by his forty years underground, with his stiff limbs, deformed body, and earthy face; and as a violent spasm of coughing took him he preferred to go and spit outside, with the idea that his black expectoration would make people uncomfortable.

Alzire received all the compliments. What an excellent little housekeeper, with her cloth! They congratulated the mother on having a little daughter so sensible for her age. And no one spoke of the hump, though looks of uneasy compassion were constantly turned towards the poor little invalid.

"Now!" concluded Madame Hennebeau, "if they ask you about our settlements at Paris you will know what to reply. Never more noise than this, patriarchal manners, all happy and well off as you see, a place where you might come to recruit a little, on account of the good air and the tranquillity."

"It is marvellous, marvellous," exclaimed the gentleman, in a final burst of enthusiasm.

They left with that enchanted air with which people leave a booth in a fair, and Maheude, who accompanied them, remained on the threshold while they went away slowly, talking very loudly. The streets were full of people, and they had to pass through several groups of women, attracted by the news of their visit, which was hawked from house to house.

Just then, Levaque, in front of her door, had stopped Pierronne, who was drawn by curiosity. Both of them affected a painful surprise. What now? Were these people going to bed at the Maheus? But it was not so very delightful a place.

"Always without a sou, with all that they earn! Lord! when people have vices!"

"I have just heard that she went this morning to beg at Piolaine, and Maigrat, who had refused them bread, has given them something. We know how Maigrat pays himself!"

"On her? Oh, no! that would need some courage. It's Catherine that he's after."

"Why, didn't she have the cheek to say just now that she would strangle Catherine if she were to come to that? As if big Chaval for ever so long had not put her backside on the shed!"

"Hush! here they are!"

Then Levaque and Pierronne, with a peaceful air and without impolite curiosity, contented themselves with watching the visitors out of the corners of their eyes. Then by a gesture they quickly called Maheude, who was still carrying Estelle in her arms. And all three, motionless, watched the well-dressed backs of Madame Hennebeau and her visitors slowly disappear. When they were some thirty paces off the gossiping recommenced with redoubled vigour.

"They carry plenty of money on their skins; worth more than themselves, perhaps."

"Ah, sure. I don't know the other, but the one that belongs here, I wouldn't give four sous for her, big as she is. They do tell stories——"

"Eh? What stories?"

"Why, she has men! First, the engineer."

"That lean, little creature! Oh, he's too small! She would lose him in the sheets."

"What does that matter, if it amuses her? I don't trust a woman who puts on such proud airs and never seems to be pleased where she is. Just look how she wags her rump, as if she felt contempt for us all. Is that nice?"

The visitors went along at the same slow pace, still talking, when a carriage stopped in the road, before the church. A gentleman of about forty-eight got out of it, dressed in a black frock-coat, and with a very dark complexion and an authoritative, correct expression.

"The husband," murmured Levaque, lowering her voice, as if he could hear her, seized by that hierarchical fear which the manager inspired in his ten thousand work-people. "It's true, though, that he has a cuckold's head, that man."

Now the whole settlement was out of doors. The curiosity of the women increased. The groups approached each other, and were melted into one crowd; while bands of urchins, with unwiped noses and gaping mouths, dawdled along the pavements. For a moment the schoolmaster's pale head was also seen behind the school-house hedge. Among the gardens, the man who was digging stood with one foot on his spade, and with rounded eyes. And the murmur of gossiping gradually increased, with a sound of rattles, like a gust of wind among dry leaves.

It was especially before the Levaques' door that the crowd was thickest. Two women had come forward, then ten, then twenty. Pierronne was prudently silent now that there were too many ears about. Maheude, one of the more reasonable, also contented herself with looking on; and to calm Estelle, who was awake and screaming, she had tranquilly drawn out her suckling animal's breast, which hung as if pulled down by the continual running of its milk. When M. Hennebeau had seated the ladies in the carriage, which went off in the direction of Marchiennes, there was a final explosion of clattering voices, all the women gesticulating and talking in each other's faces in the midst of a tumult as of an ant-hill in revolution.

But three o'clock struck. The workers of the earth-cutting, Bouteloup and the others, had set out. Suddenly around the church appeared the first colliers returning from the pit with black faces and damp garments, crossing their arms and expanding their backs. Then there was confusion among the women: they all began to run home with the terror of housekeepers who had been led astray by too much coffee and too much tattle, and one heard nothing more than this restless cry, pregnant with quarrels:

"Good Lord, and my soup! and my soup which isn't ready!"

## CHAPTER IV

WHEN MAHEU CAME IN after having left Étienne at Rasseneur's he found Catherine, Zacharie, and Jeanlin seated at the table finishing their soup. On returning from the pit they were always so hungry that they ate in their damp clothes, without even cleaning themselves; and no one was waited for, the table was laid from morning to night; there was always someone there swallowing his portion, according to the chances of work.

As he entered the door Maheu saw the provisions. He said nothing, but his uneasy face lighted up. All the morning the emptiness of the cupboard, the thought of the house without coffee and without butter, had been troubling him; the recollection came to him painfully while he was hammering at the seam, stifled at the bottom of the cutting. What would his wife do, and what would become of them if she were to return with empty hands? And now, here was everything! She would tell him about it later on. He laughed with satisfaction.

Catherine and Jeanlin had risen, and were taking their coffee standing; while Zacharie, not filled with the soup, cut himself a large slice of bread and covered it with butter. Although he saw the chitterlings on the plate he did not touch them, for meat was for the father, when there was only enough for one. All of them had washed down their soup with a big bumper of fresh water, the good, clear drink of the fortnight's end.

"I have no beer," said Maheude, when the father had seated himself in his turn. "I wanted to keep a little money. But if you would like some the little one can go and fetch a pint."

He looked at her in astonishment. What! she had money, too!

"No, no," he said, "I've had a glass, it's all right."

And Maheu began to swallow by slow spoonfuls the paste of bread, potatoes, leeks, and onions piled up in the bowl which served him as a plate. Maheude, without putting Estelle down, helped Alzire to give him all that he required, pushed near him the butter and meat, and put his coffee on the fire to keep it quite warm.

In the meanwhile, beside the fire, they began to wash themselves in the half of a barrel transformed into a tub. Catherine, whose turn came first, had filled it with warm water; and she undressed herself tranquilly, took off her cap, her jacket, her breeches and even her chemise, habituated to this since the age of eight, having grown up without seeing any harm in it. She only turned with her stomach to the fire, then rubbed herself vigorously with black soap. No one looked at her, even Lénore and Henri were no longer inquisitive to see how she was made. When she was clean she went up the stairs quite naked, leaving her damp chemise and other garments in a heap on the floor. But a quarrel broke out between the two brothers: Jeanlin had hastened to jump into the tub under the pretence that Zacharie was still eating; and the latter hustled him, claiming his turn, and calling out that he was polite enough to allow Catherine to wash herself first, but he did not wish to have the rinsings of the young urchins, all the less since, when Jeanlin had been in, it would do to fill the school ink-pots. They ended by washing themselves together, also turning towards the fire, and they even helped each other, rubbing one another's backs. Then, like their sister, they disappeared up the staircase naked.

"What a slop they do make!" murmured Maheude, taking up

their garments from the floor to put them to dry. "Alzire, just sponge up a bit."

But a disturbance on the other side of the wall cut short her speech. One heard a man's oaths, a woman's crying, a whole stampede of battle, with hollow blows that sounded like the shock of an empty gourd.

"Levaque's wife is catching it," Maheu peacefully stated as he scraped the bottom of his bowl with the spoon. "It's queer; Bouteloup made out that the soup was ready."

"Ah, yes! ready," said Maheude. "I saw the vegetables on the table, not even cleaned."

The cries redoubled, and there was a terrible push which shook the wall, followed by complete silence. Then the miner, swallowing the last spoonful, concluded, with an air of calm justice:

"If the soup is not ready, one can understand."

And after having drunk a glassful of water, he attacked the chitterlings. He cut square pieces, put the point of his knife into them and ate them on his bread without a fork. There was no talking when the father was eating. He himself was hungry in silence; he did not recognise the usual taste of Maigrat's provisions; this must come from somewhere else; however, he put no questions to his wife. He only asked if the old man was still sleeping upstairs. No, the grandfather had gone out for his usual walk. And there was silence again.

But the odour of the meat made Lénore and Henri lift up their heads from the floor, where they were amusing themselves with making rivulets with the spilt water. Both of them came and planted themselves near their father, the little one in front. Their eyes followed each morsel, full of hope when it set out from the plate and with an air of consternation when it was engulfed in the mouth. At last the father noticed the gluttonous desire which made their faces pale and their lips moist.

"Have the children had any of it?" he asked.

And as his wife hesitated:

"You know I don't like injustice. It takes away my appetite when I see them there, begging for bits."

"But they've had some of it," she exclaimed, angrily. "If you were to listen to them you might give them your share and the others, too; they would fill themselves till they burst. Isn't it true, Alzire, that we have all had some?"

"Sure enough! mother," replied the little hump-back, who under such circumstances could tell lies with the self-possession of a grown-up person.

Lénore and Henri stood motionless, shocked and rebellious at such lying, when they themselves were whipped if they did not tell the truth. Their little hearts began to swell, and they longed to protest, and to say that they, at all events, were not there when the others had some.

"Get along with you," said the mother, driving them to the other end of the room. "You ought to be ashamed of being always in your father's plate; and even if he was the only one to have any, doesn't he work, while all you, a lot of good-for-nothings, can't do anything but spend! Yes, and the more the bigger you are."

Maheu called them back. He seated Lénore on his left thigh, Henri on the right; then he finished the chitterlings by playing at dinner with them. He cut small pieces, and each had his share. The children devoured with delight.

When he had finished, he said to his wife:

"No, don't give me my coffee. I'm going to wash first; and just give me a hand to throw away this dirty water."

They took hold of the handles of the tub and emptied it into the gutter before the door, when Jeanlin came down in dry breeches, and a woollen blouse, too large for him, which was weary of fading on his brother's back. Seeing him sulkily going out through the open door, his mother stopped him:

"Where are you off to?"

"Over there."

"Where? Over there! Listen to me. You go and gather a dandelion salad for this evening. Eh, do you hear? If you don't bring a salad back you'll have to deal with me."

"All right!"

Jeanlin set out with his hands in his pockets, trailing his sabots and slouching along, with his slender loins of a ten-year-old shrimp, like an old miner. In his turn, Zacharie came down, more carefully dressed, his body covered by a black woollen knitted jacket with blue stripes. His father called out to him not to return late; and he left, nodding his head with his pipe between his teeth, without replying. Again the tub was filled with warm water. Maheu was already slowly taking off his jacket. At a look, Alzire led Lénore and Henri outside to play. The father did not like washing *en famille,* as was practised in many houses in the settlement. He blamed no one, however; he simply said that it was good for the children to dabble together.

"What are you doing up there?"cried Maheude, up the staircase.

"I'm mending my dress that I tore yesterday," replied Catherine.

"Very well. Don't come down, your father's washing."

Then Maheu and Maheude were left alone. The latter decided to place Estelle on a chair, and by a miracle, finding herself near the fire the child did not scream, but turned towards her parents the vague eyes of a little creature without intelligence. He was crouching before the tub quite naked, having first plunged his head into it, well rubbed with that black soap of which the constant use discoloured and made yellow the hair of the race. Afterwards he got into the water, lathered his chest, belly, arms, and thighs, scraping them energetically with both fists. His wife, standing by, watched him.

"Well, then," she began, "I saw your eye when you came in. You were bothered, eh? and it eased you, those provisions. Fancy! those Piolaine people didn't give me a sou! Oh! they are kind enough; they have dressed the little ones and I was ashamed to ask them, for it crosses me to ask for things."

She interrupted herself a moment to wedge Estelle into the chair lest she should tip over. The father continued to work away at his skin, without hastening by a question this story which interested him, patiently waiting for light.

"I must tell you that Maigrat had refused me, oh! straight! like one kicks a dog out of doors. Guess if I was on a spree. They keep you warm, woollen garments, but they don't put anything into your stomach, eh?"

He lifted his head, still silent. Nothing at Piolaine, nothing at

Maigrat's: then where? But, as usual, she was pulling up her sleeves to wash his back and those parts which he could not himself easily reach. Besides, he liked her to soap him, to rub him everywhere till she almost broke her wrists. She took soap and worked away at his shoulders while he held himself stiff so as to resist the shock.

"Then I returned to Maigrat's, and said to him, ah, I said something to him! And that it didn't do to have no heart, and that evil would happen to him if there were any justice. That bothered him; he turned his eyes and would like to have got away."

From the back she had got down to the buttocks and was pushing into the folds, not leaving any part of the body without passing over it, making him shine like her three saucepans on Saturdays after a big clean. Only she began to sweat with this tremendous exertion of her arms, so exhausted and out of breath that her words were choked.

"At last he called me an old nuisance. We shall have bread until Saturday, and the best is that he has lent me five francs. I have got butter, coffee, and chicory from him. I was even going to get the meat and potatoes there, only I saw that he was grumbling. Seven sous for the chitterlings, eighteen for the potatoes, and I've got three francs seventy-five left for a ragoût and a meat soup. Eh, I don't think I've wasted my morning!"

Now she began to wipe him, plugging with a towel the parts that would not dry. Feeling happy and without thinking of the future debt, he burst out laughing and took her in his arms.

"Leave me alone, stupid! You are damp, and wetting me. Only I'm afraid Maigrat has an idea——"

She was about to speak of Catherine, but she stopped. What was the good of disturbing him? It would only lead to endless discussion.

"What idea?" he asked.

"Why, ideas of robbing us. Catherine will have to pluck the bill carefully."

He took her in his arms again, and this time did not let her go. The bath always finished in this way: she enlivened him by the hard rubbing, and then by the towels which tickled the hairs of his arms and chest. Besides, among all his mates of the settlement it was the hour for stupidities, when more children were planted than were wanted. At night all the family were about. He pushed her towards the table, jesting like a worthy man who was enjoying the only good moment of the day, calling that taking his dessert, and a dessert which cost nothing. She, with her loose figure and breast, struggled a little for fun.

"You are stupid! My Lord! you are stupid! And there's Estelle looking at us. Wait till I turn her head."

"Oh, bosh! at three months; as if she understood!"

When he got up Maheu simply put on a dry pair of breeches. He liked, when he was clean and had taken his pleasure with his wife, to remain naked for a while. On his white skin, the whiteness of an anæmic girl, the scratches and gashes of the coal left tattoo-marks, grafts as the miners called them; and he was proud of them, and exhibited his big arms and broad chest shining like veined marble. In summer all the miners could be seen in this condition at their doors. He even went there for a moment now, in spite of the wet weather, and shouted out a rough joke to a comrade, whose breast was also naked, on the other side of the gardens. Others also appeared. And the children, trailing along the pathways, raised their heads and also laughed with delight at all this weary flesh of workers displayed in the open air.

While drinking his coffee, without yet putting on a shirt, Maheu told his wife about the engineer's anger over the planking. He was calm and unbent, and listened with a nod of approval to the sensible advice of Maheude, who showed much common sense in such affairs. She always repeated to him that nothing was gained by struggling against the Company. She afterwards told him about Madame Hennebeau's visit. Without saying so, both of them were proud of this.

"Can I come down yet?" asked Catherine, from the top of the staircase.

"Yes, yes; your father is drying himself."

The young girl had put on her Sunday dress, an old frock of rough blue poplin, already faded and worn in the folds. She had on a very simple bonnet of black tulle.

"Hallo! you're dressed. Where are you going to?"

"I'm going to Montsou to buy a ribbon for my bonnet. I've taken off the old one; it was too dirty."

"Have you got money, then?"

"No! but Mouquette promised to lend me half a franc."

The mother let her go. But at the door she called her back.

"Here! don't go and buy that ribbon at Maigrat's. He will rob you, and he will think that we are rolling in wealth."

The father, who was crouching down before the fire to dry his neck and shoulders more quickly, contented himself with adding:

"Try not to dawdle about at night on the road."

In the afternoon, Maheu worked in his garden. Already he had sown there potatoes, beans, and peas; and he now set about replanting cabbage and lettuce plants, which he had kept fresh from the night before. This bit of garden furnished them with vegetables, except potatoes of which they never had enough. He understood gardening very well, and could even grow artichokes, which was treated as sheer display by the neighbours. As he was preparing the bed, Levaque just then came out to smoke a pipe in his own square, looking at the cos lettuce which Bouteloup had planted in the morning; for without the lodger's energy in digging nothing would have grown there but nettles. And a conversation arose over the trellis. Levaque, refreshed and excited by thrashing his wife, vainly tried to take Maheu off to Rasseneur's. Why, was he afraid of a glass? They could have a game at skittles, lounge about for a while with the mates, and then come back to dinner. That was the way of life after leaving the pit. No doubt there was no harm in that, but Maheu was obstinate; if he did not replant his lettuces they would be faded by to-morrow. In reality he refused out of good sense, not wishing to ask a farthing from his wife out of the change of the five-franc piece.

Five o'clock was striking when Pierronne came to know if it was with Jeanlin that her Lydie had gone off. Levaque replied that it must be something of that sort, for Bébert had also disappeared, and those rascals always went prowling about together. When Maheu had quieted them by speaking of the dandelion salad, he and his comrade set about joking the young woman with the coarseness of good-natured devils. She was angry, but did not go away, in reality tickled by the strong words which made her scream with her hands to her sides. A lean woman came to her aid, stammering with anger like the clucking of a hen. Others in the distance on their doorsteps confided their alarms. Now the school was closed; all the children were running about, there was a rumbling of little creatures shouting and tumbling and fighting; while those fathers who were not at the public-house were resting in groups of three or four, crouching on their heels as they did in the mine, smoking their pipes with an occasional word in the shelter of a wall. Pierronne went off in a fury when Levaque wanted to feel if her thighs were firm; and he himself decided to go alone to Rasseneur's, since Maheu was still planting.

Twilight suddenly came on; Maheude lit the lamp, irritated because neither her daughter nor the boys had come back. She could have guessed as much; they never succeeded in taking together the only meal of the day at which it was possible for them to be all round the table. Then she was waiting for the dandelion salad. What could he be gathering at this hour, in this blackness of an oven, that nuisance of a child! A salad would accompany so well the stew which was simmering on the fire—potatoes, leeks, sorrel, fricassed with fried onion. The whole house smelt of that fried onion, that good odour which gets rank so soon, and which penetrates the bricks of the settlements with such infection that one perceives it far off in the country, the violent flavour of the poor man's kitchen.

Maheu, when he left the garden at nightfall, at once fell into a chair with his head against the wall. As soon as he sat down in the evening he went to sleep. The clock struck seven; Henri and Lénore had just broken a plate by persisting in helping Alzire, who was laying the table, when Father Bonnemort came in first, in a hurry to dine and go back to the pit. Then Maheude woke up Maheu.

"Come and eat! So much the worse! They are big enough to find the house. The nuisance is the salad!"

## CHAPTER V

AT RASSENEUR'S, AFTER HAVING eaten his soup, Étienne went back into the small chamber beneath the roof and facing the Voreux, which he was to occupy, and fell on to his bed dressed as he was, overcome with fatigue. For two days he had only slept four hours. When he awoke in the twilight he was dazed for a moment, not recognising his surroundings; and he felt such uneasiness and his head was so heavy that he rose, painfully, with the idea of getting some fresh air before having his dinner and going to bed for the night.

Outside, the weather was becoming milder: the sooty sky was growing copper-coloured, laden with one of those warm rains of the Nord, the approach of which one feels by the moist warmth of the air, and the night was coming on in great mists which drowned the distant landscape of the plain. Over this immense sea of reddish earth the low sky seemed to melt into black dust, without a breath of wind now to animate the darkness. It was the wan and deathly melancholy of a funeral.

Étienne walked straight ahead at random, with no other aim but to shake off his fever. When he passed before the Voreux, already growing gloomy at the bottom of its hole and with no lantern yet shining from it, he stopped a moment to watch the departure of the day-workers. No doubt six o'clock had struck; landers, porters from the pit-eye, and grooms were going away in bands, mixed with the vague and laughing figures of the screening girls in the shade.

At first it was Brûlé and her son-in-law, Pierron. She was abusing him because he had not supported her in a quarrel with an overseer over her reckoning of stones.

"Get along! damned good-for-nothing! Do you call yourself a man to lower yourself like that before one of these beasts who devour us?"

Pierron followed her peacefully, without replying. At last he said:

"I suppose I ought to jump on a boss? Thanks for showing me how to get into a mess!"

"Bend your backside to them, then," she shouted. "By God! if my daughter had listened to me! It's not enough for them to kill the father. Perhaps you'd like me to say 'thank-you.' No, I'll have their skins first!"

Their voices were lost. Étienne saw her disappear, with her eagle nose, her flying white hair, her long, lean arms that gesticulated furiously. But the conversation of two young people behind caused him to listen. He had recognised Zacharie, who was waiting there, and who had just been addressed by his friend Mouquet.

"Are you here?" said the latter. "We will have something to eat, and then off to the Volcan."

"Directly. I've something to attend to."

"What, then?

The lander turned and saw Philomène coming out of the screening shed. He thought he understood.

"Very well, if it's that. Then I go ahead."

"Yes, I'll catch you up."

As he went away, Mouquet met his father, old Mouque, who was also coming out of the Voreux. The two men simply wished each other good evening, the son taking the main road while the father went along by the canal.

Zacharie was already pushing Philomène in spite of her resistance into the same solitary path. She was in a hurry, another time; and they both disputed like old housemates. There was no fun in only seeing one another out of doors, especially in winter, when the earth is moist and there are no wheat fields to lie in.

"No, no, it's not that," he whispered impatiently. "I've something to say to you." He led her gently with his arm round her waist. Then, when they were in the shadow of the pit-bank, he asked if she had any money.

"What for?" she demanded.

Then he became confused, spoke of a debt of two francs which had reduced his family to despair.

"Hold your tongue! I've seen Mouquet; you're going again to the Volcan with him, where those dirty singer-women are."

He defended himself, struck his chest, gave his word of honour. Then, as she shrugged her shoulders, he said suddenly:

"Come with us if it will amuse you. You see that you don't put me out. What do I want to do with them singers? Will you come?"

"And the little one?" she replied. "How can one stir with a child that's always screaming? Let me go back, I guess they're not getting on at the house."

But he held her and entreated. See! it was only not to look foolish before Mouquet to whom he had promised. A man could not go to bed every evening like the fowls. She was overcome, and pulled up the skirt of her gown; with her nail she cut the thread and drew out some half-franc pieces from a corner of the hem. For fear of being robbed by her mother she hid there the profit of the overtime work she did at the pit.

"I've got five, you see," she said, "I'll give you three. Only you must swear that you'll make your mother decide to let us marry. We've had enough of this life in the open air. And mother reproaches me for every mouthful I eat. Swear first."

She spoke with the soft voice of a big, delicate girl, without passion, simply tired of her life. He swore, exclaimed that it was a sacred promise; then, when he had got the three pieces, he kissed her, tickled her, made her laugh, and would have pushed things to an extreme in this corner of the pit-bank, which was the winter chamber of their household, if she had not again refused, saying that it would not give her any pleasure. She went back to the settlement alone, while he cut across the fields to rejoin his companion.

Étienne had followed them mechanically, from afar, without understanding, regarding it as a simple rendezvous. The girls were precocious in the pits; and he recalled the Lille work-girls whom he had waited for behind the factories, those bands of girls, corrupted at fourteen, in the abandonment of their wretchedness. But another meeting surprised him more. He stopped.

At the bottom of the pit-bank, in a hollow into which some large stones had slipped, little Jeanlin was violently snubbing Lydie and Bébert, seated one at his right, the other at his left.

"What do you say? Eh? I'll slap each of you, if you want more. Who thought of it first, eh?"

In fact, Jeanlin had had an idea. After having rolled about in the meadows, along the canal, for an hour, gathering dandelions with the two others, it had occurred to him, before this pile of salad, that they would never eat all that at home; and instead of going back to the settlement he had gone to Montsou, keeping Bébert to watch, and making Lydie ring at the houses and offer the dandelions. He was experienced enough to know, as he said, that girls could sell what they liked. In the ardour of business, the entire pile had disappeared; but the girl had gained eleven sous. And now, with empty hands, the three were dividing the profits.

"That's not fair!" Bébert declared. "Must divide into three. If you keep seven sous we shall only have two each."

"What? not fair!" replied Jeanlin furiously. "I gathered more first of all."

The other usually submitted with timid admiration and a credulity which always made him the dupe. Though older and stronger, he even allowed himself to be struck. But this time the sight of all that money excited him to rebellion.

"He's robbing us, Lydie, isn't he? If he doesn't share, we'll tell his mother."

Jeanlin at once thrust his fist beneath the other's nose.

"Say that again! I'll go and say at your house that you sold my mother's salad. And then, you silly beast, how can I divide eleven sous into three? Just try and see, if you're so clever. Here are your two sous each. Just look sharp and take them, or I'll put them in my pocket."

Bébert was vanquished and accepted the two sous. Lydie, who was trembling, had said nothing, for with Jeanlin she experienced the fear and the tenderness of a little beaten woman. When he held out the two sous to her she advanced her hand with a submissive laugh. But he suddenly changed his mind.

"Eh! what will you do with all that? Your mother will nab them, sure enough, if you don't know how to hide them from her. I'd better keep them for you. When you want money you can ask me for it."

And the nine sous disappeared. To shut her mouth he had put his arms round her and was rolling with her over the pit-bank. She was his little wife, and in dark corners they used to try together the love which they heard and saw in their homes, behind partitions, through the cracks of doors. They knew everything, but they were able to do nothing, being too young, fumbling and playing for hours at the games of vicious puppies. He called that playing at papa and mamma; and when he chased her she ran away and let herself be caught with the delicious trembling of instinct, often angry, but always yielding, in the expectation of something which never came.

As Bébert was not admitted to these games and received a cuffing whenever he wanted to touch Lydie, he was always constrained, agitated by anger and uneasiness when the other two were amusing themselves, which they did not hesitate to do in his presence. His one idea, therefore, was to frighten them and disturb them, calling out that someone could see them.

"It's all up! There's a man looking."

This time he told the truth; it was Étienne, who had decided to continue his walk. The children jumped up and ran away, and he passed by round the bank, following the canal, amused at the terror of these little rascals. No doubt it was too early, at their age, but they saw and heard so much that one would have to tie them up to restrain them. Yet Étienne became sad.

A hundred paces farther on he came across more couples. He had arrived at Réquillart, and there, around the old ruined mine, all the girls of Montsou prowled about with their lovers. It was the common rendezvous, the remote and deserted spot to which the putters came to get their first child when they dared not risk the shed. The broken palings opened to everyone the old yard now became a nondescript piece of ground, obstructed by the ruins of the two sheds which had fallen in, and by the skeletons of the large buttresses which were still standing. Unused trams were lying about, and piles of old rotting wood, while a dense vegetation was re-conquering this corner of ground, displaying itself in thick grass, and springing up in young trees that were already vigorous. Every girl found herself at home here; there were concealed holes for all; their lovers placed them over beams, behind the timber, in the trams; they even lay elbow to elbow without troubling about their neighbours. And it seemed that around this extinguished engine, near this shaft weary of disgorging coal, there was a revenge of creation in the free love which, beneath the lash of instinct, planted children in the bellies of these girls who were yet hardly women.

Yet a caretaker lived there, old Mouque, to whom the Company had given up, almost beneath the destroyed tower, two rooms which were constantly threatened by destruction from the expected fall of the last walls. He had even been obliged to support a part of the roof, and he lived there very comfortably with his family, he and Mouquet in one room, Mouquette in the other. As the windows no longer possessed a single pane, he had decided to close them by nailing up boards; one could not see well, but it was warm. For the rest, this caretaker cared for nothing; he went to look after his horses at the Voreux, and never troubled himself about the ruins of Réquillart, of which the shaft only was preserved, in order to serve as a chimney in connection with the ventilation of the neighbouring pit.

It was thus that Father Mouque was ending his old age in the midst of love. Ever since she was ten Mouquette had been lying about in all the corners of the ruins, not as a timid and still green little urchin like Lydie, but as a girl who was already big, and a mate for bearded lads. The father had nothing to say, for she was considerate, and never introduced a lover into the house. Then he was used to this sort of accident. When he went to the Voreux, when he came back, whenever he came out of his hole, he could scarcely put a foot down without treading on a couple in the grass; and it was worse if he wanted to gather wood to heat his soup or look for burdocks for his rabbit at the other end of the enclosure. Then he saw one by one the voluptuous noses of all the girls of Montsou rising up around him, while he had to be careful not to knock against the limbs stretched out level with the paths. Besides, these meetings had gradually ceased to disturb either him who was simply taking care not to stumble, or the girls whom he allowed to finish their affairs, going away with discreet little steps like a worthy man who was at peace with the ways of Nature. Only just as they now knew him he at last also knew them, as one knows the rascally magpies who become corrupted in the pear-trees in the garden. Ah! youth! youth! how it goes on, how wild it is! Sometimes he wagged his chin with silent regret, turning away from the noisy wantons who were breathing too loudly in the darkness. Only one thing put him out of temper: two lovers had acquired the bad habit of embracing outside his wall. It was not that it prevented him from sleeping, but they leaned against the wall so heavily that at last they damaged it.

Every evening old Mouque received a visit from his friend, Father Bonnemort, who regularly before dinner took the same walk. The two old men spoke little, scarcely exchanging ten words during the half hour that they spent together. But it cheered them thus to think over the days of old, to chew their recollections over again without need to talk of them. At Réquillart they sat on a beam side by side, saying a word and then sinking into their dreams, with faces bent towards the earth. No doubt they were becoming young again. Around them lovers were turning over their sweethearts; there was a murmur of kisses and laughter; the warm odour of the girls arose in the freshness of the trodden grass. It was now forty-three years since Father Bonnemort had taken his wife behind the pit; she was a putter, so slight that he had placed her on a tram to embrace her at ease. Ah! those were fine days. And the two old men, shaking their heads, at last left each other, often without saying good-night.

That evening, however, as Étienne arrived, Father Bonnemort, who was getting up from the beam to return to the settlement, said to Mouque:

"Good-night, old man. I say, you knew Roussie?"

Mouque was silent for a moment, rocked his shoulders; then, returning to the house:

"Good-night, good-night, old man."

Étienne came and sat on the beam, in his turn. His sadness was increasing, though he could not tell why. The old man, whose disappearing back he watched, recalled his arrival in the morning, and the flood of words which the piercing wind had dragged from his silence. What wretchedness! And all these girls, worn out with fatigue, who were still animal enough in the evening to fabricate little ones, to yield flesh for labour and suffering! It would never come to an end if they were always filling themselves with starvelings. Would it not be better if they were to shut up their bellies, and press their thighs together, as at the approach of misfortune? Perhaps these gloomy ideas only stirred confusedly in him because all the others, at this hour, were going about taking their pleasure in couples. The mild weather stifled him a little, occasional drops of rain fell on his feverish hands. Yes, they all came to it; it was something stronger than reason.

Just then, as Étienne remained seated motionless in the shadow, a couple who came down from Montsou rustled against him without seeing him as they entered the uneven Réquillart ground. The girl, certainly a virgin, was struggling and resisting with low whispered supplications, while the lad in silence was pushing her towards the darkness of a corner of the shed, still upright, under which there were piles of old mouldly rope. It was Catherine and the tall Chaval. But Étienne had not recognised them in passing, and his eyes followed them; he was watching for the end of the story, touched by a sensuality which changed the course of his thoughts. Why should he interfere? When girls refuse it is because they like first to be forced.

On leaving the settlement of the Deux-Cent-Quarante, Catherine had gone to Montsou along the road. From the age of ten, since she had earned her living at the pit, she went about the country alone in the complete liberty of the colliers' families; and if no man had possessed her at fifteen it was owing to the tardy awakening of her puberty, the crisis of which had not yet arrived. When she was in front of the Company's Yards she crossed the road and entered a laundress's where she was certain to find Mouquette; for the latter stayed there from morning till night, among women who treated each other with coffee all round. But she was disappointed; Mouquette had just then been regaling them in her turn so thoroughly that she was not able to lend the half-franc she had promised. To console her they vainly offered a glass of warm coffee. She was not even willing that her companion should borrow from another woman. An idea of economy had come to her, a sort of superstitious fear, the certainty that that ribbon would bring her bad luck if she were to buy it now.

She hastened to regain the road to the settlement, and had reached the last houses of Montsou when a man at the door of the Piquette Estaminet called her.

"Eh! Catherine! where are you off to so quick?"

It was lanky Chaval. She was vexed, not because he displeased her, but because she was not inclined to joke.

"Come in and have a drink. A little glass of sweet, won't you?"

She refused politely; the night was coming on, they were expecting her at home. He had advanced, and was entreating her in a low voice in the middle of the road. It had been his idea for a long time to persuade her to come up to the room which he occupied on the first storey of the Piquette Estaminet, a fine room for a household, with a large bed. Did he frighten her that she always refused? She laughed good-naturedly, and said that she would come up some day when children didn't grow. Then, from one thing to another, she told him, without knowing how, about the blue ribbon which she had not been able to buy.

"But I'll pay for it," he exclaimed.

She blushed, feeling that it would be best to refuse again, but possessed by a strong desire to have the ribbon. The idea of a loan came back to her, and at last she accepted on condition that she should return to him what he spent on her. They began to joke again: it was agreed that if she did not sleep with him she should return him the money. But there was another difficulty when he talked of going to Maigrat's.

"No, not Maigrat's; mother won't let me."

"Why? is there any need to say where one goes? He has the best ribbons in Montsou."

When Maigrat saw lanky Chaval and Catherine coming to his shop like two lovers who are buying their engagement gifts, he became very red, and exhibited his pieces of blue ribbon with the rage of a man who is being made fun of. Then, when he had served the young people, he planted himself at the door to watch them disappear in the twilight; and when his wife came to ask him a question in a timid voice, he fell on her, abusing her, and exclaiming that he would make them repent some day, the filthy creatures, who had no gratitude, when they ought all to be on the ground licking his feet.

Lanky Chaval accompanied Catherine along the road. He walked beside her, swinging his arms; only he pushed her by the hip, conducting her without seeming to do so. She suddenly perceived that he had made her leave the pavement and that they were taking the narrow Réquillart road. But she had no time to be angry; his arm was already round her waist, and he was dazing her with a constant caress of words. How stupid she was to be afraid! Did he want to hurt such a little darling, who was as soft as silk, so tender that he could have devoured her? And he breathed behind her ear, in her neck, so that a shudder passed over the skin of her whole body. She felt stifled, and had nothing to reply. It was true that he seemed to love her. On Saturday evenings, after having blown out the candle, she had asked herself what would happen if he were to take her in this way; then, on going to sleep, she had dreamed that she would no longer refuse, quite overcome by pleasure. Why, then, at the same idea to-day did she feel repugnance and something like regret? While he was tickling her neck with his moustache so softly that she closed her eyes, the shadow of another man, of the lad she had seen that morning, passed over the darkness of her closed eyelids.

Catherine suddenly looked around her. Chaval had conducted her into the ruins of Réquillart and she recoiled, shuddering, from the darkness of the fallen shed.

"Oh! no! oh, no!" she murmured, "please let me go!"

The fear of the male had taken hold of her, that fear which stiffens the muscles in an impulse of defence, even when girls are willing, and feel the conquering approach of man. Her virginity which had nothing to learn took fright as at a threatening blow, a wound of which she feared the unknown pain.

"No, no! I don't want to! I tell you that I am too young. It's true! Another time, when I am quite grown up."

He growled in a low voice:

"Stupid! There's nothing to fear. What does that matter?"

But without speaking more he had seized her solidly and pushed her beneath the shed, and she fell on her back on the old ropes; she ceased to protest, yielding to the male before her time, with that hereditary submission which from childhood had thrown down in the open air all the girls of her race. Her frightened stammering grew faint, and only the ardent breath of the man was heard.

Étienne, however, had listened without moving. Another who was taking the leap! And now that he had seen the comedy he got up, overcome by uneasiness, by a kind of jealous excitement in which there was a touch of anger. He no longer restrained himself; he stepped over the beams, for those two were too much occupied now to be disturbed. He was surprised, therefore, when he had gone a hundred paces along the path, to find that they were already standing up, and that they appeared, like himself, to be returning to the settlement. The man again had his arm round the girl's waist, and was squeezing her, with an air of gratitude, still speaking in her neck; and it was she who seemed in a hurry, anxious to return quickly, and annoyed at the delay.

Then Étienne was tormented by the desire to see their faces. It was foolish, and he hastened his steps, so as not to yield to it; but his feet slackened of their own accord, and at the first lamp-post he concealed himself in the shade. He was petrified by horror when he recognised Catherine and lanky Chaval. He hesitated at first: was it indeed she, that young girl in the coarse blue dress, with that bonnet? Was that the urchin whom he had seen in breeches, with her head in the canvas cap? That was why she could pass so near him without his recognising her. But he no longer doubted; he had seen her eyes again, with their greenish limpidity of spring water, so clear and so deep. What a harlot! And he experienced a furious desire to avenge himself on her with contempt, without any motive. Besides, he did not like her as a girl: she was frightful.

Catherine and Chaval had passed him slowly. They did not know that they were watched. He held her to kiss her behind the ear, and she began to slacken her steps beneath his caresses, which made her laugh. Left behind, Étienne was obliged to follow them, irritated because they barred the road and because in spite of himself he had to witness these things which exasperated him. It was true, then, what she had sworn to him in the morning: she was not anyone's mistress; and he, who had not believed her, who had deprived himself of her in order not to act like the other! and who had let her be taken beneath his nose, pushing his stupidity so far as to be dirtily amused at seeing them! It made him mad! he clenched his hands, he could have devoured that man in one of those impulses to kill in which he saw everything red.

The walk lasted for half-an-hour. When Chavel and Catherine approached the Voreux they slackened their pace still more; they stopped twice beside the canal, three times along the pit-bank, very cheerful now and occupied with little tender games. Étienne was obliged to stop also when they stopped for fear of being perceived. He endeavoured to feel nothing but a brutal regret: that would teach him to treat girls with consideration through being well brought up! Then, after passing the Voreux, and at last free to go and dine at Rasseneur's, he continued to follow them, accompanying them to the settlement where he remained standing in the shade for a quarter of an hour, waiting until Chaval left Catherine to enter her home. And when he was quite sure that they were no longer together, he set off walking afresh, going very far along the Marchiennes road, stamping, and thinking of nothing, too stifled and too sad to shut himself up in a room.

It was not until an hour later, towards nine o'clock, that Étienne again passed the settlement, saying to himself that he must eat and sleep, if he was to be up again at four o'clock in the morning. The village was already asleep, and looked quite black in the night. Not a gleam shone from the closed shutters, the long fronts slept, with the heavy sleep of snoring barracks. Only a cat escaped through the empty gardens. It was the end of the day, the collapse of workers falling from the table to the bed, overcome with weariness and food.

At Rasseneur's, in the lighted room, an engine-man and two day-workers were drinking. But before going in Étienne stopped to throw one last glance into the darkness. He saw again the same black immensity, as in the morning when he had arrived in the wind. Before him the Voreux was crouching, with its air of an evil beast, its dimness pricked with a few lantern lights. The three braziers of the bank were burning in the air, like bloody moons, now and then showing the vast silhouettes of Father Bonnemort and his yellow horse. And beyond, in the flat plain, shade had submerged everything, Montsou, Marchiennes, the forest of Vandame, the immense sea of beetroot and of wheat, in which there only shone, like distant lighthouses, the blue fires of the blast furnaces, and the red fires of the coke ovens. Gradually the night came on, the rain was now falling slowly, continuously, burying this void in its monotonous streaming. Only one voice was still heard, the thick, slow respiration of the pumping engine, breathing both by day and by night.

# *PART THREE*

## CHAPTER I

ON THE NEXT DAY, and the days that followed, Étienne continued his work at the pit. He grew accustomed to it; his existence became regulated by this labour and to these new habits which had seemed so hard to him at first. Only one episode interrupted the monotony of the first fortnight: a slight fever which kept him in bed for forty-eight hours with aching limbs and throbbing head, dreaming in a state of semi-delirium that he was pushing his tram in a passage that was so narrow that his body would not pass through. It was simply the exhaustion of his apprenticeship, an excess of fatigue from which he quickly recovered.

And days followed days, until weeks and months had slipped by. Now, like his mates, he got up at three o'clock, drank his coffee, and carried off the double slice of bread and butter which Madame Rasseneur had prepared for him the evening before. Regularly as he went every morning to the pit, he met old Bonnemort who was going home to sleep, and on leaving in the afternoon he crossed Bouteloup who was going to his task. He had his cap, his breeches, and the canvas jacket, and he shivered and warmed his back in the shed before the large fire. Then came the waiting with naked feet in the receiving-room, swept by furious currents of air. But the engine, with its great steel limbs starred with copper shining up above in the shade, no longer attracted his attention, nor the cables which flew by with the black and silent motion of a nocturnal bird, nor the cages rising and plunging unceasingly in the midst of the noise of signals, of shouted orders, of trams shaking the metal floor. His lamp burnt badly. That confounded lamp-man could not have cleaned it, and it only revived when Mouquet sent them all packing, and roguishly smacked the girls' flanks. The cage was unfastened, and fell like a stone to the bottom of a hole without causing him even to lift his head to see the daylight vanish. He never thought of a possible downfall; he felt himself at home as he sank into the darkness beneath the falling rain. Below at the pit-eye, when Pierron had unloaded them with his air of hypocritical mildness, there was always the same tramping as of a flock, the yard-men each going away to his cutting with trailing steps. He now knew the mine galleries better than the streets of Montsou; he knew where he had to turn, where he had to stoop, and where he had to avoid a puddle. He had grown so accustomed to these two kilomètres beneath the earth, that he could have traversed them without a lamp, with his hands in his pockets. And every time the same meetings took place: a captain lighting up the faces of the passing workmen, Father Mouque leading a horse, Bébert conducting the snorting Bataille, Jeanlin running behind the train to close the ventilation doors, and big Mouquette and lean Lydie pushing their trams.

After a time, also, Étienne suffered much less from the damp and closeness of the cutting. The chimney or ascending passage seemed to him more convenient for climbing up, as if he had melted and could pass through cracks where before he would not have risked a hand. He breathed the coal-dust without difficulty, saw clearly in the obscurity, and sweated tranquilly, having grown accustomed to the sensation of wet garments on his body from morning to night. Besides, he no longer spent his energy recklessly; he had gained skill so rapidly that he astonished the whole stall. In three weeks he was named among the best putters in the pit; no one pushed a tram more rapidly to the up-brow, nor loaded it afterwards so correctly. His small figure allowed him to slip about everywhere, and though his arms were as delicate and white as a woman's, they seemed to be made of iron beneath the smooth skin, so vigorously did they perform their task. He never complained, out of pride no doubt, even when he was panting with fatigue. The only thing they had against him was that he could not take a joke, and grew angry as soon as anyone trod on his toes. In all other respects he was looked upon as a real miner, reduced beneath this pressure of habit, little by little, to a machine.

Maheu regarded Étienne with special friendship for he respected work that was well done. Then, like the others, he felt that this lad had more education than himself; he saw him read, write and draw little plans; he heard him talking of things of which he himself did not know even the existence. This caused him no astonishment, for miners are rough fellows who have thicker heads than engine-men; but he was surprised at the courage of this little chap, and at the cheerful way he had bitten into the coal to avoid dying of hunger. He had never met a workman who grew accustomed to it so quickly. So when hewing was urgent, and he did not wish to disturb a pikeman, he gave the timbering over to the young man, being sure of the neatness and solidity of his work. The bosses were always bothering him about that damned planking question; he feared every hour the appearance of the engineer Négrel, followed by Dansaert, shouting, discussing, ordering everything to be done over again, and he remarked that his putter's timbering gave greater satisfaction to these gentlemen, in spite of their air of never being pleased with anything, and their repeated assertions that the Company would one day or another take radical measures. Things dragged on; a deep discontent was fomenting in the pit, and Maheu himself, in spite of his calmness, was beginning to clench his fists.

There was at first some rivalry between Zacharie and Étienne. One evening they were even coming to blows. But the former, a good lad though careless of everything but his own pleasure, was quickly appeased by the friendly offer of a glass, and soon yielded to the superiority of the new-comer. Levaque was also on good terms with him, talking politics with the putter, who, as he said, had his own ideas. The only one of the men in whom he felt a deep hostility was lanky Chaval: not that they were cool towards each other, for, on the contrary, they had become companions; only when they joked their eyes seemed to devour each other. Catherine continued to move among them as a tired, resigned girl, bending her back, pushing her tram, always good-natured with her companion in the putting, who aided her in his turn, and submissive to the wishes of her lover, whose caresses she now received openly. It was an accepted situation, a recognised domestic arrangement to which the family itself closed its eyes to such a degree that Chaval every evening led away the putter behind the pit-bank, then brought her back to her parents' door, where he finally embraced her before the whole settlement. Étienne, who believed that he had reconciled himself to the situation, often teased her about these walks, making crude remarks by way of joke, as lads and girls will at the bottom of the cuttings; and she replied in the same tone, telling in a swaggering way what her lover had done to her, yet disturbed and growing pale when the young man's eyes chanced to meet hers. Then both would turn away their heads, not speaking again, perhaps, for an hour, looking as if they hated each other because of something buried within them and which they could never explain to each other.

The spring had come. On emerging from the pit one day Étienne had received in his face a warm April breeze, a good odour of young earth, of tender greenness, of large open air; and now, every time he came up the spring felt better, and warmed him more, after his ten hours of labour in the eternal winter at the bottom, in the midst of that damp darkness which no summer had ever dissipated. The days grew longer and longer; at last, in May, he went down at sunrise when a vermilion sky lit up the Voreux with a mist of dawn in which the white vapour of the pumping-engine became rose-coloured. There was no more shivering, a warm breath blew across the plain, while the larks sang far above. Then at three o'clock he was dazzled by the now burning sun which set fire to the horizon, and reddened the bricks beneath the filth of the coal. In June the wheat was already high, of a blue green, which contrasted with the black green of the beetroots. It was an endless vista undulating beneath the slightest breeze; and he saw it spread and grow from day to day, and was sometimes surprised, as if he had found it in the evening more swollen with verdure than it had been in the morning. The poplars along the canal were putting on their plumes of leaves. Grass was invading the pit-bank, flowers were covering the meadows, a whole life was germinating and pushing up from this earth beneath which he was groaning in misery and fatigue.

When Étienne now went for a walk in the evening he no longer startled lovers behind the pit-bank. He could follow their track in the wheat and divine their wanton bird's nests by eddies among the yellowing blades and the great red poppies. Zacharie and Philomène came back to it out of old domestic habit; Mother Brûlé, always on Lydie's heels, was constantly hunting her out with Jeanlin, buried so deeply together that one had to tread on them before they made up their minds to get up; and as to Mouquette, she was lying everywhere—one could not cross a field without seeing her head plunge down while only her feet emerged as she lay at full length. But all these were quite free; the young man found nothing guilty there except on the evenings when he met Catherine and Chaval. Twice he saw them on his approach tumble down in the midst of a field, where the motionless stalks afterwards remained dead. Another time, as he was going along a narrow path, Catherine's clear eyes appeared before him, level with the wheat, and immediately sank. Then the immense plain seemed to him too small, and he preferred to pass the evening at Rasseneur's, in the Avantage.

"Give me a glass, Madame Rasseneur. No, I'm not going out to-night; my legs are too stiff."

And he turned towards a comrade, who always sat at the bottom table with his head against the wall.

"Souvarine, won't you have one?"

"No, thanks; nothing."

Étienne had become acquainted with Souvarine[1] through living there side by side. He was an engine-man at the Voreux, and occupied the furnished room upstairs next to his own. He must have been about thirty years old, fair and slender, with a delicate face framed by thick hair and a slight beard. His white, pointed teeth, his thin mouth and nose, with his rosy complexion gave him a girlish appearance, an air of obstinate gentleness, across which the grey reflection of his steely eyes threw savage gleams. In his poor workman's room there was nothing but a box of papers and books. He was a Russian, and never spoke of himself, so that many stories were afloat concerning him. The colliers, who are very suspicious with strangers, guessing from his small middle-class hands that he belonged to another caste, had at first imagined a romance, some assassination, and that he was escaping punishment. But then he had behaved in such a fraternal way with them, without any pride, distributing to the youngsters of the settlement all the sous in his pockets, that they now accepted him, reassured by the term "political refugee" which circulated about him—a vague term, in which they saw an excuse even for crime, and, as it were, a companionship in suffering.

During the first weeks, Étienne had found him timid and reserved, so that he only discovered his history later on. Souvarine was the latest born of a noble family in the Government of Tula. At St. Petersburg, where he studied medicine, the social enthusiasm which then carried away all the youth in Russia had decided him to learn a manual trade, that of a mechanic, so that he could mix with the people, in order to know them and help them as a brother. And it was by this trade that he was now living after having fled, in consequence of an unsuccessful attempt against the Czar's life: for a month he had lived in a fruiterer's cellar, hollowing out a mine underneath the road, and charging bombs, with the constant risk of being blown up with the house. Renounced by his family, without money, expelled from the French workshops as a stranger who was regarded as a spy, he was dying of starvation when the Montsou Company had at last taken him on at a moment of pressure. For a year he had laboured there as a good, sober, silent workman, doing day-work one week and night-work the next week, so regularly that the masters referred to him as an example to the others.

"Are you never thirsty?" said Étienne to him, laughing.

And he replied with his gentle voice, almost without an accent:

"I am thirsty when I eat."

His companion also joked him about the girls, declaring that he had seen him with a putter in the wheat on the Bas-de-Soie side. Then he shrugged his shoulders with tranquil indifference. What should he do with a putter? Woman was for him a boy, a comrade, when she had the fraternal feeling and the courage of a man. What was the good of having a possible act of cowardice on one's conscience? He desired no bond, either woman or friend; he would be free over his own life and over those of others.

Every evening towards nine o'clock, when the inn was emptying, Étienne remained thus talking with Souvarine. He drank his beer in small sips, while the engine-man smoked constant cigarettes, of which the tobacco had at last reddened his slender fingers. His vague mystic's eyes followed the smoke in the midst of a dream; his left hand sought occupation by nervously twitching; and he usually ended by installing a tame rabbit on his knees, a large mother always full, who lived at liberty in the house. This rabbit, which he had named Poland,[2] had grown to worship him; she would come and smell his trousers, fawn on him and scratch him with her paws until he took her up like a child. Then, lying in a heap against him, she would close her eyes; and without growing tired, with an unconscious caressing gesture, he would pass his hand over her grey silky fur, calmed by that warm living softness.

"You know I have had a letter from Pluchart," said Étienne one evening.

Only Rasseneur was there. The last client had departed for the settlement, which was now going to bed.

"Ah!" exclaimed the inn-keeper, standing up before his two lodgers. "How are things going with Pluchart?"

During the last two months, Étienne had kept up a constant correspondence with the Lille mechanician, to whom he had told his Montsou engagement, and who was now indoctrinating him, having been struck by the propaganda which might be carried on among the miners.

"The association is getting on very well. It seems that they are coming in from all sides."

"What have you got to say, eh, about their society?" asked Rasseneur of Souvarine.

The latter, who was softly scratching Poland's head, blew out a puff of smoke and muttered, with his tranquil air:

"More foolery!"

But Étienne grew enthusiastic. A predisposition for revolt was throwing him, in the first illusions of his ignorance, into the struggle of labour against capital. It was the International Association of Workers[3] that they were concerned with, that famous International which had just been founded at London. Was not that a superb effort, a campaign in which justice would at last triumph? No more frontiers; the workers of the whole world rising and uniting to assure to the labourer the bread that he has earned. And what a simple and great organisation! Below, the section which represents the commune; then the federation which groups the sections of the same province; then the nation; and then, at last, humanity incarnated in a general council in which each nation was represented by a corresponding secretary. In six months it would conquer the world, and would be able to dictate laws to the masters should they prove obstinate.

"Foolery!" repeated Souvarine. "Your Karl Marx is still only thinking about letting natural forces act. No politics, no conspiracies, is it not so? Everything in the light of day, and simply to raise wages. Don't bother me with your evolution! Set fire to the four corners of the towns, mow down the people, level everything, and when there is nothing more of this rotten world left standing, perhaps a better one will grow up in its place."

Étienne began to laugh. He did not always take in his comrade's sayings; this theory of destruction seemed to him an affectation. Rasseneur, who was still more practical, like a man of solid common sense did not condescend to get angry. He only wanted to have things clear.

"Then, what? Are you going to try and create a section at Montsou?"

This was what was desired by Pluchart, who was secretary to the Federation of the Nord. He insisted especially on the services which the association would render to the miners should they go out on strike. Étienne believed that a strike was imminent: this timbering business would turn out badly; any further demands on the part of the Company would cause rebellion in all the pits.

"It's the subscriptions that's the nuisance," Rasseneur declared, in a judicial tone. "Half-a-franc a year for the general fund, two francs for the section; it looks like nothing, but I bet that many will refuse to give it."

"All the more," added Étienne, "because we must first have here a Provident Fund which we can use if need be as an emergency fund. No matter, it is time to think about these things. I am ready if the others are ready."

There was silence. The petroleum lamp smoked on the counter. Through the large open door they could distinctly hear the shovel of a stoker at the Voreux stoking the engine.

"Everything is so dear!" began Madame Rasseneur, who had entered, and was listening with a gloomy air, as if she had grown in her everlasting black dress. "When I tell you that I've paid twenty-two sous for eggs! it will have to burst up."

All three men this time were of the same opinion. They spoke one after the other in a despairing voice, giving expression to their complaints. The workers could not hold out; the Revolution had only aggravated their wretchedness; only the bourgeois had grown fat since '89, so greedily that they had not even left the bottom of the plates to lick. Who could say that the workers had had their reasonable share in the extraordinary increase of wealth and comfort during the last hundred years? They had made fun of them by declaring them free. Yes, free to starve, a freedom of which they fully availed themselves. It put no bread into your cupboard to go and vote for fine fellows who went away and enjoyed themselves, thinking no more of the wretched voters than of their old boots. No! one way or another it would have to come to an end, either quietly by laws, by an understanding in good fellowship, or like savages by burning everything and devouring one another. Even if they never saw it, their children would certainly see it, for the century could not come to an end without another revolution, that of the workers this time, a general hustling which would cleanse society from top to bottom, and rebuild it with more cleanliness and justice.

"It will have to burst up," Madame Rasseneur repeated energetically.

"Yes, yes," they all three cried. "It will have to burst up."

Souvarine was now tickling Poland's ears, and her nose was curling with pleasure. He said in a low voice, with abstracted gaze, as if to himself:

"Raise wages—how can you? They're fixed by an iron law to the smallest possible sum,[4] just the sum necessary to allow the workers to eat dry bread and make children. If they fall too low, the workers die, and the demand for new men makes them rise. If they rise too high more men come, and they fall. It is the balance of empty bellies, a sentence to a perpetual prison of hunger."

When he thus forgot himself, entering into the questions that stir an educated socialist, Étienne and Rasseneur became restless, disturbed by his despairing statements which they were unable to answer.

"Do you understand?" he said again, gazing at them with his habitual calmness, "we must destroy everything, or hunger will re-appear. Yes, anarchy and nothing more; the earth washed in blood and purified by fire! Then we shall see!"

"Monsieur is quite right," said Madame Rasseneur, who, in her revolutionary violence, was always very polite.

Étienne, in despair at his ignorance, would argue no longer. He rose, remarking:

"Let's go to bed. All this won't save one from getting up at three o'clock."

Souvarine, having blown away the cigarette end which was sticking to his lips, was already gently lifting the big rabbit beneath the belly to place it on the ground. Rasseneur was shutting up the house. They separated in silence with buzzing ears, as if their heads had swollen with the grave questions they had been discussing.

And every evening there were similar conversations in the bare room around the single glass which Étienne took an hour to empty. A crowd of obscure ideas, asleep within him, were stirring and expanding. Especially consumed by the need of knowledge, he had long hesitated to borrow books from his neighbour, who unfortunately only possessed German and Russian works. At last he had borrowed a French book on Cooperative Societies,[5] mere foolery, said Souvarine; and he also regularly read a newspaper which the latter received, the *Combat*, an Anarchist journal published at Geneva. In other respects, notwithstanding their daily relations, he found him as reserved as ever, with his air of camping in life, without interests or feelings or possessions of any kind.

Towards the first days of July, Étienne's situation began to improve. In the midst of this monotonous life, always beginning over again, an accident had occurred. The stalls in the Guillaume seam had come across a shifting of the strata, a general disturbance in the layers, which certainly announced that they were approaching a fault; and, in fact, they soon came across this fault which the engineers, in spite of considerable knowledge of the soil, were still ignorant of. This upset the pit; nothing was talked of but the lost seam, which was to be found, no doubt, lower down on the other side of the fault. The old miners were already expanding their nostrils, like good dogs, in a chase for coal. But, meanwhile, the hewers could not stand with folded arms, and placards announced that the Company would put up new workings to auction.

Maheu, on coming out one day, accompanied Étienne and offered to take him on as a pikeman in his working, in place of Levaque who had gone to another yard. The matter had already been arranged with the head captain and the engineer, who were very pleased with the young man. So Étienne merely had to accept this rapid promotion, glad of the growing esteem in which Maheu held him.

In the evening they returned together to the pit to take note of the placards. The cuttings put up to auction were in the Filonnière seam in the north gallery of the Voreux. They did not seem very advantageous, and the miner shook his head when the young man read out the conditions. On the following day when they had gone down, he took him to see the seam, and showed him how far away it was from the pit-eye, the crumbly nature of the earth, the thinness and hardness of the coal. But if they were to eat they would have to work. So on the following Sunday they went to the auction which took place in the shed, and was presided over by the engineer of the pit, assisted by the head captain, in the absence of the divisional engineer. From five to six hundred miners were there in front of the little platform which was placed in the corner, and the fixtures went on so rapidly that one only heard a deep tumult of voices, of shouted figures drowned by other figures.

For a moment Maheu feared that he would not be able to obtain one of the forty workings offered by the Company. All the rivals went lower, disquieted by the rumours of a crisis and the panic of a lock-out. Négrel, the engineer, did not hurry in the face of this panic, and allowed the offers to fall to the lowest possible figures, while Dansaert, anxious to push matters still further, lied with regard to the quality of the workings. In order to get his fifty mètres, Maheu struggled with a comrade who was also obstinate; in turn they each took off a centime from the tram; and if he conquered in the end it was only by lowering the wage to such an extent, that the captain, Richomme, who was standing behind him muttered between his teeth, and pushed him with the elbow, growling that he could never do it at that price.

When they came out Étienne was swearing. And he broke out before Chaval who was returning from the wheat-fields in company with Catherine, amusing himself while his father-in-law was absorbed in serious business.

"By God!" he exclaimed, "it's simply slaughter! To-day it is the worker who is forced to devour the worker!"[6]

Chaval was furious. He would never have lowered it, he wouldn't! And Zacharie who had come out of curiosity, declared that it was disgusting. But Étienne with a violent gesture silenced them.

"It will end some day, we shall be the masters!"

Maheu, who had been mute since the auction, appeared to wake up. He repeated:

"Masters! ah! bad luck! and not too soon either."

## CHAPTER II

IT WAS MONTSOU FEAST-DAY,* the last Sunday in July. Since Saturday evening the good housekeepers of the settlement had deluged their parlours with water, throwing bucketfuls over the flags and against the walls; and the floor was not yet dry, in spite of the white sand which had been sown over it, an expensive luxury for the purses of the poor. But the day promised to be very warm; it was one of those heavy skies threatening storm, which in summer stifle this flat bare country of the Nord.

Sunday upset the hours for rising, even among the Maheus. While the father, after five o'clock, grew weary of his bed and dressed himself, the children lay in bed until nine. On this day

*La Ducasse, a traditional festival specific to the Nord department of France.

Maheu went to smoke a pipe in his garden, and then came back to eat his bread and butter alone, while waiting. He thus passed the morning in a random manner; he mended the tub, which leaked; stuck up beneath the clock a portrait of the Prince Imperial which had been given to the little ones. However, the others came down one by one. Father Bonnemort had taken a chair outside, to sit in the sun, while the mother and Alzire had at once set about cooking. Catherine appeared, pushing before her Lénore and Henri, whom she had just dressed. Eleven o'clock struck, and the odour of the rabbit, which was boiling with potatoes, was already filling the house when Zacharie and Jeanlin came down last, still yawning and with swollen eyes.

The settlement was now in a flutter, excited by the Feast-day, and in expectation of dinner, which was being hastened for the departure in bands to Montsou. Troops of children were rushing about. Men in their shirt-sleeves were trailing their old shoes, with the lazy gait of days of rest. Windows and doors, opened wide in the fine weather, gave glimpses of rows of parlours, which were filled with movement and shouts and the chatter of families. And from one end to the other of the frontages, there was a smell of rabbit, a rich kitchen smell which on this day struggled with the inveterate odour of fried onion.

The Maheus dined at mid-day. They made little noise in the midst of the chatter from door to door, in the coming and going of women in a constant rumour of appeals and replies, of objects borrowed, of youngsters hunted away or brought back with a slap. Besides, they had not been on good terms during the last three weeks with their neighbours, the Levaques, on the subject of the marriage of Zacharie and Philomène. The men passed the time of day, but the women pretended not to know each other. This quarrel had strengthened the relations with Pierronne, only Pierronne had left Pierron and Lydie with her mother, and set out early in the morning to spend the day with a cousin at Marchiennes; and they joked, for they knew this cousin; she had a moustache, and was head captain of the Voreux. Maheude declared that it was not proper to leave one's family on a Feast-day Sunday.

Beside the rabbit with potatoes, a rabbit which had been fattening in the shed for a month, the Maheus had meat soup and beef. The fortnight's wages had just fallen due the day before. They could not recollect such a spread. Even at the last St. Barbe's Day, that fête of the miners when they do nothing for three days, the rabbit had not been so fat nor so tender. So the ten pairs of jaws, from little Estelle, whose teeth were beginning to appear, to old Bonnemort, who was losing his, worked so heartily that the bones themselves disappeared. The meat was good, but they could not digest it well; they saw it too seldom. Everything disappeared; there only remained a piece of boiled beef for the evening. They could add bread and butter if they were hungry.

Jeanlin went out first. Bébert was waiting for him behind the school, and they prowled about for a long time before they were able to entice away Lydie, whom Brûlé, who had decided not to go out, was trying to keep with her. When she perceived that the child had fled, she shouted and brandished her lean arms, while Pierron, annoyed at the disturbance, strolled quietly away with the air of a husband who can amuse himself with a good conscience, knowing that his wife also has her little amusements.

Old Bonnemort set out at last, and Maheu decided to have a little fresh air after asking Maheude if she would come and join him down below. No, she couldn't at all, it was nothing but drudgery with the little ones; but perhaps she would, all the same; she would think about it: they could easily find each other. When he got outside he hesitated, then he went into the neighbour's to see if Levaque was ready. There he found Zacharie, who was waiting for Philomène, and the Levaque woman started again on that everlasting subject of marriage, saying that she was being made fun of and that she would have an explanation with Maheude once and for all. Was life worth living when one had to keep one's daughter's fatherless children while she went off with her lover? Philomène quietly finished putting on her bonnet, and Zacharie took her off, saying that he was quite willing if his mother was willing. As Levaque had already gone, Maheu referred his angry neighbour to his wife and hastened to depart. Bouteloup, who was finishing a fragment of cheese with both elbows on the table, obstinately refused the friendly offer of a glass. He would stay in the house like a good husband.

Gradually the settlement was emptied; all the men went off one behind the other, while the girls, watching at the doors, set out from the opposite side on the arms of their lovers. As her father turned the corner of the church, Catherine perceived Chaval, and, hastening to join him, they took together the Montsou road. And the mother remained alone, in the midst of her disorganised children, without strength to leave her chair, where she was pouring out a second glass of boiling coffee, which she drank in little sips. In the settlement there were only the women left, inviting each other to finish the dregs of the coffee-pots around the tables that were still warm and greasy with the dinner.

Maheu had guessed that Levaque was at the Avantage, and he slowly went down to Rasseneur's. In fact, behind the bar, in the little garden shut in by a hedge, Levaque was having a game of skittles with some mates. Standing by, and not playing, Father Bonnemort and old Mouque were following the ball, so absorbed that they even forgot to nudge each other with their elbows. A burning sun struck down on them perpendicularly; there was only one streak of shade by the side of the inn; and Étienne was there drinking his glass before a table, annoyed because Souvarine had just left him to go up to his room. Nearly every Sunday the engine-man shut himself up to write or to read.

"Will you have a game?" asked Levaque of Maheu.

But he refused: it was too hot, he was already dying of thirst.

"Rasseneur," called Étienne, "bring a glass, will you?"

And turning towards Maheu:

"I'll stand it, you know."

They now all treated each other familiarly. Rasseneur did not hurry himself; and Madame Rasseneur at last brought some luke-warm beer. The young man had lowered his voice to complain about the house: they were worthy people, certainly, people with good ideas, but the beer was worthless and the soup abominable! He would have changed his lodgings ten times over only the thought of the walk from Montsou held him back.

One day or another he would go and live with some family at the settlement.

"Sure enough!" said Maheu in his slow voice, "sure enough, you would be better in a family."

But shouts now broke out. Levaque had overthrown all the skittles at one stroke. Mouque and Bonnemort, with their faces towards the ground, in the midst of the tumult preserved a silence of profound approbation. And the joy at this stroke found vent in jokes, especially when the players perceived Mouquette's radiant face behind the hedge. She had been prowling about there for an hour, and at last ventured to come near on hearing the laughter.

"What! are you alone?" shouted Levaque. "Where are your sweethearts?"

"My sweethearts! I've stabled them," she replied, with a fine impudent gaiety. "I'm looking for one."

They all offered themselves, throwing coarse jokes at her. She refused with a gesture and laughed louder, playing the fine lady. Besides, her father was assisting at the game without even taking his eyes from the fallen skittles.

"Ah!" Levaque went on, throwing a look towards Étienne: "one can tell where you're casting sheep's eyes, my girl! You'll have to take him by force."

Then Étienne looked amused. It was in fact around him that the putter was revolving. And he refused, amused indeed, but without having the least desire for her. She remained planted behind the hedge for some minutes longer, looking at him with large fixed eyes; then she slowly went away, and her face suddenly became serious as if she were overcome by the powerful sun.

In a low voice Étienne was again giving long explanations to Maheu regarding the necessity for the Montsou miners to establish a Provident Fund.[7] Since the Company professes to leave us free, he repeated, what is there to fear? We only have their pensions and they distribute them according to their own taste, from the moment when they hold back no reserve. Well, it will be prudent to form, outside their good pleasure, an association of mutual help on which we can count at least in cases of immediate need.

And he gave details, and discussed the organisation, promising to undertake the labour of it.

"I am willing enough," said Maheu, at last convinced, "But there are the others; get them to make up their minds."

Levaque had won, and they left the skittles to empty their glasses. But Maheu refused to drink a second glass; he would see later on, the day was not yet done. He was thinking about Pierron. Where could he be? No doubt at the Enfant Estaminet. And, having persuaded Étienne and Levaque, the three set out for Montsou, at the same moment as a new band took possession of the skittles at the Avantage.

On the road they had to enter at the Casimir Bar, and then at the Estaminet du Progrès. Comrades called them through the open doors, and there was no way of refusing. Each time it was a glass, two if they were polite enough to return the invitation. They remained there ten minutes, exchanging a few words, and then began again, a little farther on, knowing the beer, with which they could fill themselves without any other discomfort than having to piss it out again in the same measure as clear as rock water. At the Estaminet l'Enfant they came right upon Pierron, who was finishing his second glass, and who in order not to refuse to touch glasses, swallowed a third. They naturally drank theirs also. Now there were four of them, and they set out to see if Zacharie was not at the Estaminet Tison. It was empty, and they called for a glass, in order to wait for him a moment. Then they thought of the Estaminet Saint-Éloi and accepted there a round from Captain Richomme. Then they rambled from bar to bar, without any pretext, simply saying that they were having a stroll.

"We must go to the Volcan!" suddenly said Levaque, who was getting excited.

The others began to laugh, and hesitated. Then they accompanied their comrade in the midst of the growing crowd. In the long narrow room of the Volcan, on a platform raised at the end, five singers, the scum of the Lille prostitutes, were walking about, low-necked and with monstrous gestures, and the customers gave ten sous when they desired to have one behind the stage. There was especially a number of putters and landers, even trammers of fourteen, all the youth of the pit, drinking more gin than beer. A few old miners also ventured there, and the lewd husbands of the settlements, those whose households were falling into ruin.

As soon as the band was seated round a little table, Étienne took possession of Levaque to explain to him his idea of the Provident Fund. Like all new converts who have found a mission, he had become an obstinate propagandist.

"Every member," he repeated, "could easily pay in twenty sous per month. As these twenty sous accumulated they would form a nice little sum in twenty-four years, and when one has money one is strong, eh, for everything that turns up? Eh, what do you say to it?"

"I've nothing to say against it," replied Levaque, with an abstracted air. "We will talk about it."

He was excited by an enormous fair woman, and determined to remain behind when Maheu and Pierron, after drinking their glasses, set out without waiting for a second romance.

Outside, Étienne who had gone with them found Mouquette, who seemed to be following them. She was always there, looking at him with her large fixed eyes, laughing her good-natured laugh, as if to say: "Are you willing?" The young man joked and shrugged his shoulders. Then, with a gesture of anger, she was lost in the crowd.

"Where, then, is Chaval?" asked Pierron.

"True!" said Maheu. "He must surely be at Piquette's. Let us go to Piquette's."

But as they all three arrived at the Estaminet Piquette, sounds of a quarrel arrested them at the door; Zacharie with his fist was threatening a thick-set phlegmatic Walloon* nail-maker, while Chaval, with his hands in his pockets, was looking on.

"Hullo! there's Chaval," said Maheu quietly; "he is with Catherine."

For five long hours the putter and her lover had been walk-

---

*A person from the French-speaking region of Belgium.

ing about the fair. It was along the Montsou road, that wide road with low bedaubed houses descending like a braid, a crowd of people disporting in the sun, like a trail of ants, lost in the flat, bare plain. The eternal black mud had dried, a black dust was rising and floating about like a storm-cloud.

On both sides the public houses were crowded; there were rows of tables to the street, where stood a double rank of hucksters at stalls in the open air, selling neck-handkerchiefs and looking-glasses for the girls, knives and caps for the lads; without counting sweetmeats, sugar-plums, and biscuits. In front of the church archery was going on. Opposite the Yards they were playing at bowls. At the corner of the Joiselle road, beside the Administration buildings, in a spot enclosed by fences, crowds were going to a cock-fight, two large red cocks, armed with steel spurs, and with open bleeding breasts. Farther on, at Maigrat's, aprons and trousers were being won at billiards. And there were long silences; the crowd drank and stuffed itself without a sound; a mute indigestion of beer and fried potatoes was expanding in the great heat, still further increased by the frying-pans bubbling in the open air.

Chaval bought a looking-glass for nineteen sous and a handkerchief for three francs, to give to Catherine. At every turn they met Mouque and Bonnemort, who had come to the fair, and who, with their stiff legs, went from side to side in a reflective manner. Another meeting made them angry; they caught sight of Jeanlin persuading Bébert and Lydie to steal bottles of gin from an extemporised bar installed at the edge of an open piece of ground. Catherine succeeded in boxing her brother's ears; the little girl had already run away with a bottle. These imps of Satan would certainly end in a prison. Then, as they arrived before another bar, the Tête-Coupée, it occurred to Chaval to take his sweetheart in to a competition of chaffinches[8] which had been announced on the door for the past week. Fifteen nailmakers from the Marchiennes nail works had responded to the appeal, each with a dozen cages; and the gloomy little cages in which the blinded finches were motionless, were already fastened to a paling in the inn yard. It was a question as to which, in the course of an hour, should repeat the phrase of its song the greatest number of times. Each nail-maker with a slate stood near his cages to mark, watching his neighbours and watched by them. And the chaffinches had begun, the *chichouïeux* with the deeper note, the *batisecouics* with their shriller note, all at first timid, and only risking a rare phrase, then being excited by each other's songs, increasing the pace, then, at last carried away by such a rage of rivalry that they would even fall and die. The nail-makers violently whipped them on with their voices, shouting out to them in Walloon to sing more, still more, yet a little more, while the spectators, about a hundred people, stood by in mute fascination in the midst of this infernal music of a hundred-and-eighty chaffinches all repeating the same cadence out of time. It was a *batisecouic* which gained the first prize, a metal coffee-pot.

Catherine and Chaval were there when Zacharie and Philomène entered. They shook hands, and all stayed together. But suddenly Zacharie became angry, for he discovered that a nail-maker, who had come in with his mates out of curiosity, was pinching his sister's thigh. She blushed and tried to make him be silent, trembling at the idea that all these nail-makers would throw themselves on Chaval and kill him if he did not like her to be pinched. She had felt the pinch, but said nothing out of prudence. Her lover, however, merely made a grimace, and as they all four now went out the affair seemed to be finished. But hardly had they entered Piquette's to drink a glass, when the nail-maker re-appeared, making fun of them and coming close up to them with an air of provocation. Zacharie, insulted in his good family feelings, threw himself on the insolent intruder.

"That's my sister, you bugger! Just wait a bit, and I'm damned if I don't make you respect her."

The two men were separated, while Chaval, who was quite calm, only repeated:

"Let be! it's my concern. I tell you I don't care a damn for him."

Maheu now arrived with his party, and quieted Catherine and Philomène who were in tears. The nail-maker had disappeared, and there was laughter in the crowd. To finally conclude the episode, Chaval, who was at home at the Estaminet Piquette, called for drinks. Étienne had touched glasses with Catherine, and all drank together—the father, the daughter and her lover, the son and his mistress—saying politely: "To your good health!" Pierron afterwards persisted in paying for more drinks. And they were all in good humour, when Zacharie, at the sight of his comrade Mouquet, called him, as he said, to go and finish his affair with the nail-maker.

"I shall have to go and do for him! Here, Chaval, keep Philomène with Catherine. I'm coming back."

Maheu offered drinks in his turn. After all, if the lad wished to avenge his sister it was not a bad example. But as soon as she had seen Mouquet, Philomène felt at rest, and nodded her head. Sure enough the two chaps would be off to the Volcan!

On the evening of feast-days the fair was terminated in the ball-room of the Bon-Joyeux. It was a widow, Madame Désir, who kept this ball-room, a fat matron of fifty, as round as a tub, but so fresh that she still had six lovers, one for every day of the week, she said, and the six together for Sunday. She called all the miners her children; and grew tender at the thought of the flood of beer which she had poured out for them during the last thirty years; and she boasted also that a putter never became pregnant without having first stretched her legs at her establishment. There were two rooms in the Bon-Joyeux: the bar which contained the counter and tables; then, communicating with it on the same floor by a large arch, was the ballroom, a large hall only planked in the middle, being paved with bricks round the sides. It was decorated with two garlands of paper flowers which crossed one another, and were united in the middle by a crown of the same flowers; while along the walls were rows of gilt shields bearing the names of saints—St. Éloi, patron of the ironworkers; St. Crispin, patron of the shoemakers; St. Barbe, patron of the miners; the whole calendar of corporations. The ceiling was so low that the three musicians on their platform, which was about the size of a pulpit, knocked their heads against it. When it became dark four petroleum lamps were fastened to the four corners of the room.

On this Sunday there was dancing from five o'clock with the full daylight through the windows, but it was not until towards seven that the rooms began to fill. Outside, a gale was rising, blowing great black showers of dust which blinded people and sleeted into the frying-pans. Maheu, Étienne, and Pierron having come in to sit down, found Chaval at the Bon-Joyeux dancing with Catherine, while Philomène by herself was looking on. Neither Levaque nor Zacharie had re-appeared. As there were no benches around the ball-room, Catherine came after each dance to rest at her father's table. They called Philomène, but she preferred to stand up. The twilight was coming on; the three musicians played furiously; one could only see in the hall the movement of hips and breasts in the midst of a confusion of arms. The appearance of the four lamps was greeted noisily, and suddenly everything was lit up—the red faces, the dishevelled hair sticking to the skin, the flying skirts spreading abroad the strong odour of perspiring couples. Maheu pointed out Mouquette to Étienne: she was as round and greasy as a bladder of lard, revolving violently in the arms of a tall, lean lander. She had been obliged to console herself and take a man.

At last, at eight o'clock, Maheude appeared with Estelle at her breast, followed by Alzire, Henri and Lénore. She had come there straight to her husband without fear of missing him. They could sup later on; as yet nobody was hungry, with their stomachs soaked in coffee and thickened with beer. Other women came in, and they whispered together when they saw, behind Maheude, the Levaque woman enter with Bouteloup, who led in by the hand Achille and Desirée, Philomène's little ones. The two neighbours seemed to be getting on well together, one turning round to chat with the other. On the way there had been a great explanation, and Maheude had resigned herself to Zacharie's marriage, in despair at the loss of her eldest son's wages, but overcome by the thought that she could not hold it back any longer without injustice. She was trying, therefore, to put a good face on it, though with an anxious heart, as a housekeeper who was asking herself how she could make both ends meet now that the best part of her purse was going.

"Place yourself there, neighbour," she said, pointing to a table near that where Maheu was drinking with Étienne and Pierron.

"Is not my husband with you?" asked the Levaque woman.

The others told her that he would soon come. They were all

seated together in a heap, Bouteloup and the youngsters, so tightly squeezed among the drinkers that the two tables only formed one. There was a call for drinks. Seeing her mother and her children Philomène had decided to come near. She accepted a chair, and seemed pleased to hear that she was at last to be married; then, as they were looking for Zacharie, she replied in her soft voice:

"I am waiting for him; he is over there."

Maheu had exchanged a look with his wife. She had then consented? He became serious and smoked in silence. He also felt anxiety for the morrow in face of the ingratitude of these children, who got married one by one leaving their parents in wretchedness.

The dancing still went on, and the end of a quadrille drowned the ball-room in red dust; the walls cracked, a piston produced shrill whistling sounds like a locomotive in distress; and when the dancers stopped they were smoking like horses.

"Do you remember?" said the Levaque woman, bending towards Maheude's ear; "you talked of strangling Catherine if she did anything foolish!"

Chaval brought Catherine back to the family table, and both of them standing behind the father finished their glasses.

"Bah!" murmured Maheude, with an air of resignation, "one says things like that——. But what quiets me is that she will not have a child; I feel sure of that. You see if she is confined, and I am obliged to marry her, what shall we do for a living then?"

Now the piston was whistling a polka, and as the deafening noise began again, Maheu, in a low voice, communicated an idea to his wife. Why should they not take a lodger. Étienne, for example, who was looking out for quarters? They would have room since Zacharie was going to leave them, and the money that they would lose in that direction would be in part regained in the other. Maheude's face brightened; certainly it was a good idea, it must be arranged. She seemed to be saved from starvation once more, and her good-humour returned so quickly that she ordered a new round of drinks.

Étienne, however, was seeking to indoctrinate Pierron, to whom he was explaining his plan of a Provident Fund. He had made him promise to subscribe, when he was imprudent enough to reveal his real aim.

"And if we go out on strike you can see how useful that fund will be. We can snap our fingers at the Company, we shall have there a fund to fight against them. Eh? don't you think so?"

Pierron lowered his eyes and grew pale; he stammered:

"I'll think over it. Good conduct, that's the best Provident Fund."

Then Maheu took possession of Étienne, and squarely, like a worthy man, proposed to take him as a lodger. The young man accepted at once, anxious to live in the settlement with the idea of being nearer to his mates. The matter was settled in three words, Maheude declaring that they would wait for the marriage of the children.

Just then, Zacharie at last came back, with Mouquet and Levaque. The three brought in the odours of the Volcan, a breath of gin, a musky acidity of ill-kept girls. They were very tipsy and seemed well pleased with themselves, pushing their elbows into each other and grinning. When he knew that he was at last to be married Zacharie began to laugh so loudly that he choked. Philomène peacefully declared that she would rather see him laugh than cry. As there were no more chairs Bouteloup had moved so as to give up half of his to Levaque. And the latter, suddenly much affected by realising that the whole family party was there, once more had beer served out.

"By the Lord! we don't amuse ourselves so often!" he roared.

They remained there till ten o'clock. Women continued to arrive, either to join or to take away their men; bands of children followed in rows, and the mothers no longer troubled themselves, pulling out their long pale breasts, like sacks of oats, and smearing their chubby babies with milk; while the little ones who were already able to walk, gorged with beer and on all-fours beneath the table, relieved themselves without shame. It was a rising sea of beer, from Madame Désir's disembowelled barrels; the beer enlarged every belly, flowing from noses, eyes, and everywhere. So puffed out was the crowd that everyone had a shoulder or knee poking into his neighbour; all were cheerful and merry in thus feeling each other's elbows. A continuous laugh kept their mouths open from ear to ear. The heat was like an oven; they were roasting and felt themselves at ease with protruding flesh, gilded in a thick smoke from the pipes; the only discomfort was when one had to move away; from time to time a girl rose, went to the other end, near the pump, lifted her clothes, and then came back. Beneath the garlands of painted paper the dancers could no longer see each other, they perspired so much; this encouraged the trammers to tumble over the putters, catching them at chance by the hips. But where a girl tumbled with a man over her, a piston covered their fall with its furious music; the swirl of feet rolled round them as if the ball had covered them.

Someone who was passing warned Pierron that his daughter Lydie was sleeping at the door, across the pavement. She had drunk her share of the stolen bottle and was tipsy. He had to carry her away in his arms while Jeanlin and Bébert, who were more solid, followed him behind, thinking it a great joke. This was the signal for departure, and several families came out of the Bon-Joyeux, the Maheus and the Levaques deciding to return to the settlement. At the same moment Father Bonnemort and old Mouque also left Montsou, walking in the same somnambulistic manner, preserving the obstinate silence of their recollections. And they all went back together, passing for the last time through the fair, where the frying-pans were coagulating, and by the estaminets, from which the last glasses were flowing in a stream towards the middle of the road. The storm was still threatening, and sounds of laughter arose as they left the lighted houses to lose themselves in the dark country around. Panting breaths arose from the ripe wheat; many children must have been made on that night. They arrived in confusion at the settlement. Neither the Levaques nor the Maheus supped with appetite, and the latter went to bed on finishing their morning's boiled beef.

Étienne had led away Chaval for one more drink at Rasseneur's.

"I am with you!" said Chaval, when his mate had explained the matter of the Provident Fund. "Strike away at it; you're a fine fellow!"

The beginning of drunkenness was flaming in Étienne's eyes. He exclaimed:

"Yes, let's join hands. As for me, you know I would give up everything for the sake of justice, both drink and girls. There's only one thing that warms my heart, and that is the thought that we are going to sweep away these bourgeois."

## CHAPTER III

TOWARDS THE MIDDLE OF August, Étienne settled with the Maheus, Zacharie having married and obtained from the Company a vacant house in the settlement for Philomène and the two children. During the first days, the young man experienced some constraint in the presence of Catherine. There was a constant intimacy, as he everywhere replaced the elder brother, sharing Jeanlin's bed in front of the big sister. Going to bed and getting up he had to dress and undress near her, and see her take off and put on her garments. When the last skirt fell from her, she appeared of pallid whiteness, that transparent snow of anæmic blondes; and he experienced a constant emotion in finding her, with hands and face already spoilt, as white as if dipped in milk from her heels to her neck, where the line of tanning turned suddenly into a necklace of amber. He pretended to turn away; but little by little he knew her: the feet at first which his lowered eyes met; then a glimpse of a knee when she slid beneath the coverlet; then her bosom with little rigid breasts as she leant over the bowl in the morning. She would hasten without looking at him, and in ten seconds was undressed and stretched beside Alzire, with so supple and snake-like a movement that he had scarcely taken off his shoes when she disappeared, turning her back and only showing her heavy knot of hair.

She never had any reason to be angry with him. If a sort of obsession made him watch her in spite of himself from the moment when she lay down, he avoided all practical jokes or dangerous pastimes. The parents were there, and besides he still had for her a feeling, half of friendship and half of spite, which prevented him from treating her as a girl to be desired, in the midst of the abandonment of their now common life in dressing, at meals, during work, where nothing of them remained secret, not even their most intimate needs. All the modesty of the family had taken refuge in the daily bath for which the young girl now went upstairs alone, while the men bathed below one after the other.

At the end of the first month, Étienne and Catherine seemed no longer to see each other when in the evening, before extinguishing the candle, they moved about the room, undressed. She had ceased to hasten, and resumed her old custom of doing up her hair at the edge of her bed, while her arms, raised in the air, lifted her chemise to her thighs, and he, without his trousers, sometimes helped her, looking for the hairpins that she had lost. Custom killed the shame of being naked; they found it natural to be like this, for they were doing no harm, and it was not their fault if there was only one room for so many people. Sometimes, however, a trouble came over them suddenly, at moments when they had no guilty thought. After some nights when he had not seen her pale body, he suddenly saw her white all over, with a whiteness which shook him with a shiver, which obliged him to turn away for fear of yielding to the desire to take her. On other evenings, without any apparent reason, she would be overcome by a panic of modesty and hasten to slip between the sheets as if she felt the hands of this lad seizing her. Then, when the candle was out, they both knew that they were not sleeping but were thinking of each other in spite of their weariness. This made them restless and sulky all the following day; they liked best the tranquil evenings when they could behave together like comrades.

Étienne only complained of Jeanlin who slept like a cocked pistol. Alzire slept lightly, and Lénore and Henri were found in the morning, in each other's arms, exactly as they had gone to sleep. In the dark house there was no other sound than the snoring of Maheu and Maheude, rolling out at regular intervals like a forge bellows. On the whole, Étienne was better off than at Rasseneur's; the bed was tolerable and the sheets were changed every month. He had better soup, too, and only suffered from the rarity of meat. But they were all in the same condition, and for forty-five francs he could not demand rabbit to every meal. These forty-five francs helped the family and enabled them to make both ends meet, though always leaving some small debts and arrears; so the Maheus were grateful to their lodger; his linen was washed and mended, his buttons sewn on, and his affairs kept in order; in fact he felt all around him a woman's neatness and care.

It was at this time that Étienne began to understand the ideas that were buzzing in his brain. Up till then he had only felt an instinctive revolt in the midst of the inarticulate fomentation among his mates. All sorts of confused questions came before him: why are some miserable? why are others rich? why are the former beneath the heel of the latter without hope of ever taking their own place? And his first stage was to understand his ignorance. A secret shame, a hidden annoyance, gnawed him from that time; he knew nothing, he dared not talk about these things which were working in him like a passion—the equality of all men, and the equity which demanded a fair division of the earth's wealth. He thus took to the methodless study of those who in ignorance feel the fascination of knowledge. He now kept up a regular correspondence with Pluchart, who was better educated than himself and more advanced in the Socialist movement. He had books sent to him, and his ill-digested reading still further excited his brajn, especially a medical book entitled "Hygiène du Mineur,"[9] in which a Belgian doctor had summed up the evils of which the people in coal mines were dying, without counting treatises on political economy, incomprehensible in their technical dryness, Anarchist pamphlets which upset his ideas, and old numbers of newspapers which he preserved as irrefutable arguments for possible discussions. Souvarine also lent him books, and the work on co-operative societies had made him dream for a month of an universal exchange association abolishing money and basing the whole social life on work. The shame of his ignorance left him, and a certain pride came to him now that he felt himself thinking.

During these first months Étienne retained the ecstasy of a novice; his heart was bursting with generous indignation against the oppressors, and looking forward to the approaching triumph of the oppressed. He had not yet manufactured a system, his reading had been too vague. Rasseneur's practical demands were mixed up in his mind with Souvarine's violent and destructive methods, and when he came out of the Avantage, where he was to be found nearly every day railing with them against the Company, he walked as if in a dream, assisting at a radical regeneration of nations to be effected without one broken window or a single drop of blood. The methods of execution remained obscure; he preferred to think that things would go very well, for he lost his head as soon as he tried to formulate a programme of reconstruction. He even showed himself full of illogical moderation; he often said that we must banish politics from the social question, a phrase which he had read and which seemed a useful one to repeat among the phlegmatic colliers with whom he lived.

Every evening now, at the Maheus', they delayed half-an-hour before going up to bed. Étienne always introduced the same subject. As his nature became more refined he found himself wounded by the promiscuity of the settlement. Were they beasts to be thus penned together in the midst of the fields, so tightly packed that one could not change one's shirt without exhibiting one's backside to the neighbours? And how bad it was for health; and boys and girls were forced to grow corrupt together.

"Lord!" replied Maheu, "if there were more money there would be more comfort. All the same it's true enough that it's good for no one to live piled up like that. It always ends with making the men drunk and the girls big-bellied."

And the family began from there, each having his say, while the petroleum lamp vitiated the air of the room, already stinking of fried onion. No, life was certainly not a joke. One had to work like a brute at labour which was once a punishment for convicts; one left one's skin there oftener than was one's turn, all that without even getting meat on the table in the evening. No doubt one had one's feed; one ate, indeed, but so little, just enough to suffer without dying, overcome with debts and pursued as if one had stolen the bread. When Sunday came one slept from weariness. The only pleasures were to get drunk and to make a child with one's wife; then the beer fattened the belly too much, and the child, later on, left you to go to the dogs. No, it was certainly not a joke.

Then Maheude joined in.

"The bother is, you see, when you have to say to yourself that it won't change. When you're young you think that happiness will come some time, you hope for things; and then the wretchedness begins always over again, and you get shut up in it. Now, I don't wish harm to anyone, but there are times when this injustice makes me mad."

There was silence; they were all breathing with the vague discomfort of this closed-in horizon. Father Bonnemort only, if he was there, opened his eyes with surprise, for in his time people used not to worry about things; they were born in the coal and they hammered at the seam, without asking for more; while now there was an air passing which made the colliers ambitious.

"It don't do to spit at anything," he murmured. "A good glass is a good glass. As to the masters, they're often rascals; but there always will be masters, won't there? What's the use of breaking your head by thinking about those things?"

Étienne at once became animated. What! The worker was to be forbidden to think! Why! that was just it; things would change now because the worker had begun to think. In the old man's time the miner lived in the mine like a brute, like a machine for extracting coal, always under the earth, with ears and eyes stopped to outward events. So the rich, who governed, found it easy to sell him and buy him, and to devour his flesh; he did not even know what was going on. But now the miner was waking up down there, germinating in the earth[10] just as a grain germinates; and some fine day he would spring up in the midst of the fields: yes, men would spring up, an army of men who would reestablish justice. Is it not true that all citizens are equal since the Revolution, because they vote together? Why should the worker remain the slave of the master who pays him? The big companies with their machines were crushing everything, and one no longer had against them the ancient guarantees when people of the same trade, united in a body, were able to defend themselves. It was that, by God, and for no other reason, that all would burst up one day, thanks to education. One had only to look into the settlement itself: the grandfathers could not sign their names, the fathers could do so, and as for the sons, they read and wrote like schoolmasters. Ah! it was springing up, it was springing up, little by little, a rough harvest of men who would ripen in the sun! From the moment when they were no longer each of them stuck to his place for his whole existence, and that they had the ambition to take a neighbour's place, why should they not play out with their fists and try for the mastery?

Maheu was shaken but remained full of doubts.

"As soon as you move they give you back your certificate,"[11] he said. "The old man is right; it will always be the miner who gets all the trouble, without chance of a leg of mutton now and then as a reward."

Maheude, who had been silent for a while, awoke as from a dream.

"But if what the priests tell is true, if the poor people in this world become the rich ones in the next!"

A burst of laughter interrupted her; even the children shrugged their shoulders, being incredulous in the open air, keeping a secret fear of ghosts in the pit, but glad of the empty sky.

"Ah! bosh! the priests!" exclaimed Maheu. "If they believed that, they'd eat less and work more, so as to reserve a better place for themselves up there. No, when one's dead, one's dead."

Maheude sighed deeply.

"Oh! Lord, Lord!"

Then her hands fell on to her knees with a gesture of immense dejection:

"Then if that's true, we are done for, we are."

They all looked at one another. Father Bonnemort spat into his handkerchief, while Maheu sat with his extinguished pipe, which he had forgotten, in his mouth. Alzire listened between Lénore and Henri, who were sleeping on the edge of the table. But Catherine, with her chin in her hand, never took her large clear eyes off Étienne while he was protesting, declaring his faith, and opening out the enchanting future of his social dream. Around them the settlement was asleep; one only heard the stray cries of a child or the complaints of a belated drunkard. In the parlour the clock ticked slowly, and a damp freshness arose from the sanded floor in spite of the stuffy air.

"Fine ideas!"said the young man, "why do you need a good God and his Paradise to make you happy? Haven't you got it in your power to make yourselves happy on the earth?"

With his enthusiastic voice he spoke on and on. The closed horizon was bursting out; a gap of light was opening in the sombre lives of these poor people. The eternal wretchedness, beginning over and over again, the brutalising labour, the fate of a beast who gives his wool and has his throat cut, all the misfortune disappeared, as though swept away by a great flood of sunlight; and beneath the dazzling gleam of fairyland justice descended from heaven. Since the good God was dead, Justice would assure the happiness of men, and Equality and Brotherhood would reign. A new society would spring up in a day just as in dreams, an immense town with the splendour of a mirage, in which each citizen lived by his work, and took his share in the common joys. The old rotten world had fallen to dust; a young humanity purged from its crimes formed but a single nation of workers, having for their motto: "To each according to his deserts, and to each desert according to its performance." And this dream grew continually larger and more beautiful and more seductive as it mounted higher in the impossible.

At first Maheude refused to listen, possessed by a deep dread. No, no, it was too beautiful; it would not do to embark in these ideas for they made life seem abominable afterwards, and one would have destroyed everything in the effort to be happy. When she saw Maheu's eyes shine, and that he was troubled and won over, she became restless, and exclaimed, interrupting Étienne:

"Don't listen, my man! You can see he's only telling us fairy-tales. Do you think the bourgeois would ever consent to work as we do?"

But little by little the charm worked on her also. Her imagination was roused and she smiled at last, entering this marvellous world of hope. It was so sweet to forget for a while the sad reality! When one lives like the beasts with faces bent towards the earth, one needs a corner for falsehood where one can amuse oneself by regaling on the things one will never possess. And what made her enthusiastic and brought her into agreement with the young man was the idea of justice.

"Now, there you're right!" she exclaimed. "When a thing's just I don't mind being cut to pieces for it. And it's true enough! it would be just for us to have a turn."

Then Maheu ventured to become excited.

"Blast it all! I am not rich, but I would give five francs to keep alive to see that. What a hustling, eh? Will it be soon? And how can we set it about?"

Étienne began talking again. The old social system was cracking; it could not last more than a few months, he affirmed roundly. As to the methods of execution he spoke more vaguely, mixing up his reading, and fearing before ignorant hearers to enter on explanations where he might lose himself. All the systems had their share in it, softened by the certainty of easy triumph, a universal kiss which would bring to an end all class misunderstandings; without taking count, however, of the recalcitrant heads among the masters and bourgeois whom it would perhaps be necessary to bring to reason by force. And the Maheus looked as if they understood, approving and accepting miraculous solutions with the blind faith of new believers, like those Christians of the early days of the Church, who awaited the coming of a perfect society on the dung-hill of the ancient world. Little Alzire picked up a few words, and imagined happiness under the form of a very warm house, where children could play and eat as long as they liked. Catherine, without moving, her chin always resting in her hand, kept her eyes fixed on Étienne, and when he stopped a slight shudder passed over her, and she was quite pale as if she felt the cold.

But Maheude looked at the clock.

"Past nine! Can it be possible? We shall never get up tomorrow."

And the Maheus left the table with hearts ill at ease and in despair. It seemed to them that they had just been rich and that they had now suddenly fallen back into the mud. Father Bonnemort, who was setting out for the pit, growled that those sort of stories wouldn't make the soup better; while the others went upstairs in single file, noticing the dampness of the walls and the pestiferous stuffiness of the air. Upstairs, amid the heavy slumber of the settlement, when Catherine had got into bed last and blown out the candle, Étienne heard her tossing feverishly before getting to sleep.

Often at these conversations the neighbours came in: Levaque, who grew excited at the idea of a general sharing; Pierron, who prudently went to bed as soon as they attacked the Company. At long intervals Zacharie came in for a moment; but politics bored him, he preferred to go off and drink a glass at the Avantage. As to Chaval, he would go to extremes and wanted to draw blood. Nearly every evening he passed an hour with the Maheus; in this assiduity there was a certain unconfessed jealousy, the fear that he would be robbed of Catherine. This girl, of whom he was already growing tired, had become precious to him now that a man slept near her and could take her at night.

Étienne's influence increased; he gradually revolutionised the settlement. His propaganda was unseen, and all the more sure since he was growing in the estimation of all. Maheude, notwithstanding the caution of a prudent housekeeper, treated him with consideration, as a young man who paid regularly and neither drank nor gambled, with his nose always in a book; she spread abroad his reputation among the neighbours as an educated lad, a reputation which they abused by asking him to write their letters. He was a sort of business man, charged with correspondences and consulted by households in affairs of difficulty. Since September he had thus at last been able to establish his famous Provident Fund, which was still very precarious, only including the inhabitants of the settlement; but he hoped to be able to obtain the adhesion of the miners at all the pits, especially if the Company, which had remained passive, continued not to interfere. He had been made secretary of the association and he even received a small salary for the clerking. This made him almost rich. If a married miner can with difficulty make both ends meet, a sober lad who has no burdens can even manage to save.

From this time a slow transformation took place in Étienne. Certain instincts of refinement and comfort which had slept during his poverty were now revealed. He began to buy cloth garments; he also bought a pair of elegant boots; he became a big man. The whole settlement grouped round him. The satisfaction of his self-love was delicious; he became intoxicated with this first enjoyment of popularity, to be at the head of others, to command; he who was so young, and but the day before had been a mere labourer. This filled him with pride, and enlarged his dream of an approaching revolution in which he was to play a part. His face changed; he became serious and took on airs, while his growing ambition inflamed his theories and pushed him to ideas of violence.

But autumn was advancing, and the October cold had blighted the little gardens of the settlement. Behind the thin lilacs the trammers no longer tumbled the putters over on the shed, and only the winter vegetables remained, the cabbages pearled with white frost, the leeks and the salads. Once more the rains were beating down on the red tiles and flowing down into the tubs beneath the gutters with the sound of a torrent. In every house the stove piled up with coal was never cold, and poisoned the close parlours. It was the season of wretchedness beginning once more.

In October, on one of the first frosty nights, Étienne, feverish after his conversation below, could not sleep. He had seen Catherine glide beneath the coverlet and then blow out the candle. She also appeared to be quite overcome, and tormented by one of those fits of modesty which still made her hasten sometimes, and so awkwardly that she only uncovered herself more. In the darkness she lay as though dead; but he knew that she also was awake, and he felt that she was thinking of him just as he was thinking of her: this mute exchange of their beings had never before filled them with such trouble. The minutes went by and neither he nor she moved, only their breathing was embarrassed in spite of their efforts to retain it. Twice over he was on the point of rising and taking her. It was idiotic to have such a strong desire for each other and never to satisfy it. Why should they thus sulk against what they desired? The children were asleep, she was quite willing; he was certain that she was waiting for him and stifling, that she would close her arms round him in silence with clenched teeth. Nearly an hour passed. He did not go to take her, and she did not turn round for fear of calling him. The more they lived side by side, the more a barrier was raised of shames, repugnancies, delicacies of friendship, which they could not explain even to themselves.

## CHAPTER IV

"LISTEN," SAID MAHEUDE TO her man, "when you go to Montsou for the pay, just bring back a pound of coffee and a kilo of sugar."

He was sewing one of his shoes, in order to spare the cobbling.

"Good!" he murmured, without leaving his task.

"I should like to get you to go to the butcher's. A bit of veal, eh? It is so long since we saw it."

This time he raised his head.

"Do you think, then, that I've got thousands coming in? The fortnight's pay is too little as it is, with their confounded idea of always stopping work."

They were both silent. It was after breakfast, one Saturday, at the end of October. The Company, under the pretext of the derangement caused by payment, had on this day once more suspended the output in all their pits. Seized by panic at the growing industrial crisis, and not wishing to augment their already considerable stock, they profited by the smallest pretexts to force their ten thousand workers to rest.

"You know that Étienne is waiting for you at Rasseneur's," began Maheude again. "Take him with you; he'll be more clever than you are in clearing up matters if they haven't counted all your hours."

Maheu nodded approval.

"And just talk to those gentlemen about your father's affair. The doctor's on good terms with the directors. It's true, isn't it, old un, that the doctor's mistaken, and that you can still work?"

For ten days Father Bonnemort, with benumbed paws, as he said, had remained nailed to his chair. She had to repeat her question, and he growled:

"Sure enough, I can work. One isn't done for because one's legs are bad. All that is just stories they make up, so as not to give one the hundred-and-eighty franc pension."

Maheude thought of the old man's forty sous, which he would, perhaps, never bring in any more, and she uttered a cry of anguish.

"My God! we shall soon be all dead if this goes on."

"When one is dead," said Maheu, "one doesn't get hungry."

He put some nails into his shoes, and decided to set out. The Deux-Cent-Quarante settlement would not be paid till towards four o'clock. The men did not hurry, therefore, but waited about, going off one by one, beset by the women, who implored them to come back at once. Many gave them commissions, to prevent them forgetting themselves in public-houses.

At Rasseneur's Étienne had received news. Disquieting rumours were flying about; it was said that the Company were more and more discontented over the timbering. They were overwhelming the workmen with fines, and a conflict appeared inevitable. That was, however, only the avowed dispute; beneath it there were grave and secret causes of complication.

Just as Étienne arrived, a comrade, who was drinking a glass on his return from Montsou, was telling that an announcement had been stuck up at the cashier's; but he did not quite know what was on the announcement. A second entered, then a third, and each brought a different story. It seemed certain, however, that the Company had taken a resolution.

"What do you say of it, eh?" asked Étienne, sitting down near Souvarine at a table where nothing was to be seen but a packet of tobacco.

The engine-man did not hurry, but finished rolling his cigarette.

"I say that it was easy to foresee; They want to push you to extremes."

He alone had a sufficiently keen intelligence to analyse the situation. He explained it in his quiet way. The Company, suffering from the crisis, had been forced to reduce their expenses if they were not to succumb, and it was naturally the workers who would have to tighten their bellies; under some pretext or another the Company would nibble at their wages. For two months the coal had been remaining at the surface of their pits, and nearly all the work-shops were resting. As the Company did not dare to rest in this way, terrified at the ruinous inaction, they were meditating a middle course, perhaps a strike, from which the miners would come out crushed and worse paid. Then the new Provident Fund was disturbing them, as it was a threat for the future, while a strike would relieve them of it, by exhausting it when it was still small.

Rasseneur had seated himself beside Étienne, and both of them were listening in consternation. They could talk in a loud voice, because there was no one there but Madame Rasseneur, seated at the counter.

"What an idea!" murmured the innkeeper; "what's the good of it? The Company has no interest in a strike, nor the men either. It would be best to come to an understanding."

This was very sensible. He was always on the side of reasonable demands. Since the rapid popularity of his old lodger, he had even exaggerated this system of reasonable progress, saying they would obtain nothing if they wished to have everything at once. In his fat, good-humoured nature, nourished on beer, a secret jealousy was forming, increased by the desertion of his bar, into which the workmen from the Voreux now came more rarely to drink and to listen; and he thus sometimes even began to defend the Company, forgetting the rancour of an old miner who had been turned off.

"Then you are against the strike?" cried Madame Rasseneur, without leaving the counter.

And as he energetically replied, "Yes!" she made him hold his tongue.

"Bah! you have no courage; let these gentlemen speak."

Étienne was meditating, with his eyes fixed on the glass which she had served to him. At last he raised his head.

"I daresay it's all true what our mate tells us, and we must get resigned to this strike if they force it on us. Pluchart has just written me some very sensible things on this matter. He's against the strike too, for the men would suffer as much as the masters, and it wouldn't come to anything decisive. Only it seems to him a capital chance to get our men to make up their minds to go into his big machine. Here's his letter."

In fact, Pluchart, in despair at the suspicion which the International aroused among the miners at Montsou, was hoping to see them enter in a mass if they were forced to fight against the Company. In spite of his efforts, Étienne had not been able to place a single member's card, and he had given his best efforts to his Provident Fund, which was much better received. But this fund was still so small that it would be quickly exhausted, as Souvarine said, and the strikers would then inevitably throw themselves into the association of workers so that their brothers in every country could come to their aid.

"How much have you in the Fund?" asked Rasseneur.

"Hardly three thousand francs," replied Étienne, "and you know that the directors sent for me yesterday. Oh! they were very polite; they repeated that they wouldn't prevent their men from forming a reserve fund. But I understood that they wanted to control it. We are bound to have a struggle over that."

The innkeeper was walking up and down, whistling contemptuously. "Three thousand francs! what can you do with that! It wouldn't yield six days' bread; and if one took strangers into account, the people living in England, one might go to bed at once and swallow one's tongue. No, it was too foolish, this strike!"

Then for the first time bitter words passed between these two men who usually always agreed together at last in their common hatred of capital.

"We shall see! and you; what do you say of it?" repeated Étienne, turning towards Souvarine.

The latter replied with his usual phrase of habitual contempt.

"A strike? Foolery!"

Then, in the midst of the angry silence, he added gently:

"On the whole, I shouldn't say no if it amuses you; it ruins the one side and kills the other, and that is always so much cleared away. Only in that way it will take quite a thousand years to renew the world. Just begin by blowing up this prison in which you are all being done to death!"

With his delicate hand he pointed out the Voreux, the buildings of which could be seen through the open door. But an unforeseen drama interrupted him: Poland, the big tame rabbit, which had ventured outside, came bounding back, fleeing from the stones of a band of trammers; and in her terror, with fallen ears and raised tail, she took refuge against his legs, imploring and scratching for him to take her up. When he had placed her on his knees, he sheltered her with both hands, and fell into that kind of dreamy somnolence into which the caress of this soft warm fur always plunged him.

Almost at the same time Maheu came in. He would drink nothing, in spite of the polite insistance of Madame Rasseneur, who sold her beer as though she made a present of it. Étienne had risen, and both of them set out for Montsou.

On pay-day at the Company's Yards, Montsou seemed to be in the midst of a fête as on fine Sunday Feast-days. Bands of miners arrived from all the settlements. The cashier's office being very small, they preferred to wait at the door, stationed in groups on the pavement, barring the way in a crowd that was constantly renewed. Hucksters profited by the occasion and installed themselves with their movable shops exhibiting even pottery and pork. But it was especially the estaminets and the bars which did a good trade, for the miners before being paid went to the counters to get patience, and returned to them to wet their pay as soon as they had it in their pockets. But they were very sensible, except when they finished it at the Volcan. As Maheu and Étienne advanced among the groups they felt that on that day a deep exasperation was rising up. It was not the ordinary indifference with which the money was taken and curtailed at the publics. Fists were clenched and violent words were passing from mouth to mouth.

"Is it true, then," asked Maheu of Chaval, whom he met before the Estaminet Piquette, "that they've played the dirty trick?"

But Chaval contented himself by replying with a furious growl, throwing a sidelong look on Étienne. Since the working had been renewed he had hired himself on with others, more and more bitten by envy against this comrade, the new-comer who posed as a boss and whose boots, as he said, were licked by the whole settlement. This was complicated by a lover's jealousy. He never took Catherine to Réquillart now or behind the pit-bank without accusing her in abominable language of sleeping with her mother's lodger; then, seized by savage desire he would stifle her with caresses.

Maheu asked him another question.

"Is it the Voreux's turn now?"

And when he turned his back, nodding affirmatively, both men decided to enter the Yards.

The counting-house was a small rectangular room, divided in two by a grating. On the forms along the wall five or six miners were waiting; while the cashier assisted by a clerk was paying another who stood before the wicket with his cap in his hand. Above the form on the left, a yellow placard was stuck up, quite fresh against the smoky grey of the plaster, and it was in front of this that the men had been constantly passing all the morning. They entered two or three at a time, stood in front of it, and then went away without a word, shrugging their shoulders as if their backs were crushed.

Two colliers were just then standing in front of the announcement, a young one with a square brutish head and on old one very lean, his face dull with age. Neither of them could read; the young one spelt, moving his lips, the old one contented himself with gazing stupidly. Many came in thus to look, without understanding.

"Read us that there!" said Maheu, who was not very strong either in reading, to his companion.

Then Étienne began to read him the announcement. It was a notice from the Company to the miners of all the pits, informing them that in consequence of the lack of care bestowed on the timbering, and being weary of inflicting useless fines, the Company had resolved to apply a new method of payment for the extraction of coal. Hence forward they would pay for the timbering separately, by the cubic mètre of wood taken down and used, based on the quantity necessary for good work. The price of the tub of coal extracted would naturally be lowered, in the proportion of fifty centimes to forty, according to the nature and distance of the cuttings, and a somewhat obscure calculation endeavoured to show that this diminution of ten centimes would be exactly compensated by the price of the timbering. The Company added also that, wishing to leave everyone time to convince himself of the advantages presented by this new scheme, they did not propose to apply it till Monday, the 1st of December.

"If you would not read so loud over there," shouted the cashier, "we could hear what we are saying here."

Étienne finished reading without paying attention to this observation. His voice trembled, and when he had reached the end they all continued to gaze steadily at the placard. The old miner and the young one looked as though they expected something more; then they went away with depressed shoulders.

"Good God!" muttered Maheu.

He and his companions sat down absorbed, with lowered heads, and while files of men continued to pass before the yellow paper they made calculations. Were they being made fun of? They could never make up with the timbering for the ten centimes taken off the tram. At most they could only get to eight centimes, so the Company would be robbing them of two centimes, without counting the time taken by careful work. This, then, was what this disguised lowering of wages really came to. The Company was economising out of the miners' pockets.

"Good Lord! Good Lord!" repeated Maheu, raising his head. "We should be bloody fools if we took that."

But the wicket being free they came up to be paid. The heads only of the workings presented themselves at the desk and then divided the money between their men to save time. "Maheu and associates," said the clerk, "Filonnière seam, cutting No. 7."

He searched through the lists which were prepared from the inspection of the tickets on which the captains stated every day for each yard the number of trams extracted. Then he repeated:

"Maheu and associates, Filonnière seam, cutting No. 7. One hundred and thirty-five francs."

The cashier paid.

"Beg pardon, sir," stammered the pikeman in surprise. "Are you sure you have not made a mistake?"

He looked at this small sum of money without picking it up, frozen by a shudder which went to his heart. It was true he was expecting bad payment, but it could not come to so little or he must have calculated wrong. When he had given their shares to Zacharie, Étienne and the other mate who replaced Chaval, there would remain at most fifty francs for himself, his father, Catherine and Jeanlin.

"No, no, I've made no mistake," replied the clerk. "There are two Sundays and four rest days to be taken off; that makes you nine days of work." Maheu followed this calculation in a low voice: nine days gave him about thirty francs, eighteen to Catherine, nine to Jeanlin. As to Father Bonnemort, he only had three days. No matter, by adding the ninety francs of Zacharie and the two mates that would surely make more.

"And don't forget the fines," added the clerk. "Twenty francs for fines for defective timbering."

The pikeman made a gesture of despair. Twenty francs of fines, four days of rest! That made out the account. To think that he had once brought back a fortnight's pay of even a hundred and fifty francs when Father Bonnemort was working and Zacharie was not yet in the household!

"Well, are you going to take it?" cried the cashier impatiently. "You can see there's someone else waiting. If you don't want it, say so."

As Maheu decided to pick up the money with his large trembling hand the clerk stopped him.

"Wait: I have your name here. Toussaint Maheu, is it not? The general secretary wishes to speak to you. Go in, he is alone."

The stunned workman found himself in an office furnished with old mahogany, upholstered with faded green rep. And he listened for five minutes to the general secretary, a tall sallow gentleman, who spoke to him over the papers of his bureau without rising. But the buzzing in his ears prevented him from hearing. He understood vaguely that the question of his father's retirement would be taken into consideration with reference to the pension of a hundred and fifty francs, fifty years of age and forty years' service. Then it seemed to him that the secretary's voice became harder. There was a reprimand: he was accused of occupying himself with politics; an allusion was made to his lodger and the Provident Fund; finally, he was advised not to compromise himself in these follies, he, who was one of the best workmen in the mine. He wished to protest, but could only pronounce words at random, twisting his cap between his feverish fingers, and he retired, stuttering:

"Certainly, sir—I can assure you, sir——"

Outside, when he had found Étienne who was waiting for him, he broke out:

"Well, I am a bloody fool, I ought to have replied! Not enough money to get bread, and insults as well! Yes, he has been talking against you; he told me the settlement was being poisoned. And what's to be done? Good God! bend one's back and say thank-you. He's right, that's the wisest plan."

Maheu was silent, overcome at once by rage and fear. Étienne was gloomily thinking. Once more they traversed the groups who blocked the road. The exasperation was growing, the exasperation of a calm race, the muttered warning of a storm, without violent gestures, terrible to see above this stolid mass. A few heads understanding accounts had made calculations, and the two centimes gained by the Company over the wood were rumoured about, and excited the hardest heads. But it was especially the rage over this disastrous pay, the rebellion of hunger against the rest days and the fines. Already there was not enough to eat, and what would happen if wages were still further lowered? In the estaminets the anger grew loud, and fury so dried their throats that the little money taken went over the counters.

From Montsou to the settlement Étienne and Maheu never exchanged a word. When the latter entered, Maheude, who was alone with the children, noticed immediately that his hands were empty.

"Well, you're a nice one!" she said. "Where's my coffee and my sugar and the meat? A bit of veal wouldn't have ruined you."

He made no reply, stifled by the emotion he had been keeping back. Then the coarse face of this man hardened to work in the mines became swollen with despair, and large tears broke from his eyes and fell in a warm rain. He had thrown himself into a chair, weeping like a child, and throwing fifty francs on the table:

"Here," he stammered. "That's what I've brought you back. That's our work for all of us."

Maheude looked at Étienne, and saw that he was silent and overwhelmed. Then she also wept. How were nine people to live for a fortnight on fifty francs? Her eldest son had left them, the old man could no longer move his legs: it would soon mean death. Alzire threw herself round her mother's neck, overcome on hearing her weep. Estelle was howling, Lénore and Henri were sobbing.

And from the entire settlement there soon arose the same cry of wretchedness. The men had come back, and each household was lamenting the disaster of this bad pay. The doors opened, women appeared, crying aloud outside, as if their complaints could not be held beneath the ceilings of these small houses. A fine rain was falling, but they did not feel it, they called one another from the pavements, they showed one another in the hollow of their hands the money they had received.

"Look! they've given him this. Do they went to make fools of people?"

"As for me, see, I haven't got enough to pay the fortnight's bread with."

"And just count mine! I should have to sell my shifts!"

Maheude had come out like the others. A group had formed around the Levaque woman, who was shouting loudest of all, for her drunkard of a husband had not even turned up, and she knew that, large or small, the pay would melt away at the Volcan. Philomène watched Maheu so that Zacharie should not get hold of the money. Pierronne was the only one who seemed fairly calm, for that hypocritical Pierron always arranged things, no one knew how, so as to have more hours on the captain's ticket than his mates. But Mother Brûlé thought this cowardly of her son-in-law; she was among the enraged, lean and erect in the midst of the group, with her fists stretched towards Montsou.

"To think," she cried, without naming the Hennebeaus, "that this morning I saw their servant go by in a carriage! Yes, the cook in a carriage with two horses, going to Marchiennes to get fish, sure enough!"

A clamour arose, and the abuse began again. That servant in a white apron taken to the market of the neighbouring town in her master's carriage aroused indignation. While the workers were dying of hunger they must then have their fish, at all costs! Perhaps they would not always be able to eat their fish: the turn of the poor people would come. And the ideas sown by Étienne sprang up and expanded in this cry of revolt. It was impatience before the promised age of gold, a haste to get a share of the happiness beyond this horizon of misery, closed in like the grave. The injustice was becoming too great; at last they would demand their rights, since the bread was being taken out of their mouths. The women especially would have liked at once to take by assault this ideal city of progress, in which there was to be no more wretchedness. It was almost night, and the rain increased while they were still filling the settlement with their tears in the midst of the screaming helter-skelter of the children.

That evening at the Avantage the strike was decided. Rasseneur no longer struggled against it, and Souvarine accepted it as a first step. Étienne summed up the situation in a word: if the Company really wanted a strike, then the Company should have a strike.

## CHAPTER V

A WEEK PASSED, AND work went on suspiciously and mournfully, in expectation of the conflict.

Among the Maheus the fortnight threatened to be more meagre than ever. Maheude grew bitter, in spite of her moderation and good sense. Her daughter Catherine, too, had taken it into her head to stay out one night. On the following morning she came back so weary and ill after this adventure that she was not able to go to the pit; and she told with tears that it was not her fault, for Chaval had kept her, threatening to beat her if she ran away. He was becoming mad with jealousy, and wished to prevent her from returning to Étienne's bed, where he well knew, he said, that the family made her sleep. Maheude was furious, and, after forbidding her daughter ever to see such a brute again, talked of going to Montsou to box his ears. But, all the same, it was a day lost, and the girl, now that she had this lover, preferred not to change him.

Two days after there was another incident. On Monday and Tuesday Jeanlin, who was supposed to be quietly engaged on his task at the Voreux, had escaped, to run away into the marshes and the forest of Vandame with Bébert and Lydie. He had seduced them; no one knew to what plunder or to what games of precocious children they had all three given themselves up. He received a vigorous punishment, a whipping which his mother applied to him on the pavement outside before the children of the terrified settlement. Who could have thought such a thing of children belonging to her, who had cost so much since their birth, and who ought now to be bringing something in? And in this cry there was the remembrance of her own hard youth, of the hereditary misery which made of each little one in the brood a livelihood later on.

That morning, when the men and the girl set out for the pit, Maheude sat up in her bed to say to Jeanlin:

"You know that if you begin that game again, you little beast, I'll take the skin off your bottom!"

In the Maheu's new stall work was painful. This part of the Filonnière seam was so thin that the pikemen, squeezed between the wall and the roof, grazed their elbows at their work. It was, too, becoming very damp; from hour to hour they feared a stream of water, one of those sudden torrents which burst through rocks and carry away men. The day before, as Étienne was violently driving in his pick and drawing it out, he had received a jet of water in his face; but this was only an alarm; the cutting had simply become damper and more unwholesome. Besides, he now thought nothing of possible accidents; he forgot himself there with his mates, careless of peril. They lived in fire-damp without even feeling its weight on their eyelids, the spider's web veil which it left on the eyelashes. Sometimes when the flame of the lamps grew paler and bluer than usual it attracted attention, and a miner would put his head against the seam to listen to the low noise of the gas, a noise of air-bubbles escaping from each crack. But the constant threat was of land-slips; for, besides the insufficiency of the timbering, all was patched up too quickly, and the soil, soaked with water, would not hold.

Three times during the day Maheu had been obliged to add to the planking. It was half-past two, and the men would soon have to ascend. Lying on his side, Étienne was finishing the cutting of a block, when the distant growl of thunder shook the whole mine.

"What's that, then?" he cried, putting down his axe to listen.

He had at first thought that the gallery was falling in behind his back.

But Maheu had already glided along the slope of the cutting, saying:

"It's a fall! Quick, quick!"

All tumbled down and hastened, carried away by a restless movement of fraternity. Their lamps danced at their wrists in the deathly silence which had fallen; they rushed in single file along the passages with bent backs, as though they were galloping on all-fours; and without slowing this gallop they asked each other questions and threw brief replies. Where was it, then? In the cuttings, perhaps. No, it came from below; no, from the haulage. When they arrived at the chimney passage they threw themselves into it, tumbling one over the other without troubling about bruises.

Jeanlin, with skin still red from the whipping of the day before, had not run away from the pit on this day. He was trotting with naked feet behind his train, closing the ventilation doors one by one; when he was not afraid of meeting a captain he jumped on to the last tram, which he was not allowed to do for fear he should go to sleep. But his great amusement was, whenever the train was shunted to let another one pass, to go and join Bébert, who was holding the reins in front. He would come up slily without his lamp and vigorously pinch his companion, inventing a mischievous monkey's tricks, with his yellow hair, his large ears, his lean muzzle, lit up by little green eyes shining in the darkness. With morbid precocity, he seemed to have the obscure intelligence and the quick skill of a human abortion which had returned to its animal ways.

In the afternoon, Mouque brought Bataille, whose turn it was, to the trammers; and as the horse was snuffing in the shunting, Jeanlin, who had glided up to Bébert, asked him:

"What's the matter with the old hack to stop short like that? He'll break my legs."

Bébert could not reply; he had to hold in Bataille, who was growing lively at the approach of the other train. The horse had smelled from afar his comrade, Trompette, for whom he had felt great tenderness ever since the day when he had seen him disembarked in the pit. One might say that it was the affectionate pity of an old philosopher anxious to console a young friend by imparting to him his own resignation and patience; for Trompette did not become reconciled, drawing his trams without any taste for the work, standing with lowered head blinded by the darkness, and forever regretting the sun. So every time that Bataille met him he put out his head snorting, and moistened him with an encouraging caress.

"By God!" swore Bébert, "there they are, sucking each other's skins again!"

Then, when Trompette had passed, he replied on the subject of Bataille:

"Oh, he's a cunning old beast! When he stops like that it's because he guesses there's something in the way, a stone or a hole, and he takes care of himself; he doesn't want to break his bones. To-day I don't know what was the matter with him down there after the door. He pushed it, and stood stock still. Did you see anything?"

"No," said Jeanlin. "There's water, I've got it up to my knees."

The train set out again. And, on the following journey, when he had opened the ventilation door with a blow from his head, Bataille again refused to advance, neighing and trembling. At last he made up his mind, and set off with a bound.

Jeanlin, who closed the door, had remained behind. He bent down and looked at the mud through which he was paddling; then, raising his lamp, he saw that the wood had given way beneath the continual bleeding of a spring. Just then a pikeman, one Berloque, who was called Chicot, had arrived from his cutting in a hurry, to go to his wife who had just been confined. He also stopped and examined the planking. And suddenly, as the boy was starting to rejoin his train, a tremendous cracking sound was heard, and a land-slip engulfed the man and the child.

There was deep silence. A thick dust raised by the wind of the fall passed through the passages. Blinded and choked the miners came from every part, even from the farthest stalls, with their dancing lamps which feebly lighted up this gallop of black men at the bottom of these mole-hills. When the first men tumbled against the land-slip, they shouted out and called their mates. A second band, come from the cutting below, found themselves on the other side of the mass of earth which stopped up the gallery. It was at once seen that the roof had fallen in for a dozen mètres at most. The damage was not serious. But all hearts were contracted when a death-rattle was heard from the ruins.

Bébert, leaving his train, ran up, repeating:

"Jeanlin is underneath! Jeanlin is underneath!"

Maheu, at this very moment, had come out of the passage with Zacharie and Étienne. He was seized with the fury of despair, and could only utter oaths.

"My God! my God! my God!"

Catherine, Lydie, and Mouquette, who had also rushed up, began to sob and shriek with terror in the midst of the fearful disorder which was increased by the darkness. The men tried to make them be silent, but they shrieked louder as each groan was heard.

The captain, Richomme, had come up running, in despair that neither Négrel, the engineer, nor Dansaert were at the pit. With his ear pressed against the rocks he listened; and, at last, said that those sounds could not come from a child. A man must certainly be there. Maheu had already called Jeanlin twenty times over. Not a breath was heard. The little one must have been smashed up.

And still the groans continued monotonously. They spoke to the agonised man, asking him his name. The groaning alone replied.

"Look sharp!" repeated Richomme, who had already organised a rescue, "we can talk afterwards."

From each end the miners attacked the landslip with pick and shovel. Chaval worked without a word beside Maheu and Étienne, while Zacharie superintended the removal of the earth. The hour for ascent had come, and no one had touched food; but they could not go up for their soup while their mates were in peril. They realised, however, that the settlement would be disturbed if no one came back, and it was proposed to send off the women. But neither Catherine nor Mouquette, nor even Lydie would move, nailed to the spot with a desire to know what had happened, and to help. Levaque then accepted the commission of announcing the landslip—a simple accident, which was being repaired. It was nearly four o'clock; in less than an hour the men had done a day's work; half the earth would have already been removed if more rocks had not slid from the roof. Maheu persisted with such energy that he refused, with a furious gesture, when another man approached to relieve him for a moment.

"Gently!" said Richomme at last, "we are getting near. We must not finish them off."

In fact the groaning was becoming more and more distinct. It was a continuous rattling which guided the workers; and now it seemed to be beneath their very picks. Suddenly it stopped.

In silence they all looked at one another, and shuddered as they felt the coldness of death pass in the darkness. They dug on, soaked in sweat, their muscles tense to breaking. They came upon a foot, and then began to remove the earth with their hands, freeing the limbs one by one. The head was not hurt. They turned their lamps on it, and Chicot's name went round. He was quite warm, with his spinal column broken by a rock.

"Wrap him up in a covering, and put him in a tram," ordered the Captain. "Now for the lad; look sharp."

Maheu gave the first blow, and an opening was made, communicating with the men who were clearing away the soil from the other side. They shouted out that they had just found Jeanlin, unconscious, with both legs broken, still breathing. It was the father who took up the little one in his arms, with clenched jaws constantly uttering, "My God!" to express his grief, while Catherine and the other women again began to shriek.

A procession was quickly formed. Bébert had taken away Bataille, who was harnessed to the trams. In the first lay Chicot's corpse, supported by Étienne; in the second, Maheu was seated with Jeanlin, still unconscious, on his knees, covered by a fragment of wool torn from the ventilation-door. They started at a walking-pace. On each tram was a lamp like a red star. Then behind followed the row of miners, some fifty shadows in single file. Now that they were overcome by fatigue, they trailed their feet, slipping in the mud with the mournful melancholy of a flock stricken by an epidemic. It took them nearly half-an-hour to reach the pit-eye. This procession beneath the earth, in the midst of deep darkness, seemed never to end through galleries which bifurcated and turned and unrolled.

At the pit-eye Richomme, who had gone on before, had ordered an empty cage to be reserved. Pierron immediately loaded the two trams. In the first Maheu remained with his wounded little one on his knees, while in the other Étienne kept Chicot's corpse between his arms to hold it in. When the men had piled themselves up in the other decks the cage rose. It took two minutes. The rain from the tubbing fell very cold and the men looked up towards the air impatient to see daylight.

Fortunately a trammer sent to Dr. Vanderhagen's had found him and brought him back. Jeanlin and the dead man were placed in the captain's room, where, from year's end to year's end, a large fire burnt. A row of buckets with warm water was ready for washing feet; and after having spread two mattresses on the floor the man and the child were placed on them. Maheu and Étienne alone entered. Outside, putters, miners and boys were running about, forming groups and talking in a low voice.

As soon as the doctor had glanced at Chicot:

"Done for! You can wash him."

Two overseers undressed and then washed with a sponge this corpse blackened with coal and still dirty with the sweat of work.

"Nothing wrong with the head," said the doctor again, kneeling on Jeanlin's mattress. "Nor the chest either. Ah! it's the legs which have given."

He himself undressed the child, unfastening the cap, taking off the jacket, drawing off the breeches and shirt with the skill of a nurse. And the poor little body appeared, as lean as an insect, stained with black dust and yellow earth, marbled by bloody patches. Nothing could be made out, and they had to wash him also. He seemed to grow leaner beneath the sponge, the flesh so pallid and transparent that one could see the bones. It was a pity to look on this last degeneration of a wretched race, this mere nothing that was suffering and half-crushed by the falling of the rocks. When he was clean they perceived the bruises on the thighs, two red patches on the white skin.

Jeanlin, awaking from his faint, moaned. Standing up at the foot of the mattress with hands hanging down, Maheu was looking at him and large tears rolled from his eyes.

"Eh, are you the father?" said the doctor, raising his eyes, "no need to cry then, you can see he is not dead. Help me instead."

He found two simple fractures. But the right leg gave him some anxiety, it would probably have to be cut off.

At this moment the engineer, Négrel, and Dansaert, who had been informed, came up with Richomme. The first listened to the captain's narrative with an exasperated air. He broke out: Always this cursed timbering! Had he not repeated a hundred times that they would leave their men down there! and those brutes who talked about going out on strike if they were forced to timber more solidly. The worst was that now the Company would have to pay for the broken pots. M. Hennebeau would be pleased!

"Who is it?" he asked of Dansaert, who was standing in silence before the corpse which was being wrapped up in a sheet.

"Chicot! one of our good workers," replied the chief captain. "He has three children. Poor chap!"

Dr. Vanderhagen ordered Jeanlin's immediate removal to his parents'. Six o'clock struck, twilight was already coming on, and they would do well to remove the corpse also; the engineer gave orders to harness the van and to bring a stretcher. The wounded child was placed on the stretcher while the mattress and the dead body were put into the van.

Some putters were still standing at the door talking with some miners who were waiting about to look on. When the captain's room opened there was silence in the group. A new procession was then formed, the van in front, then the stretcher, and then the train of people. They left the mine square and went slowly up the road to the settlement. The first November cold had denuded the immense plain; the night was now slowly burying it like a shroud fallen from the livid sky.

Étienne then in a low voice advised Maheu to send Catherine on to warn Maheude so as to soften the blow. The overwhelmed father, who was following the stretcher, agreed with a nod; and the young girl set out running, for they were now near. But the van, that gloomy well-known box, was already signalled. Women came out wildly on to the paths; three or four rushed about in anguish without their bonnets. Soon there were thirty of them, then fifty, all choking with the same terror. Then someone was dead? Who was it? The story told by Levaque, after first reassuring them, now exaggerated their nightmare: it was not one man, it was ten who had perished, and who were now being brought back in the van one by one.

Catherine found her mother agitated by a presentiment; and after hearing the first stammered words Maheude cried:

"The father's dead!"

The young girl protested in vain, speaking of Jeanlin. Without hearing her, Maheude had rushed forward. And on seeing the van, which was passing before the church, she grew faint and pale. The women at their doors, mute with terror, were stretching out their necks, while others followed, trembling as they wondered before whose house the procession would stop.

The vehicle passed; and behind it Maheude saw Maheu, who was accompanying the stretcher. Then, when they had placed the stretcher at her door and when she saw Jeanlin alive with his legs broken, there was so sudden a reaction in her that she choked with anger, stammering, without tears:

"Is this it? They cripple our little ones now! Both legs! My God! What do they want me to do with him?"

"Be still, then," said Dr. Vanderhagen, who had followed to attend to Jeanlin. "Would you rather he had remained below?"

But Maheude grew more furious, while Alzire, Lénore, and

Henri were crying around her. As she helped to carry up the wounded boy and to give the doctor what he needed, she cursed fate, and asked where she was to find money to feed invalids. The old man was not then enough, and now this rascal too had lost his legs! And she never ceased; while other cries, more heart-breaking lamentations, were heard from a neighbouring house: Chicot's wife and children were weeping over the body. It was now quite night, the exhausted miners were at last eating their soup, and the settlement had fallen into a melancholy silence, only disturbed by these loud outcries.

Three weeks passed. It was found possible to avoid amputation; Jeanlin kept both his legs, but he remained lame. On investigation the Company had resigned itself to giving a donation of fifty francs. It had also promised to find employment for the little invalid at the surface as soon as he was well. All the same their misery was aggravated, for the father had received such a shock that he was seriously ill with fever.

Since Thursday Maheu had been back at the pit and it was now Sunday. In the evening Étienne talked of the approaching date of the 1st of December, pre-occupied in wondering if the Company would execute its threat. They sat up till ten o'clock waiting for Catherine, who must have been delaying with Chaval. But she did not return. Maheude furiously bolted the door without a word. Étienne was long in going to sleep, restless at the thought of that empty bed in which Alzire occupied so little room.

Next morning she was still absent; and it was only in the afternoon, on returning from the pit, that the Maheus learnt that Chaval was keeping Catherine. He created such abominable scenes with her that she had decided to stay with him. To avoid reproaches he had suddenly left the Voreux and had been taken on at Jean-Bart, M. Deneulin's mine, and she had followed him as a putter. The new household still inhabited Montsou, at Piquette's.

Maheu at first talked of going to fight the man and of bringing his daughter back with a kick in the backside. Then he made a gesture of resignation: what was the good? It always turned out like that; one could not prevent a girl from sticking to a man when she wanted to. It was much better to wait quietly for the marriage. But Maheude did not take things so easily.

"Did I beat her when she took this Chaval?" she cried to Étienne, who listened in silence, very pale. "See now, tell me! you, who are a sensible man. We have left her free, haven't we? because, my God! they all come to it. Now, I was in the family-way when the father married me. But I didn't run away from my parents, and I should never have done so dirty a trick as to carry the money I earned to a man who had no want of it. Ah! it's disgusting, you know. People will leave off getting children!"

And as Étienne still replied only by nodding his head, she insisted:

"A girl who went out every evening where she wanted to! What has she got in her skin, then, not to be able to wait till I married her after she had helped to get us out of difficulties? Eh? it's natural, one has a daughter to work. But there! we have been too good, we ought not to let her go and amuse herself with a man. Give them an inch and they take an ell."

Alzire nodded approvingly. Lénore and Henri, overcome by this storm, cried quietly, while the mother now enumerated their misfortunes: first Zacharie who had to get married; then old Bonnemort who was there on his chair with his twisted feet; then Jeanlin who could not leave the room for ten days, with his badly-united bones; and now, as a last blow, this jade Catherine, who had gone away with a man! The whole family was breaking up. There was only the father left at the pit. How were they to live, seven persons without counting Estelle, on his three francs? They might as well jump into the canal in a band.

"It won't do any good to worry yourself," said Maheu in a low voice, "perhaps we have not got to the end."

Étienne, who was looking fixedly at the flags on the floor, raised his head, and murmured with eyes lost in a vision of the future:

"Ah! it is time! it is time!"

# *PART FOUR*

## CHAPTER I

On that Monday the Hennebeaus had invited the Grégoires and their daughter, Cécile, to lunch. They had formed their plans: on rising from table, Paul Négrel was to take the ladies to a mine, Saint Thomas, which had been luxuriously reinstalled. But this was only an amiable pretext; this party was an invention of Madame Hennebeau's to hasten the marriage of Cécile and Paul.

Suddenly, on this very Monday, at four o'clock in the morning, the strike broke out.[1] When, on the 1st of December, the Company had adopted the new wage system, the miners remained calm. At the end of the fortnight not one made the least protest on pay-day. Everybody, from the manager down to the last overseer, considered the tariff as accepted; and great was their surprise in the morning at this declaration of war, made with a tactical unity which seemed to indicate energetic leadership.

At five o'clock Dansaert woke M. Hennebeau to inform him that not a single man had gone down at the Voreux. The settlement of the Deux-Cent-Quarante, which he had passed through, was sleeping deeply, with closed windows and doors. And as soon as the manager had jumped out of bed, his eyes still swollen with sleep, he was overwhelmed. Every quarter of an hour messengers came in, and despatches fell on his desk as thick as hail. At first he hoped that the revolt was limited to the Voreux; but the news became more serious every minute. There was the Mirou, the Crèvecœur, the Madeleine, where only the grooms had appeared; the Victoire and Feutry-Cantel, the two best disciplined pits, where the men had been reduced by a third; Saint-Thomas alone numbered all its people, and seemed to be outside the movement. Up to nine o'clock he dictated despatches, telegraphing in all directions, to the prefect of Lille, to the directors of the Company, warning the authorities, and asking for orders. He had sent Négrel to go round the neighbouring pits to obtain precise information.

Suddenly M. Hennebeau recollected the lunch; and he was about to send the coachman to tell the Grégoires that the party had been put off, when a certain hesitation and lack of will stopped him—the man who in a few brief phrases had just made military preparations for a field of battle. He went up to Madame Hennebeau, whose hair had just been done by her lady's maid, in her dressing-room.

"Ah! they are on strike," she said quietly, when he had told her. "Well, what has that to do with us? We are not going to leave off eating, I suppose?"

And she was obstinate; it was vain to tell her that the lunch would be disturbed, and that the visit to Saint-Thomas could not take place. She found an answer to everything. Why lose a lunch that was already on the fire? And as to visiting the pit, they could give that up afterwards if the walk was really imprudent.

"Besides," she added, when the maid had gone out, "you know that I am anxious to receive these good people. This marriage ought to affect you more than the follies of your men. I want to have it, don't contradict me."

He looked at her, agitated by a slight trembling, and the hard firm face of the man of discipline expressed the secret grief of a wounded heart. She had remained with naked shoulders, already over-mature, but still imposing and desirable with the broad bust of a Ceres gilded by the Autumn. For a moment he felt a brutal desire to seize her, and to roll his head between the breasts she was exposing in this warm room, which exhibited the private luxury of a sensual woman and which had about it an irritating perfume of musk, but he recoiled; for ten years they had occupied separate rooms.

"Good!" he said, leaving her. "Do not make any alterations."

M. Hennebeau had been born in the Ardennes. In his early life he had undergone the hardships of a poor boy thrown as an orphan on the Paris streets. After having painfully followed the courses of the École des Mines, at the age of twenty-four he had gone to the Grand' Combe as engineer to the Sainte-Barbe mine. Three years later he became divisional engineer in the Pas-de-Calais, at the Marles mines. It was there that he married, wedding, by one of those strokes of fortune which are the rule among the Corps des Mines, the daughter of the rich owner of a spinning factory at Arras. For fifteen years they lived in the same small provincial town, and no event broke the monotony of existence, not even the birth of a child. An increasing irritation detached Madame Hennebeau, who had been brought up to respect money, and was disdainful of this husband who gained a small salary with such difficulty, and who enabled her to gratify none of the satisfactions of vanity which she had dreamed of at school. He was a man of strict honesty, who never speculated, but stood at his post like a soldier. The lack of harmony had only increased, aggravated by one of those curious misunderstandings of the flesh which freeze the most ardent; he adored his wife, she had the sensuality of a greedy blonde, and already they slept apart, ill at ease and wounded. From that time she had a lover of whom he was ignorant. At last he left the Pas-de-Calais to occupy a situation in an office at Paris, with the idea that she would be grateful to him. But Paris only completed their separation, that Paris which she had desired since her first doll, and where she washed away her provincialism in a week, becoming a woman of fashion at once, and throwing herself into all the luxurious follies of the period. The ten years which she spent there were filled by a great passion, a public intrigue with a man whose desertion nearly killed her. This time the husband had not been able to keep his ignorance, and after some abominable scenes he resigned himself, disarmed by the quiet unconsciousness of this woman who took her happiness where she found it. It was after the rupture, and when he saw that she was ill with grief, that he had accepted the management of the Montsou mines, still hoping also that she would be changed down there in that desolate black country.

The Hennebeaus, since they had lived at Montsou, returned to the irritated boredom of their early marriage days. At first she seemed consoled by the great quiet, soothed by the flat monotony of the immense plain; she buried herself in it as a woman who has done with the world; she affected a dead heart, so detached from life that she did not even mind growing stout. Then, beneath this indifference a final fever declared itself, the need to live once more, and she deluded herself for six months by organising and furnishing to her taste the little villa belonging to the management. She said it was frightful, and filled it with upholstery, bric-à-brac, and all sorts of artistic luxuries which were talked of as far as Lille. Now the country exasperated her, those stupid fields spread out to infinity, those eternal black roads without a tree, swarming with a horrid population which disgusted and frightened her. Complaints of exile began; she accused her husband of having sacrificed her to a salary of forty thousand francs, a trifle which hardly sufficed to keep the house up. Why could he not imitate others, demand a part for himself, obtain shares, succeed in something at last? And she insisted with the cruelty of an heiress who has brought her own fortune. He, always restrained, and taking refuge in the deceptive coldness of a man of business, was torn by desire for this creature, one of those late desires which are so violent and which increase with age. He had never possessed her as a lover; he was haunted by a continual image, to have her once to himself as she had given herself to another. Every morning he dreamed of winning her in the evening; then, when she looked at him with her cold eyes, and when he felt that everything within her denied itself to him, he even avoided touching her hand. It was a suffering without possible cure, hidden beneath the stiffness of his attitude, the suffering of a tender nature in secret anguish at the lack of domestic happiness. At the end of six months, when the house, being definitely furnished, no longer occupied Madame Hennebeau, she fell into the languor of boredom, a victim who was being killed by exile, and who said that she was glad to die of it.

Just then Paul Négrel landed at Montsou. His mother, the widow of a Provence captain, living at Avignon on a slender income, had had to content herself with bread and water to enable him to reach the École Polytechnique. He had come out in a low rank, and his uncle, M. Hennebeau, had enabled him to leave by offering to take him as engineer at the Voreux. From that time he was treated as one of the family; he even had his room there, his meals there, lived there, and was thus enabled to send to his mother half his salary of three thousand francs. To disguise this kindness M. Hennebeau spoke of the embarrassment to a young man of setting up a household in one of those little villas reserved for the mine engineers. Madame Hennebeau had at once taken the part of a good aunt, treating her nephew with familiarity and watching over his comfort. During the first months, especially, she exhibited an overwhelming maternity with her advice regarding the smallest subjects. But she remained a woman, however, and slid into personal confidences. This lad, so young and so practical, with his unscrupulous intelligence, professing a philosopher's theory of love, amused her with the vivacity of the pessimism which had sharpened his thin face and pointed nose. One evening he naturally found himself in her arms, and she seemed to give herself up out of kindness, while saying to him that she had no heart left, and wished only to be his friend. In fact, she was not jealous; she joked him about the putters, whom he declared to be abominable, and she almost sulked because he had no young man's pranks to narrate to her. Then she was carried away by the idea of getting him married; she dreamed of sacrificing herself and of finding a rich girl for him. Their relations continued, a plaything for recreation, in which she felt the last tenderness of a lazy woman who had done with the world.

Two years had passed by. One night M. Hennebeau had a suspicion when he heard naked feet passing his door. But this new adventure revolted him, in his own house, between this mother and this son! And besides, on the following day his wife spoke to him about the choice of Cécile Grégoire which she had made for her nephew. She occupied herself over this marriage with such ardour that he blushed at his own monstrous imagination. He only felt gratitude towards the young man who, since his arrival, had made the house less melancholy.

As he came down from the dressing-room, M. Hennebeau found that Paul, who had just returned, was in the vestibule. He seemed to be quite amused by the story of this strike.

"Well?" asked his uncle.

"Well, I've been round the settlements. They seem to be quite sensible in there. I think they will first send you a deputation."

But at that moment Madame Hennebeau's voice called from the first storey.

"Is that you, Paul? Come up, then, and tell me the news. How queer they are to make such a fuss, these people who are so happy!"

And the manager had to renounce further information, since his wife had taken his messenger. He returned and sat before his desk, on which a new packet of despatches was placed.

At eleven o'clock the Grégoires arrived, and were astonished when Hippolyte, the footman, who was placed as sentinel, hustled them in after an anxious glance at the two ends of the road. The drawing-room curtains were drawn, and they were taken at once into the study, where M. Hennebeau apologised for their reception; but the drawing-room looked over the street and it was undesirable to seem to offer provocations.

"What! you don't know?" he went on, seeing their surprise.

M. Grégoire, when he heard that the strike had at last broken out, shrugged his shoulders in his placid way. Bah! it would be nothing, the people were honest. With a movement of her chin, Madame Grégoire approved his confidence in the everlasting resignation of the colliers; while Cécile, who was very cheerful that day, feeling that she looked well in her capucine cloth costume, smiled at the word "strike," which reminded her of visits to the settlements and the distribution of charities.

Madame Hennebeau now appeared in black silk, followed by Négrel.

"Ah! isn't it annoying!" she said, at the door. "As if they couldn't wait, those men! You know that Paul refuses to take us to Saint-Thomas."

"We can stay here," said M. Grégoire, obligingly. "We shall be quite pleased."

Paul had contented himself by formally saluting Cécile and her mother. Angry at this lack of demonstrativeness, his aunt sent him with a look to the young girl; and when she heard them laughing together she enveloped them in a maternal glance.

M. Hennebeau, however, finished reading his despatches and prepared a few replies. They talked near him; his wife explained that she had not paid attention to this study, which, in fact, retained its faded old red paper, its heavy mahogany furniture, its cardboard boxes, scratched by use. Three-quarters of an hour passed and they were about to seat themselves at table when the footman announced M. Deneulin. He entered in an excited way and bowed to Madame Hennebeau.

"Ah! you here!" he said, seeing the Grégoires.

And he quickly spoke to the manager:

"It has come, then? I've just heard of it through my engineer. With me, all the men went down this morning. But the thing may spread. I'm not at all at rest. How is it with you?"

He had arrived on horseback, and his anxiety betrayed itself in his loud speech and emphatic gesture, which made him resemble a retired cavalry officer.

M. Hennebeau was beginning to inform him regarding the precise situation, when Hippolyte opened the dining-room door. Then he interrupted himself to say:

"Lunch with us. I will tell you more at dessert."

"Yes, as you please," replied Deneulin, so full of his thoughts that he accepted without ceremony.

He was, however, conscious of his impoliteness and turned towards Madame Hennebeau with apologies. She was very charming however. When she had had a seventh plate laid she placed her guests: Madame Grégoire and Cécile by her husband, then M. Grégoire and Deneulin at her own right and left; then Paul, whom she put between the young girl and her father. As they attacked the *hors-d'œuvre* she said, with a smile:

"You must excuse me; I wanted to give you oysters. On Monday, you know, there was an arrival of Ostend oysters at Marchiennes, and I meant to send the cook with the carriage. But she was afraid of being stoned——"

They all interrupted her with a great burst of gaiety. They thought the story very funny.

"Hush!" said M. Hennebeau, vexed, looking at the windows, through which the road could be seen. "We need not tell the whole country that we have company this morning."

"Well, here is a slice of sausage which they shan't have," M. Grégoire declared.

The laughter began again, but with greater restraint. Each guest made himself comfortable, in this room upholstered with Flemish tapestry and furnished with old oak chests. The silver shone behind the panes of the sideboards; and polished surfaces of red copper reflected a palm and an aspidistra growing in majolica pots. Outside, the December day was frozen by a keen north-east wind. But not a breath of it entered; a greenhouse warmth developed the delicate odour of the pineapple, which was cut in a crystal bowl.

"Suppose we were to draw the curtains," proposed Négrel, who was amused at the idea of frightening the Grégoires.

The housemaid, who was helping the footman, treated this as an order and went and closed one of the curtains. This led to interminable jokes: not a glass or a plate could be put down without precaution; every dish was hailed as a waif escaped from the pillage in a conquered town; and behind this forced gaiety there was a certain fear which betrayed itself in involuntary glances towards the road, as though a band of starvelings were watching the table from outside.

After the jumbled eggs with truffles, trout came on. The conversation then turned to the industrial crisis, which had become aggravated during the last eighteen months.

"It was inevitable," said Deneulin, "the excessive prosperity of recent years was bound to bring us to it. Think of the enormous capital which has been sunk, the railways, harbours, and canals, all the money buried in the maddest speculations. Among us alone sugar works have been set up as if the department could furnish three beetroot harvests. Good heavens! and to-day money is scarce, and we have to wait to catch up the interest of the expended millions; so there is a mortal congestion and a final stagnation of business."

M. Hennebeau disputed this theory, but he agreed that the fortunate years had spoilt the men.

"When I think," he exclaimed, "that these chaps in our pits used to gain six francs a day, double what they gain now! And they lived well, too, and acquired luxurious tastes. To-day, naturally, it seems hard to them to go back to their old frugality."

"Monsieur Grégoire," interrupted Madame Hennebeau, "let me persuade you, a little more trout. They are delicious, are they not?"

The manager went on:

"But, as a matter of fact, is it our fault? We, too, are cruelly struck. Since the factories have closed, one by one, we have had a deuce of a difficulty getting rid of our stock; and in face of the growing reduction in demand we have been forced to lower our net prices. It is just this that the men won't understand."

There was silence. The footman presented roast partridge, while the housemaid began to pour out Chambertin to the guests.

"There has been a famine in India," said Deneulin in a low voice, as though he were speaking to himself. "America, by ceasing to order iron, has struck a rough blow at our furnaces. Everything holds together; a distant shock is enough to disturb the world. And the Empire, which was so proud of this hot fever of industry!"

He attacked his partridge wing. Then, raising his voice:

"The worst is that to lower the net prices we ought logically to produce more; otherwise the reduction bears on wages, and the worker is right in saying that he has to pay the damage."

This confession, the outcome of his frankness, raised a discussion. The ladies were not at all interested. Besides, all were occupied with their plates, in the first zest of appetite. When the footman came back he seemed about to speak, then he hesitated.

"What is it?" asked M. Hennebeau. "If there are letters, give them to me. I am expecting replies."

"No, sir. It is Monsieur Dansaert, who is in the porch. But he doesn't wish to disturb you."

The manager excused himself, and had the head captain brought in. The latter stood upright, a few paces from the table, while all turned to see him, swollen and out of breath with the news he was bringing. The settlements were quiet; only it was now decided to send a deputation. It would, perhaps, be there in a few minutes.

"Very well; thank you," said M. Hennebeau. "I want a report morning and evening, you understand."

And as soon as Dansaert had gone, they began to joke again, and hastened to attack the Russian salad, declaring that not a moment was to be lost if they wished to finish it. The mirth was unbounded when Négrel, having asked the housemaid for bread, she replied, "Yes, sir," in a voice as low and terrified as if she had behind her a troop ready for murder and rape.

"You may speak," said Madame Hennebeau complacently. "They are not here yet."

The manager, who now received a packet of letters and despatches, wished to read one of his letters aloud. It was from Pierron, who, in respectful phrases, gave notice that he was obliged to go out on strike with his comrades, in order to avoid ill-treatment; and he added that he had not even been able to avoid taking part in the deputation, although he blamed that step.

"So much for liberty of work!" exclaimed M. Hennebeau.

Then they returned to the strike, and asked him his opinion.

"Oh!" he replied, "we have had them before. It will be a week, or, at most, a fortnight, of idleness, as it was last time. They will go and wallow in the public-houses, and then, when they are hungry, they will go back to the pits."

Deneulin shook his head:

"I'm not so satisfied; this time they appear to be better organised. Have they not a Provident Fund?"

"Yes, scarcely three thousand francs. What do you think they can do with that? I suspect a man called Étienne Lantier of being their leader. He is a good workman; it would vex me to have to give him his certificate back, as we did of old to the famous Rasseneur, who still poisons the Voreux with his ideas and his beer. No matter, in a week half the men will have gone down, and in a fortnight the ten thousand will be below."

He was convinced. His only anxiety was concerning his own possible disgrace should the directors put the responsibility of the strike on him. For some time he had felt that he was diminishing in favour. So leaving the spoonful of Russian salad which he had taken, he read over again the despatches received from Paris, endeavouring to penetrate every word. His guests excused him; the meal was becoming a military lunch, eaten on the field of battle before the first shots were fired.

The ladies then joined in the conversation. Madame Grégoire expressed pity for the poor people who would suffer from hunger; and Cécile was already making plans for distributing gifts of bread and meat. But Madame Hennebeau was astonished at hearing of the wretchedness of the Montsou colliers.

Were they not very fortunate? People who were lodged and warmed and cared for at the expense of the Company! In her indifference for the herd, she only knew the lessons she had learnt, and with which she had surprised the Parisians who came for a visit. She believed them at last, and was indignant at the ingratitude of the people.

Négrel, meanwhile, continued to frighten M. Grégoire. Cécile did not displease him, and he was quite willing to marry her, to be agreeable to his aunt, but he showed no amorous fever; like a youth of experience, who, he said, was not easily carried away now. He professed to be a Republican, which did not prevent him from treating his men with extreme severity, or from making fun of them in the company of the ladies.

"Nor have I my uncle's optimism, either," he continued. "I fear there will be serious disturbances. So I should advise you, Monsieur Grégoire, to lock up Piolaine. They may pillage you."

Just then, still retaining the smile which illuminated his good-natured face, M. Grégoire was going beyond his wife in paternal sentiments with regard to the miners.

"Pillage me!" he cried, stupefied. "And why pillage me?"

"Are you not a shareholder in Montsou? You do nothing; you live on the work of others. In fact you are an infamous capitalist, and that is enough. You may be sure that if the revolution triumphs, it will force you to restore your fortune as stolen money."

At once he lost his child-like tranquillity, his serene unconsciousness. He stammered:

"Stolen money, my fortune! Did not my grandfather gain, and hardly, too, the sum originally invested? Have we not run all the risks of the enterprise, and do I to-day make a bad use of my income?"

Madame Hennebeau, alarmed at seeing the mother and daughter also white with fear, hastened to intervene, saying:

"Paul is joking, my dear sir."

But M. Grégoire was carried out of himself. As the servant was passing round the crabs he took three of them without knowing what he was doing and began to break their claws with his teeth.

"Ah! I don't say but what there are shareholders who abuse their position. For instance, I have been told that ministers have received shares from Montsou for services rendered to the Company. It is like a nobleman whom I will not name, a duke, the biggest of our shareholders, whose life is a scandal of prodigality, millions thrown into the street on women, feasting, and useless luxury. But we who live quietly, like good citizens as we are, who do not speculate, who are content to live wholesomely on what we have, giving a part to the poor! Come now! your men must be mere brigands if they came and stole a pin from us!"

Négrel himself had to calm him, though amused at his anger. The crabs were still going round; the little crackling sound of their carapaces could be heard, while the conversation turned to politics. M. Grégoire, in spite of everything and though still trembling, called himself a Liberal and regretted Louis Philippe. As for Deneulin, he was for a strong Government; he declared that the Emperor was gliding down the slope of dangerous concessions.

"Remember '89," he said. "It was the nobility who made the Revolution possible, by their complicity and its taste for philosophic novelties. Very well! the middle class to-day are playing the same silly game with their furious Liberalism, their rage for destruction, their flattery of the people. Yes, yes, you are sharpening the teeth of the monster that will devour us. It will devour us, rest assured!"

The ladies bid him be silent, and tried to change the conversation by asking him news of his daughters. Lucie was at Marchiennes, where she was singing with a friend; Jeanne was painting an old beggar's head. But he said these things in a distracted way; he constantly looked at the manager, who was absorbed in the reading of his despatches and forgetful of his guests. Behind those thin leaves he felt Paris and the directors' orders, which would decide the strike. At last he could not help yielding to his pre-occupation.

"Well, what are you going to do?" he asked suddenly.

M. Hennebeau started; then turned off the question with a vague phrase.

"We shall see."

"No doubt you are solidly placed, you can wait," Deneulin began to think aloud. "But as for me, I shall be done for if the strike reaches Vandame. I shall have re-installed Jean-Bart in vain; with a single pit, I can only get along by constant production. Ah! I am not in a very pleasant situation, I can assure you!"

This involuntary confession seemed to strike M. Hennebeau. He listened and a plan formed within him: in case the strike turned out badly, why not utilise it by letting things run down until his neighbour was ruined, and then buy up his concession at a low price? That would be the surest way of regaining the good graces of the directors, who for years had dreamed of possessing Vandame.

"If Jean-Bart bothers you as much as that," said he, laughing, "why don't you give it up to us?"

But Deneulin was already regretting his complaints. He exclaimed:

"Never, never!"

They were amused at his vigour and had already forgotten the strike by the time the dessert appeared. An apple-Charlotte meringue was overwhelmed with praise. Afterwards the ladies discussed a recipe with respect to the pineapple which was declared equally exquisite. The grapes and pears completed their happy abandonment at the end of this copious lunch. All talked excitedly at the same time, while the servant poured out Rhine wine to replace champagne which was looked upon as commonplace.

And the marriage of Paul and Cécile certainly made a forward step in the sympathy produced by dessert. His aunt had thrown such urgent looks in his direction, that the young man showed himself very amiable, and in his knowing way reconquered the Grégoires, who had been cast down by his stories of pillage. For a moment M. Hennebeau, seeing the close understanding between his wife and his nephew, felt that abominable suspicion again revive, as if in this exchange of looks he had surprised a physical contact. But again the idea of the marriage, made here before his face, reassured him.

Hippolyte was serving the coffee when the housemaid entered in a fright.

"Sir, sir, they are here!"

It was the delegates. Doors banged; a breath of terror was passing through the neighbouring rooms.

"Take them into the drawing room," said M. Hennebeau.

Around the table the guests were looking at one another with restless vacillation. There was silence. Then they tried to resume their jokes: they pretended to put the rest of the sugar in their pockets, and talked of hiding the plate. But the manager remained grave; and the laughter fell and their voices sank to a whisper, while the heavy feet of the delegates who were being shown in tramped over the carpet of the next room.

Madame Hennebeau said to her husband, lowering her voice:

"I hope you will drink your coffee."

"Certainly," he replied. "Let them wait."

He was nervous, listening to every sound, though apparently occupied with his cup.

Paul and Cécile got up, and he made her venture an eye to the keyhole. They were stifling their laughter and talking in a low voice.

"Do you see them?"

"Yes, I see a big man and two small ones behind."

"Haven't they ugly faces?"

"Not at all; they are very nice."

Suddenly M. Hennebeau left his chair, saying the coffee was too hot and he would drink it afterwards. As he went out he placed a finger to his mouth to recommend prudence. They all sat down again and remained at table in silence, no longer daring to move, listening from afar with intent ears jarred by these coarse male voices.

## CHAPTER II

THE PREVIOUS DAY, AT a meeting held at Rasseneur's, Étienne and some comrades had chosen the delegates who were to proceed on the following day to the manager's house. When, in the evening, Maheude learnt that her man was one of them, she was in despair, and asked him if he wanted them to be thrown on to the street. Maheu himself had agreed with reluctance. Both of them, when the moment of action came, in spite of the injustice of their wretchedness fell back on to the resignation of their race, trembling before the morrow, preferring still to bend their backs to the yoke. In the management of affairs he usually gave way to his wife whose advice was sound. This time, however, he grew angry at last, all the more so since he secretly shared her fears.

"Just leave me alone, will you?" he said, going to bed and turning his back. "A fine thing to leave the mates now! I'm doing my duty."

She went to bed in her turn. Neither of them spoke. Then, after a long silence, she replied:

"You're right; go. Only, poor old man, we are done for."

Mid-day struck while they were at lunch, for the rendezvous was at one o'clock at the Avantage, from which they were to go together to M. Hennebeau's. They were eating potatoes. As there was only a small morsel of butter left, no one touched it. They would have bread and butter in the evening.

"You know that we reckon on you to speak," said Étienne suddenly to Maheu.

The latter was so overcome that he was silent from emotion.

"No, no! that's too much," cried Maheude. "I'm quite willing he should go there, but I don't allow him to go at the head. Why him, more than anyone else?"

Then Étienne, with his fiery eloquence, began to explain. Maheu was the best worker in the pit, the most liked, and the most respected; whose good sense was always spoken of. In his mouth the miners' claims would carry decisive weight. At first Étienne had arranged to speak, but he had been at Montsou for too short a time. One who belonged to the country would be better listened to. In fact, the comrades were confiding their interests to the most worthy; he could not refuse, it would be cowardly.

Maheude made a gesture of despair.

"Go, go, my man; go and be killed for the others. I'm willing, after all!"

"But I could never do it," stammered Maheu. "I should do something stupid."

Étienne, glad to have persuaded him, struck him on the shoulder.

"Say what you feel, and you won't go wrong."

Father Bonnemort, whose legs were now less swollen, was listening with his mouth full, shaking his head. There was silence. When potatoes were being eaten, the children were subdued and behaved well. Then, having swallowed his mouthful, the old man muttered slowly:

"You can say what you like, and it will be all the same as if you said nothing. Ah! I've seen these affairs, I've seen them! Forty years ago they kicked us out of the manager's house, and with sabres too! Now they may receive you, perhaps, but they won't answer you any more than that wall. Lord! they have money, why should they care?"

There was silence again; Maheu and Étienne rose, and left the family in gloom before the empty plates. On going out they called for Pierron and Levaque, and then all four went to Rasseneur's, where the delegates from the neighbouring settlements were arriving in little groups. When the twenty members of the deputation had assembled there, they settled on the terms which they opposed to the Company's, and then set out for Montsou. The keen north-east wind was sweeping the street. As they arrived, it struck two.

At first the servant told them to wait, and shut the door on them; then, when he came back, he introduced them into the drawing-room, and opened the curtains. A soft daylight entered, sifted through the lace. And the miners, when left alone, in their embarrassment did not dare to sit; all of them very clean, dressed in cloth, shaven that morning, with their yellow hair and moustaches. They twisted their caps between their fingers, and looked sideways at the furniture, which was in every variety of style, as a result of the taste for the old-fashioned: Henri II easy chairs, Louis XV chairs, an Italian cabinet of the 17th century, a Spanish contador of the 15th century, with an altar-front serving as a chimney-piece, and ancient chasuble trimmings re-applied to the curtains. This old gold and these old silks, with their tawny tones, all this luxurious church furniture, had overwhelmed them with respectful discomfort. The Eastern carpets with their long wool seemed to bind their feet. But what especially suffocated them was the heat, heat like that of a hot-air stove, which surprised them as they felt it with cheeks frozen from the wind of the road. Five minutes passed by and their awkwardness increased in the comfort of this rich room so pleasantly warm. At last M. Hennebeau entered, buttoned up in a military manner and wearing on his frock- coat the correct little knot of his decoration. He spoke first.

"Ah! here you are! You are in rebellion, it seems."

He interrupted himself to add with polite stiffness:

"Sit down, I desire nothing better than to talk things over."

The miners turned round looking for seats. A few of them ventured to place themselves on chairs, while the others, disturbed by the embroidered silks, preferred to remain standing.

There was a period of silence. M. Hennebeau, who had drawn his easy chair up to the fireplace, was rapidly looking them over and endeavouring to recall their faces. He had recognised Pierron, who was hidden in the last row, and his eyes rested on Étienne who was seated in front of him.

"Well," he asked, "what have you to say to me?"

He had expected to hear the young man speak and he was so surprised to see Maheu come forward that he could not avoid adding again:

"What! you, a good workman who have always been so sensible, one of the old Montsou people whose family has worked in the mine since the first stroke of the axe! Ah! it's a pity, I'm sorry that you are at the head of the discontented."

Maheu listened with his eyes down. Then he began, at first in a low and hesitating voice.

"It is just because I am a quiet man, sir, whom no one has anything against, that my mates have chosen me. That ought to show you that it isn't just a rebellion of blusterers, badly-disposed men who want to create disorder. We only want justice, we are tired of starving, and it seems to us that the time has come when things ought to be arranged so that we can at least have bread every day."

His voice grew stronger. He lifted his eyes and went on while looking at the manager.

"You know quite well that we cannot agree to your new system. They accuse us of bad timbering. It's true we don't give the necessary time to the work. But if we gave it, our day's work would be still smaller, and as it doesn't give us enough food at present, that would mean the end of everything, the sweep of the clout that would wipe off all your men. Pay us more and we will timber better, we will give the necessary hours to the timbering instead of putting all our strength into the picking, which is the only work that pays. There's no other arrangement possible; if the work is to be done it must be paid for. And what have you invented instead? A thing which we can't get into our heads, don't you see? You lower the price of the tram and then you pretend to make up for it by paying for the timbering separately. If that was true we should be robbed all the same, for the timbering would still take us more time. But what makes us mad is that it isn't true; the Company compensates nothing at all, it simply puts two centimes a tram into its pocket, that's all."

"Yes, yes, that's it," murmured the other deputies, noticing M. Hennebeau make a violent movement as if to interrupt.

But Maheu cut short the manager's speech. Now that he had set out his words came by themselves. At times he listened to himself with surprise as though a stranger were speaking within him.[2] It was the things amassed within his breast, things he did not even know were there, and which came out in an expansion of his heart. He described the wretchedness that was common to all of them, the hard toil, the brutal life, the wife and little ones crying from hunger in the house. He quoted the recent disastrous payments, the absurd fortnightly wages, eaten up by fines and rest days and brought back to their families in tears. Was it resolved to destroy them?

"Then, sir," he concluded, "we have come to tell you that if we've got to starve we would rather starve doing nothing. It will be a little less trouble. We have left the pits and we don't go down again unless the Company agrees to our terms. The Company wants to lower the price of the tram and to pay for the timbering separately. We ask for things to be left as they were, and we also ask for five centimes more the tram. Now it is for you to see if you are on the side of justice and work."

Voices rose among the miners.

"That's it—he has said what we all feel—we only ask what's reason."

Others, without speaking, showed their approval by nodding their heads. The luxurious room had disappeared, with its gold and its embroideries, its mysterious piling up of ancient things; and they no longer even felt the carpet which they crushed beneath their heavy boots.

"Let me reply, then," at last exclaimed M. Hennebeau, who was growing angry. "First of all, it is not true that the Company gains two centimes the tram. Let us look at the figures."

A confused discussion followed. The manager, trying to divide them, appealed to Pierron, who hid himself, stammering. Levaque, on the contrary, was at the head of the more aggressive, muddling up things and affirming facts of which he was ignorant. The loud murmurs of their voices were stifled beneath the hangings in the hothouse atmosphere.

"If you all talk at the same time," said M. Hennebeau, "we shall never come to an understanding."

He had regained his calmness again, the rough politeness, without bitterness, of an agent who has received his instructions, and means that they shall be respected. From the first word he never took his eye off Étienne, and manœuvred to draw the young man out of his obstinate silence. Leaving the discussion about the two centimes, he suddenly enlarged the question:

"No, acknowledge the truth: you are yielding to abominable incitations. It is a plague which is now blowing over the workers everywhere, and corrupting the best. Oh! I have no need for anyone to confess. I can see well that you have been changed, you who used to be so quiet. Is it not so? You have been promised more butter than bread, and you have been told that now your turn has come to be masters. In fact, you have been enrolled in that famous International, that army of brigands who dream of destroying society."

Then Étienne interrupted him.

"You are mistaken, sir. Not a single Montsou collier has yet enrolled. But if they are driven to it, all the pits will enroll themselves. That depends on the Company."

From that moment the struggle went on between M. Hennebeau and Étienne as though the other miners were no longer there.

"The Company is a Providence for the men, and you are wrong to threaten it. This year it has spent three hundred thousand francs in building settlements which only return two per cent., and I say nothing of the pensions which it pays, nor of the coals and medicines which it gives. You who seem to be intelligent, and who will become in a few months one of our most skilful workmen, would it not be better if you were to spread these truths, rather than to ruin yourself by associating with people of bad reputation? Yes, I mean Rasseneur, whom we had to turn off in order to save our pits from socialistic corruption. You are constantly seen with him, and it is certainly he who has induced you to form this Provident Fund, which we would willingly tolerate if it were merely a means of saving, but which we feel to be a weapon turned against us, a reserve fund to pay the expenses of the war. And in this connection I ought to add that the Company means to control that fund."

Étienne allowed him to continue, fixing his eyes on him, while a slight nervous quiver moved his lips. He smiled at the last remark, and simply replied:

"Then that is a new demand, for until now, sir, you have neglected to claim that control. Unfortunately, we wish the Company to occupy itself less with us, and instead of playing the part of Providence to be merely just with us, giving us our due, the profits which it appropriates. Is it honest, whenever a crisis comes, to leave the workers to die with hunger in order to save the shareholders' dividends? Whatever you may say, sir, the new system is a disguised reduction of wages, and that is what we are rebelling against, for if the Company wants to economise it acts very badly by only economising on the men."

"Ah! there we are!" cried M. Hennebeau. "I was expecting that—the accusation of starving the people and living by their sweat. How can you talk such folly, you who ought to know the enormous risks which capital runs in industry—in the mines, for example? A well-equipped pit to-day costs from fifteen hundred thousand francs to two millions; and it is difficult enough to get a moderate interest on the vast sum that is thus swallowed. Nearly half the mining companies in France are bankrupt. Besides, it is stupid to accuse those who succeed of cruelty. When their workers suffer, they suffer themselves. Can you believe that the Company has not as much to lose as you have in the present crisis? It does not govern wages; it obeys competition under pain of ruin. Look to the facts, and not to it. But you don't wish to hear, you don't wish to understand."

"Yes," said the young man, "we understand very well that our lot will never be bettered as long as things go on as they are going; and that is the reason why some day or another the workers will end by arranging that things shall go differently."

This sentence, so moderate in form, was pronounced in a low voice, but with such conviction, tremulous in its menace, that a deep silence followed. A certain constraint, a breath of fear passed through the pensive drawing-room. The other delegates, though scarcely understanding, felt that their comrade had been demanding their share of this comfort; and they began again to cast side-long looks over the warm hangings, the comfortable seats, all this luxury of which the least nick-nack would have bought them soup for a month.

At last M. Hennebeau, who had remained thoughtful, rose as a sign for them to depart. All imitated him. Étienne had lightly pushed Maheu's elbow, and the latter, his tongue once more thick and awkward, again spoke.

"Then, sir, that is all that you reply? We must tell the others that you reject our terms."

"I, my good fellow!" exclaimed the manager, "I reject nothing. I am paid just as you are. I have no more power in the matter than the smallest of your trammers. I receive my orders, and my only duty is to see that they are executed. I have told you what I thought I ought to tell you, but I have nothing to decide. You have brought me your demands. I will make them known to the directors, then I will tell you their reply."

He spoke with the correct air of a high official avoiding any passionate interest in the matter, with the courteous dryness of a simple instrument of authority. And the miners now looked at him with distrust, asking themselves what interest he might have in lying, and what he would get by thus putting himself between them and the real masters. A schemer, perhaps, this man who was paid like a worker, and who lived so well!

Étienne ventured to intervene again.

"You see, sir, how unfortunate it is that we cannot plead our cause in person. We could explain many things, and bring forward many reasons of which you could know nothing, if we only knew where we ought to go."

M. Hennebeau was not at all angry. He even smiled.

"Ah! it gets complicated as soon as you have no confidence in me; you will have to go over there."

The delegates had followed the vague gesture of his hand towards one of the windows. Where was it, over there? Paris, no doubt. But they did not know exactly; it seemed to fall back into a terrible distance, in an inaccessible religious country, where an unknown god sat on his throne crouching down at the bottom of his tabernacle. They would never see him; they only felt him as a force far off, which weighed on the ten thousand colliers of Montsou. And when the director spoke he had that hidden force behind him delivering oracles.

They were overwhelmed with discouragement; Étienne himself signified by a shrug of the shoulders that it would be best to go; while M. Hennebeau touched Maheu's arm in a friendly way and asked after Jeanlin.

"That is a severe lesson now, and it is you who defend bad timbering. You must reflect, my friends; you must realise that a strike would be a disaster for everybody. Before a week you would die of hunger. What would you do? I count on your good sense, anyhow; and I am convinced that you will go down on Monday, at the latest."

They all left, going out of the drawing-room with the tramping of a flock and rounded backs, without replying a word to this hope for submission. The manager, who accompanied them, was obliged to continue the conversation. The Company, on the one side, had its new tariff; the workers, on the other, their demand for an increase of five centimes the tram. In order that they might have no illusions, he warned them that their terms would certainly be rejected by the directors.

"Reflect before committing any follies," he repeated, disturbed at their silence.

In the porch Pierron bowed very low, while Levaque pretended to adjust his cap. Maheu was trying to find something to say before leaving, when Étienne again touched his elbow. And they all left in the midst of this threatening silence. The door closed with a loud bang.

When M. Hennebeau re-entered the dining-room he found his guests motionless and silent before the liqueurs. In two words he told his story to Deneulin, whose face grew still more gloomy. Then, as he drank his cold coffee, they tried to speak of other things. But the Grégoires themselves returned to the subject of the strike, expressing their astonishment that no laws existed to prevent workmen from leaving their work. Paul reassured Cécile, stating that they were expecting the police.

At last Madame Hennebeau called the servant.

"Hippolyte, before we go into the drawing-room just open the windows and let in a little air."

## CHAPTER III

FIFTEEN DAYS HAD PASSED, and on the Monday of the third week the lists sent up to the managers showed a fresh decrease in the number of the miners who had gone down. It was expected that on that morning work would be resumed, but the obstinacy of the directors in not yielding exasperated the miners. The Voreux, Crèvecœur, Mirou, and Madeleine were not the only pits resting; at the Victoire and at Feutry-Cantel only about a quarter of the men had gone down; even Saint-Thomas was effected. The strike was gradually becoming general.

At the Voreux a heavy silence hung over the pit mouth. It was a dead workshop, the great empty abandoned Yards where work was sleeping. In the grey December sky, along the high footbridges three or four empty trains bore witness to the mute sadness of things. Underneath, between the slender posts of the platforms, the stock of coal was diminishing, leaving the earth bare and black; while the supplies of wood were mouldering beneath the rain. At the quay on the canal a barge was moored, half-laden, lying drowsily in the murky water; and on the deserted pit-bank in which the decomposed sulphates smoked in spite of the rain, a melancholy cart showed its shafts erect. But the buildings especially were growing torpid, the screening shed with closed shutters, the steeple in which the rumbling of the receiving room no more arose, and the machine room grown cold, and the giant chimney too large for the occasional smoke. The winding engine was only heated in the morning. The grooms sent down fodder for the horses, and the captains worked alone at the bottom, having become labourers again, watching over the damages that took place in the passages as soon as they ceased to be repaired; then, after nine o'clock the rest of the service was carried on by the ladders. And above these dead buildings, buried in their garment of black dust, there was only heard the escapement of the pumping engine, breathing with its thick, long breath all that was left of the life of the pit, which the water would destroy if that breathing should cease.

On the plain opposite, the settlement of the Deux-Cent-Quarante seemed also to be dead. The prefect of Lille had come in haste and the police had tramped all the roads; but in face of the calmness of the strikers, prefect and police had decided to go home again. Never had the settlement given so splendid an example in the vast plain. The men, to avoid going to the public-house, slept all day long; the women while dividing the coffee became reasonable, less anxious to gossip and quarrel; and even the troops of children seemed to understand it all, and were so good that they ran about with naked feet, smacking each other silently. The word of command had been repeated and circulated from mouth to mouth; they wished to be sensible.

There was, however, a continuous coming and going of people in the Maheus' house. Étienne, as secretary, had divided the three thousand francs of the Provident Fund among the needy families; afterwards from various sides several hundred francs had arrived, yielded by subscriptions and collections. But now all their resources were exhausted; the miners had no more money to keep up the strike, and hunger was there threatening them. Maigrat, after having promised credit for a fortnight, had suddenly altered his mind at the end of a week and cut off provisions. He usually took his orders from the Company; perhaps the latter wished to bring the matter to an end by starving the settlements. He acted besides like a capricious tyrant, giving or refusing bread according to the face of the girl who was sent by her parents for provisions; and he especially closed his door spitefully to Maheude, wishing to punish her because he had not been able to get Catherine. To complete their misery it was freezing very hard, and the women were obliged to diminish their piles of coal, thinking anxiously that they could no longer renew them at the pits now that the men were not going down. It was not enough to die of hunger, they must also die of cold.

Among the Maheus everything was already running short. The Levaques could still eat on the strength of a twenty-franc piece lent by Bouteloup. As to the Pierrons, they always had money; but in order to appear as needy as the others, for fear of loans, they got their supplies on credit from Maigrat, who would have thrown his shop at Pierronne if she had held out her petticoat to him. Since Saturday many families had gone to bed without supper, and in face of the terrible days that were beginning not a complaint was heard, all obeyed the word of command with quiet courage. There was an absolute confidence in spite of everything, a religious faith, the blind gift of a population of believers. Since an era of justice had been promised to them they were willing to suffer for the conquest of universal happiness. Hunger exalted their heads; never had the low horizon opened a larger Beyond to these people in the hallucination of their misery. They saw again over there, when their eyes were dimmed by weakness, the ideal city of their dream, but now growing near and seeming to be real, with its population of brothers, its golden age of labour and meals in common. Nothing overcame their conviction that they were at last entering it. The Fund was exhausted; the Company would not yield; every day must aggravate the situation; and they preserved their hope and showed a smiling contempt for facts. If the earth opened beneath them a miracle would save them. This faith replaced bread and warmed their stomachs. When the Maheus and the others had too quickly digested their soup, made with clear water, they thus rose into a state of semi-giddiness, the ecstasy of a better life which has flung martyrs to the beasts.

Étienne was henceforth the unquestioned leader. In the evening conversations he gave forth oracles, in the degree to which study had refined him and made him able to enter into various matters. He spent the nights reading, and received a large number of letters; he even subscribed to the *Vengeur*, a Belgian socialistic paper, and this journal, the first to enter the settlement, gained for him extraordinary consideration among his mates. His growing popularity excited him more every day. To hold an extended correspondence, to discuss the fate of the workers in the four corners of the province, to give advice to the Voreux miners, especially to become a centre and to feel the world rolling round himself, was continually swelling the vanity of the former engine-man, the pikeman with greasy black hands. He was climbing a ladder, he was entering this execrated middle class, with a satisfaction to his intelligence and comfort which he did not confess to himself. He had only one trouble, the consciousness of his lack of education, which made him embarrassed and timid as soon as he was in the presence of a gentleman in a frock-coat. If he went on instructing himself, devouring everything, the lack of method would render assimilation very slow, and would produce such confusion that at last he would know much more than he could understand. So at certain hours of good sense he experienced a restlessness with regard to his mission—a fear that he was not the man for the task. Perhaps it required a lawyer, a learned man, able to speak and act without compromising the mates? But an outcry soon restored his assurance. No, no; no lawyers! They are all rascals; they profit by their knowledge to fatten on the people. Let things turn out how they will, the workers must manage their own affairs. And his dream of popular leadership again soothed him: Montsou at his feet, Paris in the misty distance, who knows? The elections some day, the tribune in a gorgeous hall, where he could thunder against the middle class in the first speech pronounced by a workman in a parliament.

During the last few days Étienne had been perplexed. Pluchart wrote letter after letter, offering to come to Montsou to quicken the zeal of the strikers. It was a question of organising a private meeting over which the mechanic would preside; and beneath this plan lay the idea of exploiting the strike, to gain over to the International these miners who so far had shown themselves suspicious. Étienne feared a disturbance, but he would, however, have allowed Pluchart to come if Rasseneur had not violently blamed this proceeding. In spite of his power, the young man had to reckon with the innkeeper, whose services were of older date, and who had faithful followers among his clients. So he still hesitated, not knowing what to reply.

On this very Monday, towards four o'clock, a new letter came from Lille as Étienne was alone with Maheude in the lower room. Maheu, weary of idleness had set out fishing; if he had the luck to catch a fine fish under the sluice of the canal, they could sell it to buy bread. Old Bonnemort and little Jeanlin had just gone off to try their legs, which were now restored; while the children had departed with Alzire, who spent hours on the pit-bank collecting cinders. Seated near the miserable fire, which they no longer dared to keep up, Maheude, with her dress unbuttoned and one breast hanging out to her belly, was suckling Estelle.

When the young man had folded the letter, she questioned him:

"Is the news good? Are they going to send us any money?"

He shook his head, and she went on:

"I don't know what we shall do this week. However, we'll hold on all the same. When one has right on one's side, don't you think that gives you heart, and one ends always by being the strongest?"

At the present time she was, to a reasonable extent, in favour of the strike. It would have been better to force the Company to be just without leaving off work. But since they had left it they ought not to go back to it without obtaining justice. On this point she was relentless. Better to die than to show oneself in the wrong when one was right!

"Ah!" exclaimed Étienne, "if a fine old cholera was to break out, that would free us of all these Company exploiters."

"No, no," she replied, "we must not wish anyone dead. That wouldn't help us at all; plenty more would spring up. Now I only ask that they should get sensible ideas, and I expect they will, for there are worthy people everywhere. You know I'm not at all for your politics."

In fact she always blamed his violent language, and thought him aggressive. It was good that they should want their work paid for what it was worth, but why occupy oneself with such things as the *bourgeois* and Government? Why mix oneself up with other people's affairs, when one would get nothing out of it but hard knocks? And she kept her esteem for him because he did not get drunk, and regularly paid his forty-five francs for board and lodging. When a man behaves well one can forgive him the rest.

Étienne then talked about the Republic, which would give bread to everybody. But Maheude shook her head, for she remembered 1848, an awful year,[3] which had left them as bare as worms, her and her man, in their early house-keeping years. She forgot herself in describing its horrors, her eyes lost in space, her breast open; while her infant, Estelle, without letting it go, had fallen asleep on her knees. And Étienne, also absorbed in thought, had his eyes fixed on this enormous breast, of which the soft whiteness contrasted with the muddy yellowish complexion of her face.

"Not a farthing," she murmured, "nothing to put between one's teeth, and all the pits stopped. Just the same destruction of poor people as to-day."

But at that moment the door opened, and they remained mute with surprise before Catherine, who then came in. Since her flight with Chaval she had not reappeared at the settlement. Her emotion was so great that, trembling and silent, she forgot to shut the door. She expected to find her mother alone, and the sight of the young man put out of her head the phrases she had prepared on the way.

"What on earth have you come here for?" cried Maheude,

without even moving from her chair. "I don't want to have anything more to do with you; get along."

Then Catherine tried to find words:

"Mother, it's some coffee and sugar; yes, for the children. I've been thinking of them and done over-time."

She drew out of her pockets a pound of coffee and a pound of sugar, and took courage to place them on the table. The strike at the Voreux troubled her while she was working at Jean-Bart, and she had only been able to think of this way of helping her parents a little, under the pretext of caring for the little ones. But her good-nature did not disarm her mother, who replied:

"Instead of bringing us sweets, you would have done better to stay and earn bread for us."

She overwhelmed her with abuse, relieving herself by throwing in her daughter's face all that she had been saying against her for the past month. To go off with a man, to hang on to him at sixteen, when the family was in want! Only the most degraded of unnatural children could do it. One could forgive a folly, but a mother never forgot a trick like that. There might have been some excuse if they had held her tightly. Not at all; she was as free as air, and they only asked her to come in to sleep.

"Tell me, what have you got in your skin, at your age?"

Catherine, standing beside the table, listened with lowered head. A quiver shook her thin girlish body, and she tried to reply in broken words:

"Oh! if it was only me, and the amusement that I get! It's him. What he wants I'm obliged to want too, aren't I? because, you see, he's the strongest. How can one tell how things are going to turn out? Anyhow it's done and can't be undone; it may as well be him as another now. He'll have to marry me."

She defended herself without a struggle, with the passive resignation of a girl who has submitted to the male at an early age. Was it not the common lot? She had never dreamed of anything else; violence behind the pit-bank, a child at sixteen, and then a wretched household if her lover married her. And she did not blush with shame; she only quivered like this at being treated like a bitch before this lad, whose presence oppressed her to despair.

Étienne had risen, however, and was pretending to stir up the early extinct fire in order not to interrupt the explanation. But their looks met; he found her pale and exhausted; pretty, indeed, with her clear eyes in the face which had grown vexed; and he experienced a singular feeling; his spite had vanished; he simply desired that she should be happy with this man whom she had preferred to him. He felt the need to occupy himself with her still, a longing to go to Montsou and force the other man to his duty. But she only saw pity in his constant tenderness; he must feel contempt for her to gaze at her like that. Then her heart contracted so that she choked, without being able to stammer any more words of excuse.

"That's it, you'd best hold your tongue," began the implacable Maheude. "If you've come back to stay, come in; else get along with you at once, and think yourself lucky that I'm not free just now, or I should have put my foot into you somewhere before now."

As if this threat had suddenly been realised, Catherine received a vigorous kick right behind, so violent that she was stupefied with surprise and pain. It was Chaval who had leapt in through the open door to give her this lunge of a vicious beast. For a moment he had watched her from outside.

"Ah! slut," he yelled, "I've followed you. I knew well enough you were coming back here to get him to fill you. And it's you that pay him, eh? You pour coffee down him with my money!"

Maheude and Étienne were stupefied, and did not stir. With a furious movement Chaval chased Catherine towards the door.

"Out you go, by God!"

And as she took refuge in a corner he turned on her mother.

"A nice business, to look after the house while your whore of a daughter is kicking up her legs upstairs!"

At last he held Catherine's wrist, shaking her and dragging her out. At the door he again turned towards Maheude, who was nailed to her chair. She had forgotten to fasten up her breast. Estelle had gone to sleep, and her face had slipped down into the woollen petticoat; the enormous breast was hanging free and naked like the udder of a powerful cow.

"When the daughter is not at it, it's the mother who gets herself plugged," cried Chaval. "Go on, show him your meat! He isn't disgusted—your dirty lodger!"

At this Étienne was about to strike his mate. The fear of arousing the settlement by a fight had kept him back from snatching Catherine from Chaval's hands. But rage was now carrying him away, and the two men were face to face with inflamed eyes. It was an old hatred, a jealousy long unacknowledged, which was breaking out. One of them now must do for the other.

"Take care!" stammered Étienne, with clenched teeth. "I'll do for you."

"Try!" replied Chaval.

They looked at one another for some seconds longer, so close that their hot breath burnt each others faces. And it was Catherine who suppliantly took her lover's hand again to lead him away. She dragged him out of the settlement, fleeing without turning her head.

"What a brute!" muttered Étienne, banging the door, and so shaken by anger that he was obliged to sit down.

Maheude, in front of him, had not stirred. She made a vague gesture, and there was silence, a silence which was painful and heavy with unspoken things. In spite of an effort his gaze again returned to her breast, that expanse of white flesh, the brilliance of which now made him uncomfortable. No doubt she was forty, and had lost her shape, like a good female who had produced too much; but many would still desire her, strong and solid, with the large long face of a woman who had once been beautiful. Slowly and quietly she was putting back her breast with both hands. A rosy corner was still obstinate, and she pushed it back with her finger, and then buttoned herself up, and was now quite black and shapeless in her own gown.

"He's a filthy beast," she said at last. "Only a filthy beast could have such nasty ideas. I don't care a hang what he says; it isn't worth notice."

Then in a frank voice she added, fixing her eyes on the young man:

"I have my faults, sure enough, but not that one. Only two men have touched me—a putter, long ago, when I was fifteen, and then Maheu. If he had left me like the other, Lord! I don't quite know what would have happened; and I don't pride myself either on my good conduct with him since our marriage, because, when one hasn't gone wrong, it's often because one hasn't had the chance. Only I say things as they are, and I know neighbours who couldn't say as much, don't you think?"

"That's true enough," replied Étienne.

And he rose while she decided to light the fire again, after having placed the sleeping Estelle on two chairs. If the father caught and sold a fish they could manage to have some soup.

Outside night was already coming on, a frosty night; and with lowered head Étienne walked along, sunk in dark melancholy. It was no longer anger against the man, or pity for the poor ill-treated girl. The brutal scene was effaced and lost, and he was thrown back on to the sufferings of all, the abominations of wretchedness. He thought of the settlement without bread, these women and little ones who would not eat that evening, all this struggling race with empty bellies. And the doubt which sometimes touched him awoke again in the frightful melancholy of the twilight, and tortured him with a discomfort which he had never felt so strongly before. With what a terrible responsibility he had burdened himself! Must he still push them on in obstinate resistance, now that there was neither money nor credit? And what would be the end of it all if no help arrived, and starvation came to beat down their courage? He had a sudden vision of disaster; of dying children and sobbing mothers, while the men, lean and pale, went down once more into the pits. He went on walking, his feet stumbling against the stones, and the thought that the Company would be found strongest, and that he would have brought misfortune on his comrades, filled him with insupportable anguish.

When he raised his head he saw that he was in front of the Voreux. The gloomy mass of buildings looked sombre beneath the growing darkness. The deserted square, obstructed by great motionless shadows, seemed like the corner of an abandoned fortress. As soon as the winding engine stopped the soul left the place. At this hour of the night nothing was alive, not a lantern, not a voice; and the sound of the pump itself was only a distant moan, coming one could not say whence, in this annihilation of the whole pit.

As Étienne gazed the blood flowed back to his heart. If the workers were suffering hunger, the Company was encroaching on its millions. Why should it prove stronger in this war of work against gold? In any case, the victory would cost it dear. They would have their corpses to count. He felt the fury of battle again, the fierce desire to have done with misery, even at the price of death. It would be as well for the settlement to die at one stroke as to go on dying in detail of famine and injustice. His ill-digested reading came back to him, examples of nations who had burnt their towns to arrest the enemy, vague histories of mothers who had saved their children from slavery by crushing their heads against the pavement, of men who had died of want rather than eat the bread of tyrants. His head became exalted, a red gaiety arose out of his crisis of black sadness, chasing away doubt, and making him ashamed of this passing cowardice of an hour. And in this revival of his faith, gusts of pride reappeared and carried him still higher; the joy of being leader, of seeing himself obeyed, even to sacrifice, the enlarged dream of his power, the evening of triumph. Already he imagined a scene of simple grandeur, his refusal of power, authority placed in the hands of the people when he would be master.

But he awoke and started at the voice of Maheu, who was narrating his luck, a superb trout which he had fished up and sold for three francs.

They would have their soup. Then he left his mate to return alone to the settlement, saying that he would follow him; and he entered and sat down in the Avantage, awaiting the departure of a client to tell Rasseneur decisively that he should write to Pluchart to come at once. His resolution was taken; he would organise a private meeting, for victory seemed to him certain if the Montsou colliers adhered in a mass to the International.

## CHAPTER IV

IT WAS AT THE Bon-Joyeux, Widow Désir's, that the private meeting was organised for Thursday, at two o'clock. The widow, incensed at the miseries inflicted on her children, the colliers, was in a constant state of anger, especially as her inn was emptying. Never had there been a less thirsty strike; the drunkards had shut themselves up at home for fear of disobeying the sensible word of command. Thus Montsou, which swarmed with people on feast-days, now exhibited its wide street in mute and melancholy desolation. No beer flowed from counters or bellies, the gutters were dry. On the pavement at the Casimir bar and the Estaminet du Progrès one only saw the pale faces of the landladies, looking enquiringly into the street; then in Montsou itself the whole desert line extended from the Estaminet l'Enfant to the Estaminet Tison, passing by the Estaminet Piquette and the Tête-Coupée bar; only the Estaminet Sainte-Éloi, which was frequented by captains, still drew occasional glasses; the solitude even extended to the Volcan, where the ladies were resting for lack of admirers, although they would have lowered their price from ten sous to five in view of the hard times. A deep mourning was breaking the heart of the entire country.

"By God!" exclaimed Widow Désir, slapping her thighs with both hands, "it's the fault of the gendarmes! Let them run me in, devil take them, if they like, but I must plague them."

For her, all authorities and masters were gendarmes; it was a term of general contempt in which she enveloped all the enemies of the people. She had greeted Étienne's request with transport; her whole house belonged to the miners, she would lend her ball-room gratuitously, and would herself issue the invitations since the law required it. Besides, if the law was not pleased, so much the better! She would give them a bit of her mind. Since yesterday the young man had brought her some fifty letters to sign; he had had them copied by neighbours in the settlement who knew how to write, and these letters were sent around among the pits to delegates and to men of whom they were sure. The avowed order of the day was a discussion regarding the continuation of the strike; but in reality they were expecting Pluchart, and reckoning on a discourse from him which would cause a general adhesion to the International.

On Thursday morning Étienne was disquieted by the non-appearance of his old foreman, who had promised by letter to arrive on Wednesday evening. What, then, was happening? He was annoyed that he would not be able to come to an understanding with him before the meeting. At nine o'clock he went to Montsou, with the idea that the mechanic had, perhaps, gone there direct without stopping at the Voreux.

"No, I've not seen your friend," replied Widow Désir. "But everything is ready. Come and see."

She led him into the ball-room. The decorations were the same, the garlands which supported at the ceiling a crown of painted paper flowers, and the gilt cardboard scutcheons in a line along the wall with the names of saints, male and female. Only the musicians' place had been replaced by a table and three chairs in one corner; and the room was garnished with forms ranged along the floor.

"It's perfect," Étienne declared.

"And you know," said the widow, "that you're at home here. Yell as much as you like. The gendarmes will have to pass over my body if they do come!"

In spite of his anxiety, he could not help smiling when he looked at her, so vast did she appear, with a pair of breasts so huge that one alone would require a man to embrace it, which now led to the saying that of her six week-day lovers she had to take two every evening on account of the work.

But Étienne was astonished to see Rasseneur and Souvarine enter; and as the widow left them all three in the large empty hall he exclaimed:

"What! you here already!"

Souvarine, who had worked all night at the Voreux, the engine-men not being on strike, had merely come out of curiosity. As to Rasseneur, he had seemed constrained during the last two days, and his fat round face had lost its good-natured laugh.

"Pluchart has not arrived, and I am very anxious," added Étienne.

The innkeeper turned away his eyes, and replied between his teeth:

"I'm not surprised; I don't expect him."

"What!"

Then he made up his mind, and looking the other man in the face bravely:

"I, too, have sent him a letter, if you want me to tell you; and in that letter I have begged him not to come. Yes, I think we ought to manage our own affairs ourselves, without turning to strangers."

Étienne, losing his self-possession and trembling with anger, turned his eyes on his mate's and stammered:

"You've done that, you've done that?"

"I have done that, certainly! and you know that I trust Pluchart; he's a knowing fellow and reliable, one can get on with him. But you see I don't care a damn for your ideas, I don't! Politics, Government, and all that, I don't care a damn for it! What I want is for the miner to be better treated. I have worked down below for twenty years, I've sweated down there with fatigue and misery, and I've sworn to make it easier for the poor buggers who are there still; and I know well enough you'll never get anything with all your ideas, you'll only make the men's fate more miserable still. When they are forced by hunger to go down again, they will be more crushed than ever; the Company will pay them with strokes of the stick, like a runaway dog who is brought back to his tricks. That's what I want to prevent, do you see!"

He raised his voice, protruding his belly and squarely planted on his big legs. The patient, reasonable man's whole nature was revealed in clear phrases, which flowed abundantly without an effort. Was it not absurd to believe that with one stroke one could change the world, putting the workers in the place of the masters and dividing gold as one divides an apple? It would, perhaps, take thousands and thousands of years for that to be realised. There, hold your tongue, with your miracles! The most sensible plan was, if one did not wish to break one's nose, to go straight forward, to demand possible reforms, in short, to improve the lot of the workers on every occasion. He did his best, so far as he occupied himself with it, to bring the Company to better terms; if not, damn it all! they would only starve by being obstinate.

Étienne had let him speak, his own speech cut short by indignation. Then he cried:

"Haven't you got any blood in your veins, by God?"

At one moment he would have struck him, and to resist the temptation he rushed about the hall with long strides, venting his fury on the benches through which he made a passage.

"Shut the door, at all events," Souvarine remarked. "There is no need to be heard."

Having himself gone to shut it, he quietly sat down in one of the office chairs. He had rolled a cigarette, and was looking at the other two men with his mild subtle eye, his lips drawn by a slight smile.

"You won't get any farther by being angry," said Rasseneur judiciously. "I believed at first that you had good sense. It was sensible to recommend calmness to the mates, to force them to keep indoors, and to use your power to maintain order. And now you want to get them into a mess!"

At each turn in his walks among the benches, Étienne returned towards the inn-keeper, seizing him by the shoulders, shaking him, and shouting out his replies in his face.

"But, blast it all! I mean to be calm. Yes, I have imposed order on them! Yes, I do advise them still not to stir! only it doesn't do to be made a joke of after all! You are lucky to remain cool. Now there are hours when I feel that I am losing my head."

This was a confession on his part. He jested over his illusions of a novice, his religious dream of a city in which justice would soon reign among men who had become brothers. A fine method truly! to cross one's arms and wait, if one wished to see men eating each other to the end of the world like wolves. No! one must interfere, or injustice would be eternal, and the rich would for ever suck the blood of the poor. Therefore he could not forgive himself the stupidity of having said formerly that politics ought to be banished from the social question. He knew nothing then; now he had read and studied, his ideas were ripe, and he boasted that he had a system. He explained it badly, however, in confused phrases which contained a little of all the theories[4] he had successively passed through and abandoned. At the summit Karl Marx's idea remained standing: capital was the result of spoliation, it was the duty and the privilege of work to re-conquer that stolen wealth. In practice he had at first, with Proudhon, been captured by the chimera of a mutual credit, a vast bank of exchange which suppressed middlemen; then Lasalle's co-operative societies, endowed by the state, gradually transforming the earth into a single industrial town, had aroused his enthusiasm until he grew disgusted in face of the difficulty of controlling them; and he had arrived recently at collectivism, demanding that all the instruments of production should be restored to the community. But this remained vague; he knew not how to realise this new dream, still hindered by scruples of reason and good sense, not daring to risk the secretary's absolute affirmations. He simply said that it was a question of getting possession of the Government first of all. Afterwards they would see.

"But what has taken you? Why are you going over to the bourgeois?" he continued violently, again planting himself before the inn-keeper. "You said yourself it would have to burst up!"

Rasseneur blushed slightly.

"Yes, I said so. And if it does burst up, you will see that I am not more of a coward than anyone else. Only I refuse to be among those who increase the mess in order to fish out a position for themselves."

Étienne blushed in his turn. The two men no longer shouted, having become bitter and spiteful, conquered by the coldness of their rivalry. It was at bottom that which always strains systems, making one man revolutionary in the extreme, pushing the other to an affectation of prudence, carrying them, in spite of themselves, beyond their true ideas into the fatality of those parts which men do not choose for themselves. And Souvarine, who was listening, exhibited on his pale, girlish face a silent contempt—the crushing contempt of the man who was willing to yield his life in obscurity without even gaining the splendour of martyrdom.

"Then it's at me that you're saying that?" asked Étienne; "you're jealous!"

"Jealous of what?" replied Rasseneur. "I don't pose as a big man; I'm not trying to create a section at Montsou for the sake of being made secretary."

The other man wanted to interrupt him, but he added:

"Why don't you be frank? You don't care a damn for the International; you're only burning to be at our head, the gentleman who corresponds with the famous Federal Council of the Nord!"

There was silence. Étienne replied, quivering:

"Good! I don't think I have anything to reproach myself with. I always asked your advice, for I knew that you had fought here long before me. But since you can't endure anyone by your side, I'll act alone in future. And first I warn you that the meeting will take place even if Pluchart does not come, and the mates will join in spite of you."

"Oh! join!" muttered the innkeeper; "that's not enough. You'll have to get them to pay their subscriptions."

"Not at all. The International grants time to workers on strike. It will at once come to our help, and we shall pay later on."

Rasseneur was carried beyond himself.

"Well, we shall see. I belong to this meeting of yours, and I shall speak. I shall not let you turn our friends' heads, I shall let them know where their real interests lie. We shall see whom they mean to follow—me, whom they have known for thirty years, or you, who have turned everything upside down among us in less than a year. No, no! damn it all! We shall see which of us is going to crush the other."

And he went out, banging the door. The garlands of flowers swayed from the ceiling, and the gilt shields jumped against the walls. Then the great room fell back into its heavy calm.

Souvarine was smoking in his quiet way, seated before the table. After having walked for a moment in silence, Étienne began to relieve his feelings at length. Was it his fault if they had left that fat lazy fellow to come to him? And he defended himself from having sought popularity. He knew not even how it had happened, this friendliness of the settlement, the confidence of the miners, the power which he now had over them. He was indignant at being accused of wishing to bring everything to confusion out of ambition; he struck his chest, protesting his brotherly feelings.

Suddenly he stopped before Souvarine and exclaimed:

"Do you know, if I thought I should cost a drop of blood to a friend, I would go off at once to America!"

The engine-man shrugged his shoulders, and a smile again came on his lips.

"Oh! blood!" he murmured. "What does that matter? The earth has need of it."

Étienne, growing calm, took a chair, and put his elbows on the other side of the table. This fair face, with the dreamy eyes, which sometimes grew savage with its clear blush, disturbed him, and exercised a singular power over his will. In spite of his comrade's silence, conquered even by that silence, he felt himself gradually absorbed.

"Well," he asked, "what would you do in my place? Am I not right to act as I do? Isn't it best for us to join this association?"

Souvarine, after having slowly ejected a jet of smoke replied by his favourite word:

"Oh, foolery! but meanwhile it's always so. Besides, their International will soon begin to move. He has taken it up."

"Who, then?"

"He!"

He had pronounced this word in a whisper, with religious fervour, casting a glance towards the east. He was speaking of the master, Bakounine the destroyer.[5]

"He alone can give the thunderclap," he went on, "while your learned men, with their evolution, are mere cowards. Before three years are passed, the International, beneath his orders, will crush the old world."

Étienne pricked up his ears in attention. He was burning to gain knowledge, to understand this worship of destruction, regarding which the engine-man only uttered occasional obscure words, as though he kept certain mysteries to himself.

"Well, but explain to me. What is your aim?"

"To destroy everything. No more nations, no more governments, no more property, neither God nor worship."

"I quite understand. Only what will that lead you to?"

"To the primitive formless Commune, to a new world, to the renewal of everything."

"And the means of execution? How do you reckon to set about it?"

"By fire, by poison, by the sword. The brigand is the true hero, the popular avenger, the revolutionary in action, with no phrases drawn out of books. We need a series of tremendous outrages to frighten the powerful and to arouse the people."

As he talked, Souvarine grew terrible. An ecstasy raised him on his chair, a mystic flame darted from his pale eyes, and his delicate hands gripped the edge of the table almost to breaking. The other man looked at him in fear, and thought of the stories of which he had received vague intimation, of the mines charged beneath the Czar's palace, of chiefs of police struck down by knives like wild boars, of his mistress, the only woman he had loved, hanged at Moscow[6] one rainy morning, while in the crowd he kissed her with his eyes for the last time.

"No! no!" murmured Étienne, as with a gesture he pushed away these abominable visions, "we haven't got to that yet over here. Murder and fire, never! It is monstrous, unjust, all the mates would rise and strangle the guilty one!"

And besides, he could not understand; the instincts of his race refused to accept this sombre dream of the extermination of the world, mown level like a rye field. Then what would they do afterwards? How would the nations spring up again? He wanted a reply.

"Tell me your programme. We should like to know where we are going to."

Then Souvarine concluded peacefully, with his gaze fixed on space:

"All reasoning about the future is criminal, because it prevents pure destruction, and interferes with the progress of revolution."

This made Étienne laugh, in spite of the cold shiver which passed over his flesh. Besides, he willingly acknowledged that there was something in these ideas, which attracted him by their fearful simplicity. Only it would be playing into Rasseneur's hands if he were to repeat such things to his comrades. It was necessary to be practical.

Widow Désir proposed that they should have lunch. They agreed, and went into the inn-parlour, which was separated from the ball-room on week-days by a movable partition. When they had finished their omelette and cheese, the engine-man proposed to depart; and, as the other tried to detain him:

"What for? To listen to you talking useless foolery? I've seen enough of it. Good day."

He went off in his gentle, obstinate way, with a cigarette between his lips.

Étienne's anxiety increased. It was one o'clock, and Pluchart was decidedly breaking his promise. Towards half-past one the delegates began to appear, and he had to receive them, for he wished to see who entered, for fear that the Company might send its usual spies. He examined every letter of invitation, and took note of those who entered; many came in without a letter, as they were admitted provided he knew them. As two o'clock struck Rasseneur entered, finishing his pipe before the counter, and chatting without haste. This provoking calmness still further disturbed Étienne, all the more as many had come merely for fun—Zacharie, Mouquet, and others. These cared little about the strike, and found it a great joke to do nothing. Seated at tables, and spending their last two sous on drink, they grinned and bantered their mates, the serious ones, who had come to make fools of themselves.

Another quarter of an hour passed; there was impatience in the hall. Then Étienne, in despair, made a gesture of resolution. And he had decided to enter, when Widow Désir, who was putting her head outside, exclaimed:

"But here he is, your gentleman!"

It was, in fact, Pluchart. He came in a cab drawn by a broken-winded horse. He jumped at once on to the pavement, a thin, insipidly handsome man, with a large square head, and in his black cloth frock-coat he had the Sunday air of a well-to-do workman. For five years he had not done a stroke with the file, and he took care of his appearance, especially combing his hair in a correct manner, vain of his successes on the platform; but his limbs were still stiff, and the nails of his large hands, eaten by the iron, had not grown again. Very active, he worked out his ambitions, scouring the province unceasingly in order to place his ideas.

"Ah! don't be angry with me," he said, anticipating questions and reproaches. "Yesterday, lecture at Preuilly in the morning, meeting in the evening at Valençay. To-day, lunch at Marchiennes with Sauvagnat. Then I had to take a cab. I'm worn out; you can tell by my voice. But that's nothing; I shall speak all the same."

He was on the threshold of the Bon-Joyeux, when he bethought himself.

"By Jingo! I'm forgetting the tickets. We should be in a fine fix!"

He went back to the cab, which the cabman drew up again, and he pulled out a little black wooden box, which he carried off under his arm.

Étienne walked radiantly in his shadow, while Rasseneur, in consternation, did not dare to offer his hand. But the other was already pressing it, and saying a rapid word or two about the letter. What a rum idea! Why not hold this meeting? One should always hold a meeting when possible. Widow Désir asked if he would take anything, but he refused. No need; he spoke without drinking. Only he was in a hurry, because in the evening he reckoned on pushing as far as Joiselle, where he wished to come to an understanding with Legoujeux. Then they all entered the ball-room together. Maheu and Levaque, who had arrived late, followed them. The door was then locked, in order to be at home. This made the jokers laugh, Zacharie shouting to Mouquet that perhaps they were going to get them all with child in here.

About a hundred miners were waiting on the benches in the close air of the room, with the warm odours of the last ball rising from the floor. Whispers ran round and all heads turned, while the new-comers sat down in the empty places. They gazed at the Lille gentleman, and the black frock-coat caused a certain surprise and discomfort.

But on Étienne's proposition the meeting was at once constituted. He gave out the names, while the others approved by lifting their hands. Pluchart was nominated chairman, and Maheu and Étienne himself were voted stewards. There was a movement of chairs and the officers were installed; for a moment they watched the chairman disappear beneath the table under which he slid the box, which he had not let go. When he reappeared he struck lightly with his fist to call attention; then he began in a hoarse voice:

"Citizens."

A little door opened and he had to stop. It was Widow Désir who, coming round by the kitchen, brought in six glasses on a tray.

"Don't put yourself out," she said. "When one talks one gets thirsty."

Maheu relieved her of the tray and Pluchart was able to go on. He said how very touched he was at his reception by the Montsou workers, he excused himself for his delay, mentioning his fatigue and his sore throat, then he gave place to Citizen Rasseneur, who wished to speak.

Rasseneur had already planted himself beside the table near the glasses. The back of a chair served him as a rostrum. He seemed very moved, and coughed before starting in a loud voice:

"Mates."

What gave him his influence over the workers at the pit was the facility of his speech, the good-natured way with which he could go on talking to them by the hour without ever growing weary. He never ventured to gesticulate, but stood stolid and smiling, drowning them and dazing them, until they all shouted: "Yes, yes, that's true enough, you're right!" However, on this day, from the first word, he felt that there was a sullen opposition. This made him advance prudently. He only discussed the continuation of the strike, and waited for applause before attacking the International. Certainly honour prevented them from yielding to the Company's demands; but how much misery! what a terrible future if it was necessary to persist much longer! and without deciding for submission he damped their courage, he showed them the settlements dying of hunger, he asked on what resources the partisans of resistance were counting. Three or four friends tried to applaud him, but this accentuated the cold silence of the majority, and the rather irritated disapprobation which greeted his phrases. Then despairing of winning them over he was carried away by anger, he foretold misfortune if they allowed their heads to be turned at the invitation of strangers. Two-thirds of the audience had risen indignantly, trying to silence him, since he insulted them by treating them like children unable to lead themselves. But he went on speaking in spite of the tumult, taking repeated gulps of beer, and shouting violently that the man was not born who would prevent him from doing his duty.

Pluchart had risen. As he had no bell he struck his fist on the table, repeating in his hoarse voice:

"Citizens, citizens!"

At last he obtained a little quiet and the meeting, when consulted, brought Rasseneur's speech to an end. The delegates who had represented the pits in the interview with the manager led the others, all enraged by starvation and agitated by new ideas. The voting was decided in advance.

"You don't care a damn, you don't! you can eat!" yelled Levaque, thrusting out his fist at Rasseneur.

Étienne leaned over behind the chairman's back to appease Maheu, who was very red, and carried out of himself by this hypocritical discourse.

"Citizens!" said Pluchart, "allow me to speak!"

There was deep silence. He spoke. His voice sounded painful and hoarse; but he was used to it on his journeys, and took his laryngitis about him with his programme. Gradually his voice expanded and he produced pathetic effects with it. With open arms and accompanying his periods with a swaying of his shoulders, he had an eloquence which recalled the pulpit, a religious method of sinking the ends of his sentences with a monotonous roll which at last carried conviction.

His discourse centred on the greatness and the advantages of the International; it was that with which he always started in every new locality. He explained its aim, the emancipation of the workers; he showed its imposing structure—below the Commune, higher the Province, still higher the Nation, and at the summit Humanity. His arms moved slowly at each stage, preparing the immense cathedral of the future world. Then there was the interior administration: he read the statutes, spoke of the congresses, pointed out the growing importance of the work, the enlargement of the programme, which, starting from the discussion of wages, was now working towards a social liquidation, to have done with the wage system. No more nationalities. The workers of the whole world would be re-united by a common need for justice, sweeping away the middle-class corruption, founding, at last, a free society, in which he who did not work should not reap! He roared; his breath startled the flowers of painted paper beneath the low smoky ceiling which sent back the sounds of his voice.

A wave passed through the audience. Some of them cried:

"That's it! We're with you."

He went on. The world will be conquered before three years. And he enumerated the nations already conquered. From all sides adhesions are raining in. Never had a young religion counted so many disciples. Then, when they had the upper hand they would dictate terms to the masters, who, in their turn, would have a fist at their throats.

"Yes, yes! they'll have to go down!"

With a gesture he enforced silence. Now he was entering on the strike question. In principle he disapproved of strikes; it was a slow method, which aggravated the sufferings of the worker. But before better things arrived, and when they were inevitable, one must make up one's mind to them, for they had the advantage of disorganising capital. And in this case he showed the International as a Providence for strikers, and quoted examples: in Paris, during the strike of the bronze-workers, the masters had granted everything at once, terrified at the news that the International was sending help; in London it had saved the miners at a colliery, by sending back, at its own expense, a ship-load of Belgians who had been brought over by the coal-owner. It was sufficient to join and the Companies trembled, for the men entered the great army of workers who were resolved to die for one another rather than to remain the slaves of a capitalistic society.

Applause interrupted him. He wiped his forehead with his handkerchief, at the same time refusing a glass which Maheu passed to him. When he was about to continue fresh applause cut short his speech.

"It's all right," he said rapidly to Étienne. "They've had enough. Quick! the cards!"

He had plunged beneath the table, and reappeared with the little black wooden box.

"Citizens!" he shouted, dominating the disturbance, "here are the cards of membership. Let your delegates come up, and I will give them to them to be distributed. Later on we can arrange everything."

Rasseneur rushed forward and again protested. Étienne was also agitated, having to make a speech. Extreme confusion followed. Levaque jumped up with his fists out, as if to fight. Maheu was up and speaking, but nobody could distinguish a single word. In the growing tumult the dust rose from the floor, a floating dust of former balls, poisoning the air with a strong odour of putters and trammers.

Suddenly the little door opened, and Widow Désir filled it with her belly and breast, shouting in a thundering voice:

"Good God! Silence! The gendarmes!"

It was the commissioner of the district, who had arrived rather late to prepare a report and to break up the meeting. Four gendarmes accompanied him. For five minutes the widow had delayed them at the door, replying that she was at home, and that she had a perfect right to entertain her friends. But they had hustled her away, and she had rushed in to warn her children.

"Must clear out through here," she said again. "There's a dirty gendarme guarding the court. It doesn't matter; my little woodhouse opens into the alley. Quick, then!"

The commissioner was already knocking with his fist, and as the door was not opened, he threatened to force it. A spy must have spoken, for he cried that the meeting was illegal, a large number of miners being there without any letter of invitation.

In the hall the trouble was growing. They could not escape thus; they had not even voted either for adhesion or for the continuation of the strike. All persisted in talking at the same time. At last the chairman suggested a vote by acclamation. Arms were raised, and the delegates declared hastily that they would join in the name of their absent mates. And it was thus that the ten thousand colliers of Montsou became members of the International. However, the retreat began. In order to cover it, Widow Désir had propped herself up against the door, which the butt end of the gendarmes' muskets were crushing on her back. The miners jumped over the benches, and escaped, one by one, through the kitchen and the wood-yard. Rasseneur disappeared among the first, and Levaque followed him, forgetful of his abuse, and planning how he could get an offer of a glass to pull himself together. Étienne, after having seized the little box, waited with Pluchart and Maheu, who considered it a point of honour to emerge last. As they disappeared the lock gave, and the commissioner found himself in the presence of the widow, whose breast and belly still formed a barricade.

"It doesn't help you much to smash everything in my house," she said. "You can see there's nobody here."

The commissioner, a slow man who did not care for scenes, simply threatened to take her off to prison. And he then went away with his four gendarmes to prepare a report, beneath the jeers of Zacharie and Mouquet, who were full of admiration for the way in which their mates had humbugged this armed force, for which they themselves did not care a hang.

In the alley outside Étienne, embarrassed by the box, was rushing along, followed by the others. He suddenly thought of Pierron, and asked why he had not turned up. Maheu, also running, replied that he was ill—a convenient illness, the fear of compromising himself. They wished to retain Pluchart, but, without stopping, he declared that he must set out at once for Joiselle, where Legoujeux was awaiting his orders. Then, as they ran, they shouted out to him their wishes for a pleasant journey, and rushed through Montsou with their heels in the air. A few words were exchanged, broken by the panting of their chests. Étienne and Maheu were laughing confidently, henceforth certain of victory. When the International had sent help, it would be the Company that would beg them to resume work. And in this burst of hope, in this gallop of big boots sounding over the pavement of the streets, there was something else also, something sombre and fierce, a gust of violence which would inflame the settlements in the four corners of the country.

## CHAPTER V

ANOTHER FORTNIGHT HAD PASSED by. It was the beginning of January and cold mists benumbed the immense plain. The misery had grown still greater, and the settlements were in agony from hour to hour beneath the increasing famine. Four thousand francs sent by the International from London had scarcely supplied bread for three days, and then nothing had come. This great dead hope was beating down their courage. On what were they to count now since even their brothers had abandoned them? They felt themselves separated from the world and lost in the midst of this deep winter.

On Tuesday no resources were left in the Deux-Cent-Quarante settlement. Étienne and the delegates had multiplied their energies. New subscriptions were opened in the neighbouring towns, even at Paris; collections were made and lectures organised. These efforts came to nothing. Public opinion, which had at first been moved, grew indifferent now that the strike dragged on for ever, and so quietly, without any dramatic incidents. Small charities scarcely sufficed to maintain the poorer families. The others lived by pawning their clothes and selling up the household piece by piece. Everything went to the brokers, the wool of the mattresses, the kitchen utensils, even the furniture. For a moment they thought themselves saved, for the small retail shopkeepers of Montsou, killed out by Maigrat, had offered credit to try and get back their custom; and for a week Verdonck, the grocer, and the two bakers, Carouble and Smelten, kept open shop, but when their advances were exhausted all three stopped. The bailiffs were rejoicing; there only resulted a piling up of debts which would for a long time weigh over the miners. There was no more credit to be had anywhere and not an old saucepan to sell; they might lie down in a corner to die like mangy dogs.

Étienne would have sold his flesh. He had given up his salary and had gone to Marchiennes to pawn his trousers and cloth coat, happy to set the Maheus' pot boiling once more. His boots alone remained, and he retained these to keep a firm foothold, he said. His grief was that the strike had come on too early, before the Provident Fund had had time to swell. He regarded this as the only cause of the disaster, for the workers would surely triumph over the masters on the day when they had saved enough money to resist. And he recalled Souvarine's words accusing the Company of pushing forward the strike to destroy the fund at the beginning.

The sight of the settlement and of these poor people without bread or fire overcame him. He preferred to go out and to weary himself with distant walks. One evening, as he was coming back and passing near Réquillart, he perceived an old woman who had fainted by the road-side. No doubt she was dying of hunger; and having raised her he began to shout to a girl whom he saw on the other side of the paling.

"Why! is it you?" he said, recognising Mouquette. "Come and help me then, we must give her something to drink."

Mouquette, moved to tears, quickly went into the shaky hovel which her father had set up in the midst of the ruins. She came back at once with gin and a loaf. The gin revived the old woman, who without speaking bit greedily into the bread. She was the mother of a miner who lived at the settlement on the Cougny side, and she had fallen there on returning from Joiselle, where she had in vain attempted to borrow half-a-franc from a sister. When she had eaten she went away dazed.

Étienne stood in the open field of Réquillart, where the crumbling sheds were disappearing beneath the brambles.

"Well, won't you come in and drink a little glass?" asked Mouquette merrily.

And as he hesitated:

"Then you're still afraid of me?"

He followed her, won by her laughter. This bread, which she had given so willingly, moved him. She would not take him into her father's room, but led him into her own room where she at once poured out two little glasses of gin. The room was very neat and he complimented her on it. Besides, the family seemed to want for nothing; the father continued his duties as a groom at the Voreux while she, saying that she could not live with folded arms, had become a laundress, which brought her in thirty sous a day. One may amuse oneself with men, but one isn't lazy for all that.

"I say," she murmured, all at once coming and putting her arms round him prettily, "why don't you like me?"

He could not help laughing, she had done this in so charming a way.

"But I like you very much," he replied.

"No, no, not like I mean. You know that I am dying of longing. Do you know that would give me so much pleasure?" It was true she had desired him for six months. He still looked at her as she clung to him, pressing him with her two tremulous arms, her face raised with such supplicating love that he was deeply moved. There was nothing beautiful in her large round face, with its yellow complexion eaten by the coal; but her eyes shone with flame, a charm rose from her skin, a trembling of desire which made her rosy and young. In the face of this gift which was so humble and so ardent he no longer dared to refuse.

"Oh! you are willing," she stammered, delighted. "Oh! you are willing!"

And she gave herself up with the fainting awkwardness of a virgin, as if it was for the first time, and she had never before known a man. Then when he left her, it was she who was overcome with gratitude; she said "Thank-you" to him and kissed his hands.

Étienne remained rather ashamed of this good fortune. Nobody boasted of having had Mouquette. As he went away he swore that it should not occur again, but he preserved a friendly remembrance of her; she was a capital girl.

When he got back to the settlement, he found serious news

which made him forget the adventure. The rumour circulated that the Company would, perhaps, agree to make a concession if the delegates made a fresh attempt with the manager. At all events some captains had spread this rumour. The truth was, that in this struggle the mine was suffering even more than the miners. On both sides obstinacy was piling up ruin: while work was dying of hunger, capital was being destroyed. Every day of rest carried away hundreds of thousands of francs. Every machine which stops is a dead machine. Tools and material are impaired, the money that is sunk melts away like water drunk by the sand. Since the small stock of coal at the surface of the pits was exhausted, customers talked of going to Belgium, so that in future they would be threatened from that quarter. But what especially frightened the Company, although the matter was carefully concealed, was the increasing damage to the galleries and workings. The captains did not suffice for repairs, the timber was falling everywhere, and landslips were taking place constantly. Soon the disasters became so serious that long months would be needed for repairs before hewing could be resumed. Already stories went about the country: at Crèvecœur three hundred mètres of road had subsided in a mass, stopping up access to the Cinq-Paumes; at Madeleine the Maugrétout seam was crumbling away and filling with water. The management refused to admit this, but suddenly two accidents, one after the other, had forced them to avow it. One morning, near Piolaine, the ground was found cracked above the north gallery of Mirou which had fallen in the day before; and on the following day the ground subsided within the Voreux, shaking the corner of a suburb to such an extent that two houses nearly disappeared.

Étienne and the delegates hesitated to risk any steps without knowing the directors' intentions. Dansaert, whom they questioned, avoided replying: certainly, the misunderstanding was deplored, and everything would be done to bring about an agreement; but he could say nothing definitely. At last, they decided that they would go to M. Hennebeau in order to have reason on their side; for they did not wish to be accused, later on, of having refused the Company an opportunity of acknowledging that it had been in the wrong. Only they vowed to yield nothing and to maintain, in spite of everything, the terms which were alone just.

The interview took place on Thursday morning when the settlement was sinking to desperate wretchedness. It was less cordial than the first interview. Maheu was still the speaker, and he explained that their mates had sent them to ask if these gentlemen had anything new to say. At first M. Hennebeau affected surprise: no order had reached him, nothing could be changed so long as the miners persisted in their detestable rebellion; but this official stiffness produced the worst effects, so that if the delegates had gone out of their way to offer conciliation, the way in which they were received only served to make them more obstinate. Afterwards the manager tried to seek a basis of mutual concession; thus, if the men would accept the separate payment for timbering, the Company would raise that payment by the two centimes which they were accused of profiting by. Besides, he added that he would take the offer on himself, that nothing was settled, but that he flattered himself he could obtain this concession from Paris. But the delegates refused, and repeated their demands: the retention of the old system, with a rise of five centimes a tram. Then he acknowledged that he could treat with them at once, and urged them to accept in the name of their wives and little ones dying of hunger. And with eyes on the ground and stiff heads they said "No," always "No," with fierce vigour. They separated curtly. M. Hennebeau banged the doors. Étienne, Maheu, and the others went off stamping with their great heels on the pavement in the mute rage of the vanquished pushed to extremes. Towards two o'clock the women of the settlement, on their side, made an application to Maigrat. There was only this hope left, to bend this man and to wrench from him another week's credit. The idea originated with Maheude, who often counted too much on people's good-nature. She persuaded the Brûlé and the Levaque to accompany her; as to Pierronne, she excused herself, saying that she could not leave Pierron, whose illness still continued. Other women joined the band till they numbered quite twenty. When the inhabitants of Montsou saw them arrive, gloomy and wretched, occupying the whole width of the road, they shook their heads anxiously. The doors were closed, and one lady hid her plate. It was the first time they had been seen thus, and there could not be a worse sign: usually, everything was going to ruin when the women thus scoured the streets. At Maigrat's there was a violent scene. At first, he had made them go in, jeering and pretending to believe that they had come to pay their debts: that was nice of them to have agreed to come and bring the money all at once. Then, as soon as Maheude began to speak he pretended to be enraged. Were they making fun of people? More credit! Then they wanted to turn him into the streets? No, not a single potato, not a single crumb of bread! And he sent them off to the grocer, Verdonck, and to the bakers, Carouble and Smelten, since they now dealt with them. The women listened with timid humility, apologising, and watching his eyes to see if he would relent. He began to joke, offering his shop to the Brûlé if she would have him as a lover. They were all so cowardly that they laughed at this; and the Levaque improved on it, declaring that she was willing, she was. But he at once became abusive, and pushed them towards the door. As they insisted, suppliantly, he treated one brutally. The others on the pavement shouted that he had sold himself to the Company, while Maheude, with her arms in the air, in a burst of avenging indignation, cried out on death, exclaiming that such a man did not deserve to eat.

The return to the settlement was melancholy. When the women came back with empty hands, the men looked at them and then lowered their heads. There was nothing more to be done, the day would end without a spoonful of soup; and the other days extended in an icy shadow, without a ray of hope. They had made up their minds to it, and no one spoke of surrender. This excess of misery made them still more obstinate, mute as tracked beasts, resolute to die at the bottom of their hole rather than come out. Who would dare to speak first of submission? They had sworn with their mates to hold together, and hold together they would, as they held together at the pit when one of them was beneath a landslip. It was as it ought to be; it was a good school for resignation down there. They might well tighten their belts for a week, when they had been swallowing fire and water ever since they were twelve years of age; and their devotion was thus augmented by the pride of soldiers, of men proud of their profession, who in their daily struggle with death had gained a pride in sacrifice.

With the Maheus it was a terrible evening. They were all silent, seated before the dying fire in which the last cinders were smoking. After having emptied the mattresses, handful by handful, they had decided the day before to sell the clock for three francs; and the room seemed bare and dead now that the familiar tick-tock no longer filled it with sound. The only object of luxury now, in the middle of the sideboard, was the rose cardboard box, an old present from Maheu, which Maheude treasured like a jewel. The two good chairs had gone; Father Bonnemort and the children were squeezed together on an old mossy bench brought in from the garden. And the livid twilight now coming on seemed to increase the cold.

"What's to be done?" repeated Maheude, crouching down in the corner by the oven.

Étienne stood up, looking at the portraits of the Emperor and Empress stuck against the wall. He would have torn them down long since if the family had not preserved them for ornament. So he murmured, with clenched teeth:

"And to think that we can't get two sous out of these damned idiots, who are watching us starve!"

"If I were to take the box?" said the woman, very pale, after some hesitation.

Maheu, seated on the edge of the table, with hanging legs, and his head on his chest, sat up.

"No! I won't have it!"

Maheude painfully rose and walked round the room. Good God! was it possible that they were reduced to such misery? The cupboard without a crumb, nothing more to sell, no notion where to get a loaf! And the fire, which was nearly out! She became angry with Alzire, whom she had sent in the morning to glean on the pit-bank, and who had come back with empty hands, saying that the Company would not allow gleaning. Did it matter a hang what the Company wanted? As if they were robbing anyone by picking up the bits of lost coal! The little girl, in despair, told how a man had threatened to hit her; then she promised to go back next day, even if she was beaten.

"And that imp, Jeanlin," cried the mother; "where is he now I should like to know? He ought to have brought the salad; we can browse on that like beasts, at all events! You will see, he won't come back. Yesterday, too, he slept out. I don't know what he's up to; the rascal always looks as though his belly were full."

"Perhaps," said Étienne, "he picks up sous on the road."

She suddenly lifted both fists furiously.

"If I knew that! My children beg! I'd rather kill them and myself too."

Maheu had again sunk down at the edge of the table. Lénore and Henri, astonished that they had nothing to eat, began to moan; while old Bonnemort, in silence, philosophically rolled his tongue in his mouth to deceive his hunger. No one spoke any more; all were becoming benumbed beneath this aggravation of their evils; the grandfather, coughing and spitting out the black phlegm, taken again by rheumatism which was turning to dropsy; the father asthmatic, and with knees swollen with water; the mother and the little ones scarred by scrofula and hereditary anæmia. No doubt their work made this inevitable; they only complained when the lack of food killed them off; and already they were falling like flies in the settlement. But something must be found for supper. My God! where was it to be found, what was to be done?

Then, in the twilight, which made the room more and more gloomy with its dark melancholy, Étienne, who had been hesitating for a moment, at last decided with aching heart.

"Wait for me," he said. "I'll go and see somewhere."

And he went out. The idea of Mouquette had occurred to him. She would certainly have a loaf, and would give it willingly. It annoyed him to be thus forced to return to Réquillart; this girl would kiss his hands with her air of an affectionate servant; but one did not leave one's friends in trouble; he would still be kind with her if need be.

"I will go and look round, too," said Maheude, in her turn. "It's too stupid."

She re-opened the door after the young man and closed it violently, leaving the others motionless and mute in the faint light of a candle-end which Alzire had just lighted. Outside she stopped and thought for a moment. Then she entered the Levaques' house.

"Tell me, I lent you a loaf the other day. Could you give it me back?"

But she stopped herself. What she saw was far from encouraging; the house spoke of misery even more than her own.

The Levaque woman, with fixed eyes, was gazing into her burst-out fire, while Levaque, made drunk on his empty stomach by some nail-makers, was sleeping on the table with his back to the wall. Bouteloup was mechanically rubbing his shoulders with the amazement of a good-natured fellow who has eaten up his savings, and is astonished at having to tighten his belt.

"A loaf! ah! my dear," replied the Levaque woman, "I wanted to borrow another from you!"

Then, as her husband groaned with pain in his sleep, she pushed his face against the table.

"Hold your row, bloody beast! So much the better if it burns your guts! Instead of being paid to drink, you ought to have asked twenty sous from a friend."

She went on relieving herself by swearing, in the midst of this dirty household, already abandoned so long that an unbearable smell was exhaling from the floor. Everything might smash up, she didn't care a hang! Her son, that rascal Bébert, had also disappeared since morning, and she shouted that it would be a good riddance if he never came back. Then she said that she would go to bed. At least she could get warm. She hustled Bouteloup.

"Come along, up we go. The fire's out. No need to light the candle to see the empty plates. Well, are you coming, Louis? I tell you that we must go to bed. We can stick together there, that's a comfort. And let this damned drunkard die here of cold by himself!"

When she found herself outside again, Maheude struck resolutely across the gardens to go to Pierron's house. She heard laughter. As she knocked there was sudden silence. It was a full minute before the door was opened.

"What! is it you?" exclaimed Pierronne with affected surprise. "I thought it was the doctor."

Without allowing her to speak, she went on, pointing to Pierron, who was seated before a large coal fire:

"Ah! he makes no progress, he makes no progress at all. His face looks all right; it's in his belly that it takes him. Then he must have heat. We burn all that we've got."

Pierron, in fact, looked very well; his complexion was good and his flesh fat. It was in vain that he breathed hard in order to play the sick man. Besides, as Maheude came in she perceived a strong smell of rabbit; they had certainly put the dish out of the way. There were crumbs strewed over the table, and in the very midst she saw a forgotten bottle of wine.

"Mother has gone to Montsou to try and get a loaf," said Pierronne again. "We are chilled with waiting for her."

But her voice choked; she had followed her neighbour's glance, and her eyes also fell on the bottle. Immediately she began again, and narrated the story. Yes, it was wine; the Piolaine people had brought her that bottle for her man, who had been ordered by the doctor to take claret. And her thankfulness poured forth in a stream. What good people they were! The young lady especially; she was not proud, going into workpeople's houses and distributing her charities herself.

"I see," said Maheude; "I know them."

Her heart ached at the idea that the good things always go to the least poor. It was always so, and these Piolaine people would have carried water to the river. Why had she not seen them in the settlement? Perhaps, all the same, she might have got something out of them.

"I had come," she confessed at last, "to know if there was more going with you than with us. Have you just a little vermicelli by way of loan?"

Pierronne expressed her grief noisily.

"Nothing at all, my dear. Not what you can call a grain of semolina. If mother hasn't come back, it's because she hasn't succeeded. We must go to bed supperless."

At this moment crying was heard from the cellar, and she grew angry and struck her fist against the door. It was that gadabout Lydie, whom she had shut up, she said, to punish her for not having returned until five o'clock, after having been roaming about the whole day. One could not subdue her; she was constantly disappearing.

Maheude, however, remained standing; she could not make up her mind to leave. This large fire filled her with a painful sensation of comfort; the thought that they were eating there enlarged the void in her stomach. Evidently they had sent away the old woman and shut up the child, to blow themselves out with their rabbit. Ah! whatever people may say, when a woman behaves ill that brings luck to her house.

"Good-night," she said, suddenly.

Outside night had come on, and the moon behind the clouds was lighting up the earth with a dubious glow. Instead of traversing the gardens, Maheude went around, despairing, afraid to go home again. But along the dead frontages all the doors smelled of famine, and sounded hollow. What was the good of knocking? There was wretchedness everywhere. For weeks since they had had nothing to eat. Even the odour of onion had gone, that strong odour which revealed the settlement from afar across the country; now there was nothing but the smell of old vaults, the dampness of holes in which nothing lives. Vague sounds were dying out, stifled tears, lost oaths; and in the silence which slowly grew heavier one could hear the sleep of hunger coming on, the throwing of bodies across beds in the nightmares of empty bellies.

As she passed before the church she saw a shadow slip rapidly by. A gleam of hope made her hasten, for she had recognised the Montsou priest, Abbé Joire, who said mass on Sundays at the settlement chapel. No doubt he had just come out of the sacristy, where he had been called to settle some affair. With rounded back he moved quickly on, a fat gentleman, anxious to live at peace with everybody. If he had come at night it must have been in order not to compromise himself among the miners. It was said, too, that he had just obtained promotion. He had even been seen walking about with his successor, a lean man, with eyes like live coals.

"Sir, sir!" stammered Maheude.

But he would not stop.

"Good-night, good-night, my good woman."

She found herself before her own door. Her legs would no longer carry her, and she went in.

No one had stirred, Maheu was still at the edge of the table in dejection. Old Bonnemort and the little ones were squeezed together on the bench for the sake of warmth. And they had not said a word, and the candle had burnt so low that even light would soon fail them. At the sound of the door the children turned their heads; but seeing that their mother brought nothing back, they looked down at the earth again, repressing the longing to cry, for fear of being scolded. Maheude fell back into her place near the dying fire. They asked her no questions, and the silence continued. All had understood, and they thought it useless to weary themselves more by talking; they were now waiting, despairing and without courage, in the last expectation that perhaps Étienne would unearth help somewhere. The minutes went by, and at last they no longer reckoned on this.

When Étienne re-appeared, he held a cloth containing a dozen potatoes, cooked but cold.

"That's all that I've found," he said.

With Mouquette also bread was wanting; it was her dinner which she had forced him to take in this cloth, kissing him with all her heart.

"Thanks," he said to Maheude, who offered him his share; "I've eaten over there."

It was not true, and he gloomily watched the children throw themselves on the food. The father and mother also restrained themselves, in order to leave more; but the old man greedily swallowed everything. They had to take a potato away from him for Alzire.

Then Étienne said that he had heard news. The Company, irritated by the obstinacy of the strikers, talked of giving back their certificates to the compromised miners. Certainly, the Company was for war. And a more serious rumour circulated; they boasted of having persuaded a large number of men to go down again. On the next day the Victoire and Feutry-Cantel would be complete; even at Madeleine and Mirou there would be a third of the men. The Maheus were exasperated.

"By God!" shouted the father, "if there are traitors, we must settle their account."

And standing up, yielding to the fury of his suffering:

"To-morrow evening, to the forest! Since they won't let us come to an understanding at the Bon-Joyeux, we can be at home in the forest!"

This cry had aroused old Bonnemort, who had grown drowsy after his gluttony. It was the old rallying cry, the rendezvous where the miners of old days used to plot their resistance to the King's soldiers.

"Yes, yes, to Vandame! I'm with you if you go there!"

Maheude made an energetic gesture.

"We will all go. That will finish these injustices and treacheries."

Étienne decided that the rendezvous should be announced to all the settlements for the following evening. But the fire was dead, as with the Levaques, and the candle suddenly went out. There was no more coal and no more oil; they had to feel their way to bed in the intense cold which contracted the skin. The little ones were crying.

## CHAPTER VI

JEANLIN WAS NOW WELL and able to walk; but his legs had united so badly that he limped both on the right and left sides, and moved with the gait of a duck, though running as fast as formerly, with the skill of a mischievous and thieving animal.

On this evening, in the dusk on the Réquillart road, Jeanlin, accompanied by his inseparable friends, Bébert and Lydie, was on the watch. He had taken ambush in a vacant space, behind a paling opposite an obscure grocery shop, situated at the corner of a lane. An old woman who was nearly blind displayed there three or four sacks of lentils and haricots; and it was an ancient dried codfish, hanging by the door and stained with fly-blows, to which his eyes were directed. Twice already he had sent Bébert to unhook it. But each time someone had appeared at the bend in the road. Always intruders in the way, one could not attend to one's affairs.

A gentleman went by on horseback, and the children flattened themselves at the bottom of the paling, for they recognised M. Hennebeau. Since the strike he was often thus seen along the roads, riding alone amid the rebellious settlements, ascertaining, with quiet courage, the condition of the country. And never had a stone whistled by his ears; he only met men who were silent and slow to salute him; most often he came upon lovers, who cared nothing for politics and took their fill of pleasure in holes and corners. He passed by on his trotting mare with head directed straight forward, so as to disturb nobody, while his heart was swelling with an unappeased desire amid this gormandising of free love. He distinctly saw these small rascals, the little boys on the little girl in a heap. Even the youngsters were already amusing themselves by rubbing their misery! His eyes grew moist, and he disappeared, sitting stiffly on his saddle, with his frock-coat buttoned up in a military manner.

"Damned luck!" said Jeanlin. "This will never finish. Go on, Bébert! Pull on to the tail!"

But two men once more appeared, and the child again stifled an oath when he heard the voice of his brother Zacharie narrating to Mouquet how he had discovered a two-franc piece sewn into one of his wife's petticoats. They both grinned with satisfaction, striking each other on the shoulder. Mouquet proposed a game of crosse for the next day; they would leave the Avantage at two o'clock, and go to the Montoire side, near Marchiennes. Zacharie agreed. What was the good of bothering over the strike? as well amuse oneself, since there's nothing to do. And they turned the corner of the road, when Étienne, who was coming along the canal, stopped them and began to talk.

"Are they going to bed here?" said Jeanlin, in exasperation. "Nearly night; the old woman will be taking in her sacks."

Another miner came down towards Réquillart. Étienne went off with him, and as they passed the paling the child heard them speak of the forest; they had been obliged to put off the rendezvous to the following day, for fear of not being able to announce it in one day to all the settlements.

"I say, there," he whispered to his two mates, "the big affair is for to-morrow. We'll go, eh? We can get off in the afternoon."

And the road being at last free, he sent off Bébert.

"Courage! hang on to its tail. And look out! the old woman's got her broom."

Fortunately the night had grown dark. Bébert, with a leap, hung on to the cod so that the string broke. He ran away, waving it like a kite, followed by the two others, all three galloping. The woman came out of her shop in astonishment, without understanding or being able to distinguish this band now lost in the darkness.

These scoundrels had become the terror of the country. They gradually spread themselves over it like a horde of savages. At first they had been satisfied with the yard at the Voreux, tumbling into the stock of coal, from which they would emerge looking like negroes, playing at hide-and-seek amid the supply of wood, in which they lost themselves as in the depths of a virgin forest. Then they had taken the pit-bank by assault; they would seat themselves on it and slide down the bare portions still boiling with interior fires; they glided among the briars in the older parts, hiding for the whole day, occupied in the quiet little games of mischievous mice. And they were constantly enlarging their conquests, scuffling among the piles of bricks until blood came, running about the fields and eating without bread all sorts of milky herbs, searching the banks of the canals to take fish from the mud and swallow them raw; and pushing still farther, they travelled for kilomètres as far as the thickets of Vandame, under which they gorged themselves with strawberries in the spring, with nuts and bilberries in summer. Soon the immense plain belonged to them.

What drove them thus from Montsou to Marchiennes, constantly on the roads with the eyes of young wolves, was the growing love of plunder. Jeanlin remained the captain of these expeditions, leading the troop on to all sorts of prey, ravaging the onion fields, pillaging the orchards, attacking shop windows. In the country, people accused the miners on strike, and talked of a vast organised band. One day even, he had forced Lydie to steal from her mother, and made her bring him two dozen sticks of barley-sugar, which Pierronne kept in a bottle on one of the boards in her window; and the little girl, who was well beaten, had not betrayed him because she trembled so before his authority. The worst was that he always gave himself the lion's share. Bébert also had to bring him the booty, happy if the captain did not hit him and keep it all.

For some time Jeanlin had abused his authority. He would beat Lydie as one beats one's lawful wife, and he profited by Bébert's credulity to send him on unpleasant adventures, amused at making a fool of this big boy, who was stronger than himself, and could have knocked him over with a blow of his fist. He felt contempt for both of them and treated them as slaves, telling them that he had a princess for his mistress and that they were unworthy to appear before her. And, in fact, during the past week he would suddenly disappear at the end of a road or a turning in a path, no matter where it might be, after having ordered them with a terrible air to go back to the settlement. But first he would pocket the booty.

This was what happened on the present occasion.

"Give it up," he said, snatching the cod from his mate's hands when they stopped, all three, at a bend in the road near Réquillart.

Bébert protested.

"I want some, you know. I took it."

"Eh! what!" he cried. "You'll have some if I give you some. Not to-night, sure enough; to-morrow, if there's any left."

He pushed Lydie, and placed both of them in line like soldiers shouldering arms. Then, passing behind them:

"Now, you must stay there five minutes without turning. By God! if you do turn, there will be beasts that will eat you up. And then you will go straight back, and if Bébert touches Lydie on the way, I shall know it and I shall hit you."

Then he disappeared in the shadow, so lightly that the sound of his naked feet could not be heard. The two children remained motionless for the five minutes without looking round, for fear of receiving a blow from the invisible. Slowly a great affection had grown up between them in their common terror. He was always thinking of taking her and pressing her very tight between his arms, as he had seen others do; and she, too, would have liked it, for it would have changed her to be so nicely caressed. But neither of them would have allowed themselves to disobey. When they went away, although the night was very dark, they did not even kiss each other; they walked side by side, tenderly and despairingly, certain that if they touched one another the captain would strike them from behind.

Étienne, at the same hour, had entered Réquillart. The evening before Mouquette had begged him to return, and he returned, ashamed, feeling an inclination which he refused to acknowledge, for this girl who adored him like a Christ. It was, besides, with the intention of breaking it off. He would see her; he would explain to her that she ought no longer to pursue him, on account of the mates. It was not a time for pleasure; it was dishonest to thus amuse oneself when people were dying of hunger. And not having found her at home, he had decided to wait and watch the shadows of the passers-by.

Beneath the ruined steeple the old shaft opened, half blocked up above the black hole. A beam stood erect, and with a fragment of roof at the top it had the profile of a gallows; in the broken walling of the kerbs stood two trees—a mountain ash and a plane—which seemed to grow from the depths of the earth. It was a corner of abandoned wildness, the grassy and fibrous entry of a gulf, embarrassed with old wood, planted with hawthorns and sloe trees, which were peopled in the spring by warblers in their nests. Wishing to avoid the great expense of keeping it up, the Company, for the last ten years, had proposed to fill up this dead pit; but they were waiting to install an air-shaft in the Voreux, for the ventilation furnace of the two pits, which communicated, was placed at the foot of Réquillart, of which the former winding shaft served as a conduit. They were content to consolidate the tubbing by beams placed across, preventing extraction, and they had neglected the upper galleries to watch only over the lower gallery, in which blazed the furnace, the enormous coal fire, with so powerful a draught that the rush of air produced the wind of a tempest from one end to the other of the neighbouring mine. As a precaution, in order that they could still go up and down, the order had been given to furnish the conduit with ladders; only, as no one took charge of them, the ladders were rotting with dampness, and in some places had already given way. Above, a large briar stopped the entry of the passage, and, as the first ladder had lost some rungs, it was necessary, in order to reach it, to hang on to the root of the mountain ash, and to take one's chance and fall into the blackness.

Étienne was waiting patiently, hidden behind a bush, when he heard a long rustling. He thought at first that it was the timid flight of a snake. But the sudden gleam of a match astonished him, and he was stupefied on recognising Jeanlin, who was lighting a candle, and now burying himself in the earth. He was seized with curiosity, and approached the hole; the child had disappeared, and a faint gleam came from the second ladder. Étienne hesitated a moment, and then let himself go, holding on to the roots. He thought for a moment that he was about to leap down the whole five hundred and eighty mètres of the mine, but at last he felt a rung, and descended gently. Jeanlin had evidently heard nothing. Étienne constantly saw the light sinking beneath him, while the little one's shadow, colossal and disturbing, danced with the deformed gait of his distorted limbs. He kicked about his legs with the skill of a monkey, catching on with hands, feet, or chin where the rungs were wanting. Ladders, seven mètres in length, followed one another, some still firm, others shaky, yielding and almost broken; the steps were narrow and green, so rotten that one seemed to walk in moss; and the heat was suffocating as the descent continued; the heat of an oven proceeding from the air-shaft which was, fortunately, not very active now the strike was on, for when the furnace devoured its five thousand kilogrammes of coal a day, one could not have risked oneself there without roasting one's hair.

"What a damned little toad!" exclaimed Étienne in a stifled voice, "where the devil is he going to?"

Twice he had nearly fallen. His feet slid over the damp wood. If he had only had a candle like the child! but he struck himself every minute; he was only guided by the vague gleam that fled beneath him. He had already reached the twentieth ladder, and the descent still continued. Then he counted them: twenty-one, twenty-two, twenty-three, and he still went down and down. His head seemed to be swelling with the heat and the thought that he was falling into a furnace. At last he reached a landing-place, and he saw the candle going off along the gallery. Thirty ladders, that made about two hundred and ten mètres.

"Is he going to drag me about long?" he thought. "He must be going to bury himself in the stable."

But on the left, the path which led to the stable was closed by a landslip. The journey began again, now more painful and more dangerous. Frightened bats flew about and clung to the roof of the gallery. He had to hasten so as not to lose sight of the light; only where the child passed with ease, with the suppleness of a serpent, he could not glide through without bruising his limbs. This gallery, like all the older passages, was narrow, and grew narrower every day from the constant fall of soil; at certain places it was a mere tube which would eventually be effaced. In this strangling labour the torn and broken wood became a peril, threatening to saw into his flesh, or to run him through with the points of splinters, sharp as swords. He could only advance with precaution, on his knees or belly, feeling in the darkness before him. Suddenly a band of rats stamped over him, running from his neck to his feet in their galloping flight.

"Blast it all! haven't we got to the end yet?" he grumbled, with aching back and out of breath.

They were there. At the end of a kilomètre the tube enlarged, they reached a part of the gallery which was admirably preserved. It was the end of the old haulage passage cut across the bed like a natural grotto. He was obliged to stop, he saw the child afar, placing his candle between two stones, and putting himself at ease with the quiet and relieved air of a man who is glad to be at home again. This gallery-end was completely changed into a comfortable dwelling. In a corner on the ground, a pile of hay made a soft couch; on some old planks, placed like a table, there were bread, potatoes, and bottles of gin already opened; it was a real brigand's cavern, with booty piled up for weeks, even useless booty like soap and blacking, stolen for the pleasure of stealing. And the child, quite alone in the midst of this plunder, was enjoying it like a selfish brigand.

"I say, then, is this how you make fun of people?" cried Étienne, when he had breathed for a moment. "You come and gorge yourself here, when we are dying of hunger up above!"

Jeanlin, astounded, was trembling. But recognising the young man, he quickly grew calm.

"Will you come and dine with me?" he said at last. "Eh? a bit of grilled cod? You shall see."

He had not let go his cod, and he began to scrape off the fly-blows properly with a fine new knife, one of those little dagger knives, with bone handles, on which mottoes are inscribed. This one simply bore the word, "Amour."

"You have a fine knife," remarked Étienne.

"It's a present from Lydie," replied Jeanlin, who neglected to add that Lydie had stolen it, by his orders, from a huckster at Montsou, stationed before the Tête-Coupée bar.

Then, as he still scraped, he added proudly:

"Isn't it comfortable in my house? It's a bit warmer than up above, and it feels a lot better!"

Étienne had seated himself, and was amused in making him talk. He was no longer angry, he felt interested in this debauched child, who was so brave and so industrious in his vices. And, in fact he tasted a certain comfort in the bottom of this hole; the heat was not too great, an equal temperature reigned here at all seasons, the warmth of a bath, while the rough December wind was chapping the skins of the miserable people on the earth. As they grew old, the galleries became purified from noxious gases, all the fire-damp had gone, and one only smelled now the odour of old fermented wood, a subtle ethereal odour, as if sharpened with a dash of cloves. This wood, besides, had become curious to look at, with a yellowish pallor of marble, fringed with whitish thread lace, flaky vegetations which seemed to drape it with an embroidery of silk and pearls. In other places the timber was bristling with toadstools. And there were flights of white butterflies, snowy flies and spiders, a decolourised population for ever ignorant of the sun.

"Then you're not afraid?" asked Étienne.

Jeanlin looked at him in astonishment.

"Afraid of what? I am quite alone."

But the cod was at last scraped. He lighted a little fire of wood, brought out the pan, and grilled it. Then he cut a loaf into two. It was a terribly salt feast, but exquisite all the same for strong stomachs.

Étienne had accepted his share.

"I am not astonished you get fat, while we are all growing lean. Do you know that it is beastly to stuff yourself like this? And the others? you don't think of them!"

"Oh! why are the others such fools?"

"Well, you're right to hide yourself, for if your father knew you stole he would settle you."

"What! when the bourgeois are stealing from us! It's you who are always saying so. If I nabbed this loaf at Maigrat's, you may be pretty sure it's a loaf he owed us."

The young man was silent, with his mouth full, and felt troubled. He looked at him, with his muzzle, his green eyes, his large ears, a degenerate abortion, with an obscure intelligence and savage cunning, slowly gaining back the animality of old. The mine which had made him had just finished him by breaking his legs.

"And Lydie?" asked Étienne again, "do you bring her here sometimes?"

Jeanlin laughed contemptuously.

"The little one? Ah, no, not I; women blab."

And he went on laughing, filled with immense disdain for Lydie and Bébert. Who had ever seen such boobies? To think that they swallowed all his humbug, and went away with empty hands while he ate the cod in this warm place, tickled his sides with amusement. Then he concluded, with the gravity of a little philosopher:

"Much better be alone, then there's no falling out."

Étienne had finished his bread. He drank a gulp of the gin. For a moment he asked himself if he ought not to make a bad return for Jeanlin's hospitality by bringing him up to daylight by the ear, and forbidding him to plunder any more by the threat of telling everything to his father. But as he examined this deep retreat, an idea occurred to him. Who knows if there might not be need for it, either for mates or for himself, in case things should come to the worst up above! He made the child swear not to sleep out, as had sometimes happened when he forgot himself in his hay, and taking a candle-end, he went away first, leaving him to pursue quietly his domestic arrangements.

Mouquette, seated on a beam in spite of the great cold, had grown desperate in waiting for him. When she saw him she leapt on his neck; and it was as though he had plunged a knife into her heart when he said that he wished to see her no more. Good God! why? Did she not love him enough? Fearing to yield to the desire to enter with her, he drew her towards the road, and explained to her as gently as possible that she was compromising him in the eyes of his mates, that she was compromising the political cause. She was astonished; what had that got to do with politics? At last the thought occurred to her that he blushed at being seen with her. She was not wounded, however; it was quite natural; and she proposed that he should rebuff her before people, so as to seem to have broken with her. But he would see her just once sometimes. In distraction she implored him; she swore to hide things; she would not keep him five minutes. He was touched, but still refused. It was necessary. Then, as he left her, he wished at least to kiss her. They had gradually reached the first houses of Montsou, and were standing with their arms round one another beneath a large round moon, when a woman passed near them with a sudden start, as though she had knocked against a stone.

"Who is that?" asked Étienne, anxiously.

"It's Catherine," replied Mouquette. "She's coming back from Jean-Bart."

The woman now was going away, with lowered head and feeble limbs, looking very tired. And the young man gazed at her, in despair at having been seen by her, his heart aching with an unreasonable remorse. Had she not been with a man? Had she not made him suffer with the same suffering here, on this Réquillart road, when she had given herself to that man? But, all the same, he was grieved to have done the like to her.

"Shall I tell you what it is?" whispered Mouquette, in tears, as she left him. "If you don't want me it's because you want someone else."

On the next day the weather was superb; it was one of those clear frosty days, the beautiful winter days when the hard earth rings like crystal beneath the feet. Jeanlin had gone off at one o'clock, but he had to wait for Bébert behind the church, and they nearly set out without Lydie, whose mother had again shut her up in the cellar, and only now liberated her to put a basket on her arm, telling her that if she did not bring it back full of dandelions she would be shut up with the rats all night long. She was frightened, therefore, and wished to go at once for the salad. Jeanlin dissuaded her; they would see later on. For a long time Poland, Rasseneur's big rabbit, had attracted his attention. He was passing before the Avantage when, just then, the rabbit came out on to the road. With a leap he seized her by the ears, stuffed her into the little girl's basket, and all three rushed away. They would amuse themselves finely by making her run like a dog as far as the forest.

But they stopped to gaze at Zacharie and Mouquet, who, after having drunk a glass with two other mates, had begun their big game of crosse. The stake was a new cap and a red handkerchief, deposited with Rasseneur. The four players, two at a time, were taking the first turn from the Voreux to the Paillot farm, nearly three kilomètres; and it was Zacharie who won, with seven strokes, while Mouquet required eight. They had placed the ball, the little box-wood egg, on the pavement with one point in the air. Each was holding his crosse, the mallet with its bent iron, long handle, and tightly-drawn network. Two o'clock struck as they set out. Zacharie, in a masterly manner, at his first stroke, composed of a series of three, sent the ball more than four hundred yards across the beetroot fields; for it was forbidden to play in the villages and on the streets, where people might be killed. Mouquet, who was also a good player, sent off the ball with so vigorous an arm that his single stroke brought the ball a hundred and fifty mètres behind. And the game went on, one side playing against the other side, always running, their feet bruised by the frozen ridges of the ploughed fields.

At first Jeanlin, Bébert and Lydie had trotted behind the players, delighted with their vigorous strokes. Then they remembered Poland, whom they were shaking up in the basket; and, leaving the game in the open country, they took out the rabbit, inquisitive to see how fast she could run. She went off, and they fled after her; it was a chase lasting an hour at full speed, with constant turns, with shouts to frighten her, and arms opened and closed on emptiness. If she had not been at the beginning of pregnancy they would never have caught her again.

As they were panting, the sound of oaths made them turn their heads. They had just come upon the crosse party again, and Zacharie had nearly split open his brother's skull. The players were now at their fourth turn. From the Paillot farm they had gone off to the Quatre-Chemins, then from the Quatre-Chemins to Montoire; and now they were going in six strokes from Montoire to Pré-des-Vaches. That made two leagues and a half in an hour; and, besides, they had had drinks at the Estaminet Vincent and at the Trois-Sages bar. Mouquet this time was ahead. He had two more strokes to play, and his victory was certain, when Zacharie, grinning as he availed himself of his privilege, played with so much skill that the ball rolled into a deep pit. Mouquet's partner could not get it out; it was a disaster. All four shouted; the party was excited, for they were neck to neck; it was necessary to begin again. From the Pré-des-Vaches it was not two kilomètres to the point of Herbes-Rousses, in five strokes. There they would refresh themselves at Lerenard's.

But Jeanlin had an idea. He let them go on, and pulled out of his pocket a piece of string which he tied to one of Poland's legs, the left hind leg. And it was very amusing. The rabbit ran before the three young rascals drawing the thigh in such an extraordinary manner that they had never laughed so much before. Afterwards they fastened it round the neck, and let her run off; and, as she grew tired, they dragged her on her belly or on her back, just like a little carriage. That lasted for more than an hour. She was moaning when they quickly put her back into the basket, near the wood at Cruchot, on hearing the players whose game they had once more come across.

Zacharie, Mouquet, and the two others took two kilomètres, with no other rest than the time for a drink at all the inns which they had fixed on as their goals. From the Herbes-Rousses they had gone on to Buchy, then to Croix-de-Pierre, then to Chamblay. The earth rang beneath the helter-skelter of their feet, rushing untiringly after the ball, which bounded over the ice; it was a good time, only they ran the risk of breaking their legs. In the dry air the great crosse blows exploded like firearms. Their muscular hands grasped the strong handle; their entire bodies were bent forward, as though to slay an ox. And this went on for hours, from one end of the plain to the other, over ditches and hedges and the slopes of the road, the low walls of the enclosures. One needed to have good bellows in one's chest and iron hinges in one's knees. The pikemen thus rubbed off the rust of the mine with impassioned zeal. There were some so enthusiastic at twenty-five that they could do ten leagues. At forty they played no more; they were too heavy.

Five o'clock struck; the twilight was already coming on. One more turn before the Forest of Vandame, to decide who had gained the cap and the handkerchief. And Zacharie joked with his chaffing indifference for politics; it would be fine to tumble down over there in the midst of the mates. As to Jeanlin, ever since leaving the settlement he had been aiming at the forest, though apparently only scouring the fields. With an indignant gesture he threatened Lydie, who was full of remorse and fear, and talked of going back to the Voreux to gather her dandelions. Were they going to abandon the meeting? he wanted to know what the old people would say. He pushed Bébert, and proposed to enliven the end of the journey as far as the trees by detaching Poland and pursuing her with stones. His real idea was to kill her; he wanted to take her off and eat her at the bottom of his hole at Réquillart. The rabbit ran ahead, with nose in the air and ears back; a stone grazed her back, another cut her tail, and, in spite of the growing darkness, she would have remained there if the young rogues had not noticed Étienne and Maheu standing in the middle of a glade. They threw themselves on the animal in fear, and put her back again into the basket. Almost at the same minute Zacharie, Mouquet, and the two others, with their last blow at crosse, drove the ball within a few mètres of the glade. They all came into the midst of the rendezvous.

Through the whole country, by the roads and pathways of the flat plain, ever since twilight, there had been a long procession, a rustling of silent shadows, moving separately or in groups towards the violet thickets of the forest. Every settlement was emptied, the women and children themselves set out as if for a walk beneath the great clear sky. Now the roads were growing dark; this walking crowd, all gliding towards the same goal, could no longer be distinguished. But one felt it, the confused tramping moved by one soul. Between the hedges, among the bushes, there was everywhere a light rustling, a vague rumour of the voices of the night.

M. Hennebeau, who was at this hour returning home, mounted on his mare, listened to these vague sounds. He had met couples, long rows of strollers, on this beautiful winter night. Mere lovers, who were going to take their pleasure, mouth to mouth, behind the walls. Was it not what he always met, girls tumbled over at the bottom of every ditch, beggars who crammed themselves with the only joy that costs nothing? And these fools complained of life, when they could take their fill of this supreme happiness of love! Willingly would he have starved as they did if he could begin life again with a woman who would give herself to him on a heap of stones, with all her strength and with all her heart. His misfortune was without consolation, and he envied these wretches. With lowered head he went back, riding his horse at a slackened pace, rendered desperate by these long sounds, lost in the depth of the black country, in which he only heard kisses.

## CHAPTER VII

IT WAS THE PLACE-des-Dames, that vast glade[7] just opened up by the felling of trees. It spread out in a gentle slope, surrounded by tall thickets and superb beeches with straight regular trunks, which formed a white colonnade patched with green lichens; fallen giants were also lying in the grass, while on the left a mass of logs formed a geometrical cube. The cold was sharpening with the twilight and the frozen moss crackled beneath the feet. There was black darkness on the earth while the white branches showed against the pale sky, where a full moon coming above the horizon would soon extinguish the stars.

Nearly three thousand colliers had come to the rendezvous, a swarming crowd of men, women and children, gradually filling the glade and spreading out afar beneath the trees. Late arrivals were still coming up, a flood of heads drowned in shadow, and stretching as far as the neighbouring copses. A rumbling arose from them, like that of a storm, in this motionless and frozen forest.

At the top, dominating the slope, Étienne stood with Rasseneur and Maheu. A quarrel had broken out, one could hear their voices in sudden bursts. Near them some men were listening: Levaque, with clenched fists; Pierron, turning his back and much annoyed that he had no longer been able to feign a fever. There were also Father Bonnemort and old Mouque, seated side by side on a stump, lost in deep meditation. Then behind were the chaffers, Zacharie, Mouquet and others, who had come to make fun of the thing; while gathered together in a very different spirit the women in a group were as serious as if at church. Maheude silently shook her head at the Levaque woman's muttered oaths. Philomène was coughing, her bronchitis having come back with the winter. Only Mouquette was showing her teeth with laughter, amused at the way in which Mother Brûlé was abusing her daughter, an unnatural creature who had sent her away that she might gorge herself with rabbit, a creature who had sold herself and who fattened on her man's cowardice. And Jeanlin had planted himself on the pile of wood, hoisting up Lydie and making Bébert follow him, all three higher up in the air than anyone else.

The quarrel was raised by Rasseneur, who wished to proceed formally to the election of officers. He was enraged by his defeat at the Bon-Joyeux, and had sworn to have his revenge, for he flattered himself that he could regain his old authority when he was once face to face, not with the delegates, but with the miners themselves. Étienne was disgusted, and thought that the idea of officers was ridiculous in this forest. They ought to act in a revolutionary fashion, like savages, since they were tracked like wolves.

As the dispute threatened to drag on, he took possession of the crowd at once by jumping on to the trunk of a tree and shouting:

"Comrades! comrades!"

The confused roar of the crowd died down into a long sigh, while Maheu stifled Rasseneur's protestations. Étienne went on in a loud voice:

"Comrades, since they forbid us to speak, since they send the police after us as if we were robbers, we have come to talk here! Here we are free, we are at home. No one can silence us any more than they can silence birds and beasts!"

A thunder of cries and exclamations responded to him.

"Yes, yes! the forest is ours, we can talk here. Go on."

Then Étienne stood for a moment motionless on the tree-trunk. The moon, still beneath the horizon, only lit up the topmost branches, and the crowd, remaining in the darkness, gradually grew calm and silent. He, also in darkness, stood above it at the top of the slope like a bar of shadow.

He raised his arm with a slow movement and began. But his voice was not fierce; he spoke in the cold tones of a simple envoy of the people, who was rendering his account. He was delivering the discourse which the commissioner of police had cut short at the Bon-Joyeux; and he began by a rapid history of the strike, affecting a certain scientific eloquence—facts, nothing but facts. At first he spoke of his dislike to the strike; the miners had not desired it, it was the management which had provoked it with the new timbering tariff. Then he recalled the first step taken by the delegates in going to the manager, the bad faith of the directors; and, later on, the second step, the tardy concession, the ten centimes given up, after the attempt to rob them. Now he showed by figures the exhaustion of the Provident Fund, and pointed out the use that had been made of the help sent, briefly excusing the International, Pluchart and the others, for not being able to do more for them in the midst of the cares of their conquest of the world. So the situation was getting worse every day; the Company was giving back certificates and threatening to hire men from Belgium; besides, it was intimidating the weak, and had forced a certain number of miners to go down again. He preserved his monotonous voice, as if to insist on the bad news; he said that hunger was victorious, that hope was dead, and that the struggle had reached the last feverish efforts of courage. And then he suddenly concluded, without raising his voice:

"It is in these circumstances, mates, that you have to take a decision to-night. Do you want the strike to go on? and if so, what do you expect to do to beat the Company?"

A deep silence fell from the starry sky. The crowd, which could not be seen, was silent in the night beneath these words which choked every heart, and a sigh of despair could be heard through the trees.

But Étienne was already continuing, with a change in his voice. It was no longer the secretary of the association who was speaking; it was the chief of a band, the apostle who was bringing truth. Could it be that any were cowardly enough to go back on their word? What! They were to suffer in vain for a month, and then to go back to the pits, with lowered heads, so that the everlasting wretchedness might begin over again! Would it not be better to die at once in the effort to destroy this tyranny of capital, which was starving the worker? Always to submit to hunger up to the moment when hunger will again throw the calmest into revolt, was it not a foolish game which could not go on for ever? And he pointed to the exploited miners, bearing alone the disasters of every crisis, reduced to go without food as soon as the necessities of competition lowered net prices. No, the timbering tariff could not be accepted; it was only a disguised effort to economise on the Company's part; they wanted to rob every man of an hour's work a day. It was too much this time; the day was coming when the miserable, pushed to extremity, would wreak justice.

He stood with his arms in the air. At the word "justice" the crowd, shaken by a long shudder, broke out into applause which rolled along with the sound of dry leaves. Some voices cried:

"Justice! it is time! Justice!"

Gradually Étienne grew heated. He had not Rasseneur's easy flowing abundance. Words often failed him, he had to force his phrases, bringing them out with an effort which he emphasised by a movement of his shoulders. Only in these continual shocks he came upon familiar images which seized on his audience by their energy; while his workman's gestures, his elbows drawn in and then extended, with his fists thrust out, his jaw suddenly advanced as if to bite, had also an extraordinary effect on his mates. They all said that if he was not big he made himself heard.

"The wage system is a new form of slavery," he began again, in a more sonorous voice. "The mine ought to belong to the miner, as the sea belongs to the fisherman, and the earth to the peasant. Do you see? The mine belongs to you, to all of you who, for a century, have paid for it with so much blood and misery!"

He boldly entered on the obscure questions of law, and lost himself in the difficulties of the special regulations concerning mines. The sub-soil, like the soil, belonged to the nation; only an odious privilege gave the monopoly of it to the Companies; all the more since, at Montsou, the pretended legality of the concessions was complicated by treāties formally made with the owners of the old fiefs, according to the ancient custom of Hainault. The miners, then, had only to reconquer their property; and with extended hands he indicated the whole country beyond the forest. At this moment the moon, which had risen above the horizon, lit him up as it glided from behind the high branches. When the crowd, which was still in shadow, thus saw him, white with light, distributing fortune with his open hands, they applauded anew by prolonged clapping.

"Yes, yes, he's right. Bravo!"

Then Étienne trotted out his favourite subject, the assumption of the instruments of production by the collectivity, as he repeated it in a phrase of which the pedantry greatly pleased him. At the present time his evolution was completed. Having set out with the sentimental fraternity of the novice and the need for reforming the wage system, he had reached the political idea of its suppression. Since the meeting at the Bon-Joyeux his collectivism, still humanitarian and without a formula, had stiffened into a complicated programme[8] which he discussed scientifically, article by article. First, he affirmed that freedom could only be obtained by the destruction of the state. Then, when the people had obtained possession of the government, reforms would begin: return to the primitive commune, substitution of an equal and free family for the moral and oppressive family; absolute equality, civil, political and economic; individual independence guaranteed, thanks to the possession and the integral product of the instruments of work; finally, free and professional education, paid for by the collectivity. This led to the total reconstruction of the old rotten society; he attacked marriage, the right of testament, he regulated everyone's fortune, he threw down the iniquitous monument of the dead centuries with a great movement of his arm, always the same movement, the movement of the reaper who is cutting down a ripe harvest. And then with the other hand he reconstructed; he built up the future of humanity, the edifice of truth and justice rising in the dawn of the twentieth century. In this state of mental tension reason trembled, and only the sectarian's fixed idea was left. The scruples of sensibility and of good sense were lost; nothing seemed easier than the realisation of this new world. He had foreseen everything; he spoke of it as of an engine which he could get up in two hours, and neither fire nor blood cost him anything.

"Our turn is come," he broke out for the last time. "Now it is for us to have power and wealth!"

The cheering rolled up to him from the depths of the forest. The moon now whitened the whole of the glade, and cut into living waves the sea of heads, as far as the confused copses between the great grey trunks in the distance. And in the icy air there was a fury of faces, of gleaming eyes, of open mouths, a rut of famishing men, women and children, let loose on the just pillage of the ancient wealth they had been deprived of. They no longer felt the cold, these burning words had warmed them to the bone. Religious exaltation raised them from the earth, a fever of hope like that of the Christians of the early Church awaiting the near coming of justice. Many obscure phrases had escaped them, they could not at all understand this technical and abstract reasoning; but the very obscurity and abstraction still further enlarged the field of promise and lifted them into a dazzling region. What a dream! to be masters, to suffer no more, to enjoy at last!

"That's it, by God! it's our turn now! Down with the exploiters."

The women were delirious; Maheude, losing her calmness, was seized with the vertigo of hunger, the Levaque woman shouted, old Brûlé, carried out of herself, was brandishing her witch-like arms, Philomène was shaken by a spasm of coughing, and Mouquette was so excited that she cried out words of tenderness to the orator. Among the men, Maheu was won over and shouted with anger, between Pierron who was trembling and Levaque who was talking too much; while the chaffers, Zacharie and Mouquet, though trying to make fun of things, were feeling uncomfortable and were surprised that their mate could talk on so long without having a drink. But on top of the pile of wood, Jeanlin was making more noise than anyone, egging on Bébert and Lydie and shaking the basket in which Poland lay.

The clamour began again. Étienne was enjoying the intoxication of his popularity. He held his power, as it were, materialised in these three thousand chests, whose hearts he could move with a word. Souvarine, if he had cared to come, would have applauded his ideas so far as he recognised them, pleased with his pupil's progress in anarchy and satisfied with the programme, except the article on education, a relic of silly sentimentality, for men needed to be dipped in a bath of holy and salutary ignorance. As to Rasseneur, he shrugged his shoulders with contempt and anger.

"You shall let me speak," he shouted to Étienne.

The latter jumped from the tree-trunk.

"Speak, we shall see if they'll hear you."

Already Rasseneur had replaced him, and with a gesture demanded silence. But the noise did not cease; his name went round from the first ranks, who had recognised him, to the last, lost beneath the beeches, and they refused to hear him; he was an overturned idol, the mere sight of him angered his old disciples. His facile elocution, his flowing, good-natured speech, which had so long charmed them, was now treated like warm gruel made to put cowards to sleep. In vain he talked through the noise, trying to take up again his discourse of conciliation, the impossibility of changing the world by a stroke of law, the necessity of allowing the social evolution time to accomplish itself; they joked him, they damned him; his defeat at the Bon-Joyeux was now beyond repair. At last they threw handfuls of frozen moss at him, and a woman cried in a shrill voice:

"Down with the traitor!"

He explained that the miner could not be the proprietor of the mine, as the weaver who owns his trade, and he said that he preferred sharing in the benefits,[9] the interested worker becoming the child of the house.

"Down with the traitor!" repeated a thousand voices, while stones began to whistle by.

Then he turned pale, and despair filled his eyes with tears. His whole existence was crumbling down; twenty years of ambitious comradeship were breaking down beneath the ingratitude of the crowd. He came down from the tree-trunk, with no strength to go on, struck to the heart.

"That makes you laugh," he stammered, addressing the triumphant Étienne. "Good! I hope that your turn will come. It will come, I tell you!"

And as if to reject all responsibility for the evils which he foresaw, he made a large gesture, and went away alone across the country, pale and silent.

Hoots arose, and then they were surprised to see Father Bonnemort standing on the trunk and about to speak in the midst of the tumult. Up till now Mouque and he had seemed absorbed, with that air that they always had of reflecting on former things. No doubt he was yielding to one of those sudden crises of garrulity which sometimes made the past stir in him so violently that recollections rose and flowed from his lips for hours at a time. There was deep silence, and they listened to this old man, who was like a pale spectre beneath the moon, and as he narrated things without any immediate relation with the discussion—long histories which no one could understand—the impression was increased. He was talking of his youth; he described the death of his two uncles who were crushed at the Voreux; then he turned to the inflammation of the lungs which had carried off his wife. He kept to a main idea, however: things had never gone well and never would go well. Thus in the forest five hundred of them had come together because the king would not lessen the hours of work; but he stopped short, and began to tell of another strike—he had seen so many! They all broke out under these trees, here at the Place-des-Dames, lower down at the Charbonnerie, still further towards the Saut-du-Loup. Sometimes it froze, sometimes it was hot. One evening it had rained so much that they had gone back again without being able to say anything, and the king's soldiers came up and it finished with volleys of musketry.

"We raised our hands like this, and we swore not to go back again. Ah! I have sworn; yes, I have sworn!"

The crowd listened gapingly, feeling disturbed, when Étienne, who had watched the scene, jumped on to the fallen tree, keeping the old man at his side. He had just recognised Chaval among their friends in the first row. The idea that Catherine must be there had roused a new ardour within him, the desire to be applauded in her presence.

"Mates, you have heard; this is one of our old men, and this is what he has suffered, and what our children will suffer if we don't have done with the robbers and butchers."

He was terrible; never had he spoken so violently. With one arm he supported old Bonnemort, exhibiting him as a banner of misery and mourning, and crying for vengeance. In a few rapid phrases he went back to the first Maheu. He showed the whole family used-up at the mine, devoured by the Company, hungrier than ever after a hundred years of work; and contrasting with the Maheus he pointed to the big bellies of the directors sweating with gold, a whole band of kept shareholders, going on for a century like kept women, doing nothing but enjoy with their bodies. Was it not fearful? a race of men dying down below, from father to son, so that bribes of wine could be given to ministers, and generations of great lords and bourgeois could give feasts or fatten by their firesides! He had studied the diseases of the miners. He made them all march past with their awful details: anæmia, scrofula, black bronchitis, the asthma which chokes, and the rheumatism which paralyses. These wretches were thrown as food to the engines and penned up like beasts in the settlements. The great companies slowly absorbed them, regulating their slavery, threatening to enroll all the workers of the nation, millions of hands, to bring fortune to a thousand idlers. But the miner was no longer an ignorant brute, crushed within the bowels of the earth. An army was springing up from the depths of the pits, a harvest of citizens whose seed would germinate and burst through the earth some sunny day. And they would see then if, after forty years of service, anyone would dare to offer a pension of a hundred and fifty francs to an old man of sixty who spat out coal and whose legs were swollen with the water from the cuttings. Yes! work would demand an account from capital: that impersonal god, unknown to the worker, crouching down somewhere in his mysterious sanctuary, where he sucked the life out of the starvelings who nourished him! They would go down there; they would at last succeed in seeing his face by the gleam of incendiary fires, they would drown him in blood, that filthy sow, that monstrous idol, gorged with human flesh!

He was silent, but his arm, still extended in space, indicated the enemy, down there, he knew not where, from one end of the earth to the other. This time the clamour of the crowd was so great that people at Montsou heard it, and looked towards Vandame, seized with anxiety at the thought that some terrible landslip had occurred. Night-birds rose above the trees in the clear open sky.

He now concluded his speech.

"Mates, what is your decision? Do you vote for the strike to go on?"

Their voices yelled, "Yes! yes!"

"And what steps do you decide on? We are sure of defeat if cowards go down to-morrow."

Their voices rose again with the sound of a tempest:

"Kill the cowards!"

"Then you decide to call them back to duty and to their sworn word. This is what we could do: present ourselves at the pits, bring back the traitors by our presence, show the Company that we are all agreed, and that we are going to die rather than yield."

"That's it. To the pits! to the pits!"

While he was speaking Étienne had looked for Catherine among the pale shouting heads before him. She was certainly not there, but he still saw Chaval, affecting to jeer, shrugging his shoulders, but devoured by jealousy and ready to sell himself for a little of this popularity.

"And if there are any spies among us, mates," Étienne went on, "let them look out; they're known. Yes, I can see Vandame colliers here who have not left their pit."

"Is that meant for me?" asked Chaval, with an air of bravado.

"For you, or for anyone else. But, since you speak, you ought to understand that those who eat have nothing to do with those who are starving. You work at Jean-Bart."

A chaffing voice interrupted:

"Oh! he work! he's got a wife who works for him."

Chaval swore, while the blood rose to his face.

"By God! is it forbidden to work, then?"

"Yes!" said Étienne, "when your mates are enduring misery for the good of all, it is forbidden to go over, like a selfish sneaking coward, to the masters' side. If the strike had been general we should have got the best of it long ago. Not a single man at Vandame ought to have gone down when Montsou is resting. To accomplish the great stroke, work should be stopped in the entire country, at Monsieur Deneulin's as well as here. Do you understand? there are only traitors in the Jean-Bart cuttings; you're all traitors!"

The crowd around Chaval grew threatening, and fists were raised and cries of: Kill them! kill them! began to be uttered. He had grown pale. But, in his infuriated desire to triumph over Étienne, an idea restored him.

"Listen to me, then! come to-morrow to Jean-Bart, and you shall see if I'm working! We're on your side; they've sent me to tell you so. The fire shall be extinguished, and the enginemen, too, must go on strike. All the better if the pumps do stop! the water will destroy the pits and everything will be done for!"

He was furiously applauded in his turn, and now Étienne himself was out-flanked. Other orators succeeded each other from the tree-trunk, gesticulating amid the tumult, and throwing out wild propositions. It was a mad outburst of faith, the impatience of a religious sect which, tired of hoping for the expected miracle, had at last decided to provoke it. These heads, emptied by famine, saw everything red, and dreamed of fire and blood in the midst of a glorious apotheosis from which would arise universal happiness. And the tranquil moon bathed this sea, the deep forest encircled with its vast silence this cry of massacre. The frozen moss crackled beneath the heels of the crowd, while the beeches, erect in their strength, with the delicate tracery of their black branches against the white sky, neither saw nor heard the miserable beings who writhed at their feet.

There was some pushing, and Maheude found herself near Maheu. Both of them, driven out of their ordinary good sense, and carried away by the slow exasperation which had been working within them for months, approved Levaque, who went to extremes by demanding the heads of the engineers. Pierron had disappeared. Bonnemort and Mouque were both talking together, saying vague violent things which nobody heard. For a joke Zacharie demanded the demolition of the churches, while Mouquet, with his crosse in his hand, was beating it against the ground for the sake of increasing the row. The women were furious. The Levaque, with her fists to her hips, was setting to with Philomène, whom she accused of having laughed; Mouquette talked of attacking the gendarmes by kicking them somewhere; Mother Brûlé, who had just slapped Lydie on finding her without either basket or salad, went on striking into space for all the masters whom she would like to have got at. For a moment Jeanlin was in terror, Bébert having learned through a trammer that Madame Rasseneur had seen them steal Poland; but when he had decided to go back and quietly release the beast at the door of the Avantage, he shouted louder than ever, and opened his new knife, brandishing the blade and proud of its glitter.

"Mates! mates!" repeated the exhausted Étienne, hoarse with

the effort to obtain a moment's silence for a definite understanding.

At last they listened.

"Mates! to-morrow morning at Jean-Bart, is it agreed?"

"Yes! yes! at Jean-Bart! death to the traitors!"

The tempest of these three thousand voices filled the sky, and was extinguished in the pure brightness of the moon.

# *PART FIVE*

## CHAPTER I

AT FOUR O'CLOCK THE moon had set, and the night was very dark. Everything was still asleep at Deneulin's; the old brick house stood mute and gloomy, with closed doors and windows, at the end of the large ill-kept garden which separated it from the Jean-Bart mine. The other frontage faced the deserted road to Vandame, a large country town, about three kilomètres off, hidden behind the forest.

Deneulin, tired after a day spent in part below, was snoring with his face towards the wall, when he dreamt that he had been called. At last he awoke, and really hearing a voice, got out and opened the window. One of the captains was in the garden.

"What is it, then?" he asked.

"There's a rebellion, sir;[1] half the men will not work, and are preventing the others from going down."

He scarcely understood, with head heavy and dazed with sleep, and the great cold struck him like an icy douche.

"Then make them go down, by George!" he stammered.

"It's been going on an hour," said the captain. "Then we thought it best to come for you. Perhaps you will be able to persuade them."

"Very good; I'll go."

He quickly dressed himself, his mind quite clear now, and very anxious. The house might have been pillaged; neither the cook nor the man-servant had stirred. But from the other side of the staircase alarmed voices were whispering; and when he came out he saw his daughters' door open, and they both appeared in white dressing-gowns, slipped on in haste.

"Father, what is it?"

Lucie, the elder, was already twenty-two, a tall dark girl, with a haughty air; while Jeanne, the younger, as yet scarcely nineteen years old, was small, with golden hair and a certain caressing grace.

"Nothing serious," he replied, to re-assure them. "It seems that some blusterers are making a disturbance down there. I am going to see."

But they exclaimed that they would not let him go before he

had taken something warm. If not he would come back ill, with his stomach out of order, as he always did. He struggled, gave his word of honour that he was too much in a hurry.

"Listen!" said Jeanne, at last, hanging to his neck, "you must drink a little glass of rum and eat two biscuits, or I shall remain like this, and you'll have to take me with you."

He resigned himself, declaring that the biscuits would choke him. They had already gone down before him, each with her candlestick. In the dining-room below they hastened to serve him, one pouring out the rum, the other running to the pantry for the biscuits. Having lost their mother when very young, they had been rather badly brought up alone, spoilt by their father, the elder haunted by the dream of singing on the stage, the younger mad over painting in which she showed a singular boldness of taste. But when they had to retrench, after the embarrassment in their affairs, these apparently extravagant girls had suddenly developed into very sensible and shrewd managers, with an eye for errors of centimes in accounts. To-day, with their boyish and artistic demeanour, they kept the purse, were careful over sous, haggled with the tradesmen, renovated their dresses unceasingly, and, in fact, succeeded in rendering decent the growing embarrassment of the house.

"Eat, papa," repeated Lucie.

Then, remarking his silent gloomy pre-occupation, she was again frightened.

"It is serious, then, that you look at us like this? Tell us; we will stay with you, and they can do without us at that lunch."

She was speaking of a party which had been planned for the morning. Madame Hennebeau was to go in her carriage, first for Cécile, at the Grégoires, then to call for them, so that they could all go to Marchiennes to dine at the Forges, where the manager's wife had invited them. It was an opportunity to visit the workshops, the blast furnaces and the coke ovens.

"We will certainly remain," declared Jeanne, in her turn.

But he grew angry.

"A fine idea! I tell you that it is nothing. Just be so good as to get back into your beds again, and dress yourselves for nine o'clock, as was arranged."

He kissed them and hastened to leave. They heard the noise of his boots vanishing over the frozen earth in the garden.

Jeanne carefully placed the stopper in the rum bottle, while Lucie locked up the biscuits. The room had the cold neatness of dining-rooms where the table is but meagrely supplied. And both of them took advantage of this early descent to see if anything had been left uncared for the evening before. A serviette lay about, the servant should be scolded. At last they went upstairs again.

While he was taking the shortest cut through the narrow paths of his kitchen garden, Deneulin was thinking of his compromised fortune, this Montsou denier, this million which he had realised, dreaming to multiply it tenfold, and which was today running such great risks. It was an uninterrupted course of ill-luck, enormous and unforseen repairs, ruinous conditions of exploitation, then the disaster of this industrial crisis, just when the profits were beginning to come in. If the strike broke out here, he would be overthrown. He pushed a little door: the buildings of the pit could be divined in the black night, by the deepening of the shadow, starred by a few lanterns.

Jean-Bart was not so important as the Voreux, but its renewed installation made it a pretty pit, as the engineers say. They had not been contented by enlarging the shaft one mètre and a-half, and deepening it to seven hundred and eight mètres, they had equipped it afresh with a new engine, new cages, entirely new material, all set up according to the latest scientific improvements; and even a certain seeking for elegance was visible in the constructions, a screening shed with carved scallops, a steeple adorned with a clock, a receiving room and an engine room both rounded into an apse like a Renaissance chapel, and surmounted by a chimney with a mosaic spiral made of black bricks and red bricks. The pump was placed on the other shaft of the concession, the old Gaston-Marie pit, reserved solely for this purpose. Jean-Bart, to right and left of the winding shaft, only had two conduits, that for the steam ventilator and that for the ladders.

In the morning, ever since three o'clock, Chaval, who had arrived first, had been seducing his comrades, convincing them that they ought to imitate those at Montsou, and demand an increase of five centimes a tram. Soon four hundred workmen had passed from the shed into the receiving room, in the midst of a tumult of gesticulation and shouting. Those who wished to work stood with their lamps, barefooted, with shovel or pick beneath their arms; while the others, still in their sabots, with their overcoats on their shoulders because of the great cold, were barring the shaft; and the captains were growing hoarse in the effort to restore order, begging them to be reasonable and not to prevent those who wanted from going down.

But Chaval was furious when he saw Catherine in her trousers and jacket, her head tied up in the blue cap. On getting up, he had roughly told her to stay in bed. In despair at this arrest of work she had followed him all the same, for he never gave her any money; she often had to pay both for herself and him; and what was to become of her if she earned nothing? She was overcome by fear, the fear of a brothel at Marchiennes,[2] which was the end of putter-girls without bread and without lodging.

"By God!" cried Chaval, "what the devil have you come here for?"

She stammered that she had no income to live on and that she wanted to work.

"Then you put yourself against me, wench? Back you go at once, or I'll go back with you and kick my sabots into your backside!"

She recoiled timidly but she did not leave, resolved to see how things would turn out. Deneulin had arrived by the screening stairs. In spite of the weak light of the lanterns, with a quick look he took in the scene, with this troop drowned in shade; he knew every face, the pikemen, the porters, the landers, the putters, even the trammers. In the nave, still new and clean, the arrested task was waiting; the steam in the engine, under pressure, made slight whistling sounds; the cages were hanging motionless to the cables; the trains abandoned on the way were encumbering the metal floors. Scarcely eighty lamps had been taken; the others were flaming in the lamp cabin. But no doubt a word from him would suffice, and the whole life of work would begin again.

"Well, what's going on then, my lads?" he asked in a loud

voice. "What are you angry about? Just explain to me and we will see if we can agree."

He usually behaved in a paternal way towards his men, while at the same time demanding hard work. With an authoritative, rough manner, he had tried to conquer them by good-nature which had its outbursts of passion, and he often gained their love; the men especially respected in him his courage, always in the cuttings with them, the first in danger whenever an accident terrified the pit. Twice, after fire-damp explosions, he had been let down, fastened by a rope under his arm pits, when the bravest drew back.

"Now," he began again, "you are not going to make me repent having trusted you. You know that I have refused a body of police. Talk quietly and I will hear you."

All were now silent and awkward, moving away from him; and it was Chaval who at last said:

"Well, Monsieur Deneulin, we can't go on working; we must have five centimes more the tram."

He seemed surprised.

"What! five centimes! and why this demand? I don't complain about your timbering, I don't want to impose a new tariff on you like the Montsou directors."

"Maybe! but the Montsou mates are right, all the same. They won't have the tariff, and they want a rise of five centimes because it is not possible to work properly at the present rates. We want five centimes more, don't we, you others?"

Voices approved, and the noise began again in the midst of violent gesticulation. Gradually they drew near, forming a small circle.

A flame came into Deneulin's eyes, and his fist, that of a man who liked strong government, was clenched, for fear of yielding to temptation of seizing one of them by the neck. He preferred to discuss on the basis of reason.

"You want five centimes, and I agree that the work is worth it. Only I can't give it. If I gave it I should simply be done for. You must understand that I have to live first in order for you to live, and I've got to the end, the least rise in net prices will upset me. Two years ago, you remember, at the time of the last strike, I yielded, I was able to then. But that rise of wages was not the less ruinous, for these two years have been a struggle. To-day I would rather let the whole thing go than not be able to tell next month where to get the money to pay you."

Chaval laughed roughly in the face of this master who told them his affairs so frankly. The others lowered their faces, obstinate and incredulous, refusing to take into their heads the idea that a master did not gain millions out of his men.

Then Deneulin, persisting, explained his struggle with Montsou, always on the watch and ready to devour him if, some day, he had the stupidity to come to grief. It was a savage competition which forced him to economise, the more so since the depth of Jean-Bart increased the price of extraction, an unfavourable condition hardly compensated by the great thickness of the coal-beds. He would never have raised wages after the last strike if it had not been necessary for him to imitate Montsou, for fear of seeing his men leave him. And he threatened them with the morrow; a fine result it would be for them, if they obliged him to sell, to pass beneath the terrible yoke of the directors! He did not sit on a throne far away in an unknown sanctuary; he was not one of those shareholders who pay agents to shave close the miner who has never seen them; he was a master, he risked something besides his money, he risked his intelligence, his health, his life. Stoppage of work would simply mean death, for he had no stock, and he must fulfil orders. Besides, his standing capital could not sleep. How could he keep his engagements? Who would pay the interest on the sums his friends had confided to him? It would mean bankruptcy.

"That's where we are, my good fellows," he said, in conclusion. "I want to convince you. We don't ask a man to cut his own throat, do we? and if I give you your five centimes, or if I let you go out on strike, it's the same as if I cut my throat."

He was silent. Grunts went round. A party among the miners seemed to hesitate. Several went back towards the shaft.

"At least," said a captain, "let everyone be free. Who are those who want to work?"

Catherine had advanced among the first. But Chaval fiercely pushed her back, shouting:

"We are all agreed; it's only bloody fools who'll leave their mates!"

After that, conciliation appeared impossible. The cries began again, and men were hustled away from the shaft, at the risk of being crushed against the walls. For a moment the manager, in despair, tried to struggle alone, to reduce the crowd by violence; but it was useless madness, and he retired. For a few minutes he rested, out of breath, on a chair in the receiver's office, so overcome by his powerlessness that no ideas came to him. At last he grew calm, and told an inspector to go and bring Chaval; then, when the latter had agreed to the interview, he motioned the others away.

"Leave us."

Deneulin's idea was to see what this fellow was after. At the first words he felt that he was vain, and was devoured by passionate jealousy. Then he attacked him by flattery, affecting surprise that a workman of his merit should so compromise his future. It seemed as though he had long had his eyes on him for rapid advancement; and he ended by squarely offering to make him captain later on. Chaval listened in silence, with his fists at first clenched, but then gradually unbent. Something was working in the depths of his skull; if he persisted in the strike he would be nothing more than Étienne's lieutenant, while now another ambition opened, that of passing into the ranks of the bosses. The heat of pride rose to his face and intoxicated him. Besides, the band of strikers whom he had expected since the morning had not arrived; some obstacle must have stopped them, perhaps the police; it was time to submit. But all the same he shook his head; he acted the incorruptible man, striking his breast indignantly. Then, without mentioning to the master the rendezvous he had given to the Montsou men, he promised to calm his mates, and to persuade them to go down.

Deneulin remained hidden, and the captains themselves stood aside. For an hour they heard Chaval perorating and discussing, standing on a tram in the receiving-room. Some of the men hooted him; a hundred and twenty went off exasperated, persisting in the resolution which he had made them take. It was already past seven. The sun was rising brilliantly; it was a bright day of hard frost; and all at once movement began again in the pit, and the arrested labour went on. First the crank of the engine plunged, rolling and unrolling the cables on the drums. Then, in the midst of the tumult of the signals, the descent took place. The cages filled and were engulfed, and rose again, the shaft swallowing its ration of trammers and putters and pikemen; while on the metal floors the landers pushed the trains with a sound of thunder.

"By God! What the devil are you doing there?" cried Chaval to Catherine, who was awaiting her turn. "Will you just go down and not laze about!"

At nine o'clock, when Madame Hennebeau arrived in her carriage with Cécile, she found Lucie and Jeanne quite ready and very elegant, in spite of their toilets having been done up for the twentieth time. But Deneulin was surprised to see Négrel accompanying the carriage on horseback. What! were the men also in the party? Then Madame Hennebeau explained in her maternal way that they had frightened her by saying that the streets were full of evil faces, and so she preferred to bring a defender. Négrel laughed and re-assured them: nothing to cause anxiety, threats of brawlers as usual, but not one of them would dare to throw a stone at a window-pane. Still pleased with his success, Deneulin related the repressed rebellion at Jean-Bart. He said that he was now quite at rest. And on the Vandame road, while the young ladies got into the carriage, all congratulated themselves on the superb day, without guessing afar off in the country the long swelling shudder of the marching people, though they might have heard the sound of it if they had pressed their ears against the earth.

"Well! it is agreed," repeated Madame Hennebeau. "This evening you will call for the young ladies and dine with us. Madame Grégoire has also promised to come for Cécile."

"You may reckon on me," replied Deneulin.

The carriage went off towards Vandame, Jeanne and Lucie leaning down to laugh once more to their father, who was standing by the roadside; while Négrel gallantly trotted behind the fleeing wheels.

They crossed the forest, taking the road from Vandame to

Marchiennes. As they approached Tartaret, Jeanne asked Madame Hennebeau if she knew Côte-Verte, and the latter, in spite of her stay of five years in the country, acknowledged that she had never been on that side. Then they made a *détour.* Tartaret, on the outskirts of the forest, was an uncultivated moor, of volcanic sterility, under which for ages a coal mine had been burning. Its history was lost in legend. The miners of the place said that fire from Heaven had fallen on this Sodom in the bowels of the earth, where the putter-girls had committed abominations together, so that they had not even had the time to come to the surface, and to-day were still burning at the bottom of this hell. The calcined rocks, of a sombre red, were covered by an efflorescence of alum as by a leprosy. Sulphur grew like a yellow flower at the edge of the fissures. At night, those who were brave enough to venture to look into these holes declared that they saw flames there, sinful souls shrivelling in the furnace within. Wandering lights moved over the soil and hot vapours; the poisons from the devil's ordure and his dirty kitchen were constantly smoking. And like a miracle of eternal spring, in the midst of this accursed moor of Tartaret, Côte-Verte appeared, with its meadows for ever green, its beeches with leaves unceasingly renewed, its fields where three harvests grew ripe. It was a natural hot-house, warmed by the fire in the deep strata beneath. The snow never lay on it. The enormous bouquet of verdure, beside the leafless forest trees, blossomed on this December day, and the frost had not even scorched the edge of it.

Soon the carriage was passing over the plain. Négrel joked over the legend, and explained that a fire often occurred at the bottom of a mine from the fermentation of the coal dust; if not mastered it would burn on for ever, and he mentioned a Belgian pit which had been cleansed by turning a river and throwing it into the pit. But he became silent. For the last few minutes groups of miners had been constantly passing the carriage; they went by in silence, with side-long looks at the luxurious equipage which forced them to stand aside. Their number went on increasing. The horses were obliged to cross the little bridge of the Scarpe at walking pace. What was going on, then, to bring all these people into the roads? The young ladies became frightened, and Négrel began to smell out some fray in the excited country; it was a relief when they at last arrived at Marchiennes. The batteries of coke ovens and the chimneys of the blast furnaces, beneath a sun which seemed to extinguish them, were belching out smoke and raining their everlasting soot through the air.

## CHAPTER II

AT JEAN-BART, CATHERINE had already been at work for an hour, pushing trams as far as the relays; and she was soaked in such a bath of perspiration that she stopped a moment to wipe her face.

At the bottom of the cutting, where he was hammering at the seam with his mates, Chaval was astonished when he no longer heard the rumble of the wheels. The lamps burnt badly, and the coal dust made it impossible to see.

"What's up?" he shouted.

When she answered that she was sure she would melt, and that her heart was going to stop, he replied furiously:

"Do like us, stupid! Take off your shift."

They were seven hundred and eight mètres to the north in the first passage of the Désirée seam, which was at a distance of three kilomètres from the pit-eye. When they spoke of this part of the pit, the miners of the region grew pale, and lowered their voices, as if they had spoken of hell; and most often they were content to shake their heads as men who would rather not speak of these depths of fiery furnace. As the galleries sank towards the north, they approached Tartaret, penetrating to that interior fire which calcined the rocks above. The cuttings at the point at which they had arrived had an average temperature of forty-five degrees. They were there in the accursed city, in the midst of the flames which the passers-by on the plain could see through the fissures, spitting out sulphur and poisonous vapours.

Catherine, who had already taken off her jacket, hesitated, then took off her trousers also; and with naked arms and naked thighs, her chemise tied round her hips by a cord like a blouse, she began to push again.

"Anyhow, that's better," she said aloud.

In the stifling heat she still felt a vague fear. Ever since they began working here, five days ago, she had thought of the stories told her in childhood, of those putter-girls of the days of old who were burning beneath Tartaret, as a punishment for things which no one dared to repeat. No doubt she was too big now to believe such silly stories; but still, what should she do if she were suddenly to see coming out of the wall a girl as red as a stove, with eyes like live coals? The idea made her perspire still more.

At the relay, eighty mètres from the cutting, another putter took the tram and pushed it eighty mètres farther to the upbrow, so that the receiver could forward it with the others which came down from the upper galleries.

"Gracious! you're making yourself comfortable!" said this woman, a lean widow of thirty, when she saw Catherine in her chemise. "I can't do it, the trammers at the brow bother me with their dirty tricks."

"Ah, well!" replied the young girl. "I don't care about the men! I feel too bad."

She went off again, pushing an empty tram. The worst was that in this bottom passage another cause joined to the neighbourhood of Tartaret to make the heat unbearable. They were by the side of old workings, a very deep abandoned gallery of Gaston-Marie, where, ten years earlier, an explosion of firedamp had set alight the seam; and it was still burning behind the clay wall which had been built there, and was kept constantly repaired, in order to limit the disaster. Deprived of air, the fire ought to have become extinct, but no doubt unknown currents kept it alive; it had gone on for ten years, and heated the clay wall like the bricks of an oven, so that those who passed felt half-roasted. It was along this wall, for a length of more than a hundred mètres, that the haulage was carried on, in a temperature of sixty degrees.

After two journeys, Catherine again felt stifled. Fortunately, the passage was large and convenient in this Désirée seam, one of the thickest in the district. The bed was one mètre ninety in height, and the men could work standing. But they would rather have worked with twisted necks and a little fresh air.

"Hallo, there! are you asleep?" said Chaval again, roughly, as soon as he no longer heard Catherine moving. "How the devil did I come to get such a jade? Will you just fill your tram and push?"

She was at the bottom of the cutting, leaning on her shovel; she was feeling ill, and she looked at them all with a foolish air without obeying. She scarcely saw them by the reddish gleam of the lamps, entirely naked like animals, so black, so encrusted in sweat and coal, that their nakedness did not frighten her. It was a confused task, the bending of ape-like backs, an infernal vision of reddish limbs, spending their strength amid deep blows and groans. But they could see her better, no doubt, for the axes left off hammering, and they joked her about taking off her trousers.

"Eh! you'll catch cold; look out!"

"It's because she's got such fine legs! I say, Chaval, there are enough for two."

"Oh! we must see. Lift up! Higher! higher!"

Then Chaval, without growing angry at these jokes, turned on to her.

"That's it, by God! Ah! she likes dirty jokes. She'd stay there to listen till to-morrow."

Catherine had painfully decided to fill her tram, then she pushed it. The gallery was too wide for her to buttress herself to the timber on both sides; her naked feet were twisted in the rails where she sought a point of support, while she slowly moved on, her arms stiffened in front, and her back breaking. As soon as she came up to the clay wall, the fiery torture again began, and the sweat fell from her whole body in enormous drops, as from a storm cloud. She had scarcely got a third of the way before she streamed, blinded, soiled also by the black mud. Her narrow chemise, as though dipped in ink, was sticking to her skin, and rising up to her waist with the movement of her thighs; it bridled her so painfully that she had once more to stop her task.

What was the matter with her, then, to-day? Never before had she felt as if there were wool in her bones. It must be the bad air.

The ventilation did not reach to the bottom of this distant passage. One breathed there all sorts of vapours, which came out of the coal with the low bubbling sound of a spring, so abundantly sometimes that the lamps would not burn; to say nothing of fire-damp, which nobody noticed, for from one week's end to the other the men were always breathing it into their noses throughout the seam. She knew that bad air well; dead air the miners called it;[3] it was below the heavy asphyxiating gases, above the light gases which catch fire and blow up all the stalls of a pit, with hundreds of men, in a single burst of thunder. From her childhood she had swallowed so much that she was surprised she bore it so badly, with buzzing ears and burning throat.

Unable to go further, she felt the need of taking off her chemise. It was beginning to torture her, this garment of which the least folds cut and burnt her. She resisted the longing, and tried to push again, but was forced to stand upright. Then quickly, saying to herself that she would cover herself at the relay, she took off everything, the cord and the chemise, so feverishly that she would have torn off her skin if she could. And now, naked and pitiful, brought down to the level of the female animal seeking its living in the mire of the streets, with rump covered with soot and mud up to the belly, she laboured on like a cab-hack. On all-fours she pushed onwards.

But despair came; it gave her no relief to be naked. What more could she take off? The buzzing in her ears deafened her; she seemed to feel a vice pressing in her temples. She fell on her knees. The lamp, wedged into the coal in the tram, seemed to her to be going out. The intention to turn up the wick alone survived in the midst of her confused ideas. Twice she tried to examine it, and both times when she placed it before her on the earth she saw it turn pale, as though it also lacked breath. Suddenly the lamp went out. Then everything whirled around her in the darkness; a millstone turned in her head, her heart grew weak and left off beating, numbed in its turn by the immense weariness which was putting her limbs to sleep. She had fallen back in anguish amid the asphyxiating air close to the ground.

"By God! I believe she's lazing again," growled Chaval's voice.

He listened from the top of the cutting, and could hear no sound of wheels.

"Eh, Catherine! you damned sluggard!"

His voice was lost afar in the black gallery, and not a breath replied.

"I'll come and make you move, I will!"

Nothing stirred, there was only the same silence, as of death. He came down furiously, rushing along with his lamp so violently that he nearly fell over the putter's body which barred the way. He looked at her in stupefaction. What was the matter, then? was it humbug, a pretence of going to sleep? But the lamp which he had lowered to light up her face threatened to go out. He lifted it and lowered it afresh, and at last understood: it must be a gust of bad air. His violence disappeared; the devotion of the miner in face of a comrade's peril was awaking within him. He shouted for her chemise to be brought; and seized the naked and fainting girl in his arms, holding her as high as possible. When their garments had been thrown over their shoulders he set out running, supporting his burden with one hand, and carrying the two lamps with the other. The deep galleries unrolled before him as he rushed along, turning to the right, then to the left, seeking life in the frozen air of the plain which blew down the air-shaft. At last the sound of a spring stopped him, the rustling of water flowing through the rock. He was at a square in the great haulage gallery which formerly led to Gaston-Marie. The air here blew in like a tempest, and was so fresh that a shudder went through him as he seated himself on the earth against the props; his mistress was still unconscious, with closed eyes.

"Catherine, come now, by God! no humbug. Hold yourself up a bit while I dip this in the water."

He was frightened to find her so limp. However, he was able to dip her chemise in the spring, and to bathe her face with it. She was like a corpse, already buried at the bottom of the earth, with her slender girlish body which seemed to be still hesitating before swelling to the form of puberty. Then a shudder ran over her childish breast, over the belly and thighs of the poor little creature deflowered before her time. She opened her eyes and stammered:

"I'm cold."

"Ah! that's better now!" cried Chaval, relieved.

He dressed her, slipped on the chemise easily, but swore over the difficulty he had in getting on the trousers, for she could not help much. She remained dazed, not understanding where she was, nor why she was naked. When she remembered she was ashamed. How had she dared to take everything off! And she questioned him; had she been seen so, without even a handkerchief around her waist to cover her? He joked, and made up stories, saying that he had just brought her there in the midst of all the mates standing in a row. What an idea, to have taken his advice and exhibit her! Afterwards he declared that the mates could not even know whether she was round or square, he had rushed along so swiftly.

"The deuce! but I'm dying of cold," he said, dressing himself in turn.

Never had she seen him so kind. Usually, for one good word that he said to her she received at once two bullying ones. It would have been so pleasant to live in agreement; a feeling of tenderness went through her in the languor of her fatigue. She smiled at him, and murmured:

"Kiss me."

He embraced her, and lay down beside her, waiting till she was able to walk.

"You know," she said again, "you were wrong to shout at me over there, for I couldn't do more, true! Even in the cutting you're not so hot; if you only knew how it roasts you at the bottom of the passage!"

"Sure enough," he replied, "it would be better under the trees. You feel bad, in that stall, I'm afraid, my poor girl."

She was so touched at hearing him agree with her that she tried to be brave.

"Oh! it's a bad place. Then, to-day the air is poisoned. But you shall see soon if I'm a sluggard. When one has to work, one works; isn't it true? I'd die rather than stop."

There was silence. He held her with one arm round her waist, pressing her against his breast to keep her from harm. Although she already felt strong enough to go back to the stall, she forgot everything in her delight.

"Only," she went on in a very low voice, "I should like it so much if you were kinder. Yes, it is so good when we love each other a little."

And she began to cry softly.

"But I do love you," he cried, "for I've taken you with me."

She only replied by shaking her head. There are often men who take women just in order to have them, caring mighty little about their happiness. Her tears flowed more hotly; it made her despair now to think of the happy life she would have led if she had chanced to fall to another lad, whose arm she would always have felt thus round her waist. Another? and the vague image of that other arose from the depth of her emotion. But it was done with; she only desired now to live to the end with this one, if he would not hustle her about too much.

"Then," she said, "try to be like this sometimes."

Sobs cut short her words, and he embraced her again.

"You're a stupid! There, I swear to be kind. I'm not worse than anyone else, go on!"

She looked at him, and began to smile through her tears. Perhaps he was right; one never met women who were happy. Then, although she distrusted his oath, she gave herself up to the joy of seeing him affectionate. Good God! if only that could last! They had both embraced again, and as they were pressing each other in a long clasp they heard steps, which made them get up. Three mates who had seen them pass had come up to know how she was.

They set out together. It was nearly ten o'clock, and they took their lunch into a fresh corner before going back to sweat at the bottom of the cutting. They were finishing the double slice of bread-and-butter, their brick, and were about to drink the coffee from their tin, when they were disturbed by a noise coming from stalls in the distance. What then? was it another accident? They got up and ran. Pikemen, putters, trammers crossed them at every step; no one knew anything; all were shouting that it must be some great misfortune. Gradually the whole mine was in terror, frightened shadows emerged from the galleries, lanterns danced and flew away in the darkness. Where was it? Why could no one say?

All at once a captain passed, shouting:

"They are cutting the cables![4] they are cutting the cables!"

Then the panic increased. It was a furious gallop through the gloomy passages. Their heads were confused. Why cut the cables? And who was cutting them, when the men were down below? It seemed monstrous.

But the voice of another captain was heard and then lost.

"The Montsou men are cutting the cables! Let everyone go up!"

When he had understood, Chaval stopped Catherine short. The idea that he would meet the Montsou men up above, should he get out, paralysed his legs. It had come, then, that band which he thought had got into the hands of the police. For a moment he thought of retracing his path and ascending through Gaston-Marie, but that was no longer possible. He swore, hesitating, hiding his fear, repeating that it was stupid to run like that. They would not, perhaps, leave them at the bottom.

The captain's voice echoed anew, now approaching them.

"Let everyone go up! To the ladders! to the ladders!"

And Chaval was carried away with his mates. He pushed Catherine and accused her of not running fast enough. Did she want, then, to remain in the pit to die of hunger? For those Montsou brigands were capable of breaking the ladders without waiting for people to come up. This abominable suggestion finished driving them wild. Along the galleries there was now only a furious rush, helter-skelter; a race of madmen, each striving to arrive first and mount before the others. Some men shouted that the ladders were broken and that no one could come out. And then in frightened groups they began to reach the pit-eye, where they were all engulfed. They threw themselves toward the shaft, they crushed through the narrow door to the ladder passage; while an old groom who had prudently led back the horses to the stable, looked at them with an air of contemptuous indifference, accustomed to spend nights in the pit and certain that he could always be drawn out of it.

"By God! will you climb up in front of me?" said Chaval to Catherine. "At least I can hold you if you fall."

Out of breath, and suffocated by this race of three kilomètres which had once more bathed her in sweat, she gave herself up, without understanding, to the eddies of the crowd. Then he pulled her by the arm, almost breaking it; and she cried with pain, her tears bursting out. Already he was forgetting his oath, never would she be happy.

"Go on, then!" he roared.

But he frightened her too much. If she went first he would bully her the whole time. So she resisted, while the wild flood of their comrades pushed them to one side. The water that filtered from the shaft was falling in great drops, and the floor of the pit-eye, shaken by this tramping, was trembling over the sump, the muddy cesspool ten mètres deep. At Jean-Bart, two years earlier, a terrible accident had happened just here; the breaking of a cable had precipitated the cage to the bottom of the sump, in which two men had been drowned. And they all thought of this; everyone would be left down there if they all crowded on to the planks.

"Confounded dunderhead!" shouted Chaval. "Die then; I shall be rid of you!"

He climbed up and she followed.

From the bottom to daylight there were a hundred and two ladders, about seven mètres in length, each placed on a narrow landing which occupied the breadth of the passage and in which a square hole scarcely allowed the shoulders to pass. It was like a flat chimney, seven hundred mètres in height, between the wall of the shaft and the brattice of the winding-cage, a damp pipe, black and endless, in which the ladders were placed one above the other, almost straight, in regular stages. It took a strong man twenty-five minutes to climb up this giant column. The passage, however, was no longer used except in cases of accident.

Catherine at first climbed bravely. Her naked feet were used to the hard coal on the floors of the passages, and did not suffer from the square rungs, covered with iron rods to prevent them from wearing away. Her hands, hardened by the haulage, grasped without fatigue the uprights that were too big for her. And it even interested her and took her out of her grief, this unforeseen ascent, this long serpent of men flowing on and hoisting themselves up three on a ladder, so that even when the head would emerge in daylight the tail would still be trailing over the sump. They were not there yet, the first could hardly have ascended a third of the shaft. No one spoke now, only their feet moved with a low sound; while the lamps, like travelling stars, spaced out from below upward, formed a continually increasing line.

Catherine heard a trammer behind her counting the ladders. It gave her the idea of counting them also. They had already mounted fifteen, and were arriving at a landing-place. But at that moment she fell between Chaval's legs. He swore, shouting to her to look out. Gradually the whole column stopped and became motionless. What then? had something happened? and everyone recovered his voice to ask questions and to express fear. Their anxiety had increased since leaving the bottom; their ignorance as to what was going on above oppressed them more as they approached daylight. Someone announced that they would have to go down again, that the ladders were broken. That was the thought that pre-occupied them all, the fear of finding themselves face to face with space. Another explanation came down from mouth to mouth, there had been an accident, a pikeman slipped from a rung. No one knew exactly, the shouts made it impossible to hear: were they going to bed there? At last, without any precise information being obtained, the ascent began again, with the same slow, painful movement, in the midst of the rolling of feet and the dancing of lamps. It must certainly be higher up that the ladders were broken.

At the thirty-second ladder, as they passed a third landing-stage, Catherine felt her legs and arms grow stiff. At first she had felt a slight tingling in her skin. Now she lost the sensation of the iron and the wood beneath her feet and in her hands. A vague pain, which gradually became burning, heated her muscles. And in the dizziness which came over her, she recalled her grandfather Bonnemort's stories of the days when there was no passage; and little girls often used to take out the coal on their shoulders[5] along bare ladders; so that if one of them slipped, or a fragment of coal simply rolled out of a basket, three or four children would fall down head first from the blow. The cramp in her limbs became unbearable, she would never reach the end.

Fresh stoppages allowed her to breathe. But the terror which was communicated every time from above dazed her still more. Above and below her, respiration became more difficult. This interminable ascent was causing giddiness, and the nausea affected her with the others. She was suffocating, intoxicated with the darkness, exasperated with the walls which crushed against her flesh, and shuddering also with the dampness, her body perspiring beneath the great drops which fell on her. They were approaching a level where so thick a rain fell that it threatened to extinguish their lamps.

Chaval twice spoke to Catherine without obtaining any reply. What the devil was she doing down there? Had she let her tongue fall? She might just tell him if she was all right. They had been climbing for half-an-hour, but so heavily that he had only reached the fifty-ninth ladder; there were still forty-three. Catherine at last stammered that she was getting on all right. He would have treated her as a sluggard if she had acknowledged her weariness. The iron of the rungs must have cut her feet; it seemed to her that it was sawing in up to the bone. After every grip she expected to see her hands leave the uprights; they were so peeled and stiff that she could not close her fingers, and she feared she would fall backward with torn shoulders and disjointed thighs in this continual effort. It was especially the defective slope of the ladders from which she suffered, the almost perpendicular position which obliged her to hoist herself up by the strength of her wrists, with her belly against the wood. The panting of many breaths now drowned the sound of the feet, forming an enormous moan, multiplied tenfold by the partition of the passage, arising from the depths and expiring towards the light. There was a groan; word ran along that a trammer had just cut open his head at the edge of a stair.

And Catherine went on climbing. They had passed the level.

The rain had ceased; a mist made heavy the cellar-like air, poisoned with the odour of old iron and damp wood. Mechanically she continued to count in a low voice—eighty-one, eighty-two, eighty-three; still nineteen. The repetition of these figures supported her merely by their rhythmic balance; she had no further consciousness of her movements. When she lifted her eyes the lamps turned in a spiral. Her blood was flowing; she felt that she was dying; the least breath would have knocked her over. The worst was that those below were now pushing, and that the entire column was rushing on, yielding to the growing anger of its fatigue, the furious need to see the sun again. The first mates had emerged; there were, then, no broken ladders; but the idea that they might yet be broken to prevent the last from coming up, when others were already breathing up above, nearly drove them mad. And when a new stoppage occurred oaths broke out, and all went on climbing, hustling each other, passing over each other's bodies to arrive at all costs.

Then Catherine fell. She had cried Chaval's name in despairing appeal. He did not hear; he was struggling, digging his heels into a comrade's ribs to get before him. And she was rolled down and trampled over. As she fainted she dreamed. It seemed to her that she was one of the little putter girls of old days, and that a fragment of coal, fallen from the basket above her, had thrown her to the bottom of the shaft, like a sparrow struck by a flint. Five ladders only remained to climb. It had taken nearly an hour. She never knew how she reached daylight, carried up by the shoulders, supported by the throttling narrowness of the passage. Suddenly she found herself in the dazzling sunlight, in the midst of a yelling crowd who were hooting her.

## CHAPTER III

FROM EARLY MORNING, BEFORE daylight, a tremor had agitated the settlements, and that tremor was now swelling through the roads and over the whole country. But the departure had not taken place as arranged, for the news had spread that cavalry and police were scouring the plain. It was said that they had arrived from Douai during the night, and Rasseneur was accused of having betrayed his mates by warning M. Hennebeau; a putter even swore that she had seen the servant taking a despatch to the telegraph office. The miners clenched their fists and watched the soldiers from behind their shutters by the pale light of the early morning.

Towards half-past seven, as the sun was rising, another rumour circulated, reassuring the impatient. It was a false alarm, a simple military promenade, which the General occasionally ordered since the strike had broken out, at the desire of the Prefect of Lille. The strikers detested this official; they reproached him with deceiving them by the promise of a conciliatory intervention, which was limited to a march of troops into Montsou every week, to overawe them. So when the cavalry and police quietly took the road back to Marchiennes, after contenting themselves with deafening the settlements by the stamping of their horses over the hard earth, the miners jeered at this innocent prefect and his soldiers who turned on their heels when things were beginning to get hot. Up till nine o'clock they stood peacefully about, in good humour, before their houses, following with their eyes up the streets the compliant backs of the last gendarmes. In the depths of their large beds the good people of Montsou were still sleeping, with their heads among the feathers. At the manager's house, Madame Hennebeau had just been seen setting out in the carriage, leaving M. Hennebeau at work, no doubt, for the closed and silent villa seemed dead. Not one of the pits had any military guard; it was a fatal lack of foresight in the hour of danger, the natural stupidity which accompanies catastrophes, the fault which a Government commits whenever there is need of precise knowledge of the facts. And nine o'clock was striking when the colliers at last took the Vandame road, to repair to the rendezvous decided on the day before in the forest.

Étienne had very quickly perceived that he would certainly not find over at Jean-Bart the three thousand comrades on whom he was counting. Many believed that the demonstration was put off, and the worst was that two or three bands, already on the way, would compromise the cause if he did not at all costs put himself at their head. Almost a hundred, who had set out before daylight, were taking refuge beneath the forest beeches, waiting for the others. Souvarine, whom the young man went up to consult, shrugged his shoulders; ten resolute fellows could do more work than a crowd; and he turned back to the open book before him, refusing to join in. The thing threatened to turn into sentiment when it would have been enough to adopt the simple method of burning Montsou. As Étienne left the house he saw Rasseneur, seated before the metal stove and looking very pale, while his wife, in her everlasting black dress, was abusing him in polite and cutting terms.

Maheu was of opinion that they ought to keep their promise. A rendezvous like this was sacred. However, the night had calmed their fever; he was now fearing misfortune, and he explained that it was their duty to go over there to maintain their mates in the right path. Maheude approved with a nod. Étienne repeated complacently that it was necessary to adopt revolutionary methods, without attempting any person's life. Before setting out he refused his share of a loaf that had been given him the evening before, together with a bottle of gin; but he drank three little glasses, one after the other, saying that he wanted to keep out the cold; he even carried away a tinful. Alzire would look after the children. Old Bonnemort, whose legs were suffering from yesterday's walk, remained in bed.

They did not go away together, from motives or prudence. Jeanlin had disappeared long ago. Maheu and Maheude went off on the side sloping towards Montsou; while Étienne turned towards the forest, where he proposed to join his mates. On the way he caught up a band of women, among whom he recognised Mother Brûlé and the Levaque woman; as they walked they were eating chestnuts which Mouquette had brought; they swallowed the skins so as to feel more in their stomachs. But in the forest he found no one; the men were already at Jean-Bart. He took the same course, and arrived at the pit at the moment when Levaque and some hundred others were penetrating into the square. Miners were coming up from every direction—the men by the main road, the women by the fields, all at random, without leaders, without weapons, flowing naturally there like water which runs down a slope. Étienne perceived Jeanlin, who had climbed up the foot-bridge, installed as though at a theatre. He ran faster, and entered among the first. There were scarcely three hundred of them.

There was some hesitation when Deneulin showed himself at the top of the staircase which led to the receiving-room.

"What do you want?" he asked in a loud voice.

After having watched the disappearance of the carriage from which his daughters were still laughing towards him, he had returned to the pit overtaken by a vague anxiety. Everything, however, was found in good order. The men had gone down; the cage was working, and he became reassured again, and was talking to the head captain when the approach of the strikers was announced to him. He had placed himself at a window of the screening-shed; and in the face of this increasing flood which filled the square, he at once felt his impotence. How could he defend these buildings, open on every side? he could scarcely group some twenty of his workmen round himself. He was lost.

"What do you want?" he repeated, pale with repressed anger, making an effort to accept his disaster courageously.

There were pushes and growls amid the crowd. Étienne at last came forward, saying:

"We do not come to injure you, sir, but work must cease everywhere."

Deneulin frankly treated him as an idiot.

"Do you think you will benefit me if you stop work at my place? You might just as well fire a gun off into my back. Yes, my men are below, and they shall not come up, unless you mean to murder me first!"

These rough words raised a clamour. Maheu had to hold back Levaque, who was pushing forward in a threatening manner, while Étienne, always acting in a parliamentary fashion, tried to convince Deneulin of the lawfulness of their revolutionary conduct. But the latter replied by the right to work. Besides, he refused to discuss such folly; he meant to be master in his own place. His only regret was that he had not four gendarmes here to sweep away this mob.

"To be sure, it is my fault; I deserve what has happened to me.

With fellows of your sort force is the only argument. The Government thinks to buy you by concessions. You will throw it down, that's all, when it has given you weapons."

Étienne was quivering, but still held himself in. He lowered his voice.

"I beg you, sir, give the order for your men to come up. I cannot answer for my mates. You may avoid a disaster."

"No! be good enough to let me alone! Do I know you? You do not belong to my works, you have no quarrel with me. It is only brigands who thus scour the country to pillage houses."

Loud vociferations now drowned his voice, the women especially abused him. But he continued to hold his own, experiencing a certain relief in this frankness with which he expressed his disciplinarian's nature. Since he was ruined in any case, he thought platitudes a useless cowardice. But their number went on increasing; nearly five hundred were pushing towards the door, and he might have been torn to pieces if his head captain had not pulled him violently back.

"If you please, sir! There will be a massacre. What is the good of letting men be killed for nothing?"

He struggled and protested in one last cry thrown at the crowd.

"You set of brigands, you will know what, when we are strongest again!"

They led him away; the hustling of the crowd had thrown the first ranks against the staircase so that the rail was twisted. It was the women who pushed and screamed and urged on the men. The door yielded at once; it was a door without a lock, simply closed by a latch. But the staircase was too narrow for the pushing crowd, which would have taken long to get in if the rear of the besiegers had not gone off to enter by other openings. Then they poured in on all sides—by the shed, the screening place, the boiler buildings. In less than five minutes the whole pit belonged to them; they swarmed at every storey in the midst of furious gestures and cries, carried away by their victory over this master who resisted.

Maheu, in terror, had rushed forward among the first, saying to Étienne:

"They must not kill him!"

The latter was already running; then, when Étienne understood that Deneulin had barricaded himself in the captains' room, he replied:

"Well, would it be our fault? such a madman!"

He was feeling anxious, however, being still too calm to yield to this outburst of anger. His pride of leadership also suffered on seeing the band escape from his authority and become enraged, going beyond the cold execution of the will of the people, such as he had anticipated. In vain he called for coolness, he shouted that they must not put right on their enemies' side by acts of useless destruction.

"To the boilers!" shouted Mother Brûlé. "Put out the fires!"

Levaque, who had found a file, was brandishing it like a dagger, dominating the tumult with a terrible cry:

"Cut the cables! cut the cables!"

Soon they all repeated this; only Étienne and Maheu continued to protest, dazed, and talking in the tumult without attaining silence. At last the former was able to say:

"But there are men below, mates!"

The noise redoubled and voices arose from all sides.

"So much the worse!—Ought not to go down!—Serve the traitors right!—Yes, yes, let them stay there!—And then, they have the ladders!"

Then, when this idea of the ladders had made them still more obstinate, Étienne saw that he would have to yield. For fear of a greater disaster he hastened towards the engine, wishing at all events to bring the cages up, so that the cables, being cut above the shaft, should not smash them by falling down with their enormous weight. The engine-man had disappeared as well as the few daylight workers; and he took hold of the starting lever, manipulating it while Levaque and two others climbed up the metal scaffold which supported the pulleys. The cages were hardly fixed on the keeps when the strident sound was heard of the file biting into the steel. There was deep silence, and this noise seemed to fill the whole pit; all raised their heads, looking and listening, seized by emotion. In the first rank Maheu felt a fierce joy possess him, as if the teeth of the file would deliver them from misfortune by eating into the cable of one of these dens of wretchedness, into which they would never descend again.

But Mother Brûlé had disappeared by the shed stairs, still shouting:

"The fires must be put out! To the boilers! to the boilers!"

Some women followed her. Maheude hastened to prevent them from smashing everything, just as her husband had tried to reason with the men. She was the calmest of them; one could demand one's rights without making a mess in people's places. When she entered the boiler building the women were already chasing away the two stokers, and the Brûlé, armed with a large shovel, and crouching down before one of the stoves, was violently emptying it, throwing the red-hot coke on to the brick floor, where it continued to burn with black smoke. There were ten stoves for the five boilers. Soon the women warmed to the work, the Levaque manipulating her shovel with both hands, Mouquette raising her clothes up to her thighs so as not to catch fire, all looking red in the reflection of the flames, sweating and dishevelled in this witch's kitchen. The piles of coal increased, and the burning heat cracked the ceiling of the vast hall.

"Enough, now!" cried Maheude; "the storeroom is afire."

"So much the better," replied Mother Brûlé. "That will do the work. Ah, by God! haven't I said that I would pay them out for the death of my man!"

At this moment Jeanlin's shrill voice was heard.

"Look out! I'll put it out, I will! I'll let it all off!"

He had come in among the first, and had kicked his legs about among the crowd, delighted at the fray and seeking out what mischief he could do; the idea had occurred to him to turn on the discharge taps to let off steam.

The jets came out with the violence of volleys; the five boilers were emptied with the sound of a tempest, whistling in such a roar of thunder that one's ears seemed to bleed. Everything had disappeared in the midst of the vapour, the hot coal grew pale, and the women were nothing more than shadows with broken gestures. The child alone appeared mounted on the gallery, behind the whirlwinds of white steam, filled with delight and with wide-grinning mouth in the joy of unchaining this hurricane.

This lasted nearly a quarter of an hour. A few buckets of water had been thrown over the heaps to complete their extinction; all danger of a fire had gone by, but the anger of the crowd had not subsided; on the contrary, it had been whipped up. The men went down with hammers, even the women armed themselves with iron bars; and they talked of smashing boilers, of breaking engines, and of demolishing the mine.

Étienne, forewarned, hastened to come up with Maheu. He himself was becoming intoxicated and carried away by this hot fever of revenge. He struggled, however, and entreated them to be calm, now that, with cut cables, extinguished fires, and empty boilers, work was impossible. He was not always listened to; and was again about to be carried away by the crowd, when hoots arose outside at a little low door where the ladder passage emerged.

"Down with the traitors!—Oh! the dirty chops of the cowards!—Down with them! down with them!"

The men were beginning to come up from below. The first arrivals, blinded by the daylight, stood there with quivering eyelids. Then they moved away, trying to gain the road and flee.

"Down with the cowards! down with the traitors!"

The whole band of strikers had run up. In less than three minutes there was not a man left in the buildings; the five hundred Montsou men were ranged in two rows, and the Vandame men, who had had the treachery to go down, were forced to pass between this double hedge. And as every fresh miner appeared at the door of the passage, covered with the black mud of work and with garments in rags, the hooting redoubled, and ferocious jokes arose. Oh! look at that one!—three inches of legs and then her arse! and this one with his nose eaten by those Volcan girls! and this other, with eyes pissing out enough wax to furnish ten cathedrals! and this other, the tall fellow without a rump and as long as a Lent! An enormous putter-woman, who rolled out with her breast to her belly and her belly to her backside, raised a furious laugh. They wanted to handle them, the joking increased and was turning to cruelty, blows would soon have rained; while the row of poor devils came out shivering and silent beneath the abuse, with sidelong looks in expectation of blows, glad when they could at last rush away out of the mine.

"Hallo! how many are there in there?" asked Étienne.

He was astonished to see them still coming out, and irritated at the idea that it was not a mere handful of workers, terrorised by the captains. They had lied to him, then, in the forest; nearly all Jean-Bart had gone down. But a cry escaped from him and he rushed forward when he saw Chaval standing on the threshold.

"By God! is this the rendezvous you called us to?"

Imprecations broke out and there was a movement of the crowd towards the traitor. What! he had sworn with them the day before, and now they found him down below with the others! Was he, then, making fools of people?

"Off with him! To the shaft! to the shaft!"

Chaval, white with fear, stammered and tried to explain. But Étienne cut him short, carried out of himself and sharing the fury of the band.

"You wanted to be in it, and you shall be in it. Come on! take your damned snout along!"

Another clamour covered his voice. Catherine, in her turn, had just appeared, dazzled by the bright sunlight, and frightened at falling into the midst of these savages. She was panting, with legs aching from the hundred and two ladders, and with bleeding palms, when Maheude, seeing her, rushed forward with her hand up.

"Ah! slut! you, too! When your mother is dying of hunger you betray her for your bully!"

Maheu held back her arm, and stopped the blow. But he shook his daughter; he was enraged, like his wife; he threw up her conduct in her face, and both lost their heads, shouting louder than their mates.

The sight of Catherine had completed Étienne's exasperation. He repeated:

"On we go to the other pits, and you come with us, you dirty devil!"

Chaval had scarcely time to get his sabots from the shed and to throw his woollen jacket over his frozen shoulders. They all dragged him on, forcing him to run in the midst of them. Catherine was dazed and also put on her sabots, buttoning at her neck her man's old jacket, with which she kept off the cold; and she ran behind her lover, she would not leave him, for surely they were going to murder him.

Then in two minutes Jean-Bart was emptied. Jeanlin had found a horn and was blowing it, producing hoarse sounds, as though he were gathering together oxen. The women—Mother Brûlé, the Levaque and Mouquette—raised their skirts to run, while Levaque, with an axe in his hand, manipulated it like a drum-major's stick. Other men continued to arrive; they were nearly a thousand, without order, again flowing on to the road like a torrent let loose. The gates were too narrow, and the palings were broken down.

"To the pits!—Down with the traitors!—No more work!"

And Jean-Bart fell suddenly into great silence. Not a man was left, not a breath was heard. Deneulin came out of the captains' room, and quite alone, with a gesture forbidding anyone to follow him, he went over the pit. He was pale and very calm. At first he stopped before the shaft, lifting his eyes to look at the cut cables; the steel ends hung useless, the bite of the file had left a living scar, a fresh wound which gleamed in the black grease. Afterwards he went up to the engine, and looked at the crank, which was motionless, like the joint of a colossal limb struck by paralysis. He touched the metal, which had already cooled, and the cold made him shudder as though he had touched a corpse. Then he went down to the boiler-room, walked slowly before the extinguished stoves, yawning and inundated, and struck his foot against the boilers, which sounded hollow. Come! it was quite finished; his ruin was complete. Even if he mended the cables and lit the fires, where would he find men? Another fortnight's strike and he would be bankrupt. And in this certainty of disaster he no longer felt any hatred of the Montsou brigands; he felt that all had a complicity in it, that it was a general age-long fault. They were brutes, no doubt, but brutes who could not read, and who were dying of hunger.

## CHAPTER IV

AND THE TROOP WENT off over the flat plain, white with frost beneath the pale winter sun, and overflowed the path as they passed through the beetroot fields.

From the Fourche-aux-Bœufs, Étienne had assumed command. He cried his orders while the crowd moved on, and organised the march. Jeanlin galloped at the head, performing a barbarous music on his horn. Then the women came in the first ranks, some of them armed with sticks: Maheude, with wild eyes which seemed to be seeking afar for the promised city of justice, Mother Brûlé, the Levaque woman, Mouquette, striding along beneath their rags, like soldiers betting out for the seat of war. If they had any encounters, we should see if the police dared to strike women. And the men followed in a confused flock, with a roar that grew larger and larger, bristling with iron bars and dominated by Levaque's single axe, with its blade glistening in the sun. Étienne, in the middle, kept Chaval in sight, forcing him to walk before him; while Maheu, behind, gloomily kept an eye on Catherine, the only woman among these men, obstinately trotting near her lover for fear that he would be hurt. Bare heads were dishevelled in the air; only the clank of sabots could be heard, like the movement of released cattle, carried away in Jeanlin's wild trumpeting.

But suddenly a new cry arose:

"Bread! bread! bread!"[6]

It was mid-day; the hunger of six weeks on strike was awaking in these empty stomachs, whipped up by this race across the fields. The few crusts of the morning and Mouquette's chestnuts had long been forgotten; their stomachs were crying out, and this suffering was added to their fury against the traitors.

"To the pits! No more work! Bread!"

Étienne, who had refused to eat his share at the settlement, felt an unbearable tearing sensation in his chest. He made no complaint, but mechanically took his tin from time to time and swallowed a gulp of gin, shaking so much that he thought he needed it to carry him to the end. His cheeks were heated and his eyes inflamed. He kept his head, however, and still wished to avoid needless destruction.

As they arrived at the Joiselle road a Vandame pikeman, who had joined the band for revenge on his master, impelled the men towards the right, shouting:

"To Gaston-Marie! Must stop the pump! Let the water ruin Jean-Bart!"

The mob was already turning, in spite of the protests of Étienne, who begged them to let the water be drawn up. What was the good of destroying the galleries? It offended his workman's heart, in spite of his resentment. Maheu also thought it unjust to take revenge on a machine. But the pikeman still shouted his cry of vengeance, and Étienne had to cry still louder:

"To Mirou! There are traitors down there! To Mirou! to Mirou!"

With a gesture, he had turned the crowd towards the left road; while Jeanlin, going ahead, was blowing louder than ever. An eddy was produced in the crowd; this time Gaston-Marie was saved.

And the four kilomètres which separated them from Mirou were traversed in half-an-hour, almost at running pace, across the interminable plain. The canal on this side cut it with a long icy ribbon. The leafless trees on the banks, changed by the frost into giant candelabra, alone broke this pale uniformity, prolonged and lost in the sky at the horizon as in a sea. An undulation of the ground hid Montsou and Marchiennes; there was nothing but bare immensity.

They reached the pit, and found a captain standing on a footbridge at the screening shed to receive them. They all well knew Father Quandieu, the dean of the Montsou captains, an old man whose skin and hair were quite white, and who was in his seventies, a miracle of fine health in the mines.

"What have you come after here, you pack of meddlers?" he shouted.

The band stopped. It was no longer a master, it was a mate; and a certain respect held them back before this old workman.

"There are men down below," said Étienne. "Make them come up."

"Yes, there are men there," said Father Quandieu, "some six dozen; the others were afraid of you evil buggers! But I warn you that not one comes up, or you will have to deal with me!"

Exclamations arose, the men pushed, the women advanced. Quickly coming down from the footbridge, the captain now barred the door.

Then Maheu tried to interfere.

"It is our right, old man. How can we make the strike general if we don't force all the mates to be on our side?"

The old man was silent a moment. Evidently his ignorance on the subject of coalition equalled the pikeman's. At last he replied:

"It may be your right, I don't say. But I only know my orders. I am alone here; the men are down till three, and they shall stay there till three."

The last words were lost in hooting. Fists were threateningly advanced, the women deafened him, and their hot breath blew in his face. But he still held out, his head erect, and his beard and hair white as snow; his courage had so swollen his voice that he could be heard distinctly over the tumult.

"By God! you shall not pass! As true as the sun shines, I would rather die than let you touch the cables. Don't push any more, or I'm damned if I don't fling myself down the shaft before you!"

The crowd drew back shuddering and impressed. He went on:

"Where is the beast who does not understand that? I am only a workman like you others. I have been told to guard here, and I'm guarding."

That was as far as Father Quandieu's intelligence went, stiffened by his obstinacy of military duty, his narrow skull, and eyes dimmed by the black melancholy of half a century spent underground. The men looked at him moved, feeling within them an echo of what he said, this military obedience, the sense of fraternity and resignation in danger. He saw that they were hesitating still, and repeated:

"I'm damned if I don't fling myself down the shaft before you!"

A great shock carried away the mob. They all turned, and the rush went on to the right hand road, which stretched far away through the fields. Again cries arose:

"To Madeleine! to Crèvecœur! no more work! Bread! bread!"

But in the centre, as they went on, there was hustling. It was Chaval, they said, who was trying to take advantage of an opportunity to escape. Étienne had seized him by the arm, threatening to do for him if he was planning some treachery. And the other struggled and protested furiously:

"What's all this for? Isn't a man free? I've been freezing the last hour. I want to clean myself. Let me go!"

He was, in fact, suffering from the coal glued to his skin by sweat, and his woollen garment was no protection.

"On you go, or we'll clean you," replied Étienne. "Don't expect to get your life at a bargain."

They were still running, and he turned towards Catherine, who was keeping up well. It annoyed him to feel her so near him, so miserable, shivering beneath her man's old jacket and her muddy trousers. She must be nearly dead of fatigue, but she was running all the same.

"You can go off, you can," he said, at last.

Catherine seemed not to hear. Her eyes, on meeting Étienne's, only flamed with reproach for a moment. She would not stop. Why did he want her to leave her man? Chaval was not at all kind, it was true; he would even beat her sometimes. But he was her man, the one who had had her first; and it enraged her that they should throw themselves on him—more than a thousand of them. She would have defended him without any tenderness at all, out of pride.

"Off you go!" repeated Maheu, violently.

Her father's order slackened her course for a moment. She trembled, and her eyelids swelled with tears. Then, in spite of her fear, she came back to the same place again, still running. Then they let her be.

The mob crossed the Joiselle road, went a short distance up the Cron road and then mounted towards Cougny. On this side, factory chimneys striped the flat horizon; wooden sheds, brick workshops with large dusty recesses, appeared along the street.

They passed one after another the low buildings of two settlements—that of the Cent-Quatre-Vingts, then that of the Soixante-Seize; and from each of them, at the sound of the horn and the clamour arising from every mouth, whole families came out—men, women and children—running to join their mates in the rear. When they came up to Madeleine there were at least fifteen hundred. The road descended in a gentle slope; the rumbling flood of strikers had to turn round the pit-bank before they could spread over the mine square.

It was now not more than two o'clock. But the captains had been warned and were hastening the ascent as the band arrived. The men were all up, only some twenty remained and were now disembarking from the cage. They fled and were pursued with stones. Two were struck, another left the sleeve of his jacket behind. This man-hunt saved the material, and neither the cables nor the boilers were touched. The flood was already moving away, rolling on towards the next pit.

This one, Crèvecœur, was only five hundred mètres away from Madeleine. There, also, the mob arrived in the midst of the ascent. A putter-girl was taken and whipped by the women, with her breeches split open and her buttocks exposed before the men who were laughing. The trammer-boys had their ears boxed, the pikemen got away, their sides blue from blows and their noses bleeding. And in this growing ferocity, in this old need of revenge which was turning every head with madness, the choked cries went on, death to traitors, hatred against ill-paid work, the roaring of bellies after bread. They began to cut the cables, but the file would not bite, and the task was too long now that the fever was on them for moving onward, for ever onward. At the boilers a tap was broken; while the water, thrown by bucketsful into the stoves, made the metal gratings burst.

Outside they were talking of marching on Saint-Thomas. This was the best disciplined pit. The strike had not touched it, and nearly seven hundred men must have gone down there. This exasperated them; they would wait for these men with sticks, ranged for battle, just to see who would get the best of it. But the rumour ran along that there were gendarmes at Saint-Thomas, the gendarmes of the morning whom they had made fun of.

How was this known? nobody could say. No matter! they were seized by fear and decided on Feutry-Cantel. Their giddiness carried them on, all were on the road, clanking their sabots, rushing forward. To Feutry-Cantel! to Feutry-Cantel! The cowards there were certainly four hundred in number and there would be fun! Situated three kilomètres away, this pit lay in a fold of the ground near the Scarpe. They were already climbing the slope of the Plâtrières, beyond the road to Beaugnies, when a voice, no one knew from whom, threw out the idea that the soldiers were, perhaps, down there at Feutry-Cantel. Then from one end to the other of the column it was repeated that the soldiers were down there. They slackened their march, panic gradually spread. In the country, sleeping without work, which they had been scouring for hours, why had they not come across the soldiers? This impunity troubled them, the thought of the repression which they felt to be coming.

Without anyone knowing where it came from, a new word of command turned them towards another pit.

"To the Victoire! to the Victoire!"

Were there, then, neither soldiers nor police at the Victoire? Nobody knew. All seemed reassured. And turning round they descended from the Beaumont side and cut across the fields to reach the Joiselle road. The railway line barred their passage, and they crossed it, pulling down the palings. Now they were approaching Montsou, the gradual undulation of the landscape grew less, the sea of beetroot fields enlarged, reaching far away to the black houses at Marchiennes.

This time it was a march of five good kilomètres. So strong an impulse pushed them on that they had no feeling of their terrible fatigue, or of their bruised and wounded feet. The rear continued to lengthen, increased by mates enlisted on the roads and in the settlements. When they had passed the canal at the Magache bridge, and appeared before the Victoire, there were two thousand of them. But three o'clock had struck, the ascent was completed, not a man remained below. Their disappointment was spent in vain threats; they could only heave broken bricks at the workmen who had arrived to take their duty at the earth-cutting. There was a rush, and the deserted pit belonged to them. And in their rage at not finding a traitor's face to strike, they attacked things. A rankling abscess was bursting within them, a poisoned boil of slow growth. Years and years of hunger tortured them with a thirst for massacre and destruction.

Behind a shed Étienne saw some porters filling a wagon with coal.

"Will you just clear out of the bloody place!" he shouted. "Not a bit of coal goes out!"

At his orders some hundred strikers ran up, and the porters only had time to escape. Men unharnessed the horses which were frightened and some set off, struck in the haunches, while others, overturning the wagon, broke the shafts.

Levaque, with violent blows of his axe, had thrown himself on the platforms to break down the foot-bridges. They resisted, and it occurred to him to tear up the rails, destroying the line from one end of the square to the other. Soon the whole band set to this task. Maheu made the metal chairs leap up, armed with his iron bar which he used as a lever. During this time Mother Brûlé led away the women and invaded the lamp cabin, where their sticks covered the soil with a carnage of lamps. Maheude, carried out of herself, was laying about her as vigorously as the Levaque women. All were soaked in oil, and Mouquette dried her hands on her skirt, laughing to find herself so dirty. Jeanlin, for a joke, had emptied a lamp down her neck. But all this revenge produced nothing to eat. Stomachs were crying out louder than ever. And the great lamentation dominated still: "Bread! bread! bread!"

A former captain at the Victoire kept a stall near by. No doubt he had fled in fear, for his shed was abandoned. When the women came back, and the men had finished destroying the railway, they besieged the stall, the shutters of which yielded at once. They found no bread there; there were only two pieces of raw flesh and a sack of potatoes. But in the pillage they discovered some fifty bottles of gin, which disappeared like a drop of water drunk up by the sand.

Étienne, having emptied his tin, was able to refill it. Little by little a terrible drunkenness, the drunkenness of the starved, was inflaming his eyes and showing his teeth like a wolf's teeth between his pallid lips. Suddenly he perceived that Chaval had gone off in the midst of the tumult. He swore, and men ran to seize the fugitive, who was hiding with Catherine behind the timber supply.

"Ah! you dirty bugger; you are afraid of getting into trouble!" shouted Étienne. "It was you in the forest who called for a strike of the engine-men, to stop the pumps, and now you want to play us a filthy trick! Very well! By God! we will go back to Gaston-Marie. I will have you smash the pump; yes, by God! you shall smash it!"

He was drunk; he was urging his men against this pump which he had saved a few hours earlier.

"To Gaston-Marie! to Gaston-Marie!"

They all cheered, and rushed on, while Chaval, seized by the shoulders, was drawn and pushed violently along, while he constantly asked to be allowed to wash.

"Will you take yourself off, then?" cried Maheu to Catherine, who had also begun to run again.

This time she did not even draw back, but turned her burning eyes on her father, and went on running.

Once more the mob ploughed through the flat plain. They were retracing their steps over the long straight paths, by the fields endlessly spread out. It was four o'clock; the sun, which approached the horizon, lengthened the shadows of this horde with their furious gestures over the frozen soil.

They avoided Montsou, and farther on rejoined the Joiselle road; to spare the journey round Fourche-aux-Bœufs, they passed beneath the walls of Piolaine. The Grégoires had just gone out, having to visit a lawyer before going to dine with the Hennebeaus, where they would find Cécile. The estate seemed asleep, with its avenue of deserted limes, its kitchen-garden and its orchard bared by the winter. Nothing was stirring in the house, and the closed windows were dulled by the warm steam within. Out of the profound silence an impression of good-natured comfort arose, the patriarchal sensation of good beds and a good table, the wise happiness of the proprietor's existence.

Without stopping, the band cast gloomy looks through the

grating and at the length of protecting walls, bristling with broken bottles. The cry arose again:

"Bread! bread! bread!"

The dogs alone replied, by barking ferociously, a pair of big Danes, with rough coats, who stood with open jaws. And behind the closed blind there were only the servants, Mélanie the cook and Honorine the housemaid, attracted by this cry, pale and perspiring with fear at seeing these savages go by. They fell on their knees, and thought themselves killed on hearing a single stone breaking a pane of a neighbouring window. It was a joke of Jeanlin's; he had manufactured a sling with a piece of cord, and had just sent a little passing greeting to the Grégoires. Already he was again blowing his horn, and the band was lost in the distance, and the cry grew fainter:

"Bread! bread! bread!"

They arrived at Gaston-Marie in still greater numbers, more than two thousand five hundred madmen, breaking everything, sweeping away everything, with the force of a torrent which gains strength as it moves. The police had passed here an hour earlier, and had gone off towards Saint-Thomas, led astray by some peasants; in their haste they had not even taken the precaution of leaving a few men behind to guard the pit. In less than a quarter of an hour the fires were overturned, the boilers emptied, the buildings torn down and devastated. But it was the pump which they specially threatened. It was not enough to stop it in the last expiring breath of its steam; they threw themselves on it as on a living person whose life they required.

"The first blow is yours!" repeated Étienne, putting a hammer into Chaval's hand. "Come! you have sworn with the others!"

Chaval drew back trembling, and in the hustling the hammer fell; while other men, without waiting, murdered the pump with blows from iron bars, blows from bricks, blows from anything they could lay their hands on. Some even broke sticks over it. The nuts leapt off, the pieces of steel and copper were dislocated like torn limbs. The blow of a shovel, delivered with full force, fractured the metal body; the water escaped and emptied itself, and there was a supreme gurgle like an agonising death-rattle.

That was the end, and the mob found themselves outside again, madly pushing on behind Étienne, who would not let Chaval go.

"Kill him! the traitor! To the shaft! to the shaft!"

The livid wretch, clinging with imbecile obstinacy to his fixed idea, continued to stammer his need of cleaning himself.

"Wait, if that bothers you," said the Levaque woman. "Here! here's a bucket!"

There was a pond there, an infiltration of the water from the pump. It was white with a thick layer of ice; and they struck it and broke the ice, forcing him to dip his head in this cold water.

"Jump in then," repeated Mother Brûlé. "By God! if you don't jump in we'll shove you in. And now you shall have a drink of it; yes, yes, like a beast, with your jaws in the trough!"

He had to drink on all-fours. They all laughed, with cruel laughter. One woman pulled his ears, another woman threw in his face a handful of dung found fresh on the road. His old woollen jacket in tatters no longer held together. He was haggard, stumbling, and with struggling movements of his hips he tried to flee.

Maheu had pushed him, and Maheude was among those who grew furious, both of them satisfying their old spite; even Mouquette, who generally remained such good friends with her old lovers, was wild with this one, treating him as a good-for-nothing, and talking of taking his breeches down to see if he was still a man.

Étienne made her hold her tongue.

"That's enough. There's no need for all to set to it. If you like, you, we will just settle it together."

His fists closed and his eyes were lit up with homicidal fury; his intoxication was turning into the desire to kill.

"Are you ready? One of us must stay here. Give him a knife; I've got mine."

Catherine, exhausted and terrified, gazed at him. She remembered his confidences, his desire to devour a man when he had drunk, poisoned after the third glass, to such an extent had his drunkards of parents put this beastliness into his body. Suddenly she leapt forward, struck him with both her woman's hands, and choking with indignation shouted into his face:

"Coward! coward! coward! Isn't it enough, then, all these abominations? You want to kill him now that he can't stand upright any longer!"

She turned towards her father and her mother; she turned towards the others. "You are cowards! cowards! Kill me, then, with him! I will tear your eyes out, I will, if you touch him again. Oh! the cowards!"

And she planted herself before her man to defend him, forgetting the blows, forgetting the life of misery, lifted up by the idea that she belonged to him since he had taken her, and that it was a shame for her when they so crushed him.

Étienne had grown pale beneath this girl's blows. At first he had been about to knock her down; then, after having wiped his face with the movement of a man who is recovering from intoxication, he said to Chaval, in the midst of deep silence:

"She is right; that's enough. Off you go."

Immediately Chaval was away, and Catherine galloped behind him. The crowd gazed at them as they disappeared round a corner of the road; but Maheude muttered:

"You were wrong; ought to have kept him. He is sure to be after some treachery."

But the mob began to march on again. Five o'clock was about to strike. The sun, as red as a furnace on the edge of the horizon, seemed to set fire to the whole plain. A pedlar who was passing informed them that the military were descending from the Crèvecœur side. Then they turned. An order ran:

"To Montsou! To the manager!—Bread! bread! bread!"

## CHAPTER V

M. HENNEBEAU HAD PLACED himself in front of his study window to watch the departure of the carriage which was taking away his wife to lunch at Marchiennes. His eyes followed Négrel for a moment, as he trotted beside the carriage door. Then he quietly returned and seated himself at his desk. When neither his wife nor his nephew animated the place with their presence the house seemed empty. On this day the coachman was driving his wife; Rose, the new housemaid, had leave to go out till five o'clock; there only remained Hippolyte, the *valet de chambre*, trailing about the rooms in slippers, and the cook, who had been occupied since dawn in struggling with her saucepans, entirely absorbed in the dinner which was to be given in the evening. So M. Hennebeau promised himself a day of serious work in this deep calm of the deserted house.

Towards nine o'clock, although he had received orders to send everyone away, Hippolyte took the liberty of announcing Dansaert, who was bringing news. The manager then heard, for the first time, of the meeting in the forest the evening before; the details were very precise, and he listened while thinking of the intrigue with Pierronne, so well known that two or three anonymous letters every week denounced the licentiousness of the head captain. Evidently the husband had talked, for this action revealed the domestic secret. He even took advantage of the occasion; he let the head captain know that he was aware of everything, contenting himself with recommending prudence for fear of a scandal. Startled by these reproaches in the midst of his report, Dansaert denied, stammered excuses, while his great nose confessed the crime by its sudden redness. He did not insist, however, glad to get off so easily; for, as a rule, the manager displayed the implacable severity of the virtuous man whenever an employee allowed himself the indulgence of a pretty girl in the pit. The conversation continued concerning the strike; that meeting in the forest was only the swagger of blusterers; nothing seriously threatened. In any case, the settlements would surely not stir for some days, beneath the impression of respectful fear which must have been produced by the military promenade of the morning.

When M. Hennebeau was alone again he was, however, on the point of sending a telegram to the prefect. Only the fear of uselessly showing a sign of anxiety held him back. Already he could not forgive himself his lack of insight in saying everywhere, and even writing to the directors, that the strike would last at most a fortnight. It had been going on and on for nearly two months, to his great surprise, and he was in despair over it; he felt himself every day diminished and compromised, and was forced to imagine some brilliant achievement which would bring him back into favour with the directors. He had just asked them for orders in the case of a skirmish. There was delay over the reply, and he was expecting it by the afternoon post. He said to himself that there would be time then to send out telegrams, and to obtain the military occupation of the pits, if such was the desire of those gentlemen. In his own opinion there would certainly be a battle and an expenditure of blood. This responsibility troubled him in spite of his habitual energy.

Up to eleven o'clock he worked peacefully; there was no sound in the dead house except Hippolyte's waxing-stick, which was rubbing a floor far away on the first storey. Then, one after the other, he received two messages, the first announcing the attack on Jean-Bart by the Montsou band, the second telling of the cut cables, the overturned fires, and all the destruction. He could not understand. Why had the strikers gone to Deneulin instead of attacking one of the Company's pits? Besides, they were quite welcome to sack Vandame; that would merely ripen the plan of conquest which he was meditating. And at mid-day he lunched alone in the large dining-room, served so quietly by the servant that he could not even hear his slippers. This solitude rendered his pre-occupations more gloomy; he was feeling cold at the heart when a captain, who had arrived running, was shown in, and told him of the mob's march on Mirou. Almost immediately, as he was finishing his coffee, a telegram informed him that Madeleine and Crèvecœur were in their turn threatened. Then his perplexity became extreme. He was expecting the postman at two o'clock: ought he at once to ask for troops? or would it be better to wait patiently, and not to act until he had received the directors' orders? He went back into his study; he wished to read a report which he had asked Négrel to prepare the day before for the prefect. But he could not put his hand on it; he reflected that perhaps the young man had left it in his room, where he often wrote at night, and without taking any decision, pursued by the idea of this report, he went upstairs to look for it in the room.

As he entered, M. Hennebeau was surprised: the room had not been done, no doubt through Hippolyte's forgetfulness or laziness. There was a moist heat there, the close heat of the past night, made heavier from the mouth of the hot-air stove being left open; and he was suffocated, too, with the penetrating perfume, which he thought must be the odour of the toilet waters with which the basin was full. There was great disorder in the room—garments scattered about, damp towels thrown on the backs of chairs, the bed yawning, with a sheet drawn back and draggling on the carpet. But at first he only glanced round with an abstracted look as he went towards a table covered with papers to look for the missing report. Twice he examined the papers one by one, but it was certainly not there. Where the devil could that mad-cap Paul have stuffed it?

And as M. Hennebeau went back into the middle of the room, giving a glance at each article of furniture, he noticed in the open bed a bright point which shone like a star. He approached mechanically and put out his hand. It was a little gold scent-bottle lying between two folds of the sheet. He at once recognised a scent-bottle belonging to Madame Hennebeau, the little ether bottle which was always with her. But he could not understand its presence here: how could it have got into Paul's bed? And suddenly he grew terribly pale. His wife had slept there.

"Beg your pardon, sir," murmured Hippolyte's voice through the door. "I saw you going up."

The servant entered and was thrown into consternation by the disorder.

"Lord! Why, the room is not done! So Rose has gone out, leaving all the house on my shoulders!"

M. Hennebeau had hidden the bottle in his hand and was pressing it almost to breaking.

"What do you want?"

"It's another man, sir; he comes from Crèvecœur with a letter."

"Good! Leave me alone; tell him to wait."

His wife had slept there! When he had bolted the door he opened his hand again and looked at the little bottle which had left its image in red on his flesh. Suddenly he saw and understood; this filthiness had been going on in his house for months. He recalled his old suspicion, the rustling against the doors, the naked feet at night through the silent house. Yes, it was his wife who went up to sleep there!

Falling into a chair opposite the bed, which he gazed at fixedly, he remained some minutes as though crushed. A noise aroused him; someone was knocking at the door, trying to open it. He recognised the servant's voice.

"Sir——Ah! you are shut in, sir."

"What is it now?"

"There seems to be a hurry; the men are breaking everything. There are two messengers below. There are also some telegrams."

"You just leave me alone! I am coming directly."

The idea that Hippolyte would himself have discovered the scent-bottle, had he done the room in the morning, had just frozen him. And besides, this man must know; he must have found the bed still hot with adultery twenty times over, with madame's hairs trailing on the pillow. The man kept interrupting him, and it could only be out of inquisitiveness. Perhaps he had stayed with his ear stuck to the door, excited by the debauchery of his masters.

M. Hennebeau did not move. He still gazed at the bed. His long past of suffering unrolled before him: his marriage with this woman, their immediate misunderstanding of the heart and of the flesh, the lovers whom she had had unknown to him, and the lover whom he had tolerated for ten years, as one tolerates an impure taste in a sick woman. Then came their arrival at Montsou, the mad hope of curing her, months of languor, of sleepy exile, the approach of old age which would, perhaps, at last give her back to him. Then their nephew arrived, this Paul to whom she became a mother, and to whom she spoke of her dead heart buried for ever beneath the ashes. And he, the imbecile husband, foresaw nothing; he adored this woman who was his wife, whom other men had possessed, but whom he alone could not possess! He adored her with shameful passion, so that he would have fallen on his knees if she would but have given him the leavings of other men! The leavings of the others she gave to this child.

The sound of a distant gong at this moment made M. Hennebeau start. He recognised it; it was struck, by his orders, when the postman arrived. He rose and spoke aloud, breaking into the flood of coarseness with which his parched throat was bursting in spite of himself.

"Ah! I don't care a bloody hang for their telegrams and their letters! not a bloody hang!"

Now he was carried away by rage, the need of some sewer in which to stamp down all this filthiness with his heels. This woman was a vulgar drab; he sought for crude words and buffeted her image with them. The sudden idea of the marriage between Cécile and Paul, which she was arranging with so quiet a smile, completed his exasperation. There was, then, not even passion, not even jealousy at the bottom of this persistent sensuality? It was now a perverse plaything, the habit of the woman, a recreation taken like an accustomed dessert. And he put all the responsibility on her, he regarded as almost innocent the lad at whom she had bitten in this reawakening of appetite, just as one bites at an early green fruit, stolen by the wayside. Whom would she devour, on whom would she fall, when she no longer had complacent nephews, sufficiently practical to accept in their own family the table, the bed and the wife?

There was a timid scratch at the door, and Hippolyte allowed himself to whisper through the keyhole:

"The postman, sir. And Monsieur Dansaert, too, has come back, saying that they are killing one another."

"I'm coming down, good God!"

What should he do to them? Chase them away on their return from Marchiennes, like stinking animals whom he would no longer have beneath his roof? He would take a cudgel, and would tell them to carry elsewhere their poisonous coupling. It was with their sighs, with their mixed breaths, that the damp warmth of this room had grown heavy; the penetrating odour which had suffocated him was the odour of musk which his wife's skin exhaled, another perverse taste, a fleshly need of violent perfumes; and he seemed to feel also the heat and odour of fornication, of living adultery, in the pots which lay about, in the basins still full, in the disorder of the linen, of the furniture of the entire room tainted with vice. The fury of impotence threw him on to the bed, which he struck with his fists, belabouring the places where he saw the imprint of their two bodies, enraged with the disordered coverlets and the crumpled sheets, soft and inert beneath his blows, as though exhausted themselves by the embraces of the whole night.

But suddenly he thought he heard Hippolyte coming up again. He was arrested by shame. For a moment he stood panting, wiping his forehead, calming the bounds of his heart. Standing before a mirror he looked at his face, so changed that he did not recognise himself. Then, when he had watched it gradually grow calmer by an effort of supreme will, he went downstairs.

Five messengers were standing below, not counting Dansaert. All brought him news of increasing gravity concerning the march of the strikers among the pits; and the chief captain told him at length what had gone on at Mirou and the fine behaviour of Father Quandieu. He listened, nodding his head, but he did not hear; his thoughts were in the room upstairs. At last he sent them away, saying that he would take due measures. When he was alone again, seated before his desk, he seemed to grow drowsy, with his head between his hands, covering his eyes. His mail was there, and he decided to look for the expected letter, the directors' reply. The lines at first danced before him, but he understood at last that these gentlemen desired a skirmish; certainly they did not order him to make things worse, but they allowed it to be seen that disturbances would hasten the conclusion of the strike by provoking energetic repression. After this, he no longer hesitated, but sent off telegrams on all sides—to the prefect of Lille, to the corps of soldiery at Douai, to the police at Marchiennes. It was a relief; he had nothing to do but shut himself in; he even spread the report that he was suffering from gout. And all the afternoon he hid himself in his study, receiving no one, contenting himself with reading the telegrams and letters which continued to rain in. He thus followed the mob from afar, from Madeleine to Crèvecœur, from Crèvecœur to the Victoire, from the Victoire to Gaston-Marie. Information also reached him concerning the panic of the police and the troops, wandering along the roads, and always with their backs to the pit attacked. They might kill one another, and destroy everything! He put his head between his hands again, with his fingers over his eyes, and buried himself in the deep silence of the empty house, where he only heard now and then the noise of the cook's saucepans at her large fire, preparing the evening's dinner.

The twilight was already darkening the room; it was five o'clock when a disturbance made M. Hennebeau jump, as he sat dazed and inert with his elbows in his papers. He thought that it was the two wretches coming back. But the tumult increased, and a terrible cry broke out just as he was going to the window.

"Bread! bread! bread!"

It was the strikers, now invading Montsou, while the police, expecting an attack on the Voreux, were galloping off in the opposite direction to occupy that pit.

Just then, two kilomètres away from the first houses, a little beyond the crossways where the main road cut the Vandame road, Madame Hennebeau and the young ladies had witnessed the passing of the mob. The day had been spent pleasantly at Marchiennes; it had been a delightful lunch with the manager of the Forges, then an interesting visit to the workshops and to the neighbouring glassworks to occupy the afternoon; and as they were now going home in the limpid decline of the beautiful winter day, Cécile had had the whim to drink a glass of milk, as she noticed a little farm near the edge of the road. They all then got down from the carriage, and Négrel gallantly leapt off his horse; while the peasant-woman, alarmed by all these fine people, rushed about, and spoke of laying a cloth before serving the milk. But Lucie and Jeanne wanted to see the cow milked, and they went into the cattle-shed with their cups, making a little rural party, and laughing greatly at the litter, in which they buried themselves.

Madame Hennebeau, with her complacent maternal air, was drinking with the edge of her lips, when a strange snorting noise from without disturbed her.

"What is that, then?"

The cattle-shed, built at the edge of the road, had a large door for carts, for it was also used as a barn for hay. The young girls, who had put out their heads, were astonished to see on the left a black flood, a shouting band which was moving along the Vandame road.

"The deuce!" muttered Négrel, who had also gone out. "Are our brawlers getting angry at last?"

"It is perhaps the colliers again," said the peasant woman. "This is twice they've passed. Seems things are not going well; they're masters of the country."

She uttered every word prudently, watching the effect on their faces; and when she noticed the fright of all of them, and their deep anxiety at this encounter, she hastened to conclude:

"Oh, the rascals! the rascals!"

Négrel, seeing that it was too late to get into their carriage and reach Montsou, ordered the coachman to bring the vehicle into the farmyard, where it would remain hidden behind a shed. He himself fastened his horse, which a lad had been holding, beneath the shed. When he came back he found his aunt and the young girls distracted, and ready to follow the peasant-woman, who proposed that they should take refuge in her house. But he was of opinion that they would be safer where they were, for certainly no one would come and look for them in the hay. The door, however, shut very badly, and had such large cracks in it, that the road could be seen between the worm-eaten wood.

"Come, courage!" he said. "We will sell our lives dearly."

This joke increased their fear. The noise grew louder, but nothing could yet be seen; along the vacant road the wind of a tempest seemed to be blowing, like those sudden gusts which precede great storms.

"No, no! I don't want to look," said Cécile, going to hide herself in the hay.

Madame Hennebeau, who was very pale and felt angry with these people who had spoilt her pleasure, stood in the background with a sidelong look of repugnance; while Lucie and

Jeanne, though trembling, had placed their eyes at a crack, anxious to lose nothing of the spectacle.

A sound of thunder came near, the earth was shaken, and Jeanlin galloped up first, blowing into his horn.

"Take out your scent-bottles, the sweat of the people is passing by!" murmured Négrel, who, in spite of his republican convictions, liked to make fun of the populace when he was with ladies.

But his wit was carried away in the hurricane of gestures and cries. The women had appeared, nearly a thousand of them, with outspread hair dishevelled by running, the naked skin appearing through their rags, the nakedness of females weary with giving birth to starvelings. A few held their little ones in their arms, raising them and shaking them like banners of mourning and vengeance. Others, who were younger, with the swollen breasts of amazons, brandished sticks; while frightful old women were yelling so loudly that the cords of their fleshless necks seemed to be breaking. And then the men came up, two thousand madmen—trammers, pikemen, menders—a compact mass which rolled along like a single block in confused serried rank, so that it was impossible to distinguish their faded trousers or ragged woollen jackets, all effaced in the same earthly uniformity. Their eyes were burning, and one only distinguished the holes of black mouths singing the Marseillaise;[7] the stanzas were lost in a confused roar, accompanied by the clang of sabots over the hard earth. Above their heads, amid the bristling iron bars, an axe passed by, carried erect; and this single axe, which seemed to be the standard of the band, showed in the clear air the sharp profile of a guillotine-blade.

"What atrocious faces!" stammered Madame Hennebeau.

Négrel said between his teeth:

"Devil take me if I can recognise one of them! Where do the bandits spring from?"

And in fact anger, hunger, these two months of suffering and this enraged helter-skelter through the pits had lengthened the placid faces of the Montsou colliers into the muzzles of wild beasts. At this moment the sun was setting; its last rays of sombre purple cast a gleam of blood over the plain. The road seemed to be full of blood; men and women continued to rush by, bloody as butchers in the midst of slaughter.

"Oh! superb!" whispered Lucie and Jeanne, stirred in their artistic tastes by the beautiful horror of it.

They were frightened, however, and drew back close to Madame Hennebeau, who was leaning on a trough. She was frozen at the thought that a glance between the planks of that disjointed door might suffice to murder them. Négrel also, who was usually very brave, felt himself grow pale, seized by a terror that was superior to his will, the terror which comes from the unknown. Cécile, in the hay, no longer stirred; and the others, in spite of the wish to turn away their eyes, could not do so: they were compelled to gaze.

It was the red vision of the revolution, which would one day inevitably carry them all away, on some bloody evening at the end of the century. Yes, some evening the people, unbridled at last, would thus gallop along the roads, making the blood of the middle-class flow. They would hang up heads and sprinkle about gold from disembowelled coffers. The women would yell, the men would have these wolf-like jaws open to bite. Yes, there would be the same rags, the same thunder of great boots, the same terrible troop, with dirty skins and tainted breath, sweeping away the old world beneath an overflowing flood of barbarians. Fires would flame; they would not leave standing one stone of the towns; they would return to the savage life of the woods, after the great rut, the great feast-day, when the poor in one night would reduce women to leanness and rich men's cellars to emptiness. There would be nothing left, not a sou of the great fortunes, not a title-deed of acquired properties; until the day dawned and a new earth would perhaps spring up once more. Yes, it was these things which were passing along the road; it was the force of Nature herself, and they were receiving the terrible wind of it in their faces.

A great cry rose, dominating the Marseillaise:

"Bread! bread! bread!"

Lucie and Jeanne pressed themselves against Madame Hennebeau, who was almost fainting; while Négrel placed himself before them as though to protect them by his body. Was the old social order cracking this very evening? And what they saw immediately after completed their stupefaction. The band had nearly passed by, there were only a few stragglers left, when Mouquette came up. She was delaying, watching the bourgeois at their garden gates or the windows of their houses; and whenever she saw them, as she was not able to spit in their faces, she showed them what for her was the climax of contempt. Doubtless she perceived someone now, for suddenly she raised her skirts, bent her back, and showed her enormous buttocks, naked beneath the last rays of the sun. There was nothing obscene in those fierce buttocks, and nobody laughed.

Everything disappeared; the flood rolled on to Montsou along the turns of the road, between the low houses streaked with bright colours. The carriage was drawn out of the yard, but the coachman would not take it upon him to convey back madame and the young ladies without delay; the strikers occupied the street. And the worst was there was no other road.

"We must go back, however, for dinner will be ready," said Madame Hennebeau, exasperated by annoyance and fear. "These dirty workpeople have again chosen a day when I have visitors. How can you do good to such creatures?"

Lucie and Jeanne were occupied in pulling Cécile out of the hay. She was struggling, believing that those savages were still passing by, and repeating that she did not want to see them. At last they all took their places in the carriage again. It then occurred to Négrel, who had remounted, that they might go through the Réquillart lanes.

"Go gently," he said to the coachman, "for the path is atrocious. If any groups prevent you from returning to the road over there, you can stop behind the old pit, and we will return on foot through the little garden door, while you can put up the carriage and horses anywhere, in some inn out-house."

They set out. The band, far away, was streaming into Montsou. As they had twice seen police and military, the inhabitants were agitated and seized by panic. Abominable stories were circulating; it was said that written placards had been set up threatening the inhabitants to rip open their bellies. Nobody had read them, but all the same they were able to quote the exact words. At the lawyer's especially the terror was at its height, for he had just received by post an anonymous letter warning him that a barrel of powder was buried in his cellar, and that it would be blown up if he did not declare himself on the side of the people. Just then the Grégoires, prolonging their visit on the arrival of this letter, were discussing it, and decided that it must be the work of a joker, when the invasion of the mob completed the terror of the house. They, however, smiled, drawing back a corner of the curtain to look out, and refused to admit that there was any danger, certain, they said, that all would finish up well. Five o'clock struck, and they had time to wait until the street was free for them to cross the road to dine with the Hennebeaus, where Cécile, who had surely returned, must be waiting for them. But no one in Montsou seemed to share their confidence. People were wildly running about; doors and windows were banged to. They saw Maigrat, on the other side of the road, barricading his shop with a large supply of iron bars, and looking so pale and trembling that his feeble little wife was obliged to fasten the screws. The band had come to a halt before the manager's villa, and the cry echoed:

"Bread! bread! bread!"

M. Hennebeau was standing at the window when Hippolyte came in to close the shutters, for fear the windows would be broken by stones. He closed all on the ground floor, and then went up to the first floor; the creak of the window-fasteners was heard and the clack of the shutters one by one. Unfortunately, it was not possible to shut the kitchen window in the area in the same way, a disturbing window made ruddy by the gleams from the saucepans and the brioche.

Mechanically, M. Hennebeau, who wished to look out, went up to Paul's room on the second floor: it was on the left, the best situated, for it commanded the road as far as the Company's Yards. And he stood behind the blind overlooking the crowd. But this room had again overcome him, the toilet table sponged and in order, the cold bed with neat and well-drawn sheets. All his rage of the afternoon, that furious battle in the depths of his silent solitude, had now turned to an immense fatigue. His whole being was now like this room, grown cold, swept of the filth of the morning, returned to its habitual correctness. What was the good of a scandal? had anything really changed in his house? his wife had simply taken another lover; it scarcely aggravated the fact that she had chosen him in the family; perhaps even it was an advantage, for she thus preserved appearances. He pitied himself when he thought of his mad jealousy. How ridiculous to have struck that bed with his fists! Since he had tolerated another man, he could certainly tolerate this one. It was only a matter of a little more contempt. A terrible bitterness was poisoning his mouth, the uselessness of everything, the eternal pain of existence, shame for himself who always adored and desired this woman in the dirt in which he had abandoned her.

Beneath the window the yells broke out with increased violence.

"Bread! bread! bread!"

"Idiots!" said M. Hennebeau between his clenched teeth.

He heard them abusing him for his large salary, calling him a bloated idler, a bloody beast who stuffed himself to indigestion with good things, while the worker was dying of hunger. The women had noticed the kitchen, and there was a tempest of imprecations against the pheasant roasting there, against the sauces that with fat odours irritated their empty stomachs. Ah! the stinking bourgeois, they should be stuffed with champagne and truffles till their guts burst.

"Bread! bread! bread!"

"Idiots!" repeated M. Hennebeau; "am I happy?"

Anger arose in him against these people who could not understand. He would willingly have made them a present of his large salary to possess their hard skin and their facility of coupling without regret. Why could he not seat them at his table and stuff them with his pheasant, while he went to fornicate behind the hedges, to tumble over the girls, making fun of those who had tumbled them over before him! He would have given everything, his education, his comfort, his luxury, his power as manager, if he could be for one day the last of the wretches who obeyed him, free of his flesh, enough of a blackguard to beat his wife and to take his pleasure with his neighbours' wives. And he longed also to be dying of hunger, to have an empty belly, a stomach twisted by cramps that would make his head turn with giddiness: perhaps that would have killed the eternal pain. Ah! to live like a brute, to possess nothing, to scour the fields with the ugliest and dirtiest putter, and to be able to be happy!

"Bread! bread! bread!"

Then he grew angry and shouted furiously in the tumult:

"Bread! is that enough, idiots!"

He could eat, and all the same he was groaning with torment. His desolate household, his whole wounded life, choked him at the throat like a death agony. Things were not for the best because one had bread. Who was the fool who placed earthly happiness in the partition of wealth? These revolutionary dreamers might demolish society and re-build another society; they would not add one joy to humanity, they would not take away one pain, by cutting bread-and-butter for everybody. They would even enlarge the unhappiness of the earth; they would one day make the very dogs howl with despair when they had taken them out of the tranquil satisfaction of instinct, to raise them to the unappeasable suffering of passion. No, the one good thing was not to exist, and if one existed to be a tree, a stone, less still, a grain of sand, which cannot bleed beneath the heels of the passers-by.

And in this exasperation of his torment, tears swelled in M. Hennebeau's eyes, and broke in burning drops on his cheeks. The twilight was drowning the road when stones began to riddle the front of the villa. With no anger now against these starving people, only enraged by the burning wound at his heart, he continued to stammer in the midst of his tears:

"Idiots! idiots!"

But the cry of the belly dominated, and a roar blew like a tempest, sweeping everything before it.

"Bread! bread! bread!"

## CHAPTER VI

SOBERED BY CATHERINE'S BLOWS, Étienne had remained at the head of his mates. But while he was hoarsely urging them on to Montsou, he heard another voice within him, the voice of reason, asking, in astonishment, the meaning of all this. He had not intended any of these things; how had it happened that, having set out for Jean-Bart with the object of acting calmly and preventing disaster, he had finished this day of increasing violence by besieging the manager's villa?

He it certainly was, however, who had just cried, "Halt!" Only at first his only idea had been to protect the Company's Yards, which there had been talk of sacking. And now that stones were already grazing the façade of the villa, he sought in vain for some lawful prey on which to throw the band, so as to avoid greater misfortunes. As he thus stood alone, powerless, in the middle of the road, he was called by a man standing on the threshold of the Estaminet Tison, where the landlady had just put up the shutters in haste, leaving only the door free.

"Yes, it's me. Will you listen?"

It was Rasseneur. Some thirty men and women, nearly all belonging to the settlement of the Deux-Cent-Quarante, who had remained at home in the morning and had come in the evening for news, had invaded this estaminet on the approach of the strikers. Zacharie occupied a table with his wife, Philomène. Farther on, Pierron and Pierronne, with their backs turned, were hiding their faces. No one was drinking, they had simply taken shelter.

Étienne recognised Rasseneur and was turning away, when the latter added:

"You don't want to see me, eh? I warned you, things are getting awkward. Now you may ask for bread, they'll give you lead."

Then he came back and replied:

"What troubles me is, the cowards who cross their arms and watch us risking our skins."

"Your notion is, then, to pillage over there?" asked Rasseneur.

"My notion is to remain to the last with our friends, quit by dying together."

In despair, Étienne went back into the crowd, ready to die. On the road, three children were throwing stones, and he gave them a good kick, shouting out to his comrades that it was no good breaking windows.

Bébert and Lydie, who had rejoined Jeanlin, were learning

from him how to work the sling. They each sent a flint, playing at who could do the most damage. Lydie had awkwardly cracked the head of a woman in the crowd, and the two boys were loudly laughing. Bonnemort and Mouque, seated on a bench, were gazing at them behind. Bonnemort's swollen legs bore him so badly, that he had great difficulty in dragging himself as far; no one knew what curiosity impelled him, for his face had the earthy look of those days when he never spoke a word.

Nobody, however, any longer obeyed Étienne. The stones, in spite of his orders, went on hailing, and he was astonished and terrified by these brutes he had unmuzzled, who were so slow to move and then so terrible, so ferociously tenacious in their rage. All the old Flemish blood was there, heavy and placid, taking months to get heated, and then giving itself up to abominable savagery, listening to nothing until the beast was glutted by atrocities. In his Southern land crowds flamed up more quickly, but they did not effect so much. He had to struggle with Levaque to obtain possession of his axe, and he knew not how to keep back the Maheus, who were throwing flints with both hands. The women, especially, terrified him—the Levaque, Mouquette and the others—who were agitated by murderous fury, with teeth and nails out, barking like bitches, and driven on by Mother Brûlé, whose lean figure dominated them.

But there was a sudden stop; a moment's surprise brought a little of that calmness which Étienne's supplications could not obtain. It was simply the Grégoires, who had decided to bid farewell to the lawyer, and to cross the road to the manager's house; and they seemed so peaceful, they so clearly had the air of believing that the whole thing was a joke on the part of their worthy miners, whose resignation had nourished them for a century, that the latter, in fact, left off throwing stones, for fear of hitting this old gentleman and old lady who had fallen from the sky. They allowed them to enter the garden, mount the steps, and ring at the barricaded door, which was by no means opened in a hurry. Just then, Rose, the housemaid, was returning, laughing at the furious workmen, all of whom she knew, for she belonged to Montsou. And it was she who, by striking her fists against the door, at last forced Hippolyte to set it ajar. It was time, for as the Grégoires disappeared, the hail of stones began again. Recovering from its astonishment, the crowd was shouting louder than ever:

"Death to the bourgeois! Hurrah for the people!"

Rose went on laughing, in the hall of the villa, as though amused by the adventure, and repeated to the terrified manservant:

"They're not bad-hearted; I know them."

M. Grégoire methodically hung up his hat. Then, when he had assisted Madame Grégoire to draw off her thick cloth mantle, he said, in his turn:

"Certainly, they have no malice at bottom. When they have shouted well they will go home to supper with more appetite."

At this moment M. Hennebeau came down from the second storey. He had seen the scene, and came to receive his guests in his usual cold and polite manner. The pallor of his face alone revealed the grief which had shaken him. The man was tamed: there only remained in him the correct administrator resolved to do his duty.

"You know," he said, "the ladies have not yet come back."

For the first time some anxiety disturbed the Grégoires. Cécile not come back! How could she come back now if the miners were to prolong their joking?

"I thought of having the place cleared," added M. Hennebeau. "But the misfortune is that I'm alone here, and, besides, I do not know where to send my servant to bring me four men and a corporal to clear away this mob."

Rose, who had remained there, ventured to murmur anew:

"Oh, sir! they are not bad-hearted!"

The manager shook his head, while the tumult increased outside, and they could hear the faint crash of the stones against the house.

"I don't wish to be hard on them, I can even excuse them; one must be as foolish as they are to believe that we are anxious to injure them. But it is my duty to prevent disturbance. To think that there are police all along the roads, as I am told, and that I have not been able to see a single man since the morning!"

He interrupted himself, and drew back before Madame Grégoire, saying:

"Let me beg you, madam, do not stay here, come into the drawing-room."

But the cook, coming up from below in exasperation, kept them in the hall a few minutes longer. She declared that she could no longer accept any responsibility for the dinner, for she was expecting from the Marchiennes pastry-cook some *vol-au-vent* which she had ordered for four o'clock. The pastry-cook had evidently stayed on the road for fear of these bandits. Perhaps they had even pillaged his hampers. She saw the *vol-au-vent* blockaded behind a bush, besieged, going to swell the bellies of the three thousand wretches who were asking for bread. In any case, monsieur was warned; she would rather pitch her dinner into the fire if it was to be spoilt because of the revolt.

"Patience, patience," said M. Hennebeau. "Nothing is lost, the pastry-cook may come."

And as he turned toward Madame Grégoire, opening the drawing-room door himself, he was very surprised to observe, seated on the hall bench, a man whom he had not distinguished before in the deepening shade.

"What! you, Maigrat! what is it, then?"

Maigrat arose; his fat, pale face was changed by terror. He no longer possessed his usual calm stolidity; he humbly explained that he had slipped into the manager's house to ask for aid and protection should the brigands attack his shop.

"You see that I am threatened myself, and that I have no one," replied M. Hennebeau. "You would have done better to stay at home and guard your property."

"Oh! I have put up iron bars, and then I have left my wife."

The manager showed impatience, and did not conceal his contempt. A fine guard, that poor creature worn out by blows!

"Well, I can do nothing; you must try to defend yourself. I advise you to go back at once, for there they are again demanding bread. Listen!"

In fact, the tumult began again, and Maigrat thought he heard his own name in the midst of the cries. To go back was no longer possible, they would have torn him to pieces. Besides, the idea of his ruin overcame him. He pressed his face to the glass panel of the door, perspiring and trembling in anticipation of disaster, while the Grégoires decided to go into the drawing-room.

M. Hennebeau quietly endeavoured to do the honours of his house. But he begged his guests in vain to sit down; the close, barricaded room, lighted by two lamps in the daytime, was filled with terror at each new clamour from without. Amid the stuffy hangings the fury of the mob rolled more disturbingly, with vague and terrible menace. They talked, however, constantly brought back to this inconceivable revolt. He was astonished at having foreseen nothing; and his information was so defective that he specially talked against Rasseneur, whose detestable influence, he said, he was able to recognise. Besides, the gendarmes would come; it was impossible that he should be thus abandoned. As to the Grégoires, they only thought about their daughter, the poor darling who was so quickly frightened! Perhaps, in face of the peril, the carriage had returned to Marchiennes. They waited on for another quarter of an hour, worn out by the noise in the street, and by the sound of the stones from time to time striking the closed shutters, which rung out like gongs. The situation was no longer bearable. M. Hennebeau spoke of going out to chase away the brawlers by himself, and to meet the carriage, when Hippolyte appeared, exclaiming:

"Sir! sir! here is madame! They are killing madame!"

The carriage had not been able to pass through the threatening groups in the Réquillart lane. Négrel had carried out his idea, walking the hundred mètres which separated them from the house, and knocking at the little door which led to the garden, near the common. The gardener would hear them, for there was always someone there to open. And, at first, things had gone perfectly; Madame Hennebeau and the young ladies were already knocking when some women, who had been warned, rushed into the lane. Then everything was spoilt. The door was not opened, and Négrel in vain sought to burst it open with his shoulder. The rush of women increased, and fearing they would be carried away, he adopted the desperate method of pushing his aunt and the young girls before him, in order to reach the front steps, by passing through the besiegers. But this manœuvre led to a hustling. They were not left free, a shouting band followed them, while the crowd floated up to right and to left, without understanding, simply astonished at these dressed-up ladies lost in the midst of the battle. At this moment the confusion was so great that it led to one of those curious mistakes which can never be explained. Lucie and Jeanne reached the steps, and slipped in through the door, which the housemaid opened; Madame Hennebeau had succeeded in following them, and behind them Négrel at last came in, and then bolted the door, feeling sure that he had seen Cécile go in first. She was no longer there, having disappeared on the way, so carried away by fear, that she had turned her back to the house, and had herself moved into the thick of danger.

At once the cry arose:

"Hurrah for the people! Death to the bourgeois! To death with them!"

A few of those in the distance, beneath the veil which hid her face, mistook her for Madame Hennebeau; others said she was a friend of the manager's wife, the young wife of a neighbouring manufacturer who was execrated by his men. And besides it mattered little, it was her silk dress, her fur mantle, even the white feather in her hat, which exasperated them. She smelled of perfume, she wore a watch, she had the delicate skin of a lazy woman who had never touched coal.

"Stop!" shouted Mother Brûlé, "we'll put it on your arse, that lace!"

"The lazy sluts steal it from us," said the Levaque. "They stick fur on to their skins while we are dying of cold. Just strip her naked, to show her how to live!"

At once Mouquette rushed forward.

"Yes, yes! whip her!"

And the women, in this savage rivalry, struggled and stretched out their rags, as though each were trying to get a morsel of this rich girl. No doubt her backside was not better made than anyone else's. More than one of them were rotten beneath their gewgaws. This injustice had lasted quite long enough; they should be forced to dress themselves like workwomen, these harlots who dared to spend half-a-franc on the washing of a single petticoat.

In the midst of these furies Cécile was shaking with paralysed legs, stammering over and over again the same phrase:

"Ladies! please! please! Ladies, please don't hurt me!"

But she suddenly uttered a shrill cry; cold hands had seized her by the neck. The rush had brought her near old Bonnemort, who had taken hold of her. He seemed drunk from hunger, stupefied by his long misery, suddenly arousing himself from the resignation of half-a-century, under the influence of no one knew what malicious impulse. After having in the course of his life saved a dozen mates from death, risking his bones in firedamps and landslips, he was yielding to things which he would not have been able to express, fascinated by this young girl's white neck. And as on this day he had lost his tongue, he clenched his fingers, with his air of an old infirm animal ruminating over his recollections.

"No! no!" yelled the women. "Uncover her arse! out with her arse!"

In the villa, as soon as they had realised the mishap, Négrel and M. Hennebeau bravely re-opened the door to run to Cécile's help. But the crowd was now pressing against the garden railings, and it was not easy to go out. A struggle took place here, while the Grégoires in terror stood on the steps.

"Let her be there, old man! It's the Piolaine young lady," cried Maheude to the grandfather, recognising Cécile, whose veil had been torn off by one of the women.

On his side, Étienne, overwhelmed at this retaliation on a child, was trying to force the band to let go their prey. An inspiration came to him; he brandished the axe, which he had snatched from Levaque's hands.

"To Maigrat's house, by God! there's bread in there! Down to the earth with Maigrat's damned shed!"

And at random he gave the first blow of the axe against the shop door. Some comrades had followed him—Levaque, Maheu, and a few others. But the women were furious, and Cécile had fallen from Bonnemort's fingers into Mother Brûlé's hands. Lydie and Bébert, led by Jeanlin, had slipped on all-fours between her petticoats to see the lady's bottom. Already the women were pulling her about; her clothes were beginning to split, when a man on horseback appeared, pushing on his animal, and using his riding-whip on those who would not stand back quick enough.

"Ah! rascals! You are going to flog our daughters, are you?"

It was Deneulin who had come to the rendezvous for dinner. He quickly jumped on to the road, took Cécile by the waist, and with the other hand manipulating his horse, with remarkable skill and strength, he used it as a living wedge to split the crowd, which drew back before the onset. At the railing the battle continued. He passed through, however, with crushing of limbs. This unforeseen assistance delivered Négrel and M. Hennebeau, who were in great danger amid the oaths and blows. And while the young man at last led in the fainting Cécile, Deneulin protected the manager with his tall body, and at the top of the steps received a stone which nearly put his shoulder out.

"That's it," he cried; "break my bones now you've broken my engines!"

He promptly pushed the door to, and a volley of flints fell against it.

"What madmen!" he exclaimed. "Two seconds more, and they would have broken my skull like an empty gourd. There is nothing to say to them; what could you do? They know nothing, you can only knock them down."

In the drawing-room the Grégoires were weeping as they watched Cécile recover. She was not hurt, there was not even a scratch to be seen, only her veil was lost. But their fright increased when they saw before them their cook, Mélanie, who described how the mob had demolished Piolaine. Mad with fear she had run to warn her masters. She had come in when the door was ajar at the moment of the fray, without anyone noticing her; and in her endless narrative the single stone with which Jeanlin had broken one window-pane became a regular cannonade which had crushed through the walls. Then M. Grégoire's ideas were altogether upset: they were murdering his daughter, they were razing his house to the ground; it was, then, true that these miners could bear him ill will, because he lived like a worthy man on their work?

The housemaid, who had brought in a towel and some eau de Cologne, repeated:

"All the same it's queer, they're not bad-hearted."

Madame Hennebeau, seated and very pale, had not recovered from the shock to her feelings; and she was only able to find a smile when Négrel was complimented. Cécile's parents especially thanked the young man, and the marriage might now be regarded as settled. M. Hennebeau looked on in silence, turning from his wife to this lover whom in the morning he had been swearing to kill, then to this young girl by whom he would, no doubt, soon be freed from him. There was no haste, only the fear remained with him of seeing his wife fall lower, perhaps to some lackey.

"And you, my little darlings," asked Deneulin of his daughters; "have they broken any of your bones?"

Lucie and Jeanne had been much afraid, but they were pleased to have seen it all. They were now laughing.

"By George!" the father went on, "we've had a fine day! If you want a dowry, you would do well to earn it yourselves, and you may also expect to have to support me."

He was joking, but his voice trembled. His eyes swelled with tears as his two daughters threw themselves into his arms.

M. Hennebeau had heard this confession of ruin. A quick thought lit up his face. Vandame would now belong to Montsou; this was the hoped-for compensation, the stroke of fortune which would bring him back to favour with the gentlemen on the directorate. At every crisis of his existence, he took refuge in the strict execution of the orders he had received; in the military discipline in which he lived he found his small share of happiness.

But they grew calm; the drawing-room fell back into a weary peacefulness, with the quiet light of its two lamps, and the warm stuffiness of the hangings. What, then, was going on outside? The brawlers were silent, and stones no longer struck the house; one only heard deep, dull blows, those blows of the hatchet which one hears in distant woods. They wished to find out, and went back into the hall to venture a glance through the glass panel of the door. Even the ladies went upstairs to post themselves behind the blinds on the first storey.

"Do you see that scoundrel, Rasseneur, over there on the threshold of the public-house?" said M. Hennebeau to Deneulin. "I had guessed as much; he must be in it."

It was not Rasseneur, however, it was Étienne, who was dealing blows from his axe at Maigrat's shop. And he went on calling to the men; did not the goods in there belong to the colliers? Had they not the right to take back their property from this thief who had exploited them so long, who was starving them at a hint from the Company? Gradually they all left the manager's house, and ran up to pillage the neighbouring shop. The cry, "Bread! bread! bread!" broke out anew. They would find bread behind that door. The rage of hunger carried them away, as if they suddenly felt that they could wait no longer without expiring on the road. Such furious thrusts were made at the door that at every stroke of the axe Étienne feared to wound someone.

Maigrat, however, who had left the hall of the manager's house, had at first taken refuge in the kitchen; but, hearing nothing there, he imagined some abominable attempt against his shop, and came up again to hide behind the pump outside, when he distinctly heard the cracking of the door and shouts of pillage in which his own name was mixed. It was not, then, a nightmare. If he could not see, he could now hear, and he followed the attack with ringing ears; every blow struck him in the heart. A hinge must have given way; five minutes more and the shop would be taken. The thing was stamped in his skull in real and terrible images—the brigands rushing forward, then the drawers broken open, the sacks emptied, everything eaten, everything drunk, the house itself carried away, nothing left, not even a stick with which he might go and beg through the villages. No, he would never allow them to complete his ruin; he would rather leave his life there. Since he had been here he noticed at a window of his house his wife's thin silhouette, pale and confused, behind the panes; no doubt she was watching the blows with her usual silent air of a poor beaten creature. Beneath there was a shed, so placed that from the villa garden one could climb it from the palings; then it was easy to get on to the tiles up to the window. And the idea of thus returning home now pursued him in his remorse at having left. Perhaps he would have time to barricade the shop with furniture; he even invented other and more heroic defences—boiling oil, lighted petroleum, poured out from above. But this love of his property struggled against his fear, and he groaned in the battle with cowardice. Suddenly, on hearing a deeper blow of the axe, he made up his mind. Avarice conquered; he and his wife would cover the sacks with their bodies rather than abandon a single loaf.

Almost immediately hooting broke out.

"Look! look!—The tom-cat's up there! After the cat! after the cat!"

The mob had just seen Maigrat on the roof of the shed. In his fever of anxiety he had climbed the palings with agility in spite of his weight, and without troubling over the breaking wood; and now he was flattening himself along the tiles, and endeavouring to reach the window. But the slope was very steep; he was incommoded by his stoutness, and his nails were torn. He would have dragged himself up, however, if he had not begun to tremble with the fear of stones; for the crowd, which he could not see, continued to cry beneath him:

"After the cat! after the cat!—Do for him!"

And suddenly both his hands let go at once, and he rolled down like a ball, leapt at the gutter, and fell across the middle wall in such a way that, by ill-chance, he rebounded on the side of the road, where his skull was broken open on the corner of a stone pillar. His brain had spurted out. He was dead. His wife up above, pale and confused behind the window-panes, still looked out.

They were stupefied at first. Étienne stopped short, and the axe slipped from his hands. Maheu, Levaque and the others forgot the shop, with their eyes fixed on the wall along which a thin red streak was slowly flowing down. And the cries ceased, and silence spread over the growing darkness.

All at once the hooting began again. It was the women, who rushed forward overcome by the drunkenness of blood.

"Then there is a good God, after all! Ah! the bloody beast, he's done for!"

They surrounded the still warm body. They insulted it with laughter, abusing his fractured head, the dirty chops, hurling in the dead man's face the long venom of their life without bread.

"I owed you sixty francs, now you're paid, thief!" said Maheude, enraged with the others. "You won't refuse me credit any more. Wait! wait! I must fatten you once more!"

With her fingers she scratched up some earth, took two handfuls and stuffed it violently into his mouth.

"There! eat that! There! eat! eat! you used to eat us!"

The abuse increased, while the dead man, stretched on his back, gazed motionless with his large fixed eyes at the immense sky from which the night was falling. This earth heaped in his mouth was the bread which he had refused to give. And henceforth he would eat of no other bread. It had not brought him luck to starve poor people.

But the women had another revenge to wreak on him.[8] They moved round, smelling him like she-wolves. They were all seeking for some outrage, some savagery that would relieve them.

Mother Brûlé's shrill voice was heard:

"Cut him like a tom-cat! Yes, yes, after the cat! after the cat! He's done too much, the dirty beast!"

Mouquette was already unfastening and drawing off the trousers, while the Levaque woman raised the legs. And Mother Brûlé, with her dry old hands, separated the naked thighs and seized this dead virility. She took hold of everything, tearing with an effort which bent her lean spine and made her long arms crack. The soft skin resisted; she had to try again, and at last carried away the fragment, a lump of hairy and bleeding flesh, which she brandished with a laugh of triumph.

"I've got it! I've got it!"

Shrill voices saluted with curses the abominable trophy.

"Ah! bugger! you won't fill our daughters any more!"

"Yes! we've done with paying on your beastly body; we shan't any more have to offer a backside in return for a loaf."

"Here, I owe you six francs; would you like to settle it? I'm quite willing, if you can do it still!"

This joke shook them all with terrible gaiety. They showed each other the bleeding fragment as an evil beast from which each of them had suffered, and which they had at last crushed, and saw before them there, inert, in their power. They spat on it, they thrust out their jaws, saying over and over again, with furious bursts of contempt:

"He can do no more! he can do no more!—It's no longer a man that they'll put away in the earth. Go and rot then, good-for-nothing!"

Mother Brûlé then planted the whole lump on the end of her stick, and holding it in the air, bore it about like a banner, rushing along the road, followed, helter-skelter, by the yelling troop of women. Drops of blood rained down, and that pitiful flesh hung like a waste piece of meat on a butcher's stall. Up above, at the window, Madame Maigrat still stood motionless; but beneath the last gleams of the setting sun, the confused faults of the window-panes deformed her white face which looked as though it were laughing. Beaten and deceived at every hour, with shoulders bent from morning to night over a ledger, perhaps she was laughing, while the band of women rushed along with that evil beast, that crushed beast, at the end of the stick.

This frightful mutilation was accomplished in frozen horror. Neither Étienne nor Maheu nor the others had had time to interfere; they stood motionless before this gallop of Furies. At the door of the Estaminet Tison a few heads were grouped—Rasseneur pale with disgust, Zacharie and Philomène stupefied at what they had seen. The two old men, Bonnemort and Mouque, were gravely shaking their heads. Only Jeanlin was making fun, pushing Bébert with his elbow, and forcing Lydie to look up. But the women were already coming back, turning round and passing beneath the manager's windows. Behind the blinds the ladies were stretching out their necks. They had not been able to observe the scene, which was hidden from them by the wall, and they could not distinguish well in the growing darkness.

"What is it they have at the end of that stick?" asked Cécile, who had grown bold enough to look out.

Lucie and Jeanne declared that it must be a rabbit-skin.

"No, no," murmured Madame Hennebeau, "they must have been pillaging a pork butcher's, it seems to be a remnant of a pig."

At this moment she shuddered and was silent. Madame Grégoire had nudged her with her knee. They both remained stupefied. The young ladies, who were very pale, asked no more questions, but with large eyes followed this red vision through the darkness.

Étienne once more brandished the axe. But the feeling of anxiety did not disappear; this corpse now barred the road and protected the shop. Many had drawn back. Satiety seemed to have appeased them all. Maheu was standing by gloomily, when he heard a voice whisper in his ear to escape. He turned round and recognised Catherine, still in her old overcoat, black and panting. With a movement he repelled her. He would not listen to her, he threatened to strike her. With a gesture of despair she hesitated, and then ran towards Étienne.

"Save yourself! save yourself! the gendarmes are coming!"

He also pushed her away and abused her, feeling the blood of the blows she had given him mounting to his cheeks. But she would not be repelled; she forced him to throw down the axe, and drew him away by both arms, with irresistible strength.

"Don't I tell you the gendarmes are coming![9] Listen to me. It's Chaval who has gone for them and is bringing them, if you want to know. It's too much for me, and I've come. Save yourself, I don't want them to take you."

And Catherine drew him away, while, at the same instant, a heavy gallop shook the street from afar. Immediately a voice arose, "The gendarmes! The gendarmes!" There was a general breaking up, so mad a rush for life that in two minutes the road was free, absolutely clear, as though swept by a hurricane. Maigrat's corpse alone made a patch of shadow on the white earth. Before the Estaminet Tison, Rasseneur only remained, feeling relieved, and with open face applauding the easy victory of the sabres; while in dim and deserted Montsou, in the silence of the closed houses, the bourgeois remained with perspiring skins and chattering teeth, not daring to look out. The plain was drowned beneath the thick night, only the blast furnaces and the coke furnaces were burning against the tragic sky. The gallop of the gendarmes heavily approached; they came up in an indistinguishable sombre mass. And behind them the Marchiennes pastry-cook's vehicle, a little covered cart which had been confided to their care, at last arrived, and a small drudge of a boy jumped down and quietly unpacked the *vol-au-vent.*

# *PART SIX*

## CHAPTER I

THE FIRST FORTNIGHT OF February passed and a black cold prolonged the hard winter without pity for the poor. Once more the authorities had scoured the roads; the prefect of Lille, an attorney, a general, and the police were not sufficient, the military had come to occupy Montsou; a whole regiment of men were camped between Beaugnies and Marchiennes. Armed pickets guarded the pits, and there were soldiers before every engine. The manager's villa, the Company's yards, even the houses of certain residents, were bristling with bayonets. Nothing was heard along the streets but the slow movement of patrols. On the pit-bank of the Voreux a sentinel was always placed in the frozen wind that blew up there, like a look-out man above the flat plain; and every two hours, as though in an enemy's country, were heard the sentry's cries:

"*Qui vive?*—Give the password!"

Nowhere had work been resumed. On the contrary, the strike had spread; Crèvecœur, Mirou, Madeleine, like the Voreux, were producing nothing; at Feutry-Cantel and the Victoire there were fewer men every morning; even at Saint-Thomas, which had been hitherto exempt, men were wanting. There was now a silent persistence in the face of this exhibition of force which exasperated the miners' pride. The settlements looked deserted in the midst of the beetroot fields. Not a workman stirred, only at rare intervals was one to be met by chance, isolated, with sidelong look, lowering his head before the red trousers. And in this deep melancholy calm, in this passive opposition to the guns, there was a deceptive gentleness, a forced and patient obedience of wild beasts in a cage, with their eyes on the tamer, ready to spring on his neck if he turned his back. The Company, who were being ruined by this death of work, talked of hiring miners from the Borinage, on the Belgian frontier, but did not dare; so that the battle continued as before between the colliers, who were shut up at home, and the dead pits guarded by soldiery.

On the morrow of that terrible day this calm had come about at once, hiding such a panic that the greatest silence possible was kept concerning the damage and the atrocities. The enquiry which had been opened showed that Maigrat had died from his fall, and the frightful mutilation of the corpse remained uncertain, already surrounded by a legend. On its side, the Company did not acknowledge the disasters it had suffered, any more than the Grégoires cared to compromise their daughter in the scandal of a trial in which she would have to give evidence. However, some arrests took place, mere supernumeraries as usual, silly and frightened, knowing nothing. By mistake, Pierron was taken off with handcuffs at his wrists as far as Marchiennes, to the great amusement of his mates. Rasseneur, also, was nearly arrested by two gendarmes. The management was content with preparing lists of names and giving back certificates in large numbers. Maheu had received his, Levaque also, as well as thirty-four of their mates in the settlement of the Deux-Cent-Quarante alone. And all the severity was directed against Étienne, who had disappeared on the evening of the fray, and who was being sought, although no trace of him could be found. Chaval, in his hatred, had denounced him, refusing to name the others at Catherine's appeal, for she wished to save her parents. The days passed, everyone felt that nothing was yet concluded; and with oppressed heart everyone was awaiting the end.

At Montsou, during this period, the inhabitants awoke with a start every night, their ears buzzing with an imaginary alarm-bell and their nostrils haunted by the smell of powder. But what completed their discomfiture was a sermon by the new curé, Abbé Ranvier,[1] that lean priest with eyes like red-hot coals who had succeeded Abbé Joire. He was indeed unlike the smiling discreet man, so fat and gentle, whose only anxiety was to live at peace with everybody. Abbé Ranvier went so far as to defend these abominable brigands who had dishonoured the district. He found excuses for the atrocities of the strikers; he violently attacked the middle class, throwing on them the whole of the responsibility. It was the middle class which, by dispossessing the Church of its ancient liberties in order to misuse them itself, had turned this world into a cursed place of injustice and suffering; it was the middle class which prolonged misunderstandings, which was pushing on towards a terrible catastrophe by its atheism, by its refusal to return to the old beliefs, to the fraternal traditions of the early Christians. And he dared to threaten the rich. He warned them that if they obstinately persisted in refusing to listen to the voice of God, God would surely put Himself on the side of the poor. He would take back their fortunes from those who faithlessly enjoyed them, and would distribute them to the humble of the earth for the triumph of His glory. The devout trembled at this; the lawyer declared that it was Socialism of the worst kind; all saw the curé at the head of a band, brandishing a cross, and with vigorous blows demolishing the bourgeois society of '89.

M. Hennebeau, when informed, contented himself with saying as he shrugged his shoulders:

"If he troubles us too much the Bishop will free us from him."

And while the breath of panic was thus blowing from one end of the plain to the other, Étienne was dwelling beneath the earth, in Jeanlin's burrow at the bottom of Réquillart. It was there that he was in hiding; no one believed him so near; the quiet audacity of that refuge, in the very mine, in that abandoned passage of the old pit, had baffled search. Above, the sloes and hawthorns growing among the fallen scaffolding of the steeple filled up the mouth of the hole. No one ventured down; it was necessary to know the trick—how to hang on to the roots of the mountain ash and to let go fearlessly, to catch hold of the rungs that were still solid. Other obstacles also protected him, the suffocating heat of the passage, a hundred and twenty mètres of dangerous descent, then the painful gliding on all-fours for a quarter of a league between the narrowed walls of the gallery before discovering the cavern of villainy full of plunder. He lived there in the midst of abundance, finding gin there, the rest of the dried cod, and provisions of all sorts. The large hay bed was excellent, and not a current of air could be felt in this equal temperature, as warm as a bath. Light, however, threatened to fail. Jeanlin, who had made himself purveyor, with the prudence and discretion of a savage and delighted to make fun of the police, had even brought him pomatum, but could not succeed in putting his hands on a packet of candles.

After the fifth day Étienne never lighted up except to eat. He could not swallow in the dark. This complete and interminable night, always of the same blackness, was his chief torment. It was in vain that he was able to sleep in safety, that he was warm and provided with bread. The night had never weighed so heavily on his brain. It seemed to him even to crush his thoughts. Now he was living on thefts. In spite of his communistic theories, old scruples of education arose, and he contented himself with gnawing his share of dry bread. But what was to be done? One must live, and his task was not yet accomplished. Another shame overcame him: remorse for that savage drunkenness from the gin, drunk in the great cold on an empty stomach, which had thrown him, armed with a knife, on Chaval. This stirred in him the whole of that unknown terror, the hereditary ill, the long ancestry of drunkenness, no longer tolerating a drop of alcohol without falling into homicidal mania. Would he then end as a murderer? When he found himself in shelter, in this profound calm of the earth, seized by satiety of violence, he had slept the sleep of a brute, gorged and overcome; and the depression continued, he lived in a bruised state with bitter mouth and aching head, as after some tremendous spree. A week passed by; the Maheus, who had been warned, were not able to send a candle; he had to give up seeing clearly, even when eating.

Now Étienne remained for hours stretched out on his hay. Vague ideas were working within him for the first time: a feeling of superiority, which placed him apart from his mates, an exaltation of his person as he grew more instructed. Never had he reflected so much; he asked himself the why of his disgust on the morrow of that furious course among the pits; and he did not dare to reply to himself, his recollections were repulsive to him, the ignoble desires, the coarse instincts, the odour of all that wretchedness shaken out to the wind. In spite of the torment of the darkness, he would come to hate the hour for returning to the settlement. How nauseous were all these wretches in a heap living at the common bucket! There was not one with whom he could seriously talk politics; it was a bestial existence, always the same air tainted by onion, in which one choked! He wished to enlarge their horizon, to raise them to the comfort and good manners of the middle class, by making them masters; but how long it would take! and he no longer felt the courage to await victory in this prison of hunger. By slow degrees his vanity of leadership, his constant preoccupation of thinking in their place, left him free, breathing into him the soul of one of those bourgeois whom he execrated.

Jeanlin one evening brought a candle-end, stolen from a carter's lantern, and this was a great relief for Étienne. When the darkness began to stupefy him, weighing on his skull almost to madness, he would light up for a moment; then, as soon as he had chased away the nightmare, he extinguished the candle, miserly of this brightness which was as necessary to his life as bread. The silence buzzed in his ears, he only heard the flight of a band of rats, the cracking of the old timber, the low sound of a spider weaving her web. And with eyes open, in this warm nothingness, he returned to his fixed idea—the thought of what his mates were doing above. Desertion on his part would have seemed to him the worst cowardice. If he thus hid himself, it was to remain free, to give counsel, or to act. His long meditations had fixed his ambition. While awaiting something better he would like to be Pluchart, leaving manual work in order to work only at politics, but alone, in a clean room, under the pretext that brain labour absorbs the entire life, and demands much quiet.

At the beginning of the second week, the child having told him that the police supposed he had gone over to Belgium, Étienne ventured out of his hole at nightfall. He wished to ascertain the situation, and to decide if it was still well to persist. He himself considered the game doubtful. Before the strike he felt uncertain of the result, and had simply yielded to facts; and now, after having been intoxicated with rebellion, he came back to this first doubt, despairing of making the Company yield. But he would not yet confess this to himself; he was tortured when he thought of the miseries of defeat, and the heavy responsibility of suffering which would weigh upon him. The end of the strike: was it not the end of his part, the overthrow of his ambition, his life falling back into the brutishness of the mine and the horrors of the settlement? And honestly, without any base calculation or falsehood, he endeavoured to find his faith again, to prove to himself that resistance was still possible, that Capital was about to destroy itself in face of the heroic suicide of Labour.

Throughout the entire country, in fact, there was nothing but a long echo of ruin. At night, when he wandered through the black country, like a wolf who has come out of his forest, he seemed to hear the crash of bankruptcies from one end of the plain to the other. He now passed by the road-side nothing but closed, dead workshops, becoming rotten beneath the dull sky. The sugar works had especially suffered: the Hoton sugar works, the Fauvelle works, after having reduced the number of their hands, had come to grief one after the other. At the Dutilleul flour works the last mill had stopped on the second Saturday of the month, and the Bleuze rope works, for mine cables, had been quite ruined by the lock-out. On the Marchiennes side the situation was growing worse every day. All the fires were out at the Gagebois glass works, men were continually being sent away from the Sonneville workshops, only one of the three blast furnaces of the Forges was alight, and not one battery of coke ovens was burning on the horizon. The strike of the Montsou colliers, born of the industrial crisis which had been growing worse for two years, had increased it and precipitated the downfall. To the other causes of suffering—the stoppage of orders from America, and the engorgement of invested capital in excessive production—was now added the unforeseen lack of coal for the few furnaces which were still kept up; and that was the supreme agony, this engine bread which the pits no longer furnished. Frightened by the general anxiety, the Company, by diminishing its output and starving its miners, inevitably found itself at the end of December without a fragment of coal at the surface of its pits. Everything held together, the plague blew from afar, one fall led to another; the industries tumbled each other over as they fell, in so rapid a series of catastrophes that the shocks echoed in the midst of the neighbouring cities, Lille, Douai, Valenciennes, where runaway bankrupts were ruining families.

At the turn of a road Étienne often stopped in the frozen night to hear the rubbish raining down. He breathed deeply in the darkness, the joy of annihilation seized him, the hope that day would dawn on the extermination of the old world, with not a single fortune left standing, the scythe of equality levelling everything to the ground. But in this massacre it was the Company's pits that especially interested him. He would continue his walk, blinded by the darkness, visiting them one after the other, glad to discover some new disaster. Landslips of increasing gravity continued to occur on account of the prolonged abandonment of the passages. Above the north gallery of Mirou the ground sank in to such an extent, that the Joiselle road, for the distance of a hundred mètres, had been swallowed up as though by the shock of an earthquake; and the Company, disturbed at the rumours raised by these accidents, paid the owners for their vanished fields without bargaining. Crèvecœur and Madeleine, which lay in very shifting rock, were becoming stopped up more and more. It was said that two captains had been buried at the Victoire; there was an inundation at Feutry-Cantel; it had been necessary to wall-up a gallery for the length of a kilomètre at Saint-Thomas, where the ill-kept timbering was breaking down everywhere. Thus every hour enormous sums were spent, making great breaches in the shareholders' dividends; a rapid destruction of the pits was going on, which must end at last by eating up the famous Montsou deniers which had been centupled in a century.

In the face of these repeated blows, hope was again born in Étienne; he came to believe that a third month of resistance would crush the monster—the weary, sated beast, crouching down there like an idol in its unknown tabernacle. He knew that after the Montsou troubles there had been great excitement in the Paris journals, quite a violent controversy between the official newspapers and the Opposition newspapers, terrible narratives, which were especially directed against the International, of which the Empire was becoming afraid after having first encouraged it; and the directors not daring to turn a deaf ear any longer, two of them had condescended to come and hold an enquiry, but with an air of regret, not appearing to care about the upshot; so disinterested, that in three days they came back again, declaring that everything was going on as well as possible. He was told, however, from other quarters that during their stay these gentlemen sat permanently, displaying feverish activity, and absorbed in transactions of which no one about them uttered a word. And he charged them with affecting confidence they did not feel, and came to look upon their departure as a nervous flight, feeling now certain of triumph since these terrible men were letting everything go.

But on the following night Étienne despaired again. The Company's back was too robust to be so easily broken; they might lose millions, but later on they would get them back again by gnawing at their men's bread. On that night, having pushed as far as Jean-Bart, he guessed the truth when an overseer told him that there was talk of yielding Vandame to Montsou. At Deneulin's house, it was said, the wretchedness was pitiful, the wretchedness of the rich; the father ill in his powerlessness, aged by his anxiety over money, the daughters struggling in the midst of tradesmen, trying to save their shifts. There was less suffering in the famished settlements than in this middle class house where they shut themselves up to drink water. Work had been resumed at Jean-Bart, and it had been necessary to replace the pump at Gaston-Marie; while, in spite of all haste, an inundation had already begun which made great expenses necessary. Deneulin had at last risked his request for a loan of one hundred thousand francs from the Grégoires, and the refusal, though he had expected it, completed his dejection: if they refused, it was for his sake, in order to save him from an impossible struggle; and they advised him to sell. He, as usual, violently refused. It enraged him to have to pay the expenses of the strike; he hoped at first to die of it, with the blood at his head, strangled by apoplexy. Then what was to be done? he had listened to the directors' offers. They wrangled with him, they depreciated this superb prey, this repaired pit, equipped anew, where the lack of capital alone paralysed the out-put. He would be lucky if he got enough out of it to satisfy his creditors. For two days he had struggled against the directors at Montsou, furious at the quiet way with which they took advantage of his embarrassment and shouting his refusals at them in his loud voice. And there the affair remained, and they had returned to Paris to await patiently his last groans. Étienne smelled out this compensation for the disasters, and was again seized by discouragement before the invincible power of the great capitalists, so strong in battle that they fattened in defeat by eating the corpses of the small capitalists who fell at their side.

The next day, fortunately, Jeanlin brought him a piece of good news. At the Voreux the tubbing of the shaft was threatening to break, and the water was filtering in from all the joints; in great haste a gang of carpenters had been set on to repair it.

Up to now Étienne had avoided the Voreux, warned by the everlasting black silhouette of the sentinel stationed on the pit-bank above the plain. He could not be avoided, he dominated in the air, like the flag of the regiment. Towards three o'clock in the morning the sky became overcast, and he went to the pit, where some mates explained to him the bad condition of the tubbing; they even thought that it would have to be done entirely over again, which would stop the output of coal for three months. For a long time he prowled round, listening to the carpenters' mallets hammering in the shaft. That wound which had to be dressed rejoiced his heart.

As he went back in the early daylight, he saw the sentinel still on the pit-bank. This time he would certainly be seen. As he walked he thought about those soldiers who were taken from the people, to be armed against the people. How easy the triumph of the revolution would be if the army were suddenly to declare for it! It would be enough if the workman and the peasant in the barracks were to remember their origin. That was the supreme peril, the great terror, which made the teeth of the middle class chatter when they thought of the possible defection of the troops. In two hours they would be swept away and exterminated with all the delights and abominations of their iniquitous life. It was already said that whole regiments were tainted with socialism. Was it true? When justice came, would it be thanks to the cartridges distributed by the middle class? And snatching at another hope, the young man dreamed that the regiment, with its posts, now guarding the pits, would come over to the side of the strikers, fusillade the Company, and at last give the mine to the miners.

He then noticed that he was ascending the pit-bank, his head filled with these reflections. Why should he not talk with this soldier? He would get to know what his ideas were. With an air of indifference, he continued to come nearer, as though he were gleaning old wood among the rubbish. The sentinel remained motionless.

"Eh! mate! damned weather," said Étienne, at last. "I think we shall have snow."

He was a small soldier, very fair, with a pale, gentle face covered with red patches. In his great cloak he showed the embarrassment of the recruit.

"Yes, perhaps we shall, I think," he murmured.

And with his blue eyes he gazed at the livid sky, the smoky dawn, with soot weighing like lead afar over the plain.

"What idiots they are to put you here to freeze!" Étienne went on. "One would think the Cossacks were coming! And then there's always wind here."

The little soldier shivered without complaining. There was certainly a little cabin of dry stones there, where old Bonnemort used to take shelter when it blew a hurricane, but the order being not to leave the summit of the pit-bank, the soldier did not stir from it, his hands so stiffened by cold that he could no longer feel his weapon. He belonged to the guard of sixty men who were protecting the Voreux, and as this cruel sentry-duty frequently came round, he had before nearly stayed there for good with his dead feet. His work demanded it; a passive obedience finished the benumbing process, and he replied to these questions by the stammered words of a sleepy child.

Étienne in vain endeavoured during a quarter of an hour to make him talk about polities. He replied "yes" or "no" without seeming to understand. Some of his comrades said that the captain was a republican; as to him, he had no idea—it was all the same to him. If he was ordered to fire, he would fire, so as not to be punished. The workman listened, seized by the popular hatred against the army—against these brothers whose hearts were changed by sticking a pair of red pantaloons on to their buttocks.

"Then what's your name?"

"Jules."

"And where do you come from?"

"From Plogof, over there."

He stretched out his arm at random. It was in Brittany, he knew no more. His small pale face grew animated; he began to laugh, and felt warmer.

"I have a mother and a sister. They are waiting for me, sure enough. Ah! it won't be for to-morrow. When I left, they came with me as far as Pont-l'Abbé. We had to take the horse to Lepalmec: it nearly broke its legs at the bottom of the Audierne Hill. Cousin Charles was waiting for us with sausages, but the women were crying too much, and it stuck in our throats. Good Lord! what a long way off our home is!"

His eyes grew moist, though he was still laughing. The desert moorland of Plogof, that wild storm-beaten point of the Raz, appeared to him beneath a dazzling sun in the rosy season of heather.

"Do you think," he asked, "if I'm not punished, that they'll give me a month's leave in two years?"

Then Étienne talked about Provence, which he had left when he was quite small. The daylight was going, and flakes of snow began to fly in the earthy sky. And at last he felt anxious on noticing Jeanlin, who was prowling about in the midst of the bushes, stupefied to see him up there. The child was beckoning to him. What was the good of this dream of fraternising with the soldiers? It would take years and years, and his useless attempt cast him down as though he had expected to succeed. But suddenly he understood Jeanlin's gesture. The sentinel was about to be relieved, and he went away, running off to bury himself at Réquillart, his heart crushed once more by the certainty of defeat; while the little scamp who ran beside him was accusing that dirty beast of a trooper of having called out the guard to fire at them.

On the summit of the pit-bank Jules stood motionless, with eyes vacantly gazing at the falling snow. The sergeant was approaching with his men, and the regulation cries were exchanged.

"*Qui vive?*—Give the password!"

And they heard the heavy steps begin again, ringing as

though on a conquered country. In spite of the growing daylight, nothing stirred in the settlements; the colliers remained in silent rage beneath the military boot.

## CHAPTER II

SNOW HAD BEEN FALLING for two days; since the morning it had ceased, and an intense frost had frozen the immense sheet. This black country, with its inky roads and walls, and trees powdered with coal-dust, was now white, a single whiteness stretching out without end. The Deux-Cent-Quarante settlement lay beneath the snow as though it had disappeared. No smoke came out of the chimneys; the houses, without fire and as cold as the stones in the street, did not melt the thick layer on the tiles. It was nothing more than a quarry of white slabs in the white plain, a vision of a dead village wound in its shroud. Along the roads the passing patrols alone made a muddy mess with their stamping.

Among the Maheus the last shovelful of cinders had been burnt the evening before, and it was no use any longer to think of gleaming on the pit-bank in this terrible weather, when the sparrows themselves could not find a blade of grass. Alzire, from the obstinacy with which her poor hands had dug in the snow, was dying. Maheude had to wrap her up in the fragment of a coverlet while waiting for Dr. Vanderhagen, for whom she had twice gone out without being able to find him. The servant had, however, promised that he would come to the settlement before night, and the mother was standing at the window watching, while the little invalid, who had wished to be downstairs, was shivering on a chair, having the illusion that it was better there near the cold grate. Old Bonnemort opposite, his legs bad once more, seemed to be sleeping; neither Lénore nor Henri had come back from scouring the roads, in company with Jeanlin, to ask for sous. Maheu alone was walking heavily up and down the bare room, stumbling against the wall at every turn, with the stupid air of an animal which can no longer see its cage. The petroleum also was finished; but the reflection of the snow from outside was so bright that it vaguely lit up the room, in spite of the deepening night.

There was a noise of sabots, and the Levaque woman pushed open the door like a gale of wind, shouting furiously from the threshold at Maheude:

"Then it's you who have said that I forced my lodger to give me twenty sous when he sleeps with me?"

The other shrugged her shoulders.

"Don't bother me. I said nothing; and who told you so?"

"They tell me you said so; it doesn't concern you who it was. You even said you could hear us at our dirty tricks behind the wall, and that the filth gets into our house because I'm always on my back. Just tell me you didn't say so, eh?"

Every day quarrels broke out as a result of the constant gossiping of the women. Especially between these households which lived door-to-door, squabbles and reconciliations took place every day. But never before had so sharp an altercation thrown them one against the other. Since the strike hunger exasperated their rancour, so that they felt the need of blows; an altercation between two gossiping women finished by a murderous onset between their two men.

Just then Levaque arrived in his turn, dragging Bouteloup.

"Here's our mate; let him just say if he has given twenty sous to my wife to sleep with her."

The lodger, hiding his timid gentleness in his great beard, protested and stammered:

"Oh! that? No! Never anything! never!"

At once Levaque became threatening, and thrust his fist beneath Maheu's nose.

"You know that won't do for me. If a man's got a wife like that, he ought to knock her ribs in. If not, then you believe what she says."

"By God!" exclaimed Maheu, furious at being dragged out of his dejection, "what is all this clatter again? Haven't we got enough to do with our misery? Just leave me alone, damn you! or I'll let you know it! And first, who says that my wife said so?"

"Who says so? Pierronne said so."

Maheude broke into a sharp laugh, and turning towards the Levaque woman:

"Ah! Pierronne is it? Well! I can tell you what she told me. Yes, she told me that you sleep with both your men—the one—and the other——!"

After that it was no longer possible to come to an understanding. They all grew angry, and the Levaques, as a reply to the Maheus, asserted that Pierronne had said a good many other things on their account; that they had sold Catherine, that they were all rotten together, even to the little ones, with a dirty disease caught by Étienne at the Volcan.

"She said that! She said that!" yelled Maheu. "Good! I'll go to her, I will, and if she says that she said that, she shall feel my hand on her chops!"

He was carried out of himself, and the Levaques followed him to see what would happen, while Bouteloup, having a horror of disputes, furtively returned home. Excited by the altercation, Maheude was also going out, when a complaint from Alzire held her back. She crossed the ends of the coverlet over the little one's quivering body, and placed herself before the window looking out vaguely. And that doctor, who still delayed!

At the Pierron's door Maheu and the Levaques met Lydie, who was stamping in the snow. The house was closed, and a thread of light came through a crack in a shutter. The child replied at first to their questions with constraint: no, her father was not there, he had gone to the wash-house to join Mother Brûlé and bring back the bundle of linen. Then she was confused, and would not say what her mother was doing. At last she let out everything with a sly, spiteful laugh: her mother had pushed her out of the door because M. Dansaert was there, and she prevented them from talking. Since the morning he had been going about the settlement with two policemen, trying to pick up workmen, imposing on the weak, and announcing everywhere that if the descent did not take place on Monday at the Voreux, the Company had decided to hire men from the Borinage. And as the night came on he sent away the policemen, finding Pierronne alone; then he had remained with her to drink a glass of gin before a good fire.

"Hush! hold your tongue! We must see them," said Levaque, with a lewd laugh. "We'll explain everything directly. Get off with you, youngster."

Lydie drew back a few steps while he put his eye to a crack in the shutter. He stifled a low cry and his back bent with a quiver. In her turn his wife looked through, but she said, as though taken by the colic, that it was disgusting. Maheu, who had pushed her, wishing also to see, then declared that he had had enough for his money. And they began again, in a row, each taking his glance as at a peep-show. The parlour, glittering with cleanliness, was enlivened by a large fire; there were cakes on the table with a bottle and glasses, in fact quite a feast. What they saw going on in there at last exasperated the two men, who under other circumstances would have laughed over it for six months. That she should let herself be stuffed up to the neck, with her skirts in the air, was funny. But, good God! was it not disgusting to do that in front of a great fire, and to get up one's strength with biscuits, when the mates had neither a slice of bread nor a fragment of coal?

"Here's father!" cried Lydie, running away.

Pierron was quietly coming back from the wash-house with the bundle of linen on his shoulder. Maheu immediately addressed him:

"Here! they tell me that your wife says that I sold Catherine, and that we are all rotten in the house. And what do they pay you in your house, your wife and the gentleman who is making use of her skin?"

The astonished Pierron could not understand, and Pierronne, seized with fear on hearing the tumult of voices, lost her head and set the door ajar to see what was the matter. They could see her, looking very red, with her dress open and her skirt tucked up at her waist; while Dansaert, in the background, was wildly fixing himself up. The head captain rushed away and disappeared, trembling with fear that this story would reach the manager's ears. Then there would be an awful scandal, laughter and hooting and abuse.

"You, who are always saying that other people are dirty!"

shouted the Levaque woman to Pierronne, "it's not surprising that you're clean when you get the bosses to scour you."

"Ah! it's fine for her to talk!" said Levaque again. "Here's a trollop who says that my wife sleeps with me and the lodger, one below and the other above! Yes! yes! that's what they tell me you say."

But Pierronne, grown calm, held her own against this abuse, very contemptuous in the assurance that she was the best looking and the richest.

"I've said what I've said; just leave me alone, will you! What have my affairs got to do with you, a pack of jealous creatures who want to get over us because we are able to save up money! Get along! get along! You can say what you like; my husband knows well enough why Monsieur Dansaert was here."

Pierron, in fact, was furiously defending his wife. The quarrel turned. They accused him of having sold himself, of being a spy, the Company's dog; they charged him with shutting himself up, to gorge himself with the good things with which the bosses paid him for his treachery. In defence, he pretended that Maheu had slipped beneath his door a threatening paper with two crossbones and a dagger above. And this necessarily ended in a struggle between the men, as the quarrels of the women always did now that famine was enraging the mildest. Maheu and Levaque rushed on Pierron with their fists, and had to be separated.

Blood was flowing from her son-in-law's nose, when Mother Brûlé, in her turn, arrived from the wash-house. When informed of what had been going on, she merely said:

"The damned beast dishonours me!"

The road was becoming deserted, not a shadow spotted the naked whiteness of the snow, and the settlement, falling back into its death-like immobility, went on starving beneath the intense cold.

"And the doctor?" asked Maheu, as he shut the door.

"Not come," replied Maheude, still standing before the window.

"Are the little ones back?"

"No, not back."

Maheu again began his heavy walk from one wall to the other, looking like a stricken ox. Father Bonnemort, seated stiffly on his chair, had not even lifted his head. Alzire also had said nothing, and was trying not to shiver, so as to avoid giving them pain; but in spite of her courage in suffering, she sometimes trembled so much that one could hear against the coverlet the quivering of the little invalid girl's lean body, while with her large open eyes she stared at the ceiling, from which the pale reflection of the white gardens lit up the room as by moonshine.

The emptied house was now in its last agony, having reached a final stage of nakedness. The mattress ticks had followed the wool to the dealers; then the sheets had gone, the linen, everything that could be sold. One evening they had sold a handkerchief of the grandfather's for two sous. Tears fell over each object of the poor household which had to go, and the mother was still lamenting that one day she had carried away in her skirt the rose cardboard box, her man's old present, as one would carry away a child to get rid of it on some doorstep. They were bare; they had only their skins left to sell, so worn-out and injured that no one would have given a farthing for them. They no longer even took the trouble to search, they knew that there was nothing left, that they had come to the end of everything, that they must not hope even for a candle, or a fragment of coal, or a potato; and they were waiting to die, only grieved about the children, for it was useless cruelty to have got the little girl ill before strangling her.

"At last! here he is!" said Maheude.

A black figure passed before the window. The door opened. But it was not Dr. Vanderhagen; they recognised the new curé, Abbé Ranvier, who did not seem surprised at coming on this dead house, without light, without fire, without bread. He had already been to three neighbouring houses, going from family to family, picking up those who were willing, like Dansaert with his two policemen; and at once he exclaimed, in his feverish fanatic's voice:

"Why were you not at Mass on Sunday, my children? You are wrong, the Church alone can save you. Now promise me to come next Sunday."

Maheu, after staring at him, went on walking heavily, without a word. It was Maheude who replied:

"To Mass, sir? What for? Isn't the good God making fun of us? Look here! what has my little girl done to Him up there to be shaking with fever? It seems that we hadn't enough misery, that He had to make her ill, too, just when I can't even give her a cup of warm gruel."

Then the priest stood and talked at length. He spoke of the strike, this terrible wretchedness, this exasperated rancour of famine, with the ardour of a missionary who is preaching to savages for the glory of religion. He said that the Church was with the poor, that she would one day cause justice to triumph by calling down the anger of God on the iniquities of the rich. And that day would come soon, for the rich had taken the place of God, and were governing without God, in their impious theft of power. But if the workers desired the fair division of the goods of the earth, they ought at once to put themselves in the hands of the priests, just as on the death of Jesus the poor and the humble grouped themselves around the Apostles. What strength the Pope would have, what an army the clergy would have under them, when they were able to command the numberless crowd of workers! In one week they would purge the world of the wicked, they would chase away the unworthy masters. Then, indeed, there would be a real reign of God, everyone recompensed according to his merits, and the law of work leading to universal happiness.

Maheude, who was listening to him, seemed to hear Étienne, in those autumn evenings when he announced to them the end of their evils. Only she had always distrusted the cloth.

"That's very well, what you say there, sir," she replied, "but that's because you no longer agree with the bourgeois. All our curés dined at the manager's, and threatened us with the devil as soon as we asked for bread."

He began again, and spoke of the deplorable misunderstanding between the Church and the people. Now, in veiled phrases, he hit at the town curés, at the bishops, at the highly-placed clergy, sated with enjoyment, gorged with domination, making pacts with the liberal middle class, in the imbecility of their blindness, not seeing that it was this middle class which had dispossessed them of the empire of the world. Deliverance would come from the country priests, who would all rise to re-establish the kingdom of Christ, with the help of the poor; and already he seemed to be at their head; he raised his bony form like the chief of a band, an evangelical revolutionary, his eyes so filled with light that they illuminated the gloomy room. This enthusiastic sermon lifted him to mystic heights, and the poor people had long ceased to understand him.

"It doesn't need so many words," growled Maheu suddenly. "You'd best begin by bringing us a loaf."

"Come on Sunday to Mass," cried the priest. "God will provide for everything."

And he went off to catechise the Levaques in their turn, so carried away by his dream of the final triumph of the Church, and so contemptuous of facts, that he would thus go through the settlements without charities, with empty hands amid this army dying of hunger, being a poor devil himself who looked upon suffering as the spur to salvation.

Maheu went on walking, and nothing was heard but his regular tramp which made the floor tremble. There was the sound of a rust-eaten pulley, old Bonnemort was spitting into the cold grate. Then the rhythm of the feet began again. Alzire, weakened by fever, was rambling in a low voice, laughing, thinking that it was warm and that she was playing in the sun.

"Good gracious!" muttered Maheude, after having touched her cheeks, "how she burns! I don't expect that damned beast now, the brigands must have stopped him from coming."

She meant the doctor and the Company. She uttered a joyous exclamation, however, when the door once more opened. But her arms fell back and she remained standing still with gloomy face.

"Good evening," whispered Étienne, when he had carefully closed the door.

He often came thus at night-time. The Maheus learnt his retreat after the second day. But they kept the secret and no one in the settlement knew exactly what had become of the young man. A legend had grown up around him. People still believed in him and mysterious rumours circulated; he would re-appear with an army and chests full of gold; and there was always the religious expectation of a miracle, the realised ideal, a sudden entry into that city of justice which he had promised them. Some said they had seen him lying back in a carriage, with three other gentlemen, in the Marchiennes road; others affirmed that he had spent two days in England. At length, however, suspicions began to arise and jokers accused him of hiding in a cellar, where Mouquette kept him warm, for this relationship, when known, had done him harm. There was a slow disaffection in the midst of his popularity, a gradual increase of the despairing among the faithful, and their number was certain, little by little, to grow.

"What brutal weather!" he added. "And you nothing new, always from bad to worse? They tell me that little Négrel has been to Belgium to get Borains. Good God! we are done for if that is true!"

He shuddered as he entered this dark icy room, where it was some time before his eyes were able to see the unfortunate people whose presence he guessed by the deepening of the shade. He was experiencing the repugnance and discomfort of the workman who has risen above his class, refined by study and stimulated by ambition. What wretchedness! and the odours! and the bodies in a heap! And a terrible pity caught him by the throat. The spectacle of this agony so overcame him that he tried to find words to advise submission.

But Maheu came violently up to him, shouting:

"Borains! They won't dare, the bloody fools! Let the Borains go down, then, if they want us to destroy the pits!"

With an air of constraint, Étienne explained that it was not possible to move, that the soldiers who guarded the pits would protect the descent of the Belgian workmen. And Maheu clenched his fists, irritated especially, as he said, by having those bayonets in his back. Then the colliers were no longer masters in their own place? They were treated, then, like convicts, forced to work by a loaded musket? He loved his pit, it was a great grief to him not to have been down for two months. He was driven wild, therefore, at the idea of this insult, these strangers whom they threatened to introduce. Then the recollection that his certificate had been given back to him struck him to the heart.

"I don't know why I'm angry," he muttered. "I don't belong to their shop any longer. When they have hunted me away from here, I may as well die on the road."

"As to that," said Étienne, "if you like, they'll take your certificate back to-morrow. People don't send away good workmen."

He interrupted himself, surprised to hear Alzire, who was laughing softly in the delirium of her fever. So far he had only made out Father Bonnemort's stiff shadow, and this gaiety of the sick child frightened him. It was indeed too much if the little ones were going to die of it. With trembling voice he made up his mind.

"Look here! this can't go on, we are done for. We must give it up."

Maheude, who had been motionless and silent up to now, suddenly broke out, and treating him familiarly and swearing like a man, she shouted in his face:

"What's that you say? It's you who say that, by God!"

He was about to give reasons, but she would not let him speak.

"Don't repeat that, by God! or, woman as I am, I'll put my fist into your face. Then we have been dying for two months, and I have sold my household, and my little ones have fallen ill of it, and there is to be nothing done, and the injustice is to begin again! Ah! do you know! when I think of that my blood stands still. No, no! I would burn everything, I would kill everything, rather than give up."

She pointed at Maheu in the darkness, with a vague, threatening gesture.

"Listen to this! If my man goes back to the pit, he'll find me waiting for him on the road to spit in his face and cry coward!"

Étienne could not see her, but he felt a heat like the breath of a barking animal. He had drawn back, astonished at this fury which was his work. She was so changed that he could no longer recognise the woman who was once so sensible, reproving his violent schemes, saying that we ought not to wish anyone dead, and who was now refusing to listen to reason and talking of killing people. It was not he now, it was she, who talked politics, who dreamed of sweeping away the bourgeois at a stroke, who demanded the Republic and the guillotine to free the earth of these rich robbers who fattened on the labour of starvelings.

"Yes, I could flay them with my fingers. We've had enough of them! Our turn is come now; you used to say so yourself. When I think of the father, the grandfather, the father's grandfather, what all of them who went before have suffered, what we are suffering, and that our sons and our sons' sons will suffer it over again, it makes me mad—I could take a knife. The other day we didn't do enough at Montsou; we ought to have pulled the bloody place to the ground, down to the last brick. And do you know I've only one regret, that we didn't let the old man strangle the Piolaine girl. Hunger may strangle my little ones for all they care!"

Her words fell like the blows of an axe in the night. The closed horizon would not open, and the impossible ideal was turning to poison in the depths of this skull which had been crushed by grief.

"You have misunderstood," Étienne was able to say at last, beating a retreat. "We ought to come to an understanding with the Company. I know that the pits are suffering much, so that it would probably consent to an arrangement."

"No, never!" she shouted.

Just then Lènore and Henri came back with their hands empty. A gentleman had certainly given them two sous, but the girl kept kicking her little brother, and the two sous fell into the snow, and as Jeanlin had joined in the search they had not been able to find them.

"Where is Jeanlin?"

"He's gone away, mother; he said he had business."

Étienne was listening with an aching heart. Once she had threatened to kill them if they ever held out their hands to beg. Now she sent them herself on to the roads, and proposed that all of them—the ten thousand colliers of Montsou—should take the sticks and wallets of the aged poor and scour the terrified country.

The anguish continued to increase in the black room. The little urchins came back hungry, they wanted to eat; why could they not have something to eat? And they grumbled, flung themselves about, and at last crushed the feet of their dying sister, who groaned. The mother furiously boxed their ears in the darkness at random. Then, as they cried still louder, asking for bread, she burst into tears, and dropped on to the floor, seizing them all in one embrace with the little invalid; then, for a long time, her tears fell in a nervous outbreak which left her limp and worn out, stammering over and over again the same phrase, calling for death:

"Oh! God! why do you not take us? Oh! God! in pity take us, to have done with it!"

The grandfather preserved his immobility, like an old tree twisted by the rain and wind; while the father continued walking between the fire-place and the cupboard, without turning his head.

But the door opened, and this time it was Doctor Vanderhagen.

"The devil!" he said. "This light won't spoil your eyes. Look sharp! I'm in a hurry."

As usual, he scolded, knocked up by work. Fortunately, he had matches with him, and the father had to strike six, one by one, and to hold them while he examined the invalid. Unwound from her coverlet, she shivered beneath this flickering light, as lean as a bird in agony in the snow, so small that one only saw her hump. But she smiled with the wandering smile of the dying, and her eyes were very large; while her poor hands were shrivelled over her hollow breast. And as the half-choked mother asked if it was right to take away from her the only child who helped in the household, so intelligent and gentle, the doctor grew vexed.

"Ah! she is going. Dead of hunger, your blessed child. And not the only one, either; I've just seen another one over there. You all send for me, but I can't do anything; it's meat that you want to cure you."

Maheu, with burning fingers, had dropped the match, and the darkness fell back over the little corpse, which was still warm.

The doctor had gone away in a hurry. Étienne heard nothing more in the black room but Maheude's sobs, repeating her cry for death, that melancholy and endless lamentation:

"Oh! God! it is my turn, take me! Oh! God! take my man, take the others, out of pity, to have done with it!"

## CHAPTER III

On that Sunday, ever since eight o'clock, Souvarine had been sitting alone in the parlour of the Avantage, at his accustomed place, with his head against the wall. Not a single collier knew where to get two sous for a drink, and never had the bars had fewer customers. So Madame Rasseneur, motionless at the counter, preserved an irritated silence; while Rasseneur, standing before the iron fireplace, seemed to be gazing with a reflective air at the red smoke from the coal.

Suddenly, in this heavy silence of an over-heated room, three light quick blows struck against one of the window-panes made Souvarine turn his head. He rose, for he recognised the signal which Étienne had already used several times before, in order to call him, when he saw him from without, smoking his cigarette at an empty table. But before the engine-man could reach the door, Rasseneur had opened it, and, recognising the man who stood there in the light from the window, he said to him:

"Are you afraid that I shall sell you? You can talk better here than on the road."

Étienne entered. Madame Rasseneur politely offered him a glass, which he refused, with a gesture. The innkeeper added:

"I guessed long ago where you hide yourself. If I was a spy, as your friends say, I should have sent the police after you a week ago."

"There is no need for you to defend yourself," replied the young man. "I know that you have never eaten that sort of bread. People may have different ideas and esteem each other all the same."

And there was silence once more. Souvarine had gone back to his chair, with his back to the wall and his eyes fixed on the smoke from his cigarette, but his feverish fingers were moving restlessly, and he pushed them over his knees, seeking the warm fur of Poland, who was absent this evening; it was an unconscious discomfort, something that was lacking, he could not exactly say what.

Seated on the other side of the table, Étienne at last said:

"To-morrow work begins again at the Voreux. The Belgians have come with little Négrel."

"Yes, they landed them at nightfall," muttered Rasseneur, who remained standing. "As long as they don't kill each other, after all!"

Then, raising his voice:

"No, you know, I don't want to begin our disputes over again, but this will end badly if you hold out any longer. Why, your story is just like that of your International. I met Pluchart the day before yesterday, at Lille, where I went on business. It's going wrong, that machine of his."

He gave details. The association, after having conquered the workers of the whole world, in an outburst of propaganda which had left the middle-class still shuddering, was now being devoured and slowly destroyed by an internal struggle[2] between vanities and ambitions. Since the anarchists had triumphed in it, chasing out the earlier evolutionists, everything was breaking up; the original aim, the reform of the wage-system, was lost in the midst of the squabbling of sects; the scientific framework was disorganised by the hatred of discipline. And already it was possible to foresee the final abortion of this general revolt which for a moment had threatened to carry away in a breath the old rotten society.

"Pluchart is ill over it," Rasseneur went on. "And he has no voice at all now. All the same, he talks on in spite of everything and wants to go to Paris. And he told me three times over that our strike was done for."

Étienne with his eyes on the ground let him talk on without interruption. The evening before he had chatted with some mates, and he felt that breaths of spite and suspicion were passing over him, those first breaths of unpopularity which forerun defeat. And he remained gloomy, he would not confess his dejection in the presence of a man who had foretold to him that the crowd would hoot him in his turn on the day when they had to avenge themselves for a miscalculation.

"No doubt the strike is done for, I know that as well as Pluchart," he said. "But we foresaw that. We accepted this strike against our wishes, we didn't count on finishing up with the Company. Only one gets carried away, one begins to expect things, and when it turns out badly one forgets that one ought to have expected that, instead of lamenting and quarrelling as if it were a catastrophe tumbled down from heaven."

"Then if you think the game's lost," asked Rasseneur, "why don't you make the mates listen to reason?"

The young man looked at him fixedly.

"Listen! enough of this. You have your ideas, I have mine. I came in here to show you that I feel esteem for you in spite of everything. But I still think that if we come to grief over this trouble, our starved carcasses will do more for the people's cause than all your common-sense politics. Ah! if one of those bloody soldiers would just put a bullet in my heart, that would be a fine way of ending!"

His eyes were moist, as in this cry there broke out the secret desire of the vanquished, the refuge in which he desired to lose his torment for ever.

"Well said!" declared Madame Rasseneur, casting on her husband a look which was full of all the contempt of her radical opinions.

Souvarine, with a vague gaze, feeling about with his nervous hands, did not appear to hear. His fair girlish face, with the thin nose and small pointed teeth, seemed to be growing savage in some mystic dream full of bloody visions. And he began to dream aloud, replying to a remark of Rasseneur's about the International which had been let fall in the course of the conversation.

"They are all cowards; there is only one man who can make their machine into a terrible instrument of destruction. It requires will, and none of them have will; and that's why the revolution will abort once more."

He went on in a voice of disgust, lamenting the imbecility of men, while the other two were rather disturbed by these somnambulistic confidences made in the darkness. In Russia there was nothing going on well, and he was in despair over the news he had received. His old companions were all turning to the politicians; the famous Nihilists who made Europe tremble—sons of popes, of the lower middle class, of tradesmen—could not rise above the idea of national liberation, and seemed to believe that the world would be delivered when they had killed their despot. As soon as he spoke to them of razing society to the ground like a ripe harvest—as soon as he even pronounced the infantile word "republic"—he felt that he was misunderstood and a disturber, henceforth unclassed, enrolled among the lost leaders of cosmopolitan revolution. His patriotic heart struggled, however, and it was with painful bitterness that he repeated his favourite expression:

"Foolery! They'll never get out of it with their foolery."

Then, lowering his voice still more, in a few bitter words he described his old dream of fraternity. He had renounced his rank and his fortune; he had gone among workmen in the hope of seeing at last the foundation of a new society of work in common. All the sous in his pockets had always gone to the urchins of the settlement; he had been as tender as a brother with the colliers, smiling at their suspicion, winning them over by his quiet workmanlike ways and his dislike of chattering. But decidedly the fusion had not taken place; he remained a stranger, with his contempt of all bonds, his desire to keep himself free of all vain-glorious enjoyments. And since this morning he had been especially exasperated by reading an incident in the newspapers.

His voice changed, his eyes grew bright, he fixed them on Étienne, directly addressing him:

"Now, do you understand that? These hat-workers at Marseilles who have won the great lottery prize of a hundred thousand francs have gone off at once and invested it, declaring that they are going to live without doing anything! Yes, that is your idea, all of you French workmen; you want to unearth a treasure in order to devour it alone afterwards in some lazy, selfish corner. You may cry out as much as you like against the rich, you haven't got courage enough to give back to the poor the money that luck brings you. You will never be worthy of happiness as long as you have anything of your own, and your hatred of the bourgeois only comes of your mad desire to be bourgeois in their place."

Rasseneur burst out laughing. The idea that the Marseilles workmen ought to renounce the big prize seemed to him absurd. But Souvarine grew pale; his face changed and became terrible in one of those religious rages which exterminate nations. He cried:

"You will all be mown down, overthrown, cast to the dung-heap. Someone will be born who will annihilate your race with its cowardly enjoyments. And look here! you see my hands; if my hands were able they would take up the earth, like that, and shake it until it was smashed to fragments, and you were all buried beneath the rubbish."

"Well said," declared Madame Rasseneur, with her polite and convinced air.

There was silence again. Then Étienne spoke once more of the Borinage men. He questioned Souvarine concerning the steps that had been taken at the Voreux. But the engine-man was still pre-occupied, and scarcely replied. He only knew that cartridges would be distributed to the soldiers who were guarding the pit; and the nervous restlessness of his fingers over his knees increased to such an extent that, at last, he became conscious of what was lacking—the soft and soothing fur of the tame rabbit.

"Where is Poland, then?" he asked.

The innkeeper laughed again as he looked at his wife. After an awkward silence he made up his mind:

"Poland? She is in the pot."

Since her adventure with Jeanlin the pregnant rabbit, no doubt wounded, had only brought forth dead young ones; and to avoid feeding a useless mouth they had resigned themselves that very day to serve her up with potatoes.

"Yes, you ate one of her legs this evening. Eh! You licked your fingers after it!"

Souvarine had not understood at first. Then he became very

pale, and his chin contracted with nausea; while, in spite of his stoicism, two large tears were swelling beneath his eyelids.

But no one had time to notice this emotion, for the door had opened roughly and Chaval had appeared, pushing Catherine before him. After having made himself drunk with beer and bluster in all the public-houses of Montsou, the idea had occurred to him to go to the Avantage to show his old friends that he was not afraid. As he came in, he said to his mistress:

"By God! I tell you you shall drink a glass in here; I'll break the jaws of the first man who looks at me askance!"

Catherine, moved at the sight of Étienne, had become very pale. When Chaval in his turn perceived him, he grinned in his evil fashion.

"Two glasses, Madame Rasseneur! We're wetting the new start of work."

Without a word she poured out, as a woman who never refused her beer to anyone. There was silence, and neither the landlord nor the two others stirred from their places.

"I know people who've said that I was a spy," Chaval went on swaggeringly, "and I expect them just to say it again to my face, so that we can have a bit of explanation."

No one replied, and the men turned their heads and gazed vaguely at the walls.

"There are some who sham, and there are some who don't sham," he went on louder. "I've nothing to hide. I've left Deneulin's dirty shop, and to-morrow I'm going down to the Voreux with a dozen Belgians, who have been given me to lead because I'm held in esteem; and if anyone doesn't like that, he can just say so, and we'll talk it over."

Then, as the same contemptuous silence greeted his provocations, he turned furiously on Catherine.

"Will you drink, by God? Drink with me to the confusion of all the dirty beasts who refuse to work."

She drank, but with so trembling a hand that the two glasses struck together with a tinkling sound. He had now pulled out of his pocket a handful of silver, which he exhibited with drunken ostentation, saying that he had earned that with his sweat, and that he defied the shammers to show ten sous. The attitude of his mates exasperated him, and he began to come to direct insults.

"Then it is at night that the moles come out? The police have to go to sleep before we meet the brigands."

Étienne had risen, very calm and resolute.

"Listen! You annoy me. Yes, you are a spy; your money now stinks of some treachery. You've sold yourself, and it disgusts me to touch your skin. No matter; I'm your man. It is quite time that one of us did for the other."

Chaval clenched his fists.

"Come along, then, cowardly bugger! I must call you so to warm you up. You all alone—I'm quite willing; and you shall pay for all the bloody tricks that have been played on me."

With suppliant arms Catherine advanced between them. But they had no need to repel her; she felt the necessity for the battle, and slowly drew back of her own accord. Standing against the wall, she remained silent, so paralysed with anguish that she no longer shivered, her large eyes gazing at these two men who were going to kill each other over her.

Madame Rasseneur simply removed the glasses from the counter for fear that they might be broken. Then she sat down again on the bench, without showing any improper curiosity. But the two old mates could not be left to murder each other like this. Rasseneur persisted in interfering, and Souvarine had to take him by the shoulder and lead him back to the table, saying:

"It doesn't concern you. There is one of them too many, and the strongest must live."

Without waiting for the attack, Chaval's fists were already dealing blows at space. He was the taller of the two, and his blows swung about aiming at the face, with furious cutting movements of both arms one after the other, as though he were manœuvring a couple of sabres. And he went on talking, playing to the gallery with volleys of abuse, which served to excite him.

"Ah! you damned devil, I'll have your nose! I'll do for your bloody nose! Just let me get at your chops, you whore's looking-glass; I'll make a hash for the bloody buggers, and then we shall see if the strumpets will run after you!"

In silence, and with clenched teeth, Étienne gathered up his small figure, according to the rules of the game, protecting his chest and face by both fists; and he watched and drove them out like a spring with terrible straight blows.

At first they did each other little damage. The whirling and blustering blows of the one, the cool watchfulness of the other prolonged the struggle. A chair was overthrown; their great boots crushed the white sand sprinkled over the floor. But they grew out of breath at last, and their panting respiration was heard, while their faces became red and swollen as from an interior fire which flamed out from the clear holes of their eyes.

"Played!" yelled Chaval; "trumps on your carcass!"

In fact his fist, like a flail working along a slope, had belaboured his adversary's shoulder. Étienne kept back a groan of pain, and there was only a soft sound, the low bruising of the muscles. He replied by a straight blow in the chest, which would have knocked the other in if he had not saved himself by his constant goat-like leaps. The blow, however, reached him in the left flank with such effect that he tottered with broken respiration. He became furious on feeling his arm grow limp with pain, and rushed like a wild beast, aiming at his adversary's belly, which he wished to crush with his heel.

"Have at your guts!" he stammered in a choked voice. "I'll pull them out and wind them for you!"

Étienne avoided the blow, so indignant at this infraction of the laws of fair fighting, that he broke silence.

"Hold your tongue, brute! And no feet, by God! or I take a chair and bash you with it!"

Then the struggle became serious. Rasseneur was disgusted, and would again have interfered, but a severe look from his wife held him back: had not two customers a right to settle an affair in the house? He simply placed himself before the fireplace, for fear lest they should tumble over into it. Souvarine, in his quiet way, had rolled a cigarette, but he forgot to light it. Catherine was motionless against the wall; only her hands had unconsciously risen to her waist, and with constant fidgeting movement were twisting and tearing at the stuff of her dress. She was striving as hard as possible not to cry out, and so, perhaps, kill one of them by declaring her preference; but she was, too, so distracted that she did not even know which she preferred.

Chaval, who was bathed in sweat and striking at random, soon became exhausted. In spite of his anger, Étienne continued to cover himself, parrying nearly all the blows, a few of which grazed him. His ear was split, a finger nail had carried away a fragment of his neck, and he was so heated that he swore in his turn as he drove out one of his terrible straight blows. Once more Chaval saved his chest by a leap, but he had lowered himself, and the fist reached his face, smashing his nose and crushing one eye. Immediately a jet of blood came from his nostrils, and his eye was swollen and bluish. Blinded by this red flood, and dazed by the shock to his skull, the wretch was beating the air with his arms at random, when another blow, striking him at last full in the chest, finished him. There was a crunching sound; he fell on his back with a heavy thud, as when a sack of plaster is emptied.

Étienne waited.

"Get up! if you want another, we'll begin again."

Without replying, Chaval, after a few minutes stupefaction, moved on the ground and stretched his limbs. He gathered himself up with difficulty, resting for a moment on his knees in a ball, doing something with his hand in the bottom of his pocket which could not be observed. Then, when he was up, he rushed forward again, his chest swelling with a savage yell.

But Catherine had seen; and in spite of herself a loud cry came from her heart, like the avowal of a preference she had herself been ignorant of.

"Take care! he's got his knife!"

Étienne had only time to parry the first blow with his arm. His woollen jacket was cut by the thick blade, one of those blades fastened by a copper ferrule into a boxwood handle. He had already seized Chaval's wrist, and a terrible struggle began; for he felt that he would be lost if he let go, while the other shook his arm in the effort to free it and strike. The weapon was gradually lowered as their stiffened limbs grew fatigued. Étienne twice felt the cold sensation of the steel against his skin; and he had to make a supreme effort, so crushing the wrist that the knife slipped from the open hand. Both of them had fallen to the earth, and it was Étienne who snatched it up, brandishing it in his turn. He held Chaval down beneath his knee and threatened to slit his throat open.

"Ah, traitor! by God! you've come to it now!"

He felt an awful voice within, deafening him. It arose from his bowels and was beating in his head like a hammer, a sudden mania of murder, a need to taste blood. Never before had the crisis so shaken him. He was not drunk, however, and he struggled against the hereditary disease with the despairing shudder of a man who is mad with lust and struggles on the verge of rape. At last he conquered himself; he threw the knife behind him, stammering in a hoarse voice:

"Get up—off you go!"

This time Rasseneur had rushed forward, but without quite daring to venture between them, for fear of catching a nasty blow. He did not want anyone to be murdered in his house, and was so angry that his wife, sitting erect at the counter, remarked to him that he always cried out too soon. Souvarine, who had nearly caught the knife in his legs, decided to light his cigarette. Was it, then, all over? Catherine was looking on stupidly at the two men, who were still both living.

"Off you go!" repeated Étienne. "Off you go, or I'll do for you!"

Chaval arose, and with the back of his hand wiped away the blood which continued to flow from his nose; with jaw smeared red and bruised eye, he went away trailing his feet, furious at his defeat. Catherine mechanically followed him. Then he turned round, and his hatred broke out in a flood of filth.

"No, no! since you want him, sleep with him, dirty jade! and don't put your bloody feet in my place again if you care about your skin!"

He violently banged the door. There was deep silence in the warm room, the low crackling of the coal was alone heard. On the ground there only remained the overturned chair and a rain of blood which the sand on the floor was drinking up.

## CHAPTER IV

WHEN THEY CAME OUT of Rasseneur's, Étienne and Catherine walked on in silence. The thaw was beginning, a slow cold thaw which stained the snow without melting it. In the livid sky a full moon could be faintly seen behind great clouds, black rags driven furiously by a tempestuous wind far above; and on the earth no breath was stirring, nothing could be heard but drippings from the roofs, the falling of white lumps with a soft thud.

Étienne was embarrassed by this woman who had been given to him, and in his disquiet he could find nothing to say. The idea of taking her with him to hide at Réquillart seemed absurd. He had proposed to lead her back to the settlement, to her parents' house, but she had refused in terror. No, no! anything rather than be a burden on them once more after having behaved so badly to them! And neither of them spoke any more; they tramped on at random through the roads which were becoming rivers of mud. At first they went down towards the Voreux; then they turned to the right and passed between the pit-bank and the canal.

"But you'll have to sleep somewhere," he said at last. "Now, if I only had a room, I could easily take you——"

But a curious spasm of timidity interrupted him. The past came back to him, their old longings for each other, and the delicacies and the shames which had prevented them from coming together. Did he still desire her that he felt so troubled, gradually warmed at the heart by a fresh longing? The recollection of the blows she had dealt him at Gaston-Marie now attracted him instead of filling him with spite. And he was surprised; the idea of taking her to Réquillart was becoming quite natural and easy to execute.

"Now, come, decide; where would you like me to take you? You must hate me very much to refuse to come with me?"

She was following him slowly, delayed by the painful slipping of her sabots into the ruts; and without raising her head she murmured:

"I have enough trouble, good God! don't give me any more.

What good would it do us, what you ask, now that I have a lover and you have a woman yourself?"

She meant Mouquette. She believed that he still went with this girl, as the rumour ran for the last fortnight; and when he swore to her that it was not so she shook her head, for she remembered the evening when she had seen them eagerly kissing each other.

"Isn't it a pity, all this nonsense?" he whispered, stopping. "We might understand each other so well."

She shuddered slightly and replied:

"Never mind, you've nothing to be sorry for; you don't lose much. If you knew what a trumpery thing I am—no bigger than two ha'porth of butter, so ill made that I shall never become a woman, sure enough!"

And she went on freely accusing herself, as though the long delay of her puberty had been her own fault. In spite of the man whom she had had, this lessened her, placed her among the urchins. One has some excuse, at any rate, when one can produce a child.

"My poor little one!" said Étienne, with deep pity, in a very low voice.

They were at the foot of the pit-bank, hidden in the shadow of the enormous pile. An inky cloud was just then passing over the moon; they could no longer even distinguish their faces, their breaths were mingled, their lips were seeking each other for that kiss which had tormented them with desire for months. But suddenly the moon reappeared, and they saw the sentinel above them, at the top of the rocks white with light, standing out erect on the Voreux. And before they had kissed an emotion of modesty separated them, that old modesty in which there was something of anger, a vague repugnance, and much friendship. They set out again heavily, up to their ankles in mud.

"Then it's settled. You don't want to have anything to do with me?" asked Étienne.

"No," she said. "You after Chaval; and after you another, eh? No, that disgusts me; it doesn't give me any pleasure. What's the use of doing it?"

They were silent, and walked some hundred paces without exchanging a word.

"But, anyhow, do you know where to go to?" he said again. "I can't leave you out in a night like this."

She replied, simply:

"I'm going back. Chaval is my man. I have nowhere else to sleep but with him."

"But he will beat you to death."

There was silence again. She had shrugged her shoulders in resignation. He would beat her, and when he was tired of beating her he would stop. Was not that better than to roam the streets, like a vagabond? Then she was used to blows; she said, to console herself, that eight out of ten girls were no better off than she was. If her lover married her some day it would, all the same, be very nice of him.

Étienne and Catherine were moving mechanically towards Montsou, and as they came nearer their silences grew longer. It was as though they had never been together. He could find no argument to convince her, in spite of the deep vexation which he felt at seeing her go back to Chaval. His heart was breaking, he had nothing better to offer than an existence of wretchedness and flight, a night with no to-morrow should a soldier's bullet go through his head. Perhaps, after all, it was wiser to suffer what he was suffering rather than risk a fresh suffering. So he led her back to her lover's, with sunken head, and made no protest when she stopped him on the main road, at the corner of the Yards, twenty mètres from the Estaminet Piquette, saying:

"Don't come any further. If he sees you it will only make things worse."

Eleven o'clock struck at the church. The estaminet was closed, but gleams came through the cracks.

"Good-bye," she murmured.

She had given him her hand; he kept it, and she had to draw it away painfully, with a slow effort, to leave him. Without turning her head, she went in through the little latched door. But he did not turn away, standing at the same place with his eyes on the house, anxious as to what was passing within. He listened, trembling lest he should hear the cries of a beaten woman. The house remained black and silent; he only saw a light appear at a first-storey window, and as this window opened, and he recognised the thin shadow that was leaning over the road, he came near.

Catherine then whispered very low:

"He's not come back. I'm going to bed. Please go away."

Étienne went off. The thaw was increasing; the rustling of a shower was falling from the roofs, a moist sweat flowed down the walls, the palings, the whole confused mass of this industrial district lost in night. At first he turned towards Réquillart, sick with fatigue and sadness, having no other desire except to disappear under the earth and to be annihilated there. Then the idea of the Voreux occurred to him again. He thought of the Belgian workmen who were going down, of his mates at the settlement, exasperated against the soldiers and resolved not to tolerate strangers in their pit. And he passed again along the canal through the puddles of melted snow.

As he stood once more near the pit-bank the moon was shining brightly. He raised his eyes and gazed at the sky. The clouds were galloping by, whipped on by the strong wind which was blowing up there; but they were growing white, and ravelling out thinly with the misty transparency of troubled water over the moon's face. They succeeded each other so rapidly that the moon, veiled at moments, constantly reappeared in limpid clearness.

With gaze full of this pure brightness, Étienne was lowering his head, when a spectacle on the summit of the pit-bank attracted his attention. The sentinel, stiffened by cold, was walking up and down, taking twenty-five paces towards Marchiennes, and then returning towards Montsou. The white glitter of his bayonet could be seen above his black silhouette, which stood out clearly against the pale sky. But what interested the young man, behind the cabin where Bonnemort used to take shelter on tempestuous nights, was a moving shadow—a crouching beast in ambush—which he immediately recognised as Jeanlin, with his long flexible spine like a martin's. The sentinel could not see him. That brigand of a child was certainly preparing some practical joke, for he was still furious against the soldiers, and asking when they were going to be freed from these murderers who had been sent here with guns to kill people.

For a moment Étienne thought of calling him to prevent the execution of some stupid trick. The moon was hidden. He had seen him draw himself up ready to spring; but the moon reappeared, and the child remained crouching. At every turn the sentinel came as far as the cabin, then turned his back and walked in the opposite direction. And suddenly, as a cloud threw its shadow, Jeanlin leapt on to the soldier's shoulders with the great bound of a savage cat, and gripping him with his claws buried his large open knife in his throat. The horsehair collar resisted; he had to apply both hands to the handle and hang on with all the weight of his body. He had often bled fowls which he had found behind farms. It was so rapid that there was only a stifled cry in the night, while the musket fell with the sound of old iron. Already the moon was shining again.

Motionless with stupor, Étienne was still gazing. A shout had been choked in his chest. Above, the pit-bank was vacant; no shadow was any longer visible against the frightened flight of clouds. He ran up and found Jeanlin on all-fours before the corpse, which was lying back with extended arms. Beneath the limpid light the red trousers and grey overcoat contrasted harshly with the snow. Not a drop of blood had flowed, the knife was still in the throat up to the handle. With a furious, unreasoning blow of the fist he threw the child down beside the body.

"What have you done that for?" he stammered wildly.

Jeanlin picked himself up and rested on his hands, with a feline movement of his thin spine; his large ears, his green eyes, his prominent jaws were quivering and aflame with the shock of his deadly blow.

"By God! why have you done this?"

"I don't know; I wanted to."

He persisted in this reply. For three days he had wanted to. It tormented him, it made his head ache. There, behind his ears, he thought about it so much. Need one be so particular with these damned soldiers who were worrying the colliers in their own homes? Of the violent speeches he had heard in the forest, the cries of destruction and death shouted among the pits, five or six words had remained with him, and these he repeated like a street urchin playing at revolution.[3] And he knew no more; no one had pushed him on, it had come to him by himself, just as the desire to steal onions from a field came to him.

Startled at this gloomy vegetation of crime at the bottom of the child's skull, Étienne again pushed him away with a kick, like an unconscious animal. He trembled lest the guard at the Voreux had heard the sentinel's stifled cry, and looked towards the pit every time the moon was uncovered. But nothing stirred, and he bent down, felt the hands that were gradually becoming icy, and listened to the heart, which had stopped beneath the overcoat. Only the bone handle of the knife could be seen with the motto on it, the simple word "Amour," engraved in black letters.

His eyes went from the throat to the face. Suddenly he recognised the little soldier; it was Jules, the recruit with whom he had talked one morning. And deep pity took him in front of this fair gentle face, marked with reddish patches. The blue eyes, widely open, were gazing at the sky with that fixed gaze with which he had before seen him searching at the horizon for the country of his birth. Where was it, that Plogof which had appeared to him beneath the dazzling sun? Over there, over there! The sea was moaning afar on this tempestuous night. That wind passing above had perhaps swept over the moors. Two women were standing there, the mother and the sister, holding on their blown hats, also looking out, as if they could see what was now happening to the little fellow through the leagues which separated them. They would always wait for him now. What an abominable thing it is for poor devils to kill each other for the sake of the rich!

But this corpse had to be disposed of. Étienne at first thought of throwing it into the canal, but was deterred from this by the certainty that it would be found there. His anxiety became extreme, every minute was of importance; what decision should he take? He had a sudden inspiration: if he could carry the body as far as Réquillart, he would be able to bury it there for ever.

"Come here," he said to Jeanlin.

The child was suspicious.

"No, you want to beat me. And then I have business. Good-night."

In fact, he had given a rendezvous to Bébert and Lydie in a hiding-place, a hole arranged under the wood supply at the Voreux. It had been arranged to sleep out, so as to be there if the Belgians' bones were to be broken by stoning when they went down the pit.

"Listen!" repeated Étienne. "Come here, or I shall call the soldiers, who will cut your head off."

And as Jeanlin was making up his mind, he rolled his handkerchief, and bound the soldier's neck tightly, without drawing out the knife, so as to prevent the blood from flowing. The snow was melting; on the soil there was neither a red patch nor the footmarks of a struggle.

"Take the legs!"

Jeanlin took the legs, while Étienne seized the shoulders, after having fastened the gun behind his back, and then they both slowly descended the pit-bank, trying to avoid rolling any rocks down. Fortunately the moon was hidden. But as they passed along the canal it reappeared brightly, and it was a miracle that the guard did not see them. Silently they hastened on, hindered by the swinging of the corpse, and obliged to place it on the ground every hundred mètres. At the corner of the Réquillart lane they heard a sound which froze them with terror, and they only had time to hide behind a wall to avoid a patrol. Farther on, a man came across them, but he was drunk, and moved away abusing them. At last they reached the old pit, bathed in perspiration, and so exhausted that their teeth were chattering.

Étienne had guessed that it would not be easy to get the soldier through the ladder passage. It was an awful task. First of all Jeanlin, standing above, had to let the body slide down, while Étienne, hanging on to the bushes, had to accompany it to enable it to free the first two ladders where the rungs were broken. Afterwards, at every ladder, he had to perform the same manœuvre over again, going down first, then receiving the body in his arms; and he had thus, through thirty ladders, two hundred and ten mètres, to feel it constantly falling over him. The gun scraped his spine; he had not allowed the child to go for the candle end, which he preserved avariciously. What was the use? The light would only embarrass them in this narrow tube. When they arrived at the pit-eye, however, out of breath, he sent the youngster for the candle. He then sat down and waited for him in the darkness, near the body, with heart beating violently. As soon as Jeanlin reappeared with the light, Étienne consulted with him, for the child had explored these old workings, even to the cracks through which men could not pass. They set out again, dragging the dead body for nearly a kilomètre, through a maze of ruinous galleries. At last the roof became low, and they found themselves kneeling beneath a sandy rock supported by half-broken planks. It was a sort of long chest in which they laid the little soldier as in a coffin; they placed his gun by his side; then with vigorous blows of their heels they finished breaking the timber at the risk of being buried themselves. Immediately the rock gave way, and they scarcely had time to crawl back on their elbows and knees. When Étienne returned, seized by the desire to look once more, the roof was still falling in, slowly crushing the body beneath its enormous weight. And then there was nothing more left, nothing but the profound mass of the earth.

Jeanlin, having returned to his own corner, his little cavern of villainy, was stretching himself out on the hay, overcome by weariness, and murmuring:

"Heigho! the brats must wait for me; I'm going to have an hour's sleep."

Étienne had blown out the candle, of which there was only a small end left. He also was worn out, but he was not sleepy; painful nightmare thoughts were beating like hammers in his skull. Only one at last remained, torturing him and fatiguing him with a question to which he could not reply: Why had he not struck Chaval when he held him beneath the knife? and why had this child just killed a soldier whose very name he did not know? It shook his revolutionary beliefs, the courage to kill, the right to kill. Was he, then, a coward? In the hay the child had begun snoring, the snoring as of a drunken man, as if he were sleeping off the intoxication of his murder. Étienne was disgusted and irritated; it hurt him to know that the boy was there and to hear him. Suddenly he started, a breath of fear passed over his face. A light rustling, a sob, seemed to him to have come out of the depths of the earth. The image of the little soldier, lying over there with his gun beneath the rocks, froze his back and made his hair stand up. It was idiotic, the whole mine seemed to be filled with voices; he had to light the candle again, and only grew calm on seeing the emptiness of the galleries by this pale light.

For another quarter of an hour he reflected, still absorbed in the same struggle, his eyes fixed on the burning wick. But there was a shrivelling, the wick was going out, and everything fell back into darkness. He shuddered again; he could have boxed Jeanlin's ears, to keep him from snoring so loudly. The neighbourhood of the child became so unbearable that he escaped, tormented by the need for fresh air, hastening through the galleries and up the passage, as though he could hear a shadow, out of breath, at his heels.

Up above, in the midst of the ruins of Réquillart, Étienne was at last able to breathe freely. Since he dared not kill, it was for him to die; and this idea of death, which had already touched him, came again and fixed itself in his head, as a last hope. To die bravely, to die for the revolution, that would end everything, would settle his account, good or bad, and prevent him from thinking more. If the men attacked the Borains, he would be in the first rank, and would have a good chance of getting a bad blow. It was with a firmer step that he returned to prowl around the Voreux. Two o'clock struck, and the loud noise of voices was coming from the captains' room, where the guards who watched over the pit were posted. The disappearance of the sentinel had overcome the guards with surprise; they had gone to arouse the captain, and after a careful examination of the place, they concluded that it must be a case of desertion. Hiding in the shade, Étienne recollected this republican captain of whom the little soldier had spoken. Who knows if he might not be persuaded to pass over to the people's side! The troop would raise their rifles, and that would be the signal for a massacre of the bourgeois. A new dream took possession of him; he thought no more of dying, but remained for hours with his feet in the mud, and a drizzle from the thaw falling on his shoulders, filled by the feverish hope that victory was still possible.

Up to five o'clock he watched for the Borains. Then he perceived that the Company had cunningly arranged that they should sleep at the Voreux. The descent had begun, and the few strikers from the Deux-Cent-Quarante settlement who had been posted as scouts had not yet warned their mates. It was he who told them of the trick, and they set out running, while he waited behind the pit-bank, on the towing-path. Six o'clock struck, and the earthy sky was growing pale and lighting up with a reddish dawn, when the Abbé Ranvier came along a path, holding up his cassock above his thin legs. Every Monday he went to say an early Mass at a convent chapel on the other side of the pit.

"Good-morning, my friend," he shouted in a loud voice, after gazing at the young man with his flaming eyes.

But Étienne did not reply. Far away between the Voreux platforms he had just seen a woman pass, and he rushed forward anxiously, for he thought he recognised Catherine. Since midnight, Catherine had been walking about the thawing roads. Chaval, on coming back and finding her in bed, had knocked her out with a blow. He shouted to her to go out at once by the door if she did not wish to go by the window; and scarcely dressed, in tears, and bruised by kicks in her legs, she had been obliged to go down, pushed outside by a final thrust. This sudden separation dazed her, and she sat down on a stone, looking up at the house, still expecting that he would call her back. It was not possible; he would surely look for her and tell her to come back when he saw her thus shivering and abandoned, with no one to take her in.

At the end of two hours she made up her mind, dying of cold and as motionless as a dog thrown into the street. She left Montsou, then retraced her steps, but dared neither to call from the pathway nor to knock at the door. At last she went off by the main road to the right with the idea of going to the settlement, to her parents' house. But when she reached it she was seized by such shame that she rushed away along the gardens for fear of being recognised by someone, in spite of the heavy sleep which weighed on all eyes behind the closed shutters. And after that she wandered about, frightened at the slightest noise, trembling lest she should be seized and led away as a strumpet to that house at Marchiennes, the threat of which had haunted her like a nightmare for months. Twice she stumbled against the Voreux, but terrified at the loud voices of the guard, she ran away out of breath, looking behind her to see if she was being pursued. The Réquillart lane was always full of drunken men; she went back to it, however, with the vague hope of meeting there him she had repelled a few hours earlier.

Chaval had to go down that morning, and this thought brought Catherine again towards the pit, though she felt that it would be useless to speak to him: all was over between them. There was no work going on at Jean-Bart, and he had sworn to kill her if she worked again at the Voreux, where he feared that she would compromise him. So what was to be done?—to go elsewhere, to die of hunger, to yield beneath the blows of every man who might pass? She dragged herself along, tottering amid the ruts, with aching legs and mud up to her spine. The thaw had now filled the streets with a flood of mire. She waded through it, still walking, not daring to look for a stone to sit on.

Day appeared. Catherine had just recognised the back of Chaval, who was cautiously going round the pit-bank, when she noticed Lydie and Bébert putting their noses out of their hiding-place beneath the wood supply. They had passed the night there in ambush, without going home, since Jeanlin's order was to await him; and while this latter was sleeping off the drunkenness of his murder at Réquillart, the two children were lying in each other's arms to keep warm. The wind blew between the planks of chestnut and oak, and they rolled themselves up as in some wood-cutter's abandoned hut. Lydie did not dare to speak aloud the sufferings of a small beaten woman, any more than Bébert found courage to complain of the captain's blows which made his cheeks swell; but the captain was really abusing his power, risking their bones in mad marauding expeditions while refusing to share the booty. Their hearts rose in revolt, and they had at last embraced each other in spite of his orders, careless of that box of the ears from the invisible with which he had threatened them. It never came, so they went on kissing each other softly, with no idea of anything else, putting into that caress the passion they had long struggled against—the whole of their martyred and tender natures. All night through they had thus kept each other warm, so happy, at the bottom of this lost hole, that they could not remember that they had ever been so happy before—not even at Sainte-Barbe, when they had eaten fritters and drunk wine.

The sudden sound of a clarion made Catherine start. She raised herself, and saw the Voreux guards taking up their arms. Étienne arrived running; Bébert and Lydie jumped out of their hiding-place with a leap. And over there, beneath the growing daylight, a band of men and women were coming from the settlement, gesticulating wildly with anger.

## CHAPTER V

ALL THE ENTRANCES TO the Voreux had been closed, and the sixty soldiers, with grounded arms, were barring the only door left free, that leading to the receiving-room by a narrow staircase into which opened the captains' room and the shed. The men had been drawn up in two lines against the brick wall, so that they could not be attacked from behind.

Maheude, who had arrived first with dishevelled hair beneath a handkerchief knotted on in haste, and having Estelle asleep in her arms, repeated in feverish tones:

"Don't let anyone in or anyone out! Shut them all in there!"

Maheu approved, and just then Father Mouque arrived from Réquillart. They wanted to prevent him from passing. But he protested; he said that his horses ate their hay all the same, and cared precious little about a revolution. Besides, there was a horse dead, and they were waiting for him to draw it up. Étienne freed the old groom, and the soldiers allowed him to go to the shaft. A quarter of an hour later, as the band of strikers, which had gradually enlarged, was becoming threatening, a large door opened on the ground floor and some men appeared drawing out the dead beast, a miserable mass of flesh still fastened in the rope-net; they left it in the midst of the puddles of melting snow. The surprise was so great that no one prevented the men from returning and barricading the door afresh. They all recognised the horse, with his head bent back and stiff against the plank. Whispers ran around.

"It's Trompette, isn't it? it's Trompette."

It was, in fact, Trompette. Ever since his descent he had never become acclimatised. He remained melancholy, with no taste for his task, as though tortured by regret for the light. In vain Bataille, the dean of the mine, would rub him with his ribs in his friendly way, softly biting his neck to impart to him a little of the resignation gained in his ten years beneath the earth. These caresses increased his melancholy, his skin quivered beneath the confidences of the comrade who had grown old in darkness; and both of them, whenever they met and snorted together, seemed to be grieving, the old one that he could no longer remember, the young one that he could never forget. At the stable they were neighbours at the manger, and lived with lowered heads, breathing in each other's nostrils, exchanging a constant dream of daylight, visions of green grass, of white roads, of infinite yellow light. Then, when Trompette, bathed in sweat, lay in agony in his litter, Bataille had smelled at him despairingly with short sniffs like sobs. He felt that he was growing cold, the mine was taking from him his last joy, that friend fallen from above, fresh with good odours, who recalled to him his youth in the open air. And he had broken his tether, neighing with fear, when he perceived that the other no longer stirred.

Mouque had indeed warned the head captain a week ago. But much they troubled about a sick horse at such a time as this! These gentlemen did not at all like moving the horses. Now, however, they had to make up their minds to take him out. The evening before the groom had spent an hour with two men tying up Trompette. They harnessed Bataille to bring him to the shaft. The old horse slowly pulled, dragging his dead comrade through so narrow a gallery that he could only shake himself at the risk of taking the skin off. And in his harness he moved his head, listening to the long rustle of this mass which was expected at the knacker's. At the pit-eye, when he was unharnessed, he followed with his melancholy eye the preparations for the ascent—the body pushed on to the crossbars over the sump, the net fastened beneath a cage. At last the porters rang meat; he lifted his neck to see it go up, at first softly, then at once lost in the darkness, flown up for ever to the top of that black hole. And he remained with neck stretched out, his vague beast's memory perhaps recalling the things of the earth. But it was all over; he would never see his comrade again, and he himself would thus be tied up in a pitiful bundle on the day when he would ascend up there. His legs began to tremble, the fresh air which came from the distant country choked him, and he seemed intoxicated when he went heavily back to the stable.

At the surface the colliers stood gloomily before Trompette's carcass. A woman said in a low voice::

"Another man; that may go down if it likes!"

But a new flood arrived from the settlement, and Levaque, who was at the head followed by his wife and Bouteloup, shouted:

"Kill them, those Borains! No blacklegs here! Kill them! Kill them!"

All rushed forward, and Étienne had to stop them. He went up to the captain, a tall thin young man of scarcely twenty-eight years, with a despairing, resolute face. He explained things to him; he tried to win him over, watching the effect of his words. What was the good of risking a useless massacre? Was not justice on the side of the miners? They were all brothers, and they ought to understand one another. When he came to use the word "republic" the captain made a nervous movement; but he preserved his military stiffness, and said suddenly:

"Keep off! Do not force me to do my duty."

Three times over Étienne tried again. Behind him his mates were growling. The report ran that M. Hennebeau was at the pit, and they talked of letting him down by the neck, to see if he would hew his coal himself. But it was a false report; only Négrel and Dansaert were there. They both showed themselves for a moment at a window of the receiving-room; the head captain stood in the background, rather out of countenance since his adventure with Pierronne, while the engineer bravely looked round on the crowd with his bright little eyes, smiling with that sneering contempt in which he enveloped men and things generally. Hooting arose, and they disappeared. And in their place only Souvarine's pale face was seen. He was just then on duty; he had not left his engine for a single day since the strike began, no longer talking, more and more absorbed by a fixed idea, the steel nail of which seemed to be shining in the depths of his pale eyes.

"Keep off!" repeated the captain loudly. "I wish to hear nothing. My orders are to guard the pit, and I shall guard it. And do not press on to my men, or I shall know how to drive you back."

In spite of his firm voice, he was growing pale with increasing anxiety, as the flood of miners continued to swell. He would be relieved at mid-day; but fearing that he would not be able to hold out until then, he had sent a trammer from the pit to Montsou to ask for reinforcements.

Shouts had replied to him:

"Kill the blacklegs! Kill the Borains! We mean to be masters in our own place!"

Étienne drew back in despair. The end had come; there was nothing more except to fight and to die. And he ceased to hold back his mates. The mob moved up to the little troop. There were nearly four hundred of them, and the people from the neighbouring settlements were all running up. They all shouted the same cry. Maheu and Levaque said furiously to the soldiers:

"Get off with you! We have nothing against you! Get off with you!"

"This doesn't concern you," said Maheude. "Let us attend to our own affairs."

And, from behind, the Levaque woman added, more violently:

"Must we eat you to get through? Just clear out of the bloody place!"

Even Lydie's shrill voice was heard. She had crammed herself in more closely, with Bébert, and was saying, in a high voice: "Oh! the pale-livered Tommies!"

Catherine, a few paces off, was gazing and listening, stupefied by new scenes of violence, into the midst of which ill-luck seemed to be always throwing her. Had she not suffered too much already? What fault had she committed, then, that misfortune would never give her any rest? The day before she had understood nothing of the fury of the strike; she thought that when one has one's share of blows it is useless to go and seek for more. And now her heart was swelling with hatred; she remembered what Étienne had once told her when they used to sit up; she tried to hear what he was now saying to the soldiers. He was treating them as mates; he reminded them that they also belonged to the people, and that they ought to be on the side of the people against those who took advantage of their wretchedness.

But a tremour ran through the crowd, and an old woman rushed up. It was Mother Brûlé, terrible in her leanness, with her neck and arms in the air, coming up at such a pace that the wisps of her grey hair blinded her.

"Ah! by God! here I am," she stammered, out of breath; "that traitor Pierron, who shut me up in the cellar!"

And without waiting she fell on to the army, her black mouth belching abuse.

"Pack of scoundrels! dirty scum! ready to lick their masters' boots, and only brave against poor people!"

Then the others joined her, and there were volleys of insults. A few, indeed, cried: "Hurrah for the soldiers! to the shaft with the officer!" but soon there was only one clamour: "Down with the red breeches!" These men, who had listened quietly, with motionless mute faces, to the fraternal appeals and the friendly attempts to win them over, preserved the same stiff passivity beneath this hail of abuse. Behind them the captain had drawn his sword, and as the crowd pressed in on them more and more, threatening to crush them against the wall, he ordered them to present bayonets. They obeyed, and a double row of steel points was placed in front of the strikers' breasts.

"Ah! the bloody buggers!" yelled Mother Brûlé, drawing back.

But already they were coming on again, in excited contempt of death. The women were throwing themselves forward, Maheude and the Levaque shouting:

"Kill us! kill us, then! We want our rights!"

Levaque, at the risk of getting cut, had seized three bayonets in his hands, shaking and pulling them in the effort to snatch them away. He twisted them in the strength of his fury; while Bouteloup, standing aside, and annoyed at having followed his mate, quietly watched him.

"Just come and look here," said Maheu; "just look a bit if you are good chaps!"

And he opened his jacket and drew aside his shirt, showing his naked breast, with his hairy skin tattooed by coal. He moved on towards the points, he obliged them to turn back, terrible in his insolence and bravado. One of them had pricked him in the chest, and he became like a madman, trying to make it enter deeper and to hear his ribs crack.

"Cowards, you don't dare! There are ten thousand behind us. Yes, you can kill us; there are ten thousand more of us to kill yet."

The position of the soldiers was becoming critical, for they had received strict orders not to make use of their weapons until the last extremity. And how were they to prevent these furious people from spitting themselves? Besides, the space was getting less; they were now pushed back against the wall, and it was impossible to draw farther back. Their little troop—a mere handful of men—opposed to the rising flood of miners, still held its own, however, and calmly executed the brief orders given by the captain. The latter, with keen eyes and nervously compressed lips, only feared lest they should be carried away by this abuse. Already a young sergeant, a tall lean fellow whose thin moustache was bristling up, was moving his eyelids in a disquieting manner. Near him an old soldier, with tanned skin and stripes won in twenty campaigns, had grown pale when he saw his bayonet twisted like a straw. Another, doubtless a recruit still smelling of field-work, became very red every time he heard himself called "scum" and "riffraff." And the violence did not cease, the stretched-out fists, the abominable words, the shovelfuls of accusations and threats which buffeted their faces. It required all the force of order to keep them thus, with mute faces, in the proud, gloomy silence of military discipline.

A collision seemed inevitable, when Captain Richomme appeared from behind the troop with his good-natured white head, overwhelmed by emotion. He spoke out loudly:

"By God! this is idiotic! such tomfoolery can't go on!"

And he threw himself between the bayonets and the miners.

"Mates, listen to me. You know that I am an old workman, and that I have always been one of you. Well, by God! I promise you, that if they're not just with you, I'm the man to go and say to the bosses how things lie. But this is too much, it does no good at all to howl bad names at these good fellows, and try to get your bellies ripped up."

They listened, hesitating. But up above, unfortunately, little Négrel's short profile reappeared. He feared, no doubt, that he would be accused of sending a captain in place of venturing out himself; and he tried to speak. But his voice was lost in the midst of so frightful a tumult that he had to leave the window again, simply shrugging his shoulders. Richomme then found it vain to entreat them in his own name, and to repeat that the thing must be arranged between mates; they repelled him, suspecting him. But he was obstinate and remained amongst them.

"By God! let them break my head as well as yours, for I don't leave you while you are so foolish!"

Étienne, whom he begged to help him in making them hear reason, made a movement of powerlessness. It was too late, there were now more than five hundred of them. And besides the madmen who were rushing up to chase away the Borains, some came out of inquisitiveness, or to joke and amuse themselves over the battle. In the midst of one group, at some distance, Zacharie and Philomène were looking on as at a theatre, so peacefully that they had brought their two children, Achille and Désirée. Another stream was arriving from Réquillart, including Mouquet and Mouquette. The former at once went on, grinning, to slap his friend Zacharie's shoulders; while Mouquette, in a very excited condition, rushed to the first rank of the evil-disposed.

Every minute, however, the captain looked down the Montsou road. The desired reinforcements had not arrived, and his sixty men could not hold out longer. At last it occurred to him to strike the imagination of the crowd and he ordered his men to load. The soldiers executed the order, but the disturbance increased, the swaggery, and the mockery.

"Ah! these shammers, they're going off to the target!" jeered the women, the Brûlé, the Levaque and the others.

Maheude, with her breast covered by the little body of Estelle, who was awake and crying, came so near that the sergeant asked her what she was going to do with that poor little brat.

"What the devil's that to do with you?" she replied. "Fire at it if you dare!"

The men shook their heads with contempt. None believed that they would fire on them.

"There are no balls in their cartridges," said Levaque.

"Are we Cossacks?" cried Maheu. "You don't fire against Frenchmen, by God!"

Others said that when people had been through the Crimean campaign they were not afraid of lead. And all continued to push themselves on to the guns. If firing had begun at this moment the crowd would have been mown down.

In the front rank Mouquette was choking with fury, thinking that the soldiers were going to gash the women's skins. She had spat out all her coarse words at them, and could find no vulgarity low enough, when suddenly, having nothing left but that mortal offence with which to bombard the faces of the troop, she exhibited her backside. With both hands she raised her skirts, bent her back, and expanded the enormous rotundity.

"Here, that's for you! and it's a lot too clean, you dirty blackguards!"

She plunged and bent down so that each might have his share, repeating after each insult: "There's for the officer! there's for the sergeant! there's for the soldiers!"

A tempest of laughter arose; Bébert and Lydie were in convulsions; Étienne himself, in spite of his sombre expectation, applauded this insulting nudity. All of them, the banterers as well as the infuriated, were now hooting the soldiers as though they had seen them stained by a splash of filth; Catherine only, standing aside on some old timber, remained silent with the blood at her heart, slowly carried away by the hatred that was rising within her.

But a hustling took place. To calm the excitement of his men, the captain decided to make prisoners. With a leap Mouquette escaped, saving herself between the legs of her comrades. Three miners, Levaque and two others, were seized among the more violent, and kept in sight at the other end of the captains' room. Négrel and Dansaert, above, were shouting to the captain to come in and take refuge with them. He refused; he felt that these buildings with their doors without locks would be carried by assault, and that he would undergo the shame of being foiled. His little troop was already growling with impatience; it was impossible to flee before these wretches in sabots. The sixty, with their backs to the wall and their rifles loaded, again faced the mob.

At first there was a recoil, followed by deep silence; the strikers were astonished at this energetic stroke. Then a cry arose calling for the prisoners, demanding their immediate release. Some voices said that they were being murdered in there. And without any attempt at concerted action, carried away by the same impulse, by the same desire for revenge, they all ran to the piles of bricks which stood near, those bricks for which the marly soil supplied the clay, and which were baked on the spot. The children brought them one by one, and the women filled their skirts with them. Every one soon had her ammunition at her feet, and the battle of stones began.

It was Mother Brûlé who set to first. She broke the bricks on the sharp edge of her knee, and with both hands she discharged the two fragments. The Levaque woman was almost pulling her shoulders out, being so large and soft that she had to come near to get her aim, in spite of Bouteloup's entreaties, and he dragged her back in the hope of being able to lead her away now that her husband had been taken off. They all grew excited, and Mouquette, tired of heating herself by breaking the bricks on her over-fat thighs, preferred to throw them whole. Even the youngsters came into line, and Bébert showed Lydie how the brick ought to be sent from under the elbow. It was a shower of enormous hailstones, producing low thuds. And suddenly, in the midst of these furies, Catherine was observed with her fists in the air also brandishing half-bricks, and throwing them with all the force of her little arms. She could not say why, she was suffocating, she was dying of the desire to kill everybody. Would it not soon be done with, this cursed life of misfortune? She had had enough of it, beaten and hunted away by her man, wandering about like a lost dog in the mud of the roads, without being able to ask a crust from her father, who was starving like herself. Things never seemed to get better; they were getting worse ever since she could remember. And she broke the bricks and threw them before her with the one idea of sweeping everything away, her eyes so blinded that she could not even see whose jaws she might be crushing.

Étienne, who had remained in front of the soldiers, nearly had his skull broken. His ear was grazed, and turning round he started when he realised that the brick had come from Catherine's feverish hands; but at the risk of being killed he remained where he was, gazing at her. Many others also forgot themselves there, absorbed in the battle, with empty hands. Mouquet criticised the blows as though he were looking on at a game of *bouchon.* Oh, that was well struck! and that other, no luck! He joked, and with his elbow pushed Zacharie, who was squabbling with Philomène because he had boxed Achille's and Désirée' s ears, refusing to put them on his back so that they could see. There were spectators crowded all along the road. And at the top of the slope near the entrance to the settlement, old Bonnemort appeared, resting on his stick, motionless against the rust-coloured sky.

As soon as the first bricks were thrown, Captain Richomme had again placed himself between the soldiers and the miners. He was entreating the one party, exhorting the other party, careless of danger, in such despair that large tears were flowing from his eyes. It was impossible to hear his words in the midst of the tumult; only his large grey moustache could be seen moving.

But the hail of bricks came faster; the men were joining in, following the example of the women.

Then Maheude noticed that Maheu was standing behind with empty hands and sombre air.

"What's up with you?" she shouted. "Are you a coward? Are

you going to let your mates be carried off to prison? Ah! only I hadn't got this child, you should see!"

Estelle, who was clinging to her neck, screaming, prevented her from joining Mother Brûlé and the others. And as her man did not seem to hear, she kicked some bricks against his legs. "By God! will you take that? Must I spit in your face before people to get your spirits up?"

Becoming very red, he broke some bricks and threw them. She lashed him on, dazing him, shouting behind him cries of death, stifling her daughter against her breast with the spasm of her arms; and he still moved forward until he was opposite the guns.

Beneath this shower of stones the little troop was disappearing. Fortunately they struck too high, and the wall was riddled. What was to be done? The idea of going in, of turning back, for a moment turned the captain's pale face purple; but it was no longer even possible, they would be torn to pieces at the least movement. A brick had just broken the peak of his cap, drops of blood were running down his forehead. Many of his men were wounded; and he felt that they were losing self-control in that unbridled instinct of self-defence when obedience to leaders ceases. The sergeant had uttered a "By God!" for his left shoulder had nearly been put out, and his flesh bruised by a shock like the blow of a washerwoman's beetle against linen. Grazed twice over, the recruit had his thumb smashed, while his right knee was burning. Were they to let themselves be worried much longer? A stone having bounded back and struck the old soldier with the stripes beneath the belly, his cheeks turned green, and his weapon trembled and was stretched out at the end of his lean arms. Three times the captain was on the point of ordering them to fire. He was choked by anguish; an endless struggle during the last few minutes was stirring up ideas and duties within him, all his beliefs as a man and as a soldier. The rain of bricks increased, and he opened his mouth and was about to shout: "Fire!" when the guns went off of themselves, three shots at first, then five, then the roll of a volley, then one by itself, some time afterwards, in the deep silence.

There was stupefaction on all sides. They had fired, and the gaping crowd stood motionless, as yet unable to believe it.[4] But heartrending cries arose while the clarion was sounding to cease firing. And there was a mad panic, the rush of cattle filled with grapeshot, a wild flight through the mud. Bébert and Lydie had fallen one on top of the other at the first three shots, the little girl struck in the face, the boy wounded beneath the left shoulder. She was crushed, and never stirred again. But he moved, seized her with both arms in the convulsion of his agony, as if he wanted to take her again, as he had taken her at the bottom of the black hiding-place where they had spent the past night. And Jeanlin, who just then ran up from Réquillart still half asleep, kicking about in the midst of the smoke, saw him embrace his little wife and die.

The five other shots had brought down Mother Brûlé and Captain Richomme. Struck in the back as he was entreating his mates, he had fallen on to his knees, and slipping on to one hip he was groaning on the ground with eyes still full of tears. The old woman, whose breast had been opened, had fallen back stiff and crackling, like a bundle of dry faggots, stammering one last oath in the gurgling of blood.

But then the volley swept the field, mowing down the inquisitive groups who were laughing at the battle a hundred paces off. A ball entered Mouquet's mouth and threw him down with fractured skull at the feet of Zacharie and Philomène, whose two youngsters were splashed with red drops. At the same moment Mouquette received two balls in the belly. She had seen the soldiers shoulder arms, and in an instinctive movement of her good nature she had thrown herself in front of Catherine, shouting out to her to take care; she uttered a loud cry and fell on to her back overturned by the shock. Étienne ran up wishing to raise her and take her away; but with a gesture she said it was all over. Then she groaned, but without ceasing to smile at both of them, as though she were glad to see them together now that she was going away.

All seemed to be over, and the hurricane of balls was lost in the distance as far as the frontages of the settlement when the last shot, isolated and delayed, was fired.

Maheu, struck in the heart, turned round and fell with his

face down into a puddle black with coal. Maheude leant down in stupefaction.

"Eh! old man, get up. It's nothing, is it?"

Her hands were engaged with Estelle, whom she had to put under one arm in order to turn her man's head.

"Say something! where are you bad?"

His eyes were vacant, and his mouth was slavered with bloody foam. She understood: he was dead. Then she remained seated in the mud with her daughter under her arm like a bundle, gazing at her old man with a besotted air.

The pit was free. With a nervous movement the captain had taken off and then put on his cap, struck by a stone; he preserved his pallid stiffness in face of the disaster of his life, while his men with mute faces were reloading. The frightened faces of Négrel and Dansaert could be seen at the window of the receiving-room. Souvarine was behind them with a deep wrinkle on his forehead, as though the nail of his fixed idea had printed itself there threateningly. On the other side of the horizon, at the edge of the plain, Bonnemort had not moved, supported by his hand on his stick, the other hand up to his eyelids to see better the murder of his people below. The wounded were howling, the dead were growing cold in twisted postures, muddy with the liquid mud of the thaw, here and there forming puddles with the inky patches of coal which reappeared beneath the tattered snow. And in the midst of these human corpses, all small, poor and lean in their wretchedness, lay Trompette's carcass, a monstrous and pitiful mass of dead flesh.

Étienne had not been killed. He was still waiting beside Catherine, who had fallen from fatigue and anguish, when a sonorous voice made him start. It was Abbé Ranvier, who was coming back after saying his mass, and who, with both arms in the air, with the inspired fury of a prophet, was calling the wrath of God down on the murderers. He foretold the era of justice, the approaching extermination of the middle class by fire from heaven, since it was bringing its crimes to a climax by massacring the workers and the disinherited of the world.

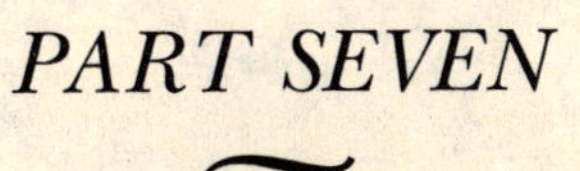

# *PART SEVEN*

## CHAPTER I

THE SHOTS FIRED AT Montsou had reached as far as Paris with a formidable echo. For four days all the opposition journals had been indignant, displaying atrocious narratives on their front pages: twenty-five wounded, fourteen dead, including three women and two children, and prisoners taken as well. Levaque had become a sort of hero, and was credited with a reply of antique sublimity to the examining magistrate. The Empire, hit in mid-career by these few balls, affected the calm of omnipotence, without itself realising the gravity of its wound. It was simply an unfortunate collision, something lost over there in the black country, very far from the Parisian boulevard which formed public opinion; it would soon be forgotten. The Company had received an official intimation to hush up the affair, and to put an end to a strike which from its irritating duration was becoming a social danger.

So on Wednesday morning three of the directors appeared at Montsou. The little town, sick at heart, which had not dared hitherto to rejoice over the massacre, now breathed again, and tasted the joy of being saved. The weather, too, had become fine; there was a bright sun—one of those first February days which, with their moist warmth, bring out the green points of the lilacs. All the shutters had been flung back at the administration building, the vast structure seemed alive again. And the best rumours were circulating; it was said that these gentlemen, deeply affected by the catastrophe, had rushed down to open their paternal arms to the wanderers from the settlements. Now that the blow had fallen—a more vigorous one doubtless than they had wished for—they were prodigal in their task of relief, and decreed measures that were excellent though tardy. First of all they sent away the Borains, and made much of this extreme concession to their workmen. Then they put an end to the military occupation of the pits, which were no longer threatened by the crushed strikers. They also obtained silence regarding the sentinel who had disappeared from the Voreux; the district had been searched without finding either the gun or the corpse, and although there was a suspicion of crime, it was decided to consider the soldier a deserter. In every way they thus tried to attenuate matters, judging it dangerous to acknowledge the irresistible savagery of a crowd set free amid the falling structure of the old world. And besides, this work of conciliation did not prevent them from bringing purely administrative affairs to a satisfactory conclusion; for Deneulin had been seen to return to the administration buildings, where he met M. Hennebeau. The negotiations for the purchase of Vandame continued, and it was considered certain that Deneulin would accept the Company's offers.

But what particularly stirred the country were the great yellow posters which the directors had stuck up in profusion on the walls. On them were to be read these few lines, in very large letters: "Workers of Montsou! We do not wish that the errors of which you have lately seen the sad effects should deprive sensible and willing workmen of their livelihood. We shall therefore reopen all the pits on Monday morning, and when work is resumed we shall examine with care and consideration those cases in which there may be room for improvement. We shall, in fact, do all that is just or possible to do." In one morning the ten thousand colliers passed before these placards. Not one of them spoke, many shook their heads, others went away with trailing steps, without changing one line in their motionless faces.

Up till now the settlement of the Deux-Cent-Quarante had persisted in its fierce resistance. It seemed that the blood of their mates, which had reddened the mud of the pit, was barricading the road against the others. Scarcely a dozen had gone down, merely Pierron and some sneaks of his sort, whose departure and arrival were gloomily watched without a gesture or a threat. Therefore a deep suspicion greeted the placard stuck on to the church. Nothing was said about the returned certificates in that. Would the Company refuse to take them on again? and the fear of retaliations, the fraternal idea of protesting against the dismissal of the more compromised men, made them all obstinate still. It was dubious; they would see. They would return to the pit, when these gentlemen were good enough to put things plainly. Silence crushed the low houses.

Hunger itself seemed nothing; all might die now that violent death had passed over their roofs.

But one house, that of the Maheus, remained especially black and mute in its overwhelming grief. Since she had followed her man to the cemetery, Maheude kept her teeth clenched. After the battle, she had allowed Étienne to bring back Catherine, muddy and half dead; and as she was undressing her, before the young man, in order to put her to bed, she thought for a moment that her daughter also had received a ball in the belly, for the chemise was marked with large patches of blood. But she soon understood that it was the flood of puberty, which was at last breaking out in the shock of this abominable day. Ah! another piece of luck, that wound! A fine present, to be able to make children for the gendarmes to kill; and she never spoke to Catherine, nor did she, indeed, talk to Étienne. The latter slept with Jeanlin, at the risk of being arrested, seized by such horror at the idea of going back to the darkness of Réquillart that he would have preferred a prison. A shudder shook him, the horror of the night after all those deaths, an unacknowledged fear of the little soldier who slept down there underneath the rocks. Besides, he dreamed of a prison as of a refuge in the midst of the torment of his defeat; but they did not trouble him, and he dragged on his wretched hours, not knowing how to weary out his body. Only at times Maheude looked at both of them, at him and her daughter, with a spiteful air, as though she were asking them what they were doing in her house.

Once more they were all snoring in a heap. Father Bonnemort occupied the former bed of the two youngsters, who slept with Catherine now that poor Alzire no longer dug her hump into her big sister's ribs. It was when going to bed that the mother felt the emptiness of the house by the coldness of her bed, which was now too large. In vain she took Estelle to fill the vacancy; that did not replace her man, and she wept quietly for hours. Then the days began to pass by as before, always without bread, but yet without the luck to die for good; things picked up here and there rendered to the wretches the poor service of keeping them alive. Nothing had changed in their existence, only her man was gone.

On the afternoon of the fifth day, Étienne, made miserable by the sight of this silent woman, left the room, and walked slowly along the paved street of the settlement. The inaction which weighed on him impelled him to take constant walks, with arms swinging idly and lowered head, always tortured by the same thought. He tramped thus for half-an-hour, when he felt, by an increase in his discomfort, that his mates were coming to their doors to look at him. His little remaining popularity had been driven to the winds by that fusillade, and he never passed now without meeting fiery looks which pursued him. When he raised his head there were threatening men there, women drawing aside the curtains from their windows; and beneath this still silent accusation and the restrained anger of these eyes, enlarged by hunger and tears, he became awkward and could scarcely walk straight. These dumb reproaches seemed to be always increasing behind him. He became so terrified, lest he should hear the entire settlement come out to shout its wretchedness at him, that he returned shuddering. But at the Maheus' the scene which met him still further agitated him. Old Bonnemort was near the cold fireplace, nailed to his chair ever since two neighbours, on the day of the slaughter, had found him on the ground, with his stick broken, struck down like an old thunder-stricken tree. And while Lénore and Henri, to cajole their hunger, were scraping, with deafening noise, an old saucepan in which cabbages had been boiled the day before, Maheude, after having placed Estelle on the table, was standing up, threatening Catherine with her fist.

"Say that again, by God! Just dare to say that again!"

Catherine had declared her intention to go back to the Voreux. The idea of not gaining her bread, of being thus tolerated in her mother's house, like a useless animal that is in the way, was becoming every day more unbearable; and if it had not been from the fear of Chaval she would have gone down on Tuesday.

She said again, stammering:

"What would you have? We can't go on doing nothing. We should get bread, anyhow."

Maheude interrupted her.

"Listen to me, the first one of you who goes to work, I'll do for you. No, that would be too much, to kill the father and go on taking it out of the children! I've had enough of it; I'd rather see you all put in your coffins, like him that's gone already."

And her long silence broke out into a furious flood of words. A fine sum that Catherine would bring her! hardly thirty sous, to which they might add twenty sous if the bosses were good enough to find work for that brigand Jeanlin. Fifty sous, and seven mouths to feed! The brats were only good to swallow soup. As to the grandfather, he must have broken something in his brain when he fell, for he seemed imbecile; unless it had turned his blood to see the soldiers firing at his mates.

"That's it, old man, isn't it? They've quite done for you. It's no good having your hands still strong; you're done for."

Bonnemort looked at her with his dim eyes without understanding. He remained for hours with fixed gaze, having no intelligence now except to spit into a plate filled with ashes, which was put beside him for cleanliness.

"And they've not settled his pension, either," she went on. "And I'm sure they won't give it, because of our ideas. No! I tell you that we've had too much to do with those people who bring ill-luck."

"But," Catherine ventured to say, "they promise on the placard——"

"Just let me alone with your damned placard! More bird-lime for catching us and eating us. They can be mighty kind now that they have ripped us open."

"But where shall we go, mother? They won't keep us at the settlement, sure enough."

Maheude made a vague, terrified gesture. Where should they go to? She did not know at all; she avoided thinking, it made her mad. They would go elsewhere—somewhere. And as the noise of the saucepan was becoming unbearable, she turned round on Lénore and Henri and boxed their ears. The fall of Estelle, who had been crawling on all-fours, increased the disturbance. The mother quieted her with a push—a good thing if it had killed her! She spoke of Alzire; she wished the others might have that child's luck. Then suddenly she burst out into loud sobs, with her head against the wall.

Étienne, who was standing by, did not dare to interfere. He no longer counted for anything in the house, and even the children drew back from him suspiciously. But the unfortunate woman's tears went to his heart, and he murmured:

"Come, come! courage! we must try to get out of it."

She did not seem to hear him, and was bemoaning herself now in a low continuous complaint.

"Ah! the wretchedness! is it possible? Things did go on before these horrors. We ate our bread dry, but we were all together; and what has happened, good God! What have we done, then, that we should have such troubles—some under the earth, and the others with nothing left but to long to get there too? It's true enough that they harnessed us like horses to work, and it's not at all a just sharing of things to be always getting the stick and making rich people's fortunes bigger without hope of ever tasting the good things. There's no pleasure in life when hope goes. Yes, that might have gone on longer; we might have breathed a bit. If we had only known! Is it possible to make oneself so wretched through wanting justice?"

Sighs swelled her breast, and her voice choked with immense sadness.

"Then there are always some clever people there who promise you that everything can be arranged by just taking a little trouble. Then one loses one's head, and one suffers so much from things as they are that one asks for things that can't be. Now, I was dreaming like a fool; I seemed to see a life of good friendship with everybody; I got off into the air, my faith! into the clouds. And then one breaks one's back when one tumbles down into the mud again. It's not true; there's nothing over there of the things that people tell of. What there is, is only wretchedness; ah! wretchedness, as much as you like of it, and bullets into the bargain."

Étienne listened to this lamentation, and every tear struck him with remorse. He knew not what to say to calm Maheude, broken by her terrible fall from the heights of the ideal. She had come back to the middle of the room, and was now looking at him; she addressed him with contemptuous familiarity in a last cry of rage:

"And you, do you talk of going back to the pit, too, after driving us out of the bloody place? I've nothing to reproach you with; but if I were in your shoes I should be dead of grief by now after causing such harm to the mates."

He was about to reply, but then shrugged his shoulders in despair. What was the good of explaining, for she would not understand in her grief? And he went away, for he was suffering too much, and resumed his wild walk outside.

There again he found the settlement apparently waiting for him, the men at the doors, the women at the windows. As soon as he appeared growls ran along, and the crowd increased. The breath of gossip, which had been swelling for four days, was breaking out in a universal malediction. Fists were stretched towards him, mothers spitefully pointed him out to their boys, old men spat as they looked at him. It was the change which follows on the morrow of defeat, the fatal reverse of popularity, an execration exasperated by all the suffering endured without result. He had to pay for famine and death.

Zacharie, who came up with Philomène, hustled Étienne as he went out, grinning maliciously.

"Well, he gets fat. It's filling, then, to live on other people's deaths?"

The Levaque woman had already come to her door with Bouteloup. She spoke of Bébert, her youngster, killed by a bullet, and cried:

"Yes, there are cowards who get children murdered! Let him go and look for mine in the earth if he wants to give it me back!"

She was forgetting her man in prison, for the household was going on since Bouteloup remained; but she thought of him, however, and went on in a shrill, voice: "Get along! rascals may walk about while good people are put away!"

In avoiding her, Étienne tumbled on to Pierronne, who was running up across the gardens. She had regarded her mother's death as a deliverance, for the old woman's violence threatened to get them hanged; nor did she weep over Pierron's little girl, that street-walker Lydie—a good riddance. But she joined in with her neighbours with the idea of gaining reconciliation.

"And my mother, eh, and the little girl? You've been seen; you were hiding yourself behind them when they caught the lead instead of you!"

What was to be done? Strangle Pierronne and the others, and fight the whole settlement? Étienne wanted to do so for a moment. The blood was throbbing in his head, he now looked upon his mates as brutes, he was irritated to see them so unintelligent and barbarous that they wanted to revenge themselves on him for the logic of facts. How stupid it all was! and he felt disgust at his powerlessness to tame them again; and satisfied himself with hastening his steps as though he were deaf to abuse. Soon it became a flight; every house hooted him as he passed, they hastened after his heels, it was a whole nation cursing him with a voice that was becoming like thunder in its overwhelming hatred. It was he, the exploiter, the murderer, who was the sole cause of their misfortune. He rushed out of the settlement, pale and terrified, with this yelling crowd behind his back. When he at last reached the main road most of them left him; but a few persisted, until at the bottom of the slope before the Avantage he met another group coming from the Voreux.

Old Mouque and Chaval were there. Since the death of his daughter Mouquette, and of his son Mouquet, the old man had continued to act as groom without a word of regret or complaint. Suddenly, when he saw Étienne, he was shaken by fury, tears broke out from his eyes, and a flood of coarse words burst from his mouth, black and bleeding from his habit of chewing tobacco.

"You devil! you bloody bugger! you filthy snout! Wait, you've got to pay me for my poor children; you'll have to come to it!"

He picked up a brick, broke it, and threw both pieces.

"Yes! yes! clear him off!" shouted Chaval, who was grinning in excitement, delighted at this vengeance. "Everyone gets his turn; now you're stuck to the wall, you dirty hound!"

And he also attacked Étienne with stones. A savage clamour arose; they all took up bricks, broke them, and threw them, to rip him open, as they would like to have done to the soldiers. He was dazed and could not flee; he faced them, trying to calm them with phrases. His old speeches, once so warmly received, came back to his lips. He repeated the words with which he had intoxicated them at the time when he could keep them in hand like a faithful flock; but this power was dead, and only stones replied to him. He had just been struck on the left arm, and was drawing back, in great peril, when he found himself hunted against the front of the Avantage.

For the last few moments Rasseneur had been at his door.

"Come in," he said simply.

Étienne hesitated; it choked him to take refuge there.

"Come in; then I'll speak to them."

He resigned himself, and took refuge at the other end of the parlour, while the innkeeper filled up the doorway with his broad shoulders.

"Look here, my friends, just be reasonable. You know very well that I've never deceived you. I've always been in favour of quietness, and if you had listened to me, you certainly wouldn't be where you are now."

Rolling his shoulders and belly, he went on at length, allowing his facile eloquence to flow with the lulling gentleness of warm water. And all his old success came back; he regained his popularity, naturally and without an effort, as if he had never been hooted and called a coward a month before. Voices arose in approval: "Very good! we are with you! that is the way to put it!" Thundering applause broke out.

Étienne, in the background, grew faint, and there was bitterness at his heart. He recalled Rasseneur's prediction in the forest, threatening him with the ingratitude of crowds. What imbecile brutality! What an abominable forgetfulness of old services! It was a blind force which constantly devoured itself. And beneath his anger at seeing these brutes spoil their own cause, there was despair at his own fall and the tragic end of his ambition. What! was it already done for? He remembered hearing beneath the beeches three thousand hearts beating to the echo of his own. On that day he had held his popularity in both hands. Those people belonged to him; he felt that he was their master. Mad dreams had then intoxicated him. Montsou at his feet, Paris beyond, becoming a deputy perhaps, crushing the middle-class in a speech, the first speech ever pronounced by a workman in a parliament. And it was all over! He awakened, miserable and detested; his people were dismissing him by flinging bricks.

Rasseneur's voice rose higher:

"Never will violence succeed; the world can't be re-made in a day. Those who have promised you to change it all at one stroke are either making fun of you or they are rascals!"

"Bravo! bravo!" shouted the crowd.

Who then was the guilty one? And this question which Étienne put to himself overwhelmed him more than ever. Was it in fact his fault, this misfortune which was making him bleed, the wretchedness of some, the murder of others, these women, these children, lean and without bread? He had had that lamentable vision one evening before the catastrophe. But then a force was lifting him, he was carried away with his mates. Besides, he had never led them, it was they who led him, who obliged him to do things which he would never have done if it were not for the shock of that crowd pushing behind him. At each new violence he had been stupefied by the course of events, for he had neither foreseen nor desired any of them. Could he anticipate, for instance, that his followers in the settlement would one day stone him? These infuriated people lied when they accused him of having promised them an existence all fodder and laziness. And in this justification, in this reasoning, in which he tried to fight against his remorse, was hidden the anxiety that he had not risen to the height of his task; it was the doubt of the half-cultured man still perplexing him. But he felt himself at the end of his courage, he was no longer at heart with his mates; he feared this enormous mass of the people, blind and irresistible, moving like a force of nature, sweeping away everything, outside rules and theories. A certain repugnance was detaching him from them—the discomfort of his new tastes, the slow movement of all his being towards a superior class.

At this moment Rasseneur's voice was lost in the midst of enthusiastic shouts:

"Hurrah for Rasseneur! he's the fellow! Bravo, bravo!"

The innkeeper shut the door, while the band dispersed; and the two men looked at each other in silence. They both shrugged their shoulders. They finished up by having a drink together.

On the same day there was a great dinner at Piolaine; they were celebrating the betrothal of Négrel and Cécile. Since the previous evening the Grégoires had had the dining-room waxed and the drawing-room dusted. Melanie reigned in the kitchen, watching over the roasts and stirring the sauces, the odour of which ascended to the attics. It had been decided that Francis, the coachman, should help Honorine to wait. The gardener's wife would wash up, and the gardener would open the gate. Never had the substantial, patriarchal old house been in such a state of gaiety.

Everything went off beautifully. Madame Hennebeau was charming with Cécile, and she smiled at Négrel when the Montsou lawyer gallantly proposed the health of the future household. M. Hennebeau was also very amiable. His smiling face struck the guests. The report circulated that he was rising in favour with the directors, and that he would soon be made an officer of the Legion of Honour, on account of the energetic manner in which he had put down the strike. Nothing was said about recent events; but there was an air of triumph in the general joy, and the dinner became the official celebration of a victory. At last, then, they were saved, and once more they could begin to eat and sleep in peace. A discreet allusion was made to those dead whose blood the Voreux mud had yet scarcely drunk up. It was a necessary lesson; and they were all affected when the Grégoires added that it was now the duty of all to go and heal the wounds in the settlements. They had regained their benevolent placidity, excusing their brave miners, whom they could already see again at the bottom of the mines, giving a good example of everlasting resignation. The Montsou notables, who had now left off trembling, agreed that this question of the wage-system ought to be studied, cautiously. The roasts came on; and the victory became complete when M. Hennebeau read a letter from the bishop, announcing Abbé Ranvier's removal.

The middle class throughout the province had been roused to anger by the story of this priest who treated the soldiers as murderers. And when the dessert appeared, the lawyer resolutely declared that he was a free-thinker. Deneulin was there with his two daughters. In the midst of the joy, he forced himself to hide the melancholy of his ruin. That very morning he had signed the sale of his Vandame concession to the Montsou Company. With the knife at his throat he had submitted to the directors' demands, at last giving up to them that prey they had been on the watch for so long, scarcely obtaining from them the money necessary to pay off his creditors. He had even accepted, as a lucky chance, at the last moment, their offer to keep him as divisional engineer, thus resigning himself to watch over, as a simple salaried servant, that pit which had swallowed up his fortune. It was the knell of small personal enterprises, the approaching disappearance of the masters, eaten up, one by one, by the ever-hungry ogre of capital, drowned in the rising flood of great companies. He alone paid the expenses of the strike; he understood that they were drinking to his disaster when they drank to M. Hennebeau's rosette. And he only consoled himself a little when he saw the fine courage of Lucie and Jeanne, who looked charming in their done-up toilettes, laughing at the downfall, like pretty boyish girls, disdainful of money. When they passed into the drawing-room for coffee, M. Grégoire drew his cousin aside and congratulated him on the courage of his decision.

"What would you have? Your real mistake was to risk the million of your Montsou denier over Vandame. You gave yourself a terrible wound, and it has melted away in that dog's labour, while mine, which has not stirred from my drawer, still nourishes me in sensibly doing nothing, as it will nourish my grandchildren's children."

## CHAPTER II

ON SUNDAY ÉTIENNE ESCAPED from the settlement at nightfall. A very clear sky, sprinkled with stars, lit up the earth with the blue haze of twilight. He went down towards the canal, and followed the bank slowly, in the direction of Marchiennes. It was his favourite walk, a grass-covered path two leagues long, passing straight beside this geometrical stream, which unrolled itself like an endless ingot of molten silver. He never met anyone there. But on this day he was vexed to see a man come up to him. Beneath the pale starlight, the two solitary walkers only recognised each other when they were face to face.

"What! is it you?" said Étienne.

Souvarine nodded his head without replying. For a moment they remained motionless, then side by side they set out towards Marchiennes. Each of them seemed to be continuing his own reflections, as though they were far away from each other.

"Have you seen in the paper about Pluchart's success at Paris?" asked Étienne, at length. "After that meeting at Belleville, they waited for him on the pavement, and gave him an ovation. Oh! he's afloat now, in spite of his sore throat. He can do what he likes in future."

The engine-man shrugged his shoulders. He felt contempt for fine talkers, fellows who go into politics as one goes to the bar, to get an income out of phrases.

Étienne was now studying Darwin. He had read fragments, summarised and popularised in a five-sou volume; and out of this ill-understood reading he had gained for himself a revolutionary idea of the struggle for existence, the lean eating the fat, the strong people devouring the pallid middle class. But Souvarine furiously attacked the stupidity of the Socialists who accept Darwin, that apostle of scientific inequality, whose famous selection was only good for aristocratic philosophers. His mate persisted, however, wishing to reason out the matter, and expressing his doubts by an hypothesis: supposing the old society were no longer to exist, swept away to the crumbs; well, was it not to be feared that the new world would grow up again, slowly spoilt by the same injustices, some sick and others flourishing, some skilful and intelligent, fattening on everything, and others imbecile and lazy, becoming slaves again? But before this vision of eternal wretchedness, the engine-man shouted out fiercely that if justice was not possible with man, then man must disappear. For every rotten society there must be a massacre, until the last creature was exterminated. And there was silence again.

For a long time, with sunken head, Souvarine walked over the short grass, so absorbed that he kept to the extreme edge, by the water, with the quiet certainty of a sleeping man, dreaming on a roof. Then he shuddered causelessly, as though he had stumbled against a shadow. His eyes lifted and his face was very pale; he said softly to his companion:

"Did I ever tell you how she died?"

"Whom do you mean?"

"My wife, over there, in Russia."

Étienne made a vague gesture, astonished at the tremor in his voice and at the sudden desire for confidence in this lad, who was usually so impassive in his stoical detachment from others and from himself. He only knew that the woman was his mistress, and that she had been hanged at Moscow.

"The affair hadn't gone off," Souvarine said, with eyes still vacantly following the white stream of the canal between the bluish colonnades of tall trees. "We had been a fortnight at the bottom of a hole undermining the railway; and it was not the imperial train that was blown up, it was a passenger train. Then they arrested Annutchka. She brought us bread every evening, disguised as a peasant woman. She lit the fusee, too, because a man might have attracted attention. I followed the trial, bidden in the crowd, for six long days."

His voice became thick, and he coughed as though he were choking.

"Twice I wanted to cry out, and to rush over the people's heads to join her. But what was the good? One man less would be one soldier less; and I could see that she was telling me not to come, when her large eyes met mine."

He coughed again.

"On the last day in the square I was there. It was raining; they stupidly lost their heads, put out by the falling rain. It took twenty minutes to hang the other four; the cord broke, they could not finish the fourth. Annutchka was standing up waiting. She could not see all, she was looking for me in the crowd. I got on to a post and she saw me, and our eyes never turned from each other. When she was dead she was still looking at me. I waved my hat; I came away."

There was silence again. The white road of the canal unrolled to the far distance, and they both walked with the same quiet step as though each had fallen back into his isolation. At the horizon, the pale water seemed to open the sky with a little hole of light.

"It was our punishment," Souvarine went on roughly. "We were guilty to love each other. Yes, it is well that she is dead; heroes will be born from her blood, and I no longer have any cowardice at my heart. Ah! nothing, neither parents, nor wife, nor friend! Nothing to make my hand tremble on the day when I must take others' lives or give up my own!"

Étienne had stopped, shuddering in the cool night. He discussed no more, he simply said:

"We have gone far; shall we go back?"

They went back towards the Voreux slowly, and he added, after a few paces:

"Have you seen the new placards?"

The Company had that morning put up some more large yellow posters. They were clearer and more conciliatory, and the Company undertook to take back the certificates of those miners who went down on the following day. Everything would be forgotten, and pardon was offered even to those who were most implicated.

"Yes, I've seen," replied the engine-man.

"Well, what do you think of it?"

"I think that it's all up. The flock will go down again. You are all too cowardly."

Étienne feverishly excused his mates: a man may be brave, a mob which is dying of hunger has no strength. Step by step they were returning to the Voreux; and before the black mass of the pit he continued swearing that he, at least, would never go down; but he could forgive those who did. Then, as the rumour ran that the carpenters had not had time to repair the tubbing, he asked for information. Was it true? Had the weight of the soil against the timber which formed the internal skirt of scaffolding to the shaft so pushed it in that the winding-cages rubbed as they went down for a length of over fifty mètres?

Souvarine, who once more became uncommunicative, replied briefly. He had been working the day before, and the cage did, in fact, jar; the engine-men had even had to double the speed to pass that spot. But all the bosses received any observations with the same irritating remark: it was coal they wanted; that could be repaired later on.

"You see that's smashing up!" Étienne murmured. "It will be a fine time!"

With eyes vaguely fixed on the pit in the shadow, Souvarine quietly concluded:

"If that does smash up, the mates will know it, since you advise them to go down again."

Nine o'clock struck at the Montsou steeple; and his companion having said that he was going to bed, he added, without putting out his hand:

"Well, good-bye. I'm going away."

"What! you're going away?"

"Yes, I've asked for my certificate back. I'm going elsewhere."

Étienne, stupefied and affected, looked at him. After walking for two hours he said that to him! And in so calm a voice, while the mere announcement of this sudden separation made his own heart ache. They had got to know each other, they had toiled together; that always makes one sad, the idea of not seeing a person again.

"You're going away! And where do you go?"

"Over there—I don't know at all."

"But I shall see you again?"

"No, I think not."

They were silent and remained for a moment facing each other without finding anything to say.

"Then good-bye."

"Good-bye."

While Étienne ascended towards the settlement, Souvarine turned and again went along the canal bank; and there, now alone, he continued to walk, with sunken head, so lost in the darkness that he seemed merely a moving shadow of the night.

Now and then he stopped, he counted the hours that struck afar. When he heard midnight strike he left the bank and turned towards the Voreux.

At that time the pity was empty, and he only met a sleepy-eyed captain. It was not until six o'clock that they would begin to get up steam to resume work. First he went to take from a cupboard a jacket which he pretended to have forgotten. Various tools—a drill armed with its screw, a small, but very strong saw, a hammer and a chisel—were rolled up in this jacket. Then he left. But instead of going out through the shed he passed through the narrow corridor which led to the ladder passage. With his jacket under his arm he quietly went down without a lamp, measuring the depth by counting the ladders. He knew that the cage jarred at three hundred and seventy-four mètres against the fifth row of the lower tubbing. When he had counted fifty-four ladders he put out his hand and was able to feel the swelling of the planking. It was there. Then with the skill and coolness of a good workman who had been reflecting over his task for a long time, he set to work. He began by sawing a panel in the brattice so as to communicate with the winding shaft. With the help of matches, quickly lighted and blown out, he was then able to ascertain the condition of the tubbing and of the recent repairs.

Between Calais and Valenciennes the sinking of mine shafts is surrounded by immense difficulties on account of the masses of subterranean water in great sheets at the level of the lowest valleys. Only the construction of tubbings, frameworks jointed like the stays of a barrel, can keep out the springs which flow in and isolate the shafts in the midst of the lakes, which with deep obscure waves beat against the walls. It had been necessary in sinking the Voreux to establish two tubbings; that of the upper level, in the shifting sands and white clays bordering the chalky stratum, and fissured in every part, swollen with water like a sponge; then that of the lower level, immediately above the coal stratum, in a yellow sand as fine as flour, flowing with liquid fluidity; it was here that the torrent was to be found, that subterranean sea so dreaded in the mine pits of the Nord, a sea with its storms and its shipwrecks, an unknown and unfathomable sea, rolling its dark floods more than three hundred mètres beneath the daylight. Usually the tubbings resisted the enormous pressure; the only thing to be dreaded was the piling up of the neighbouring soil, shaken by the constant movement of the old galleries which were filling up. In this descent of the rocks lines of fracture were sometimes produced which slowly extended as far as the scaffolding, at last perforating it and pushing it into the shaft; and there was the great danger of a landslip and a flood filling the pit with an avalanche of earth and a deluge of springs.

Souvarine, sitting astride in the opening he had made, discovered a very serious defect in the fifth row of tubbing. The wood was bellied out from the framework; several planks had even come out of their shoulder-pieces. Abundant filtrations, *pichoux* the miners call them, were jetting out of the joints through the tarred oakum with which they were caulked. The carpenters, pressed for time, had been content to place iron squares at the angles, so carelessly that all the screws were not put in. A considerable movement was evidently going on behind in the sand of the torrent.

Then with his wimble he unscrewed the squares so that another push would tear them all off. It was a foolhardy task, during which he frequently only just escaped from falling and leaping down the hundred and eighty mètres which separated him from the bottom. He had been obliged to seize the oak guides, the joists along which the cages slid; and suspended over the void he traversed the length of the cross-beams with which they were joined from point to point, slipping along, sitting down, turning over, simply buttressing himself on an elbow or a knee, with tranquil contempt of death. A breath would have sent him over, and three times he caught himself up without a shudder. First he felt with his hand and then worked, only lighting a match when he lost himself in the midst of these sticky beams. After loosening the screws he attacked the wood itself, and the peril became still greater. He had sought for the key, the piece which held the others; he attacked it furiously, making holes in it, sawing it, diminishing it so that it lost its resistance; while through the holes and the cracks the water which escaped in small jets blinded him and soaked him in icy rain. Two matches were extinguished. They all became damp and then there was night, the bottomless depth of darkness.

From this moment he was seized by rage. The breath of the invisible intoxicated him, the black horror of this rain-beaten hole urged him to mad destruction. He wreaked his fury at random against the tubbing, striking where he could with his wimble, with his saw, seized by the desire to bring the whole thing at once down on his head. He brought as much ferocity to the task as though he had been digging a knife into the skin of some execrated living creature. He would kill the Voreux at last, that evil beast with ever open jaws which had swallowed so much human flesh! The bite of his tools could be heard, his spine lengthened, he crawled, climbed down, then up again, holding on by a miracle, in continual movement, the flight of a nocturnal bird amid the scaffolding of a belfry.

But he grew calm, dissatisfied with himself. Why could not things be done coolly? Without haste he breathed, and then went back into the ladder passage, stopping up the hole by replacing the panel which he had sawn. That was enough; he did not wish to raise alarm by excessive damage which would have been repaired immediately. The beast was wounded in the belly; we should see if it was still alive at night. And he had left his mark; the frightened world would know that the beast had not died a natural death. He took his time in methodically rolling up his tools in his jacket, and slowly climbed up the ladders. Then, when he had emerged from the pit without being seen, it did not occur to him to go and change his clothes. Three o'clock struck. He remained standing on the road waiting.

At the same hour Étienne, who was not asleep, was disturbed by a slight sound in the thick night of the room. He distinguished the low breath of the children, and the snoring of Bonnemort and Maheude; while Jeanlin near him was breathing with a prolonged flute-like whistle. No doubt he had dreamed, and he was turning back when the noise began again. It was the creaking of a palliasse, the stifled effort of someone who is getting up. Then he imagined that Catherine must be ill.

"I say, is it you? What is the matter?" he asked in a low voice.

No one replied, and the snoring of the others continued. For five minutes nothing stirred. Then there was fresh creaking. Feeling certain this time that he was not mistaken, he crossed the room, putting his hands out into the darkness to feel the opposite bed. He was surprised to find the young girl sitting up, holding in her breath, awake and on the watch.

"Well! why don't you reply? What are you doing, then?"

At last she said:

"I'm getting up."

"Getting up at this hour?"

"Yes, I'm going back to work at the pit."

Étienne felt deeply moved, and sat down on the edge of the palliasse, while Catherine explained her reasons to him. She suffered too much by living thus in idleness, feeling continual looks of reproach weighing on her; she would rather run the risk of being knocked about down there by Chaval. And if her mother refused to take her money when she brought it, well! she was big enough to act for herself and make her own soup.

"Go away; I want to dress. And don't say anything, will you, if you want to be kind?"

But he remained near her; he had put his arms round her waist in a caress of grief and pity. Pressed one against the other in their shirts, they could feel the warmth of each other's naked flesh, at the edge of this bed, still moist with the night's sleep. She had at first tried to free herself; then she began to cry quietly, in her turn taking him by the neck to press him against her in a despairing clasp. And they remained, without any further desires, with the past of their unfortunate love, which they had not been able to satisfy. Was it, then, done with for ever? Would they never dare to love each other some day, now that they were free? It only needed a little happiness to dissipate their shame—that awkwardness which prevented them from coming together because of all sorts of ideas which they themselves could not read clearly.

"Go to bed, again," she whispered. "I don't want to light up, it would wake mother. It is time; leave me."

He could not hear; he was pressing her wildly, with a heart drowned in immense sadness. The need for peace, an irresistible need for happiness, was carrying him away; and he saw himself married, in a neat little house, with no other ambition than to live and to die there, both of them together. He would be satisfied with bread; and if there were only enough for one, she should have it. What was the good of anything else? Was there anything in life worth more?

But she was unfolding her naked arms.

"Please, leave me."

Then, in a sudden impulse, he said in her ear:

"Wait, I'm coming with you."

And he was himself surprised at what he had said. He had sworn never to go down again; whence then came this sudden decision, arising from his lips without thought of his, without even a moment's discussion? There was now such calm within him, so complete a cure of his doubts, that he persisted like a man saved by chance, who has at last found the only harbour from his torment. So he refused to listen to her when she became alarmed, understanding that he was devoting himself for her and fearing the ill words which would greet him at the pit. He laughed at everything; the placards promised pardon and that was enough.

"I want to work; that's my idea. Let us dress and make no noise."

They dressed themselves in the darkness, with a thousand precautions. She had secretly prepared her miner's clothes the evening before; he took a jacket and breeches from the cupboard; and they did not wash themselves for fear of knocking the bowl. All were asleep, but they had to cross the narrow passage where the mother slept. When they started, as ill-luck would have it, they stumbled against a chair. She woke and asked, drowsily:

"Eh! what is it?"

Catherine had stopped, trembling, and violently pressing Étienne's hand.

"It's me; don't trouble yourself," he said. "I feel stifled and am going outside to breathe a bit."

"Very well."

And Maheude fell asleep again. Catherine dared not stir. At last she went down into the parlour and divided a slice of bread and butter which she had reserved from a loaf given by a Montsou lady. Then they softly closed the door and went away.

Souvarine had remained standing near the Avantage, at the corner of the road. For half-an-hour he had been looking at the colliers who were returning to work in the darkness, passing by with the dull tramp of a herd. He was counting them, as a butcher counts his beasts at the entrance to the slaughter-house, and he was surprised at their number; even his pessimism had not foreseen that the number of cowards would have been so great. The stream continued to pass by, and he grew stiff, very cold, with clenched teeth and bright eyes.

But he started. Among the men passing by, whose faces he could not distinguish, he had just recognised one by his walk. He came forward and stopped him.

"Where are you going to?"

Étienne, in surprise, instead of replying, stammered:

"What! you've not set out yet!"

Then he confessed he was going back to the pit. No doubt he had sworn; only it could not be called life to wait with crossed arms for things which would perhaps happen in a hundred years; and, besides, reasons of his own had decided him.

Souvarine had listened to him, shuddering. He seized him by the shoulder, and pushed him towards the settlement.

"Go home again; I want you to. Do you understand?"

But Catherine having approached, he recognised her also. Étienne protested, declaring that he allowed no one to judge his conduct. And the engine-man's eyes went from the young girl to her companion, while he stepped back with a sudden, relinquishing movement. When there was a woman in a man's heart that man was done for; he might die. Perhaps he saw again in a rapid vision his mistress hanging over there at Moscow, that last link cut from his flesh, which had rendered him free over the lives of others and over his own life. He said simply:

"Go."

Étienne, feeling awkward, was delaying, and trying to find some friendly word, so as not to separate in this manner.

"Then you're still going?"

"Yes."

"Well, give me your hand, old chap. A pleasant journey, and no ill-feeling."

The other stretched out an icy hand. Neither friend nor wife.

"Good-bye for good this time."

"Yes, good-bye."

And Souvarine, standing motionless in the darkness, watched Étienne and Catherine entering the Voreux.

## CHAPTER III

AT FOUR O'CLOCK THE descent began. Dansaert, who was personally installed at the marker's office in the lamp cabin, wrote down the name of each worker who presented himself and had a lamp given to him. He took them all, without remark, keeping to the promise of the placards. When, however, he noticed Étienne and Catherine at the wicket, he started and became very red, and was opening his mouth to refuse their names; then, he contented himself with the triumph, and a jeer. Ah! ah! So the strong man was thrown? The Company was, then, in luck since the terrible Montsou wrestler had come back to it to ask for bread? Étienne silently took his lamp and went towards the shaft with the putter.

But it was there, in the receiving-room, that Catherine feared the mates' bad words. At the very entrance she recognised Chaval, in the midst of some twenty miners, waiting till a cage was free. He came furiously towards her, but the sight of Étienne stopped him. Then he affected to sneer with an offensive shrug of the shoulders. Very good! he didn't care a hang, since the other had come to occupy the place that was still warm; good riddance! It only concerned the gentleman if he liked the leavings; and beneath the exhibition of this contempt he was again seized by a tremor of jealousy, and his eyes flamed. For the rest, the mates did not stir, standing silent, with eyes lowered. They contented themselves with casting a sidelong look at the newcomers; then, dejected and without anger, they again stared fixedly at the mouth of the shaft, with their lamps in their hands, shivering beneath their thin jackets in the constant draughts of this large room. At last the cage was wedged on to the keeps, and they were ordered to get in. Catherine and Étienne were squeezed in one tram, already containing Pierron and two pikemen. Beside them, in the other tram, Chavel was loudly saying to Father Mouque that the directors had made a mistake in not taking advantage of the opportunity to free the pits of the blackguards who were corrupting them; but the old groom, who had already fallen back into the dog-like resignation of his existence, no longer grew angry over the death of his children, and simply replied by a gesture of conciliation.

The cage freed itself and slipped down into the darkness. No one spoke. Suddenly, when they were in the middle third of the descent, there was a terrible jarring. The iron creaked, and the men were thrown on to each other.

"By God!" growled Étienne, "are they going to flatten us? We shall end by being left here for good, with their confounded tubbing. And they talk about having repaired it!"

The cage had, however, freed the obstacle. It was now descending beneath so violent a rain, like a storm, that the workmen anxiously listened to the pouring. A number of leaks must then have appeared in the caulking of the joints.

Pierron, who had been working for several days, when asked about it did not like to show his fear, which might be considered as an attack on the management, so he only replied:

"Oh, no danger! it's always like that. No doubt, they've not had time to caulk the leaks."

The torrent was roaring over their heads, and they at last reached the pit-eye beneath a veritable waterspout. Not one of the captains had thought of climbing up the ladders to investigate the matter. The pump would be enough, the carpenters would examine the joints the following night. The reorganisation of work in the galleries gave considerable trouble. Before allowing the pikemen to return to their hewing cells, the engineer had decided that for the first five days all the men should execute certain works of consolidation which were extremely urgent. Landslips were threatening everywhere; the passages had suffered to such an extent that the timbering had to be repaired along a length of several hundred mètres. Gangs of ten men were therefore formed below, each beneath the control of a captain. Then they were set to work at the most damaged spots. When the descent was complete, it was found that three hundred and twenty-two miners had gone down, about half of those who worked there when the pit was in full swing.

Chaval belonged to the same gang as Catherine and Étienne. This was not by chance; he had at first hidden behind his mates, and had then forced the captain's hand. This gang went to the end of the north gallery, nearly three kilomètres away, to clear out a landslip which was stopping up a gallery in the Dix-Huit-Pouces seam. They attacked the fallen rocks with shovel and pick. Étienne, Chaval, and five others cleared away the rubbish, while Catherine, with the trammers, wheeled the earth to the upbrow. They seldom spoke, and the captain never left them. The putter's two lovers, however, were on the point of coming to blows. While growling that he had had enough of this trollop, Chaval was still thinking of her, and slily hustling her about, so that Étienne had threatened to settle him if he did not leave her alone. They eyed each other fiercely, and had to be separated.

Towards eight o'clock Dansaert passed to give a glance at the work. He appeared to be in a very bad humour, and was furious with the captain; nothing had gone well, what was the meaning of such work, the planking would everywhere have to be done over again! And he went away declaring that he would come back with the engineer. He had been waiting for Négrel since morning, and could not understand the cause of this delay.

Another hour passed by. The captain had stopped the removal of the rubbish to employ all his people in supporting the roof. Even the putter and the two trammers left off wheeling to prepare and bring pieces of timber. At this end of the gallery the gang formed a sort of advance guard at the very extremity of the mine, now without communication with the other stalls. Three or four times strange noises, distant rushes, made the workers turn their heads to listen. What was it, then? One would have said that the passages were being emptied and the mates already returning at a running pace. But the sound was lost in the deep silence, and they set to wedging their wood again, dazed by the loud blows of the hammer. At last they returned to the rubbish, and the wheeling began once more. Catherine came back from her first journey, in terror, saying that no one was to be found at the upbrow.

"I called, but there was no reply. They've all cleared out of the place."

The bewilderment was so great that the ten men threw down their tools to rush away. The idea that they were abandoned, left alone at the bottom of the mine, so far from the pit-eye, drove them wild. They only kept their lamps and ran in single file—the men, the boys, the putter; the captain himself lost his head and shouted out appeals, more and more frightened at the silence in this endless desert of galleries. What then had happened that they did not meet a soul? What accident could thus have driven away their mates? Their terror was increased by the uncertainty of the danger, this threat which they felt there without knowing what it was.

When they at last came near the pit-eye, a torrent barred their road. They were at once in water to the knees, and were no longer able to run, painfully fording the flood with the thought that one minute's delay might mean death.

"By God! it's the tubbing that's given way," cried Étienne. "I said we should be left here for good."

Since the descent Pierron had anxiously observed the increase of the deluge which fell from the shaft. As with two others he loaded the trams he raised his head, his face covered with large drops, and his ears ringing with the roar of the tempest above. But he trembled especially when he noticed that the sump beneath him, that pit ten mètres deep, was filling; the water was already spurting through the floor and covering the metal plates. This showed that the pump was no longer sufficient to fight against the leaks. He heard it out of breath, with the groan of fatigue. Then he warned Dansaert, who swore angrily, replying that they must wait for the engineer. Twice he returned to the charge without extracting anything else but exasperated shrugs of the shoulder. Well! the water was rising; what could he do?

Mouque appeared with Bataille, whom he was leading to work, and he had to hold him with both hands, for the sleepy old horse had suddenly reared up, and, with a death-like neigh, was stretching his head towards the shaft.

"Well, philosopher, what troubles you? Ah! it's because it rains. Come along, that doesn't concern you."

But the beast quivered all over his skin, and Mouque forcibly drew him to the haulage gallery.

Almost at the same moment as Mouque and Bataille were disappearing at the end of a gallery, there was a crackling in the air, followed by the prolonged noise of a fall. It was a piece of the tubbing which had got loose and was falling a hundred and eighty mètres down, rebounding against the walls. Pierron and the other porters were able to get out of the way, and the oak plank only smashed an empty tram. At the same time, a mass of water, the leaping flood of a broken dyke, rushed down. Dansaert proposed to go up and examine; but, while he was still speaking, another piece rolled down. And in terror before the threatening catastrophe, he no longer hesitated, but gave the order to go up, sending captains to warn the men in their stalls.

Then a terrible hustling began. From every gallery rows of workers came rushing up, trying to take the cages by assault. They crushed madly against each other in order to be taken up at once. Some who had thought of trying the ladder-passage came down again shouting that it was already stopped up. That was the terror they all felt each time that the cage rose; this time it was able to pass, but who knew if it would be able to pass again in the midst of the obstacles obstructing the shaft? The downfall must be continuing above, for a series of low detonations was heard, the planks were splitting and bursting amid the continuous and increasing roar of a storm. One cage soon became useless, broken in and no longer sliding between the guides, which were doubtless broken. The other jarred to such a degree that the cable would certainly break soon. And there remained a hundred men to be taken up, all panting, clinging to one another, bleeding and half drowned. Two were killed by falls of planking. A third, who had seized the cage, fell back fifty mètres up and disappeared in the sump.

Dansaert, however, was trying to arrange matters in an orderly manner. Armed with a pick he threatened to open the skull of the first man who refused to obey; and he tried to arrange them in file, shouting that the porters were to go up last after having sent up their mates. He was not listened to, and he had to prevent the pale and cowardly Pierron from entering among the first. At each departure he pushed him aside with a blow. But his own teeth were chattering, a minute more and he would be swallowed up; everything was smashing up there, a flood had broken loose, a murderous rain of scaffolding. A few men were still running up when, mad with fear, he jumped into a tram, allowing Pierron to jump in behind him. The cage rose.

At this moment the gang to which Étienne and Chaval belonged had just reached the pit-eye. They saw the cage disappear and rushed forward, but they had to draw back from the final downfall of the tubbing; the shaft was stopped up and the cage would not come down again. Catherine was sobbing, and Chaval was choked with shouting oaths. There were twenty of them; were those bloody bosses going to abandon them thus? Father Mouque, who had brought back Bataille without hurrying, was still holding him by the bridle, both of them stupefied, the man and the beast, in the face of this rapid flow of the inundation. The water was already rising to their thighs. Étienne in silence, with clenched teeth, supported Catherine between his arms. And the twenty yelled with their faces turned up, obstinately gazing at the shaft like imbeciles, that shifting hole which was belching out a flood and from which no help could henceforth come to them.

At the surface, Dansaert, on arriving, perceived Négrel running up. By some fatality, Madame Hennebeau had that morning delayed him on rising, turning over the leaves of catalogues for the purchase of wedding presents. It was ten o'clock.

"Well! what's happening, then?" he shouted from afar.

"The pit is ruined," replied the head captain.

And he described the catastrophe in a few stammered words, while the engineer incredulously shrugged his shoulders. What! could tubbing be demolished like that? It was exaggerated; he would make an examination.

"I suppose no one has been left at the bottom?"

Dansaert was confused. No, no one; at least, so he hoped. But some of the men might have been delayed.

"But," said Négrel, "what in the name of creation have you come up for, then? You can't leave your men!"

He immediately gave orders to count the lamps. In the morning three hundred and twenty-two had been distributed, and now only two hundred and fifty-five could be found; but several men acknowledged that in the hustling and panic they had dropped theirs and left them behind. An attempt was made to call over the men, but it was impossible to establish the exact number. Some of the miners had gone away, others did not hear their names. No one was agreed as to the number of the missing mates. It might be twenty, perhaps forty. And the engineer could only make out one thing with certainty: there were men down below, for their yells could be distinguished through the sound of the water and the fallen scaffolding, on leaning over the mouth of the shaft.

Négrel's first care was to send for M. Hennebeau, and to try to close the pit; but it was already too late. The colliers who had rushed to the Deux-Cent-Quarante settlement, as though pursued by the crackling tubbing, had frightened the families; and bands of women, old men, and little ones came up running, shaken by cries and sobs. They had to be pushed back, and a line of overseers was formed to keep them off, for they would have interfered with the manœuvres. Many of the men who had come up from the shaft remained there stupidly without thinking of changing their clothes, riveted by fear before this terrible hole in which they had nearly remained for ever. The women, rushing wildly around them, implored them for names. Was so-and-so among them? and that one? and this other? They did not know, they stammered; they shuddered terribly, and made gestures like mad men, gestures which seemed to be pushing away some abominable vision which was always present to them. The crowd rapidly increased, and lamentations arose from the roads. And up there on the pit bank, in Bonnemort's cabin, on the earth was seated a man, Souvarine, who had not gone away, who was looking on.

"The names! the names!" cried the women, with voices choked by tears.

Négrel appeared for a moment, and said hurriedly:

"As soon as we know the names they shall be given out, but nothing is lost so far: everyone will be saved. I am going down."

Then, silent with anguish, the crowd waited. The engineer, in fact, with quiet courage was preparing to go down. He had had the cage unfastened, giving orders to replace it at the end of the cable by a tub; and as he feared that the water would extinguish his lamp, he had another fastened beneath the tub, which would protect it.

Several captains, trembling and with white, disturbed faces, assisted in these preparations.

"You will come with me, Dansaert," said Négrel, abruptly.

Then, when he saw them all without courage, and that the head captain was tottering, giddy with terror, he pushed him aside with a movement of contempt.

"No, you will be in my way. I would rather go alone."

He was already in the narrow bucket, which swayed at the end of the cable; and holding his lamp in one hand and the signal-cord in the other, he shouted to the engine-man:

"Gently!"

The engine set the drums in movement, and Négrel disappeared in the gulf, from which the yells of the wretches below still arose.

At the upper part nothing had moved. He found that the tubbing here was in good condition. Balanced in the middle of the shaft he lighted up the walls as he turned round; the leaks between the joints were so slight that his lamp did not suffer. But at three hundred mètres, when he reached the lower tubbing, the lamp was extinguished, as he expected, for a jet had filled the tub. After that he was only able to see by the hanging lamp which preceded him in the darkness, and, in spite of his courage, he shuddered and turned pale in face of the horror of the disaster. A few pieces of timber alone remained; the others had fallen in with their frames. Behind, enormous cavities had been hollowed out, and the yellow sand, as fine as flour, was flowing in considerable masses; while the waters of the torrent, that subterranean sea with its unknown tempests and shipwrecks, was expanding and discharging like a millstream. He went down lower, lost in the centre of this space which continued to increase, beaten and turned round by the waterspout of the springs, so badly lighted by the red star of the lamp moving on below, that he seemed to distinguish the roads and squares of some destroyed town far away in the play of the great moving shadows. No human work was any longer possible. His only remaining hope was to attempt to save the men in peril. As he sank down he heard the cries becoming louder, and he was obliged to stop; an impassable obstacle barred the shaft—a mass of scaffolding, the broken joists of the guides, the split brattices entangled with the metal-work torn from the pump. As he looked on for a long time with aching heart, the yelling suddenly ceased. No doubt, the rapid rise of the water had forced the wretches to flee into the galleries, if, indeed, the flood had not already filled their mouths.

Négrel resigned himself to pulling the signal-cord as a sign to draw up. Then he had himself stopped again. He could not conceive the cause of this sudden accident. He wished to investigate it, and examined those pieces of the tubbing which were still in place. At a distance the tears and cuts in the wood had surprised him. His lamp, drowned in dampness, was going out, and, touching with his fingers, he clearly recognised the marks of the saw and of the wimble—the whole abominable labour of destruction. Evidently this catastrophe had been intentionally produced. He was stupefied, and the pieces of timber cracking and falling down with their frames in a last slide nearly carried him with them. His courage fled. The thought of the man who had done that made his hair stand on end, and froze him with a supernatural fear of evil, as though, mixed with the darkness, the man were still there paying for his immeasurable crime. He shouted and shook the signal furiously; and it was, indeed, time, for he perceived that the upper tubbing, a hundred mètres higher, was in its turn beginning to move. The joints were opening, losing their oakum caulking, and streams were rushing through. It was now only a question of hours before the tubbing would all fall down.

At the surface M. Hennebeau was anxiously waiting for Négrel.

"Well, what?" he asked.

But the engineer was choked, and could not speak; he felt faint.

"It is not possible; such a thing was never seen. Have you examined?"

He nodded with a cautious look. He refused to talk in the presence of the captains, who were listening, and led his uncle ten mètres away, and not thinking this far enough, drew still further back; then, in a low whisper, he at last told the attempt, the torn and sawn planks, the pit bleeding at the neck and groaning. Turning pale, the manager also lowered his voice, with that instinct we need of silence in face of the monstrosity of great orgies and great crimes. It was useless to look as though they were trembling before the ten thousand Montsou men; later on they would see. And they both continued whispering, overcome at the thought that a man had had the courage to go down, to hang in the midst of space, to risk his life twenty times over in this terrible task. They could not even understand this mad courage in destruction; they refused to believe, in spite of the evidence, just as we doubt those stories of celebrated escapes of prisoners who fly through windows thirty mètres above the ground.

When M. Hennebeau came back to the captains a nervous spasm was drawing his face. He made a gesture of despair, and gave orders that the mine should be evacuated at once. It was a kind of funeral procession, in silent abandonment, with glances thrown back at those great masses of bricks, empty and still standing, but which nothing henceforth could save.

And as the manager and the engineer came down last from the receiving-room, the crowd met them with its clamour, repeating obstinately:

"The names! the names! Tell us the names!"

Maheude was now there, among the women. She recollected the noise in the night; her daughter and the lodger must have gone away together, and they were certainly down at the bottom. And after having cried that it was a good thing, that they deserved to stay there, the heartless cowards, she had run up, and was standing in the first row, trembling with anguish. Besides, she no longer dared to doubt; the discussion going on around her informed her as to the names of those who were down. Yes, yes, Catherine was among them, Étienne also—a mate had seen them. But there was not always agreement with regard to the others. No, not this one; on the contrary, that one, perhaps Chaval, with whom, however, a trammer declared that he had ascended. The Levaque and Pierronne, although none of their people were in danger, cried out and lamented as loudly as the others. Zacharie, who had come up among the first, in spite of his inclination to make fun of everything had weepingly kissed his wife and mother, and remained near the latter, quivering, and showing an unexpected degree of affection for his sister, refusing to believe that she was below so long as the bosses made no authoritative statement.

"The names! the names! For pity's sake, the names!"

Négrel, who was exhausted, shouted to the overseers:

"Can't you make them be still? It's enough to kill one with vexation! We don't know the names!"

Two hours passed away in this manner. In the first terror no one had thought of the other shaft at the old Réquillart mine. M. Hennebeau was about to announce that the rescue would be attempted from that side, when a rumour ran round: five men had just escaped the inundation by climbing up the rotten ladders of the old unused passage, and Father Mouque was named. This caused surprise, for no one knew he was below. But the narrative of the five who had escaped increased the weeping; fifteen mates had not been able to follow them, having gone astray, and been walled up by falls. And it was no longer possible to assist them, for there was already ten mètres of water in Réquillart. All the names were known, and the air was filled with the groans of a nation that was being slaughtered.

"Will you make them be still?" Négrel repeated furiously. "Make them draw back! Yes, yes, to a hundred mètres! There is danger; push them back, push them back!"

It was necessary to struggle against these poor people. They were imagining all sorts of misfortunes, and they had to be driven away so that the deaths might be concealed; the captains explained to them that the shaft would destroy the whole mine. This idea rendered them mute with terror, and they at last allowed themselves to be driven back step by step; the guards, however, who kept them back had to be doubled, for they were fascinated by the spot and continually returned. Thousands of people were hustling each other along the road; they were running up from all the settlements, and even from Montsou. And the man above, on the pit bank, the fair man with the girlish face, smoked cigarettes to occupy himself, keeping his clear eyes fixed on the pit.

Then the wait began. It was mid-day; no one had eaten, but no one moved away. In the misty sky, of a dirty grey colour, rusty clouds were slowly passing by. A big dog, behind Rasseneur's hedge, was barking furiously without cessation, irritated by the living breath of the crowd. And the crowd had gradually spread over the neighbouring ground, forming a circle at a hundred mètres round the pit. The Voreux arose in the centre of the great space. There was not a soul there, not a sound; it was a desert. The windows and the doors, left open, showed the abandonment within; a forgotten red cat, divining the peril in this solitude, jumped from a staircase and disappeared. No doubt the stoves of the boilers were scarcely extinguished, for the tall brick chimney gave out a light smoke beneath the dark clouds; while the weather cock on the steeple creaked in the wind with a short, shrill cry, the only melancholy voice of these vast buildings which were about to die.

At two o'clock nothing had moved. M. Hennebeau, Négrel and other engineers who had hastened up, formed a group in black coats and hats standing in front of the crowd; and they, too, did not move away though their legs were aching with fatigue, and they were feverish and ill at their impotence in the face of such a disaster, only whispering occasional words as though at a dying person's bedside. The upper tubbing must nearly all have fallen in, for sudden echoing sounds could be heard as of deep broken falls, succeeded by silence. The wound was constantly enlarging; the landslip which had begun below was rising and approaching the surface. Négrel was seized by nervous impatience; he wanted to see, and he was already, advancing alone into this awful void when he was seized by the shoulders. What was the good? he could prevent nothing. An old miner, however, circumventing the overseers, rushed into the shed; but he quietly reappeared, he had gone for his sabots.

Three o'clock struck. Still nothing. A falling shower had soaked the crowd, but they had not withdrawn a step. Rasseneur's dog had begun to bark again. And it was at twenty minutes past three only that the first shock was felt. The Voreux trembled, but continued solid and upright. Then a second shock followed immediately, and a long cry came from open mouths; the tarred screening-shed, after having tottered twice, was falling down with a terrible crash. Beneath the enormous pressure the structures broke and jarred each other so powerfully that sparks leapt out. From this moment the earth continued to tremble, the shocks succeeded one another, subterranean downfalls, the rumbling of a volcano in eruption. Afar the dog was no longer barking, but he howled plaintively as though announcing the oscillations which he felt coming; and the women, the children, all these people who were looking on, could not keep back a clamour of distress at each of these blows which shook them. In less than ten minutes the slate roof of the steeple fell in, the receiving-room and the engine-room were split open, leaving a considerable breach. Then the sounds ceased, the downfall stopped, and there was again deep silence.

For an hour the Voreux remained thus, broken into, as though bombarded by an army of barbarians. There was no more crying out; the enlarged circle of spectators merely looked on. Beneath the piled-up beams of the sifting-shed, fractured tipping-cradles could be made out with broken and twisted hoppers. But the rubbish had especially accumulated at the receiving-room, where there had been a rain of bricks, and large portions of wall and masses of plaster had fallen in. The iron scaffold which bore the pulleys had bent, half buried in the pit; a cage was still suspended, a torn cable end was hanging; then there was a hash of trams, metal plates, and ladders. By some chance the lamp-cabin remained standing, exhibiting on the left its bright rows of little lamps. And at the end of its disembowelled chamber, the engine could be seen seated squarely on its massive foundation of masonry; its copper was shining, and its huge steel limbs seemed to possess indestructible muscles. The enormous crank, bent in the air, looked like the powerful knee of some giant quietly reposing in his strength.

After this hour of respite, M. Hennebeau's hopes began to rise. The movement of the soil must have come to an end, and there would be some chance of saving the engine and the remainder of the buildings. But he would not yet allow anyone to approach, considering another half-hour's patience desirable. This waiting became unbearable; the hope increased the anguish, and all hearts were beating quickly. A dark cloud, growing large at the horizon, hastened the twilight, a sinister day-fall over this wreck of earth's tempests. Since seven o'clock they had been there without moving or eating.

And suddenly, as the engineers were cautiously advancing, a supreme convulsion of the soil put them to flight. Subterranean detonations broke out; a whole monstrous artillery was cannonading in the gulf. At the surface, the last buildings were tipped over and crushed. At first a sort of whirlwind carried away the rubbish from the sifting-shed and the receiving-room. The boiler buildings afterwards burst and disappeared. Then it was the low square tower, where the pumping engine was groaning, which fell on its face like a man mown down by a bullet. And then a terrible thing was seen; the engine, dislocated from its massive foundation, with outspread limbs was struggling against death; it moved, it extended its crank, its giant's knee, as though to rise; but crushed and swallowed up, it was dying. The chimney, alone, thirty mètres high, still remained standing, though shaken, like a mast in the tempest. It was thought that it would be crushed to fragments and fly to powder, when suddenly it sank in one block, drunk down by the earth, melted like a colossal candle; and nothing was left, not even the point of the lightning conductor. It was done for; the evil beast crouching in this hole, gorged with human flesh, was no longer breathing with its thick, long respiration. The Voreux had been swallowed whole by the abyss.

The crowd rushed away yelling. The women hid their eyes as they ran. Terror drove the men along like a pile of dry leaves. They wished not to shout and they shouted, with swollen breasts, and arms in the air, before the immense hole which had been hollowed out. This crater, as of an extinct volcano, fifteen mètres deep, extended from the road to the canal for a space of at least forty mètres. The whole square of the mine had followed the buildings, the gigantic platforms, the foot-bridges with their rails, a complete train of trams, three wagons; without counting the wood supply, a forest of cut timber, gulped down like straw. At the bottom it was only possible to distinguish a confused mass of beams, bricks, iron, plaster, frightful remains, piled up, entangled, soiled in the fury of the catastrophe. And the hole became rounder, cracks started from the edges, reaching afar, across the fields. A fissure ascended as far as Rasseneur's bar, and his front wall had cracked. Would the settlement itself pass into it? How far ought they to flee to reach shelter at the end of this abominable day, beneath this leaden cloud which also seemed about to crush the earth?

A cry of pain escaped Négrel. M. Hennebeau, who had drawn back, was in tears. The disaster was not complete; one bank of the canal gave way, and the canal emptied itself like one bubbling sheet through one of the cracks. It disappeared there, falling like a cataract down a deep valley. The mine drank down this river; the galleries would now be submerged for years. Soon the crater was filled and a lake of muddy water occupied the place where once stood the Voreux, like one of those lakes beneath which sleep accursed towns. There was a terrified silence, and nothing now could be heard but the fall of this water rumbling in the bowels of the earth.

Then on the shaken pit-bank Souvarine rose up. He had recognised Maheude and Zacharie sobbing before this downfall, the weight of which was so heavy on the heads of the wretches who were in agony beneath. And he threw down his last cigarette; he went away, without looking back, into the now dark night. Afar his shadow diminished and mingled with the darkness. He was going over there, to the unknown. He was going tranquilly to extermination, wherever there may be dynamite to blow up towns and men. He will be there, without doubt, when the middle class in agony shall hear the pavement of the streets bursting up beneath their feet.

## CHAPTER IV

On the night that followed the collapse of the Voreux M. Hennebeau started for Paris, wishing to inform the directors in person before the newspapers published the news. And when he returned on the following day he was found to be quite calm, with his usual correct administrative air. He had evidently freed himself from responsibility; he did not appear to have decreased in favour. On the contrary, the decree appointing him officer of the Legion of Honour was signed twenty-four hours afterwards.

But if the manager remained safe, the Company was tottering beneath the terrible blow. It was not the few million francs that had been lost, it was the wound in the flank, the deep incessant fear of the morrow in face of this massacre of a mine. The Company was so impressed that once more it felt the need of silence. What was the good of stirring up this abomination? If the villain were discovered, why make a martyr of him in order that his awful heroism might turn other heads, and give birth to a long line of incendiaries and murderers? Besides, the real culprit was not suspected. The Company came to think that there was an army of accomplices, not being able to believe that a single man could have had courage and strength for such a task; and it was precisely this thought which weighed on them, this thought of an ever increasing threat to the existence of their mines. The manager had received orders to organise a vast system of espionage, and then to dismiss quietly, one by one, the dangerous men who were suspected of having had a hand in the crime. They contented themselves with this method of purification—a prudent and politic method.

There was only one immediate dismissal, that of Dansaert, the head captain. Ever since the scandal at Pierronne's house he had become impossible. A pretence was made of his attitude in danger, the cowardice of a captain abandoning his men. This was also a prudent sop thrown to the miners, who hated him.

Among the public, however, many rumours had circulated, and the directors had to send a letter of correction to one newspaper, contradicting a story in which mention was made of a barrel of powder lighted by the strikers. After a rapid enquiry the Government inspector had concluded that there had been a natural rupture of the tubbing, occasioned by the piling up of the soil; and the Company had preferred to be silent, and to accept the blame of a lack of superintendence. In the press at Paris, after the third day, the catastrophe had served to increase the stock of general news; nothing was talked of but the men in agony at the bottom of the mine, and the telegrams published every morning were eagerly read. At Montsou people grew pale and speechless at the very name of the Voreux, and a legend had formed which made the boldest tremble as they whispered it. The whole country showed great pity for the victims; visits were organised to the destroyed pit, and whole families hastened up to shudder at the ruins which lay so heavily over the heads of the buried wretches.

Deneulin, who had been appointed divisional engineer, came upon the midst of the disaster on beginning his duties; and his first care was to turn the canal back into its bed, for this torrent increased the damage every hour. Extensive works were necessary, and he at once set a hundred men to construct a dyke. Twice over the impetuosity of the stream carried away the first dams. Now pumps were set up and a furious struggle was going on; step by step the vanished soil was being violently reconquered.

But the rescue of the engulfed miners was a still more absorbing work. Négrel was appointed to attempt a supreme effort, and arms were not lacking to help him; all the colliers rushed to offer themselves in an outburst of brotherhood. They forgot the strike, they did not trouble themselves at all about payment; they might get nothing, they only asked to risk their lives as soon as there were mates in danger of death. They were all there with their tools, shuddering as they waited to know where they ought to strike. Many of them, sick with fright after the accident, shaken by nervous tremors, soaked in cold sweats, and the prey of continual nightmares, got up in spite of everything, and were as eager as any in their desire to fight against the earth, as though they had a revenge to take on it. Unfortunately, the difficulty began when the question arose, What could be done? how could they go down? from what side could they attack the rocks?

Négrel's opinion was that not one of the unfortunate people was alive; the fifteen had surely perished, drowned or suffocated. But in these mine catastrophes the rule is always to assume that buried men are alive, and he acted on this supposition. The first problem which he proposed to himself was to decide where they could have taken refuge. The captains and old miners whom he consulted were agreed on one point: in the face of the rising water the men had certainly come up from gallery to gallery to the highest cuttings, so that they were, without doubt, driven to the end of the upper passages. This agreed with Father Mouque's information, and his confused narrative even gave reason to suppose that in the wild flight the band had separated into smaller groups, leaving fugitives on the road at every level. But the captains were not unanimous when the discussion of possible attempts at rescue arose. As the passages nearest to the surface were a hundred and fifty mètres down, there could be no question of sinking a shaft. Réquillart remained the one means of access, the only point by which they could approach. The worst was that the old pit, now also inundated, no longer communicated with the Voreux; and above the level of the water only a few ends of galleries belonging to the first level were left free. The pumping process would require years, and the best plan would be to visit these galleries and ascertain if any of them approached the submerged passages at the end of which the distressed miners were suspected to be. Before logically arriving at this point, much discussion had been necessary to dispose of a crowd of impracticable plans.

Négrel now began to stir up the dust of the archives; he discovered the old plans of the two pits, studied them, and decided on the points at which their investigations ought to be carried on. Gradually this hunt excited him; he was, in his turn, seized by a fever of devotion, in spite of his ironical indifference to men and things. The first difficulty was in going down at Réquillart; it was necessary to clear out the rubbish from the mouth of the shaft, to pull down the mountain ash, and raze the sloes and the hawthorns; they had also to repair the ladders. Then they began to feel around. The engineer, having gone down with ten workmen, made them strike the iron of their tools against certain parts of the seam which he pointed out to them; and in deep silence they each placed an ear to the coal, listening for any distant blows to reply. But they went in vain through every practicable gallery; no echo returned to them. Their embarrassment increased. At what spot should they cut into the bed? Towards whom should they go, since no one appeared to be there? They persisted in seeking, however, notwithstanding the exhaustion produced by their growing anxiety.

On the first day, Maheude came in the morning to Réquillart. She sat down on a beam in front of the shaft, and did not stir from it till the evening. When a man came up, she rose and questioned him with her eyes: Nothing? No, nothing! And she sat down again, and waited still, without a word, with hard, fixed face. Jeanlin also, seeing that his den was invaded, prowled around with the frightened air of a beast of prey whose burrow will betray his booty. He thought of the little soldier lying beneath the rocks, fearing lest they should trouble his sound sleep; but that side of the mine was beneath the water; and, besides, their investigations were directed more to the left, in the west gallery. At first, Philomène had also come, accompanying Zacharie, who was one of the gang; then she became wearied at catching cold, without need or result, and went back to the settlement, dragging through her days, a limp indifferent woman, occupied from morning to night in coughing. Zacharie, on the contrary, lived for nothing else; he would have devoured the soil to get back his sister. At night he shouted out that he saw her, he heard her, very lean from hunger, her chest sore with calling for help. Since that he had tried to dig without orders, saying that it was there, that he was sure of it. The engineer would not let him come down any more, and he would not go away from the pit, from which he was driven off; he could not even sit down and wait near his mother, he was so deeply stirred by the need to act, which drove him constantly on.

It was the third day. Négrel, in despair, had resolved to abandon the attempt in the evening. At mid-day, after lunch, when he came back with his men to make one last effort, he was surprised to see Zacharie, red and gesticulating, come out of the mine shouting:

"She's there! She's replied to me! Come along, quickly!"

He had slid down the ladders, in spite of the watchman, and was declaring that he had heard hammering over there, in the first passage of the Guillaume seam.

"But we have already been twice in that direction," Négrel observed sceptically. "Anyhow, we'll go and see."

Maheude had risen, and had to be prevented from going down. She waited, standing at the edge of the shaft, gazing down into the darkness of the hole.

Négrel, down below, himself struck three blows, at long intervals. He then applied his ear to the coal, cautioning the workers to be very silent. Not a sound reached him, and he shook his head; evidently the poor lad was dreaming. In a fury, Zacharie struck in his turn, and listened anew with bright eyes and limbs trembling with joy. Then the other workmen tried the experiment, one after the other, and all grew animated, hearing the distant reply, very far away. The engineer was astonished; he again applied his ear, and was at last able to catch a sound of aerial softness, a rhythmical roll scarcely to be distinguished, the well-known cadence beaten by the miners when they are fighting against the coal in the midst of danger. The coal transmits the sound with crystalline limpidity for a very great distance. A captain who was there estimated that the thickness of the block which separated them from their mates could not be less than fifty mètres. But it seemed as if they could already stretch out a hand to them, and general gladness broke out. Négrel had to begin at once the work of approach.

When Zacharie, up above, saw Maheude again, they embraced each other.

"It won't do to get excited," Pierronne, who had come for a

visit of inquisitiveness, was cruel enough to say. "If Catherine isn't there, it would be such a grief afterwards!"

That was true; Catherine might be somewhere else.

"Just leave me alone, will you? Damn it!" cried Zacharie, in a rage. "She's there; I know it!"

Maheude sat down again in silence, with motionless face, continuing to wait.

As soon as the story was spread at Montsou, a new crowd arrived. Nothing was to be seen; but they remained there all the same, and had to be kept at a distance. Down below, the work went on day and night. For fear of meeting an obstacle, the engineer had had three descending galleries opened in the seam, converging to the point where the enclosed miners were supposed to be. Only one pikeman could hew at the coal on the narrow face of the tube; he was relieved every two hours, and the coal piled in was passed up, from hand to hand, by a chain of men, increased as the hole was hollowed out. The work at first proceeded very quickly; they did six mètres a day.

Zacharie had secured a place among the workers chosen for the hewing. It was a post of honour which was disputed over, and he became furious when they wished to relieve him after his two hours of regulation labour. He robbed his mates of their turn, and refused to let go the axe. His gallery was soon in advance of the others. He fought against the coal so fiercely that his breath could be heard coming from the tube like the roar of a forge within his breast. When he came out, black and muddy, dizzy with fatigue, he fell to the ground and had to be wrapped up in a covering. Then, still tottering, he plunged back again, and the struggle began anew—the low, deep blows, the stifled groans, the victorious fury of massacre. The worst was that the coal now became hard; he twice broke his tool, and was exasperated that he could not get on so fast. He suffered also from the heat, which increased with every mètre of advance, and was unbearable at the end of this narrow hole where the air could not circulate. A hand ventilator worked well, but aeration was so inadequate that on three occasions it was necessary to take out fainting hewers who were being asphyxiated.

Négrel lived below with his men. His meals were sent down to him, and he sometimes slept for a couple of hours on a truss of straw, rolled in a cloak. The one thing that kept them up was the supplication of the wretches beyond, the call which was sounded ever more distinctly to hasten on the rescue. It now rang very clearly with a musical sonority, as though struck on the plates of a harmonica. It led them on; they advanced to this crystalline sound as men advance to the sound of cannon in battle. Every time that a pikeman was relieved, Négrel went down and struck, then applying his ear; and every time, so far, the reply had come, rapid and urgent. He had no doubt remaining, they were advancing in the right direction, but with what fatal slowness! They would never arrive soon enough. On the first two days they had indeed hewn through thirteen mètres; but on the third day they fell to five, and then on the fourth to three. The coal was becoming closer and harder, to such an extent that they now with difficulty struck through two mètres. On the ninth day, after superhuman efforts, they had advanced thirty-two mètres, and calculated that some twenty must still be left before them. For the prisoners it was the beginning of the twelfth day; twelve times over had they passed twenty-four hours without bread, without fire, in that icy darkness! This awful idea moistened the eyelids and stiffened the arms of the workers. It seemed impossible that Christians could live longer. The distant blows had become weaker since the previous day, and every moment they trembled lest they should stop.

Maheude came regularly every morning to sit at the mouth of the shaft. In her arms she brought Estelle, who could not remain alone from morning to night. Hour by hour she followed the workers, sharing their hopes and fears. There was feverish expectation among the groups standing around, and even as far as Montsou, with endless discussion. Every heart in the district was beating down there beneath the earth.

On the ninth day, at the breakfast hour, no reply came from Zacharie when he was called for the relay. He was like a madman, working on furiously with oaths. Négrel, who had come up for a moment, was not there to make him obey, and only a captain with three miners were below. No doubt Zacharie, infuriated with the feeble vacillating light, committed the imprudence of opening his lamp, although severe orders had been given, for leakages of fire-damp had taken place, and the gas remained in enormous masses in these narrow, unventilated passages. Suddenly, a roar of thunder was heard, and a spout of fire darted out of the tube as from the mouth of a cannon charged with grapeshot. Everything flamed up and the air caught fire like powder, from one end of the galleries to the other. This torrent of flame carried away the captain and three workers, ascended the pit, and leapt up to the daylight in an eruption which hid the rocks and the ruins around. The inquisitive fled, and Maheude arose, pressing the frightened Estelle to her breast.

When Négrel and the men came back they were seized by a terrible rage. They struck their heels into the earth, as a stepmother who was killing her children at random in the imbecile whims of her cruelty. They were devoting themselves, they were coming to the help of their mates, and still they must lose some of their men! After three long hours of effort and danger they reached the galleries once more, and the melancholy ascent of the victims took place. Neither the captain nor the workers were dead, but they were covered by awful wounds which gave out an odour of grilled flesh; they had drunk of fire, the burns had got into their throats, and they constantly moaned and prayed to be left alone. One of the three miners was the man who had smashed the pump at Gaston-Marie with a final blow of the shovel during the strike; the two others still had scars on their hands, and grazed torn fingers from the energy with which they had thrown bricks at the soldiers. The pale and shuddering crowd took off their hats when they were carried by.

Maheude stood waiting. Zacharie's body at last appeared. The clothes were burnt, the body was nothing but black charcoal, calcined and unrecognisable. The head had been smashed by the explosion and no longer existed. And when these awful remains were placed on a stretcher, Maheude followed them mechanically, her burning eyelids without a tear. With Estelle drowsily lying in her arms, she went along, a tragic figure, her hair lashed by the wind. At the settlement Philomène seemed stupid; her eyes were turned into fountains and she was quickly relieved. But the mother had already returned with the same step to Réquillart; she had accompanied her son, she was returning to wait for her daughter.

Three days more passed by. The rescue work had been resumed amid incredible difficulties. The galleries of approach had fortunately not fallen after the fire-damp explosion; but the air was so heavy and so vitiated that more ventilators had to be installed. Every twenty minutes the pikemen relieved one another. They were advancing; scarcely two mètres separated them from their mates. But now they worked feeling cold at their hearts, striking hard only out of vengeance; for the noises had ceased, and the low, clear cadence of the call no longer sounded. It was the twelfth day of their labours, the fifteenth since the catastrophe; and since the morning there had been a death-like silence.

The new accident increased the curiosity at Montsou, and the inhabitants organised excursions with such spirit that the Grégoires decided to follow the fashion. They arranged a party, and it was agreed that they should go to the Voreux in their carriage, while Madame Hennebeau took Lucie and Jeanne there in hers. Deneulin would show them over his yards, and then they would return by Réquillart, where Négrel would tell them the exact state of things in the galleries, and if there was still hope. Finally, they would dine together in the evening.

When the Grégoires and their daughter Cécile arrived at the ruined mine, towards three o'clock, they found Madame Hennebeau already there, in a sea-blue dress, protecting herself under her parasol from the pale February sun. The warmth of spring was in the clear sky. M. Hennebeau was there with Deneulin, and she was listening, with listless ear, to the account which the latter gave her of the efforts which had been made to dam up the canal. Jeanne, who always carried a sketch-book with her, began to draw, carried away by the horror of the subject; while Lucie, seated beside her on the remains of a waggon, was crying out with pleasure, and finding it awfully jolly. The incomplete dam allowed numerous leaks, and frothy streams fell in a cascade down the enormous hole of the engulfed mine. The crater was being emptied, however, and the water, drunk by the earth, was sinking, and revealing the fearful ruin at the bottom. Beneath the tender azure of this beautiful day there lay a sewer, the ruins of a town drowned and melted in mud.

"And people came out of their way to see that!" exclaimed M. Grégoire, disillusioned.

Cécile, rosy with health and glad to breathe so pure an air, was cheerfully joking, while Madame Hennebeau made a little grimace of repugnance as she murmured:

"The fact is, this is not pretty at all."

The two engineers laughed. They tried to interest the visitors, taking them round and explaining to them the working of the pumps and the manipulation of the stamper which drove in the piles. But the ladies became anxious. They shuddered when they knew that the pumps would have to work for six or seven years before the shaft was reconstructed and all the water exhausted from the mine. No, they would rather think of something else; this destruction was only good to give bad dreams.

"Let us go," said Madame Hennebeau, turning towards her carriage.

Lucie and Jeanne protested. What! so soon! and the drawing, which was not finished! They wanted to remain; their father would bring them to dinner in the evening. M. Hennebeau alone took his place with his wife in the carriage, for he wished to question Négrel.

"Very well! go on before," said M. Grégoire. "We will follow you; we have a little visit of five minutes to make over there at the settlement. Go on, go on! we shall be at Réquillart as soon as you."

He got up behind Madame Grégoire and Cécile, and while the other carriage went along by the canal, theirs gently ascended the slope.

Their excursion was to be completed by a visit of charity. Zacharie's death had filled them with pity for this tragical Maheu family, about whom the whole country was talking. They had no pity for the father, that brigand, that slayer of soldiers, who had had to be struck down like a wolf. But the mother touched them, that poor woman who had just lost her son after having lost her husband, and whose daughter was perhaps a corpse beneath the earth; to say nothing of an invalid grandfather, a child who was lame as the result of a landslip, and a little girl, who died of starvation during the strike. So that, though this family had in part deserved its misfortunes by the detestable spirit it had shown, they had resolved to assert the breadth of their charity, their desire for forgetfulness and conciliation by themselves bringing an alms. Two parcels, carefully wrapped up, had been placed beneath a seat of the carriage.

An old woman pointed out to the coachman Maheude's house, No. 16 in the second block. But when the Grégoires alighted with the parcels, they knocked in vain and at last struck their fists against the door, still without reply; the house echoed mournfully, like a house emptied by grief, frozen and black, long since abandoned.

"There's no one there," said Cécile, disappointed. "What a nuisance! What shall we do with all this?"

Suddenly the door at the side opened, and the Levaque woman appeared.

"Oh, sir! I beg pardon, ma'am. Excuse me, miss. It's the neighbour that you want? She's not there; she's at Réquillart."

With a flow of words she told them the story, repeating to them that people must help one another, and that she was keeping Lénore and Henri in her house to allow the mother to go and wait over there. Her eyes had fallen on the parcels, and she began to talk about her poor daughter, who had become a widow, displaying her own wretchedness, while her eyes shone with covetousness. Then, in a hesitating way, she muttered:

"I've got the key. If the lady and gentleman would really like——The grandfather is there."

The Grégoires looked at her in stupefaction. What! The grandfather was there! But no one had replied. He was sleeping, then? And when the Levaque made up her mind to open the door, what they saw stopped them on the threshold. Bonnemort was there alone, with large fixed eyes, nailed to his chair in front of the cold fireplace. Around him the room appeared larger without the clock or the polished deal furniture which formerly animated it; there only remained against the green crudity of the walls the portraits of the Emperor and Empress, whose rosy lips were smiling with official benevolence. The old man did not stir nor wink his eyelids beneath the sudden light from the door; he seemed imbecile, as though he had not seen all these people come in. At his feet lay his plate, garnished with ashes, such as is placed for cats for ordure.

"Don't mind if he's not very polite," said the Levaque woman, obligingly. "Seems he's broken something in his brain. It's a fortnight since he left off speaking."

But Bonnemort was shaken by some agitation, a deep scraping which seemed to arise from his belly, and he expectorated into the plate a thick black expectoration. The ashes were soaked into a coaly mud, all the coal of the mine which he drew from his chest. He had already resumed his immobility. He stirred no more, except at intervals, to spit.

Uneasy, and with stomachs turned, the Grégoires endeavoured to utter a few friendly and encouraging words.

"Well, my good man," said the father, "you have a cold, then?"

The old man, with his eyes to the wall, did not turn his head. And a heavy silence fell once more.

"They ought to make you a little gruel," added the mother.

He preserved his mute stiffness.

"I say, papa," murmured Cécile, "they certainly told us he was an invalid; only we did not think of it afterwards——"

She interrupted herself, much embarrassed. After having placed on the table a *pot-au-feu* and two bottles of wine, she undid the second parcel and drew from it a pair of enormous boots. It was the present intended for the grandfather, and she held one boot in each hand, in confusion, contemplating the poor man's swollen feet, which would never walk more.

"Eh! they come a little late, don't they, my worthy fellow?" said M. Grégoire again, to enliven the situation. "It doesn't matter, they're always useful."

Bonnemort neither heard nor replied, with his terrible face as cold and as hard as a stone.

Then Cécile furtively placed the boots against the wall. But in spite of her precautions the nails clanked; and those enormous boots stood oppressively in the room.

"He won't say thank you," said the Levaque woman, who had

cast a look of deep envy on the boots. "Might as well give a pair of spectacles to a duck, asking your pardon."

She went on; she was trying to draw the Grégoires into her own house, where she hoped to gain their pity. At last she thought of a pretext; she praised Henri and Lénore, who were so good, so gentle and so intelligent, answering like angels the questions that they were asked. They would tell the lady and gentleman all that they wished to know.

"Will you come for a moment, my child?" asked the father, glad to get away.

"Yes, I'll follow you," she replied.

Cécile remained alone with Bonnemort. What kept her there, trembling and fascinated, was the thought that she seemed to recognise this old man: where then had she met this square livid face, tatooed with coal? Suddenly she remembered; she saw again a mob of shouting people who surrounded her, and she felt cold hands pressing her neck. It was he; she saw the man again; she looked at his hands placed on his knees, the hands of an invalid workman whose whole strength is in his wrists, still firm in spite of age. Gradually Bonnemort seemed to awake; he perceived her and examined her in his turn. A flame mounted to his cheeks, a nervous spasm drew his mouth, from which flowed a thin streak of black saliva. Fascinated, they remained opposite each other—she flourishing, plump and fresh from the long idleness and sated comfort of her race; he swollen with water, with the pitiful ugliness of a foundered beast, destroyed from father to son by a century of work and hunger.

At the end of ten minutes, when the Grégoires, surprised at not seeing Cécile, came back into the Maheus' house, they uttered a terrible cry. Their daughter was lying on the ground, with livid face, strangled. At her neck fingers had left the red imprint of a giant's hand. Bonnemort, tottering on his dead legs, had fallen beside her without power to rise. His hands were still hooked, and he looked round with his imbecile air and large open eyes. In his fall he had broken his plate, the ashes were spread round, the mud of the black expectoration had stained the floor; while the pair of large boots, safe and sound, stood side by side against the wall.

It was never possible to establish the exact facts. Why had Cécile come near? How could Bonnemort, nailed to his chair, have been able to seize her throat? Evidently, when he held her, he must have become furious, constantly pressing, overthrown with her, and stifling her cries to the last groan. Not a sound, not a moan had traversed the thin partition to the neighbouring house. It seemed to be an outbreak of sudden madness, an inexplicable longing to murder before this white girl's neck. Such savagery was stupefying in an old invalid, who had lived like a worthy man, an obedient brute, opposed to new ideas. What rancour, unknown to himself, by some slow process of poisoning, had risen from his bowels to his brain? The horror of it led to the conclusion that he was unconscious, that it was the crime of an idiot.

The Grégoires, however, on their knees, were sobbing, choked with grief. Their idolised daughter, that daughter desired so long, on whom they had lavished all their goods, whom they used to watch sleeping, on tiptoe, whom they never thought sufficiently well nourished, never sufficiently plump! It was the downfall of their very life; what was the good of living, now that they would live without her?

The Levaque woman in distraction cried:

"Ah, the old bugger! what's he done there? Who would have expected such a thing? And Maheude, who won't come back till evening! Shall I go and fetch her?"

The father and mother were crushed, and did not reply.

"Eh? It will be better. I'll go."

But, before going, the Levaque woman looked at the boots. The whole settlement was excited, and a crowd was already hustling around. Perhaps they would get stolen. And then the Maheus had no man, now, to put them on. She gently carried them away. They would just fit Bouteloup's feet.

At Réquillart the Hennebeaus, with Négrel, waited a long time for the Grégoires. Négrel, who had come up from the pit, gave details. They hoped to communicate that very evening with the prisoners, but they would certainly find nothing but corpses, for the death-like silence continued. Behind the engineer Maheude, seated on the beam, was listening with white face, when the Levaque woman came up and told her the old man's strange deed. And she only made a sweeping gesture of impatience and irritation. She followed her, however.

Madame Hennebeau was much affected. What an abomination! That poor Cécile, so merry this very day, so full of life an hour before! M. Hennebeau had to lead his wife for a moment into old Mouque's hovel. With his awkward hands, he unfastened the dress, troubled by the odour of musk which her open bodice exhaled. And as with streaming tears she clasped Négrel, terrified at this death which cut short the marriage, the husband watched them lamenting together, and was delivered from one anxiety. This misfortune would arrange everything; he preferred to keep his nephew for fear of his coachman.

## CHAPTER V

AT THE BOTTOM OF the shaft the abandoned wretches were yelling with terror. The water now came up to their hips. The noise of the torrent dazed them, the final falling in of the tubbing sounded like the last crack of doom; and their bewilderment was completed by the neighing of the horses shut up in the stable, the terrible unforgettable death-cry of an animal that is being slaughtered.

Mouque had let go Bataille. The old horse was there trembling, with its dilated eye fixed on this water which was constantly rising. The pit-eye was rapidly filling; the greenish flood slowly enlarged under the red gleam of the three lamps which were still burning under the roof. And suddenly, when he felt this ice soaking his coat, he set out in a furious gallop, and was engulfed and lost at the end of one of the haulage galleries.

Then there was a general rush, the men following the beast.

"Nothing more to be done in this damned hole!" shouted Mouque. "We must try at Réquillart."

This idea, that they might get out by the old neighbouring pit if they arrived before the passage was cut off, now carried them away. The twenty hustled one another as they went in single file, holding their lamps in the air so that the water should not extinguish them. Fortunately, the gallery rose with an imperceptible slope, and they proceeded for two hundred mètres struggling against the flood, which was not now gaining on them. Sleeping beliefs re-awakened in these distracted souls; they invoked the earth, for it was the earth that was avenging herself, liberating the blood from the vein because they had cut one of her arteries. An old man stammered forgotten prayers, bending his thumbs backwards to appease the evil spirits of the mine.

But at the first turning disagreement broke out; the groom proposed turning to the left, others declared that they could make a short cut by going to the right. A minute was lost.

"Well, die there! what the devil does it matter to me?" Chaval brutally exclaimed. "I go this way."

He turned to the right, and two mates followed him. The others continued to rush behind Father Mouque, who had grown up at the bottom of Réquillart. He himself hesitated, however, not knowing where to turn. They lost their heads; even the old men could no longer recognise the passages, which lay like a tangled skein before them. At every bifurcation they were pulled short by uncertainty, and yet they had to decide.

Étienne was running last, delayed by Catherine, who was paralysed by fatigue and fear. He would have gone to the right with Chaval, for he thought that the better road; but he had left him, careless whether he remained behind. The rush continued, however; some of the mates had gone from their side, and only seven were left behind old Mouque.

"Hang on to my neck and I will carry you," said Étienne to the young girl, seeing her grow weak.

"No, let me be," she murmured. "I can't do more; I would rather die at once."

They delayed and were left fifty mètres behind; he was lifting her, in spite of her resistance, when the gallery was suddenly stopped up; an enormous block fell in and separated them from the others. The inundation was already soaking the soil, which was shifting on every side. They had to retrace their steps; then they no longer knew in what direction they were going. There was an end of all hope of escaping by Réquillart. Their only remaining hope was to gain the upper workings, from which they might perhaps be delivered if the water sank.

Étienne at last recognised the Guillaume seam.

"Good!" he exclaimed. "Now I know where we are. By God! we were in the right road; but we may go to the devil. now! Here, let us go straight on; we will climb up the passage."

The flood was beating against their breasts, and they walked very slowly. As long as they had light they did not despair, and they blew out one of the lamps to economise the oil, meaning to empty it into the other lamp. They had reached the chimney passage, when a noise behind made them turn. Was it some mates, then, who had also found the road barred and were returning? A roaring sound came from afar; they could not understand this tempest which approached them, bespattering foam. And they cried out when they saw a gigantic whitish mass coming out of the shadow and trying to rejoin them between the narrow timbering in which it was crushed.

It was Bataille. On leaving the pit-eye he had wildly galloped along the dark galleries. He seemed to know his road in this subterranean town which he had inhabited for eleven years, and his eyes saw clearly in the depths of the eternal night in which he had lived. He galloped on and on, bending his head, drawing up his feet, passing through these narrow tubes in the earth, filled by his great body. Road succeeded to road, and the forked turnings were passed without any hesitation. Where was he going? Over there, perhaps, towards that vision of his youth, to the mill where he had been born on the bank of the Scarpe, to the confused recollection of the sun burning in the air like a great lamp. He desired to live, his beast's memory awoke; the longing to breathe once more the air of the plains drove him straight onwards to the discovery of that hole, the exit beneath the warm sun into light. Rebellion carried away his ancient resignation; this pit was murdering him after having blinded him. The water which pursued him was lashing him on the flanks and biting him on the crupper. But as he went deeper in the galleries became narrower, the roofs lower, and the walls protruded. He galloped on in spite of everything, grazing himself, leaving fragments of his limbs on the timber. From every side the mine seemed to be pressing on to him to take him and to stifle him.

Then Étienne and Catherine, as he came near them, perceived that he was strangling between the rocks. He had stumbled and broken his two front legs. With a last effort, he dragged himself a few mètres, but his flanks could not pass; he remained wrapped up and garrotted by the earth. With his bleeding head stretched out, he still sought for some crack with his great troubled eyes. The water was rapidly covering him; he began to neigh with that terrible prolonged death-rattle with which the other horses had already died in the stable. It was a sight of fearful agony, this old beast fractured and motionless, struggling at this depth, far from the daylight. The flood was drowning his mane, and his cry of distress never ceased; he uttered it more hoarsely, with his large open mouth stretched out. There was a last rumble, the hollow sound of a cask which is being filled; then deep silence fell.

"Oh, my God! take me away!" Catherine sobbed. "Ah, my God! I'm afraid; I don't want to die. Take me away! take me away!"

She had seen death. The fallen shaft, the inundated mine, nothing had seized her with such terror as this clamour of Bataille in agony. And she constantly heard it; her ears were ringing with it; all her flesh was shuddering with it.

"Take me away! take me away!"

Étienne had seized her and lifted her; it was, indeed, time. They ascended the chimney passage, soaked to the shoulders. He was obliged to help her, for she had no strength to cling to the timber. Three times over he thought that she was slipping from him and falling back into that deep sea of which the tide was roaring beneath them. However, they were able to breathe for a few minutes when they reached the first gallery, which was still free. The water reappeared, and they had to hoist themselves up again. And for hours this ascent continued, the flood chasing them from passage to passage, and constantly forcing them to ascend. At the sixth level a respite rendered them feverish with hope, and it seemed that the waters were becoming stationary. But a more rapid rise took place, and they had to climb to the seventh and then to the eighth levels. Only one remained, and when they had reached it they anxiously watched each centimètre by which the water gained on them. If it did not stop they would then die like the old horse, crushed against the roof, and their chests filled by the flood.

Landslips echoed every moment. The whole mine was shaken, and its distended bowels burst with the enormous flood which gorged them. At the end of the galleries the air, driven back, pressed together and crushed, exploded terribly amid split rocks and overthrown soil. It was a terrifying uproar of interior cataclysms, a remnant of the ancient battle when deluges overthrew the earth, burying the mountains beneath the plains.

And Catherine, shaken and dazed by this continuous downfall, joined her hands, stammering the same words without cessation:

"I don't want to die! I don't want to die!"

To reassure her, Étienne declared that the water was not now moving. Their flight had lasted for fully six hours, and they would soon be rescued. He said six hours without knowing, for they had lost all count of time. In reality, a whole day had already passed in their climb up through the Guillaume seam.

Damp and shivering, they settled themselves down. She undressed herself without shame and wrung her clothes; then she put on again the jacket and breeches, and let them finish drying on her. As her feet were bare, he made her take his own sabots. They could wait patiently now; they had lowered the wick of the lamp, leaving only the feeble gleam of a night-light. But their stomachs were torn by cramp, and they both realised that they were dying of hunger. Up till now they had not felt that they were living. The catastrophe had occurred before breakfast, and they now found their bread-and-butter, swollen by the water and changed into sop. She had to become angry before he would accept his share. As soon as she had eaten she fell asleep from weariness, on the cold earth. He was devoured by insomnia, and watched over her with fixed eyes and forehead between his hands.

How many hours passed by thus? He would have been unable to say. All that he knew was that before him, through the hole they had ascended, he had seen the flood disappear, black and moving, the beast whose back was ceaselessly swelling out to reach them. At first it was only a thin line, a supple serpent stretching itself out; then it enlarged into a crawling, crouching flank; and soon it reached them, and the sleeping young girl's feet were touched by it. In his anxiety he yet hesitated to wake her. Was it not cruel to snatch her from this repose of unconscious ignorance, which was, perhaps, lulling her with a dream of the open air and of life beneath the sun? Besides, where could they fly? And he thought and remembered that the upbrow established at this part of the seam communicated end to end with that which served the upper level. That would be a way out. He let her sleep as long as possible, watching the flood gain on them, waiting for it to chase them away. At last he lifted her gently, and a great shudder passed over her.

"Ah, my God! it's true! it's beginning again, my God!"

She remembered, she cried out, again finding death so near.

"No! calm yourself," he whispered. "We can pass, upon my word!"

To reach the upbrow they had to walk doubled up, again wetted to the shoulders. And the climbing began anew, now more dangerous, through this hole entirely of timber, a hundred mètres long. At first they wished to pull the cable so as to fix one of the carts below, for if the other should come down during their ascent, they would have been crushed. But nothing moved, some obstacle interfered with the mechanism. They ventured in, not daring to make use of the cable which was in their way, and tearing their nails against the smooth framework. He came behind, supporting her by his head when she slipped with torn hands. Suddenly they came across the splinters of a beam which barred the way. A portion of the soil had fallen down and prevented them from going any higher. Fortunately, a door opened here and they passed into a passage. They were stupefied to see the flicker of a lamp in front of them. A man cried wildly to them:

"More clever people as big fools I am!"

They recognised Chaval, who had found himself blocked by the landslip which filled the upbrow; and his two mates who had set out with him had been left on the way with fractured skulls. He was wounded in the elbow, but he had had the courage to go back on his knees, take their lamps, and search them to steal their bread-and-butter. As he escaped, a final downfall behind his back had closed the gallery.

He immediately swore that he would not share his victuals with these people who came up out of the earth. He would sooner knock their brains out. Then he, too, recognised them; his anger fell, and he began to laugh with a laugh of evil joy.

"Ah! it's you, Catherine! you've broken your nose, and you want to join your man again. Well, well! We'll play out the game together."

He pretended not to see Étienne. The latter, overwhelmed by this encounter, made a gesture as though to protect the putter, who was pressing herself against him. He must, however, accept the situation. Speaking as though they had left each other good friends an hour before, he simply asked:

"Have you looked down below? We can't pass through the cuttings, then?"

Chaval still grinned.

"Ah, bosh! the cuttings! They've fallen in too; we are between two walls, a real mousetrap. But you can go back by the brow if you are a good diver."

The water, in fact, was rising; they could hear it rippling. Their retreat was already cut off. And he was right; it was a mousetrap, a gallery end obstructed before and behind by considerable falls of earth. There was not one issue; all three were walled up.

"Then you'll stay?" Chaval added, jeeringly. "Well, it's the best you can do, and if you'll just leave me alone, I shan't even speak to you. There's still room here for two men. We shall soon see which will die first, provided they don't come to us, which seems to me a tough job."

The young man said:

"If we were to hammer, they would, perhaps hear us."

"I'm tired of hammering. Here, try yourself with this stone."

Étienne picked up the fragment of sandstone which the other had already broken off, and against the seam at the end he struck the miner's call, the prolonged roll by which workmen in peril signal their presence. Then he placed his ear to listen. Twenty times over he persisted; no sound replied.

During this time Chaval affected to be coolly attending to his little household. First he arranged the three lamps against the wall; only one was burning, the others could be used later on. Afterwards, he placed on a piece of timber the two slices of bread-and-butter which were still left. That was the sideboard; he could last quite two days with that, if he were careful. He turned round saying:

"You know, Catherine, there will be half for you when you are famished."

The young girl was silent. It completed her unhappiness to find herself again between these two men.

And their awful life began. Neither Chaval nor Étienne opened their mouths, seated on the earth a few paces from each other. At a hint from the former the latter extinguished his lamp, a piece of useless luxury; then they sank back into silence. Catherine was lying down near Étienne, restless under the glances of her former lover. The hours passed by; they heard the low murmur of the water for ever rising; while from time to time deep shocks and distant echoes announced the final settling down of the mine. When the lamp was empty and they had to open another to light it, they were, for a moment, disturbed by the fear of fire-damp; but they would rather have been blown up at once than live on in darkness. Nothing exploded, however; there was no fire-damp. They stretched themselves out again, and the hours continued to pass by.

A noise aroused Étienne and Catherine, and they raised their heads. Chaval had decided to eat; he had cut off half of a slice of bread-and-butter, and was chewing it slowly, to avoid the temptation of swallowing it all. They gazed at him, tortured by hunger.

"Well, do you refuse?" he said to the putter, in his provoking way. "You're wrong."

She had lowered her eyes, fearing to yield; her stomach was torn by such cramps that tears were swelling beneath her eyelids. But she understood what he was asking; in the morning he had breathed over her neck; he was seized again by one of his old furies of desire on seeing her near the other man. The glances with which he called her had a flame in them which she knew well, the flame of his crisis of jealousy when he would fall on her with his fists, accusing her of committing abominations with her mother's lodger. And she was not willing; she trembled lest, by returning to him, she would throw these two men on to each other in this narrow cave, where they were all in agony together. Good God! why could they not end together in comradeship!

Étienne would have died of inanition rather than beg a mouthful of bread from Chaval. The silence became heavy; an eternity seemed to be prolonging itself with the slowness of monotonous minutes which passed by, one by one, without hope. They had now been shut up together for a day. The second lamp was growing pale, and they lighted the third.

Chaval started on his second slice of bread-and-butter, and growled:

"Come, then, stupid!"

Catherine shivered. Étienne had turned away in order to leave her free. Then, as she did not stir, he said to her in a low voice:

"Go, my child."

The tears which she was stifling then rushed forth. She wept for a long time, without even strength to rise, no longer knowing if she was hungry, suffering with pain which she felt all over her body. He was standing up, going backwards and forwards, vainly beating the miner's call, enraged at this remainder of life which he was obliged to live here tied to a rival whom he detested. Not even enough space to die away from each other! As soon as he had gone ten paces he must come back and knock up against this man. And she, this sorrowful girl whom they were disputing over even in the earth! She would belong to the one who lived longest; that man would still steal her from him should he go first. There was no end to it; the hours followed the hours; the revolting promiscuity became worse, with the poison of their breaths and the ordure of their necessities satisfied in common. Twice he rushed against the rocks as though to open them with his fists.

Another day was done, and Chaval had seated himself near Catherine, sharing with her his last half slice. She was chewing the mouthfuls painfully; he made her pay for each with a caress, in his jealous obstinacy not willing to die until he had had her again in the other man's presence. She abandoned herself in exhaustion. But when he tried to take her she complained.

"Oh, leave me! you're breaking my bones."

Étienne, with a shudder, had placed his forehead against the timber so as not to see. He came back with a wild leap.

"Leave her, by God!"

"Does it concern you?" said Chaval. "She's my wife; I suppose she belongs to me!"

And he took her again and pressed her, out of bravado, crushing his red moustaches over her mouth, and continuing:

"Will you leave us alone, eh? Will you be good enough to look over there if we are at it?"

But Étienne, with white lips, shouted:

"If you don't let her go, I'll do for you!"

The other quickly stood up, for he had understood by the hiss of the voice that his mate was in earnest. Death seemed to them too slow; it was necessary that one of them should immediately yield his place. It was the old battle beginning over again, down in the earth where they would soon sleep side by side; and they had so little room that they could not swing their fists without grazing them.

"Look out!" growled Chaval. "This time I'll have you."

From that moment Étienne became mad. His eyes seemed drowned in red vapour, his chest was congested by the flow of blood. The need to kill seized him irresistibly, a physical need, the bloody stimulus of mucus which causes a violent spasm of coughing. It rose and broke out beyond his will, beneath the pressure of the hereditary disease. He had seized a sheet of slate in the wall and he shook it and tore it out, a very large, heavy piece. Then with both hands and with exaggerated strength he brought it down on Chaval's skull.

The latter had no time to jump backwards. He fell, his face

crushed, his skull broken. The brain had bespattered the roof of the gallery, and a purple jet flowed from the wound, like the continuous jet of a spring. Immediately there was a pool, which reflected the smoky star of the lamp. Darkness was invading the walled-up cave, and this body, lying on the earth, looked like the black boss of a mass of rough coal.

Leaning over, with wide eyes, Étienne looked at him. It was, then, done; he had killed. All his struggles came back to his memory confusedly, that useless fight against the poison which slept in his muscles, the slowly accumulated alcohol of his race. He was, however, only intoxicated by hunger; the remote intoxication of his parents had been enough. His hair stood up before the horror of this murder; and yet, in spite of the revolt which came from his education, a certain gladness made his heart beat, the animal joy of an appetite at length satisfied. He felt pride, too, the pride of the stronger man. The little soldier appeared before him, with his throat opened by a knife, killed by a child. Now he, too, had killed.

But Catherine, standing erect, uttered a loud cry:

"My God! he is dead!"

"Are you sorry?" asked Étienne, fiercely.

She was choking, she stammered. Then, tottering, she threw herself into his arms.

"Ah, kill me too! Ah, let us both die!"

She clasped him, hanging to his shoulders, and he clasped her; and they hoped that they would die. But Death was in no hurry, and they unlocked their arms. Then, while she hid her eyes, he dragged away the wretch, and threw him down the upbrow, to remove him from the narrow space in which they still had to live. Life would no longer have been possible with that corpse beneath their feet. And they were terrified when they heard it plunge into the midst of the foam which leapt up. The water had, then, already filled that hole? They saw it; it was entering the gallery.

Then there was a new struggle. They had lighted the last lamp; it was becoming exhausted in illuminating this flood, with its regular, obstinate rise which never ceased. At first the water came up to their ankles; then it wetted their knees. The passage sloped up, and they took refuge at the end. This gave them a respite for some hours. But the flood caught them up, and bathed them to the waist. Standing up, brought to bay, with their spines close against the rock, they watched it ever and ever increasing. When it should reach their mouths, all would be over. The lamp, which they had fastened up, threw a yellow light on the rapid surge of the little waves. It was becoming pale; they could distinguish no more than a constantly diminishing semicircle, as though eaten away by the darkness which seemed to grow with the flood; and suddenly the darkness enveloped them. The lamp had gone out, after having spit forth its last drop of oil. There was now complete and absolute night, that night of the earth which they would have to sleep through without ever again opening their eyes to the brightness of the sun.

"By God!" Étienne swore, in a low voice.

Catherine, as though she had felt the darkness seize her, sheltered herself against him. She repeated, in a whisper, the miner's saying:

"Death is blowing out the lamp."

Yet in the face of this threat their instincts struggled, the fever of living animated them. He violently set himself to hollow out the slate with the hook of the lamp, while she helped him with her nails. They formed a sort of elevated bench, and when they had both hoisted themselves up to it, they found themselves seated with hanging legs and bent backs, for the vault forced them to lower their heads. They now only felt the icy water at their heels; but before long the cold was at their ankles, their calves, their knees, with its invincible, truceless movement. The bench, not properly smoothed, was soaked in moisture, and so slippery that they had to hold themselves on vigorously to avoid slipping off. It was the end; what could they expect, reduced to this niche where they dared not move, exhausted, starving, having neither bread nor light? and they suffered especially from the darkness, which would not allow them to see the coming of death. There was deep silence; the mine, being gorged with water, no longer stirred. They had nothing beneath them now but the sensation of that sea, swelling out from the depths of the galleries its silent tide.

The hours succeeded one another, all equally black; but they were not able to measure their exact duration, becoming more and more vague in their calculation of time. Their tortures, which might have been expected to lengthen the minutes, rapidly bore them away. They thought that they had only been shut up for two days and a night, when in reality the third day had already come to an end. All hope of help had gone; no one knew they were there, no one could come down to them. And hunger would finish them off if the inundation spared them. For one last time it occurred to them to beat the call, but the stone was lying beneath the water. Besides, who would hear them?

Catherine was leaning her aching head against the seam, when she sat up with a start.

"Listen!" she said.

At first Étienne thought she was speaking of the low noise of the ever rising water. He lied in order to quiet her.

"It's me you hear; I'm moving my legs."

"No, no; not that! Over there, listen!"

And she placed her ear to the coal. He understood, and did likewise. They waited for some seconds, with stifled breath. Then, very far away and very weak, they heard three blows at long intervals. But they still doubted; their ears were ringing; perhaps it was the cracking of the soil. And they knew not what to strike with in answer.

Étienne had an idea.

"You have the sabots. Take your feet out and strike with the heels."

She struck, beating the miner's call; and they listened and again distinguished the three blows far off. Twenty times over they did it, and twenty times the blows replied. They wept and embraced each other, at the risk of losing their balance. At last the mates were there, they were coming. An over-flowing joy and love carried away the torments of expectation and the rage of their vain appeals, as though their rescuers had only to split the rock with a finger to deliver them.

"Eh!" she cried merrily; "wasn't it lucky that I leant my head?"

"Oh, you've got an ear!" he said, in his turn. "Now, *I* heard nothing."

From that moment they relieved each other, one of them always listening, ready to answer at the least signal. They soon caught the sounds of the pick; the work of approaching them was beginning, a gallery was being opened. But their joy sank. In vain they laughed to deceive each other; despair was gradually seizing them. At first they entered into long explanations; evidently they were being approached from Réquillart. The gallery descended in the bed; perhaps several were being opened, for there were always three men hewing. Then they talked less, and were at last silent when they came to calculate the enormous mass which separated them from their mates. They continued their reflections in silence, counting the days and days that a workman would take to penetrate such a block. They would never be reached soon enough; they would have time to die twenty times over. And no longer venturing to exchange a word in this redoubled anguish, they gloomily replied to the appeals by a roll of the sabots, without hope, only retaining the mechanical need to tell the others that they were still alive.

Thus passed a day, two days. They had been at the bottom six days. The water had stopped at their knees, neither rising nor falling, and their legs seemed to be melting away in this icy bath. They could certainly keep them out for an hour or so, but their position then became so uncomfortable that they were twisted by horrible cramps, and were obliged to let their feet fall in again. Every ten minutes they hoisted themselves back by a jerk on the slippery rock. The fractures of the coal struck into their spines, and they felt at the back of their necks a fixed intense pain, through having to keep constantly bent in order to avoid striking their heads. And their suffocation increased; the air, driven back by the water, was compressed into a sort of bell, in which they were shut up. Their voices were muffled, and seemed to come from afar. Their ears began to buzz, they heard the peals of a furious tocsin, the tramp of a flock beneath a storm of hail, going on unceasingly.

At first Catherine suffered horribly from hunger. She pressed her poor shrivelled hands against her breasts, her breathing was deep and hollow, a continuous tearing moan, as though tongs were tearing her stomach.

Étienne, choked by the same torture, was feeling feverishly round him in the darkness, when his fingers came upon a half-rotten piece of timber, which his nails could crumble. He gave a handful of it to the putter, who swallowed it greedily. For two days they lived on this worm-eaten wood, devouring it whole, in despair when it was finished, grazing their hands in the effort to crush the other planks which were still solid with resisting fibres. Their torture increased, and they were enraged that they could not chew the cloth of their clothes. A leather girdle, which he wore round the waist, relieved them a little. He bit small pieces from it with his teeth, and she chewed them, and endeavoured to swallow them. This occupied their jaws, and gave them the illusion of eating. Then, when the girdle was finished, they went back to their clothes, sucking them for hours.

But soon these violent crises grew calm; hunger became only a low deep ache with the slow progressive languor of their strength. No doubt they would have succumbed if they had not had as much water as they desired. They merely bent down and drank from the hollow of the hand, and that very frequently, parched by a thirst which all this water could not quench.

On the seventh day Catherine was bending down to drink, when her hand struck some floating body before her.

"I say, look! What's this?"

Étienne felt in the darkness.

"I can't make out; it seems like the cover of the ventilation door."

She drank, but as she was drawing up a second mouthful the body came back; striking her hand. And she uttered a terrible cry.

"My God! it's he!"

"Whom do you mean?"

"Him! You know well enough. I felt his moustache."

It was Chaval's corpse, risen from the upbrow and pushed on to them by the flow. Étienne stretched out his arm; he, too, felt the moustache and the crushed nose, and shuddered with disgust and fear. Seized by horrible nausea, Catherine had spat out the water which was still in her mouth. It seemed to her that she had been drinking blood, and that all the deep water before her was now that man's blood.

"Wait!" stammered Étienne. "I'll push him off!"

He kicked the corpse, which moved off. But soon they felt it again striking against their legs.

"By God! Get off!"

And the third time Étienne had to leave it. Some current always brought it back. Chaval would not go; he desired to be with them, against them. It was an awful companion, at last poisoning the air. All that day they never drank, struggling, preferring to die. It was not until the next day that their suffering decided them: they pushed away the body at each mouthful and drank in spite of it. It had not been worth while to knock his brains out, for he came back between him and her, obstinate in his jealousy. To the very end he would be there, even though he was dead, preventing them from coming together.

A day passed, and again another day. At every shiver of the water Étienne received a slight blow from the man he had killed, the simple elbowing of a neighbour who is reminding you of his presence. And every time it came he shuddered. He continually saw it there, swollen, greenish, with the red moustache and the crushed face. Then he no longer remembered; he had not killed him; the other man was swimming and trying to bite him. Catherine was now shaken by long endless fits of crying, after which she was completely prostrated. She fell at last into a condition of irresistible drowsiness. He would arouse her, but she stammered a few words and at once fell asleep again without even raising her eyelids; and fearing lest she should be drowned, he put his arm round her waist. It was he now who replied to the mates. The blows of the axe were now approaching, he could hear them behind his back. But his strength, too, was diminishing; he had lost all courage to strike. They were known to be there; why weary oneself more? It no longer interested him whether they came or not. In the stupefaction of waiting he would forget for hours at a time what he was waiting for.

One relief comforted them a little: the water sank, and Chaval's body moved off. For nine days the work of their deliverance had been going on, and they were for the first time taking a few steps in the gallery when a fearful commotion threw them to the ground. They felt for each other and remained in each other's arms like mad people, not understanding, thinking the catastrophe was beginning over again. Nothing more stirred, the sound of the picks had ceased.

In the corner where they were seated holding each other, side by side, a low laugh came from Catherine.

"It must be good outside. Come, let's go out of here."

Étienne at first struggled against this madness. But the contagion was shaking his stronger head, and he lost the exact sensation of reality. All their senses seemed to go astray, especially Catherine's. She was shaken by fever, tormented now by the need to talk and move. The ringing in her ears had become the murmur of flowing water, the song of birds; she smelled the strong odour of crushed grass, and could see clearly great yellow patches floating before her eyes, so large that she thought she was out of doors, near the canal, in the meadows on a fine summer day.

"Eh? how warm it is! Take me, then; let us keep together. Oh, always, always!"

He pressed her, and she rubbed herself against him for a long time, continuing to chatter like a happy girl:

"How silly we have been to wait so long! I would have liked you at once, and you did not understand; you sulked. Then, do you remember, at our house at night, when we could not sleep, with our faces out listening to each other's breathing, with such a longing to come together?"

He was won by her gaiety, and joked over the recollection of their silent tenderness.

"You struck me once. Yes, yes, blows on both cheeks!"

"It was because I loved you," she murmured. "You see, I prevented myself from thinking of you. I said to myself that it was quite done with, and all the time I knew that one day or another we should get together. It only wanted an opportunity—some lucky chance. Wasn't it so?"

A shudder froze him. He tried to shake off this dream; then he repeated slowly:

"Nothing is ever done with; a little happiness is enough to make everything begin again."

"Then you'll keep me, and it will be all right this time?"

And she slipped down fainting. She was so weak that her low voice died out. In terror he kept her against his heart.

"Do you ache?"

She sat up surprised.

"No, not at all. Why?"

But this question aroused her from her dream. She gazed at the darkness with distraction, wringing her hands in another fit of sobbing.

"My God, my God, how black it is!"

It was no longer the meadows, the odour of the grass, the song of larks, the great yellow sun; it was the fallen, inundated mine, the stinking night, the melancholy dripping of this cellar where they had been groaning for so many days. Her perverted senses now increased the horror of it; her childish superstitions came back to her; she saw the Black Man, the old dead miner who returns to the pit to twist naughty girls' necks.

"Listen! did you hear?"

"No, nothing; I heard nothing."

"Yes, the Man you know? Look! he is there. The earth has let all the blood out of the vein to revenge itself for being cut into; and he is there—you can see him—look! blacker than night. Oh, I'm so afraid, I'm so afraid!"

She became silent, shivering. Then in a very low voice she whispered:

"No, it's always the other one."

"What other one?"

"Him who is with us; who is not alive."

The image of Chaval haunted her, she talked of him confusedly, she described the dog's life she led with him, the only day when he had been kind to her at Jean-Bart, the other days of follies and blows, when he would kill her with caresses after having covered her with kicks.

"I tell you that he's coming, that he will still keep us from being together! His jealousy is coming on him again. Oh, push him off! Oh, keep me, keep me close!"

With a sudden impulse she hung on to him, seeking his mouth and pressing her own passionately to it. The darkness lighted up, she saw the sun again, and she laughed a quiet laugh of love. He shuddered to feel her thus against his flesh, half naked beneath the tattered jacket and trousers, and he seized her with a reawakening of his virility. It was at length their wedding night, at the bottom of this tomb, on this bed of mud, the longing not to die before they had had their happiness, the obstinate longing to live and make life one last time. They loved each other in despair of everything, in death.

After that there was nothing more. Étienne was seated on the ground, always in the same corner, and Catherine was lying motionless on his knees. Hours and hours passed by. For a long time he thought she was sleeping; then he touched her; she was very cold, she was dead. He did not move her, however, for fear of arousing her. The idea that he was the first who had possessed her as a woman, and that she might be pregnant, filled him with tenderness. Other ideas, the desire to go away with her, joy at what they would both do later on, came to him at moments, but so vaguely that it seemed only as though his forehead had been touched by a breath of sleep. He grew weaker, he only had strength to make a little gesture, a slow movement of the hand, to assure himself that she was certainly there, like a sleeping child in her frozen stiffness. Everything was being annihilated; the night itself had disappeared, and he was nowhere, out of space, out of time. Something was certainly striking beside his head, violent blows were approaching him; but he had been too lazy to reply, benumbed by immense fatigue; and now he knew nothing, he only dreamed that she was walking before him, and that he heard the slight clank of her sabots. Two days passed; she had not stirred; he touched her with his mechanical gesture, reassured to find her so quiet.

Étienne felt a shock. Voices were sounding, rocks were rolling to his feet. When he perceived a lamp he wept. His blinking eyes followed the light, he was never tired of looking at it, enraptured by this reddish point which scarcely stained the darkness. But some mates carried him away, and he allowed them to introduce some spoonfuls of soup between his clenched teeth. It was only in the Réquillart gallery that he recognised someone standing before him, the engineer, Négrel; and these two men, who felt contempt for each other—the rebellious workman and the sceptical master—threw themselves on each other's necks, sobbing loudly in the deep upheaval of all the humanity within them. It was an immense sadness, the misery of generations, the extremity of grief to which life can fall.

At the surface, Maheude, stricken down near dead Catherine, uttered a cry, then another, then another—very long, deep, incessant moans. Several corpses had already been brought up, and placed in a row on the ground: Chaval, who was thought to have been crushed beneath a landslip, a trammer, and two hewers, also crushed, with brainless skulls and bellies swollen with water. Women in the crowd went out of their minds, tearing their skirts and scratching their faces. When Étienne was at last taken out, after having been accustomed to the lamps and fed a little, he appeared fleshless, and his hair was quite white. People turned away and shuddered at this old man. Maheude left off crying to stare at him stupidly with her large fixed eyes.

## CHAPTER VI

IT WAS FOUR O'CLOCK in the morning, and the fresh April night was growing warm at the approach of day. In the limpid sky the stars were twinkling out, while the east grew purple with dawn. And a slight shudder passed over the drowsy black country, the vague rumour which precedes awakening.

Étienne, with long strides, was following the Vandame road. He had just passed six weeks at Montsou, in bed at the hospital. Though very thin and yellow, he felt strength to go, and he went. The Company, still trembling for its pits, was constantly sending men away, and had given him notice that he could not be kept on. He was offered the sum of one hundred francs, with the paternal advice to leave off working in mines, as it would now be too severe for him. But he refused the hundred francs. He had already received a letter from Pluchart, calling him to Paris, and enclosing money for the journey. His old dream would be realised. The night before, on leaving the hospital, he had slept at the Bon-Joyeux, Widow Désir's. And he rose early; only one desire was left, to bid his mates farewell before taking the eight o'clock train at Marchiennes.

For a moment Étienne stopped on the road, which was now becoming rose-coloured. It was good to breathe that pure air of the precocious spring. It would turn out a superb day. The sun was slowly rising, and the life of the earth was rising with it. And he set out walking again, vigorously striking down his briar stick, watching the plain afar, as it rose from the vapours of the night. He had seen no one; Maheude had come once to the hospital, and, probably, had not been able to come again. But he knew that the whole settlement of the Deux-Cent-Quarante was now going down at Jean-Bart, and that she too had taken work there. Little by little the deserted roads were peopled, and colliers constantly passed Étienne with pallid silent faces. After two and a half months of strike, when they had returned to the pits, conquered by hunger, they had been obliged to accept the timbering tariff, that disguised decrease in wages, now the more hateful because stained with the blood of their mates. They were being robbed of an hour's work, they were being made false to their oath never to submit; and this imposed perjury stuck in their throats like gall. Work was beginning again everywhere, at Mirou, at Madeleine, at Crèvecœur, at the Victoire. Everywhere, in the morning haze, along the roads lost in darkness, the flock was tramping on, rows of men trotting with faces bent towards the earth, like cattle led to the slaughter-house. They shivered beneath their thin garments, crossing their arms, rolling their hips, expanding their backs with the humps formed by the brick between the shirt and the jacket. And in this wholesale return to work, in these mute shadows, all black, without a laugh, without a look aside, one felt the teeth clenched with rage, the hearts swollen with hatred, a simple resignation to the necessity of the belly.

The nearer Étienne approached the pit the more their number increased. They nearly all walked alone; those who came in groups were in single file, already exhausted, tired of one another and of themselves. He noticed one who was very old, with eyes that shone like hot coals beneath his livid forehead. Another, a young man, was panting with the restrained fury of a storm. Many had their sabots in their hands; one could scarcely hear the soft sound of their coarse woollen stockings on the ground. It was an endless rustling, a general downfall, the forced march of a beaten army, moving on with lowered heads, sullenly absorbed in the desire to renew the struggle and achieve revenge.

When Étienne arrived, Jean-Bart was emerging from the shade; the lanterns, hooked on to the platform, were still burning in the growing dawn. Above the obscure buildings a trail of steam arose like a white plume delicately tinted with carmine. He passed up the sifting staircase to go to the receiving-room.

The descent was beginning, and the men were coming from the shed. For a moment he stood by, motionless amid the noise and movement. The rolling of the trains shook the metal floor, the drums were turning, unrolling the cables in the midst of cries from the trumpet, the ringing of bells, blows of the mallet on the signal block; he found the monster again swallowing his daily ration of human flesh, the cages rising and plunging, engulfing their burden of men, without ceasing, with the facile gulp of a voracious giant. Since his accident he had a nervous horror of the mine. The cages, as they sank down, tore his bowels. He had to turn away his head; the pit exasperated him.

But in the vast and still sombre hall, feebly lighted up by the exhausted lanterns, he could perceive no friendly face. The miners, who were waiting there with bare feet and their lamps in their hands, looked at him with large restless eyes, and then lowered their faces, drawing back with an air of shame. No doubt they knew him and no longer had any spite against him; they seemed, on the contrary, to fear him, blushing at the thought that he would reproach them with cowardice. This attitude made his heart swell; he forgot that these wretches had stoned him, he again began to dream of changing them into heroes, of directing a whole people, this force of Nature which was devouring itself. A cage was embarking its men, and the batch disappeared; as others arrived he saw at last one of his lieutenants in the strike, a worthy fellow who had sworn to die.

"You, too!" he murmured, with aching heart.

The other turned pale and his lips trembled; then, with a movement of excuse:

"What would you have? I've got a wife."

Now in the new crowd coming from the shed he recognised them all.

"You too!—you too!—you too!"

And all shrank back, stammering in choked voices:

"I have a mother."—"I have children."—"One must get bread."

The cage no longer reappeared; they waited for it mournfully, with such sorrow at their defeat that they avoided meeting each other's eyes, obstinately gazing at the shaft.

"And Maheude?" Étienne asked.

They made no reply. One made a sign that she was coming. Others raised their arms, trembling with pity. Ah, poor woman! what wretchedness! The silence continued, and when Étienne stretched out his hand to bid them farewell, they all pressed it vigorously, putting into that mute squeeze their rage at having yielded, their feverish hope of revenge. The cage was there; they got into it and sank, devoured by the gulf.

Pierron had appeared with his free captain's lamp fixed into the leather of his cap. For the past week he had been chief of the gang at the pit-eye, and the men moved away, for promotion had rendered him bossy. The sight of Étienne annoyed him; he came up, however, and was at last reassured when the young man announced his departure. They talked. His wife now kept the Estaminet du Progrès, thanks to the support of all those gentlemen who had been so good to her. But he interrupted himself and turned furiously on to Father Mouque, whom he accused of not sending up the dung-heap from his stable at the regulation hour. The old man listened with bent shoulders. Then, before going down, suffering from this reprimand, he, too, gave his hand to Étienne, with the same long pressure as the others, warm with restrained anger and quivering with future rebellion. And this old hand which trembled in his, this old man who was forgiving him for the loss of his dead children, affected

Étienne to such a degree that he watched him disappear without saying a word.

"Then Maheude is not coming this morning?" he asked Pierron after a time.

At first the latter pretended not to understand, for there was ill-luck even in speaking of her. Then, as he moved away, under the pretext of giving an order, he said at last:

"Eh! Maheude? There she is."

In fact, Maheude had reached the shed with her lamp in her hand, dressed in trousers and jacket, with her head confined in the cap. It was by a charitable exception that the Company, pitying the fate of this unhappy woman, so cruelly afflicted, had allowed her to go down again at the age of forty; and as it seemed difficult to set her again at haulage work, she was employed to manipulate a small ventilator which had been installed in the north gallery, in those infernal regions beneath Tartaret, where there was no movement of air. For ten hours, with aching back, she turned her wheel at the bottom of a burning tube, baked by forty degrees of heat. She earned thirty sous.

When Étienne saw her, a pitiful sight in her male garments, her breast and belly seeming to be swollen by the dampness of the cuttings, he stammered with surprise, trying to find words to explain that he was going away and that he wished to say goodbye to her.

She looked at him without listening, and said at last, speaking familiarly:

"Eh? it surprises you to see me. It's true enough that I threatened to wring the neck of the first of my children who went down again; and now that I'm going down I ought to wring my own, ought I not? Ah, well! I should have done it by now if it hadn't been for the old man and the little ones at the house."

And she went on in her low, fatigued voice. She did not excuse herself, she simply narrated things—that they had been nearly starved, and that she had made up her mind to it, so that they might not be sent away from the settlement.

"How is the old man?" asked Étienne.

"He is always very gentle and very clean. But he is quite off his nut. He was not brought up for that affair, you know. There was talk of shutting him up with the madmen, but I was not willing; they would have done for him in his soup. His story has, all the same, been very bad for us, for he'll never get his pension; one of those gentlemen told me that it would be immoral to give him one."

"Is Jeanlin working?"

"Yes, those gentlemen found something for him to do at the top. He gets twenty sous. Oh! I don't complain; the bosses have been very good, as they told me themselves. The brat's twenty sous and my thirty, that makes fifty. If there were not six of us we should get enough to eat. Estelle devours now, and the worst is that it will be four or five years before Lénore and Henri are old enough to come to the pit."

Étienne could not restrain a movement of pain.

"They, too!"

Maheude's pale cheeks turned red, and her eyes flamed. But her shoulders sank as if beneath the weight of destiny.

"What would you have? They after the others. They have all been done for there; now it's their turn."

She was silent; some landers, who were rolling trams, disturbed them. Through the large dusty windows the early sun was entering, drowning the lanterns in grey light; and the engine moved every three minutes, the cables unrolled, the cages continued to swallow down men.

"Come along, you loungers, look sharp!" shouted Pierron. "Get in; we shall never have done with it to-day."

Maheude, whom he was looking at, did not stir. She had already allowed three cages to pass, and she said, as though arousing herself and remembering Étienne's first words:

"Then you're going away?"

"Yes, this morning."

"You're right; better be somewhere else if one can. And I'm glad to have seen you, because you can know now, anyhow, that I've nothing on my mind against you. For a moment I could have killed you, after all that slaughter. But one thinks, doesn't one? One sees that when all's reckoned up it's nobody's fault. No, no! it's not your fault; it's the fault of everybody."

Now she talked with tranquillity of her dead, of her man, of

Zacharie, of Catherine; and tears only came into her eyes when she uttered Alzire's name. She had resumed her calm reasonableness, and judged things sensibly. It would bring no luck to the middle class to have killed so many poor people. Sure enough, they would be punished for it one day, for everything has to be paid for. There would even be no need to interfere; the whole thing would explode by itself. The soldiers would fire on the masters just as they had fired on the men. And in her everlasting resignation, in that hereditary discipline under which she was again bowing, a conviction had established itself, the certainty that injustice could not last longer, and that, if there were no good God left, another would spring up to avenge the wretched.

She spoke in a low voice, with suspicious glances round. Then, as Pierron was coming up, she added, aloud:

"Well, if you're going, you must take your things from our house. There are still two shirts, three handkerchiefs, and an old pair of trousers."

Étienne, with a gesture, refused these few things saved from the dealers.

"No, it's not worth while; they can be for the children. At Paris I can arrange for myself."

Two cages had once more gone down, and Pierron decided to speak straight to Maheude.

"I say now, over there, they are waiting for you! Is that little chat nearly done?"

But she turned her back. Why should he be so zealous, this man who had sold himself? The descent didn't concern him. His men hated him enough already on his level. And she persisted, with her lamp in her hand, frozen amid the draughts in spite of the mildness of the season. Neither Étienne nor she found anything more to say. They remained facing each other with hearts so full that they would like to speak once more.

At last she spoke for the sake of speaking.

"The Levaque is in the family-way. Levaque is still in prison; Bouteloup is taking his place meanwhile."

"Ah, yes! Bouteloup."

"And, listen! did I tell you? Philomène has gone away."

"What! gone away?"

"Yes, gone away with a Pas-de-Calais miner. I was afraid she would leave the two brats on me. But no, she took them with her. Eh? A woman who spits blood and looks as if she were always swallowing her tongue!"

She mused for a moment, and then went on in a slow voice:

"There's been talk on my account. You remember they said I slept with you. Lord! After my man's death that might very well have happened if I had been younger. But now I'm glad it wasn't so, for we should have regretted it, sure enough."

"Yes, we should have regretted it," Étienne repeated, simply.

That was all; they spoke no more. A cage was waiting for her; she was being called angrily, threatened with a fine. Then she made up her mind, and pressed his hand. Deeply moved, he still looked at her, so worn and worked out, with her livid face, her discoloured hair escaping from the blue cap, her body as of a good over-fruitful beast, deformed beneath the jacket and trousers. And in this last pressure of the hands, he felt again the long, silent pressure of his mates, giving him a rendezvous for the day when they would begin again. He understood perfectly. There was a tranquil faith in the depths of her eyes. It would be soon, and that time it would be the final blow.

"A damned shammer!" exclaimed Pierron.

Pushed and hustled, Maheude squeezed into a tram, with four others. The signal-cord was drawn to strike for meat, the cage was unhooked and fell into the night, and there was nothing more but the rapid flight of the cable.

Then Étienne left the pit. Below, beneath the screening-shed, he noticed a creature seated on the earth, with legs stretched out, in the midst of a thick pile of coal. It was Jeanlin, who was employed there to clean the large coal. He held a block of coal between his thighs, and freed it with a hammer from the fragments of slate. A fine powder drowned him in such a flood of soot that the young man would never have recognised him if the child had not lifted his ape-like face, with the protruding ears and small greenish eyes. He laughed, with a joking air, and, giving a final blow to the block, disappeared in the black dust which arose.

Outside, Étienne followed the road for a while, absorbed in his thoughts. All sorts of ideas were buzzing in his head. But he felt the open air, the free sky, and he breathed deeply. The sun was appearing in glory at the horizon, there was a reawakening of gladness over the whole country. A flood of gold rolled from the east to the west in the immense plain. This heat of life was expanding and extending in a tremor of youth, in which vibrated the sighs of the earth, the song of birds, all the murmuring sounds of the waters and the woods. It was good to live, and the old world wanted to live through one more spring.

And penetrated by that hope, Étienne slackened his walk, his eyes wandering to right and to left amid the gaiety of the new season. He thought about himself, he felt himself strong, seasoned by his hard experiences at the bottom of the mine. His education was complete, he was going away armed, a rational soldier of the revolution, having declared war against society as he saw it and as he condemned it. The joy of rejoining Pluchart and of being, like Pluchart, a leader who was listened to, inspired him with speeches, and he began to arrange the phrases. He was meditating an enlarged programme; that middle-class refinement, which had raised him above his class, had deepened his hatred of the middle class. He felt the need of glorifying these workers, whose odour of wretchedness was now unpleasant to him; he would show that they alone were great and stainless, the only nobility and the only strength in which humanity could be dipped afresh. He already saw himself in parliament, triumphing with the people, if the people had not devoured him.

The loud song of a lark made him look up towards the sky. Little red clouds, the last vapours of the night, were melting in the limpid blue; and the vague faces of Souvarine and Rasseneur came to his memory. Decidedly, all was spoilt when each man tried to get power for himself. Thus that famous International which was to have renewed the world had impotently aborted, and its formidable army had been cut up and crumbled away from internal dissensions. Was Darwin right, then, and the world only a battlefield, where the strong ate the weak for the sake of the beauty and continuance of the race? This question troubled him, although he settled it like a man who is satisfied with his knowledge. But one idea dissipated his doubts and enchanted him—that of taking up his old explanation of the theory the first time that he should speak. If any class must be devoured, would not the people, still new and full of life, devour the middle class, exhausted by enjoyment? The new society would arise from new blood. And in this expectation of an invasion of barbarians, regenerating the old decayed nations, reappeared his absolute faith in an approaching revolution, the real one—that of the workers—the fire of which would inflame this century's end with that purple of the rising sun which he saw like blood on the sky. He still walked, dreaming, striking his briar stick against the flints on the road, and when he glanced around him he recognised the various places. Just there, at the Fourche-aux-Bœufs, he remembered that he had taken command of the band that morning when the pits were sacked. Today the brutish, deathly, ill-paid work was beginning over again. Beneath the earth, down there at seven hundred mètres, it seemed to him he heard low, regular, continuous blows; it was the men he had just seen go down, the black workers, who were hammering in their silent rage. No doubt they were beaten. They had left their dead and their money on the field; but Paris would not forget the volleys fired at the Voreux, and the blood of the Empire, too, would flow from that incurable wound. And if the industrial crisis was drawing to an end, if the workshops were opening again one by one, a state of war was not less declared, and peace was henceforth impossible. The colliers had reckoned up their men; they had tried their strength, with their cry for justice arousing the workers all over France. Their defeat, therefore, reassured no one. The Montsou bourgeois, in their victory, were carried away by their deep anxiety over to-morrow's strike, looking behind them to see if their end did not lie inevitably over there, in spite of all, beyond that great silence. They understood that the revolution would be born again unceasingly, perhaps to-morrow, with a general strike—the common understanding of all workers having general funds, and so able to hold out for months, eating their own bread. This time a push only had been given to a ruinous society, but they had heard the rumbling beneath their feet, and they felt more shocks arising, and still more, until the old edifice would be crushed, fallen in and swallowed, going down like the Voreux to the abyss.

Étienne took the Joiselle road, to the left. He remembered that he had prevented the band from rushing on to Gaston-Marie. Afar, in the clear sky he saw the steeples of several pits—Mirou to the right, Madeleine and Crèvecœur side by side. Work was going on everywhere; he seemed to be able to catch the blows of the axe at the bottom of the earth, striking now from one end of the plain to the other, one blow, and another blow, and yet more blows, beneath the fields and roads and villages which were laughing in the light, all the obscure labour of the underground prison, so crushed by the enormous mass of the rocks that one had to know it was underneath there to distinguish its great painful sigh. And he now thought that, perhaps, violence would not hasten things. Cutting cables, tearing up rails, breaking lamps, what a useless task it was! It was not worth while for three thousand men to rush about in a devastating band doing that. He vaguely divined that lawful methods might one day be more terrible. His reason was ripening, he had sown the wild oats of his spite. Yes, Maheude had well said, with her good sense, that that would be the great blow—to organise quietly, to know one another, to unite in Associations when the laws would permit it;[1] then, on the morning when they felt their strength, and millions of workers would be face to face with a few thousand idlers, to take the power into their own hands and become the masters. Ah! what a reawakening of truth and justice! The sated and crouching god would at once get his deathblow, the monstrous idol hidden in the depths of his sanctuary, in that unknown distance where poor wretches fed him with their flesh without ever having seen him.

But Étienne, leaving the Vandame road, now came on to the paved street. On the right he saw Montsou, which was lost in the valley. Opposite were the ruins of the Voreux, the accursed hole where three pumps worked unceasingly. Then there were the other pits at the horizon, the Victoire, Saint-Thomas, Feutry-Cantel; while, towards the north, the tall chimneys of the blast furnaces, and the batteries of coke ovens, were smoking in the transparent morning air. If he was not to lose the eight o'clock train he must hasten, for he had still six kilomètres before him.

And beneath his feet, the deep blows, those obstinate blows of the pick, continued. The mates were all there; he heard them following him at every stride. Was not that Maheude beneath the beetroots, with bent back and hoarse respiration accompanying the rumble of the ventilator? To left, to right, farther on, he seemed to recognise others beneath the wheatfields, the hedges, the young trees. Now the April sun, in the open sky, was shining in his glory, and warming the pregnant earth. From its fertile flanks life was leaping out, buds were bursting into green leaves, and the fields were quivering with the growth of the grass. On every side seeds were swelling, stretching out, cracking the plain filled by the need of heat and light. An overflow of sap was mixed with whispering voices, the sound of the germs expanding in a great kiss. Again and again, more and more distinctly, as though they were approaching the soil, the mates were hammering. In the heated rays of the sun on this youthful morning the country seemed full of that sound. Men were springing forth,[2] a black avenging army, germinating slowly in the furrows, growing towards the harvests of the next century, and this germination would soon overturn the earth.

THE END

# *Endnotes*

## PART ONE

**1.** (p. 1) *Germinal:* The title suggests the rebirth of plants in the spring, as well as revolution. Germinal was the name of the "seed-time" month of the Revolutionary calendar (March 21–April 19). During the month of Germinal, *an* (year) III (1795) there were bread riots in Paris, and popular protests brought down the government of the National Convention.

**2.** (p. 5) *Montsou:* The name of this fictional mining town ("mountain of pennies") suggests ideas of greed as well as poverty—rather than centimes, the miners count in sous, the old currency for small change.

**3.** (p. 6) *Étienne Lantier:* The hero of *Germinal* is the son of Gervaise Macquart, the heroine of Zola's 1877 novel *L'Assommoir* (*The Drunkard*); see endnote 14 to part one, below. Étienne's brother Claude, an archetypal Impressionist painter, is the hero of Zola's next novel, *L'Oeuvre* (1886; *The Masterpiece*).

**4.** (p. 7) *The Voreux:* Named with another highly suggestive word, the Voreux is an anthropomorphic monster of a mine that devours human flesh.

**5.** (p. 8) *"why should he go and fight in America?":* This is a reference to the disastrous Mexican expedition that ended in 1867 with the victory of Benito Juárez (later elected president of the Mexican republic) over the French. Maximilian of Austria, the puppet emperor that Napoléon III had tried to impose on Mexico, was executed in the same year. In addition to foreign policy reversals, the 1860s were marred by an economic crisis and a cholera epidemic in 1866 in the Lille and Valenciennes region where the novel is set (2,000 people died in Lille alone). Insufficient hygiene and sanitation, combined with malnutrition, respiratory diseases, unsafe working conditions, and alcoholism, accounted for the low life expectancy (twenty-four years) and the high infant mortality rate (40 percent of children died before their fifth birthdays) in the mining regions of France.

6. (p. 10) *Bonnemort:* The old man's nickname, "Good Death," points to the grisly reality of working conditions in the mining industry. A living dead man, pulled out of the mine alive after three horrific accidents and plagued by all the common diseases of the miners, he is a sort of ghost of the mine. As the first person that Étienne meets in Montsou, he also has a symbolic role as an intermediary, facilitating Étienne's entry into the world of the mine.
7. (p. 10) *a terrible spasm of coughing:* Bonnemort, who has spent forty-five years working underground, has contracted an assortment of respiratory diseases from prolonged coal dust inhalation, and his skeletal deformity is characteristic of anemia, malnutrition, and prolonged exposure to humidity in the mine tunnels. Zola used information from several medical treatises on common mining ailments, in particular Doctor H. Boëns-Boisseau's *Traité pratique des maladies, des accidents et des difformités des houilleurs* (1862; *Practical Treatise on the Illnesses, Accidents and Deformities of Miners*).
8. (p. 12) *their history:* The Maheu family is meant to be a typical one, with several generations slaving in the mines and most of the men succumbing to mining accidents. Bonnemort himself seems unaware of how sick he really is.
9. (p. 14) *the Deux-Cent-Quarante settlement:* The village built by the Company is not a real living community evolving naturally with time, but a geometric row of mass-produced identical houses, without as much as a name. Zola was struck by the rectilinear brick lodgings, stuck back to back in parallel rows, and he drew a picture of them in his "Notes sur Anzin" ("Notes on Anzin"; see the Gallimard edition of *Les Rougon-Macquart,* listed in "For Further Reading"), which he wrote after personal observations of the mining town of Anzin.
10. (p. 19) *"still six days before the fortnight's out":* The miners were paid every second week, a system that was more advantageous to the Company than weekly payment—since payday meant a day off—but highly inconvenient to the miners, who found it difficult to budget their expenses.
11. (p. 21) *hard slaty coal:* Zola mentions in his "Notes on Anzin" the poor-quality coal—actually, debris swept out from the tunnels—that the Company gave to the miners to heat their homes.
12. (p. 29) *Davy lamps:* Introduced in 1815, these oil lamps used a metal gauze to prevent the flame of the lamp from igniting flammable gases in the mines.
13. (p. 35) *"These men are eating the bread of girls":* In 1874 France

passed a law that forbade women from working underground, and children under age twelve from working in the mines altogether. *Germinal* is set in the last years of the Second Empire, in the late 1860s. Resistance to prohibiting or regulating female and child labor came from the workers themselves. Although women and children earned only about half of a man's wages, the extra income was indispensable to families.

**14.** (p. 43) *"Laundress, Rue de la Goutte-d'or":* Étienne Lantier's mother is the unfortunate heroine of *The Drunkard,* the novel about alcoholism in the urban slums that made Zola a celebrity in 1877. At the opening of *Germinal,* she is only beginning her descent into dereliction, but readers of the Rougon-Macquart novels would have already known about her squalid death.

**15.** (p. 57) *The Volcan:* The name of the pub makes clear its attraction for the workers—a combination of cheap liquor and cheap sex. The sheer number of pubs mentioned in the novel for the Montsou area alone indicates the extent of the problem of alcoholism.

**16.** (p. 61) *Rasseneur:* In the political configuration of *Germinal,* Rasseneur represents the moderates, the pragmatic supporters of compromise with the authorities and collaboration between Labor and Capital. Rasseneur was modeled on several historical figures, including Paul Brousse, head of the reformist Federation of Socialist Workers, and Émile Basly, whom Zola met at Anzin. Similar to Rasseneur, Basly was an ex-miner who became a pub owner and the leader of the miners' union in Denain. Eventually—in 1885, the year of *Germinal*'s publication—he became a member of Parliament.

## PART TWO

**1.** (p. 73) *acquired as national property:* During the Revolution, much of the land belonging to the aristocracy and the church was confiscated and sold to members of the bourgeoisie at very affordable prices.

**2.** (p. 73) *Napoleon's bloody fall:* The Emperor Napoléon I was defeated in 1814 by allied opposition armies; then, after his attempted return from his first exile, on the island of Elba, he was defeated again at Waterloo in 1815. He was sent to Saint Helena, where he died in 1821.

**3.** (p. 76) *the Salon:* This was an annual exhibit of paintings in Paris. So many works were rejected by the very traditional jury of the salon that in 1863 Napoléon III authorized the creation of a Salon des Refusés, an exhibit of works not selected for the official Salon. Claude Lantier, Étienne's brother, an Impressionist painter and the hero of Zola's novel *The Masterpiece*, is repeatedly turned down by the Salon jury.

**4.** (p. 86) *"Seven children! But why?":* The little dialogue between Maheude and the Grégoires illustrates the difference between the bourgeoisie, who protect their fortune by reducing the number of their children, and the proletariat, whose only source of income is children who can bring home supplemental wages when they are old enough to work (typically, in the mining industry, around eight or nine years of age).

**5.** (p. 89) *The poor starving urchins went off, holding the brioche:* Zola's text reads literally "the poor kids, who lacked bread, went away holding the brioche"—a line that is meant to suggest Marie-Antoinette's famous remark about starving Parisians when she was told they had no bread: "Then let them eat cake."

## PART THREE

**1.** (p. 129) *Souvarine:* Zola's character is based on the Russian nihilist Mikhail Bakunin and his followers, whose mystical brand of anarchism advocated the violent destruction of the old society and refused to imagine anything beyond apocalypse. The nihilists attempted to take Czar Alexander II's life several times; the last attempt, in 1881, was successful.

**2.** (p. 131) *This rabbit, which he had named Poland:* Souvarine's fondness for his pet rabbit is his last connection to the realm of human affections. The rabbit's name is suggestive. Throughout the nineteenth century Poland's aspiration to independence was brutally suppressed by Russia and there were many Polish refugees in France. The rabbit's fate—tormented by the sadistic Jeanlin, then eaten by the strikers—will be accordingly harsh.

**3.** (p. 131) *the International Association of Workers:* Founded in London in 1864 by Karl Marx and others, the International Workingmen's Association attempted to organize workers internationally by federating national sections. Its goal was the revolutionary overthrow of the bourgeoisie and the seizure of power by the socialist workers. Pluchart is the leader of the French section. His historical model is probably in part Jules Guesde, who was, under Marx's guidance, the founder in 1879 of the *Parti des Travailleurs Socialistes* (Socialist Workers Party).

**4.** (p. 133) *"They're fixed by an iron law to the smallest possible sum":* Souvarine is echoing British economist David Ricardo's theory on minimum salaries (he called it the Iron Law of Wages), that they always will be set at the lowest possible level that allows the worker to survive. Zola found a summary of this thesis in E. de Laveleye's *Le Socialisme contemporain* (second edition, 1883; *The Socialism of Today*), which he read and annotated extensively in preparation for *Germinal*.

**5.** (p. 134) *At last he had borrowed a French book on Cooperative Societies:* Here Étienne appears influenced by Pierre-Joseph Proudhon, whose *Philosophie de la misère* (1846; *The Philosophy of Poverty*) advocated a brand of anarchism that was much less violent than Bakunin's, relying on unions and cooperatives. Marx, in *Misère de la philosophie* (1847; *The Poverty of Philosophy*), attacked Proudhon's socialism for not being revolutionary enough.

**6.** (p. 136) *"To-day it is the worker who is forced to devour the worker":* In his "Notes on Anzin," Zola summarized the miners' complaints about this bidding system, which pitted workers against one another and brought down the wages. The system was one of the causes of the 1884 strike at Anzin.

**7.** (p. 140) *establish a Provident Fund:* This is another key idea in Proudhon's system, which envisioned a society structured around small-scale self-help societies of workers. Since the fund could also be used to support strikers, mining companies would typically attempt to gain control of it. This is indeed what Monsieur Hennebeau demands on p. 202 during the first confrontation with the miners.

**8.** (p. 143) *competition of chaffinches:* Finches were used in the early mining days to warn of escaped gas. Zola described the very popular finch competitions in his "Notes on Anzin."

**9.** (p. 152) *Hygiène du Mineur:* This fictional book is a composite of three different treatises, written by French and Belgian doctors on the subject of miners' ailments. Zola read the books on which it is based in preparation for writing *Germinal*; see endnote 7 to part one.

**10.** (p. 154) *germinating in the earth:* This is the first occurrence of the title metaphor. Here it is linked explicitly with progress in the education of the working classes, a key nineteenth-century idea. The underlying Greek myth, that an army is sprung from a dragon's teeth sown into the earth, is one of the structuring myths of the narrative. See endnote 2 to part seven.

**11.** (p. 155) *"As soon as you move they give you back your certificate":* From 1803 on, every worker had to carry a certificate (*livret ouvrier*, or "worker's booklet"), signed by the municipal authorities, to be given to successive employers, who would hand it back when the worker was dismissed. This practice was abolished in 1869. Pierre Larousse describes the *livret* in the entry for *grève* (strike) in his encyclopedia, the *Grand dictionnaire universel du XIX*[e] *siècle* (1866–1876), as an annoying measure seeking to place an entire class under direct police control.

## PART FOUR

**1.** (p. 183) *the strike broke out:* The strike at Anzin lasted from February to April 1884. It was caused by a new wage system. See endnote 6 to part three.

**2.** (p. 200) *as though a stranger were speaking within him: Germinal* is also the story of the people learning to find their own voices. The typical miners, embodied by Toussaint Maheu, are on the whole a docile lot, with a long tradition of humility and resignation compounded by the awareness of their own ignorance; however, in this scene Maheu is able to overcome his shyness and speak in simple and powerful words for all of his fellow workers. None of the ambivalence expressed elsewhere in the book about professional leaders—even Étienne, the hero—is felt here.

**3.** (p. 210) *1848, an awful year:* The revolution that broke out in February 1848, putting an end to Louis-Philippe's constitutional monarchy, was fueled by political dissent from the middle class as well as popular anger over growing inequality and demands for social justice. The government that followed, the Second Republic, attempted radical social measures but failed to prevent unemployment and famine. A conservative Assembly, elected in April 1848, used the troops to crush a popular insurrection in June—hence Maheude's disillusionment with the Republic.

**4.** (p. 220) *confused phrases which contained a little of all the theories:* Étienne has subscribed successively to several incompatible versions of socialism. Proudhon repudiated property, which he equated with theft (*Qu'est-ce que la propriété?* [1840]; *What Is Property?*), and advocated a society based on barter. German socialist Ferdinand Lassalle (1825–1864) thought that cooperatives endowed by the state could reform society. Marx criticized Proudhon's rejection of the state as a governing power and advocated collective ownership of the means of production.

**5.** (p. 222) *Bakounine the destroyer:* Mikhail Bakunin (1814–1876; also spelled Bakounine) was a Russian anarchist leader and author of *Statism and Anarchy* (1873). His theory of cooperative units was close to Proudhon's, but he advocated the violent destruction of the State as a prerequisite to any socialist society. His rivalry with Karl Marx led to his exclusion from the First International (formally, the International Workingmen's Association) in 1872. Souvarine's chilling conclusion—"All reasoning about the future is criminal, because it prevents pure destruction, and interferes with the progress of revolution" (p. 223)—directly echoes Bakunin's theories and his famous 1842 aphorism: "The passion for destruction is also a creative passion."

**6.** (p. 223) *His mistress . . . hanged at Moscow:* Sophia Perovskaya, one of five co-conspirators in the murder of Czar Alexander II, was hanged in Saint Petersburg on April 15, 1881.

**7.** (p. 256) *the Place-des-Dames, that vast glade:* Since public meetings were illegal, miners held secret meetings in the woods at Anzin in 1878 and at Monceau-les-Mines in 1882.

**8.** (p. 261) *his collectivism . . . has stiffened into a complicated programme:* In Étienne's vision, Bakunin's anarchism (the immediate destruction of the State) is combined with Proudhon's influence (the primitive commune) and Marxist doctrine (collective ownership of the instruments of work). His "sectarianism" (p. 261) is perceptible in the way true obstacles no longer seem to apply. Interestingly, his brother Claude undergoes a similar "stiffening" of his aesthetic theories in the middle of his unhappy career as a painter (see *The Masterpiece*, chapter 9).

**9.** (p. 263) *The miner could not be the proprietor of the mine . . . he preferred sharing in the benefits:* Rasseneur is advocating the cooperation between Labor and Capital and the sharing of profits, whereas the miners have been won over by a Marxist view of history based on class warfare.

## PART FIVE

**1.** (p. 271) *"There's a rebellion, sir":* This is another allusion to a famous episode from the Revolution. When the Bastille was taken on July 14, 1789, Louis XVI's naive question "Is it a rebellion?" provoked the answer "No, Sire, it is a revolution."

**2.** (p. 274) *She was overcome by fear . . . of a brothel at Marchiennes:* Prostitution was tolerated only in special places euphemistically called *maisons de tolerance,* where prostitutes, registered with the police, were forced to reside and submit to regular medical inspections. When Chaval throws Catherine out, she is in danger of being forcibly registered at the local brothel by the police (p. 386).

**3.** (p. 283) *dead air the miners called it:* This is a reference to carbon dioxide, which is heavier than air. Its presence in the mine explains why Catherine is in danger of suffocating to death when she faints. Chaval has to lift her up above the deadly gas.

**4.** (p. 287) *"They are cutting the cables!":* Strikers are trapping working miners at the bottom. Zola is using the notes he took on strikes at the end of the Second Empire. This same action had been taken during strikes at Monceau-les-Mines in 1882 and at Denain in 1884.

**5.** (p. 290) *little girls often used to take out the coal on their shoulders:* Zola is using Louis-Laurent Simonin's 1867 study on mines, *Le Monde souterrain* (*Underground Life*), in which the author describes the dangerous work little girls did in Scottish mines. Their job was to carry baskets of coal on their backs up the ladders, and deadly accidents were frequent.

**6.** (p. 301) *"Bread! Bread! Bread!":* In October 1789 a starving mob led by the women of Paris marched on Versailles to demand the return to Paris of "the Baker" (the King) and his family. This hostage-taking by the starving people of Paris was the beginning of the end for the monarchy and the royal family. Then, on 12 and 13 Germinal, *an* (year) III (April 1 and 2, 1795), a popular riot caused by famine brought down the National Convention government (see endnote 1 to part one).

**7.** (p. 320) *singing the Marseillaise:* The current French national hymn was composed by Claude-Joseph Rouget de l'Isle during the Revolution, in 1792. It rapidly became the anthem of French Republicans and accordingly was banned under the Second Empire. It was reinstated as the national anthem in 1879.

**8.** (p. 337) *the women had another revenge to wreak on him:* Zola's initial intention was to have the rampaging miners commit murder. He then decided to avoid murder while still writing an episode of extreme violence. Maigrat is already dead when the women take graphic revenge on the man who has starved and raped them for years. This shocking scene is reduced to a brief modest paragraph in the expurgated Vizetelly translation, which censured all sexual details (see "A Note on the Translation").

**9.** (p. 339) *"Don't I tell you the gendarmes are coming!":* Strikes were routinely broken up by the army. In the following chapter (p. 343), the army occupies the mine, something that had actually happened at Anzin in 1884.

## PART SIX

**1.** (p. 344) *Abbé Ranvier:* This socialist priest is one of the last characters Zola added to his story. One of Zola's sources, Laveleye's *The Socialism of Today* (see endnote 4 to part three), mentions evangelical socialism and the worker priest phenomenon. The curé here is so out of touch with his starving parishioners that, while he preaches an apocalyptic end of capitalism to them, he does not even think of helping them in a material way.

**2.** (p. 367) *The association . . . was now being devoured and slowly destroyed by an internal struggle:* The First International (formally, the International Workingmen's Association) collapsed in 1876 following a conflict between Bakunin's anarchist followers and Marxists. Bakunin was expelled from the organization in 1872.

**3.** (p. 381) *a street urchin playing at revolution:* Jeanlin is a kind of perverted version of Victor Hugo's Gavroche, the endearing urchin of *Les Misérables,* who dies a hero's death on the barricades. Jeanlin's repulsive ugliness is in keeping with the key theme of the complete degeneration, both physical and moral, of the miners. On the one hand, Jeanlin has regressed to animality (he is compared to unfriendly animals throughout), which suggests ideas of fate and irresponsibility; on the other hand, he is simply acting out Étienne's fiery attacks on bourgeois society.

**4.** (pp. 397–398) *They had fired, and the gaping crowd stood motionless . . . unable to believe it:* The episode is inspired by very similar historical events. In 1869, at La Ricamarie, the troops had fired and killed thirteen miners, including two women; a few months later, at Aubin, fourteen strikers were killed.

## PART SEVEN

**1.** (p. 483) *to unite in Associations when the laws would permit it:* Trade unions and strikes were illegal during the Second Empire. They were finally legalized by the Waldeck-Rousseau law in 1884.

**2.** (p. 484) *Men were springing forth:* This is the final occurrence of the title metaphor (see endnote 10 to part three). The mythical motif used by Zola refers to similar variants of the myth in Ovid's *Metamorphoses.* Cadmos, the mythical founder of Thebes, sows the dragon's teeth, which bring forth armed men who fight one another; the survivors found the city (book 3). In the story of the Argonauts, Jason forms an army by sowing the dragon's teeth (book 7). The secondary motif of the men fighting one another could be read in the light of the political and ideological divisions among the miners, compared by Étienne to "a blind force which constantly devoured itself" (p. 411).

# *Inspired by* Germinal

*"Burn the books of the hypocrites, the shams . . . and let their pages warm the bones of a man of truth."*

—Paul Muni as Émile Zola

## FILM

Warner Brothers' production of *The Life of Émile Zola* (1937), directed by William Dieterle, came just a year after the studio's widely successful *Story of Louis Pasteur.* Paul Muni headed the cast for both screen biographies, but his portrayal of the author and social critic was the more nuanced performance. Muni plays Zola as a struggling young novelist as well as a settled older man who reluctantly enters the Dreyfus Affair, all the while surrounded by such luminaries as Anatole France and Paul Cézanne. Dieterle is faithful both to Zola's life and to the period in which he lived, and the film proceeds with little contrivance. Most significantly, it connects the man who spun brilliant fictions with the author of one of history's most famous political writings, Zola's open letter to France's president, "J'accuse." Though it avoids delving into the anti-Semitism at the heart of the Dreyfus Affair, *The Life of Émile Zola* provides a thrilling courtroom climax to showcase Zola's impassioned defense.

In addition to winning Academy Awards for Best Picture, Best Supporting Actor (Joseph Schildkraut as Dreyfus), and Best Screenplay (Heinz Herald, Geza Herczeg, and Norman Reilly Rane), *The Life of Émile Zola* earned a number of Oscar nominations, including Dieterle for his direction, Anton Grot for his art direction, the studio for both its sound recording and score, and Paul Muni for his portrayal of Zola.

One of France's highest-grossing films of all time, Claude

Berri's *Germinal*, premiered in 1993. Adapted by Berri and Arlette Langmann, *Germinal* maintains an epic sweep while focusing on the personal struggle of Maheu (played by Gérard Depardieu), the valiant father of Zola's poor coal-mining family. Depardieu's honest portrayal forms the moral center of the film, peopled with broken characters who must work from dawn till dusk to eke out meager livings. Miou-Miou stars as Maheu's fiery wife, Maheude, and Renaud takes the role of student and activist Étienne Lantier, who falls in love with Maheu's daughter Catherine (Judith Henry).

*Germinal* culminates with the violent strike in which soldiers brought in to defend the mine start firing on the workers. Even more powerful are the scenes that quietly portray the grueling tedium of working underground with only oil lamps for light. The film's claustrophobic cinematography tunnels its way through the mine shafts, which Berri recaptures with accuracy. Despite the palette of browns and charcoals, which help convey the coal miners' drab lives, the film remains lively throughout. The scene in which Maheu and Lantier rally the miners to strike incorporates more than 800 extras descended from the original laborers whom Zola took as the inspiration for his story.

## NATURALISM IN AMERICA

Émile Zola is considered the father of French naturalism, whose practitioners include the writers Alphonse Daudet, Edmond and Jules de Goncourt, and Guy de Maupassant. The tenets of the movement, as codified by Zola, are a meticulous attention to detail, with an eye toward great historical accuracy; a focus on contending societal forces, inherited from naturalism's forerunners—Stendhal, Honoré de Balzac, and Gustave Flaubert; and a near-scientific approach to human nature that borrows from the ideas of Charles Darwin and Karl Marx. This literary movement first spread to England and then across the Atlantic to America, where it helped motivate significant social change. American critic and writer of realist novels William Dean Howells was devoted to Zola and the French naturalists, and helped import their ideals and techniques. In his influential 1891 work *Criticism and Fiction,* Howells wrote:

> No author is an authority except in those moments when he held his ear close to Nature's lips and caught her very accent. These moments are not continuous with any authors in the past, and they are rare with all. Therefore I am not afraid to say now that the greatest classics are sometimes not at all great, and that we can profit by them only when we hold them, like our meanest contemporaries, to a strict accounting, and verify their work by the standard of the arts which we all have in our power, the simple, the natural, and the honest. . . . Let fiction cease to lie about life; let it portray men and women as they are, actuated by the motives and the passions in the measure we all know; let it leave off painting dolls and working them by springs and wires; let it show the different interests in their true proportions; let it forbear to preach pride and revenge, folly and insanity, egotism and prejudice, but frankly own these for what they are, in whatever figures and occasions they appear; let it not put on fine literary airs; let it speak the dialect, the language, that most Americans know—the language of unaffected people everywhere—and there can be no doubt of an unlimited future, not only of delightfulness but of usefulness, for it.

Howells is remembered not just for his own literary and critical works, but for encouraging the efforts of several young writers, among them Stephen Crane and Frank Norris. Crane, the prodigal author of *The Red Badge of Courage* (1895), was the first author in America to apply the techniques of naturalism to literature, with *Maggie: A Girl of the Streets* (1893). In *Maggie*—a gritty portrait of the filth, chaos, destruction, and anger pervading American cities—Crane renders the slum life of America's industrialized cities with realism and a lack of moralizing sentiment. Frank Norris became an important figure in American naturalism with the publication in 1899 of his novel *McTeague,* which details the life of an unlicensed dentist who murders his miserly wife and attempts an escape to Death Valley, where he dies of thirst. Norris followed this book with his best-remembered work, *The Octopus* (1901), the first volume of an unfinished trilogy, *The Epic of the Wheat.* With environmental determinism as a template, Norris explores the conflict between simple wheat farmers and the all-powerful railroad monopoly.

Theodore Dreiser's novel *Sister Carrie* was first published in 1900 but was generally suppressed until 1907. The novel, which largely concerns the profound gulf between the rich and the poor, is widely considered the first masterpiece of naturalism in America. Dreiser, a sober, uncompromising realist, excelled at compassionately portraying characters who must flout convention to survive. About his method, Dreiser remarked in a 1907 *New York Times* interview that *Sister Carrie* was "intended not as a piece of literary craftsmanship, but as a picture of conditions done as simply and effectively as the English language will permit." Most critics eventually agreed that Dreiser had in fact taken Howells's idea—that fiction should present life unadorned—a step further. As Sinclair Lewis put it in 1930, in the speech he gave upon accepting the Nobel Prize, "Usually unappreciated, often hounded, [Dreiser] has cleared the trail from Victorian Howellsian timidity and gentility in American fiction to honesty, boldness, and passion of life."

The most famous of the muckraking journalists, Upton Sinclair, made his reputation not with a nonfiction exposé, but with a naturalistic novel, *The Jungle,* published in book form in 1906 after appearing the previous year in the socialist magazine *Appeal to Reason.* The novel centers on Jurgis Rudkus, a Lithuanian immigrant working in Chicago's infamous Packingtown. Instead of finding the American Dream, Rudkus and his family inhabit a brutal, soul-crushing urban jungle dominated by greedy bosses, pitiless con men, and corrupt politicians. The novel, dedicated to the "Workingmen of America," depicts the appalling conditions in American packing plants. The grisliness of the account, which eventually led to an official investigation and the passage of the Pure Food and Drug Act, nearly prevented Sinclair from getting his novel published. Fortunately, he got a significant push in the form of backing by fellow socialists, including America's highest-paid novelist, Jack London, a leading figure in American naturalism. His 1913 novel *The Valley of the Moon* chronicles the on-the-road adventures of Billy and Saxon Roberts, who manage to escape their labor woes in Oakland, California. Trading the dehumanizing effects of urban life for the pastoral wonders of agriculture, Billy and Saxon establish an idyllic ranch called "The Valley of the Moon." The novel reflects London's deep concerns for social progress while conveying the waning of his trust in the ideals of socialism.

# *Comments & Questions*

*In this section, we aim to provide the reader with an array of perspectives on the text, as well as questions that challenge those perspectives. The commentary has been culled from sources as diverse as reviews contemporaneous with the work, letters written by the author, literary criticism of later generations, and appreciations written throughout the work's history. Following the commentary, a series of questions seeks to filter Émile Zola's* Germinal *through a variety of points of view and bring about a richer understanding of this enduring work.*

## COMMENTS

***THE NATION***

On being interviewed, recently, by a Parisian reporter, the author of 'Germinal' said: "I wished to paint the miner, and in order to do so truthfully I consulted documents everywhere. The Parliamentary inquiry into the condition of the English miners has been of much service to me. I believe I have described the miners as they are." And further: "My book is a work of pity, nothing more, and I shall be content if my readers experience this sensation." It is well that we should know from M. Zola's own lips what his object was in writing 'Germinal,' for, if we discover no literary merit in the vulgar style he adopts whenever he is not describing nature, we may still ask, Has he attained that commendable object? The picture he draws of the wretchedness of the poor miners and their families is certainly calculated to excite pity, but this feeling gives way to one of disgust when he describes the sufferers as living in a state of moral depravation too general, too complete, to be true. Not one of the numerous characters—miners or bourgeois—has the faintest notion of virtue, of chastity, of common decency. . . . Neither in England nor in France could there be found a community so depraved, so utterly God-forsaken as that of M. Zola's miners. A picture of wickedness without a single redeeming feature is not true art; much less is it true to nature. Where the shadow is darkest it is made so by contrast with the light. There is no such thing as utter darkness.

—April 2, 1885

**BRANDER MATTHEWS**

I have the highest respect for the strong work of M. Zola, and for the charming subtlety of M. Daudet; the shriek of horror with which British journalists are wont to greet French novels strikes me to be only too often the violent reaction of a guilty enjoyment. But there is no denying that a man may write in his study, and you may read by the fireside, what you do not wish to hear him say aloud on the stage of a crowded theater. M. Zola, for example, delights in describing the undescribable, and he takes rude pleasure in violating all the decencies of civilized life; rank strength is perhaps his chief characteristic. On the stage he is shaven and shorn perforce, and the result is not wholly satisfactory. I arrived in Paris last spring just too late to see *Germinal*, but I hardly regret it. M. Zola does not seem to me a born dramatist, and he is hopelessly unwilling to accept or even to understand the conditions of the theater, the limitations under which the dramatist must work. *Germinal* was the strongest story of the past ten years; there was in it not a little of the magnificent sweep of a great epic; it had the irresistible and inevitable movement of a solemn tragedy. Taken from the pages of the book and put on the boards of a theater, all this evaporated, and there was left nothing but a rather vulgar panorama of violence and suffering.

—from *Harper's Weekly* (May 18, 1889)

**WILLIAM DEAN HOWELLS**

The critics know now that Zola is not the realist he used to fancy himself, and he is full of the best qualities of the romanticism he has hated so much; but for what he is, there is but one novelist of our time, or of any, that outmasters him, and that is Tolstoy. For my own part, I think that the books of Zola are not immoral, but they are indecent through the facts that they nakedly represent; they are infinitely more moral than the books of any other French novelist. This may not be saying a great deal, but it is saying the truth, and I do not mind owning that he has been one of my great literary passions, almost as great as Flaubert, and greater than Daudet and Maupassant, though I have profoundly appreciated the exquisite artistry of both these.

—from *My Literary Passions: Criticism and Fiction* (1895)

**FRANCIS GRIBBLE**

As all the world knows, the Rougon-Macquart books were originally announced as a library written to illustrate the author's views on the subject of heredity. So far as one can judge from the novels, Zola neither knew anything about heredity, in the sense in which the man of science understands knowledge, nor had any views about it worthy of the name of views. The only possible scientific criticism on his labours in this direction is that his premises are assumed and that his conclusions do not follow from them. . . . The great scheme was presently supplanted, in effect, if not ostensibly, by a still greater plan. The study of heredity soon led up to the study of the reaction of environment upon it; and the study of the environment came to be found the more interesting study of the two. Though old machinery was still used, it was turned to a more ambitious purpose. The study of the fortunes of a family grew by insensible degrees to be the study of the psychological condition of contemporary France. Zola aspired to take all the departments of French life in turn—the life of the peasants, of the *bourgeoisie*, of the miners, of the financiers, of the gilded youth, and the *haute cocotterie*—and so to produce a library which should be the complete tableau of the social organism as he saw it through his temperament. No man ever lived who possessed the knowledge really needed for the adequate execution of such a task. Zola probably started with less of the knowledge than most people.

—from the *Fortnightly Review* (November 1, 1902)

**HENRY JAMES**

Grant—and the generalisation may be emphatic—that the shallow and the simple are *all* the population of [Zola's] richest and most crowded pictures, and that his "psychology," in a psychologic age, remains thereby comparatively coarse, grant this and we but get another view of the miracle. We see enough of the superficial among novelists at large, assuredly, without deriving from it, as we derive from Zola at his best, the concomitant impression of the solid. It is in general—I mean among the novelists at large—the impression of the cheap, which the author of Les Rougon-Macquart, honest man, never faithless for a moment to his own stiff standard, manages to spare us even in the prolonged sandstorm of "Vérité." The Common is another matter; it is one of the forms of the superficial—pervading and consecrating all things in such a book as "Germinal"—and it only adds to the number of our critical questions. How in the world is it made, this deplorable democratic malodorous Common, so strange and so interesting? How is it taught to receive into its loins the stuff of the epic and still, in spite of that association with poetry, never depart from its nature? It is in the great lusty game he plays with the shallow and the simple that Zola's mastery resides, and we see of course that when values are small it takes innumerable items and combinations to make up the sum. In "L'Assommoir" and in "Germinal," to some extent even in "La Débâcle," the values are all, morally, personally, of the lowest—the highest is poor Gervaise herself, richly human in her generosities and follies—yet each is as distinct as a brass-headed nail.

—from *Notes on Novelists, with Some Other Notes* (1914)

## QUESTIONS

**1.** Henry James asked, "How in the world is it made, this deplorable democratic malodorous Common, so strange and so interesting?" How would you answer this question? Is James's attitude one of pure disdain, or is it deeper than that?

**2.** Does Zola seem to endorse one political movement among the great number that he describes in the novel?

**3.** Zola tries to fix his characters at the intersection of heredity, environment, and the historical moment. Does this method make for good art, convincing psychology, vivid characters, and a panoramic view of characters and events that is historically plausible?

**4.** Despite Zola's use of "naturalism"—a term he coined—much in the novel is symbolic, mythic, and broadly figurative in both language and action. Do the naturalism and symbolism clash, support each other, or interact in some other way? Given the symbolism, can we believe Zola's claim of fidelity to the facts? Or is reality full of natural symbols that an author merely has to report?

# *For Further Reading*

## ZOLA'S *ROUGON-MACQUART* CYCLE

*La Fortune des Rougon* (1871; *The Fortune of the Rougons*)
*La Curée* (1872; *The Kill*)
*Le Ventre de Paris* (1873; *The Belly of Paris*)
*La Conquête de Plassans* (1874; *The Conquest of Plassans*)
*La Faute de l'Abbé Mouret* (1875; *The Sin of the Abbé Mouret*)
*Son Excellence Eugène Rougon* (1876; *His Excellency Eugène Rougon*)
*L'Assommoir* (1877; *The Drunkard*)
*Une Page d'amour* (1878; *A Love Affair*)
*Nana* (1880)
*Pot-Bouille* (1882; *Restless House*)
*Au Bonheur des Dames* (1883; *The Ladies' Paradise*)
*La Joie de vivre* (1884; *Zest for Life*)
*Germinal* (1885)
*L'Oeuvre* (1886; *The Masterpiece*)
*La Terre* (1887; *The Earth*)
*La Rêve* (1888; *The Dream*)
*La Bête Humaine* (1890; *The Beast in Man*)
*L'Argent* (1891; *Money*)
*La Débâcle* (1892; *The Debacle*)
*Le Docteur Pascal* (1893; *Doctor Pascal*)

## BIOGRAPHIES

Mitterand, Henri. *Zola.* 3 vols. Paris: Fayard, 1999–2002. The second volume—*L'Homme de Germinal* (1871–1893)—covers the *Germinal* years. Unfortunately, this comprehensive biography by the greatest Zola expert is not yet available in English.

Brown, Frederick. *Zola: A Life.* New York: Farrar, Strauss and Giroux, 1995.

Hemmings, F. W. J. *The Life and Times of Émile Zola.* New York: Scribner, 1977.

Josephson, Matthew. *Zola and His Time.* London: V. Gollancz, 1929.

Schom, Alan. *Émile Zola: A Bourgeois Rebel.* London: Queen Anne Press, 1987.

Walker, Philip D. *Zola.* London and Boston: Routledge and Kegan Paul, 1985.

## STUDIES ON ZOLA

Baguley, David. *Naturalist Fiction: The Entropic Vision.* Cambridge and New York: Cambridge University Press, 1990.

Baguley, David, ed. *Critical Essays on Émile Zola.* Boston, MA: G. K. Hall, 1986.

Berg, William J. *The Visual Novel: Émile Zola and the Art of His Times.* University Park: Pennsylvania State University Press, 1992.

Berg, William J., and Laurey K. Martin, *Émile Zola Revisited.* Twayne's World Author Series. New York: Twayne Publishers, 1992.

Bloom, Harold, ed. *Émile Zola.* Modern Critical Views. Philadelphia, PA: Chelsea House, 2004.

Hemmings, F. W. J. *Émile Zola.* 1966. New York: Oxford University Press, 1970.

King, Graham. *Garden of Zola: Émile Zola and His Novels for English Readers.* London: Barrie and Jenkins, 1978.

Knapp, Bettina L. *Émile Zola.* New York: Frederick Ungar, 1980.

Lethbridge, Robert, and Terry Keefe, eds. *Zola and the Craft of Fiction.* Leicester, UK, and New York: Leicester University Press, 1990.

Levin, Harry. "Zola." In his *The Gates of Horn: A Study of Five French Realists.* New York: Oxford University Press, 1963, pp. 305–371.

Mitterand, Henri. *Émile Zola: Fiction and Modernity.* Translated and edited by Monica Lebron and David Baguley. London: Émile Zola Society, 2000.

Nelson, Brian. *Zola and the Bourgeoisie: A Study of Themes and Techniques in Les Rougon-Macquart.* London: Macmillan, 1983.

Patterson, J. G. *A Zola Dictionary: The Characters of the Rougon-Macquart Novels of Émile Zola.* 1912. Detroit: Gale Research, 1969.

Schor, Naomi. *Zola's Crowds.* Baltimore, MD: Johns Hopkins University Press, 1978.

Wilson, Angus. *Émile Zola: An Introductory Study of his Novels.* London: Mercury Books, 1965.

## STUDIES ON GERMINAL

Grant, Elliot M. *Zola's "Germinal": A Critical and Historical Study.* Leicester University Press, 1962. An analysis of the composition of *Germinal* that shows in detail how Zola wove fact and fiction into the novel.

Zakarian, Richard H. *Zola's "Germinal": A Critical Study of Its Primary Sources.* Geneva: Librairie Droz, 1972. This study provides the historical documents—quoted extensively in French, with good summaries in English—that Zola used as the basis for his fiction.

Zola, Émile. *Les Rougon-Macquart.* Volume 3. Paris: Gallimard, Bibliothèque de la Pléiade, 1965. This standard French scholarly edition, prepared by Henri Mitterand, the greatest Zola expert, offers a comprehensive presentation on the making of the novel *Germinal*, including the preliminary sketches and generous excerpts from Zola's "Notes sur Anzin" ("Notes on Anzin").

## RECEPTION IN ENGLAND OF ZOLA'S WORKS AND *GERMINAL*

Speirs, Dorothy E. "Émile Zola's Novels." In *Vizetelly & Companies): A Complex Tale of Victorian Printing and Publishing*, pp. 79–105. This is the catalog for an exhibition at the Thomas Fisher Rare Book Library, University of Toronto, 2003.

Vizetelly, Ernest. *Émile Zola: Novelist and Reformer.* 1904. Freeport, NY: Books for Libraries Press, 1971. A personal account of the obscenity trial of Henry Vizetelly (see "Note on the Translation"), written by his son.

## HISTORICAL BACKGROUND FOR ZOLA AND *GERMINAL*

Furet, François. *Revolutionary France, 1770–1880.* Translated by Antonia Nevill. Oxford and Cambridge, MA: Blackwell, 1992.

Lough, John, and Muriel Lough. *An Introduction to Nineteenth-Century France.* London: Longman, 1978.

Magraw, Roger. *France 1815–1914: The Bourgeois Century.* London: Fontana, 1987.

McPhee, Peter. *A Social History of France, 1789–1914.* New York: Palgrave Macmillan, 2004.

Rancière, Jacques. *The Nights of Labor: The Workers' Dream in Nineteenth-Century France.* Translated by John Drury. Philadelphia, PA: Temple University Press, 1989.